ROME BURNING

Also by Sophia McDougall

Romanitas

ROME BURNING

SOPHIA McDOUGALL

First published in Great Britain in 2007 by Orion Books,
an imprint of the Orion Publishing Group Ltd,
Orion House, 5 Upper Saint Martin's Lane,
London, WC2H 9EA.
An Hachette Livre UK Company

1 3 5 7 9 10 8 6 4 2

A CIP catalogue record for this book is
available from the British Library.

ISBN (Hardback): 978 0 7528 6079 4
ISBN (Export Trade Paperback): 978 0 7528 7427 2

Typeset by Deltatype Ltd, Birkenhead, Merseyside

Set in Trump Mediaeval

Printed in Great Britain by Clays Ltd, St Ives plc

The Orion Publishing Group's policy is to use papers that
are natural, renewable and recyclable products and made
from wood grown in sustainable forests. The logging and
manufacturing processes are expected to conform to the
environmental regulations of the country of origin.

www.orionbooks.co.uk

For Masie

This is the second of three books set in a Roman Empire which never fell but spread to take in half the world.

CONTENTS

THE MAP OF THE WORLD

THULE MAIOR

THULE MINOR
Nova Deva

Colonia
Vincia

GOT

Suionic

BRITANNIA
HIBERNIA
London

GERMAN

VENDATIA
ABENACIA

LACOTA
Stadacona
Cayarta
Mixigana

ALGONQUIANA

Moguntiacum

RHAETIA
PANN
GAUL
Lugdunum
Convenarum
ITALI
DA
Sirmium

ARCANSA
Augusta
Tuscarorum

Cathocia

Tarraco
Rome

ANASASIA
Sievibacum

CALUSA

HISPANIA

Carthage
Lepcis
Magna

MEXICA

Tecesta

TERRANOVA

TRIPOLITAN

MAURETANIA

Garama

LIBY

Cinitisia

Tenaclanum

MAIA

MASAESYLIA

GAETUL

Asantium
Daura

Bacata

ARAVACIA

IND

Caesarea
Incarum

TUPIA

Xavantium

ARAUCANIA

GARANIA

Diaquitia

HARPEIA

処金 TOKOGANE
TERRANOVA

HYOUDEN 氷田 霜湖 SOUKO

YUKIMIJI 雪美地 AOKUSAHARA 青草原 IWATOUGEN 岩凍原 VENDATIA ABENACIA

夕陽川 ENKONO 塩湖野 GREAT WALL OF TERRANOVA LACOTA Cavarta Stadacona

Yuuhigawa SORASANMYAKU 空山脈 Wall breached Mixigana ALGONQUIANA

ANASASIA ARCANSA Augusta Tuscarorum

東海 TOUKAI Sievibacum Cathocia CALUSA

MEXICA ATLANTIC OCEAN

Tecesta

Cinitisia

TEST SITE 火山諸島 Tenaclanum

KAZANSHOTOU MAIA

PROMETHEAN OCEAN

CHARACTER LIST

(All characters *named* in the text. All dates are in A.U.C – e.g, 2757 = 2004 AD.)

A

Acchan – A slave in the palace longdictor exchange.

'Amaryllis' – A name for a slave-girl owned by **Drusus**.

Ananias – A slave.

Anna – A slave.

Aoi – A senior concubine at the Nionian court.

Atronius – A slave supervisor at Veii Imperial Arms factory, formerly a vigile officer.

Aulus – A doctor working at the slave clinic in Transtiberina.

B

Baro – A slave.

Bupe – A slave from Veii Imperial Arms factory.

C

Cleomenes – A vigile commander.

Clodia Aurelia – Mother of **Marcus**, wife of **Leo**, supporter of the abolition of slavery. Murdered in 2757 along with her husband.

Cosmas – A slave.

D

Dama – A slave, crucified for murder in 2753, but taken down from the cross alive by **Delir**. Instrumental in establishing the slave-refuge in the Pyrenees. Involved in the rescue of **Marcus** from the Galenian Sanctuary in 2757. Unaccounted for since.

Delir – A former merchant from Persia, subsequently a fugitive. Established a slave refuge camp in the Holzarta gorge in the Pyrenees, after rescuing the slave **Dama** from crucifixion. Roman citizenship revoked.

Drusilla Terentia – divorced wife of **Lucius,** mother of **Drusus.**

Drusus – see **Novii.**

E

Edda – A slave owned by **Epimachus.**

Epimachus – Divorced husband of **Tancorix,** living in Novomagius, Germany.

Erastus – A slave.

Eudoxius – A Senator.

F

Falx – A Roman intelligence specialist on Nionia.

Faustus – See **Novii**.

Fenius – A member of the Praetorian Guard.

Florens – See **Sing-Ji**

G

Gabinius – A construction magnate, involved in the pro-slavery conspiracy that killed **Leo, Clodia** and **Gemella.** Illegally detained **Varius** at his house for some weeks after the disappearance of **Marcus.** Killed attempting to flee by boat in 2757.

Galla – A gladiatrix in the same troop as **Ziye.**

Gemella – Wife of **Varius,** poisoned in mistake for **Marcus** by **Tulliola** in 2757.

Geng – A peasant farmer in the Jiangsu region of Sina. Son of **Mrs. Su.**

Glycon – Faustus' *cubicularius,* or private secretary.

Go-Natoku – Regnal name of the current Nionian Emperor.

H

Helena – A fugitive slave, formerly resident at the Holzarta refuge camp

Huang – A trader exporting Sinoan slaves into the Roman Empire.

Hypatia – A friend of **Makaria** living on Siphnos.

J

Jun Shen also (to the Romans) **Junosena** – Dowager Empress of Sina.

K

Kato-no-Masaru also (to the Romans) **Masarus Cato** – Lord of Tokogane.

Kiyowara-no-Sanetomo – Lord of Goshu.

L

Lal – Daughter of **Delir**, also a fugitive. Roman citizenship revoked.

Laureus – A young Roman aristocrat.

Leo – See **Novii.**

Liuyin – Son of an official, living in Jiangning.

Lucius – See **Novii.**

M

Maecilii, The – A Senatorial family.

Makaria – See **Novii.**

Marcus – See **Novii.**

Marinus – A fugitive slave, formerly resident at the Holzarta refuge camp.

Matho – A fugitive Roman slave, working as a shopkeeper in Jiangning.

Mazatl – ?

Mei – Purchased as a child along with **Ziye** by **Huang.**

Mimana-no-Fusahira – Lord of Corea.

Mizuki – A lady-in-waiting at the Nionian court.

Mouli – A contact of **Delir** living in a village near Wuhu, has assisted fugitive Roman slaves travelling through Sina in the past.

N

Noriko – ?

Novii, The – The Roman Imperial family.

Novia Faustina, nicknamed **Makaria** – only child of **Faustus.**

Drusus Novius Faustus – Son of **Lucius** and **Drusilla Terentia**, cousin of **Makaria** and **Marcus.**

Lucius Novius Faustus – Brother of **Faustus** and **Leo,** father of **Drusus,** uncle of **Marcus** and **Makaria.** Suffers from the 'Novian curse' – excluded from succession.

Marcus Novius Faustus Leo – Son of **Leo** and **Clodia**, nephew of **Faustus** and **Lucius,** cousin of **Makaria** and **Drusus.** Heir Apparent to the Roman throne.

Oppius Novius Faustus – The first member of the **Novii** to become Emperor in 2509.

Tertius Novius Faustus Leo – Youngest brother of **Faustus** and **Lucius,** father of **Marcus.** Heir presumptive to the Roman throne, supporter of the abolition of slavery, murdered along with his wife **Clodia Aurelia** in 2757.

Titus Novius Faustus Augustus – Emperor of Rome.

O

Octavia – A divorcée living in the same block of flats as **Varius**.
Oppius – See **Novii**.

P

Paccia – A slave.
Probus – A Senator acting as minister for Terranova.
Proculus – Manager of Veii Imperial Arms Factory.

Q

Quentin, Memmius, – an advisor to Faustus.

R

Rong – Purchased as a child along with **Ziye** by **Huang.**

S

Salvius – General of the Legions of the Roman Empire.
Sakura – A lady-in-waiting at the Nionian court.
Sibyl, The – The Pythia at Delphi.
Sing-ji – The Sinoan Emperor, son of the Dowager Empress **Jun Shen**.
  Also (to the Romans) **Florens**. [興智, in Pinyin: Xing Zhi]
Sohaku – A retainer to **Kato-no-Masaru.**
Su, Mrs. – A peasant farmer, mother of **Geng.**
Sulien – Brother of **Una**. A former slave with strange abilities born in
  London. Sentenced to crucifixion for rape in 2757, but rescued by Una
  and later exonerated by the testimony of **Tancorix.**

T

Tadahito also (to the Romans) **Tadasius** – The Nionian Crown Prince,
  eldest son of the **Go-Natoku Emperor.**
Taira – a Nionian Lord.
Tancorix – The daughter of the London family that owned **Sulien**.
  Formerly married to **Epimachus**, disgraced by admission of an affair
  with a slave. Now living as a singer in Rome.
Tiro – A fugitive slave, formerly resident at the Holzarta refuge camp.
Tomoe – A lady-in-waiting at the Nionian court.
Tulliola (Tullia Marciana) – Former wife of **Faustus**. Arrested for
  involvement in the pro-slavery conspiracy that killed **Leo**, **Clodia** and
  Gemella. Died in custody, apparently by suicide, in 2757.

U

Ulpia – Nurse to **Lucius.**

Una – Sister of **Sulien.** A former slave with strange abilities born in London.

V

Varius, Caius – Director of a free clinic for slaves in Transtiberine Rome. Former private secretary to **Leo**, widower of **Gemella.** Charged with murder and treason in 2757, but later exonerated.

W

Weigi – An interpreter at the Sinoan court.

X

Xanthe – Daughter of **Tancorix**.

Y

Yanisen, Marcus Vesnius – Head Governor of Terranova.

Z

Ziye – A former gladiatrix of Sinoan origin. Escaped to the Holzarta refuge camp in 2754, now a fugitive.

THE NOVIAN DYNASTY
AN IMPERIAL FAMILY TREE

✶

Gaius Novius Faustus Augustus

[m]

Sextilia Gratiana

✶
Titus Novius
Faustus Augustus
(Emperor of Rome)

[m]

Julia Sabina

✶
Novia Faustina
(**Makaria**)

✶
Lucius Novius
Faustus

[m]

Drusilla Terentia

✶
Drusus Novius
Faustus

✶
Tertius Novius
Faustus **Leo**

[m]

Clodia Aurelia

✶
Marcus Novius
Faustus

How is it that a mortal can wish for another mortal the annihilation of his body, or of his soul, or death for his children or for his cattle, if he has sense enough to know that he himself is mortal?

For he is pitiless to himself, and none of the others shall pity him.

Avesta, Fragments 48-49
Tr. James Darmesteter

I

YELLOW FIRE

She had barely slept. The single damp sheet that lay over her was smothering, a heavy pelt, but when she pushed it off she felt exposed, a little panting grey animal, curled up in the heat. The windows were all open, but when the air moved it made no difference; it was like moist wool brushing over her. Summers had not always been like this, had they? She thought she could feel the bricks of the house, the trees outside and the miles of dry ground, hurt with heat, straining and creaking.

But after all she must have been more than half-asleep, or stunned with the nights she had already lost, though she kept moaning and shifting in the bed; for she was very late noticing the sound, or the scent.

She thought that perhaps something had moved in the corner of the room, near the door: an animal, or a person. She blinked heavily and pressed her cheek to the pillow, not afraid; it did not really occur to her to believe there was anything there. She lay, possibly asleep, eyes open or shut, she could not tell. The heat puffed and crept.

Then again she had the impression of motion, in the air above her this time – a dark ripple – and she smelt it now.

She sat up, and the gasp she made brought the bitterness in the air far more sharply into her throat. She had seen smoke moving, and there were flames like small creatures skittering on the floor.

She ran shufflingly across the room. The door led into her sitting room, the stairs down into the rest of the house were beyond it. The little flames by the door were not, in themselves, terrifying, but when she pushed the door open, the room was bright with yellow fire, and a thick hovering flood of hot gas and dust struck her face.

She choked and cried out, backing away into the bedroom. She groped towards the window, at first only for the air that now seemed clean and cool. Then she looked down and saw the thick red flames, gushing like a liquid, like blood, upwards out of the lower windows. Her brother and sister-in-law, and their children – they were out, weren't they? She could see dim figures in the garden, but there was no light except that of the fire.

She could not climb down or jump. Her rooms were on the third floor, out of the family's way. She had not meant to end up surviving on goodwill like this, but she'd always lived in this house, and now, even as she leant out, calling for help, she wanted to weep with grief for it, for the *things*, furniture her parents had bought, pictures—

A rich fountain of black smoke, fast and bloated, rolled up to her window from below and forced her back into her bedroom.

The vigiles, surely, must be nearly here.

She stood for a moment, coughing, clasping her hands near her face, crying with helplessness, and then plunged through the burning doorway into the other room. Down near the floor there was still some air, though her palms and knees were seared at once. She crawled into the cavern of heat, whimpering with pain and horror, and at the sight of her own possessions blazing – hidden in the drawers of the burning writing-desk – her bundles of *letters*. Some of them thirty years old, some of them she could almost never bear to read over, but they were terribly important, necessary.

It was dark, formless. She could not understand how the familiarity of the room's shape could be burning away with everything else, how hard it was even to remember the way to the door, but she saw in despair that even if she reached it, it would be no good; of course the stairs would be impassable with flame. And she could not breathe; the fire encroached towards her from all sides, it steered her, so that she had to scramble backwards again, and could barely make it into the bedroom once more, in pain, her hair already singed and eaten to rags by the fire.

But this room too was soaking with heat and poison; she could not even try to get near the window again: the curtains were moving murderously and dropping away in flakes as they burnt. Flame was beginning to pool on the ceiling.

'If there is ever a fire, don't hide, children die in fires because they hide from them.' Her parents had told her this. She crept under her bed. It was decades since she had been a child, and there was nowhere else to go. She lay there on her stomach and saw the carpet steam or smoke. She could feel that she would probably lose consciousness soon, and was afraid that even if the vigiles came in now they wouldn't find her; they wouldn't know she was there.

But nothing was ever found of her. She was dead before the orange flame burst from the floor, from the bed, before the roof fell through, crushing the shell of her body into black crumbs of bone that later could not be told from those of the slaves, or even, at first, from the scorched chips of plaster and wood.

II

TOKOGANE

The heat exhausted Faustus, heaped viscously over his body, gripped his head, a bottling, fermenting feeling. It was hard to think clearly, but the month's meetings kept multiplying, swelling: there were forest fires, more this year and worse than any he could remember, huge red flotillas, crescent-shaped on Terranova, advancing on tall sails of smoke towards the cities on the west coast. And also in Gaul, and even in Italy itself, to the north. And Nionia – how serious the threat was, how fast it was growing – just for an hour he should be allowed to forget it all but he could not, and he could not sleep.

His eyes pulsed redly against his shut lids.

The woman trying to rub the ache out of his shoulders was young, with long dark hair which sometimes he felt whisk against his skin. Not really like Tulliola, except in that. A slight pleasure glowed in his scalp as her fingers moved up into his hair, but the tiredness had only retreated from her a little, she could not do more than touch the surface of it.

He felt a very faint, very perfunctory excitement, mingled with a stronger boredom at the knowledge that, if he wanted, he could turn over, reach for her. He was the Emperor, she would have to ...

But he did not want to. Because of Tulliola, and because he was so tired.

There was a slight noise, a tap, a warning, recognisable clearing of the throat at the door to which Faustus uttered a vague grunt of mingled assent and protest, knowing at once that it was Glycon, his cubicularius or private secretary. The girl draped a towel over him, and he raised himself, embarrassed, not by his nakedness, but by the slowness with which he did it, the little groan, a creaking 'mmm ...' His eyes were still shut.

'Sir.'

Faustus opened his eyes, knowing the tone of voice. He had of course heard it several times, but worst of all and most repeatedly during the terrible summer and autumn of three years before, beginning with the news that his youngest brother was dead. Then everything with his nephew Marcus, and finally that they had found Tulliola, dead under house arrest.

How should he think of Tulliola now? As little as possible, and not, if he could, as having been his wife; he was so ashamed of her. He did not know why she had done such terrible things, and he never wanted to find out; and she had been so beautiful. He was almost grateful to her for having killed herself. It was better than having to have her executed.

So, his first thought was that, again, he was going to hear that something had happened to one of his family. Marcus, who was his heir now. Or even worse, his daughter Makaria – no, please, not her. Or it could be both of them, they were both in Greece.

'We need you downstairs,' said Glycon. 'There has been a massacre.'

Oh, thank goodness for that, thought Faustus, disgracefully, glad that no one would ever know. He sat up and punitive pain flowed back into his head.

It eased off. 'What do you mean by a massacre? How many people?'

He felt sorry for Glycon, knowing he would hate giving a straight answer. He saw Glycon flinch, resist the urge to dodge the question altogether and settle on saying softly, 'The lowest figure I've heard was a hundred, the highest was four hundred. Yanisen can tell you more.'

'This is on the Wall, then, of course?' Yanisen was the Governor of Roman Terranova.

'The Wall has been breached,' said Glycon, just as gently.

Faustus felt a sharp twang of real shock for the first time. 'The Wall has been *breached*? Are you telling me about an invasion?'

Again Glycon recoiled a little. 'It's a matter of the last few hours. It's very unclear. I wouldn't like to speculate. But you will need the military options before you: I have General Salvius waiting with Probus, and Memmius Quentin, because obviously the impact on the public will become important very soon.'

'Good,' said Faustus heavily. 'You'd better get, ah ...' For an odd moment he could not get the name to form, either in his brain or on his tongue. 'Falx,' he said finally. Falx was an intelligence specialist on Nionia.

'He's on his way.'

He walked with Glycon through the palace. The massage seemed to have done no good at all. He was as sluggish as before. He felt oily under his clothes.

'We can talk to Nionia through Sina or our trade contacts,' said

Glycon. For eighteen months and more there had been, officially, only bitter silence between Nionia and Rome. The last Nionian ambassadors had been spies, or at least, the danger that they were spies had been too strong to take chances.

'Sina,' answered Faustus dully. The light through the gold-tinted glass hurt his eyes.

In the private office the doors were almost invisible when closed: carved leaves obscuring the edges, even the hinges and little handles concealed among the unbroken ivy and clematis painted in fresco round the walls, so that once inside you seemed to be within a large, cool, motionless garden, beautiful, with no way out. But there was a bright flat aperture now in the green wall opposite Faustus' desk, where the shutters that covered the longvision were folded back, displaying Yanisen.

Yanisen was Navaho, but looked – was – as essentially Roman as the men in the room: dressed in crisp white, his stiff, lead-coloured hair cut short and square above his elegant long face. Terranova was one of the few regions left in the Empire where languages other than Latin still had much currency, but the Governor's full name was Marcus Vesnius Yanisen, and he would probably have dropped or altered even the Navaho cognomen, if it had not run easily enough off tongues used only to Latin.

He and Probus should have been preparing what they would say to Faustus; instead they were in passionate argument: 'If you had given me the resources—'

'Do you – think – this is – an appropriate time – to be scoring *points*?' said Probus, in a series of low, dry, furious gulps.

'I think it's a time to remember that I've been warning about this for years!'

'Yes, we are all very aware of *that*, you've spent less time ...' he swallowed again, 'actually *doing* anything about it.'

Probus was thirty-six, a short but upright man with dark hair and a square face. He was precociously high ranking, the youngest person in the room, and the most afraid for himself; for it was true Yanisen had often complained to him, as the tension on the Wall grew and the skirmishes got worse. It was also true that Salvius and Faustus himself were just as responsible for refusing Yanisen everything he had wanted, but Probus must know he would be the easiest to blame, if it came to that.

Yanisen opened his mouth, incensed, but cut himself short, seeing Probus react as Faustus entered. The appalled, argumentative look of them brought the ache and the weariness to a peak again in Faustus. The lovely green room felt inexplicably stuffy.

Salvius made him tired too; he was sitting on one of the green couches, scowling at the argument but taking no part in it. He sprang up to greet Faustus with the energy of a charge going off. He was white-haired, but the hair was still thick, and combed to a snowy gloss, and he was as muscular and handsome as he had been at twenty-five. Leo, Faustus' dead brother, had been similarly careful of his appearance, and yet Faustus did not believe Salvius was really vain at all, as Leo certainly had been. Salvius had simply realised at some stage that to look this way helped him extract respect. He certainly had none of Leo's loucheness – he seemed to have been happily faithful to his wife for thirty years. Oddly, even though politically they must have violently disapproved of each other, Leo and Salvius had got on quite well, not only out of military fellow-feeling, but from the conscious shared possession of a certain kind of strength.

Salvius bowed. Faustus took his hand, and felt that though it gripped firmly on his own, it trembled too, but not with fear like Probus'. Faustus looked into Salvius' face and saw the spontaneous, wounded outrage there, and was surprised. Again he felt rather ashamed of himself; he just did not feel as if he personally had been attacked, when presumably of all people he ought to.

Salvius burst out, 'That's the last shred of Mixigana gone, Your Majesty, and frankly it's been a farce for years anyway: we've got no choice but to show we won't tolerate this.' Mixigana was the peace treaty that had established the Roman-Nionian border more than three hundred years before.

'That's probably the best way to let this out, it makes it clear you're still in control,' agreed Quentin, although Salvius did not seem to relish the advisor's support and glanced at him with minor distaste. Quentin was in his forties but plumply boyish looking, round-faced, with smooth chestnut hair. He did not look particularly shocked by what had happened.

'Quiet,' said Faustus. 'You may think you know what this is all about, but I don't. Yanisen?' It was principally for Salvius' benefit that he tried to sound forceful, pulled his protesting body up as straight as he could. You've got to watch people like that, he felt, deeply and instinctively. The Novii might have ruled in Rome for two hundred years now, but it would never be long enough to be completely certain they were safe; not for any Emperor.

Salvius looked at him broodingly, and he and Quentin subsided. Probus stood and clenched his teeth.

Yanisen nodded. 'Sir. Our troops came under the kind of attack they've experienced many times, especially in the last four years.'

7

Probus grimaced, longing to interrupt.

'Where?' said Faustus.

'This was in – that is, it began near Vinciana.'

'I've never heard of it.'

'No, there's no reason you would have done. But it's in Arcansa, very near the Wall, close to where it intersects the Emissourita. Of course, our troops retaliated. I think we lost four or five men at this point, sir. You must understand that with all of this – because of the way things escalated, it's hard to be precise. A detail in armoured vehicles advanced a little way into Nionian territory to disperse the enemy. It appeared they had done so successfully. But on the return they were attacked again. Sir, the Nionians must have reinforced at some point in the last month; it was much more sustained, the numbers were such that the Roman soldiers were all but wiped out. We haven't been able to recover the bodies.'

'But that can't have been a hundred people?' asked Faustus.

'No. The Nionians pursued the remnants back. And this is when they fired explosives at the Wall itself. Of course, by this time our surviving troops had called for support, but it didn't come in time, there was no way they could hold the breach. The fighting spilled into Vinciana. And then, I think they – the Nionians – must have begun simply killing people indiscriminately.'

Faustus exhaled heavily; he hadn't realised so many of the deaths were civilian. He understood Salvius' indignation better now, but he still couldn't share it, not really; he felt more depressed than anything.

'But they were driven back or killed after that? They're not still there?'

'No. The back-up from the next fort arrived; it doesn't seem there's been any more gunfire.'

'And the breach itself?'

'They've got it contained for the moment.'

'But how big is it? What does the town look like now?'

'Well, it's – the damage must be – I'm not there.'

'Then go there. But first find me someone who's there already. And decent pictures. And some idea of where these numbers are coming from.'

'Very well,' said Yanisen, his voice strained. Then, seemingly trying in vain to stop himself, he continued through his teeth. 'The town is still vulnerable, of course, and will continue to be. I am sorry, Your Majesty, I feel I *have* to say, this could have been prevented—'

'Yes, *you* could have prevented it,' exclaimed Probus savagely. 'Don't you try and lay the blame here because we weren't prepared to throw good money after bad.'

'Stop,' barked Faustus, acting fury easily enough; after all these years he could produce the right voice and expression on demand. 'You can continue this in person. Probus, you should be out there too.' Probus nodded shakily, but Faustus added, '*Now*, go now,' and felt – vague as his desire for the girl in the bath-suite – a pang of pleasure at being able to flick Probus across the globe. Infantile, really. Probus left, still swallowing dryly; Faustus thought, with mingled scorn and pity, that he might even burst into tears.

He gestured at the screen and a slave turned it off. An aide had entered and whispered something to Glycon.

'What are we hearing from Cynoto?' Faustus asked.

Glycon looked disconsolate. He was training a quietly tormented, imploring expression on a cherry tree painted on the wall, and he had to lower his hand from his mouth to speak; unconsciously, he'd been biting the flesh of his index finger. 'It's taking time,' he replied.

'They're not refusing to speak to us?'

'No. Possibly keeping us waiting to make a point.' He slipped out of the room.

Faustus and Salvius exchanged a silent look now, not quite of guilt, but both were aware that for years they had considered quietly, why lavish money on the Wall when a war with Nionia might be coming, after which the Wall would be pointless. Yanisen must have known as much.

'All right, now you can talk.'

'We have almost the numbers on the Wall to head north already; we can reinforce them within weeks. I don't believe it would take more than four months to take control of the territory.'

Faustus nodded. Glycon re-entered to interject. 'Falx is here.'

'In a minute. But could we keep the war contained in Terranova?'

'Obviously we would attack Cynoto from the air at the same time,' said Salvius.

'And their bases in Edo?'

'It goes without saying.'

Faustus nodded again, but he looked at Quentin. 'Are you sure this looks like being in control? Because you could equally well say the opposite.'

'Well,' said Quentin, 'people will want to feel *something* is being done.'

'But – not to belittle what's happened today – we don't need to overstress it to the public, do we? People are used to hearing about skirmishes.'

Quentin looked thoughtful. 'It's true that it's a long way away for most people. But it's not as easy to keep things quiet these days; and even if we were successful, they might then find it harder to accept if you did decide war was necessary.'

Salvius by this time was looking overtly disgusted. '*What?*' demanded Faustus loudly, finding with some surprise that he was contemplating Salvius almost with hatred. Oh, you think you'd do so much better, he thought sourly.

Salvius hesitated, bristling warily. 'I suppose it seems like a question of right or wrong to me. A question of the interests of Rome, at the least. I'm a little surprised it's being considered in these terms.'

'We're considering everything, I hope,' Faustus snarled.

'Of course,' said Salvius, trying to sound dispassionate.

Faustus wanted Salvius out of the room so he could release his body from the straight posture he'd hauled it into, knead his face with hands. He said, '*You* talk with Falx. Come back and tell me what we can expect from the Nionians, and what we need to do to be ready.'

Salvius was even a little appeased by this. When he and Quentin were gone, Faustus let himself sag, as he'd wanted to. He rubbed at the back of his neck and head, trying to mimic what the girl had been doing, but holding his arm aloft like that only seemed to make the muscles stiffen even more painfully and he let it drop.

He noticed Glycon, who had retreated diffidently into a chair at the edge of the room. As the conversation had gone on, he had wound himself by subtle degrees into a position that looked agonising: his legs twisted round each other, his shoulders skewed, his hands up to his face with the interlaced and steepled fingers spikily protecting the lower half of his nose, his thumbs under his chin, jutting into his neck. He might be unaware he was doing it, but Faustus was sure Glycon wanted him to say, as he did now, 'You're looking very gloomy.'

Glycon separated his hands to hold them splayed in mid-air. 'Of course,' he murmured. 'The situation ...'

'No, don't give me that,' said Faustus, tersely gentle. He dragged a chair into place to sit opposite Glycon.

Glycon unknotted himself fully, sighing. 'I think the general reaches decisions so fast,' he confessed. 'I think it ... it's possible he underestimates the cost – financially, apart from anything else. And in – destruction.'

This was an unusually strong word for Glycon: having said it he blinked and made a mute gesture, as if to rub it out of the air.

'Of course, he may very well be right,' he added quickly, which almost made Faustus want to laugh, but Glycon went on again gravely, his eyes distant.' 'But if Nionia is stronger than he thinks, then this would be something we've never seen before. A world conflict. It doesn't bear thinking about.'

'*I* haven't decided anything yet,' Faustus said quietly.

As the afternoon wore on, however, he became increasingly angry with Nionia, for still all they heard through Sina were imprecise promises that the Nionian emperor would be ready to speak with them soon. Faustus found himself roaring at Glycon, as if it were his fault: 'Make sure they know they're taking a damn stupid risk playing this game! The blind gods! He should be glad I'm willing to talk to him at all!'

Glycon only nodded, unflinching. At last he came into the private office again to tell Faustus, 'The Nionian Prince will speak with you, if you want.'

'Which one?' asked Faustus. He found the workings of the Nionian court confusing; he knew the Emperor had a lot of children. Faustus felt envious. It was curious and regrettable that he and his two brothers had only managed to produce one child each. He thought again of his daughter Makaria, and of Marcus. If Makaria had been a son – if she had married and had children like a normal woman ... how much easier everything would have been. Of course, it was still not impossible, though she was thirty-six now. But he no longer seriously expected it to happen.

If he had had a son with Tulliola – a child of six, at the oldest, now ...? Briefly, he imagined such a boy, with black hair and a crooked Novian mouth. But the idea of Tulliola jabbed at his head again, and in honesty, did he remember what you were supposed to do with a child that young? A grandchild would have been different. Very occasionally he heard rumours that Makaria had a lover out on Siphnos; if so, he wished she would produce him, Faustus would really not care who it was.

'Tadasius, the Crown Prince,' answered Glycon. But of course the Prince did not call himself Tadasius, that was only the Latin rendering of it. His name was Tadahito.

Faustus exhaled at length again, trying to puff the anger out of himself so that he could think clearly. 'Suppose that'll do,' he muttered.

The aides adjusted the longdictor and Faustus took it. 'Your Majesty,' said a voice.

For a moment Faustus thought this must be some Roman intermediary, for the Prince's Latin was disconcertingly flawless. Faustus was thrown, not only by this, but by the Prince's age, older than Marcus, true, but what – twenty-two, twenty-four? 'Your Highness,' Faustus said, 'can I not speak to your father?' and realised too late that this sounded, absurdly and offensively, like something one might say to a child – 'Is your daddy there?'

In response he heard a quiet, sharp intake of breath. 'My father trusts me to represent him accurately; I hope and believe he is right to do so. May I pass on to him your condolences for the murders of our people today? Shall I say Rome feels at last some degree of remorse for her actions?'

'Flawless' was almost an inadequate word for the Prince's fluency. And yet Faustus no longer thought he would have mistaken him for a native speaker: though the accent was exhaustively correct, it was somehow clearly not intended as a pretence or disguise of being Roman. The structure of each sentence, the resonance of the voice were all de-liberately, even insultingly perfect. Faustus felt uncomfortably aware of the very few, very faltering words of Nionian that had survived in his memory through the fifty or fifty-five years since his schooldays.

'Oh, come on,' he said, irked. 'Your troops attacked the Wall. Did you authorise that or not?'

'Our soldiers are authorised at all times to respond to Rome's per-sistent incursions into Tokogane,' replied the Prince. To Faustus' ears the sudden, soft foreign syllables, spoken so naturally, sounded bizarre, resting incongruously on the familiar frame of his own language. There was no established Latin interpretation or taming of the Nionian name for the land north of the Wall. Romans would only speak, grudgingly, of 'Nionian Terranova', But he still remembered – Tokogane, the Land of Gold. That was what the Nionian name meant.

'Yes, and you've sent in more. Even aside from what happened today, they are in violation of Mixigana simply by being there.'

'We see Rome violate the treaty daily. We see infringement on Nionian territory, kidnappings, murders, rapes committed by your soldiers, or by your citizens with their protection.'

'All that's rubbish.'

'It is possible,' suggested the Prince, with pointed, forbearing courtesy, 'that your subordinates prefer to keep these things from you, in which case your reaction is understandable. But I can give you specific instances.'

'If I'm not supposed to believe my people, why should I believe yours? Look, the point is that explosives were used on the Wall, I assume you don't dispute that much? Did this happen spontaneously, in which case we will expect the men concerned to be punished, or was this an inten-tional act of war?'

'They were repelling your army's assault. They were responding to the destruction of a village. The murders of children. Did *you* authorise *that*?'

Faustus hesitated. His head beat. He began, 'Deaths in a battle pro-voked by your troops—'

'A village *ten miles* away,' cried the Prince.

Faustus was silent, blinking, thinking first, 'I don't have to believe that.' Then: 'but *he* believes it, that much is obvious.' He pulled at his neck-cloth, which had begun to feel smothering, finally unpinned it and took it off altogether. He said quietly, 'Tell me what your intentions are.'

'The Emperor's intentions have always been to protect and uphold Nionia's side of the Mixigana treaty, despite Rome's evident contempt for it; after today, of course, he may be forced to reconsider,' said the Prince, performing the sentence with a kind of restrained, hostile flourish, and so beautifully that he was almost singing.

'This isn't helping anyone,' snapped Faustus. 'My generals are fully prepared to respond. I thought you would appreciate the chance to give me your side of it.' He glowered, angry with himself, and with the Prince for goading him into this. He had not meant to sound so schoolmasterly. It would not have come out so if the Prince had been older.

There was a silence, which he thought he could hear ringing with both rage and satisfaction. The Prince said finally, politely, 'Thank you. I *have* appreciated it. Goodbye.'

'Sir, are you all right?' asked Glycon, watching him.

'Yes,' said Faustus thickly. Shouldn't have drunk so much, he thought. But what was that supposed to mean? He hadn't had a drink since the night before – he shouldn't still be feeling that, should he? How much had it been? He couldn't remember. 'Get Salvius in here again.'

Salvius listened impassively while Faustus told him what the Prince had said. 'I think it's a good sign he felt the need to justify it. It shows they know they're in the weaker position.' Talking with Falx had made him calmer, more confident that the right thing would be done.

'You don't think there's any truth in the story about the village?'

'Well,' Salvius did lower his eyes briefly, 'I might not go as far as that, but you can't trust his account of it.'

'No, I suppose not,' said Faustus bleakly.

'In any case it hardly makes a difference. However today began, the fact is that the Nionians have proved themselves a threat, and neither the Wall nor the treaty is strong enough to protect us. And this is not just a matter of our territory in the West, sir, it's a question of whether we're willing to let Nionia overtake us as an Imperial power. Because if not, this could be our last chance to stop it.'

'Wait a minute,' said Faustus. He could see that something had gone wrong; he hadn't said it properly. He rose from his seat and tried again. 'Just wait.' He made for the hidden door because he felt it was the room that was wrong: the beautiful green room was so full of detail, and of the past, a minute or two anywhere else and he would be all right again. He reached the door, but fumbled at the familiar handles among the painted foliage.

'Sir,' Glycon was saying, coming towards him, his voice full of concern

Then abruptly the door opened, and before his foot could fall in the doorway the impact came; a huge, soundless thud, a detonation so total that he could not immediately tell that it was within the walls of his own skull, for it knocked half the floor away, so that he stepped off the remaining ground into dark air, and fell.

III

AXE AND RODS

Una could bear the sun here, where the sea blunted it a little. She was sitting with her legs drawn up protectively into the square of shade under a paper parasol on the stones, the folds of her white swimming dress stiffening around her with salt water. The dark island dropped straight down into the water with no softening of its slope. Here beneath the water it hollowed into a deep bowl, green and purple-red with floating leaves, and also there were spherical dark anemones, blood- or jewel-like and faintly sinister, fixed to the rock. Marcus was swimming back towards this bowl, and her, sitting above it. Sometimes she lifted one of the books beside her, although even in the shadow the sunlight turned the pages dazzling, sometimes she watched Marcus in the water. Her pale skin had not burnt, nor did it turn a clear brown as Marcus' had; it only, very slowly, picked up what looked to her like a faint tinge of dust.

Marcus' usually muted blond hair had been warmed to gold and amber-yellow, near the temples especially; the hair on his body had turned paler and brighter still. She knew that when he got out of the water, as his skin dried, it would look as if there was thin gold sand near this shore, instead of only rock.

They would probably never again be closer to being alone together than this: a tactful distance out there were a few Praetorian boats buzzing in circles round the island, more at the tiny port, and Marcus' cousin Makaria would have her own bodyguards at the vineyard, although Una was not planning to go there.

She looked out and everything shone, the water, Marcus' wet hair and skin, and, subtle as smoke, a little silver drift of narrow fish, only visible when they turned and caught the light. It was as if she were watching them fly; it hardly seemed natural to her that water could be so transparent – it looked less substantial almost than air, not dense enough to support either a fish or a man, and if it could it was

15

barely within reason, almost a cheat, a joke, that she should be there to see it.

They were not far from the slave market at Delos.

The books scattered around her were history books, Cossus' *Rome and Nionia*, and the older works, the Livy and Plutarch that Marcus wanted her to read, hoping that they might make her a little more forgiving of Rome. She could read as fast as anyone else now, though always with a furtive, defiant tension somewhere under her ribs, a sullen fear that there was too much lost time to make up. Marcus and the other students in Athens were reading new things all the time. Knowing she felt like this Marcus had persuaded one of his own tutors from the Academy to visit her every week, but although he tried to hide it Una knew the tutor didn't really understand what he was doing there, what the point was. And she had turned stiff, inarticulate, moody, so that he had not even thought her intelligent. It was because she didn't know how to explain herself. She wasn't preparing for anything, as Marcus was. She had told the tutor he might as well stop coming.

When she had been freed she had not, until it was done, paid much attention to the fact that her name was being altered. Someone, drawing up her freedwoman's papers, had cobbled together a bit of Marcus' name with her own to make up a citizen's name: Noviana Una. She had never been Marcus' slave, or a slave of any member of his family, but it sounded rather like that. She tried not to let this bother her. Of course it was much better than living with the name of anyone who had actually owned her, as would have been more usual, and, she told herself, she need not think of it as more than an official detail, not really a name at all. But she found she had to use it more often than she would have expected.

She knew that to look at her, it was not obvious, at least not at first, that she had ever been a slave. She was still very lean, but without the unhealthy look she realised she must have had once. She almost never curled her hair or wound it up in plaited coils, she let it hang, as she always had, pale, rabbit's-fur-coloured, straight over her shoulders; but it had been cut so that it always fell smoothly, and there was more of a shine on it now. She had good clothes, like the white dress lying now on the rocks, plain and narrow but graceful; she had jewellery, even. Marcus had given her some of these things: the necklace of pale green stones now in the pocket of her small bag (she kept checking it was safe there), but she had her own money. She was very stingy with it, partly because she had worked out that it would not be so very much if it had to last her whole life. And really the money was not all hers or her brother's. Dama had done as much; if he were alive they should share

16

it with him. Keeping a part of it for him was complicated; it comforted her fear that he was dead, but it held her in an odd state of suspense, missing him, but as much afraid as hopeful that she would have to see him again. But sometimes, as time passed and he was not found, saving the money for him began to feel more like an act of memorial than anything else. No one had found his body in the woods near the Sanctuary, but the guards there could have buried or dumped it before they either vanished or were arrested. Sometimes she thought it would be better to spend the money on something he would have liked.

But she had another, deeper-rooted motive for thrift. Even after three years, she had never relaxed completely: the paperwork that said no one could touch her, the physical ease of her life now – they were only to be trusted so far. She might suddenly need to escape, hide.

On the Aventine hill in Rome, not too far from the palace or the shadowy streets in Transtiberina where her brother lived, she'd noticed a particular bath-house, an ineffective and fallow place, just popular enough for its clients to come and go anonymously, where the staff would be uninterested and unconcerned by a slightly strange request. Una had come here, eighteen months before, driven by fierce, compelling impulse – and yet, could it really be called an impulse when it had made her act so carefully? Inside the locker that she'd used a false name to rent, under innocent towels and a strigil, under a pile of nondescript clothes, tidily rolled up and hidden in opaque little bottles meant for scented bathing-oil, were thick sheaves of cash: enough to get two or three people out of the country quickly. After Una had placed them there, she felt humiliated by what she had done. It seemed so furtive, so graceless, the dirty habit of a feral animal. She was, she thought, more like an urban fox, gnawing on rubbish out of a London bin, than a civilised woman. And she was ashamed of herself for keeping it secret from Marcus; it was unjust, when there was so little he could really hide from her. And yet she could not bring herself to tell him, or anyone, or to empty the locker; all this time later the stash was still there. Sometimes, without warning she would be struck by a lash of panic that it had been discovered, or that she had forgotten the code needed to retrieve it; sometimes at night – but not often, not often at all – she lay in bed smoothing the sequence over, like a short string of Indian prayer-beads. She was glad there was nothing visible, no key that had to be hidden or could have been lost: only the code, shameful but safe, folded tightly in her brain, as if in silk.

No, she was not altogether a Roman citizen, in spite of the name. It was not just these guilty slave's fixations; it was a matter of law too, although most of the differences were subtle enough. She could not vote, or stand for public office, but she was a woman and could not have done that anyway.

She could not marry a member of the aristocracy.

Marcus hovered easily in the water below her. Una looked at him with clear, brooding happiness and leant down, grasped his wet hand and dragged him upwards giving needless help as he pulled himself out onto the rock beside her. He flicked open one of the books and Una said, 'A lot of men killing each other.'

'No, sometimes they stop and make speeches.' He draped himself across her lap; the sun was drying his skin so fast that she didn't mind the brief film of water he spread over hers. He smiled up and coaxed her: 'Don't go back to the house tonight. Don't make me go on my own.'

The night before they'd slept in a little house Makaria owned near the harbour, but Marcus was visiting his cousin at the vineyard that evening.

'It's much better that I'm not there,' said Una, with flat certainty. 'I would make her uncomfortable.'

'She should be grateful to you.'

'Exactly.'

'All right, but that wouldn't last very long. A few minutes. Isn't it worth it? I think she'd like you, if you actually talked. It might ...' He played diffidently with her fingers. 'It might help.'

It was not exactly that Makaria or Faustus disapproved, or were particularly troubled by Marcus' loving Una. On the contrary, they extended an easy, unspoken indulgence towards the two of them, based entirely on the assumption that, at an appropriate time, Marcus would get rid of her.

Una sighed. 'But *I* don't *want* to meet her. You *know* why. How can I be there? There are slaves.'

'Not many,' said Marcus, and went on hesitantly, unhappily, embarrassed by the argument before he offered it. 'She doesn't ... They probably hardly even think of themselves as slaves.'

Una widened her eyes slightly, a strict, ascetic look. 'Well, Sulien thought that. They'll change their minds if they're ever accused of a crime, or if your cousin dies or loses her money and they're sold on.'

Marcus sat up beside her. 'I *know*, you know I know. You could talk to her – maybe we could explain it to her.'

'You want to take me to meet your cousin, and say, you remember this little vagrant I picked up, she's going to explain why she doesn't approve of your life – and then we will all sit down and have dinner.'

'Oh,' groaned Marcus, dropping his head against her shoulder in defeat. 'Stop it, don't talk like that.' He kissed the shoulder blade, ran his lips across her back to the base of her neck.

'I'm sorry,' said Una, letting her body loosen, resting her head against his.

'I'd like you to be there, that's all.'

'I know.' She turned to kiss him. 'It's only a night.' But it was one of the last nights before she left Greece; she was sometimes with Marcus in Athens at the flat near the Academy, sometimes with her brother Sulien in Rome. She did not exactly live anywhere.

She looked again across the lovely water and thought maybe Dama would want her to do something like go to Delos and see how many slaves she could buy. But it would be almost impossible to free them legally – should she just tell them to go wherever they liked, without any identity papers, with no certainty that they could live, that they wouldn't be caught and punished? There was no longer anywhere that she knew of to send them; she didn't know where Delir and the others had gone.

Was this only an excuse for doing nothing?

Her legs brushed against Marcus', entangled idly. They watched a Praetorian boat drone by, the round-backed wave it carved lolling into the cove below them. When it had passed they folded together more greedily and regretfully, for if they had really been alone they could have climbed up the slope to find shade and smoother ground, to lie down and make love.

Then, out of its rhythm, they heard the noise of the boat again, scraping through the water, growing louder. They looked up to see the Praetorians closing on them and both felt the same instinctive cramp of anxiety, not because they guessed what the men were coming to say. It was not only Una who privately nursed the possibility of catastrophe and flight.

The boat turned to jog up and down in its own wake alongside the cove. The Praetorian lieutenant standing up in it, looking at Marcus, called out to him, 'Sir, we've got to get you to Lady Novia's house immediately.'

Marcus got to his feet. Una remained huddled, feeling exposed in the pale swimming dress, but the Praetorian officers were trying to gloss over her presence by pretending she was not there.

'Why? Are you expecting something to happen here?'

'No, sir. Rome needs to talk to you on the longdictor in twenty minutes, that's all I know.'

Marcus nodded, silent at first, feeling apprehensive sickness gathering. 'Let us get changed.'

19

The Praetorian pilot drove the boat obediently around the headland. Marcus stood still on the rock and Una said, 'Of course I'll come with you.'

'Thank you.' Marcus turned shut eyes to the blue bay. 'Either it's an attack on Rome, or it's my uncle, isn't it?'

They dressed silently.

Una, sitting in the boat, stringing the green chain around her throat, felt a mess, at a disadvantage; the grace of the white dress was gone from lying crumpled on the rocks and from being thrown on so hastily. Picking at her damp and salty hair with a comb did it no good. She did not want to be in Makaria's house at all, but especially not feeling that she looked anomalously shabby, cheap, or worse than that. But thinking this made her jab the comb back into her bag with a defensive shrug, deciding crossly that there would have been no point in dressing up, even if it had been possible. She kept touching and pivoting the smooth green stones, which had lost their coolness and heated faint humid discs on her skin.

Beside her Marcus was motionless, his eyes fixed sightlessly on the water. She put her arm round him and he looked at her, but he didn't speak, all the short journey round the little coast.

A twist of white steps led up from a small quay. Stepping into the coolness of the low house, at the base of the vineyard, Una and Marcus were, for a little while, almost blind, it seemed so dark after the white-and-blue glare outside. Una's self-consciousness was slightly eased by the fact that Makaria, out on the hill somewhere, had not yet been retrieved, but the woman who let them in was a slave, and yes, it was true, she did not seem at all unhappy, and Una did not know how to look at her or what to say. Almost immediately she and Marcus were separated; the Praetorians hurried him into Makaria's study and shut the door before Marcus could protest that this was not what he wanted, and once inside, he was fixed, staring at the longdictor, and could not bring himself to order them to let her in, or to do it himself.

They were a few horrible minutes early.

Outside, Una stood on the white tiles, as aware of him behind the door as if she could see him; and yet she felt she could not force herself through into the room, although she wanted to, although she knew he wanted her there.

The house was so plain inside that she was surprised it could belong to an Emperor's daughter. There were no frescoes, the small tiles formed no pattern or picture; the atrium was stark, handsome, and slightly dirty from the scuffing of boots. She was nagged by the fear that Makaria, still innocent of what was happening, would come back and find her lingering there, alone.

She heard them beginning to speak, could not make out the words – but she felt the stroke of shock that fell on Marcus. It happened to her too, at the same moment.

Then he walked out of the room towards her, pale – the tan did not show how pale – and she asked at once, 'Is he dead?'

'No,' said Marcus. 'No, he's not dead. But he can't do anything. It was a stroke. He might never – I've got to go back and …' There was a plain black-painted chair against the wall, he dropped onto it suddenly.

He wanted to be Emperor, both for the sake of what he meant to do, and – inseparable from that – an amoral, secret and contained desire, which frightened him a little. If the waiting had gone on for twenty years or more, as it might have done – and perhaps it *still could* – he must have come to prickly impatience in the end, as Leo had, however fond he was of Faustus. But so soon as this –

He was trying so hard, as he sat there, not to even admit the risk that one way or another this was going to cost him Una. He was afraid to look at her and see her fearing this, suspecting that he feared it, or knowing that he did.

He was afraid to let himself moan, even once, 'I *can't* do this.'

Una, still immobile, suggested, 'They should get Sulien.'

'It's all right, they have,' he said blankly. He stared downward. 'I just – I thought we'd have more time.' And he looked up at her and began fervently, 'I mean, more time in Greece, time before anything like this, not—'

'I know,' she interrupted quickly. But she wished he would not look at her like that, not only stricken and aghast, but as if she were relentlessly receding from him. She went and enclosed his head in her arms.

'There could be a war,' he said. 'The Wall's been broken through. It happened today. I'm going to have to decide what to do. Or let Salvius decide. Of course he knows more than I do. But I can't do that – he'd kill so many people.'

'Well,' murmured Una sternly into his hair, 'of course I'm not glad for you, or for your uncle, but I am glad for everyone else that you'll be the one accountable; because you're good.'

Marcus blinked and embraced her in a kind of spasm, pressing a hard imprecise kiss onto her face, then clutched her thinking, no. No. No.

At that moment Makaria trudged in, sunburnt and gawky and far shabbier than Una, and yet over her unkempt clothes she wore an unconscious garment of Novian confidence, and so still looked like the aristocrat she was. She saw Una and Marcus locked in each other's arms, felt a moment's faint and unpleasant surprise that Una was there, and then said, 'It's Daddy,' and rushed into the room Marcus had left.

It was as if an invisible mechanism that had been held forcibly still was suddenly released and began to move with a pouncing, merciless speed. Makaria wept, and ran upstairs to pack clothes, and came down, looking half-tamed in a city dress. There was no need, of course, and no time, for Marcus to do anything like that: the Palace had already dispatched a squad of Praetorians to empty the Athens flat, the trunks they filled would be in Rome within days, and there was nothing in the meantime Marcus could need that the Palace could not instantly acquire for him. Una and Marcus thought of the flat ransacked, and felt at once invaded and guilty, as though the rooms were full of secrets and evidence of crimes. Una offered to go and see to it, but Marcus said, 'No, they're only things. Don't go.'

She was afraid that they would be whisked apart again, and after what had happened before, Marcus was staying stubbornly close to her to prevent it; but in fact the rush was, just in this, kind to them: it was too fast for anyone to try and decide she should be somewhere else. Makaria, hurrying out into the vineyard and back, instructing her staff, ignored her without malice or intention – having genuinely forgotten about her. Only when they went outside did she become aware of Una again, and looked at her with wet-eyed bewilderment and a polite, reflexive smile.

The green little island was suddenly helpless under an attacking sky full of aircraft, large and shining and inexorable. On the flanks of each, the image of an eagle spread triumphant metallic wings, blinding in this sharp light, above the letters S.P.Q.R: The Senate and the People of Rome. They reared down, like huge locusts, churning the hot air cold, so that birds panicked from the trees and the seagulls fled crying, over the sea.

Una and Marcus both felt their breath catch.

The machines hung, roaring. There was no room for more than one to land, so men plunged out of them on ropes, surrounding the place – surrounding Marcus. It might have been an invasion, the lightning assassination of some foreign potentate or rebel warlord.

Una murmured, trying to joke, 'We could still run.'

Marcus laughed, but said grimly, 'No.' He set his shoulders, as the central spira lowered, and their hair rose and streamed.

The spira's harsh grandeur diminished very slightly as it settled, a little awkwardly, on the dusty yard behind Makaria's house. Although Makaria could have had a landing bay on the island, she hadn't wanted one. She too winced at the sight of this military influx, but because of the damage she feared the blast from the wings had done to her plants. She muttered sourly, 'Stupid thugs. No one *thinks*.'

Glycon was standing in the hatchway, strained and ruffled by the journey, his limp fair hair fluttering. 'Glycon,' said Marcus, while he was still climbing the steps, Una following him in the continuing torrent of lashed air. 'Are there decisions I have to make at once?'

Inside, the spiralwing was lined with fat, cream-coloured seats, and there were gold crests embossed on the internal doors; yet the attempt to translate the magnificence of a palace room to a narrow and airborne space had not been perfectly successful: the large furniture looked cramped, and almost cheap, although of course it was not.

To his surprise, Marcus realised that Salvius was also there, at the far end of the chamber. Marcus assumed he must be going to tell him more about what had happened on the Wall. But Glycon was looking at Marcus with anxious pity, handing him a sheet of paper. 'There is something that has to be done, even before that.'

Marcus stopped with the page in his hand and, for a moment, could not seem to take in what it was: the paper was hastily printed in plain, smudgy black, although the edges were rimmed with gold. It was a short script. He realised now what Salvius was stiffly holding: a polished wooden box and, on top of it, a bundle of rods around an axe, or rather the bronze replica of such a thing: the rods inseparable, the curved axe-head small and ornamented and useless. And yet it looked dangerous – *because* it could have looked slightly absurd, because it was a symbol rather than a tool. Marcus knew why Salvius was here now – what he could say about Nionia was incidental: he was representing the army.

A quiet vertigo touched Marcus, as the spira lifted.

'Sit down,' said Salvius.

Marcus obeyed, warily: Salvius affected the same defensive instinct in him as in Faustus, it was only that it urged Marcus to look older, not younger. He could guess how Salvius would regret giving up what he held.

Una watched Salvius, also feeling a prickle of threat, as the green island dropped away from beneath her. As they entered the spira Salvius had stared at Marcus with mixed feelings that resolved into near-disgust when he saw that Marcus had his little girlfriend along with him. He had noticed her retreating into one of the seats at the rear, with what he thought of as a kind of demure shiftiness. She was looking at him.

Una sat by the window, masked her face with guarded blankness and, mechanically, worked a quick, cold-blooded calculation. Glycon had met her before, and did not mind her presence; Marcus, of course, wanted her here; Makaria might have sided with Salvius but was, for now at least, subdued with anxiety about Faustus. So you are outnumbered, thought Una to Salvius, and relaxed a little.

But Salvius was teeming painfully with frustration and smothered power, the little devious-looking girl was the smallest part of the problem. Marcus' face made him remember Leo with affection and sorrow, and smart at the thought of what a disaster Leo would have been as Emperor. He knew that he could, almost certainly, stop this from happening – and he must not, he was not a traitor. Or was he? What if it were treachery *not* to act, to hand Rome over to a boy at such a moment? Would they, afterwards, say, 'If Salvius had moved, then ...'? Or would the ruin be so comprehensive that he would be drowned in it, and barely remembered at all?

He and Marcus sat facing each other across a polished shelf of table and Salvius demanded, as if he were interrogating Marcus, 'Do you promise to govern Rome and her Empire, on behalf of the People and the Senate?'

'I promise this,' replied Marcus, as the script said he should.

Salvius picked up the bronze fasces, weighed it unhappily, and put it into Marcus' hands.

'Do you promise to uphold the rights and privileges of the Roman people established in custom and law?'

'I will uphold them.'

After glancing across it, Marcus didn't really need the script any longer; his part was simple enough and he felt safer and stronger when he was able to look Salvius in the eyes. Laying it down, he looked up and saw that for the first time the expression of distress or of distrustful blankness had left Una's face and she was staring – at Salvius, at himself, at the items that passed between them – with a curiosity so disconcertingly avid that she looked almost ecstatic.

Salvius nodded and removed from the box a smaller, more ornate ebony chest which he opened, swivelled to face Marcus, and pushed to him across the table.

Inside were packed rows of wooden tubes or cylinders, some plainly labelled, some darkly painted with gods, or hunting scenes, or with an enthroned Emperor. They were cases of rolled documents. Most were probably defunct and meaningless, only there because their presence had become traditional – the texts of religious rites, old prophecies – but some of the newer ones must be real and important secrets: the military codes to be used if, for example, an Emperor ever needed to order an attack on part of the Empire itself.

Marcus touched them lightly, as if they might give off electric shocks.

'Do you promise, as far as lies within you, to execute the law with justice, compassion and truth?' said Salvius, quietly appealing now, for it was far too late to go back.

'I promise to do this,' repeated Marcus.

From the box, Salvius lifted a square of gold-fringed cloth. He undid the folding carefully, a layer at a time, until the Imperial seal-ring was visible, resting on his palm.

Somehow, despite the script, despite the fact that he could have predicted all of this, Marcus was genuinely startled by every new phase of the ritual, as though he were watching a developing magic trick done with knives. The appearance of the ring almost made him jump. 'I will perform what I have promised, in the name of the gods,' he said, calmly enough.

He took the ring. The gold was dark, sullen-coloured. It seemed huge and unwieldy: both the drum-shaped boss, with the stern Eagle and laurel impressed upon it, and the band itself, widened for a heavy man's finger, so that putting it on he felt shamefully slight, almost childlike. He curled his right hand into a fist; only so, or by holding his hand out flat and balancing it, could he keep the ring from swinging upside down, or sliding off altogether. This way it was almost like a small piece of armour for the hand, or a weapon, to reinforce a punch.

'The Roman army acclaims you as Caesar and Regent, and implores the gods to grant you health and victory,' said Salvius tersely. He bowed; an uncomfortable forward jerk of the shoulders, and sat back.

Glycon also bowed, and there was silence. Marcus sat, trying not to submit to the threatening dazed feeling, wondering what he was supposed to do with the box of scrolls and the fasces. Except where Salvius had said 'Regent' and not 'Emperor', the words were exactly those of a coronation, although that would never have happened in such furtive, pared-down haste. The gold laurel wreath was not there.

'It will be altered later this evening,' said Glycon, of the ring. 'It's important that you do a broadcast quickly; you'll need it to fit for that.'

'Is it necessary that he wear it?' asked Salvius, discontentedly. 'He's not taking the wreath. This is supposed to be temporary, isn't it? Nominally at least.'

Marcus, again, suppressed a small jolt of shock.

'It can be altered back again,' said Glycon mildly.

Marcus did not want them to continue discussing him like another item of the insignia. He said, 'Tell me about Nionia.'

Later, during a lull for food and wine, he slid into the seat beside Una, and they linked fingertips, covertly. But the captivated way she'd watched the ceremony had unsettled him a little. She said, 'I couldn't help it.' Then, stealthily, afraid that she might be forbidden to touch it, she made a quick move to the table and seized upon the script of the oath with the same predatory fascination with which she'd listened to it. 'I was thinking about agreement,' she told him.

'Agreement?' echoed Marcus. He felt tired.

'I don't know. I was thinking, what changed when you said that? What do those words do? That man, Salvius, it's as if he expected it to be a spell. But ...' She tapped the paper. 'Nothing's any different. Anyone could say this. We aren't even in Rome. There's hardly anyone here to hear you.' Very softly, so that Salvius, Glycon and Makaria would not hear her, she recited: 'I promise to govern Rome and her Empire.' And she raised her face, faintly sardonic, as if waiting for something to happen. 'It doesn't mean anything when I say it. Why does it when you do? I thought, only because it's *agreed* to mean something. But who agreed to it, then? On one hand, very few people. But if consent is having the power to prevent it but allowing it to happen, then everyone ...'

'Oh,' said Marcus. 'I hope they give me a week before they start the revolution, this is enough for today.' He too had wondered, what is this doing to me, what am I doing to myself?

'And the army,' added Una, looking at Salvius.

'Don't put ideas in his head,' protested Marcus, with a forced laugh.

'It will be all right, yes it will,' she said, but if she kissed him, she knew that Salvius would think him weak. She closed her hand over the finger that wore the loose gold ring, as if smoothing a small burn.

Glycon was trying to plan Marcus' day, and the days after that; Marcus was perhaps equally occupied with that and with what Salvius said of Nionia. These were not, of course, separate subjects. For a long time Marcus listened to Salvius neutrally, almost without speaking. But after only a few seconds of this quiet, Salvius was sure that if Marcus had any instinctive feeling of what was necessary, then there must have been some sign of it by now. He overheard Glycon giving Marcus the gist of Faustus' conversation with Tadahito – as it were behind Salvius' back – and felt conspired against. He found he was trying to pound agreement out of Marcus, or at least provoke him into declaring his own folly. His voice rose helplessly louder. It was like shouting into a ravine for a non-existent echo.

And the girl kept eavesdropping; aside from his disapproval of her presence, he found the sense of a second, unacknowledged audience simply disconcerting. She and Marcus had separated strategically again, but they were still palpably in silent league; and Salvius could not keep his eyes both on her and on Marcus at once. If, as of course he must, he ignored the girl and focused on Marcus, he could not conquer the feeling that he was exposed on the other flank. He almost felt that if he looked around at her quickly he would catch her with a pen in her hand, taking down critical notes, like some kind of inspector.

Marcus waited until the hard spots of light on the Golden House and the Colosseum became visible, and the patterns of Rome spread beneath them, in intricate grids like fanning columns of Sinoan characters. Then he said, 'Salvius, I know what you want done. And I can see you've already guessed that I don't agree with you; so that might as well be said. I'm not going to order any attack. I want to meet the Nionians. I think it could happen in Sina.'

He had spent a minute or two constructing this speech. He was fairly sure his voice balanced the warning that Salvius must not hector him any more with enough sorrow that they could not agree, but he hoped it did not sound absurd to use such a tone on someone so much older than him – and taller also, and not dressed, as Marcus still was, in loose informal clothes meant for hanging around by the sea.

Salvius swivelled his head, jaw-first, from side to side, stretching the neck muscles, as if preparing to shoulder his way through a hostile crowd or break down a door. He explained, carefully, heavily, 'Of course you're reluctant to take such a step – but, so am I, I promise you. No one with any experience of war would ever want to start one without reason. But we have let them go too far already. If we don't stop them now they are certain to go further. It's unfortunate that we weren't more decisive about this in the past, then perhaps you wouldn't be in this position now. But you are.' But he felt a kind of release that Marcus had spoken at last.

'We've got the whole of the future to fight them,' answered Marcus.

'*No*,' said Salvius categorically, but did not elaborate, so Marcus went on.

'But we could never get back to here. Or even if we could, there'd be so many dead already.'

'There are four hundred dead today,' said Salvius desperately. 'And if we hesitate after this, it won't be forgotten. It isn't only Nionia. Provinces could revolt. Think of what happened in Mexica; there's always India. We are only strong if they know we're strong, we've always relied on that.'

'You make it sound as if we've always fought every possible war,' said Marcus. 'You know we haven't. This is what I'm going to do.'

Salvius muttered, trying to make the best of it, 'At least it gives us more time to prepare.'

'No,' said Marcus. 'That is, of course you must do what you need to protect the people in the territory, but no more than that, not huge numbers of troops moving in.'

This time Salvius just stared at him, appalled.

'Otherwise meeting them would be meaningless. They would mirror what we did. There'd be two armies looking at each other across the Wall, waiting. How could either we or Nionia believe they would walk away again? It would become inevitable. I've studied this ...'

But no, he shouldn't have said that, thought Una, and Marcus realised it himself at the same moment, and they couldn't prevent their eyes from meeting, both of them knowing that he shouldn't have justified himself at all, shouldn't have reminded Salvius of the Athens Academy where Marcus had been only days before. Of course he didn't have any experience of war, as Salvius had already implied. He was not even twenty years old.

Nevertheless, Salvius said nothing.

Una and Sulien watched Marcus' broadcast together, sitting on the floor, ignoring their surroundings while the heavily beautiful apartments that would be Marcus', opened out around them like a rich flower.

They'd locked themselves in, they didn't exactly know why.

'He looks different,' said Sulien.

Una's shoulders shifted upwards in a taut shrug, and didn't lower again. 'He knows what he's doing. He's all right.'

'Yeah,' agreed Sulien, glancing at her cautiously and then back at the longvision. As casually as he could, he added, 'How about you?'

Una's gaze at the screen turned warningly blank, fixed. She said levelly, 'Knew it was coming eventually.'

'But not so soon. Not like this.' He knew it was stupid to feel responsible. 'I'm just ... sorry.'

Una twitched her head and gave no answer beyond a faintly disapproving grunt.

'What?' he asked.

'Your *voice*,' she answered unexpectedly. 'What are they *doing* to you here?'

'There's nothing wrong with my voice,' said Sulien.

'Yes there is. When I was last here you still sounded a little bit like you might be my brother. I come back and you've turned into a born and bred Roman.'

'No I haven't,' he protested, the British note suddenly pushing to the surface of his voice. Una looked at him and felt her face slipping into a grin. He hardly thought about having grown up in a different country. If he remembered any other place as mattering to him it wouldn't be London – it would be the camp in the Pyrenees, and the journey there. His accent had begun to change very early, the vowels and stresses moulding to the shape of the sounds around him as pliantly as wax, before he'd been in Rome even a year. But she knew two weeks spent talking to no one except her would have colonised his voice as completely as rennet in milk, except that the process would be entirely reversible.

'Anyway, I can't help it.' Though it did seem embarrassing to be so malleable. 'So what if I do sound Roman? I like it here.'

And yet it was almost not a question of liking Rome; he fitted in as easily as into air, so that it no longer really occurred to him whether he liked it or not.

Una considered him affectionately, but with mild wonder. 'You'd like it anywhere.'

Travelling in or out of Rome, on the Appian or Ostian Way, the crosses by the roadside would still turn him sick and shaky, and his fingers would move involuntarily to the vulnerable skin of his wrist. But he wouldn't have been safe from that in any Roman city.

Her own accent was the same as ever, although only out of a kind of tone-deafness, she thought, rather than any deliberate effort to keep it. But she was sometimes confused by a furtive nostalgia for Britain, for London, where she'd suffered so much. It was not that she'd ever been fond of the feel of the air there – different from anything she'd found on the European mainland – or the shape of the ground under the city; only that they'd imprinted themselves on her as being the essential state of things. There was no reason ever to go back. She and Sulien had no family except each other. (Although this was not true, their mother was presumably still alive, but Una never wanted to think of her, would have dug the very idea of such a person out of her own memory if she could.)

And whenever she went into Rome she always drew herself up a little, combatively, as if wanting to remind the place that she was working under a truce with it, that was all.

29

They fell quiet again, watching the screen. Marcus alluded lightly to both his parents, who had been loved. Una knew that there was very little he could say, nothing firm about Nionia because there was nothing certain yet. He could only look and talk and act as if it were all right, as if it was right that he should be there, making wordless promises with the rhythm of his voice and the expression on his face. He could not have been more than a few hundred yards away, but watching him on the screen, that was hard to believe. The ring, hastily narrowed as Glycon had promised, was steady and visible on his hand, and the purple robe that had been hung over the new formal clothes was very dark, almost black, and of rough dense silk that stood around him in carved folds, constructing his body into extra, illusionary height and breadth. His hair had been trimmed and smoothed. He could have been five or six years older than he really was, or else of no specific age; young in a burnished, lacquered-over way, not raw or susceptible. He was not wearing the gold wreath, but it lay symmetrically on the desk in front of him, in the very centre, so that his body rose above it, in a column.

Of course they had known Marcus' face long before they met him. They could remember staring at him while he was asleep, that first night after finding him, that longvision face intruding into real life.

'Well,' said Sulien quietly. 'This is what he was brought up for.'

But the difference in Marcus alarmed him. He felt almost as if it were something he had inflicted upon him

When he'd first gone into the room where Faustus lay, the gilded space had been crowded with what seemed to Sulien's tired eyes a welter of important men, although some in fact were slaves, indistinguishable for a moment in the general shock from the secretaries, palace doctors, and even senators. More or less all of them were shouting at or around Sulien as he tried to concentrate, and they didn't all obey him at once when he told them to leave; one he even pushed physically from the room. Once he was alone with Faustus, lying with his face slack, still uttering a long rustling snarl, Sulien had emptied his mind of everything but his job: salvage work, trying to save a life. But when that was done he'd felt as if he had a decision to make, as if he were about to do something terrible to Marcus – and to his sister.

Really it was no choice of his, all he had to do was report how things were: that Faustus was alive, but that if Glycon – who had brought him there – had thought that Sulien could immediately wipe the injury out of Faustus' brain as if it had never been there, then he was wrong. But he had waited for a minute, as if hoping something else would happen, something to stop him, and he had watched Faustus with an attack of the too-acute pity that he often thought was a bad and amateurish feeling in any kind of physician. It was no good to get so bleeding-heart about things. In this case, for example, the pity for Faustus had become as intense and as indistinguishable from the idea of Marcus as if they were both mortally ill. He had left the room and said, 'Yes, get him.'

He rubbed his eyes and complained, 'I'm wiped out.' He'd been awake since before dawn, and when the peremptory call from the Golden House came – followed within minutes by a Palace car – he'd been about to walk the little way to his flat in Transtiberina and fall for a while onto his bed. His friends – students, apprentices, other young doctors, actresses, and, perhaps, Tancorix – would be in a wine bar somewhere, wondering where he was, but he was too tired now to worry about it much.

'Then go to sleep. They'll give you a room,' said Una.

'No.' He had left Faustus barely two hours before, before there had been time for Marcus to visit his uncle, so Sulien had not seen him. 'I want to see Marcus. Keep me awake.' But by now he had sunk from a sitting position to sprawl limply on the carpet, eyes half-closed, and grumbled when she obediently prodded his arm.

'Today I took an oath—' said Marcus, on the screen.

'Sulien,' asked Una, softly. 'How long is this going to last?'

Sulien pulled himself up onto his elbows, slowly. He did not answer at once. 'The Emperor will get tired very fast, much too tired to work,' he said, faintly defensively. 'He's lucky in that he doesn't seem to have lost any speech as such, but ordering his thoughts as he wants – he'll find that difficult. It's hard to explain. And he *can* recover. But it's hard for me to know how much, or how fast, and it's always possible it could happen again.' He recited this off pat; he'd been saying it all day.

Una frowned at the lack of a clearer answer, even though she hadn't really expected one, but she nodded silently. Sulien wasn't keeping anything back. And even that wary suggestion of an indefinite amount time meant something, she told herself. It meant no less than a year. But the upper limit ...?

Marcus' face vanished.

A grating little cry of anger and grief scraped through her teeth. She stood up, abruptly, and muttered, 'Oh, damn him.'

'Who?'

'The Emperor. Why can't he die properly?'

'Don't talk like that,' said Sulien, dismayed.

'All right, why can't he die or get better and leave us in peace? Either way would be better than this. For everyone.'

31

'Poor man,' demurred Sulien, uncomfortably, looking away from her. He was pretty sure Faustus would be dead if not for him.

'"*Poor man*,"' echoed Una, half with scoffing irony, half with a kind of experimental openness to contrition at what she'd said. She drooped a little, wearily.

She conceded, 'Yes, I suppose so.'

Sulien also got to his feet. They weren't children in a hiding place. The soft carpet under them glowed darkly with silks. Across the walls spread the coppery fresco of an orchard, the falling russet leaves touched here and there with real gold. Tending golden apples on a fragile bronze tree, the Hesperides crouched: gilded, secretive nymphs guarded by the low muscular length of a coiling dragon, rippling and cramped in its gold and auburn scales. Quite inconspicuous on a peak far in the background, Atlas could just be seen, bowed beneath the weight of the sunset sky. Two London slaves should have no right to be here. And even if Sulien had little capacity to feel out of place anywhere, he knew his sister did.

He asked, 'Will you stay here, with Marcus?'

'Yes,' said Una, her voice suddenly flat. 'At least as long as I can.'

'As long as you can? What do you mean?'

For a second her face seemed to flicker open, painfully and involuntarily, as she met his eyes, but then she looked away, at the room, and ran her finger over the arched back of a chair, trying to pinch a sardonic smile onto her lips. 'Well, I'll manage. At least they keep it clean. They obviously know where to buy decent slaves.' She held out the dustless finger, dropped it, then scrubbed at her face. 'Hundreds and hundreds of them.'

Sulien approached her, quietly. 'I just talk to them. Tell them where you come from. It's better that way.'

'But you have something to say because you're *doing* something. You can tell them about the clinic. What can I say to them? "Hold out, it's all going to change"?'

'Why not? When you were in London, when you were working in those places – if someone who'd been a slave had said that to you—'

'I'd have thought she could stick it. I'd have thought, you're out of it and I'm not, fine, but shut up and leave me to it.'

Sulien sighed. 'Is that what people think when I talk to them?'

Una looked at him quickly, suddenly remorseful. 'No. You're different.' Then Marcus came and had to knock on the locked door; they let him in, apologising, and saw that he looked exactly as he had on the longvision screen, which startled them, although of course they should have expected it.

Just before the broadcast Marcus had gone at last to see his uncle; and he came in thinking that he had to tell Una and Sulien what Faustus had said, quickly, because Una would know in a minute, anyway. He'd forgotten what he looked like until he saw the flicker of surprise on their faces. He pulled the gown off and threw it messily onto a chair, hugged Sulien, but kept on the ring because despite its weight he'd already forgotten it was there.

Faustus had fallen asleep even before Marcus had left the room. When he woke he made Makaria show him a few minutes of Marcus' speech before the longvision screen somehow dazzled him and he was knocked unwillingly again into sleep. But later he eased open his eyes slowly and peered into the hushed room. Half his body lay beside him, a weighty jumble of aching wood, the wreck of trees after a hurricane.

Marcus, sitting by his bed, had asked him, 'How do you feel?' and Faustus repeated sourly, 'How do *you* feel?' He was disgusted by the altered sound of his own voice; his tongue seemed to push against a dry barrier in his mouth, expecting every moment to clear it, but failing.

Marcus had looked confused and concerned, perhaps suspecting Faustus was parroting him mindlessly. 'I mean,' said Faustus, rankling at the idea, 'how are you taking to it? They've given you the axe and rods and everything, the ring, all of it haven't they – are you enjoying it?'

'No, of course not,' said Marcus.

'Have to enjoy it a bit, or you go under,' remarked Faustus, although he knew he was wasting time; he could feel that he had perhaps fifteen minutes to get anything serious said, before the obliterating exhaustion overtook him again. 'Oh, you'll be all right.'

'I hope so.'

'Too young though. I want Makaria and Drusus to help you.' Makaria gave an exclamation of surprise at this, but Faustus ignored it. 'And that's only fair. Got to try and be fair to Drusus, considering everything.' Because of course he knew how hurt Drusus must have been, when he named Marcus as his heir.

'All right,' agreed Marcus, though he felt a little stir of trepidation at the mention of Drusus. Marcus had barely seen his other cousin since his own return to Rome: a strained conversation on the longdictor – both of them pointedly skirting the fact of Faustus' decision – Drusus congratulating Marcus that his health was no longer in question after the horrible days he'd spent in the Galenian Sanctuary; an exchange of greetings at one of Faustus' birthday parties, that was all. Drusus was almost never in Rome now.

'And I know you've got all these plans, like Leo,' burst out Faustus suddenly. 'But you'd better remember this is a, this is a, this time is – what with the war ...'

'There isn't a war yet.'

'I *know*,' said Faustus, in almost a hoarse cry, and lay for a few seconds, glowering mutely. 'But you can't – knock it all sideways, not when things are like this.'

Marcus was silent for a while. 'You mean the slaves, don't you, Uncle?'

'It's all very well. I don't want to get back and have to deal with the mess,' said Faustus, as bullishly as his crooked voice would allow. 'Do what you like when you're Emperor, but you're not yet.'

'I know I'm not,' Marcus assured him quietly, though he was feeling more and more anxious. The truth of it was he thought Faustus was right. Rome could not bear the pressure of a possible war and the huge changes he wanted to make at the same time. He weighed what Faustus had just said and decided it was, intentionally or not, a warning: 'I don't want to get back and have to deal with the mess'. If Marcus outlawed slavery and if, during the aftershock, Faustus did indeed take power again, he might simply permit it once more. And then – Marcus wasn't even sure he could imagine becoming Emperor after such a failure, but if it did happen, how could you begin again, how would Rome tolerate it?

But he remembered himself asking Varius, 'How do I know I'd ever do the things I think I would? Perhaps it would always seem too difficult.'

Thinking stiffly over all this, it occurred to Faustus that he could just have given it up. 'Even when I get better, I won't take back the ring or the rest of it.' That would make things easier for Marcus.

Why, when he was so desperately tired, when so much of him would be so relieved to let it go, could he not bear the thought? In fact he was furious; he could have hit someone. He lay there and swore wrathfully, aloud, into the darkness. No, he did not want to! It was too bad! He wouldn't do it! He had been nearly forty when he became Emperor, but suddenly it seemed to him that between childhood and his accession, he couldn't remember much. He concentrated, alarmed that perhaps his memory had been damaged, maybe a whole third of his life was gone and he'd never get it back. Makaria's birth. Disappointment that she was a girl. Her little feet, however – yes, he could remember it, but it was hard work; he stopped and let his head fall back on the pillow with a sigh, and for some minutes had no choice but to lie waiting, empty, in the quiet dark.

Suppose he'd said he'd stay out of the way. Put out to grass. What then? He sneered at the idea of pottering around in a garden, like poor Lucius – but really all he saw when he tried to imagine a life outside the Golden House was another assault of nothing.

He pictured his nephew, and instead of the worried boy who'd been at his bedside a few hours before, he saw Marcus framed again on a screen with the ring on his hand – and despite himself, Faustus found he was overcome with dislike. A nasty little upstart; a young crook who'd done him out of his power and his health too, somehow. He knew distantly that this was cruel and unfair, that really he loved Marcus, but it didn't stop him: in his mind he shrieked viciously, 'Sorry to disappoint you, I'm still here! I'm not dying just because it's convenient!' – forgetting that he had been thinking about abdicating, not about death.

IV

DELPHI

At first the fact that his uncle was still alive seemed only a kind of technicality to Drusus; all he understood from the message was that it had happened, his cousin would be Emperor, not him, not even – for he knew what the will said – if Marcus died. He said the expected things and then, when he had turned off the longdictor, smashed the first thing that came to hand, which was a blue glass jug of wine, and he felt a moment of peace at the violence of the sound. There *must* be something that could be done, he wanted to plead. He crouched over the wet fragments and sobbed.

There was no one he could tell how wrong this was; not, above all, the one person – 'Oh, Tulliola,' he said, and pain dragged on his chest at the sound of her name, for he hardly ever dared utter it.

He stood up and destroyed the glass from which he'd been drinking as well, but it was too deliberate, there was no more relief to be had that way. There was a mirror over the mantel, and as he turned with another smothered cry, he was arrested by the sight of his own face, knotted in grief, and stared, the expression freezing there, involuntarily. So that is what you look like when you are suffering, he said to himself from far off as if watching through a telescope, as the face untwisted slowly, dully curious, gazed back.

He knew he would have to go back to Rome, but for now he assumed all that was required of him was a quick, dutiful visit, which would be painful. With Marcus victorious there and the memory of Tulliola, Rome was ruined for him.

He was in Byzantium, staying in a tall, rented mansion. He had always grown bored of houses quickly; he'd never settled anywhere even in Rome. But there the whole city had been his house, there he'd felt that there was no more need to confine himself in any one part of it than to shut himself up now, in a single room, for ever. He'd moved as he might cross the corridor or mount the stairs. It was true that Rome had a mark, a puncture at the centre of it – the shameful and ridiculous presence of his father, nestled in the Caelian house with Ulpia, coddling the stupid secret that had been inflicted also on Drusus himself. But it was Rome he loved. Now he felt driven wearily from place to place, because nowhere was right; almost every city was an imitation of Rome, but never a satisfying one. So he'd tried peace – beautiful places: the Istrian coast, Gomant in India – and he could see the beauty clearly enough; it would even lift him a little way, but what were you supposed to do in places like that? Within days he would be bored to death and lonely.

Of course he could easily surround himself with people anywhere – other young aristocrats and their lovers or slaves – but they circulated more naturally in a city, they did not turn as stagnant.

He tried calling his mother, but the slave who came to the longdictor told him she was busy and could it not wait until the usual time? She only expected to hear from her son twice a month, on the ides and the calends. Drusus blurted bitterly, 'Tell her I've got to come back to Rome and I thought she might want to see me, for appearances' sake.' But turning the longdictor off he felt angry for having forgotten himself so much – what was the use? And perhaps it was even true, perhaps she really was busy.

It was not that he did not have friends, not exactly that. But even if he really began to feel close to someone – Laureus, for instance, half-asleep on his sofa among the wreckage of a party, admitting drunkenly that he couldn't think about anything except the woman his brother had married and managing to make it sound funny. Drusus had laughed at him, but without wanting to, because for that moment he was delighted by how fond he felt of Laureus. And he had wanted intensely to offer the confidence back, almost just for the sake of fair exchange. Of course he could not. He must not say why and how much he missed his home, what he'd wanted, whom he'd loved.

He had a girl, too: 'Amaryllis' was the name she'd come with, though that was probably only a marketing gambit. He did not know what she called herself, and never used any name for her, or told her anything. As always when loss and panic hit him, he wanted her now, but he told himself, as he always did, that he wouldn't go to her, because he knew she did him no good. She was a vice, a habit. For most of the time he didn't want her in sight; she barely saw him except when he was most angry and distraught, so naturally she was afraid of him. But she wasn't so badly off, he considered. Most of the time she had only to take care of herself. He even kept away from her as much as he could. And he – he wasn't ugly, was he?

Of course, now, he did go and find her in the study, where, for all the time he didn't need her, he kept her looking busy, tending needlessly to unimportant papers. He pulled her up the stairs and to her room, paced outside her door while she got ready, shoved through the door while she was still pinning up her hair, pushed her down on the bed. They did not speak.

Afterwards he fell asleep, with her awake in his arms for a little while, but when he woke he felt worse, as he had known he would. 'You're really disgusting. You really are,' he kept repeating to himself silently, puzzled, wondering.

It had not been easy to find her. As well as the money it had taken months, repeated trips to all the markets – Delos, Sardis, Side – endless agitation and disappointment. Of course, the chances of finding something even adequate were small enough in themselves, for what he wanted was so singular, but it was harder because he didn't dare to explain very clearly. A clear, sweet, calm face, with cream-coloured skin. Darkly-fringed eyes. Black hair long and thick enough to be wound up into a high peak, and then pulled down again.

But she scared him, in some ways. For one thing, wherever he was and whatever he was doing, part of him was always rubbing anxiously at the idea of her, terrified that someone would see her and guess from her face and hair what had happened, what he had done. He was afraid someone else would see the clothes that he wanted her – just briefly, occasionally – to wear. He would have liked to believe she was slightly slow-witted and incapable of guessing herself. That was another reason that he didn't want her to talk.

For he did not want the substitution to go any further than looks, he didn't want her to *do* anything to imitate Tulliola, not even – especially not – to say 'I love you'. For one thing her voice was nothing like Tulliola's. And every time he slept with her, afterwards the resemblance would be more sickening than anything; he would realise how all the time he had been noticing all the many other things that were wrong, his body involuntarily measuring the texture and contours of hers – hips, waist, ribs, breasts, collarbone, the distribution of hard bone and soft flesh. She was slightly too tall. She was younger, yes, very young and fresh and all the things the trader had said she was, when Tulliola had been a little older than he was. There was a faint olive note to her skin – because after all, how rare to be as milk-skinned as Tulliola but with such dark hair. And Tulliola's hair had not been quite so straight. 'Amaryllis' might perhaps be partly Terranovan, though the plaited spiral he made her twist her hair into would leave an acceptable wave. Her jaw, the bridge of her nose – of course really there was not a single feature that was actually the same.

And even if she had been a perfect replica, what a strange thing to do, how horrible really. What would Tulliola think of him if she knew? But he could only manage to ration himself, he couldn't stop.

But this time, abruptly letting go of Amaryllis and standing up, he knew whom he could tell.

On the magnetway it would have been possible, though exhausting, to reach Rome in a single day. But, unlike Marcus, he had no one hurrying him back – there was no practical reason, he thought bitterly, for him to go at all. So there was no reason why he should not stop in Greece overnight, cross into Italy through the tunnel under the Hydruntum Strait the next morning.

He should have made an appointment, waited for days or even weeks, as he had done meekly enough before; but this time his name and his money were enough to let him bulldoze through all that. It was a sweaty climb in the heat, up past the treasuries of Delphi, but he did not feel his journey at all.

Far out on the sea, untouched and archaic, the sun had just thawed into a slick of fluid red, and Delphi was lighting up: a thick crust of many-coloured lava poured down to the sea. There were huge inns, and – for those who could not afford the true oracle but wanted some version of the experience – fortune-telling complexes, where one could play an electronic version of the Sinoan Book of Change, or consult crystal-gazers. Drusus could hear faint screams of excitement from the stadium above, invisible from where he stood except for its lights, where perhaps a horse race was going on. And, from the slopes below, some of the sprawling bath houses projected great water slides, winding down the mountain side and decked, in the evening, with coloured lamps, so the pilgrims to Delphi could speed deliriously past the city's sights, all the way down to the bay. Above Drusus – beyond the treasuries and the sudden stillness of the temple of Apollo itself, above the stadium – the mountainside was dark and pure for a little way, where it rose too steeply for human business to cling on. But as Drusus walked, right on the ridge of Paranassus itself, a line of hidden boilers suddenly disgorged a great screen of steam high into the dark blue air, and upon it a huge row of floating letters of light appeared, and pulsed, and changed colour – beaming the command out across the gulf of Corinth: VISITATE ORACULAM PERPETUAM.

Naturally he had a few bodyguards with him, and a pair of pilgrims, picking their way down the steps, recognised him and took his picture, though they would have got no more than a resentfully twisted pair of shoulders, a lowered dark head.

So close to the shrine itself, the relentlessness of Delphi softened a little – there were more temples, and no more places to buy holy water in bottles shaped like Apollo's lyre. But the way was nearly choked with self-promotion: outside the treasuries statues of athletes, politicians, magnates – many of whom Drusus had met – jostled close to the road, quite without order or design, grand as each work was. Some of the most recent were sculpted in chemical resin, with gleaming moist eyes and hair that stirred in the warm wind, and were shockingly lifelike, except that Drusus knew that paunches had been evaporated and jowls ignored. Images of his own ancestors should be here somewhere, near the top. Not all the figures were human; some were tributes from cities and provinces. Drusus passed between a pair of rampant bronze lions, snarling at each other across the path – nearly mythical beasts now. Drusus didn't know how much lions had really looked like that, or how big they had been, for the arenas had swallowed the last of them, and tigers too, three centuries ago or more. But Drusus had seen wonderful things done with Arctic bears, and of course with arena hounds. And once in a flooded arena he had seen men on flimsy little rafts, armed with spears and pitched against sharks.

He was supposed to tell the attendant priest his single question in advance, but all he'd say was, belligerently, 'I want to know what's going to happen.'

'Nothing more specific than that?'

'No. If there's anything in all this, then she'll know what I need to know.'

'I can interpret what she says for you. If you want it can be taken down, it can even be put into verse for you to keep.'

'*No,*' cried Drusus through his teeth, recoiling. He was already so impatient and overwrought that the priest's offer seemed like a deliberate insult or attack. 'Either I'm alone in there with her, or I go now. If you want my money you'll stop pestering me.'

The priest subsided obediently and Drusus watched with distaste while the man cut the throat of a shivering kid, averted his eye as it kicked, tapped his foot fiercely until they had finished with it and let him stride down into the chamber under the temple.

'You were wrong,' he said violently, at once. 'You remember what you told me? You got it wrong or you lied. You lied, didn't you? Do you realise what you've done? Really it's because of you ...' He stopped, shocked at himself. He'd been about to accuse her of Tulliola's death – and he could have gone on and blamed the others' on her as well, Leo and Clodia, Gabinius, and that woman – he couldn't remember her name – Varius' wife. Although most of these deaths, if he thought of them, he usually considered as immutable as if they had always already happened: acts of history, moving like a god, above human power or responsibility. It was only Tulliola who had been lost – sacrificed. The Sibyl could repeat what she'd heard, like anyone else, couldn't she? And at that it seemed ridiculous to think that she could know anything about the future, that she had ever made him believe anything.

'Wait,' said the Sibyl. She had gained weight. She had been heavy before, but her disorderly body now bulged through a shapeless pale-blue dress, somehow unabashedly naked under the cloth. The flesh on her bare legs hung in irregular mottled billows, her skin and dress visibly damp, because the day had been as sweltering as the weeks before it, and the braziers of burning laurel leaves kept the heat alive in the half-light. Her hair stood her round face in a muddy blonde frizz, but the features were harsh, hawkish, proud, an arrogantly curved mouth under vacant eyes that seemed almost the same colour as her skin and hair – a greenish, murky yellow ochre. She was pacing about, ambling barefoot in the dark. She yawned.

Drusus did not see why he was to wait; she did not seem to be doing anything. 'Do you even remember?' he demanded. 'Do you know who I am?'

'Emperor of Rome,' she answered loudly and thickly, and cleared her throat.

Drusus, despite himself, despite the cynical disgust at her and at himself, that he'd felt a moment before, shuddered with an intense pang of relieved joy. For a second a wonderful warm relaxation flowed through all his limbs, and he could almost have sunk to the dark marble floor and fallen asleep at her feet. Then he reminded himself. It must all be a sham. The priests could have told her he was coming; they could have done so even more easily the last time. He was the Emperor's nephew, it was hardly difficult to guess that he must have had some hope of being Emperor himself. That was why he was always so afraid that someone would see what he had seen, in his girl Amaryllis. He objected, but in a whisper, 'No, I'm not.'

'*Wait*,' insisted the Sibyl, forcefully, suddenly marching forward and making him start. For several minutes he was obediently silent, but so was she; she climbed heftily onto the tripod, a thin, flimsy-looking thing underneath her, and sat there, looking at him and did not speak. Her head seemed to roll a little on her neck; she blinked, her tawny-sallow face slackening.

'You mean – wait and it will happen? Still?' he ventured, at last. 'Not wait now for you to tell me? You mean – wait?'

'There's glass on the ground,' she remarked finally, her voice changing and rasping as she spoke.

Drusus felt another shock, trying to think if anyone could have told her that he'd smashed the jug and the wine glass earlier that day – one of his slaves, his bodyguards? 'The glass?'

'Wait,' she repeated, and then, on one breath, dying away to a garbled mutter, *'What you want it will be you the last one Novius it will come Emperor of Rome you.'*

It was like listening to a recording, it was almost four years since she had said that to him before. Then he thought she was beginning to say his name again: 'Novius'. And she did say it, many times, but she no longer seemed to mean it as a name, *novii, novissimi – newer, newest.*

'*The new*,' she said, a loud voice droning from deep within her chest. '*The newer newest. The newly come, no Novian but one. The newer branch of Novian stem. No Novian but another comes to ruin you. Save yourself from that, if you think you can.*'

'What do you mean?' he pressed. 'Is this someone who stops me from being Emperor? Because it's already happened.' He said this sardonically, as if it were too late even to care, but then asked, much more tentatively, afraid of being heard even by her, 'Do you mean I can still do something – I can still stop him? My cousin?'

'Your cousin, yes. Against you, afterwards—'

'You told me there'd be no one else!' protested Drusus.

'No one else left to take what you want,' she agreed, her voice sounding higher and softer, further off, and almost pitying.

Drusus shook his head. 'I don't understand,' he said. 'Are you warning me about something? My cousin won't stop me but he will?' He deliberated, and then observed coldly, 'Whether this is you, or if it's something else, a god talking – if you really know what's going to happen, why should that be the clearest you can put it? But I can see another explanation. You could just be trying to convince me you weren't wrong before. All this could be – a distraction. Perhaps you're afraid of what I'll do to punish you for what happened. Perhaps you *should* be.'

She sat passively, solid, unperturbed by this. She let her shoulders slump and her back round. The trance, if that had been real, seemed to be fading, leaving a peaceful apathy behind. She swung one large bare foot. 'What was the question?' she asked at length, sleepily.

'It wasn't a question at all, I wanted to make you answer for last time,' snapped Drusus, and then, thinking uneasily of what she'd said about the glass, 'Oh, I suppose I told the man outside that I wanted to know what's going to happen.'

The Sibyl nodded vaguely, but didn't seem to have listened. She scratched her thigh and watched her moving foot.

'It was, "Will I be Emperor? Still?"' he admitted at last, softly.

She sat up, jerking her foot still against the tripod, and looked at him again. 'And what have I said?' she demanded.

He couldn't tell whether or not she knew the answer, whether she was only trying to prompt him. '"Yes,"' whispered Drusus.

She shrugged, as if to say, there you are, then.

Drusus hesitated, opened his lips to speak, but did not. She *had* said that, hadn't she? He tried to think if she could have mistaken him for Marcus, if there were any other way he could have misunderstood her. Certainly it remained possible that she'd only ever been playing some kind unfathomable game or joke. But it was only now that he really understood that Faustus was still alive, that his cousin was not Emperor but Regent, that there was a difference. Perhaps Faustus would still change his mind – perhaps something more than that would have to happen.

She climbed down onto the ground, and yawned again. Drusus felt at a loss, seasick both with elation and with the suspicion that he was being practised upon. He did not want to leave yet, he wanted her to reassure him, clearly, lovingly. And he still felt a little like hurting her. But he'd had one question answered, and that was all he was allowed. But as he moved up the steps, something else occurred to him, and he turned back.

'How am I going to die?' he asked her, abruptly.

She blinked again and the emptiness cleared in her pale, dirty-coloured eyes; she raised her eyebrows and tilted her head, a faintly disapproving look, as if he should know it was wrong to ask her that. But she answered him anyway, quite normally and conversationally now: 'In your sleep. Of old age.'

The train sliced through the heart of the Empire, like a flexing bullet, an airborne snake, piercing the olive-clothed mountains, or lashing around their flanks like a whip. But Drusus sat, eyes unfocused, lips slightly parted, and did not see Greece and Illyricum vanish behind him. In Delphi he had commandeered three of the best-appointed carriages; his guards and the few slaves he had brought with him were divided between the front and rear, but in the centre Drusus was alone, and he barely even noticed the windows turn black when the train slid beneath the Adriatic Sea. No part of him moved except the hand that lay on the oak table, which kept drumming and tapping insistently. Several times, and almost without his knowledge, his forefinger drew out the word 'Yes' on the table top, as if in a dry and intangible ink.

Unmistakably she had said 'Yes'.

But I am not stupid, he thought grimly, as if giving an opppponent fair warning. He remembered the stories: Nero, still young, being told, 'Beware the seventy-third year' and duly expecting a long successful life. What else could Nero possibly have thought? It was Galba's seventy-third year that was meant, but there had been nothing in what was said to let Nero deduce that. So perhaps the warning the Sibyl had given Drusus was equally pointless. But if there is any way I will find it, he promised himself. And at least Nero had been Emperor first. Please, *let* me, he thought passionately. I don't care what happens in the end, I don't care if I die, just *please*.

But she had said he would not die.

So he meditated on the words of the warning for a while, but at last, with a little frustrated sigh, he decided that it was impossible that he should solve it now; the main thing was only to remember it. She had said, unmistakably, 'Emperor of Rome'. For the moment it was enough to think if it could be true.

There was Faustus' will. But if Marcus were to die in a way that was beyond suspicion – that could not possibly be blamed on himself or any Roman – surely that would be different. But – it was so unjust – even an unassisted accident would be no good to him now. And anyway, he had never been able to think of any such unimpeachable way, not after that what had happened before, not now so much was known about Leo's and Clodia's deaths.

He blinked with another start of shocked inspiration – Nionia! When the war came, as it was bound to, and Marcus died that way, surely no one would blame him for a thing like that! He saw himself standing haunted and noble amid the cracked pillars in the Forum, mourning his young cousin, promising to shoulder the burden, urging the people not to be afraid.

Drusus chuckled a little, guiltily. It was funny because it was shocking, treacherous – to be summoning a rain of Nionian bombs over his home, even in his imagination. Rome in flames, the Golden House shattered! Really it was so terrible that he giggled at himself for wishing it. Oh, no, really I would do anything to keep Rome safe, he thought, although it occurred to him in the same moment – with a bright, indistinct vision of huge unprecedented domes and arches – what I could build, afterwards!

He kept indulging himself furtively in the daydream and with each repetition, a warm swell of confidence burgeoned through him a little higher, as if he were becoming drunk. Involuntarily he added extra touches; in snatches he could hear the words he would say, the tone of voice he would say them in: 'We will always remember, but we will also ...' And less clearly – or equally clearly, perhaps, but very quietly – he allowed little swift, creeping notions of encouraging this to happen. If someone were to speak, just once, to the Nionians – if a body, dead already, were placed in a bombed building? It did not seem to him that he was contemplating having Marcus killed, or even that he had ever thought of that – it seemed that it would still all be the actions of others or of chance; he would have done nothing but place a slight pressure upon events, correcting them. At the moment he was merely trying to judge his own chances of becoming Emperor, counting the ways it could come. All this desolate, heartbroken time, when he could barely stagger from a day's beginning to its end – suppose it had all been needless, suppose he'd been only too *early*.

He blinked as the light reappeared outside the glass. He was in Italy, and nearly home. For the moment his head was completely empty of Tulliola and bliss flowed freely into the space. It grew so strong that even the secreted ideas about Marcus were silenced. It was as if he had removed restrictive clothes that he'd been wearing for years, had stepped into clean water. And of course, Marcus need not die. Perhaps the fact that he was Regent now was a good thing, the best thing that could have happened. Faustus was still alive to see that he had been wrong, and change his mind.

That morning, before he went to the temple, Drusus had called the Palace and learnt that his uncle wanted him to 'help' Marcus, somehow or other. At the time it had seemed insulting, a shabby consolation prize that made him want to shout his disgust into the longdictor. But now he thought, work! That's what I've been needing all this time! For of course there was so much to do, the whole Empire to keep steady – the war – and Marcus was so young. He could not really be more than a figurehead anyway; everything of substance would have to be done for him. He would, perhaps, even be grateful. Drusus actually began to feel rather affectionate toward Marcus; the indulgent patience appropriate to a younger relative, a harmless person.

He stepped out of the metal tube onto the platform at Vatican Field, whose mane of slim columns looked too slight and graceful to support the distant ceiling. The vast clarity of the largest magnetway station in the world was enough, already, to bring tears into his eyes. The Tiber was only yards ahead; in a moment he would see it.

A car from his father's house – his own house, really – picked him up, but Drusus did not feel like seeing his father yet; he wanted to get on with things. He told the driver to take him straight to the Golden House. A pleasant blast of cool air brushed his face as he got in, but he wouldn't have minded the natural heat, not here. He could stay in the Palace, but unless – until – it was his, he would rather have space of his own. He would have to order the place in Byzantium to be packed up. Suddenly he thought of the girl travelling to Rome with everything else, installed in his lodgings, and the image of her, the nearness of the thought of Tulliola swayed his happiness. The risk of someone interpreting the coded confession of Amaryllis' face would be so much worse in Rome. It would be safest to get rid of her altogether – sell her, free her even. But though the craving for her was not there now, he couldn't fool himself that it wouldn't come back. No, he couldn't give her up. She must never leave the house or the garden, he decided. She must never wear her hair up when he was not there.

As they drove over the Neronian Bridge, even though it was only an unattractive bundle of roads over the river, boiling with cars from the station, the feeling of joyous expectation settled over him again. He leant forward in his seat. The Golden House raised its glass towers above the Circus Maximus. The Praetorians let him through the carved façade and he bounded up the steps into the blue space behind the high windows. He went to the outer office.

'Tell my cousin I'm here – no, don't ...' he said to the aides in the same breath. 'Take me to where he is.'

He found to his surprise that he was being led downstairs again. Once they were past the hectic administrative stir on the first floor, there was a strangeness in the passages that he couldn't identify; a stillness. He walked into the banqueting hall, but the tables and couches had been pushed back against the walls, and the room was full of people. For a strange second Drusus did not recognise them – but they were the palace slaves, all of them. There must be four hundred at least. That was what he had missed in the corridors; not so much the presence of the slaves, but the subconscious sense that they had just darted out of sight. Drusus drew back a little. He felt suddenly vulnerable, outnumbered. Of course there had to be hundreds of slaves in the Palace, but not all gathered in one place like this.

Marcus stood at the far end of the room, still – as Drusus thought of it – dressed up as Emperor, with Makaria and Glycon and a few other people who did not interest him. Marcus noticed Drusus come in and managed a quick, minimal nod, without disrupting what he was saying.

'You don't have to decide now. The palace works very well because of you, so I hope you'll choose to stay. But if you don't want to work as

46

paid servants – if you've never wanted that, then from this minute you are free to leave, whether to look for other work, or for any family from whom you've been separated. We will give as much help as possible, whatever you decide.'

'Good heavens,' said Drusus ringingly from the back of the hall. 'What *are* you doing?'

Marcus frowned slightly, but did not look at Drusus again. He said straight into the crowd, 'And I apologise to each of you. I'm sorry you've had no choice but to stay here so long.'

In another mood, Drusus might have been outraged, but for now, although he was incredulous, he was amused too. It was so fantastic, so brazen as to be quite entertaining. At the same time he felt a little apprehensive, because what might the slaves do now that Marcus had said that, now they were all gathered in one place? They might riot. But even the danger seemed thrilling. He shook his head and beamed.

The slaves did not erupt into joy, as Drusus expected; they stared, nonplussed and sceptical, as if they suspected it was a joke. Then painful exhilaration did break from a few, who began to clap and hug each other and weep, and the rest picked up the applause, dutifully and doubtfully, but they were interrupted by Drusus striding through them to the head of the room, forcing them to fall aside and leave a path, instinctively.

'Drusus—' began Marcus, prepared to defend what he had done, but Drusus was already speaking loudly.

'You've got a nerve,' he said, laughing. 'They're not exactly yours to give away, are they? It's a bit – it's a bit *sly*! What do you think about this, Makaria?'

Makaria shrugged uncomfortably and said, 'I don't know.' She was looking at the slaves; not the hesitant or guarded ones, who were beginning to file out, but the others, the few ecstatic ones, who stood in small, breathless, oblivious circles. There was a woman in her thirties who no longer looked happy at all, but had buried her face in one palm, sobbing, and wrapped the other arm around her stomach, as if she were in pain there. A dark teenage girl soothed her uncertainly. Makaria muttered, 'It's going to be expensive, I know that. We'd better hope at least a tenth of them do leave.'

'Never mind!' exclaimed Drusus, and he enclosed Marcus in his arms.

Una was sitting on one of the dining chairs, watching. For three years she had been waiting with a predator's patience to see Drusus in person. Though he must have appeared in countless pictures, he was rarely the focus of the cameras which always sought out Faustus, or Leo and Clodia, or Marcus himself, so she had no strong sense of his face. But now she saw it, it was familiar. She was not prepared for how much he would look like Marcus.

Yet he was taller than Marcus, and the straight outline of his face seemed a little clearer or firmer for being framed with dark hair and eyelashes. The smile pulled higher on one side, as it seemed to do for all the Novians – on the right, in Drusus' case – and the lips were just as full, but Drusus' mouth was a long, firmly moulded double ripple, moving to a kind of deep peak at its centre. The large, heavily lidded eyes were not grey-blue but green, like Faustus' and Makaria's, and for the moment he was the more handsome, because his whole face was lit with ebullient well-being. He was slightly, becomingly flushed.

'Everyone says you were very good on the longvision,' continued Drusus. 'I wish I'd seen it, I was travelling. But I'm here now. It's so good to see you! It's been too long, we shouldn't have let that happen. But I wish it were in happier circumstances – such terrible news!' But he said all this so fast that his expression had no time to shift into appropriate sorrow.

Marcus patted his cousin's back and said, 'It's good to see you too,' but he was unpleasantly startled by the embrace. He could not remember seeing Drusus either so happy or so friendly towards him, and whether or not it was an act, he was taken aback by the cheerful force of it.

Una was startled too, because Drusus seemed not in the least un-comfortable, and the weird good humour was not only unforced but seemingly bottomless. Drusus was brimming with it: she could see nothing else in him, not guilt, not even jealousy.

Drusus noticed now that one of Marcus' hangers-on was incongru-ously young and female, and looking at him. He asked merrily, 'Who's this?'

'This is Una,' said Marcus, stepping back from him a little.

'Ah, yes,' said Drusus lightly, looking at her once and briefly wonder-ing why he had wasted curiosity on such a mousey, unattractive person. He felt mild scorn and pity for Marcus. If he had not known she had been a slave he would have looked at her quite differently, and yet this was not in the least because he considered slave-girls untouchable, of course not (there was Amaryllis) – quite the opposite. Because he knew the young woman had been a slave, he expected a higher standard of beauty from her. If Marcus was going to amuse himself with a girl like that, why choose such a pallid one when he could have got something so much better – anything he wanted? Involuntarily he drew the com-parison: he saw Amaryllis' fresh face, and winced.

'Yes,' echoed Una, smiling prettily. She looked away from him politely but went on concentrating, trying to probe after the flash of a face that had shot through the contentment, but it seemed to dive and vanish with bewildering speed before she could touch it, like a fish dodging the claws of an osprey.

She had expected that it would be easier to tell if he were a murderer.

POSSIBLE DEATHS

Marcus walked away from the hall, feeling a slight, unexpected depression, as if he'd wanted something more from the occasion. Most of the slaves' lives would probably not be much different now, he reflected. Really it was because of that he'd been able to do it. Still, Una murmured to him, 'Thank you.' They were already perfecting a way of talking to each other in short, whispered bursts that were not detectable even from quite nearby, because the movements of their faces were minimal, and they kept walking without turning to look at each other.

'I wanted to do it. I couldn't work here otherwise,' he said. This was true, but what he had done was also a kind of present and apology to her and to Sulien nonetheless.

'But when you are Emperor, then you *will* do it then?' she'd insisted the night before, when he'd told them what Faustus had said.

'Yes, I promise,' he'd answered. 'It was because of this my parents were killed, and Gemella – and us nearly – and I was stuck in that place in Tivoli. Of course I won't give it up.' He'd felt ashamed of mentioning the time in the Sanctuary alongside three deaths – he'd been there less than two days, but he still remembered it is as far longer. The drug in his blood had stretched the time unrecognisably, and the horror had been total.

He glanced at Una now, because he was aware of a small abstracted frown on her face, and though she'd said only two words, her voice sounded odd, too, faintly laboured, as if it required a deliberate allocation of effort. 'Are you all right?' he said.

Her frown deepened thoughtfully and she took a breath to answer, but she let it out silently as Drusus pushed forward to walk beside him, and only nodded.

'Was the journey horrible, Drusus?' Marcus asked.

'Oh, hellish, but it doesn't matter,' said Drusus airily. 'But you look awful, Marcus. It must be overwhelming. You didn't sleep last night, did you?'

'No, not really,' Marcus admitted. He and Una had lain all night in each other's arms, tense, eyes open.

'No, of course not,' agreed Drusus regretfully. 'I want you to tell me how I can help.'

'All right,' said Marcus. He stopped briefly to face Drusus. 'We've had as many people die in fires this summer as we lost yesterday on the Wall. We don't seem to be able to do anything about these forest fires in Terranova and Gaul, and there have been some terrible house fires around Rome, too. I don't know when I'm going to be able to read the reports. It would help if you could do that: find out if it's arson, if it's because of the heat, if there's something that's not being done. I wondered if the people who should be working on it have got too isolated from each other. Can you get them together and find out?'

Drusus did not answer at once, although his face remained fixed unnaturally in an expression of friendly eagerness to help. 'Very well,' he said at last. 'Of course I'll do that. But Nionia – what does Salvius say about our next move?'

Marcus turned away again and walked on. 'Our next move is waiting to see how the Nionians respond to the message I sent this morning.'

Drusus face began to rearrange itself slowly into a detached, quizzical look. 'Oh?'

'About peace talks in Bian,' explained Makaria.

Now it was Drusus who stopped in his tracks. He stared at Makaria. 'Is that even an option at this stage?' he demanded, and then broke briefly into a run to catch up with Marcus again.

'Well, obviously it's an option, Drusus,' retorted Makaria.

'And you won't listen to another view, Marcus?'

'I *have*, I will,' said Marcus, with faint violence.

'About rewarding them for an attack against us?'

'We seem to have killed an awful lot of them,' interjected Makaria again.

'It's hardly a reward,' said Marcus. 'I don't know if they'll even trust us enough to listen. It wasn't something they were expecting.'

'Well, how do you know that?' asked Drusus, sounding very reasonable and adult now. 'If it's because they couldn't have known you'd be in charge, then isn't that an admission that this isn't what Uncle Titus would do?'

Marcus stopped again, struggling to sound equally rational, for he felt like shouting, 'That doesn't *mean* anything.' The sleeplessness of the night before was battering his eyes. 'I don't know what he would do. I can't do things for that reason.'

Drusus passed a hand over his face. 'No, I know you can't. But there has to be – there must be – discussion. You do need advisors, Marcus.'

'I know I do,' Marcus said.

'I've been thinking. We had better meet every morning.'

Marcus began to walk again. 'I'm meeting someone now, Drusus. I'm sorry.'

'Well,' protested Drusus, 'if you're having a meeting, shouldn't I be there? If our uncle has asked me to advise you, that's an instruction to you as well, isn't it? Or do you propose to ignore it?'

'I'll be back in an hour. This isn't a Palace meeting. I'm going over to Transtiberina.'

'Oh, Marcus,' said Drusus, finally openly exasperated. 'Don't waste everyone's time. Whoever it is, pull him over *here*. He can't very well refuse, can he?'

'He might,' said Marcus, walking ahead with Una, leaving Drusus decisively behind.

Una lagged along beside him, looking back over her shoulder.

Varius was at his desk. There was no breath of air from the windows at his side, and he felt a treacherous little urge to make sure they really were wide open, to go and see if they could be pushed any further. He resisted it. He could remember opening the windows. He mustn't start doing things like that, checking things he knew he had done. He did not look up from his work.

The sterilising boiler was broken. They needed – they always needed – more money. He was trying to school himself out of a slight impatient disdain for these tasks. They were not beneath him, as he realised he was dangerously close to feeling. They were important.

In the corridor outside his office he could hear two of the doctors talking in distracting detail, because his door was gaping open too. Sulien and the others who worked in the clinic had learnt that this did not necessarily mean he wanted anyone to come in. So he got up now, went briskly to the door and pulled it to. But before he had even reached his desk again he knew it was useless; he had such an oppressive sense of being locked in that he could attempt nothing until he'd turned and pushed the door open again. He even had to walk through into the corridor, smile pleasantly at the doctors – it would be unfair to ask them to be quiet; they were tired, they weren't doing anything wrong – before turning back.

Oh, *stop this* now, he thought irritably, standing in the centre of his office. These habits that had grown upon him – it was as if someone were repeatedly making an insultingly obvious point, and would not be silenced, no matter how doggedly Varius answered yes, *yes*, all *right*, I understand.

He saw the doctors walk past his door, leaving the corridor quiet, and was able to concentrate again. He arranged for the boiler to be repaired; he wrote a letter.

His wife had died. He had been locked up, interrogated. He had expected to die as well. More than that, he'd been convinced of it, deliberately so; the certainty of death had been a weapon, a tool, a consolation, finally. But then everything, *everything*, he had expected had been overturned. Or had just been wrong, not to mince words about it. The aim of it all of course had been to make him say where Marcus was. And he had done so, in the end.

He was sick of thinking and thinking over it, for *years* now, trying to see exactly how it had been done, how it could have gone differently. He thought it was like this: like taking apart an engine, say, or a clock, neatly and methodically, breaking nothing, displaying the separated components, as he had heard torturers displayed their implements at the start of the session. But then, when each part lay tidily, separate, flat – and although all this had been done on the reasonable understanding that it was final – the pieces were somehow made to re-assemble, and they did, and the thing still largely worked. But now in each joint was the proof that this need not be so, that it was not inevitable that the clock, the engine should run. It – he – knew that it could stop at any time. Whenever it liked.

Torture had been one of the things he had expected, which had not happened. Not exactly, not as such. Varius did not think the things that had been done to him qualified. But torture, and the ways he had tried to prepare himself for it, were part of the structure of things now, subtly tangible, everywhere.

About six weeks into the foreign and inexplicable time afterwards, while he was still navigating the daytime by striding around the city, as committed as if it were a job – it was about then he'd started noticing how difficult it was to tolerate a room for long without clear and certain ways out. But he *had* tolerated it; he had made this *stop* – for months, for more than a year, which seemed to count for humiliatingly little now. He'd given himself no time, to care about windows or doors or the things he'd been forced to know about himself, because he was feeding the clinic. Marcus' parents had wanted to build a place where ill or injured slaves who might otherwise have been left to die could be treated for free. But it had nearly come to nothing after Leo and Clodia's deaths, and everything that followed. It had been left so fragile, so endlessly and querulously hungry – even more for his time and thoughts and strength than for money. And at first he did not feel that he had much of any of these things, except for time, but the need was so bad that he produced them somehow, although wearily and dutifully to begin with, as if he didn't really expect anything to come of any decision he made, any sum of money he spent. But the walls went up. The place was real, it worked. Varius was amazed, even exhilarated. And it occurred to him: no one needs to be happy, only interested. That is all that's required. And the excitement and relief at the thought were, for a little while, almost happiness in themselves.

But he kept uneasily remembering what Gabinius had promised him, during the worst time of his life: you will feel better one day. He did not entirely like the fact that the prediction seemed to be right. It was something Gabinius could not be made to surrender, even in death – a wisp of power.

Surprisingly soon after his wife's death people began encouraging him to look at other women, even tried to arrange meetings for him with sisters or friends. When a year had passed – almost the day after the anniversary, it seemed to him – this small mutter of suggestions became suddenly clamorous and insistent. To his outrage, his parents joined in. They would start dropping a young woman's name into conversation and innocently praising her, and then they would make him come to some small party and the young woman would be there. They would try and steer him towards her, leave them alone together. It was the more galling because they really seemed to believe that he did not know what they were doing. Varius resisted, out of fury at first, and later, when he was still angry but more resigned, on principle and out of habit. He reminded himself that his parents were trying to help; he did not always give the others so much grace.

He met another widower, once, who blurted out, nearly weeping, 'You lose friends, don't you? People avoid you. I suppose they think it's infectious.' Varius was surprised by this, and did not know how to answer, because though it was true that his group of friends had quietly thinned, and not only those who tried to matchmake him he knew that he was the one responsible. It wasn't that he liked being alone, quite the contrary; the little time he spent at home in the evenings before going to sleep was horrible. But it was Gemella that he wanted then; remembering what you were supposed to do with other people was possible, but tiring. He had spent most of the time in the prison, and at Gabinius' house, trying not to be a person at all. The best thing was to be – as he was at work – in a room in a building full of people that he liked, but who diluted one another.

But perhaps he had paid more attention to his parents and the rest than he'd thought, or at least that was one of the ways he could account for what he'd done. Why hurt someone so unnecessarily? Was it a sort of arrogance, that because the clinic was going so well, because all this time had passed and things were all right, he'd believed that this was another thing he could just do? As well as the more obvious reasons of physical need, and the quiet at nights.

Octavia still lived in his building. Coming and going they greeted each other civilly, but even after eight months she looked so miserable at the sight of him that he thought, sooner or later one of us will have to move. What had been between them had finished almost at once, but it had been no less disastrous for that. Even now he couldn't shake the tainted feeling that Gemella was no longer the last woman he'd touched, made love to.

She must have been in the flat next to his for weeks before he noticed her one afternoon, crouched outside her door, desperately sorting through a little heap of things she'd laid out from her bag. In a vague way he realised that she was attractive, more clearly he saw that her face was taut with panic.

'Are you locked out?' he asked.

She looked up with an agitated nod. 'Would you let me try your key …?' she began, then uttered a little gasp of angry self-reproach. 'That's not going to work, is it?' She went through her possessions again. 'My family's coming,' she said with a certain grimness. 'Oh, they'll love this. Do you know a locksmith?'

'They cost a fortune if you want it done the same day.'

'Really?'

He doubted she could afford it; the flats in the block were small and cheap. The salary he paid himself now was less than what he'd earnt as Leo's private secretary. 'Don't worry.' He opened his own door, let her follow him in and went out onto the battered little iron balcony, which overlooked only a yard with a single tree and some dusty cars.

'What are you doing?'

'I'll go through and let you in. Your windows aren't locked, are they?' He'd put his foot on the bottom rail.

'What? You're not going to climb across? You can't, you'll kill your-self,' she said.

'No, I won't.'

In fact, as he stepped over the railing onto the outside edge, he felt how it would be to drop, twist in the air; he saw an improbably garish swoop of red blood as the ground below smashed up through him. He sighed. These abrupt visions of possible deaths – always violent and usually slightly ridiculous – offered themselves to him annoyingly, on the prompting of the most ordinary incidents and sights: pens, bottles of cleaning products, razors of course, and knives of all kinds, the electric hedge-trimmer he saw a slave using on the Caelian. Often the flashes seemed to have nothing whatsoever to do with him. A fence post, for instance, flung into the air by an unexplained explosion, hurtling like a javelin across the street and pinning him to the wall through the heart – this when the sunlight was pleasant, the day was going well and he didn't especially want any such thing to happen.

'Come back. I mean it. Please,' said Octavia behind him.

'It's all right,' he assured her. He stretched his arm around the corner of the building to grasp the bars of Octavia's balcony and stepped easily across. They were only two floors up. Probably he'd do no more than break his legs. In any case he knew he wouldn't fall.

He walked through a sparsely furnished flat, bleaker-looking than his own, and opened the front door to find her standing there, looking both intensely grateful and appalled.

'Thank you. Thank you, but if you'd fallen because of a *key* ...'

'It was fine, really,' he said, walking back to his own flat and already forgetting about it.

She called after him, 'I'm Octavia, by the way.'

He told her his name, and saw her face change very slightly. She'd worked out who he was.

That week she had a copy of her key cut and gave it to him. 'I do this all the time,' she warned him.

Later he discovered that she was divorced and that her family were vocally disappointed in her because of it. And it was true, she did seem to get herself locked out a lot. She also brought round letters of his that had gone to her by mistake. It seemed idiotic now, but for months none of this meant anything at all to him. He liked Octavia; he could sit in her kitchen sometimes and listen to her, and was glad to put off shutting himself in the flat and going to bed. The nights were worse now than before, because often he heard a baby crying overhead. He and Octavia could complain companionably about it to each other. But he scarcely thought about her when she was not there. Although she was the only one of his neighbours whom he had anything to do with, still his time at home was as small a part of his life as he could make it. Even when he was there for a whole day, he only thought of it as a place to sleep.

One evening, though, home earlier than usual, he found he was climbing the stairs with a man who lived on the floor above his own. It seemed they had spoken more than once before, for this man – around his own age, with a pale, prim face – called him by name and knew about the clinic. Varius on the other hand simply couldn't remember anything about him, could not even have picked out this face as being in the least familiar. He wondered if this might be the father of the baby, in which case the decent thing would be to ask about it, but the risk that this was someone else entirely was too great. He walked up the stairs as fast as he politely could, aiming to get to his own flat without betraying the fact that he didn't know the man's name.

The man knew Octavia too, which was not unexpected, Varius knew she wanted to be friends with everyone in the building; he thought that was the main reason he saw so much of her. Because of this though, he was a little surprised that the other man should need to ask after her.

'She's well,' Varius replied.

'Are you going to make it official?' The tone was odd – trying to sound light-hearted, but faintly censorious.

Varius made an enquiring noise, not realising they were still talking about Octavia.

'Well, she's ... Octavia is a decent, a *good* – she *shouldn't* be ...' Varius' neighbour exhaled; he was genuinely bothered about this. 'She must feel – not respectable. I don't mean any criticism. But she's plainly not happy.'

'What?' asked Varius, and realised not only what the man meant, but the reasons for it, in the same instant as he saw the other man realise his assumptions were wrong. They both blinked and looked at the floor in confusion.

'Did she *say* to you that we ...?' began Varius, alarmed at the idea.

'No!' interrupted the neighbour, hastily, blushing now. 'No. But we thought – we always see you together. And she ... Well ...'

'We', noted Varius, so he was probably married, and probably the man with the baby; there weren't that many couples in the block. At least that much was cleared up. 'I see. No, Don't worry about it.'

It was December, but he went out onto the rickety balcony, looking across towards Octavia's. He thought back over her visits with the post and for her keys and saw that they were transparently excuses to see him. He seemed after all to have registered certain things about her smile and way of talking to him, and kept them stored until he could attend to them. He found he remembered their conversations more clearly now than he'd experienced them when they were actually happening. He could see her face more sharply, too, than he'd ever seen it when she was there.

When he next saw her, he watched her with more attention than

57

before, observing that he did like her, that she was pretty, intelligent. And a good person. They walked together down towards the river. Now that he was alerted to it, it was clear what the upstairs neighbour had seen. There was a vividness about her that rose when she looked at him and slackened off visibly when she looked away. It was flattering, if a little baffling, to have that effect on another person. It made Varius feel obliged to her. She didn't deserve to be unhappy because of him. When, between their two doors, they were saying goodbye, he bent his head to hers and kissed her lips. Startled and delighted she put her arms round his neck and they kissed more deeply, for longer.

A little while later she confessed to him, 'I'd been telling myself to give up.'

Varius found that the pleasure from the touch of lips on his was overwhelming, but he felt strange afterwards, a kind of dry quivering in the nerves that he couldn't name. He thought it would wear off. But it didn't. It gathered to a horrid and familiar restlessness, a fear that wherever he stood or sat or lay down might be a trap, and he could not quiet it by working, as he had done before, because there was no real urgency or difficulty left in the slave clinic now. For the first time he realised how routine his job had become, that he must have been manufacturing a burden of work that was not altogether necessary for some while.

And after they slept together for the first time it was far worse. He lay awake in her bed, with her warm arm over his chest. The baby wept and screamed somewhere on the floor above, for hours.

He had never shared the flat he lived in now with Gemella, but unlocking his door afterwards he seemed to expect to walk into their old rooms. He did not quite feel that he would find her there – she would be over in Tusculum, arranging a party perhaps, helping Clodia with a speech. Clodia would be working her hard, as ever. He would sit on their bed and wait for her to come back, trying to decide if he should tell her what he'd done. He went in and found himself in tears because it was not the same, because Gemella wouldn't come home. 'I'm sorry, I'm so sorry,' he said, aloud. Because he knew this wasn't reasonable, he carried on, although he managed to control things so that they were never in his flat together, only Octavia's.

He grew preoccupied with wondering why she wanted him, why she was, apparently, in love with him. She knew the gist of the events around Gemella's death and Marcus' disappearance. Everyone knew. Varius' picture had been screened on longvision over only a few days – not enough for people to recognise him in the street – but often his name would do it, and if not, they only needed to hear what his previous job had been, that his wife was dead, and then they would remember.

It was a fact he hated. He could *feel* people knowing, whether or not it showed in the way they treated him.

As for her, why should she have liked him so much when all she knew about him was that his wife had been killed, that he had first been said to be a murderer, then not; when – he thought resentfully – that was indeed the main fact of his life. Was *that* attractive? Perhaps to her it was. In which case the whole thing was ghoulish and unhealthy. He found himself thinking about this more and more; at first only when they were apart, but later in her presence, too. For it seemed to him the only explanation – that she *liked* the idea that something horrible had happened to him, that she found him romantic because of it. When what he had meant to be was simply a conscientious, happily married civil servant. When what he manifestly was now was unjust, ungrateful and malicious – because look at the way he was thinking about her.

She did not ask about his past – not that part of it, anyway. Sourly he wondered if she were hoping that he would break down and volunteer everything dramatically, weep and wail. He found it increasingly hard to say anything to her at all.

Gemella had been dead now longer than they had been married. The thought was intolerable, but intolerable also was the fact that it didn't seem to be true. When he slept he kept waking up as he had woken in the prison hospital. All the time that had passed since then was a delusion. He was still there. It had just happened. She had just died. And all the rest of it still to go through. He did not know how he, or anyone, managed to breathe in their sleep. It seemed to require such a conscious exertion of will, like working a stiff pair of bellows, day in and day out, without the possibility of rest.

He now neither believed that the affair with Octavia could be salvaged nor wanted to do it. He had said nothing to her of what he was thinking. But it was so constant, and the most ordinary elements of conversation – where shall we eat? What did you do today? – felt so unnatural and needed so much physical effort, that he supposed it was bitterly obvious, that she must have expected something like this. But apparently not. She was shocked; her eyes sparkled with tears, which she tried to conceal at first but had to give up because it was a long time before she would stop trying to retrieve something of him. She mentioned Gemella by name for the first time, she guessed that perhaps he felt guilty, but that he shouldn't, he was not, it would change …

No, No, he said. It would not.

'All right,' she conceded at last. 'Then I understand. But I do want to *see* you, at least – after all, we have no choice, we live next to each other. We were friends, before.'

He said that he was sorry, he didn't think this was possible. Afterwards he was not sure if this had been sensible or if he'd just rejected a reasonable human thing. She looked so grief-stricken; he was again baffled that he could have meant so much to her.

But when this was done, though there was a mild relief at one less effort to make, it went on: an unfluctuating torrent of nights where he felt his pulse go and go and go and wanted to slot his fingers between his ribs to hold it still. The only comfort was a kind of bleak satisfaction at Gabinius' expense. He thought, there, you bastard! You were wrong, I knew you were.

After eight months, it was better again, although he was not sure why or how. But he couldn't train himself again to leave doors alone. In a way he was glad of the heatwave; everyone had to have all the windows open if they were to sleep, not just him. Although really he did not need an excuse for doing as he liked, there was no one else to consider.

He had only just turned thirty. He could not quite let himself say, I will never marry again. I will never even touch another woman again. But he wanted to, in a way, to say this once and for all. It would be a relief.

An hour before he'd heard from the Palace that Marcus was coming to see him, if that was convenient, but he didn't know why. On the excuse of going to see if Marcus had arrived yet, he went downstairs, past the patients waiting in heat-weakened huddles in the lobby, out into the sunlight.

Drusus more or less dragged Makaria into a side room. 'I didn't expect this of you,' he began.

'Well, why not?' asked Makaria.

'Because you're not a child!' cried Drusus, and broke off, flushing, his eyes widening at the mistake he'd almost made. It was absurd, but he'd almost added, 'You're not a woman!' as he would have done if he'd been having this conversation with a man. For he had genuinely been talking to her as simply another person. It would have been, as far as he was concerned, an involuntary compliment to her in that she seemed partially exempt from the normal requirements for dealing with women.

He mumbled instead, because he had also been thinking resentfully of Marcus' mother, that so much of this was her fault. 'You're not Clodia.'

He surveyed his cousin anxiously. It was not that she looked like a man, of course, but, despite the plainly Novian and handsome features, despite the natural and unconscious manner of authority, she did not look like the kind of woman one might expect to meet in the Golden House. Her skin was very tanned, and so she looked, perhaps, older than she need have done. Her stiff short hair, the same colour as his own, spread in a fan around her face. She was square-shouldered and neither slim nor plump, but angularly sturdy looking. Behind her the wall was hung with glowing Scythian tapestries, an Indian carved plaque of a blue-skinned Apollo Krishna among nymphs. Against this background Makaria's clothes – a straight, calf-length skirt, a loose tunic – were weird and anomalous, being obviously expensive if looked at in any detail, but coloured and shaped like peasant's clothes. She wore a plain gold chain and little round amethyst earrings; she might have been a farmer or perhaps a colonel in the army.

Really she was a farmer. The thought depressed him. The real reason he had not expected any difficulty from her was that he could not remember a conversation about politics or warfare in which she had been more than sullenly non-commital.

Makaria said, 'No, I'm not. But look, I used to try not to get worked up about the Wall, because there wasn't a thing I could do. And I never thought people would really be this stupid when it came to it, but apparently they are.'

Drusus made an effort not to snap back angrily at the insult. 'Makaria. Sooner or later there's bound to be a war whether we like it or not; all we'll manage to do now is postpone it. And then when it does come it'll be worse; more people will die. But we can win now, and after-wards—'

'What, are you saying it'll all be over in a flash and we'll scarcely notice?'

'Of course not.'

'And everlasting peace afterwards? Well, I suppose if you managed to kill everyone, that would be true in a way.'

'No, but think of Tupia, or further back, Persia – they're integrated now, aren't they? Stable. That what Terranova needs to be – what the *world* needs to be. Look, we are really the ones your father meant to stand in for him, aren't we? To keep an eye on Marcus. So, for *his* sake we can't keep telling him different things.'

'I can't pretend I think you're right if I don't,' said Makaria.

Drusus gave up on her with a little sigh of exasperation. He went into the south-west tower of the four that rose from each corner of the Golden House, and took over the offices that had been Leo's. In dis-gruntled obedience he had the fire reports brought to him. He lifted a page and held it before him, staring at the picture of a blackened room, the husk of a villa for a moment or two, before casting them down in fury. He strode out of the room to go and see Faustus.

Marcus had just entered the clinic, and because of this the Praetorians were trying to keep someone out; the urgency and indignation with which he tried to rush between them counted against him. Marcus shouted, to little seeming effect, 'What are you doing? Is there someone hurt? Let them in!' It was finally one of the Praetorians who brought the patient in, for the man had been carrying something, someone, draped awkwardly over his shoulder, and abruptly he managed to unload the motionless body into the guard's arms and then fled.

For a while the Praetorian had to hover, reluctantly cradling the incomplete bundle of bones, before the doctors came with a stretcher and he could lay it down with an involuntary, revolted backwards step. Varius understood, because as well as the ripped and burnt flesh, what he had been holding was so filthy – Varius could guess already that the scalp and clothes would be seething with lice – that it was a moment before the eye could even judge the figure's sex. But it was a woman, or a girl; her age difficult to guess because she was so thin, and because the deep brown skin of her face crumpled and split into a terrible bedlam of raw pink and ash white, which whorled across her cheek and the torn pit of her right eye. There was an odd bloom of bright yellow staining the black hair and the flesh – where it remained intact. Her left hand, with its missing thumb, was gloved in the same violent colours. The right arm descended below the elbow into a dark spray of wet rags, and stopped. There were patches on her chest and sleeve where her clothes seemed to have melted onto her skin.

Varius saw Marcus and Una flinch. He knew, and would advise anyone that came to work in the clinic, not to let cases like the mutilated girl touch you too closely. And he found this easier himself than, in a way, he would have liked. He was certainly angry. But whatever else he felt at such spectacles of pain seemed to be happening too far off to be properly detectable, like the movement of a windmill in the distance. And he didn't feel as if he were useful to this girl, despite the fact that he was the one who'd raised the clinic. He was not a doctor. There was nothing he could do for her.

'Veii,' he said. 'Again.' He turned impatiently to the Praetorians. 'Who brought her here?'

But the man was gone.

'What's in Veii – a factory?' stammered Marcus, transfixed as the girl was borne out of sight. He felt sick.

'Yes, it produces girls with no hands and no eyes,' said Varius starkly. More evenly he explained, 'Veii Imperial Arms. The detonators go off while they're packing them – all the time.'

The first time he'd seen a slave's skin stained yellow he'd thought it must be some kind of jaundice, but it was the explosive powder, which not only dyed the skin, but raised sores on it too.

'At least someone bothered to bring her here. It won't have been the factory. They know damn well we're here, but they still just dump them outside the gates. They don't tell us.'

Part of the clinic's purpose was to stop slave-owners from doing this, to leave them no excuse – no reason. Many of the patients were house slaves, who were often treated comparatively well by their owners and came in with normal illnesses or after ordinary accidents. But the casualties from the factories were so much worse that often the proprietors evidently saw no cause to expend even small amounts of time on slaves that they plainly could not use again. Veii had always been the worst, but in the last two months or so it seemed to have been getting worse still; the injuries were even more horrific, and more frequent.

Una said, 'Sulien's got to come back here.'

Sometimes Varius saw Una at the clinic, for she would come round to meet Sulien; but he did not know her well. She seemed less uncanny when he saw her with Marcus. Alone, waiting for Sulien in the lobby or sitting outside on the steps, with her pale face and hair and her black eyes, she remained faintly disturbing. The first time he'd seen her, in Faustus' rooms at the Palace – an unexplained dishevelled girl lying asleep on the Emperor's couch – she'd woken up and turned into a kind of apparition announcing that it was Tulliola who'd killed his wife.

'He can't be here all the time,' he told her.

'I know. Has anyone died here because he's been at the Golden House?' she asked, and then added unnervingly, 'They have, haven't they?'

Varius was slightly chilled, because the memory of a livid body with only occasional patches of odd, anomalous clear skin, had jumped into his mind. He said, 'There was a man with burns. From the same place as that girl. I don't know if Sulien could have saved him, but if he could, then perhaps it's as well he wasn't here.'

He could have explained, he could have spelled out wearily, 'The man was in agony. He could never have worked again. His life was finished.' But though Marcus flinched again, Una only nodded slowly, and it seemed to Varius that he had somehow expected that of her. 'Don't tell Sulien that,' he said to her.

'No, I won't,' said Una. She remembered Varius sitting in the centre of Faustus' rooms, almost motionless in his chair but not inscrutably so, visibly tense and restless underneath it. He was better at it now, she saw. He had learnt a kind of strict economy of movement, remaining so effortlessly still that you could mistake him for an unusually peaceful man. Most of the time, he barely even moved a hand without it looking necessary – like a well-rehearsed actor.

'Can I talk to you?' said Marcus to Varius. They went upstairs and Una wandered into Sulien's empty surgery to wait.

She thought about Drusus: I *will* know all about you, soon. She needed more time, that was all.

Drusus was surrounded by a fresco of birds arrested in flight, hushed by the dimness in the room. He stood in the near dark over the wide, silk-spread bed and studied Faustus' face carefully, glad of the chance to examine him while he slept, but the truth was that at present there was little obvious sign of his illness, except a greyish pallor. The familiar vision of Tulliola in that bed, beside his uncle, in those arms, that had so often troubled Drusus when she was alive, forced itself upon him. He took and expelled a shuddering, nauseated breath.

'Uncle,' he said, unable to bear it. He tried to recall the feeling of happy receptiveness to fate that he'd felt only hours before, to clear Tulliola again from his head.

Faustus stirred and muttered, and Drusus said again, compassionately, 'Uncle.' He sat on the bed and took Faustus' hand. 'Do you feel any better than yesterday?'

Faustus gave a little grunt of helpless disgust. 'Can't walk. Can't move this side.' Yes, Drusus noticed, when he spoke the drag on one side of his face was much more obvious.

'But you will again. And you're talking – I thought you'd be worse.' This was true. And he doesn't need to walk, Drusus thought in indignation; surely if he can speak that's enough. Why let Marcus take over everything if it's no worse than this?

'My voice ...'

'It's not that bad,' urged Drusus gently. 'It's fine.'

Faustus found his eyes were wet. 'Hardly,' he said, and to his shame, and increased misery, the word prompted the tears to run faster. He swore, which was still easy enough, because he wanted to explain how his thoughts kept running into a great fist which flattened them, and he could not find the strength to think how to say it; the sense seemed to stand smugly unconquered in front of him, like a mountain.

Silently, Drusus wiped the tears away. 'Yes, yes it is. Don't let anyone make you believe you're weaker than you are, Uncle. Because Rome needs you strong. And as soon as possible.'

Sudden anxiety cleared Faustus' eyes. 'What do you mean?'

'That I want you to get well.'

Faustus made an impatient, disbelieving grunt, and queried, 'Marcus?'

Drusus gave a long sigh, and passed a hand over his face. 'Well, I am worried. Very worried. It's hard to believe he's only been here a day, with everything he's doing.'

'What—?'

'Well! He's what, nineteen, and facing a war of this scale? I ... Uncle, I truly fear he's handing away the safety of the Empire. Of course, he can't help his age, he can't help being in this position, but he seems to think he knows better than Salvius, or anyone, really.'

Faustus' breathing had become hurried, but he began, 'Drusus. I know you want ...'

'No, it's not personal, really! I know you feel that everything he went through will help him, somehow, when it comes to it. But as for now – after all, Uncle, whatever he may be capable of in the future ... Can you think of an Emperor who came to power that young and turned out well?'

'Marcus is not Emperor,' said Faustus with surprising clarity and force.

Drusus felt at once nervous and encouraged. In truth, his idea of what precisely he was trying to do had been somewhat clouded so far – he couldn't expect Faustus to alter his will and make him Caesar after only one conversation, when Drusus had never managed to persuade Faustus even to let him have the governorship of Terranova. But he did not need that to happen all at once. As things were now, it seemed to him that it would not be very hard, or even take very long, perhaps only two or three attempts, to get Faustus either to instate him as Regent now, or else to take the power back himself. Although of course his uncle would need help for some time to come.

'But he can do whatever he likes, all the same,' he said. 'Did you know he freed all your slaves, only this morning?'

'What?' exclaimed Faustus with a little jolt, 'I told him ...' His breath came quicker still, and his face was greyer than before.

Then behind Drusus, the door clicked open, making him start unpleasantly, and blood warmed his face. He turned and saw a tall young man – very young in fact, with a lot of disordered brown hair, and widely-spaced, much lighter brown eyes in a handsome triangular face that seemed designed to look guileless and trusting, but which, just now, did not look trusting at all.

'You must be Drusus Novius Faustus,' he said. As an obvious after-thought, he executed a slapdash bow towards the bed, but he did not lower his eyes from Drusus' face as he did it.

Faustus uttered a vague rumble of recognition and fell back on the pillows.

'Yes,' replied Drusus, motionless, unable to think how to react, un-sure if the alarm he felt was even justified. He turned stiffly towards the bed and asked with automatic, defensive haughtiness, 'Who is this?'

''S the doctor,' answered Faustus glumly, as the young man announced his name.

'Sulien.'

'What's happened to the usual doctor?' enquired Drusus, in as light a tone as he could muster. If it was credible that a boy so young could be some kind of doctor, he still could not understand what he should be doing treating the Emperor.

'He saved my life,' announced Faustus, adding morosely, 'For all the good that's worth.'

'Don't say that, Uncle,' said Drusus mechanically.

Sulien pushed the door wider and asked pleasantly, 'Your Highness, will you come out here, please?'

Drusus felt intensely reluctant and thought of refusing, but he must not; it was not safe to leave without knowing what the boy had heard. Which might after all be nothing. He followed.

Sulien shut the door. 'You can't come and talk to him like that,' he said.

'What do you mean by that? Were you eavesdropping?' demanded Drusus.

There was a pause. The preceding day Sulien had already taken in how the room in which they stood was utterly, eerily unchanged from its state three years before. There was the chair in which he had fallen asleep at the end of a night he hadn't believed any of them would live through. He remembered gunshots breaking through wood, inches away from him, and, almost worse, the shots he'd fired himself, and blood bubbling up from the wound in a man's throat. It wasn't a wound he'd made himself, but he had felt – he *was* – complicit in it. These days he rarely thought back over those weeks of his life, but still, they were there, like radioactivity in the bone marrow. He looked back now at the unsettling approximation of Marcus' face, and was surprised by an intense urge to hit Drusus, which was as strong as if he'd found him trying to attack Marcus physically. Drusus couldn't know what it had been like, he had just been calmly trying to wreck everything for which they had done it, for which Dama had perhaps died. Yes, Sulien had listened. He had heard everything.

He said, truthfully, and as forbearingly as he could, 'There is a good reason why he's in here and not downstairs. He could easily have another stroke. He's not strong enough to run an Empire, or to think about it. It's dangerous for him. In any case, I need to treat him now.'

'I've come a long way to see my uncle; if I really have to leave now I'll come back later,' said Drusus, in a tolerably conciliatory manner.

'No,' said Sulien. 'I'm afraid not.'

'What?'

'No,' repeated Sulien, emphatically. 'You can see him when I say.'

'What are you thinking, talking to me like that?' breathed Drusus, genuinely taken aback, so that his voice sounded almost gentle and diffident, 'You *cannot* give me orders. How dare you? I am part of the imperial family – the *only* person who can speak to me that way is in that room.' And he jerked his head at the door to the bedroom.

Sulien scowled, losing what patience he'd had. 'Look at it this way,' he retorted. 'He'll never change his will if he dies now, will he?'

Drusus parted his lips, but his power to speak seemed to escape soundlessly between them, like a thread of steam. He had gone pale. Sulien felt a moment of satisfaction at this, followed by a slight and ill-defined anxiety. He left Drusus standing there and went into Faustus' room.

'If I go over to that factory, can I use you as a threat?' asked Varius, as they went back into his office. Without even thinking about it he crossed the room to adjust the windows.

'If that will help.'

'Of course it'll help.'

Marcus said, 'It looks as though the clinic's running well, anyway.'

'Oh, it is, it is,' agreed Varius, faintly wearily. But he smiled at Marcus. He was surprised at how glad he was to see him, forgetting that he was always nervous in advance of any meeting between them. The hampering sense of other people's knowledge was naturally worse with those whose lives had also been extruded through the autumn of three years before. This was why, although he'd seen Cleomenes perhaps four or five times since his release, they couldn't really become friends. Only

Sulien was exempt from this, because Varius was used to him being part of the clinic, and because although Sulien had been there that last night in the Golden House, it was hard to believe that someone who seemed so uncontaminated could have had anything to do with such times.

But Marcus was the centre, the cause. It was not that Varius had ever blamed him, for he had done nothing, but the simple fact was that if it had not been for him, Gemella would still be alive. Varius had tried to protect him, and instead had almost caused his death. He knew Marcus didn't consider him responsible for that. Marcus had said to him, some weeks after his return to Rome, 'But I would have been killed if I'd stayed in Rome, I'm sure of that. And I would have stayed if you hadn't made me go.' He had also said, 'I think it was torture, all of it.' It had not been a conversation Varius entirely wanted to have. He'd badly needed to understand how Marcus had survived, and he hadn't been able to bear listening to the official version on the longvision. But he had not wanted to give an account of the time after he'd driven back to Rome, nor to hear what he knew Marcus would say: that he had done nothing wrong. What he blamed himself for was not so much the moment of betrayal, because yes, it was true, by that point there was no plausible way out – but he should have prevented it happening. He just should not have been there. The guilt he felt demanded to be kept controlled and self-contained and independent, not to be disturbed by anyone else.

Nevertheless it did alter things that Marcus was one of the few people to whom he'd found himself telling the full truth – although on the condition that they didn't talk of it again. And it did count for something that Marcus was the only other person who'd been there when Gemella died. What had happened to them both had been, at certain points, parallel, and it still seemed to defy sense that they were both alive.

'And the world?' he asked now.

Marcus attempted to smile and said, 'That's not going quite so well.'

'It never does,' said Varius. 'I don't know that it's meant to. So long as it goes on supporting life to some degree you can't be doing too badly.'

'I'm doing my best!' Marcus looked, for a moment, wan. Three years before, Varius had thought of Marcus as a child. In general he no longer did so now, but Marcus' age seemed to slide back, briefly, leaving him looking defenceless.

'I'm sorry it had to happen to you like this,' said Varius, quietly.

Marcus nodded. 'It's what I want to do. Not yet. Not with things this way. But still …' He shrugged a little. 'I've told Salvius we're not bringing in more troops in Terranova. Do you think the Nionians will talk to us?'

Varius considered, and sat meditatively on the edge of his desk, interested. 'I don't think they could be sure of gaining much from this war. I doubt they're eager for it.'

'Salvius is, Drusus is. There must be people like them in Cynoto.'

'Rome still has the advantage, and may lose it. That's at least part of the reason Salvius feels so strongly. I think the Nionians would prefer to avoid fighting us. That doesn't answer your question, though. The risk isn't only in their intentions, or in yours. It could be just some little mistake. A detail you don't see in time – you can lose everything over some stupid little thing.'

'Like what?' prompted Marcus.

'You've said we won't prepare an attack against them while this is happening. You had to. And obviously they'll have to make the same promise before we can enter into talks with them or your position here will become untenable. Stipulations like that do matter. But they can come to matter too much. People grow fixated with them in situations as tense as this. If there was, say, a military exercise – and the message cancelling it didn't get through – or even a general really trying to sabotage things, we could find ourselves at war, without either you or the Nionians truly wanting it to happen, because of something that doesn't really matter at all. A few men moving a few miles.'

'What should I do, then?' asked Marcus. He had seen Varius' bearing alter indefinably as he spoke, becoming subtly more alert and engaged.

'You shouldn't let it become a sequence of ultimatums in the first place,' began Varius, enjoying the flow of thought, but then stopped. 'Why am I giving you advice on this? And Marcus, I'm very glad to see you, but why are you here?'

'Because I *do* need advice,' said Marcus. 'I'd like you to come to the Palace as soon as you can, as my advisor.'

Varius leant back a little into the sunlight from the open windows, and became hard to look at, masked. Marcus, watching him, supposed he must be surprised, because of the time it took him to answer, but then some silent limit passed and it became clear that he must be deciding how to say no.

'Thank you for the offer,' he began finally.

'Why are you turning it down?'

'I have no experience of government,' said Varius reasonably.

'You expected to have, once.'

'Yes. In very different circumstances. As an extension of the job I was doing then. I'm in another line of work now.'

'And you're bored with it,' said Marcus.

There was a pause, and Varius' face surfaced from the light, looking faintly alarmed. 'No, I'm not, why do you say that?'

'I've just turned up and you've got time to see me.'

'Marcus, you can have people executed now if they don't make time to see you.'

'I promise I won't do that often,' said Marcus smiling, though he felt another flash of mute shock, as he'd had at the first sight of the ring that was now on his hand. 'Anyway, Sulien said you were bored.'

'Why?' demanded Varius. 'Is he unhappy about the way I'm doing things here?'

'No, he just said you looked bored.'

Varius sighed. 'Well, it's true, it does more or less run itself,' he confessed. 'But I've been thinking of setting up another one, so—'

'We could do that. You wouldn't have to scrape up the money. You could have it.'

'Does that only happen if I say yes?' asked Varius impassively, after a moment.

Marcus gave a helpless little laugh. 'No. I suppose I've got to do it now I've said it. But look, Varius, I'm not stupid, I know I'm too young for this.' He waved the hand that wore the ring. 'Even if I wasn't, perhaps it's too much power for one person anyway. But that doesn't mean I'm going to let Drusus have it. So, this is much more than the job you'd have had with my father. It *is* power. You must have wanted that once.'

Varius said flatly, 'I made a decision that I would have nothing to do with the Palace, ever again.'

Marcus hesitated. 'Those people are gone, Varius,' he murmured carefully.

'Are they? All of them? Are you sure?' asked Varius, in a low, grim voice, not looking at him.

'All right,' said Marcus. 'No. No, I'm not sure. But I'm very sure you're not one of them. I know you've got good reason not to trust the Golden House, but so have I. But I do trust you.'

Marcus had got Varius to look at him, and even smile. Then he lowered his head and asked, as if of himself, 'What can I say to that?'

But this was not quite an acceptance, even if it was obvious to Marcus that Varius was tempted.

'Varius, there has to be someone I can talk to openly. I *can't* get this wrong, whatever else I do. And if you tell me something – if you think I'm doing something wrong, I'd know you didn't have any other motive for saying so. I could believe you.'

Varius frowned down at the floor for a while, but when he looked up a detached, alert calm had evened out his face again. He asked reasonably, 'Why?'

'*Because* –,' began Marcus incredulously, after a moment's speechlessness.

Varius interrupted, 'All right. I know why you can trust *me*. You can trust me to mean well. But that isn't enough.'

'No, I trust your judgement,' protested Marcus.

'I can see you do,' said Varius. 'But that's why I won't do it. I'm sorry.'

Afterwards, Varius went on with his work, but he felt vaguely shaken for some hours, as if he'd been in a fight.

Sitting in the gilt cavern of the car again Marcus tried not to let himself wish that the vehicle would turn off its course and, mysteriously, take Una and himself somewhere hours and hours away. It was much worse than the day before, in the spiralwing, daunted though he'd been then. Of course the Golden House looked bigger from the city below it than it had from the air.

'I can help you,' Una said with a kind of taut, restrained ardency. 'I don't want to spend all day waiting to see you. I want to be with you. Whenever you have to decide what to do. No one will lie to you without me knowing. Glycon doesn't mind me and I think I could do some things for him, boring things like taking messages, and then that would be an excuse for me to be there—'

'I want you there,' Marcus interrupted. His face had lifted with a kind of reckless relief, but Una continued defending the proposal almost as if he hadn't spoken.

'And I would have to make myself very quiet and dull and hard to notice; you know I can do that. That way I could listen. And – and I want to see it, I *want to be there*. But I know people will think I shouldn't be there, and they'll think badly of you for letting me.'

'No, it's worth it,' he insisted.

Una hoped that this was right. He might have been warier if Varius had said yes, she thought. She smiled back at Marcus, knowing she could be sure now of the time she needed to watch Drusus.

Drusus lingered in the Palace for a while, sitting paralysed in the glazed tower, again wishing that there was someone he dared talk to, for he simply could not think what he should do. He felt another twinge of unfocused alarm and resentment when he established, by sending one of the guards that had come with him from Byzantium across to talk to the Praetorians, where Marcus had gone. Drusus could probably have found this out quite openly, but this way comforted him a little. Varius: another of the obstacles that had tripped his hopes! Without him, Marcus would be safely dead.

When Marcus returned to the Golden House, Drusus tried to think of some plan, something to go and say to him, but could not. For short spasms he managed to interest himself in the mechanics of fire, at least going through the motions of carrying out his cousin's request, but he began to feel as if the Palace was on the point of shattering into glass splinters around him. And so he fled it, back to the quiet Caelian hill, and his father's villa – or rather his own, for he had taken charge of it as soon as he was of age; his father was known to be mad.

It was a dark nest of barriers; the high, blind outer wall, the thick hedge within that, a buffer zone of land, and then the fort of the house itself – all like several pairs of hands parsimoniously clasped around the coin of the central garden.

Inside the house was full of marsh-like colours: deep green, a dark, muggy purple; reeds and shadowy willows were painted on the wall. Drusus strode through into the dining room, where, lying opposite each other on the couches, he found Lucius eating an early supper with Ulpia, a pleasant-looking, snub-nosed brunette who was supposed to be Lucius' nurse, and instead, Drusus thought disgustedly, lived with him as a kind of wife, or concubine, or a *nanny*.

'Get out,' he said to her. 'I want to talk to my father.'

Ulpia started up, distressed and hesitant, and then darted out. Lucius looked scared and saddened as he so often did, but, as Drusus expected, said nothing to rebuke him. Oh, how every act, every word to him flapped and pattered, a feeble, far-too-late apology! But instead of his usual irritation at this, Drusus felt only deep, lonely weariness. He sat down on the couch where Ulpia had lain, stared broodingly at his father with his chin propped on his fists, then sank his face into his hands.

After what seemed a long time, Lucius padded silently round the table and laid an awkward hand on Drusus' shoulder. Drusus let out a sigh that had the ghost of laughter in it and, without raising his head, lifted the hand at the wrist and plucked it away. 'Don't be so absurd,' he murmured, without aggression.

Meekly, Lucius receded. He sat humbly on the edge of his couch, poked a dish or two aside on the table and appealed timidly, 'Drusus. Drusus. It's very nice that you're in Rome. What's the matter?'

'Everything,' pronounced Drusus, simply. 'Everything is the matter.'

'Is Titus very ill?'

'You don't care anything about him,' Drusus remarked.

'I do,' ventured Lucius.

'How can that statement be reconciled with your actions?'

'I don't know,' admitted Lucius in a whisper, shifting in his seat like a scolded schoolboy. He raised both his hands to his face and peeked over them, wide-eyed and afraid. It was quite natural and instinctive to him now, and yet the sort of gesture a shy child would cultivate on purpose, to try and seem endearing, so as not to be hit. Drusus hated the sight of it. Above his hands, under the tumbled white hair, Lucius' weak green eyes begged: Please. Enough.

And Drusus gave way to it, as somehow he always did; there was a kind of sour kindness that suddenly and inexplicably overcame him when dealing with his father, and would not let him go beyond a certain point, to list the consequences of his cowardice and lies. Or tell his secret.

He summoned a slave to get him a fresh glass, poured himself wine and stretched out resignedly on his side, pillowing his head on the crook of his arm, his fingertips on the back of his head vaguely stroking and cherishing his own hair. 'He's not as ill as I expected,' he said. 'His voice sounds odd when he talks. He can't walk, though.'

'Poor Titus.'

'Yes, poor Titus. Although I'm sure he would recover better if he hadn't put himself in this position with Marcus. Because Marcus is certainly throwing his weight about; the gods know what'll be left when he's finished. It's a travesty.'

'Do you really want to be Emperor so very badly, then?' asked Lucius, with audible pity in his voice.

'What else is there?' answered Drusus, dully.

Lucius looked almost as if he would cry. 'But there must be plenty – oh you could just – Drusus. Why do you want to do that? Terrible. And so dangerous! Why would you put yourself in harm's way? Oh dear – I would hate it if anything happened to you.'

Drusus shot an indignant look at him and wanted to cry out, 'Do you think nothing has happened to me *so far!*' Always, always his father had been a weight on his life. Through his childhood, he and his mother had lived in a mute community of shame; but the humiliation she felt – understandably, given what she thought she'd signed up for, marrying a Novian – extended to Drusus too. It always had as far as he could tell. Certainly things had gone badly wrong by the time he was two years old.

Drusus had thought it would be a wonderful blessing if Lucius was not mad. But it was like the gifts of the gods in the myths – to Cassandra or Tithonus – a literal yet malicious granting of what was asked for: to get his wish, not in the form of a metamorphosis, or miraculous cure, but in the discovery that his father had only used the family blight of insanity as a cover to retreat from his name, from his marriage, from his small son. And he had kept this up nearly the whole of Drusus' life. Drusus had discovered the truth – walking in on Lucius and Ulpia repulsively half-undressed – only when he was nineteen, the age Marcus was now.

But the shock and betrayal – although it continued, even nine years later – had somehow made an intimacy between the two of them that had never existed before, incomplete and defective though it was. For years Drusus told no one the truth about Lucius, and then only Tulliola – silent partly from mortification, but partly from a bitter, unexpected feeling of duty and pity.

He contented himself now with saying, 'Not everyone feels so compelled to dodge responsibilty, Dad.' Lucius hung his head. 'In any case. The oracle told me I was to be Emperor,' went on Drusus quietly. 'You will not tell anyone that.'

Strange thing – in this Drusus did trust his father, who nodded earnestly and offered, 'Then you don't have to worry.'

'I have never believed that. Everything is stacked against me, everything is designed to keep it from happening. Who is going to change that if not myself? I can't even make my case to Uncle Titus, you realise. It's a disgrace, the things going on behind his back. Ah ...' Another tide of despair rushed over Drusus and he let himself slip lower on the couch and wrapped his arm around his face. 'There's this kid of a doctor. He listened to everything I said. And now he'll tell Marcus, so I can't even ... You see, they know exactly what they're doing. They've put him there as a spy. They're making sure I can't let the Emperor know what's really happening. Perhaps he's even keeping him ill ...' And he stopped, turned quickly onto his back, and looked up at the murky ceiling, staring as the thoughts came. Softly he muttered, '*Sulien.*' For he had only been thinking resentfully aloud, but as he heard the words he had spoken, he knew they must be true. For it was only now, suddenly, that the name meant anything to him. Sulien.

Drusus tried to remember what he had heard three years before, and it was difficult, for he had been too sick at heart to take in anything to do with the disaster. But now he thought: Yes, the people who broke into the Galenian and got Marcus out. Sulien was one of those. He was another slave. But wasn't he supposed to have been a kind of magician from London? Drusus ran over the conversation in Faustus' rooms, and thought it was possible he'd heard the faintest shadow of an accent. It must be the same person, and it was no coincidence that he was as young as Marcus; they were friends. Of course, if you were in Marcus' position, that was what you would need – a means of controlling Faustus for as long as the regency lasted. And once you had that, you had more: a means of *making* it last, or bringing it to a succession, as you saw fit. Of course you would do that. Drusus would have done the same himself.

There was no hope, then, that the boy would not think it his place to tell Marcus what he'd heard.

Drusus gave a short laugh and, sardonically, because there was no reason not to, he explained the substance of these thoughts to his father. It was odd, but although he had just realised that things were even worse than he had supposed, he felt less wretched than before, not so powerless. If nothing else, he knew now what he was up against.

VI

FURNACE

For the first time, Sulien began to wish the weight of heat held in the taut blue sky would erupt into rain. He was usually oddly impervious to the unremitting sun, and could walk about in the full glare of it as if he'd grown up in desert heat and not the wavering dampness of London. If it were not for the drought he would hardly have understood why anyone should want it to stop. But there had been more fires; a power plant had gone up and ignited a knot of streets. The number of dead would have been universally horrifying if they had not mostly been slaves. Each fire was clean of any certain sign of sabotage, every single one had immaculate credentials as an accident. It was only because there had been so many that the idea of arson was spreading, the still-soft talk of a quiet virus of culprits, whether they were separatists, or Nionian agents, or a revolutionary sect that wanted to tear down Rome for the sake of it. Sulien began to fancy that the hot air carried a faint taste of burning, a delicate smog of seige and mistrust.

It must have been affecting him more than he would have thought. A few nights ago, he had walked Tancorix home and she had stepped a little closer to him and taken his arm, although with a movement of the eyebrows to make obvious that this was partly ironic, and had said, 'Oh, look. You'll fight for my honour, won't you?'

'Isn't it too late for that?' answered Sulien. They skirted dexterously around a little heap of fresh dog shit deposited precisely in the middle of the narrow Transtiberine street.

'And whose fault would that be?' said Tancorix. Automatically she darted a look at him that began as expertly flirtatious and then, as she remembered, grew more doubtful. They crossed a little forum around a temple of Ceres, bright and crowded as noon although it was halfway towards dawn, full of people conducting various kinds of business. A group of African musicians were playing electric harps and zithers with an air of slightly frantic single-mindedness, trying to outdo a serene

Arabian flautist in the opposite corner. A woman tried to sell Tancorix one of five tamed sparrows, perched in a dutiful huddle on the outstretched stem of a rose. Moving past, shaking their heads, Sulien and Tancorix moved out of the square of man-made light, into dimness again.

She said, 'Anyway, someone's following us.'

Naturally they both assumed she was the one being followed – for, shadowy in the haphazard streetlights, there did seem to be a man walking behind at a distance of fifty yards or so. It surprised neither of them, nor were they concerned. Tancorix was living in a kind of small plot of social land hacked out by disgrace. Singing in inns and cauponas, she boosted the money her former husband gave her for the daughter he said might very well not be his. Tancorix did not really have a very good voice, although it had got better with persistence and bravado, but she was so proficient at handling and directing her beauty, like a team of horses, that she got on well enough. Sulien liked watching her perform; their friendship, his pleasure at the sight of her were more lightly touched with memory and strange guilt, when she was on a little stage and he was slightly drunk.

So they parted with the usual faint awkwardness – a glancing kiss, like friends. Sulien walked on, alone. His flat in a tall, shabbily handsome building whose faded, powdery blue walls emerged from aggressive rainbows of graffiti at its base, was towards the rear of Transtiberina, right under the sudden steep green peak of the Janiculum hill. Sulien turned a few corners, following one raggedy uphill street after another. A black curtain of hanging creeper, lovely in daylight, fell draped between buildings. Sulien crossed beneath it, beyond there was no light at all except the low, electric glare of the sky. It was strange how often, how abruptly, in Transtiberina, one could pass from light and activity into complete solitude and darkness.

Sulien found that he had fastened one hand around the wrist of the other with a sudden unaccustomed feeling of vulnerablity. He was absolutely certain that footsteps had been quietly accompanying his own since he had left Tancorix, and that, although he could see no one, as he unlocked the door someone was watching him. He shut the door behind him with a surprising little shiver of relief.

He slept badly. Half his friends said you needed a set of earplugs to get a decent night's sleep in Rome. Usually Sulien was adept at shutting out the nocturnal sounds of Transtiberina – the inexplicable bangs and thuds in the streets outside, the strange, isolated yells, the barks of dogs, but that night they all seemed louder and closer, while the feverish heat soaked into the sheets. In the morning, however, he barely even remembered the fear any more than he remembered what he'd dreamt that night, the daylight itself seemed such a strong repudiation of it.

But three days later, on the steps of the bath house he had seen a man heading in as he came out, quite unremarkable looking and surely not the same as the figure on the street that night – and yet Sulien felt that he had seen him more than once, between the clinic and here. But if he had – on the way after all to a public building – what of it? He could not think what was wrong with him.

In the clinic, Bupe, the girl from the arms factory, lay propped in a narrow bed and stared with her remaining eye. She had screamed with pain and horror for a day, but was now still, her maimed face dull with a terrible lack of surprise. The yellow was gone from her skin now, and though the wound still looked horrifying, Sulien was sure he could make the flesh heal straight, forbid the tissue to form itself into granular or fibrous knots; she would hardly be scarred. But of course the eye socket would stay empty, and there was nothing he could do about the missing hand and thumb.

'So I could still be a whore,' she said grimly, when he told her about her face. Varius, progressing moodily through the ward, felt almost relieved by the rare twinge of real shock he experienced at this.

He said, 'Bupe, we're going to Veii; we're going to stop them doing this,' but then suppressed a grimace of displeasure with himself. Why should he think that would comfort her? Even if they could stop it, what good was it to her?

Bupe's visible eyelid lifted slowly. 'I wouldn't bother,' she said flatly. And she asked Sulien, because Varius had strode away in a frustrated sweep, 'When are you going to do that?'

'This afternoon.'

Bupe looked at him and uttered a bitter little scoffing noise. 'There's no point with those places,' she announced.

Sulien said nothing else, but Bupe brought back the tension that had dogged him for the last few days. He thought of Una, because Bupe reminded him of her in a way; they were almost the same age, and there was something else, a level, bitter certainty they both had, which troubled him.

Later he went after Varius, insisting, 'There's got to be something for her. There's no rule that says her life has to be ruined. Is there? There have got to be things she could do. The factory should pay for doing that to her. They could *help* her. At least she's free, in a way, isn't she?'

It was true, in that no one would want her as a slave and officially, she hardly existed.

Varius only muttered and forced a nod. In fact he couldn't imagine a future for Bupe that seemed both tolerable and plausible. A weary quarrel resumed in his head: *This is no good*, it went. *Better than nothing*, came the answer, dully. *No, or it is such a fraction above nothing that you might as well stop.* He did not want to say this to Sulien; he did not want to make other people believe it.

'I hope my sister never worked anywhere like that,' blurted Sulien.

'Wouldn't you know?' asked Varius, slight curiosity briefly lifting his mood.

Sulien gritted his teeth. 'I don't know if I'd know,' he said. 'She was in some factories. What she's told me ... maybe it's all of it, maybe it's not. Probably not, is what I think.'

'She's not stunted, she's not disfigured. She can't have been somewhere that bad for long,' said Varius, with a kind of contained, deliberate brutality that seemed somehow directed at himself, not Sulien. He had been visibly depressed and short-tempered since Marcus' visit.

'You could tell Marcus you've changed your mind,' Sulien said, recklessly.

Varius looked sharply at him, so that Sulien half-expected a rebuke, but all he said was, 'But I haven't.'

At noon, Sulien was called to the longdictor.

The voice was female, hushed, blurred with urgency, trying, it seemed, to get as much as possible said in a desperate whisper, without being heard by someone else: '... wouldn't stop kicking him, he's only eleven. I think he'll die, oh, you've got to come.'

'All right – all right. Can't someone bring him here?' He was a little irritated at being called over to say these things, it was not his job.

'I *can't*.' There was an indistinct sound of shouting somewhere, she caught her breath in an audible flinch.

'Then we'll send someone. Where are you?'

'In the Subura but *no. No.* I'm not supposed to be doing this. They'll find out. He won't let you take him.'

'Is this the owner? We can deal with him, I'm sure. Look, we can help, but I'm going to give the longdictor to—'

'*No, I need to talk to you. No.* He said he stole – or something – I think he's mad, I think he might kill me.'

'If it's that bad then we—'

'*No, no, please,* if you do that you'll make it worse, I can manage, he'll calm down later, he'll be out, he won't even see you but *please just come I'll do anything*. This *is* Sulien, isn't it?'

Sulien said, 'Yes, it's me,' and then felt an unfamiliar stirring of vague paranoia. 'Why did you ask for me?'

'I know about you, everyone does. I know you do things – you can really help, you can save his life. The little boy—'

'I can't just walk out and—'

'Please, I think he'll die, *he's not moving – please.*'

Sulien turned off the longdictor, and sighed. He felt somehow that he should not go, but could think of no reason. He could send someone else to fetch the child, despite the woman's frantic insistance – but it was true, he was different; he could do more, and more quickly. He remembered that he had not complained about being whisked across town for Faustus, and that decided him. He sighed again, and walked out of the cool clinic into the melee of heat.

His trirota was chained outside the clinic. Sulien winced as he fired the motor – the metal was bloated with heat even though the machine had been standing in the shade. He crossed the Aemilian bridge, the cowed Tiber creeping along below, under the gold glare of light, and rode west. But as he moved into the sudden shade between tenement blocks, for no reason at all, he remembered the man on the bath-house steps, the footsteps on the way home from Tancorix's. He stopped and turned round abstractedly as if – indeed it was partly true – he was slightly uncertain of where he was going. There were people on the street behind him – he recognised none of them. He was uncomfortably aware of the dampness on his forehead and in his hair; the shade in the street seemed only a kind of formality of light, it cast a bluish, dazzled haze over his vision, but had no effect on the heat. At the next turn the hot street was emptier, and the shabby high buildings pressed closer together, crushing it. It seemed as if he was being led away from where there were people.

It occurred to him that if there were a household here who had a slave – two slaves, it seemed – it was strange that they could afford to throw them away so lightly.

He was a fool to have come alone. He'd said he was going to the Subura, but he should have left the exact address; no one would know where to look for him – why was he thinking like this, in broad daylight? What could he do except keep on?

The next street was so narrow that it was almost dark, despite the burning strip of violent blue skimming sparingly above it. At street level, the walls were ragged and blank, the windows were boarded up, the surfaces bare even of graffiti; a torn poster urging the election of an official in a contest two years over, and a young woman standing in the middle of the street, seemed almost the only signs of human life, as if it was not a street but a split in the earth, naturally formed by rain, or earthquake.

Sulien knew, even before she spoke, that the woman must be the one who'd summoned him because of her look of agitated anticipation. She clearly knew him because he was the only other person there. She certainly looked like a slave: tangled dark hair tied roughly back, a colourless dress that left her arms bare, a premature droop to the edges of the thin, dry-skinned lips. Still, she was younger than he expected, perhaps only twenty-three or -four. Talking to her before, he'd assumed she was the mother of the hurt child – it was still possible, but seemed less likely. She called out his name, and barely giving him time to prop the trirota against a wall, she ran forward, seized his wrist and fairly dragged him up the steps and through the open front door of an apartment block of dark, run-down brick, hissing at him, 'Oh, hurry. I mean thank you for coming here, but please.'

Inside, the block was almost silent. There was a lift, but the woman ignored it, rushing for the stairs, not letting go of Sulien's arm. Occasional windows, cracked and miserable, let a little bare light into the stairwell, but the lamps on the stained walls were unlit. This is a joke, Sulien thought unhappily, almost scoffing at himself: no one lives here. Or no one who can afford two slaves. Why are you going along with this? Because, although he felt the possibility of the hurt boy's existence dwindling every second, it had not disappeared altogether, and until it had he must go on, mocked with pity for what he suspected did not exist. The feeling of wrongness had to be *proven* correct, however disastrously.

But the block was not, evidently, completely empty, for just as he thought this, a man, heavy set, perhaps in his late twenties, emerged from one of the flats and pushed past them without acknowledging them or looking either in the face, and trudged downstairs.

Sulien asked, trying to sound normal, 'Where's your master?'

'He's gone – he's selling some stuff. It'll be all right. I think he'll be an hour, at least – that'll be all right, won't it?'

Out of breath on the eighth floor, she took him to the end of the corridor and opened the door of a dismal little flat. The furniture looked old and sad and perfunctory, and aside from that, there was scarcely any evidence of life, no books, pictures, or even discarded clothes, nothing personal. But there were residues of the violence she'd talked of; the white fragments of a bowl or plate had been swept into a small pile, but not removed. A chair lay overturned, which, even in her desperation, the woman darted from his side to put straight. She opened another door behind which was another sharp flight of steps, leading up steeply into what must have been loft space. He could see the upper slice of a little cell of a room, and from halfway up the steps he could see the edge of a mattress, and a shape under a blanket that did not move. For a moment

81

Sulien thought the child might be dead, but the next instant he knew it was not a human body at all; it could have been simply another blanket rolled up, or perhaps a dummy more artfully constructed of clothes that might have deceived the eye a little longer – but for Sulien it was as if he'd been asked to believe that the cold banister under his hand was the bone of an arm. He knew, before he was close enough to see, that the bulk was something dull and cheap, not flesh. And the room was windowless: once inside, and the door locked, there would be nothing he could do. He felt a tiny lapsing of tension, a sort of relief at being right, before his nerves shrilled furious warning.

As if the woman might not know, might somehow believe a child really lay there, Sulien felt a brief, ridiculous urge to announce to her what was wrong and why he had to get out, as if sudden flight might make him look stupid or callous, unless he explained himself. But he was moving nevertheless, backwards down the steps, knocking into the woman and swivelling, thudding down into the living room. She gave a wail of protest at first, but as he forced past her to the floor, she gave that up and tried to catch at him, saying clearly, 'Stop.'

He ignored her, covering the dingy ground through the flat, a tutting voice in his mind pointing out to him in slow, told-you-so tones that of course no one lived here, the furniture was perfunctory scenery, either what she – what they – had found abandoned here or rubbish that they'd managed to scramble together.

The woman called again, 'Stop.' But Sulien realised that she was striding, not running after him. She was confident that he would not get far. There were more people in the building.

Nevertheless, the door of the flat was only shut, not locked. He burst out into the corridor, and behind him, the woman shouted – but not to him, this time. Sulien pounded round the stairwell once, twice, and as he swung round the turn he looked down; the flights were placed too tightly in the shaft, one after the other, to let him see who was coming, but he saw a shadowy blur of swift movement three, two floors down? A hand briefly grabbing the banister, sliding up towards him, fast.

Sulien stopped for a second, dithering, the building had fallen oddly still so that he was aware of the greenish paint on the wall and the dank carpet under his feet, and had time to ask himself in bewilderment, what is *happening?* He charged sideways into another corridor of flats, and shoved at the nearest door – they were still so high up, but perhaps if he could get to a window he could climb down somehow, or at least call for help. But the door did not open. Sulien left it and kicked desperately at the next one, then the next. None of them moved. So there was nothing he could do but run out to the stairs again, in the weak hope that perhaps he still had time to reach the floor below and try the same thing there. But he did not have time. He got halfway down the next flight, and there they were, running to meet him. Two men – the one he'd seen before, going downstairs, and another, younger, about the same age as the woman. And he held a gun, levelled at Sulien's chest. Time stuttered: Sulien heard the shattering of gunfire in the Sanctuary bedroom three years before, as though a sound-proof door to the past had been flung open. At least back then he had understood why it was happening.

He stood on the stairs, breathless, dazed.

'Just do as we say,' the woman said, stepping down onto the landing behind him.

'All right,' said Sulien, in a friendly voice, stepping backwards towards her. 'Fine.'

The four of them moved upwards, remaining for a couple of seconds in a kind of slow formation, the gun seeming to hold them fixed in relation to one another as if on rods radiating out from it, like a model of the solar system. Sulien felt his breathing slow a little; there was almost a feeling of calm, now he had no choice but to do what they said. He could think a little more clearly. 'What's this about?' he asked the woman, in the same nice tones, although he was unsurprised when she didn't answer.

All right, he thought. Perhaps this was not too bad. Were they hoping to get a ransom for him? For he reasoned this could only be happening because he was friends with Marcus. In that case, he'd probably be all right. If they really were or had been slaves, he knew he could talk to them. They wouldn't *want* to hurt him, he was sure of it. But then, they might not be slaves at all. They had known what to say to get him to come here, the shabby, desperate look of them might only be more stage-dressing. Then it struck him that, much worse, it might not be a question of money. They might be hoping to make Marcus *do* something, something about the war with Nionia, perhaps. Something to which Marcus could not consent.

Then the man who had the gun pushed forward sharply, wanting to get a proper hold on Sulien, with the weapon against his head or back – and Sulien moved at the same time; he sprang sideways and swung himself over the handrail, not down the shaft but over it, to the foot of the flight below.

They shouted a warning and then the gun went off, a great crack, a noise that drilled through the breastbone, and kicked a little jolted noise out of Sulien, even as he hit the ground.

He fell painfully, impact bludgeoning his heels, knees, the base of his spine, his ribs; he got down the last few steps and round the corner more in a rolling continuation of the fall than anything more deliberate, dragged himself to his feet and plunged unsteadily on. The jump had happened in a blur, and he was shocked at having done it. It was as if, as had happened to him once or twice before, his body had made the decision for him. If it had occurred to him consciously, surely he wouldn't have done something so stupid – had he not just been thinking how he should act towards them, make them *like* him? But, amazingly, apparently it was not stupid, the shot hadn't hit him, and at least he had a head start.

His legs hammered downwards, not broken it seemed, but still they felt like loose stacks of smashed bricks, tumbling. His head start was only a flight and a half, and the others weren't hurt, they were faster. He did not look back, but he could hear the stairs rumbling as they ran down. Sulien skidded achingly on, but as the ground came closer he began to shout at himself silently, as if he might forget: the door at the bottom is locked. The door at the bottom is locked. For of course the man he'd seen must have done that, almost as soon as Sulien was inside.

He skidded around another landing and managed to gather himself enough to vault again over the banisters, more deliberately, landing better, although it still jarred through his bruised joints, but at once he heard a heavy thud behind as one of them copied him.

The first floor. Instead of rounding again onto the final flight, Sulien ran through again into the corridor of flats. It was darker here and, for a moment, although the three pursuers could be in no doubt where he had gone, he could look back and not see them. The illusion of completed escape was terrible. Again he rushed at a door, felt not so much frustration or rage as a kind of sad urgent disappointment when it would not give way. He heard them reach the landing outside the passage. He ducked miserably along the passage to another door, pushed it. And this time it moved under his hands, a wonderful thing, a miracle.

He pulled the door closed behind him and kept going forward, but unexpected nausea pinched at his throat and made his lips flex. A filthy smell rose from an unrecognisable moist mess that had melted or dissolved over the floor and every disordered surface; his entrance caused ripplings and contractions in a carpet of insects. Some grey mice scattered from his feet. Sulien staggered a little. There was a pounding outside the room, and to either side of it – they were trying several doors at once. Sulien ploughed through the dirt, not straight to the window before him but into a rumpled bedroom to the side. He was hoping there might be a lock on this door, but there was not. The smell here was equally sharp but sourer, fusty. He pushed aside a cobwebby drift of sagging curtain and wrenched at the window, not even sure as yet what was outside – but the handles must have rusted and stiffened in however long it had been since the room had been used. He felt with frustration that it *would* open if he had even ten seconds to spend on it. Unwillingly – because the sound would reveal where he was – he swept up a little three-legged table and hurled it through. He brushed at the teeth and scales of glass left sticking up around the sill, knowing he was bound to cut himself and feeling somehow irritable about it. He swung a leg out into space, and as he'd anticipated, pain whistled across his fingers, and he left a trail of blood on the ledge.

He heard them entering the room he'd just left.

His body dreaded a second fall, but there was no help for it, nothing to climb down. It was hard to get a decent hold on the sill with his hurt fingers, in so little time; his feet vainly scraped at the brick. He let himself drop, and rolled on the sudden pitiless concrete, groaning. Above they burst into the foul-smelling bedroom. As he rose, hobbling now, he saw that the small table he'd thrown was lying on the ground beside him with its top broken off, which seemed strange and surprising, like the blue sky and heat, that of course had been continuing all the time.

He was in a yard of patchy concrete. There was a skip in the far corner, another block of flats – were there people there? Would they see what was happening, would they help him? But he couldn't run straight into an open space like that, making such a clear target of himself. He lurched along the base of the wall as fast as he could. There was a gate out. If it was locked and he had to climb it he was probably finished, but the place looked so derelict and ignored he hoped it wouldn't be. The woman startled him by using his name again: 'Sulien, I'm warning you, *stay where you are.*' Then came another shot, bursting somewhere behind him.

He did not know what they did after that. Perhaps one of them followed him out of the window. The gate opened only into another empty little crevice of a street. But around the next corner there would be people, shops – good, explicable things. He was certain he could get that far.

He'd been away two hours by the time the vigiles took him back to the clinic. Aulus, one of his friends, found him going up the stairs and complained, 'What was that? An extended lunch?' Sulien would have told him everything at once, but Aulus was already hurrying away saying crossly, 'Well, if you're going to be here, will you please come and *help?*'

'Hang on,' muttered Sulien, rather aggrieved.

85

He went to his surgery and commenced cleaning himself up. Already the knocks he'd received no longer hurt much. It had been hard to concentrate but waiting at the vigiles' station he'd shut his eyes and tried to numb the sites of pain scattered along his body. He hadn't been badly injured, really. But he still felt faintly sick and cold, with a kind of thin continuing tremble under his skin, although he had stopped shaking visibly. His clothes and hair were dusty, so he tried to brush them down. He washed his face and cleaned the cuts on his hands to make sure.

Varius came in while he was doing this, beginning angrily, 'Sulien, it's been two hours, what the hell are you ...?' But he stopped when he saw Sulien's face. He asked quietly, 'Are you all right?'

Sulien nodded

'What happened?'

Sulien let out a long unsteady breath. 'I don't even know. Some people tried to ...' Abduct him? Kill him? What had they been trying to do? He shuddered again and mumbled through what had happened: the woman's call; how he'd felt there was something wrong but had gone anyway; the gun. Varius, who'd sat down to listen, made a low, shocked sound. Sulien said, 'I don't know – I was thinking how the best thing I could do was just go along with they said, but instead I took off over the banisters. It was weird,' he finished lamely.

Varius shook his head. 'Sulien – *why*?'

Sulien told Varius what he'd thought then said, 'If it is that, you'd better look out too. We're the easiest ones to get to.'

'You've told the vigiles?'

'Yes, for what that's worth.'

This made Varius smile slightly – neither of them could muster more than a grudging trust in the vigiles, despite the purges that had cut mercilessly through both forces for months after Tulliola's arrest. 'You'd better tell Marcus too.'

'Oh ...' said Sulien, somehow exhausted at the suggestion. 'Later. Yes, I will, but later.'

'You needn't have come back in. You should have called me from the station. The woman definitely asked for you by name? She knew who you were?'

Sulien nodded.

'Then you shouldn't go straight home.'

'No, probably not ... I mean, I wasn't going to.'

'If you want, you can go to mine,' offered Varius, willing himself past the slight reluctance to invite anyone into his flat. 'Although if they're looking for Marcus' friends, I don't know if that'll help.'

'No, I don't think it would. And don't worry about it, there are loads of people I could stay with. Maybe Tancorix. I'll sort it out later. But I'm all right here.'

Varius frowned. 'You're not going to achieve anything but taking up space. Go somewhere you can have a drink or lie down. Don't waste time proving points.'

'It's not that,' mumbled Sulien, with an uneven, self-conscious grin. 'Much more selfish. Everyone's still at work. And I don't want to be on my own.'

'You do think they'll come after you again?'

Sulien hesitated. 'Yes,' he said unwillingly, and then, as if he could trample down such a possibility by talking over it, 'Look, I was supposed to go with you to Veii anyway. I can still come. It'll be fine. It won't matter if you talk and I sit there and look stupid, will it?'

'No,' allowed Varius, finally. 'Of course it won't.'

They heard the factory before they saw it – a dull, thick boil of sound, which, as they approached through the increasingly drab streets, began to separate out and organise itself into a deep, volcanic, stamping throb, less like a heartbeat than like a giant, belligerent drum. But as they reached the gates the sounds thawed together again – not one but several hammer rhythms that sometimes overlapped as the repeated booms resounded against the surrounding walls, while unremitting whirs and clacks flowed through everything, filling every chink. The slaves slept in shifts; it never stopped. Their barracks were rows of narrow wooden huts on the opposite side of the enclosure.

The factory was a jagged mass of auburn brick, the long, high buildings at its heart incongruously handsome in a stark, sharp-edged way. The complex was framed within a tall, bristling fence, and as the car passed through it, something seemed to happen to the air – a shrillness, a choked feeling that clamped down instantly, even before Varius and Sulien saw anyone. Then a tense line of gaunt, yellow-stained women jerked past, utterly silent, not looking at them or at one another.

There was a haze of hot dust in the air, a faint metallic smell, like blood, but fibrous and powdery. Varius got out of the car. The ground around him was transected with many small sharp tramlines, like lines of stitches connecting the cautiously-spaced, stumpy little buildings on the perimeter where the explosive materials were stored, to the huge and cavernous hangars from which the bleak din came.

The gates had been closed behind them and now the fence pressed on him as if it were touching him as he had known it would. He tried to look through the fence rather than at it, refocusing his eyes to reduce the metal to a hanging grey blur over the street outside. It was controllable, but he could not altogether shed the feeling of being confined which seemed weak and detestable when he was not one of those who couldn't leave.

Sulien looked pale. He started a little as a loud bang penetrated the smog of sound coming from the testing site, over on the far edge of the complex. Varius realised he should not have let him come.

Between the entrance to the grounds and the vast workshops stood a trim, dapper building, three or four storeys high, fronted with sheets of pale marble so that it looked quite unrelated either to the structures or the dusty ground around it, almost like a mirage, blurred by the filminess in the air, almost weightless in the light. It even had a frieze of statues within its pediment, cast in polished steel: Vulcan stood in the centre, his hammer swung up to gleam in the apex of the triangle that framed him. He was top heavy; the knotted muscles of his shoulders were massive and inflated, his legs were crippled, but it did not seem to bother him. He was forging the armour of Achilles. Around him were assistant Cyclopes, bending over their tasks, obedient and absorbed. Sulien looked up at these and was reminded queasily of Bupe's one eye.

A young woman in smart, dull-textured clothes, not a slave, came out to meet them, a taut square smile pegged out on her face like a tent. She said in a similarly strained, polite voice, 'You're from Transtiberina, yes? Will you come up?'

'Not yet, we won't,' said Varius. 'You keep us very busy. I want to see how.' He walked away, towards the shell-filling shop.

Dismayed and angry, the woman followed him, 'Where do you think you're going? It's dangerous if you just … Well! No one's taking any responsibility for you going in there, I hope you realise that!'

Although he was deliberately ignoring her, by the time he reached the entrance of the workshop, Varius genuinely could not hear her. He went on, into the centre of the works, and Sulien followed, more reluctantly. The machine-driven hammers were ranged along one immense wall, gnashing beneath chimney-like shafts that bulged into bell-shaped hoods, like a street of adobe houses. The metallic scent Sulien and Varius had noticed outside was far stronger; every breath carried a drift of metal particles, filed from the casings of the shells, and the fine grey dust lay everywhere, mixed in with the general grime and darkness on the floor, which sometimes seemed to stir with possible rats.

There were ranks of slaves in the heat and dirt; pushing the hot rods of metal into the maw of the hammers, obscured, at the far end, by some jerking loom-like machinery involving vertical rods that skipped rapidly and droning leather belts; packing the shells with explosive powder at long benches. And still, although Sulien and Varius were plainly foreign to the factory, not one of the slaves did more than glance at them. Beside the benches, on low carts, the finished weapons lay in stacks, like huge, innocent vases. And it was impossible to think; the hammers seemed to flatten the very self to nothing. Although there was obvious danger everywhere, the bit of Varius' brain that sputtered reflexively with possible deaths fell silent, as if overloaded. For a few seconds he shut his eyes, the blackening sound filling his head, and for that time he felt oddly reluctant to leave. Nevertheless, they were in there only a few minutes before the angrily-smiling woman lead them out again to the management building with the frieze of Vulcan. They climbed through floors of clerks tending ledgers and records of purchases, and the woman showed them towards an office, then subsided to a desk of her own where her look of strained hostility altered slightly but did not disappear. There were very few other women.

The office was smart and pleasant, although there was a blur of dust on the windows, as well as the constant dull thudding, just palpable within the floor and walls. Presumably everyone got used to it working there, whether as a slave or a director.

Proculus, the manager of the factory's operations, sat down and nodded at them repeatedly, with a kind of grudging pulled-down smile. Still nodding, he said, 'Well. All right,' as if he'd been forced to yield a point, and then sighed and sat up, saying, 'So, why don't you tell me why you're here?'

Sulien had meant only to sit in the room and let the conversation wash past him; he still felt too shaken by what had happened earlier to do any more. But he was angry too, and found he was speaking as if on a furious physical reflex. 'Why do you *think* we're here? Do you mean you don't know what we see, week after week – the state people are in when you dump them? I should have brought pictures.'

Proculus winced, not with shame but with exasperation, and said with regretful impatience, 'Well, I know about you. You were a slave yourself, of course. You see a distorted view of the matter.'

Sulien blinked, speechless.

Proculus went on, 'Of course, there is a question of profit. But contrary to what you might think, that is not the only thing at stake. We're not turning out saucepans here. We all know this is a vulnerable time, and what we do is essential to protecting Rome. And that, I'm afraid, can't stop for anything.'

Varius told Proculus calmly, 'We're here to *help* you.'

Sulien and Proculus looked at him, both taken aback.

'In what way?' asked Proculus, guardedly.

Varius leant forward, purposeful and friendly. 'We can help you keep your slaves going longer. We think we can find a way to save you a significant proportion of what you spend on replacing and training them.'

Proculus paused. 'Look, I'm sure that works in other industries, but the reality is when they're finished here we can't use them again.'

'But,' Sulien shook his head, 'don't you feel anything for them? Any *regret*? They end up covered in burns, or blind, or dead. You *can't* just ...' He was beginning to wish he hadn't come. He felt as if he had soaked up some of the violence from the disused apartment block and it threatened to spray out of him again at the slightest touch. He was tapping his foot, trying to earth some of it.

'I've already explained,' said Proculus wearily.

'Not how you can bear it. It's getting worse all the time!'

Varius agreed, 'It's true, it is getting worse.' He was not worried by Sulien's outspokenness; it was pretty much what Proculus would have been expecting from them both. He would be the more relieved that Varius at least seemed to be talking to him dispassionately.

'Well,' said Proculus. 'We've had to increase production.'

Varius felt a small flick of attention. 'Why's that?'

Proculus looked at once amused and bewildered. 'I think we all know why. Nionia. It's only a matter of time. We've had instructions from the military.'

Varius was silent for a moment. He looked at Sulien. 'Salvius,' he said. He would have to tell Marcus about this. He did not want to. It was an uncomfortable reminder of Marcus' offer. But he carried on, evenly, 'If there's a war, then it's all the more important that you don't waste the resources you have. How many are there, working here?'

'About a thousand, give or take.'

'Not so many, really,' remarked Varius. 'And it's true, as things are now, many of the slaves you dispose of are – irreparable. But there are things you could do. You know that. There could be better shields on those machines. You could keep them healthier. The ones we see are so clapped out it's no wonder they have accidents. And then we would have a better chance of returning usable labour to you. And there may not be a war—'

'Well, all the signs say to the contrary.'

'You're probably right, but even if it's only further off than you think, as long as we don't have new shipments of prisoners of war going onto the market, then slaves are only going to become more and more expensive. Either way, you need to take steps to get more out of the ones you have.'

Proculus' face had become still and reflective. He said nothing.

'You should invest some of what you spend on new slaves with us,' said Varius.

'Then you want money?' As Varius had anticipated, Proculus looked contemptuous, and yet a little more comfortable too.

'Of course we want money,' said Varius, and gave him a sudden, broad, genial smile. To Sulien, who was watching the conversation with near-disgust, this looked bizarre and out of character, but, to his surprise, it prompted Proculus to utter a slight companionable chuckle. Varius expanded amicably, 'We have to keep the place going. We all have to have something to live on, too.'

Proculus chuckled again and said, 'Yes, we all have to do that.'

'But as I've said, I believe you'd save money overall. It's very much in your interest. From another perspective too.'

'Oh? What's that?'

Varius smiled again, more thinly. 'Our new Regent is very concerned about these things. And we both have connections with him.'

There was a silence. Proculus sat motionless, his own smile fading. 'All I can say is that I'll take this up with my superiors,' he said at last.

'I'm glad you will,' said Varius mildly. 'And what will you recommend to them?'

A trapped, unhappy ripple played over Proculus. 'That we ... make changes. I can't promise you anything about the money.'

'Good. But there are improvements you can make yourself.'

'Yes. Yes. I will think about what can be done.'

Varius extended his hand. Proculus took it, subdued. 'We'll go over to the slaves' quarters now,' Varius told him, almost kindly.

'Is that really ...?' began Proculus, sounding almost mournful.

'It may help us come up with more suggestions,' said Varius, letting go of the other man's fingers. 'It's been good to talk to you.'

Outside, the terrible noise marched up again to meet them. For minutes, they didn't speak. Varius was aware that Sulien hadn't looked at him since they'd left Proculus' office. At last he said impatiently, 'He wasn't going to get on his knees and beg forgiveness, Sulien.'

'I know,' muttered Sulien.

'I don't know how near or far off abolition is, but few more of them might live to see it. It's better than nothing.'

'I know,' repeated Sulien.

Varius walked faster, leaving Sulien a little behind. He'd said what he'd meant to; the disgust he'd felt with the words and with himself had perversely seemed to help him, like a fuel burning. It had worked as well as he could have expected, better even. There had been moments when it had seemed to him he'd heard something like his own argument before, somewhere else, a friendly ruthlessness that was not wholly like himself. As if someone were saying to him, do it like this, place this barrier here, and it will work. Where had he learnt that? Who was that like?

Gabinius, he thought, as his foot hit the dust. He stopped, briefly immobile with fury and revulsion. 'I'll *kill you*,' he told dead Gabinius in his head, and he paced on again towards the barracks, trying to check an unforeseen gust of rage about Gemella – not so much the usual, almosttedious regret that he should have seen at the time what was going to kill her and stopped it, but anger that it was not preventable *now*, that she could not be *forced* back to life. The factory crunched and roared, there was no good reason to be there.

Sulien did not try to catch him up. He was tired now, and trying to cast an understanding blur over what Varius had said to Proculus was more tiring still. Behind the barracks, all along this side of the enclosure, the fence – barb-topped and unforgiving – gave way to a flat, emphatic brick wall that rose ten feet above the barracks roof and then sprouted a crop of ferociously edged blades, curling inwards like cats' claws. The long dark shed below these skewers, windowless except for a few skylights, was divided into three sections, each with its own low pitched roof, but connected by doors. Ahead, Varius entered one of the further sections of the barracks, seemingly leaving the first partitions to him. Sulien pushed a door open cautiously, afraid of wrecking someone's sleep, if sleep were possible in the babel from outside. But the barracks seemed to be empty; no one lay in the rows of stinking beds before him. The narrow bunks were placed along the walls as regularly as the hammers in the factory, but far more tightly, scarcely a foot between them. The thin, oily mattresses bore the bleary yellowish imprints of bodies as if whenever someone rose from the bed someone else had always thrown themselves down at once, to lie and ache. Even at a glance he could see the live reddish dust of bedbugs. There was a single tap on the wall behind him, no other way of washing, it seemed, although the shed must have housed 150 people at a time. There were buckets. The smell was hot and vivid, and as nauseating as the stale odour in the room in the Subura flat. He felt too tired to think clearly about what he saw now, or even to worry about whether Una had ever had to live anywhere so horrible. It was such a long day and he still did not know what he was going to do at the end of it, if it was even safe to go home.

Varius, entering the next dormitory, could not make the door stand open and looked around in automatic frustration for something to prop it open with, then abandoned it in disgust, allowing it to swing shut behind him, even though this was more like a dungeon than anywhere he'd been, even in prison. His body was tense and his heart beat fast and bitterly. He only needed a few minutes in here, surely he could damn well stand it that long. He made himself concentrate: get Sulien to tell him about how diseases would spread here and how fast, he would concoct some exact-sounding figure of how much money this was costing Proculus, what should be done ... Then, like something he'd summoned, he heard a flaw, a burst in the heart of the noise, surely too close to be from the testing facility. Varius turned, thinking in instinctive dread of the stores of explosives around the site, and just as he was reassuring himself, the second explosion came – nearer, worse. Somehow, through the closed blinds, between the slats of the roof, he could see something like a sun hurtling across from the core of the factory. It soared with a strangely gentle, silky whispering sound, and struck the next division where Sulien was. The connecting door flew open and Varius saw the space beyond it lighting up.

As the boom slammed against him and made his bones hum, Varius felt that he was going to be paralysed with shock – was even angry in advance with his failure to do anything. But in fact, he moved immediately, down between the files of bunks towards the door, shouting Sulien's name. He heard no answer, but when he called again he could barely hear himself for the rushing of the fire and the drumming of falling embers on the roof. He got halfway to the door and knew, suddenly, that he would not make it the rest of the way in time; the little comet that had set fire to the barracks had been flung from the shell-filling shops, the mortar factory. The two blasts so far were only like the first bubbles rising from the bottom of a heated pan of water. More would come any second now, and much worse.

Quite methodically he grabbed the upright of the bunk beside him, pressed into the paltry space between two beds, towards the wall furthest from what was coming. He got up onto the lower mattress, and it came – an arm sweeping the plates off a table; a gaping force that wiped all sound before it, mauled down the walls and the roof, hurled him down on the fetid bed and pinned him there. The bed skidded back, driven hard against the wall, its foot mangling and sloping as the broken roof and the opposite row of bunks were rammed into it, cracking and tumbling. Tangled barricades of smashed wood piled themselves up on either side. The bunk above jolted and collapsed down over him. Not one explosion but a pulsing string of them, unrolling over the ground. All the light crumpled up like paper.

He could hear nothing except a cold hollow humming, cupped in each ear. He might have been blind too; the blackness was solid and total. Varius elbowed at the stuff that lay over him, struggled up onto his knees, dragged on something, a long serrated spar. The remnants of the bunk bed had left him in a little triangular space, like a cave. The back wall of the shed seemed to be still intact, but on every other side he felt a dark mass of splinters and smashed boards. The spar was wedged fast and wouldn't move. He fished around, loosened something – a slat from another bunk, a plank? – and flung it down beside him on the bed like a prize.

He was at the bottom of a newly lit bonfire. He could feel the heat of the flames overhead, fluttering on the outer shell of the wreck. And he knew, feeling something like rough fingertips on his lungs, that the black hollow where he crouched was already nearly full of smoke. Varius' head clouded, his limbs grew heavy. In a slow, sing-song voice it came to him gently: *no* one can blame *any*one for getting killed in a *fire*. As if for future reference, as if it would be helpful to tell people, he noted that it was not as bad as you might think. Certainly he would have shrunk from it happening like this. Burning was the worst kind of pain, but, as it turned out, the smoke killed you before the flames did, and mercifully fast; soaking you up swiftly and cheerfully, like alcohol. Varius blinked good humouredly in the blackness. He was coughing steadily as he worked, his eyes streaming, but it was impossible to mind that much. The half-smashed frame of the bed was supporting what was left of the ceiling, the mass on either side more loosely packed. Varius clawed, pulled, kicked. Yes, it was like getting drunk. Someone should tell people these things. And he was alone, he could do whatever he wanted. No one would know if he just lay here on the bed and waited. He had not even had to make the choice, here it came: his much-belated death – out of nowhere, a free gift.

Was Sulien going to die too? Varius felt a great rush of drunken sorrow at the idea. No, no, no. He would be all right.

He threw another dusty lath down beside him. He had a little pile there now. As he scrabbled at it, the wreckage shuddered rhythmically – he felt rather than heard that the explosions were still beating out across the compound. Still marvelling at the extraordinary kindness of death by smoke, he kicked again as the next shiver came, and something overhead dislodged and shook free. There was a fall and clattering, a few bright flakes of orange fire dropped past in the dark, and he felt a little puff of real air, clean on the edge of his lungs. For the first time, as if a severe, prompting voice had said his name, Varius noticed with disbelief what he had been doing all this time, how hard he'd been working. It was the reverse of those dreams of getting out of bed and dressing for work, while the real body still lies inert under the warm covers.

His arms, straining against the bars of wood, ached with effort. Had he been knocked out when the walls first blew in, was it possible that he could have started trying to dig his way out even before he was properly conscious again? Because he could not remember beginning.

He thought with clearer alarm of Sulien in the next dormitory, the burst of gold fire. There was a little yellow blaze somewhere below and ahead of him now, where the sparks had fallen. It was eating the air even faster than it was going already, but it let him see: he had cleared a gap in the thicket of ruined planking, crossed and hatched about though it was with fallen beams. He was aware now of the rage of his body, the horror of being trapped in this tiny and poisonous space. And yet it was almost a good feeling, like electricity. He forced himself bruisingly in among the shafts, reached and thrashed fiercely, feeling things shifting and cracking under and around him like dry bones. He got his knee onto what was left of the top bunk and pushed upwards again like a swimmer, and a fragment of the husk fell aside; his head and shoulders were in the daylight and a partial, smoke-infected air.

Heat struck his face and dabbled with his sight. There was a wall of terrible light somewhere but he couldn't look at it. He felt almost no relief, no more amazement at what had just happened. He heaved his legs free, rolled and fell; and for the moment he hardly knew where he was, what he had pulled himself out of or why there were smears of molten pain on his shins and hands – nothing, only the pitiless clutching of his lungs. Only that he would do anything to get one more breath.

He was lying between the burning remains of the barracks and the brick wall behind them, although he did not think of that. The coughing, perversely, was more painful in the air, as though sheets of sandpaper were working in and out of his chest. He rose onto his hands and knees, powerless as spasm after strangled spasm scraped through his throat; he almost thought his lungs would be forced bloodily inside out, and he wouldn't care – anything to stop the choking. As if by mere chance, he felt one palm slap blindly against the wall and he made some kicking movement on the dusty ground that levered him somehow onto his feet.

What had he just done? The violence in his lungs – the burns shrilling on his hands – a few moments before he had been in no pain at all, by now he could have been past feeling anything. Then, why? Not for his parents' sake; though was it not chiefly for them that he'd knuckled down to each successive day, that for three years he'd done his utmost not to be tempted, to ignore every means of cancelling this unchosen stretch of his life? Yet he was guiltily aware that, there in the dark, if he'd remembered them at all it had been with the almost irritable thought that they would just have to put up with it. He'd had his chance, it had seemed *allowed*. After all this time trying to resign himself to captivity, there had been peaceful, effortless freedom, and what had he done with it? He was almost calmed by the touch of the wall beside him, by looking up and seeing the palisade of barbs overhead. He was not out of it yet, not by a long way.

He stumbled forward, pushing himself along against the wall, walking, after a fashion. He croaked, 'Sulien,' and found that he could hear it, although even his own voice seemed to be happening outside a glass bubble in which his head was encased.

Well, he thought, if he had survived this far, Sulien must have done too, he must have got out of the collapsed barracks, probably some time before Varius had himself. The section where Sulien had been did not even seem as badly blown in as the ruins he'd just escaped, a quarter or so of its roof was still in place, although pale smoke was swelling steadily above it. Perhaps Sulien was round on the other side, although Varius did feel a dim warning that this did not make much sense, lingering out in the open, in the scope of the blast.

And he saw it now, as he reached the corner of the ruined barracks: a gorgeous, livid pillar of fire, continually buttressed by round explosions, casting a glowing shower of burning shreds and metal hail, rising into the sky from where the heart of the factory had been. A dome of barely penetrable heat extended around it, even to where he stood, where it met and merged with the heat of the burning sheds. Something screamed out of it, ploughing a yellow trail into the sky above the city. Varius staggered. Had Proculus really said there were a thousand people? It was not possible. In the distance he saw a small flight of figures running, stumbling over the remains of the little tramlines, but no more than ten, and no one else, and he could not see where they went. Black and white chutes of smoke rolled and glided across the ground, another powder store burst and perhaps felled them all, he didn't know.

And he could not see Sulien. Bent double, he lurched into the glare with his arms crossed over his head, along the fractured front of the sheds and shouted again, but the curious certainty that Sulien was outside somewhere evaporated completely. For a stunned moment Varius stood lurching in the heat, panting, staring at the wreck. From here, the dormitory Sulien had entered looked worse now than he'd thought – a stockade of trampled timbers and fire. The door was no longer a way in or out, only a bunch of flaming kindling, propped on the rest of the heap. He called hoarsely again and ran back round the building, knocking on the walls that still stood, and fell against the heating wood with another choking fit and a panicked feeling of helplessness. He shut his eyes as it occurred to him that even if Sulien were alive and conscious, he would be just as deafened as Varius was; they might both be shouting and not hearing each other.

There was a rain-water butt against the wall beside him. Varius reached for and fell towards it rather than walked, and hung over it, wondering if he could move it and douse the flames enough to get into the barracks. But there was nothing at the bottom but a few cupfuls of fly-blown slime, which made him utter a gasping cough that was almost a laugh. He swore hollowly. Then, with something close to exasperation at the uselessness of it, thinking clearly, Might as well, he climbed clumsily onto the edge of the barrel, teetered a little and hoisted himself up onto the roof, then crawled over to the skylight. He lay beside it for a moment, trying to get control of his protesting breath. White smoke was already seeping up around the window frame, and when he stamped it through, a pale, thick column exhaled itself from the space. He turned his face away from it, screwed shut his stinging eyes and climbed down.

The smoke seemed to have lost all its gentleness, it was like giant hands trying to hold his ribcage still; he felt the familiar haze growing in his head much faster this time, but not the vague addled pleasure at it. He'd lowered himself, as he'd hoped, on to the top of a relatively un-scathed bunk. At this end the blast seemed to have tipped the whole row of bunks back and sideways, so that they were packed, tilting, against each other, like books placed untidily on a shelf. There was no way between them and only because the opposite row had been loosened and smashed could he get down to the ground at all. Varius plunged down as fast as he could through the embrace of the smoke, on to some clear ground between the slanted uprights, sinking his face almost to the floor and gulping desperately at the air that was still there. It was amazing that there could still be such fierce light outside. It was so dark inside that at once he saw the risk of being unable to find his way back to the skylight even if he had any time or chance to do so. It was so loud, and the heat sent his burns, which for a minute or so he'd nearly forgotten, into infuriated tantrums of pain. He tried to console himself that perhaps that would keep him conscious a little longer. Grimacing, he began to feel his way along the ground in the dark, and then turned back, hesitated for a second, kicked off one of his shoes and left it there at the foot of the bunk he'd climbed down. It was probably pointless and seemed such a ludicrous thing to do that again he smiled sourly, but he hoped that at least if he crawled back this way and felt it again he'd know he was under the skylight.

He crawled again along the remants of the aisle, pushing aside or climbing over the hurdled planks. He patted around on the ground, calling, but nothing met his fingers except the sharp ends of split wood. Certainly if Sulien had been anywhere near the front wall then he was dead, Varius already knew that. It was plain now that even if he were alive and trapped in the debris at the further end of the shed, in the kind of little cavity from which Varius had forced his way out, then Varius had no real chance of finding him, let alone digging him free, before the smoke carried away first his own strength and then his life. All he could hope for was that, in the blackness, Sulien might simply not have been able to find the skylights or a break in the roof. But he neither heard anyone answering his calls nor sensed any human movement in the dark. Then the space he was crawling along narrowed and his hands met a fence of slivers and beams which he could not move.

Varius felt sideways and slid himself into the tilted space between the bottom of two beds. There was a kind of cramped road here, under the packed bunks, roofed with the slats and edges of the beds, too low for him even to crawl on his hands and knees. Varius swivelled round and pulled himself along it. Only a few minutes could have passed since the explosion, and yet he felt as if he'd been doing this for days. Again he felt the lure of lying down alone in the privacy of this dark and narrow space. The confinement he dreaded so much in normal, day-lit life, seemed to welcome him forgivingly as if it had been waiting for him. And Gemella stepped lightly, casually into his mind, bringing the feeling he'd had sometimes in prison, that there was only a little way, a few inches between them, a barrier yielding as paper. He was bewildered and distressed that he had not remembered this before.

Just then, as he crawled, he knocked again into an obstacle, something inert and soft: a shoulder, an arm in a sleeve. Varius started a little as if he'd completely ceased to expect this, and his breath accelerated with shock. 'Sulien. Sulien,' he said, sternly. He felt for the face: Sulien was breathing, but he lay still. Varius thought he must have been running down the aisle when the explosion had flung him back and slapped the bunk beds sideways above him. At least it had meant he'd been kept below the worst of the smoke, breathing quietly and slowly. Varius shook him a little and at once thought derisively to himself, 'he hasn't overslept, idiot.' He took hold of Sulien's arm and dragged, the relief and surprise he had felt at finding him slipping into near-horror, for Sulien seemed to have become impossibly heavy, and as the space would not let Varius rise higher than onto his elbows, he only succeeded in pulling himself further along the floor. He hooked his feet around the leg of a bunk further back, wincing at the friction on his burnt hands, and managed to lug Sulien a short way – less than half his body's length.

But stretched across the ground like this it was difficult even to keep a good grip on Sulien's arm, and it was far harder, far more draining, to move him than he would have expected. He thought he heard Sulien groan dully as he slid over the floor, but he remained motionless, heavy. Varius shuffled backwards, anchored himself by his feet again and tried once more. But already he found he was panting and the smoke had lowered. The coughing squeezed his chest and throat so much that he felt close to retching. He knew he would never do it this way.

He managed to surface a little, got an arm up between two beds, felt about and tugged down a filthy sheet, gathering it messily into a bunch and trailing it behind him as he crawled back to Sulien. He pushed it under Sulien's head and threw his arms awkwardly over it so that it was under Sulien's armpits, and dragged it tight again. He was surprised that it worked so well. Pulling on the ends of the sheet he found he could haul Sulien further, with much less effort. He struggled past the blockage and out into the aisle, where at last he could rise onto his feet and lift Sulien properly. Standing up meant his head was again in the thick of the smoke, but he did it anyway, trying to hold his breath, and stumbled along backwards a little way before he fell down again, choking. He cast out on the ground for the shoe he'd left as a marker, felt it for a second as his scrabbling hand flicked it away into the darkness by accident. He began trying to heave Sulien up into his arms, but this time effort made him gasp dizzily and fold up again, once more bowing his face towards the ground, trying to find air. There wasn't enough. The coughing made him shiver and reel, something crunched in the blackness, the heat rolled in and the dull reddish glow he'd seen in the far edges of the dark grew pointed and turned to clear, sharp-edged blades of light, squares and triangles of yellow and orange, as the fire worked inwards.

Varius tried to say, 'Sulien, come on, wake up,' but he couldn't speak. He knelt awkwardly, Sulien propped beside him. To get this far, he'd had wilfully to ignore how difficult it was going to be to get Sulien up to the skylight. And he realised now that it was far worse than that – he couldn't do it at all. Sulien was taller than he was, must be at least his own weight. To lift such a load over his head onto a platform, and then up through the skylight would have been impossible even with his normal strength; now, in pain and with no air to breathe, he wasn't sure he could even raise Sulien onto the lower bunk. In spite of this, he tried, but there was a muffled pressure growing fatally and rapidly in his head and his hands weakened so that he had to let Sulien down. He managed to wheeze thickly, 'I can't do it. I can't lift you, Sulien. Just get up, I can help you then, I can't do it unless you ...' Soft, muting shutters were swinging slowly closed before him; he left Sulien lying on his side with his head turned away from the fire, and dragged himself heavily up the frame of the bunk bed, through the window again. He crawled to the edge of the roof to get his face free of the smoke, and let his head hang into space. The heat in the air was brutal, and he could feel it growing underneath him too, the structure cracking and weakening. The small wooden island was shrinking around him as the flames lapped up and across the shattered roof towards it. Varius' shut eyes were bathed in a kind of gritty acidic rinse, but he found he wanted to sob, he was so exhausted and it seemed so insultingly cruel. If he and Sulien were both going to be killed in an accident or a bombing, whatever it was, if he had even given up and lain still under the bunks a few minutes ago before he'd found Sulien, then senseless as that would have been, it didn't seem *unreasonable* to him. But to be allowed to get so pointlessly close, to be given just enough time and unexpected resilience and transient luck to let him see and *think* about how worthless his efforts were, it was enough to make him believe in vindictive gods.

His eyes opened slowly and he stared at the indistinct ground; the air, however raggedly, moved in and out of his lungs. Inexplicably he felt himself relax, a kind of watchful quietness running through him like a medicine – but not the drowsy acquiescence to death that had kept drawing close and then receding, since the first explosion. All this, he thought, was still too soon. Sulien was at least not yet certainly dead. And he had only climbed out to get enough breath to try again, and he could do that now. He took another draught of the hot air, as deep as he could, and slid back again across the creaking roof, into the dark shed.

And yet it was not so dark as it had been; even in the little time he'd been outside, the fitful and dangerous light had grown markedly stronger, although it was little use for seeing by in the smoke-drenched air. Varius dropped into the shadows beneath the bunks, steadily, although the airlessness at once resumed its pummeling assault on his failing body, and felt for Sulien on the ground. He could not find him, though surely he had come down in the same place. He almost thought, for an illogical and unsteadying second, that Sulien might not merely have died but disintegrated completely. And then, faintly, he saw something move, only inches away from him and not a current of the smoke or a falling rafter. Putting out his hands doubtfully, Varius again felt Sulien's arm, this time in mid air, reaching blindly and laboriously for the edge of the capsized bed. Sulien had raised himself a little way, leaning clumsily on the bunk, his head hanging.

Varius pushed back amazement. Sulien was not fully awake. Varius gripped his arm as if arresting a criminal who might escape, and began trying brutally to force him onto his feet. Sulien swayed so that Varius staggered too and both nearly fell; he mumbled and repeated some baffled-sounding question that, in the liquid roar of the fire and the ringing in his own ears, Varius could not make out. Varius found that he was swearing viciously at Sulien and wondered faintly at the unfairness of it, but did not stop. Sulien made a clearer sound, a cry of pain as Varius drove him forward, so that Varius realised that he must be injured on his left arm, or side. For the moment he refused to feel any sympathy whatever: 'Get up there, for fuck's sake,' he rasped furiously, though probably Sulien, coughing heavily now, didn't know what was being said to him. Varius allowed him to sag against the bed and climbed onto its upper level himself, then grabbed at Sulien's arm and collar as he felt the foundering in his chest and skull grow again, almost forgetting what it was he was trying to do.

Although Sulien was still only laggingly conscious, he could feel the advancing fire as if it were something with a will and ability to hate, and he tried to obey Varius' bullying and raise his body up the frame, tripping and jarring the waking pains in his arm, side and head. He fell beside Varius, who at once hoisted him up again and felt desperately in the smoke to find the skylight, which, for a few appalling suffocating seconds, he seemed to have lost.

At last, Varius' hand touched space, and he steered Sulien towards it and pushed and bundled him upwards, until, with a dim surprise, he felt the weight on his arms and shoulders suddenly disappear. He reached forward to climb out onto the roof, scraping at its surface with a drowner's effort. But his legs crumpled under him. It was not much of a height from here – his head and shoulders were already out – but the smoke pouring up through the window, enveloping him, was now so dense that he could scarcely tell the difference, and the shuttered feeling closed inwards again while his arms pleaded to be excused any more weight, any more struggle.

But as he buckled, he felt Sulien pull weakly, one handed, at his arm, and hang onto his sleeve. He had no real strength to try and drag Varius up, the grasp only kept him from slipping back into the smoke. Varius lunged and surfaced onto the fragment of the roof, and the unsupported raft shuddered and dipped under their combined weight. Brokenly, Varius pushed Sulien towards the edge. He had forgotten the existence of the rain-water butt, and probably neither of them had enough dexterity left to climb down it even if he had remembered it. All Varius could do was try to clutch at Sulien long enough to slow his fall, then he rolled over the edge himself and dropped to the ground.

As they staggered away, convulsed with coughing, a missile ripped out of the tower of fire at the centre of the factory and a blurred and melting round of explosions rumbled outwards. Flame and metal and smashed bricks swung through the air. The force knocked them both to the dust, the roof of the barracks caved in and sparks leapt up, but neither of them noticed.

Varius didn't even try to get to his feet. The only sheltered place they had a chance of reaching was back in the little alley between the impassable brick wall and the smoking back of the barracks, although that would not stay standing for very long. He crawled towards it. Even if they could go no further, somehow it didn't seem like failure. He saw that Sulien was still alive, and heading in the same direction, faster than he was. He dragged himself behind the vestiges of the barracks, pitched down onto his side, and turned his face to the wall.

For a week Una had been clinging to her small foothold in the Imperial Office and meeting rooms of the Palace, veiled in a deliberate mousey blandness, her eyes usually inoffensively lowered. Sometimes she did minutely useful and tedious things for Glycon, forcing patience on herself, so that she was scarcely noticeable and caused only occasional sparks of unease in the senators and generals that came there, when watching, listening, she forgot to keep herself hidden and hunger bared itself on her suddenly conspicuous face. To her secret frustration, she had not seen Drusus all this time: he seemed to have retreated to his father's house, from where he had sent Marcus a single, slapdash report on his work on the fire reports. And for seven days there had been nothing from Nionia, but an icily polite acknowledgement of Marcus' offer, and with each day of silence the strain on Marcus rose like a tide, like hands joining the pull on a rope. He had done as Varius had said and set no limit by which they must respond, and now it seemed that Una was the only one left who did not tell him that he must do that, at least, that if he would not resolve that it was already too late.

Probus was in Arcansa, telling Marcus from the longvision on the wall about the state of the ravaged town, about the news from Roman spies, when Marcus heard an arms factory had been bombed at Veii, and was still burning. Una felt a strange ripple travel down her body, a cold system of collapsings and reinforcements, tendons stiffening as others went weak, her knees bracing against the sudden tug down towards the dense carpet. And she saw that Marcus had not realised yet. Abruptly, and with a curt absence of explanation, he turned off Probus' screen. Then he went to the wall, slammed the panel violently shut against the longvision and said to her, 'Then there will be a war.'

'Sulien is there,' announced Una, her voice grating and thick.

Marcus turned to her, eyes widening slightly as at something that simply defied sense.

'Sulien is there.'

Marcus glanced away instead of holding the look. It was too unreasonable; there was no room or time. He said, quite confidently, 'They will be all right,'

'What?'

'They probably weren't there. I'm sure they can't have been. Was it definitely today they were going?'

'*Yes*,' said Una, through her teeth, frightened by a gale of rage at him, a need to get away from him and look for Sulien while it was still just in her power to control it. It was not the first time that she had felt afraid that she was not entirely to be trusted with Marcus, that one day she might recklessly damage or smash him and not notice what she had done until it was too late, but it had never been so immediate or piercing. In another moment she would hate him for caring at least as much about Varius as about Sulien.

Marcus, still convinced that they would have to be all right, wanted to comfort her, but she jolted away, saying with dangerous patience, 'I'll try to find him.'

'I'll come with you,' he promised rashly, half guilty now that he somehow couldn't feel the torment she did.

'Don't be stupid. Of course you can't,' said Una, unable to keep the sneer out of her voice, moving for the door. But Glycon came through before she reached it, pale excitement on his face, and told Marcus. 'Caesar. We've got contact from the Nionians. It's Prince Tadasius.'

Despite herself, Una froze, staring at Marcus, wanting to see what would happen. 'Fine, tell Salvius to come,' said Marcus mechanically, and stopped breathing for a moment as he walked to the longdictor. The news, almost without its own shock, seemed to bring on a little of what so far he had not felt. It was suddenly more possible that Sulien and Varius could have been at the factory. He settled the longdictor circlet on his head. He tried to think what to say, and found it felt right scarcely to speak at all. He didn't know why. With as little expression as possible, then, he said, 'Yes?'

He had not heard Prince Tadahito speak before, and so, although he noticed, and was a little daunted by his command of Latin, he did not know the fierce note of near-joy in the exercise of skill that Faustus had heard, could not hear how it was absent this time, the Prince's voice remained elegant, accentless: 'Caesar. May I say I am sorry to hear of the Emperor's illness.'

'Thank you,' said Marcus, flatly.

'My father wished me to speak to you at once.'

Marcus was silent.

'We are aware of what has happened in Veii today. Of course the munitions factory would be an obvious target in the opening of a campaign against Rome. You are likely to believe you are under attack by my country.'

Still Marcus said nothing. Una continued to hover, her face a hard, white, lipless mask, helplessly watching him and unable to move. In as minimal a way as she could, she tested the idea that the small buzz of speech she could just hear from the longdictor could be a noise made by Sulien's murderer.

'We had no involvement,' said the Prince, emphatically. 'I assure you. We did not do this.' There was a faint pause, and he continued, 'I wish to respond to your message of a week ago – we are willing to discuss Terranova and Tokogane. As you suggest. We hope that war can still be avoided. We agree that it would be best to meet in Sina, rather than in Roman or Nionian territory.'

Marcus lifted his eyes to Una on a kind of sharp thrill that broke down into excitement, distrust, and worsening fear that Sulien and Varius might be dead. 'Rome will need more than your assurances to me,' he said.

From his face Una understood the sense of what he said, but not the words. Of course, until now the conversation had been entirely in Latin, but now Marcus had spoken in slow, careful Nionian.

Marcus was not entirely sure what he was doing. If he was simply trying to compete with Tadahito, he was going to fail. He had been taught Nionian since his early childhood, and he was reasonably fluent now, but he didn't have the Prince's obvious talent, and the awareness of that would probably trip him up if he tried to talk at length – he would have to think too much about the language, not about what he was saying.

But there was a confused pause at the change of language before the Prince answered in Nionian, demanding, 'Why would I contact you if we were responsible?'

'There could be many reasons.'

'None as far as I am concerned!' insisted Tadahito. 'Do you think I would lie? Either this is a mistake or you are being manipulated – do you want to start a war on those terms? We would not act and be ashamed of it afterwards.' He was speaking increasingly fast, so that Marcus began to miss words here and there.

'My generals are on their way to advise me,' said Marcus at last, grimly imagining Salvius' response to all this. 'But I know exactly what they will say.'

'That you should not believe me.' The indignation did not leave the Prince's voice, but it had grown tired, depressed.

'Yes,' answered Marcus.

'And do you?'

By now Marcus understood his own instinct to switch languages. It was nothing to do with anything he could say in Nionian himself. Listening to Tadahito speak naturally, his voice bared of the subtle lacquer of proficiency, the tightness and strain in it became more audible, the feeling far easier to gauge. Even if he had to work harder to keep up with the sense, it was as close as he could get to doing what Una could, eavesdropping on the thoughts. He did not respond to the Prince's question, even though the truthful answer was: 'Yes.' Instead he said, 'They will need proof.'

'How can one offer proof that something has not happened?' asked the Prince, sounding at once angry and helpless.

'You can disown it on longvision. You can say what you've said to me to your own people.'

'In Nionia, the Imperial family do not appear on longvision,' said the Prince, in Latin again this time, audibly trying to keep scorn out of his voice that the Romans did. 'Romans cannot understand this. But it does not happen.'

Marcus did not press this, or resist the change back to Latin. 'Fine. I'm not interested in humiliating you. Use whomever you like. I don't care how it's done, so long as it's clear.'

'It will be done. Is this sufficient?'

'No.' Of course it would not be enough, and not only for Salvius, not for anyone.

As he spoke, Una snatched a sheet of paper from the desk. The thought was cold and deliberate enough, although without the passion of dread, she would not have had the nerve to scrawl it down in furious jagged capitals and thrust it at Marcus: 'WALL. TROOPS BACK.' She was shocked at her own intrusion even as she extended her arm, and saw Marcus read it and glance up at her in surprise, still more shocked when he nodded, saying into the longdictor, in Nionian, 'Move your troops back from the wall.'

Tadahito let out an affronted breath, 'You expect us to *surrender*?'

'No. Move them back as far as the nearest towns. The people should still feel protected.'

'Why should we have to make such dangerous amends for something we did not do?'

'Asking me to believe you did not attack us today is just as large a request.'

The Prince was silent for a moment, then he asked, 'How do *I* know you have not done this to yourselves to bring us to this point?'

Marcus had been, if anything, surprised by how calm, or at least controlled, he'd felt so far. He was aware of his hands shaking slightly and had them hidden on his lap, as if the Prince was in the room and could have seen them, but it seemed like a trivial natural phenomenon, unconnected to him. But now he was unprepared for the hot anger that struck at him like nausea that he had to clamp his jaw against – a sudden sharp impression of exploding buildings and screaming people that had been completely lacking so far. 'Because two of my friends were at that factory,' he said. 'And nothing's been heard from them.'

He saw Una start, an obvious wrench of self-reproaching anguish on her face. She pulled the paper back and scratched out, barely legibly, 'If they're alive you'll probably hear before I do. I've got to go anyway,' and fled.

Alone, reading the note as the Prince hesitated, Marcus realised that a callous part of himself had judged that, as he'd been measuring the feeling in Tadahito's voice, it was no bad thing that Tadahito would have heard the anger in his own. It must have sounded convincing. He wouldn't have had a good answer if Sulien and Varius hadn't been at the factory. Again he felt sick.

Someone urged him to wake up, and after delaying for a little while, Varius did. Deep and perfect as his unconsciousness had felt, he seemed to leave it behind easily, as if he had merely been asleep. He knew at once where he was, and what had happened. His ears whistled numbly, he felt the burns ring when he flexed his hands. And there was a heat and a pain in his lungs, but still they filled and emptied, fluently enough. He observed the brickwork, in which the patterns of cracks, the shadows cast by the dessicated weeds at the wall's base seemed so intricate and extraordinary, so specific, that a long second passed before he could look away.

Smoke was fast pushing between the slats in the listing wall of the barracks and the heat was growing intolerable. There was another deep blast, and the ground shook. He looked at Sulien, who was sitting beside him, propped loosely against the wall. Varius hadn't seen him clearly since the explosions began, and he was shocked. Sulien's face was a streaked monochrome, marbled with grey and black and colour-less underneath it, except for the redness of his eyes. One hand rested lightly on the ground beside him, carefully still. With the other he'd been gently tapping at Varius' face and shoulder to wake him, but as Varius lifted his head he withdrew his hand and placed it cautiously over the dark circle of blood that spread across his side. At its centre a snapped blade of stained wood stuck out through his clothes.

Sulien looked back at Varius with half-shut eyes and said lazily, 'Why have you lost your shoe?'

Varius, somehow compelled to answer by the startling pointlessness of the question, gestured at the sheds, and then they fell for a while into a kind of sign language; talking seemed tiring and unpleasant to both of them, as their own roughened voices sounded thin and distant to their overloaded ears.

Sulien turned his hand outward slightly from his chest, towards Varius, palm up: thank you. Varius shook his head, pointing first at the turmoil of light and noise on the other side of the barracks, and then, in questioning horror, at the blood on Sulien's side.

Sulien closed his eyes and nodded slow, absent-minded reassurance. The wound wasn't so bad in itself, the splinter hadn't gone in very far, but the pain and slow seeping blood was weakening him. He'd tried to will the bleeding at least to stop, but whenever he moved the split points stirred and cut into him again, and he couldn't pick the sliver out; when he'd plucked gingerly at it he'd only caused hideous snagging pains in the flesh which he could barely find enough strength to blunt. And his left arm was broken, halfway between the elbow and shoulder, and the edges of bone had been jolted away from each other during Varius' fight to get him out of the shed, though at least they hadn't sliced through the flesh. The break hurt calmly, with a cold ache. About that, too, he felt unable to do anything. He had been afraid that Varius, lying motionless against the wall, might float quietly deeper into unconsciousness and stop breathing, as the soot and dirt settled in the little passages of his lungs. It had been all he could manage to drag himself across to him, concentrate on making sure that the other man's damaged airways were at least adequately clear. Varius looked no better than he did – his face also stained with smoke and the brown skin leached of blood to a dusty, dried-earth colour, his hair singed, a tattered mess on his lower legs – black flakes of burnt cloth on burnt skin.

'Can you walk?' said Varius aloud.

Again Sulien nodded slowly, and raised his hand to make a leisurely so-so gesture.

Varius rose unsteadily to his feet, coughing again, his head pounding.

Sulien said with effortful clarity, 'Varius. A thousand people.'

'No,' Varius told him. 'Some of them must have got out. Come on.'

107

Sulien made an ambivalent move of his head. 'But why? What happened?' he whispered. 'Today – I don't understand it.'

'Think about it later, *come on*,' urged Varius.

He had, once more, almost to lift Sulien, because as Sulien tried to shift his weight it made the muscles around the wound tense so that the tines of wood scraped against them unbearably. It eased once he was actually on his feet, although fans of milder pain opened outwards across his body when he took a step. The simple business of standing up left them both, again, speechless with effort and fatigue. Leaning back on the wall, gasping, Sulien tilted his head back to look up at its sheer height, and the defensive barbs running along its upper edge.

'No,' said Varius, breathless. 'Have to try the way we came.'

Sulien looked out across the blazing and shuddering ground, and felt immobilised with bewilderment as well as exhaustion and fear, as though a reasonable answer would make escape easier. But Varius stumbled forward, head lowered, into the open, and Sulien followed.

The rain of little globules of metal was still falling steadily, and there was no more cover, no way of avoiding the occasional burnt weals, flicked onto their arms and backs as the heated beads bounced off them. Larger and more deadly fragments continued to hurl into space and after a while Sulien concluded it was better to pretend they were not there than to think about dodging them, or you would never move at all. Still, more than once Varius and Sulien either fell or were forced to throw themselves down, jerking the broken lengths of bone in Sulien's arm, driving the splinters closer into his side and causing renewed agony when he had to get to his feet again. He tried to concentrate on something else and it occurred to him that at some point, either just before he was first thrown out into nowhere when the barracks smashed in, or, perhaps more likely, when the most recent explosions had struck him again to the powdery ground, that he'd briefly recovered a strong image of Lal, colourful and lucid – something he'd lost with a speed that had distressed him after she and Delir had disappeared from Holzarta. Though he still kept, in a drawer in his flat, the paintbrush and the bottle of ink from her smashed room in the camp, he could not pretend that he'd been continually haunted by her for three years, but still it saddened him that he could not now force the sharp detail of the memory back: each feature dissolved as he tried to focus on it.

The wall joined the fence. Varius had hoped that the frailer metal barrier might have collapsed, or at least have been damaged enough to let them force their way out, but ahead of them it ran intact until it stretched past an erupting powder shed, which had scattered itself into a wide carpet of fire that extended beyond the fence into the building site on the other side, and was still shaking the ground and kicking flames. It had blown down the fence beside it, but they could get no closer to it or even venture round to see if there were any way out on its far side, without being driven too close to the burning plume of the missile factory. Briefly, through the rolling black smoke, they saw the management building, its pediment hollowed out and cracked, the side wall brought down to show the floors within. Varius began trying to drag and rip exhaustedly at the seam of fence and wall, but the join was too firm, the stakes driven too deep. They called out, scarcely audible even to themselves. There was no one to call to; everyone who lived or worked near the factory must have fled as soon as they'd heard the first blast, primed by long unease at the dangerous thing in their midst. The vigiles would surely come, but even if they dared get close enough to the continuing blasts, it was hard to believe that they could find them in time, in so much burning space.

Varius and Sulien scraped fruitlessly at the fence, and another furrow carved itself terribly through the air, shockingly close to them and low to the earth, so that they both had to drop to the ground, trying to shield their heads. They looked at each other helplessly.

Sulien had no conscious sense that he had given up – the idea would have shocked him, but he could not see what they could do, and he was still surprised, even exasperated at the pain, when Varius started trying to drag him to his feet again. 'What?' he muttered.

'Back there. That thing could have knocked the wall down.' Varius was steering him back towards the barracks again. 'It was low enough. It must have done.'

'All right, in a minute,' Sulien wanted to say, but the words scared him as they formed. He gave an almost irritated grunt and made himself plod along beside the wall again. It seemed stupid to be heading back to where the last missile had flown, and he felt as if he just could not bear to fall over and have to get up again.

The barracks were now roaring as they were consumed, a shapeless heap of glowing timbers under a lush fleece of velvety red fire, rising to high thready peaks and thick unreeling fibres of smoke. The mass had collapsed and spread against the wall, so that there was no way between and they had to veer further into the open, blinking, with a fine smarting pain growing on their skin like sunburn, from the fires on either side. Sulien went on trying to ignore the absurd closeness of the danger, and even sang erratically to himself, almost soundlessly, occasionally hearing a tuneless note through some fluke of the heat-blown air. The flat pain in his arm was growing hotter and more jagged from launching himself down so many times, from having to crawl. Varius, beside him, seemed to keep having to slow down so as not to leave him behind, which frustrated him, and once, when they had skirted round towards the perimeter again, harassed him out of a doze he was alarmed to realise he'd allowed himself. Varius was shouting in his ear, 'The wall *is* down. Come on, you can go to sleep in a minute.'

And it was down – the wall sloped to a pyramid of blackened rubble, and beyond it a trough cut across a road, into a rank of buildings and ended in a quarried pit. But still, the shattered wall was six foot high at its lowest point, a stupid, easy little height, and not even a sheer barrier any more but a crumbled hill – but Sulien's first thought was how much it was going to hurt getting over it, and he had to prompt himself to think no, it's going to be all right, no, this is good.

They made painful, awkward, flopping progress up the wall, like singed frogs up a bank. Sulien felt warm rivulets of blood feel their way along his skin inside his clothes, as the soaked cloth fell away from the wound, and the clamping pain. He thought grimly, never mind. Never mind.

There was another long shower of crushing noise and fire.

On the other side of the wall the churned ground was scattered with burning scraps, and the very existence of this way out proved how they were not safe. But they wove haphazardly down the centre of an empty road, as if it were the middle of the night after all the bars have shut. Sometimes they had to stop; Varius was aware again of the taste of smoke and fumes in his mouth, and the small fund of extra strength burning off like an oil. His lungs squeezed bitterly until, leaning in an open doorway, he was forced to spit out a blackish paste onto the dust.

Quite suddenly they noticed noises other than the factory's roar; the air was violent with hooting, whistling, the bells of the vigiles' trucks, somewhere close. Finally they began to see a few people rushing ahead of them, clutching or dragging things – money chests, pictures, a battered private longvision – either trying to save their possessions from the fire and looters, or looters themselves. Sulien and Varius watched them run, as if they were far further away than they were, but a little way after that, when they came across a wavering crowd, standing and crying and looking back the way that they had come, they turned and saw how far the mast of fire and smoke rose into the sky. It was like an unanswerable signal to stop moving; after that, they could do nothing but collapse onto the cobbles, and wait for help.

It seemed that many of the shivering people in the street were not fleeing the explosion but gathering to watch it, wanting to do something, even though the vigiles and ambulances were coming. Varius was surprised at how swiftly Sulien and he were lifted up, helped into a shopkeeper's van, the driver and his wife both fiercely, effusively concerned about them. The man drove too fast, whenever there was a space to do so in the Roman traffic, and kept telling them almost argumentatively that they would be fine. The woman climbed into the back beside them and stroked Sulien's hair away from his forehead, nearly in tears, wanted to hold Varius' hand, making him flinch as she touched the burns. It occurred to Varius that there was something absurd, *greedy* about all this, and at the same time he found it moving and unexpected, and couldn't speak. Sulien, lying on the floor of the van, felt drowsily obliged to answer and reassure the woman; he kept murmuring wearily, 'I'm all right.'

Una rode through Rome in a slender Palace car that sliced its way through the traffic at ruthless, comforting speed. She was appalled by how quickly the fog of smoke became visible above the city, when the factory was still miles away. Bars of pressure gathered in her head, eyes, chest. She would have refused to cry here in any case, but she both wanted to and felt it physically, oppressively impossible; the grip that encased her whole body would not allow it.

Finally they could drive no further; the traffic collapsed into an impenetrable mass. There were two enmeshed currents of people and vehicles: one flowed away from the disaster, and a second, fainter but definite, towards it. Una leapt out of the car into the bitter air and ran in the direction of the smoke without a backwards look. Soon, however, she reached a second impasse, a bottleneck of people trying to get out or in, and a line of vigiles trying to push the desperate incomers back from the empty streets behind them.

A vigile officer shoved her dispassionately away. That could not have happened in the Palace. Jostled among dust-coated strangers, the Golden House seemed as distant and vague as if she'd never set foot there, while the street felt real and concrete, as if she'd been here before, often, and had finally come back. She began to say to the soldier, 'My brother's there,' and realised what a common and useless thing it was to say here. She stood back a little and looked around. Crying people, she observed, impartially. She thought, cry if you want to, go on, other people are. It was like trying to breathe while being strangled; for less than a second she managed a kind of double spasm, a choking noise, and heat and meagre wetness in her eyes that would not spill, before the sobs crammed themselves ruthlessly back, like screws of abrasive paper being shoved down her throat. The attempt only made the pressure and rawness worse.

She turned mechanically, paced back through the crowd and pressed gently on a front door as she passed it. It was locked; she ignored it and moved on to another. She walked calmly through a tattered little room, seeing nothing in front of her, and out again into the street beyond. The solitude was startling after the throng. She ran along a little way and shouted, 'Sulien,' but the roar in the air and the shriek of the alarms drank up her voice. It was useless, she'd known that really. She remembered hiding on the prison ferry and knowing the second Sulien was pushed on board, before she could see him, even after all that time. There was no chance of that now even if Sulien were alive – the ring of damage around the wrecked factory, framed in scattered and shaken people was too wide.

The scouring tightness in her eyes grew worse, although they remained stingingly dry. She looked up and watched orange belches of flame in the tower of smoke, and even here a warm snow of ash fluttered against her face. The rage with Marcus had spent itself, as she had known it would. She could feel a trapped repeated stinging of pity for him – both Sulien and Varius, and now of all times! – and she wished now that he could have been with her. It would have been good now, as it had not been before, to be told that Sulien simply could not be dead. The palace still seemed so unreachably far away that she felt as if she might never see Marcus again either.

She noticed slowly that she had an indistinct sense of people ahead somewhere, closer to the factory – were they trapped? But as she tried to focus one of the vigiles saw her. She'd come to a helpless stop, standing in the middle of the road and staring, and she stood out not only because of that, she realised, but because her clothes were all wrong, her heather-coloured dress, although it was spattered with cinders now, was too impractically decorative for her to be fleeing a home near the factory. She wished she was wearing something different. She said hoarsely, 'There are still people there, help them,' as the man grabbed her shoulder with a snort of irritation, and steered her back through the cordon. She didn't resist. The whole thing was useless.

It took her an enragingly long time to find the car again in the crush. She gave the driver taut instructions and sat rigidly in the back, trying to picture nothing but whiteness.

By the time she reached the clinic her prediction that Marcus would hear first if Varius and Sulien were alive had come true, but he'd had no way of reaching her. Una marched stiffly through the doors and a sudden hand on her arm made her body jerk, as if she'd been burnt, and

112

sent a vein-flooding shudder rocketing through her, which it took her a second to identify as relief.

Aulus, whom she must have seen fifty times before but for the moment could not recognise, was saying with strange impersonal tenderness, 'Una, he's here, he's not badly hurt. He'll be all right.' Una looked at him blankly, slowly deducing who he was. His round face was soft and honest with shock. 'We thought they were both dead,' he said, unsteadily.

Varius, it seemed, had asked to be taken back to the clinic. In a corridor, Sulien was lying on a stretcher held up on trestles. He said to her conversationally, 'Oh, you're here,' but she wasn't prepared for his bloodless, pain-stiffened appearance and at the sight of him tears did try, finally, to force their way up, but she fastened them back, seeing how they prompted Sulien's eyes also to water, in a kind of helpless sympathetic mimicry. Almost at once, though, he started trying to reassure her, 'It's nothing that bad, I should know, shouldn't I? I can fix it.' He'd managed a smile of greeting but it slid off his face at once, frictionless as a drop of liquid gas. He said, 'But I thought some of the slaves from the factory might end up here. And they haven't, have they?'

'They still might,' said Una.

Sulien nodded, lightly and reasonably, but his eyes went dull. He didn't believe it.

Bearers came to lift the stretcher and Aulus tried to steer her away – they needed to pick the fragments of wood out of the wound. Sulien grabbed at Una's hand, 'No, wait, I need to talk to her.'

There were two things he wanted to tell her: what Varius had done, and what had happened earlier in the day. Una listened with sombre attention.

'What do you think they wanted?' she asked softly.

Sulien let his head fall back, his face creasing with weariness and, again, restrained tears of shock. The question was too exhausting and so was the thought that he had to be able to answer it soon; he could not bear it otherwise. 'I don't know.'

'They're not going to get near you again.'

Sulien again constructed a smile that was incongruously sweet on his grey face, as bearers picked up the stretcher and carried him away.

Una found a silent flight of stairs, sat down and put her face into her hands. She never got much relief from crying; it annoyed her that this concession must be made at all, now the fear was over. She had no patience with the rhythm of it and stopped while she was still shaking and the muscles of her face and chest were still tight. She lifted her head, closing her eyes.

Sometimes she thought she believed in a single god, because of Dama, and Delir and Lal. She had read more since that time, about other faiths that had long since been blurred or stifled out of existence, enough to notice how often, within the Empire, it seemed to be women and slaves who, being starved of fairness, wanted to believe there was more to the world, somewhere to go after they died. Perhaps there was no more to it than that, and she didn't want to be a dupe. Nevertheless, sometimes she believed in God. In the car she had imagined a point of white that began in her head spreading to an infinite blizzard, smoothing the universe. As a slave in London, this was something she'd needed to do daily, or she'd have gone mad. Sometimes she still retreated there, when she had to. What she surveyed now with shut eyes was like that, but it was a live, fathomless space, rather than pallor. She brooded on this, not so much with thanks – which seemed senseless and irrelevant – than with steady-eyed incomprehension. She continued to feel far more outrage that this had happened at all than gratitude that Sulien was alive. She was furious about his broken arm and the wound and the smoke he'd breathed, and more than that, she was frightened by how much the day seemed to have hurt him. And people had died, for no reason. Still, this unfriendly form of praying calmed her in the same remote, measureless way as the silent floods of whiteness did, although it did not wipe out thought. And there was someone that she did want to thank.

First, though, she went and tried to call Marcus. It was frustrating that when she left Marcus at the Palace it seemed to close around him into a baffling labyrinth of pointless formalities and suspicion. It took a long time to struggle through it, which scuffed painfully at her nerves. Marcus' voice, finally, made aggravating tears harass her eyes again, because she wanted him now even more acutely than before, and they could not get to one another.

'I've got to stay here,' she muttered, and explained about the attack on Sulien in the Subura.

Marcus made a sound of sympathetic shock and asked, 'What, does he think it was connected with the factory?'

'In a way. But he can't make any sense of it and neither can I. How *can* they have anything to do with each other? But how could they happen on the same day otherwise?'

'Well – the place is still burning, the vigiles haven't had a chance to investigate. It wasn't bombed from the air, whatever else. We don't know it wasn't an accident. Varius said how dangerous it was there.'

'Come on. We do know. It just can't have been,' said Una.

Marcus sighed, uneasily. 'Stay with him, then, and I'll send an escort of Praetorians for as long as he needs them.'

114

'Thank you.'

'I wish I wasn't shut up here,' he said.

Una listened unhappily to the faint sound of his breath, knowing he wouldn't have much time to talk, unwilling to turn off the longdictor. At last she said, 'The Prince did give in, didn't he? You will go to Bian?'

'Yes, but you'll come too, won't you?

Una smiled into the unseeing air. 'If I think Sulien's safe.'

Varius was in a little room on the first floor. To Una's surprise he was not in the narrow bed that stood against the wall, but standing in the centre of the room. As he got up, a jolt of astonishment at the day had caught him in mid-step and held him motionless, making an incongruously vivid, expectant look hover over his exhausted face, so that he looked as if he'd been waiting for her. His burns had been dressed and he was wearing a combination of borrowed clothes and his own, the garments strange and inconsistent against the singed ones he'd worn to the factory. So far none of the staff would condone what he was doing by helping him get any shoes.

'You can't be meant to go yet,' said Una.

'I hate hospitals,' replied Varius. He'd found that when he spoke in a deliberate whisper the soreness in his chest was less and his voice sounded closer to normal.

Una gave a strained smile. 'But you *work* here.'

Varius' mouth flicked into a small, answering smile. He amended: 'Hospital rooms. I don't mind inflicting them on other people.'

'But will you be all right?'

'Yes,' said Varius, abstracted surprise just audible in his muted voice. 'I feel sure.' He'd been told about the remaining risk from the smoke in his lungs, but he felt, crackling over the ache and shock in his bones, a subtle electric confidence that it wasn't going to kill him. He had to get home and think, he kept telling himself, and then correcting himself dutifully, feeling the dead fatigue throb across his body – no, not think, sleep. But he couldn't sleep or think here.

'You saved Sulien's life. Thank you,' said Una, fast but very clearly and formally, as if she were projecting her voice across an auditorium, and then added abruptly, 'That is, I don't know how to thank you.'

Her face was grave and official, but Varius saw how the words made her shake. 'I – it was just lucky I wasn't knocked out at the start, that I had a chance,' he said lamely. He felt almost dismayed, not exactly at being thanked, but at the fierceness of it, and at not knowing how to answer. Nevertheless, he was not sorry she was there. She looked brittle

115

and pale and surely didn't want to be alone, and he discovered that, for now, neither did he. They stood and talked clumsily for a little while – she told him about Marcus' agreement with the Prince – tentatively proving that something as normal as that was possible. He found he wanted to lay a hand on her shoulder, and did so, even knowing it would hurt. Sharp heat glowed through the dressing on his skin.

The door had been shut while the doctors had examined him, while he'd changed into the borrowed clothes. When Una went she left it open – deliberately, for his sake, Varius was certain. He saw this and felt a quick flaring of indignation – at her knowing, at his own usual feeling of respite – and then it went out, leaving a flat calm. Well, even if he were always like this, what harm did it do, to him or anyone else?

He was so tired by the time he reached home that he might have almost admitted it had been foolish to insist on leaving the clinic. Yet, though he fell onto his bed at once, he couldn't sleep. Or rather, he kept feeling sleep float luxuriously close, enjoying its approach, but then, at the last second, he would draw back from it, his eyes springing open, his heart suddenly pumping fiercely, and he'd think, no, not yet, just a few more minutes – as though the real luxury were being awake. He thought that though the factory was gone, still he must remember to tell Marcus what he suspected he'd learnt about Salvius. And then he wondered if anyone he'd seen for the first and only time that day – the jaundiced women crossing the yard, the strained female clerk, Proculus, any of the ranks of tense and silent slaves in the workshops – if any of them were still alive. The thought made him start on the bed, and he stared into the dark, where, of all the things he had seen that day, it was something so ordinary – the section of dull brickwork he'd noticed when he'd first woken behind the burning sheds – that hung before his eyes as if on a bright screen. If he had been a good enough draughtsman he could have produced a perfect copy of the pattern of cracks and dry stems and shadows. By the time he finally let himself slip into confused dreams he'd given up trying to explain to himself what it had seemed to mean.

At one point he woke up from a chaotic nightmare of hammers and fire and lay tense, shuddering a little, but feeling the addictive tang of adrenaline in his blood. He was impatient that it was not morning, that he was still bitterly tired, and had somehow to get back to sleep. He must speak to Marcus as early as he could the next day. He knew it was a presumptuous thing to do, to ask for a job he'd rejected, but he was so excited by the idea of it now, by the talks in Bian, by being free to do more than beg men like Proculus for poor little scraps of change. He was aware of the clinic too, but now it seemed to him like it had in the beginning: a good, unlikely thing, and because of that he could leave it.

In the clinic, Una stalked restlessly for a long time, up and down the stairs, out to the lobby, peering past the Praetorians into the street. As she watched from an upstairs window, an hour after the streetlights went on, a figure walking past caught her attention, glancing once at the building, at the uniformed men standing on the steps. It was a young man, dipping in and out of shadow as he walked – she could not tell if he matched what Sulien had told her of the men in the apartment block. But even his casual, unremarkable progress down the street set suspicion blazing in her nerves – she remembered moving that way herself, running past the vigile station on the Thames, determined to take everything she needed from a single glance at it. And more than that, she *felt* the strictness of his concentration on the building. She was certain he had wanted to know if Sulien were still alive, and if he were here. And he had understood what the presence of the Praetorians meant. Another guard stood on the landing near Sulien's door, but by the time she'd got him to the window there was no one to point out – the man had gone by, and as she tried to describe him she realised in frustration how there was absolutely nothing distinctive in what she'd seen of him. She had not even been able, in the monochrome light, to tell the colour of his clothes or hair. It was hard even to make her sense of urgency explicable. All the man could do was tell the other guards to watch for such a vaguely described person approaching the clinic again. Una ran out and up the street, knowing she would recognise that tenor of mind if she came close. But she did not, and though, back in the clinic, sprawling uncomfortably in a chair for hours, she barely slept, nothing else happened, all that night.

The pain in Sulien's arm and side, and the various little burnt streaks on his skin had been hushed to a resentful murmur, but still, sleep kept eroding away from above him, too, like dry soil over roots. Of course he was afraid that the people from the Subura, or whoever they had been working for, would look for him again, but it was not so much the fear that kept this rattling of protest shaking him awake, but a terrible, vertiginous bafflement. He kept straining his memory of the few minutes they'd spent in the vast workshop, trying to hold the image still to look deeper into the hot darkness to count the people, study their faces, find something about them to remember. He even felt guilty for having hated Proculus in what must have been his unrecognised last minutes, because he could now picture a family for him, and a mitigatingly blinkered life – and then he veered back to loathing him for keeping all those people in that murderous pit. It was intolerable not to understand this. Naturally he wanted to know who had done it, but almost only as a corollary of knowing the reason for it. And the two things – the attack on him, and the explosion – he kept jamming them together and prising them apart, always recoiling from what seemed like the easiest way of connecting them: that both were attempts on his life. No, it was inconceivable. Surely no one would ever do that, destroy so much, kill a thousand people just to get to one? You would have to be mad.

VII

THE GHOST

He had, at least, the possibility of a chance, lasting perhaps a week, perhaps longer. It was bad luck that Sulien had not been killed at Veii; still, for now he was not at the Palace. Drusus decided it was worth trying again to talk seriously to his uncle.

Drusus had taken a lovely villa on the Quirinal hill, everything in it as new and perfect as an egg. And it had suitable rooms for Amaryllis, who had been conveyed across from Byzantium with the rest of his things. The clean freshness of the house had soothed him at first but then, within only a day or two, and for reasons he could not define, had made him feel isolated and panicked, and needing the girl too often, so that he had hastily constructed a party, lavishing money on it for food, drink, musicians, and gilt-skinned dancers and prostitutes. The long night passed for Drusus in a strung-out haze – of continuing nervousness as much as alcohol – and it shook the house into a foul-smelling ruin of trampled rose petals and vomit, which strangely seemed to be what he'd wanted, although the mess was such that he'd had to move back to his father's house while the slaves cleaned it up. Both during this time, and in the fortnight or so on the Caelian before he found the villa, his father kept trying in small, anxious, dog-like ways to look after him, to make him happy. Drusus was aware of these little things – Lucius' quiet enquiries about what he wanted to eat, about his health – and he thought cynically how belated and absurd it was, and yet he was confused to realise that he rather liked it too, that it was nice to be tended to in this way. He did not even mind Lucius gently asking him if he had any thoughts of getting married. 'I'm sure one of these days I'll get round to it,' Drusus had said, truthfully enough. There was no particular reason why a wife should inconvenience him.

Once – much more timidly, fear of his son cluttering his speech with half-stifled syllables that Drusus could barely understand what he was saying – Lucius tried to pick up the conversation about being Emperor again, but Drusus, gradually reassembling some sort of hope, some sort of plan, was no longer in the mood.

But when he went back to the Golden House, his hopes of Faustus came to nothing. He thought at first that he would not be allowed to see his uncle at all. Finally, the calmly obdurate doctor let him in, but would not be persuaded to leave the room and scarcely even troubled to disguise the fact that it was Drusus, not Faustus, that he was there to watch. 'I've had clear instructions,' he kept repeating. Faustus might still have countermanded all of this, but he sat listlessly in a chair and seemed reluctant to notice his nephew's urgency. His voice was thick and embarrassingly difficult to understand, but evidently he noticed Drusus' dismay and the irritable grimace on his face was clear enough. He made no effort to prevent Drusus from being hurried from the room.

Drusus wandered bleakly into one of the palace galleries. It was the feeling of being laughed at that rankled more than anything, and he was tired. It was still early but the light soaked the room with gold heat. Drusus stared heavily at a vast canvas of Oppius – the first Novian Emperor, rising in an heroic and foolhardily exposed stance atop a primitive armoured vehicle, in the act of subduing the Nionians in Abenacia. His arm was aloft and a great sweep of cloak soared from his shoulders into the snowy sky, like a flag or a pair of red wings, flooding a quarter of the canvas. Drusus found the image vaguely uplifting and encouraging, and wondered if Oppius was the one that had first gone mad. No, presumably not, or surely the dynasty wouldn't have gone any further and Drusus would not be standing here now. Would not even exist, in fact. What a strange thought that was.

Of course he knew the outline of the madness story, but he had managed to avoid ever hearing it told very clearly or fully. By the time he would have been old enough to understand, Drusus and his mother already had good reason not to want to think about it: Lucius was ill, or so they believed. Drusus could remember when he was perhaps ten and he could look down from here, and see the very place in the gardens where it had happened – Leo cornering him and hectoring him, wanting to tell him some myth of sin and retribution. Drusus had felt that Leo was trying to make a cruel point about his being Lucius' son, or perhaps punishing him unjustly for making the two-year-old Marcus cry, when that had been nothing to do with him. He'd fled, persecuted and miserable, to look for his mother.

He had another reason to be here now: he was supposed to go to a meeting about the peace talks, about who was going to Bian, who was staying. And while Drusus did not really feel like going after what had just happened, he knew he must not let himself get downhearted too easily. He needed to speak to the one other person beside himself that the picture had made him think of. So he calculated which way Salvius was likely to come, and waited, and as the senators began to gather, fell in with him on the way to the banqueting hall in the room full of mirrors. Salvius was striding along with his head lowered, his body visibly tense with a forboding that looked close to despair.

'I've just been in the gallery,' Drusus announced.

Salvius, transparently uninterested, uttered a preoccupied sound.

'I was wondering what Oppius would have made of all this,' said Drusus, allowing a little fatalistic humour into his voice. Salvius looked at him sharply and Drusus concluded sadly, 'About what you do, I should think.' And because he needed to for this conversation, Drusus felt what he knew Salvius felt: stark terror for Rome at how recklesly Marcus was gambling with it. But he remained half-aware that, despite everything, he still had faith that everything would come out as it should. The peace talks were a nonsense, a sideshow, but at least they would get Marcus away from Rome.

Salvius laughed dejectedly, which Drusus could see was a relief to him, and said, 'He'd feel able to do something.'

'Then perhaps that's a lesson,' remarked Drusus.

These words caused a small shock of mingled excitement and alarm in Salvius, before he even had a chance to decide what Drusus meant. It touched the edges of what he'd felt before, on the spiralwing, holding the axe and rods in his hands, the confused and painful thoughts about what constituted treachery. But Drusus didn't go on and his expression stayed casual. With relief, and yet reluctantly too, Salvius decided that it had probably meant nothing.

Drusus had left a second for this to happen. His instincts had told him not to look at Salvius after he spoke, not to make what he'd said seem too significant, so he could only hope that Salvius had reacted as he wanted. He said companionably, 'Well, you should know what's going on, even if I don't. Are they saying who's going to take the reins while he's in Sina?'

'I think it'll be Eudoxius. Almost certainly.'

'Oh, yes?'

'It's a good choice, in the circumstances,' said Salvius unhappily.

'You could have done it,' suggested Drusus.

'I would have been very surprised by *that*.'

'So would I, to be honest, the way things are going now. But you might have expected it, if the situation was different.' Drusus walked beside Salvius silently, aware that there was no need for him to say anything more, that his presence was enough. Eudoxius was a senator from Armenia. Drusus could see perfectly well why Marcus had picked him, and it was true, he was a good choice. He was patient and intelligent, but he had risen to the Senate through slow, unassuming effort, and was now about Faustus' age; he was unlikely to succumb to a sudden bout of ambition. He would manage, without being a threat.

'Of course,' said Salvius after a moment, becoming uncomfortable. 'You – you have the best claim of all, really. The Emperor would have wanted—'

'Wants,' corrected Drusus, very mildly, very softly.

'He's said so?'

'My uncle? Do you really think he's given a chance to say anything?'

'What do you mean by that?' asked Salvius, sounding urgent and concerned.

Drusus sighed and shook his head. 'Oh, what does it matter? I thought his intentions were clear from the start. But I don't know, perhaps it's for the best – I can't compete in terms of experience with you, any more than with Eudoxius. I'm not so much older than my cousin, I know that. I might have listened to wiser people, though. And I think I'd have been slower to believe all these claims of wounded innocence from Nionia than he has.'

He did look at Salvius now and they smiled at each other.

The wound under Sulien's ribs had healed, and he'd made the broken edges of bone knit together far quicker than they could have done alone, but, he explained to Una, it was like paint or glue, dry to a light touch after a few hours, but not perfectly solid. But there was little he couldn't do with the arm, and the minor caution with which he had to treat it would last only a few more days. And he seemed in good spirits, considering what had happened. He had always been so supply resilient, like water. Now the flat kept filling with his friends, who dragged him out to plays and races, trailing his embarrassing little retinue of guards with them, or brought wine and got him drunk where he was. Tancorix came almost at once with little Xanthe, who charged around the room trying noisily to entertain Sulien – successfully, it seemed, to Una's surprise. Still, Una kept thinking of what he'd said about half-set glue: often he would be animated and then, suddenly, lapse away for a few seconds, the muscles of his face sagging, the blood vessels emptying, while his eyes became slow and distant, shadowed as if by smoke.

It wasn't only the thought of the slaves from the factory – there were more dead. The glow of the fire had raged like a long dawn over Rome all that night; it had been late morning before the vigiles could control it, and three of them had died. But the missiles that had ploughed into the surrounding streets had killed more; the number had just reached sixty, the latest a father of two children, his lungs scalded. Sulien thought that if he'd known in time perhaps he could have got to the man and saved his life. He spent a whole day repeatedly slipping back into guilt and fury that no one had told him. Una couldn't remember seeing him so angry. He'd been frustratingly slow to blame anybody even for trying to have him crucified.

And he didn't know how many others were injured. And that sounded so weak, so uninteresting beside a given number of dead, but Sulien kept thinking about pain: about broken spines, lost limbs, scars.

He started going back to work, but erratically, for specific things he wanted to do: repair Varius' burns, do what he could to mend Bupe's dis-figured face, although once he was at the clinic, it was difficult to leave; there was always somebody that needed him. He didn't understand why this tired him so much more than he was used to, when there was virtu-ally nothing wrong with his body. One day he went in to find that Bupe had gone, it seemed she'd climbed out of a window overnight, even with her one curtailed hand. It sometimes happened. But this time Sulien felt personally unhappy as if it were his fault. He'd felt a confused fel-low feeling with Bupe and kept being surprised to remember that she'd arrived at the clinic before the disaster at the factory. He couldn't shake the false memory that that was when she'd been hurt, that she'd been there with Varius and himself.

He kept trying to remember more – just for its own sake, or the sake of all those dead, not because he really thought there was anything sig-nificant he might have missed. Una wanted to make him stop, because he was normally so bafflingly good at paring his memory down to the minimum he needed.

Marcus came to the flat as soon as he could, trying to be anonymous in the simplest of the possible cars, and informal dress, but the memory of him in the purple robe made him look slightly bizarre to Sulien now, sitting on the floor with a chipped wine glass in his hand. And of course he had guards of his own. With Sulien's, they clogged up the stairs out-side the small flat and stood, stern and awkward, by the windows.

Sulien walked into his bedroom where the one guard actually inside the flat stood watching the street. 'Why don't you just come and talk to us?'

'I can't,' the man mumbled, embarrassed at being spoken to.

Sulien shrugged and went back to Una and Marcus muttering, 'This is ridiculous, how can you live like this?'

'Longer than I would without them, supposedly. But history shows that doesn't always work,' said Marcus.

Sulien didn't smile. 'I wish something *would* happen, so they'd have some kind of point.' He thought of Leo and Clodia after speaking, and felt guilty even though Marcus was the one who'd touched on the idea of his parents, and plainly wasn't offended.

But Una flinched slightly and ordered him, 'Don't say that.'

'Oh, come on,' said Sulien, finding the annoyance he wanted. 'I mean I don't *need* them. What happened – it was probably just ...' But he couldn't find a conclusion.

'What if they leave and someone kills you? You don't have any choice,' Marcus told him, a trace too much authority in his voice for Sulien.

'You can't say that to me,' he said. He laughed, but there was a soft leather case for papers lying messily on the sofa beside him and he scooped it up and pitched it at Marcus, with a sharp incredulous smile on his face, striking Marcus' head harder than he meant to. 'I don't care if you're Emperor, you can't tell me what to do.'

Marcus threw the case back, almost as aggressively, saying, in the same grim half-joking voice, 'I *am* telling you what to do,' and they began clumsily grappling. They crashed about a little, their faces both bright with amusement and frustration until the guard from the next room came in at the sounds of violence.

'It's all right,' gasped Marcus, as Sulien let him go and threw himself back disconsolately in his chair.

'I could have the gun and let them go home,' he said. 'Then, even if something did happen ...' A small chill afflicted him, making him remember the feeling when, years before, he had actually held a gun.

'I have seen no evidence you could hit anything,' said Marcus sonorously, a deliberate parody of Imperial arrogance this time weighting his voice so that he sounded inadvertently like Drusus.

Sulien lashed out at him loosely again, in less complicated affection this time

Una said, 'Sulien, it's only until we know what happened.'

Sulien sighed again and asked Marcus, 'Do you know anything now?'

'I've only been hearing about Veii. And you are right. It could have been an accident.'

Sulien blinked, slightly alarmed to realise that he had, indeed, said that. Watching him, Una saw the dull look cross his face again. 'I don't think it was an accident,' he said flatly. 'I don't know why I said that. Don't tell me you think that.'

'I don't,' answered Marcus carefully. 'But I don't know if that's because it really is unlikely, or just because what happened was so *bad*. Of course a lot of people are telling me it must have been the Nionians. But I do believe Tadahito, unless it could have happened without his knowing – but I think not. I ...' He broke off, holding his breath against a new pang of anxious self-doubt. At least it did not come so often now, this feeling. Finally he went on. 'It could have been Africa. One of the border countries. They're not exactly comfortable with how close we are. They'd probably like to see us weaker, and concentrating on Nionia. But I think it's more likely it wasn't from outside the Empire at all. Terranova, or Ethiopia. India, even.'

'Separatists. But wouldn't they claim responsibility?'

Marcus looked almost shifty, and to Sulien's surprise answered, 'They have. But that ... happens. "We're coming, we're going to do more ..." It happened when I was missing, even. There is something, though. There was a man called Atronius, he started work at Veii about a fortnight before it happened. He was a slave manager.'

'And?'

'He was from Maia,' said Marcus.

'Is that it? Where he came from? This *is* Rome.'

'He was supposed to be connected to some faction there. Though whether he really was doesn't seem to add up to much. It could be just that he went to school with someone or was friends with someone's cousin or something. That's about as clear as it's got, so far.'

'Isn't he dead, anyway?'

'He hasn't been seen. Perhaps he is. Or he could have set it up and gone underground. If there were someone on the inside, he looks the most likely. That's all there is, really, I'm sorry.'

'But why would you need to be on the inside for a fortnight? You just get in and do it, wouldn't you, if you knew how? And why,' the words became stiff and reluctant, 'when I was there. I mean – why just after those people in the Subura ...'

'Perhaps they thought they could achieve something, either by holding you hostage or – killing you,' said Marcus, unwillingly too. 'They might have thought it would mean more, on the same day.' He was leaning against the couch where Una sat, and her hand hung down and rested on his chest. He took hold of it, looking up at her urgently. 'You must be careful too. You must.'

'I am,' she said, with unsatisfying calm.

Sulien retrieved the case he'd thrown at Marcus, felt for a pen inside it and began searching the room for a fresh sheet of paper on which to write Atronius' name.

'What are you doing?' asked Marcus, as Sulien found what he was looking for.

'I don't know. Nothing.' It was true that when he re-read the firmly printed name, he didn't know what he intended to do with it. He exhaled wearily and looked at Una and Marcus. Marcus had let go of her hand and Una was combing her fingers meditatively through his hair, while looking straight ahead of her and thinking about something, her expression absorbed and stern.

'Una, why don't you go back with him?' Sulien demanded suddenly.

She looked up. 'Because I don't think I should.'

'You want to. And you want to go to Sina.'

She said nothing but kept looking at him gravely.

Sulien sat down near Marcus and said with strained buoyancy, 'You need all the help you can get, don't you, Marcus?'

Marcus gave a small embarrassed laugh and did not actually deny it.

'I need to know you're safe,' said Una.

'How can I not be? I've got my own militia. Unless you think there's anything dodgy about any of them?'

'No,' Una conceded, wavering slightly.

Sulien made himself relax as they looked at each other. He gestured at the next room where the Praetorian kept watch. 'Well I'm stuck with them. I can *tell* you to go, I don't want you here for this reason. But as it is, please go. Really.'

Una made an uncertain sound, and went on fingering Marcus' hair. Marcus and she hadn't been apart very long, but the time seemed to count for much more when things were moving so fast, and Sulien was right to hint that Marcus felt more exposed without her. But there was more than that: she didn't want to be absent any time Drusus was near Marcus. Since the explosion at the factory she had been even more impatient for a chance to study Marcus' cousin. It was not that it had struck her that he might be responsible – in a way, it was the opposite. She did not see how she could search out and pin down whomever had threatened Sulien, but if there were dangers nearer at hand, within her reach, it seemed more urgent to know them. And if Drusus had had nothing to do with Tulliola or Gabinius or the rest of them, if Marcus was safe with him, it was important to stop wasting her time thinking about it.

Drusus mixed water with a little wine, a safe amount for this time of day – but then he noted sourly that Marcus was not touching the wine at all, not even diluted. Fine, thought Drusus, setting down his own glass untasted. If you're taking no risks then neither will I. He gestured for a slave to take it away, to be sure that he would not pick it up again absent-mindedly, and as a boy came to do it, he found himself unaccountably uneasy. The boy was fractionally late in responding, his fingers faintly careless as he grabbed the glass, his footsteps too noisy when he withdrew. And instead of a brief, gliding, impersonal presence, Drusus had an obtrusively strong sense of the boy's face: his expression was jaunty, and just possibly mocking. And there were a few other things wrong that Drusus, surprisingly slowly and laboriously, eventually connected to the fact that the attendants were no longer slaves. There was a puddle of water at the corner of the table, dripping onto the ground. A few acacia leaves, scorched early by the long summer, had fluttered in among the plates and onto the couch where Drusus lay. It was a while before Drusus even noticed these flaws, or thought of them as failures of the servants, but nothing felt quite right. He had never felt so unpleasantly conscious of how many extra people were in the room, watching him eat. He disliked the fact that he could not keep his eyes on all of them. He kept suspecting them of laughing amongst themselves.

The meeting was being held around a low table, shaded by Sinoan screens and an ivory fringed awning, in a kind of open court or garden room, open to the sky and the Palace grounds ahead of it. A pair of sparrows bounced across the paved ground. The table was spread with a light meal; dishes of pastries and fruit, decanters of chilled wine. The food somehow mitigated Una's presence, Drusus would have felt intense scorn if he'd found her among senators anywhere else. She did not, at least, appear self-satisfied at being there, or to take it for granted. She seemed unable to relax enough to stretch out loosely on the couch, resting instead in a tense, crouched curl beside Marcus, as if trying to occupy minimal space. Drusus' eyes had met hers by chance as he settled himself at the table, and unexpectedly she gave him a wide, shy, apologetic smile, then dipped her eyes modestly and barely raised them again. Drusus approved of the shyness; it seemed such a graceful admission of humility that it seemed only fair to admit to himself in turn that her precise, hard-boned little face was not quite as boring to look at as he'd thought, not when she smiled, anyway. Of course it was natural that the poor thing would be intimidated.

Salvius was less won over by her presence. Curled up like that, with glossy, dust-coloured hair falling around her face in timid curtains, letting the discussion proceed around her lowered head without even seeming to listen, she did indeed look as smooth and fragile and incapable of understanding what was being said as a pet greyhound. But Salvius thought she must have been attempting a similar effect on the journey from Siphnos, when she'd been less able to disguise an expression of underhanded watchfulness. But even with this warning in his mind, even though, beside Marcus, she was in such a position of status, it was almost hard to remember she was there.

Una did not need to look at Drusus again. She felt equipped, prepared to work, there was even a pinch of pre-emptive triumph that now she had him, and he would not escape. She looked down gently at the food with unfocused eyes, and as the couches filled around her, she began to filter away everyone in the room except the two of them, Drusus and herself.

Drusus was watching Marcus and the way the assembling people looked at him and smiled. It's started, he told himself. He noticed that the Imperial ring was not, this morning, on his cousin's hand – presumably he'd left it off by accident. But Marcus seemed to need it so much less. He had given a reasonable impression of confidence at the beginning, but it was plainly real now, and the power he held was beginning to draw a helpless tide of approval and admiration. More or less everyone seemed to like him – or to *believe* they did, Drusus thought bitterly. And Marcus was smiling, the hollow-eyed look Drusus had seen in him when he first arrived had gone. What you like is being able to order about men three times your age, Drusus accused him silently.

And it was true. It was impossible for Marcus not to enjoy it. They began to discuss how long the talks might last – at least a fortnight, they agreed, but probably a lot longer, and Marcus gave his cousin a friendly wave across the table. He was surprised and slightly ashamed at feeling like this, so soon after all those deaths in Veii and when the whole world seemed so brittle and close around him. But now that the talks were really set to happen, even though Marcus knew they might come to nothing, and feared that Salvius was right to think they were a dangerous folly to begin with, hope seemed to flicker from everything he touched. And he was no longer so isolated: Varius had found someone to manage the clinic, he was coming to the palace that same day. Already he'd been the one to suggest Eudoxius as a substitute. Marcus remembered watching Drusus across another palace table just after his parents' funeral, conducting the slaves with easy poise as if they were puppets attached to his person by hair-fine threads. And now all the harmony had gone, and there was Drusus left skulking and bewildered in the wreckage of it. Marcus could not help the pleasure he felt. He was aware of Una at his side, settling into her most guardedly impassive manner, could even guess from the decorous set of her body, at the defensive simper that would be on her lowered face, but he hoped she noticed this. He was so happy that she was there to see it.

'There are things that should be done before we go,' he said, quite naturally now, after all, he'd been preparing for this all his life, apprehensive as he might have been about it. 'Most of it will be quite routine, but not everything. I'm sure everyone knows about the illness that recurs in my family. My father always told me it began after one of our ancestors crucified a child. And you also know that three years ago I had to leave Rome very suddenly and for a while I had to live a kind of life I would never normally even have witnessed. I don't think I'd be alive now, if it were not for the people I met.'

He looked at Una here, and felt a light responsive touch on the back of his hand, but the fact that the contrived sweet, vacant look stayed on her face told him that she didn't want attention drawn to her, and he thought with regret that she was probably right.

'One of them had been convicted of a crime that had never taken place, and condemned to crucifixion. It was not the courts or any system of ours that saved his life, or by extension, mine. He might have been rearrested at any moment and subjected to what we all know was always intended to be a terrible form of death, as terrible as centuries of efficient use of technology could make it. And ...' For a second he hesitated, considering telling more, but deciding against it. 'And I was sure then that this is not, or it should not be, Roman. It's barbaric. Perhaps it is why our family has suffered so long. I think we should end it.'

This was a simplified essence of the truth. The hesitation had come when he'd wanted to talk about Dama, and the horror of what had been done to his body when he was only a few years older than the boy in the curse story; his stretched, half-dead arms and stiffened feet; four years of illegal life and continuing pain. But better not. Dama wasn't as easy or as innocent an example as Sulien. He had committed the crime for which he'd been so exhaustively punished. He could never have settled as naturally into Roman life as Sulien had, who had grown up thinking of himself as essentially a Roman citizen anyway. And Dama had certainly hated Marcus at first; if he'd softened at all it was only ever to the extent of ignoring him. Still, Dama had helped to save his life, even if not for Marcus' sake. And he'd died for it. For, unlike Una and Sulien, Marcus felt fairly certain that Dama was dead. And because of that, he tried to bring Dama's ghost close for a minute, to tell it, 'Please see this, please accept this from me. I'm sorry it was too late for you.' And somehow uneasy, he added doubtfully, 'Will you rest, now?'

There was a low swell of surprise around the table, but with a quickness that Drusus found depressingly predictable but that plainly shocked Marcus, most of the men's faces arranged themselves into a look of agreement and approval. Marcus felt dazed, and struggled to contain a little fizz of euphoria. It can't really be as easy as that, he thought.

Oh, what do you expect, Drusus wanted to say. They're all sheep. But he found he couldn't eat any more; a confused current of feeling had gone through him at the mention of the curse, a welling up of nineteen years of cringing misery about his father, and the different shame since he'd learnt the truth. He was virtually indifferent about crucifixion as far as politics went; on the whole it seemed foolish to give up a useful tool, he could have argued that passionately, not really feeling much. But he wondered painfully – even without cynicism – could this work? The fear he'd grown up with – would this make it stop?

Falx, a thin, tanned, dry-skinned man at least had the courage to say, 'Caesar, surely this will endanger Roman citizens? We need the deterrent.'

'No,' answered Memmius Quentin calmly before Marcus could speak. 'Our slaves and any barbarian residents will have more reason to comply with an authority that treats them fairly. It will make the Empire safer.' He smiled, his face aglow with totally impartial satisfaction at this piece of ingenuity, as if he had solved a puzzle. Salvius was certain that Quentin had no real opinion and could not prevent a grimace of contempt.

'What do you propose instead?' asked Eudoxius without rancour.

Marcus' exhilaration faded. He'd tried to summon Dama's ghost a minute before, now he imagined an anonymous legion of phantoms, filling the room, and the palace and its ground, rushing the Palatine hill; he could not evade a slow, incredulous feeling that, in a sense, he was about to kill an unknown number of unknown people. 'I don't see that we need inventive methods,' he said more quietly. 'When citizens are executed we use ... firing squads.'

'The Nionians do it – crucifixion,' remarked Salvius suddenly, and there was a pause as it was not clear, even to Salvius himself as he spoke, whether he meant this in support or in opposition. He looked down, discomfited. Perhaps, he thought, the boy was even right on this, perhaps abandoning a form of torture Nionia still practised would prove which Empire was truly civilised. In any case, it wasn't worth squandering whatever power he had, better to save himself for more important things.

Something obvious suddenly occurred to Drusus. Why was Marcus really doing this? Why would anyone? Well, he'd as good as admitted it openly: 'Perhaps it is why our family has suffered so long.' Marcus was afraid of going mad. Well, they all were, but perhaps Marcus even felt it germinating in himself. Drusus looked up in excitement but could see no obvious sign of disorder in Marcus' expression, still, that was surely the answer and it gave him a boost of hope.

Una stared at the reflection in a dish of olive oil, mechanically swirling a piece of bread around in it, concentrating on her quarry, intent but baffled. Something incredible, something she'd fiercely wanted, was happening around her, and she was missing it, but she could not stop although the pursuit grew maddening. She had thought these minutes would be all the time she needed to be sure about Drusus – why was she not? This time, she could see the tendrils of resentment in Drusus that flexed when Marcus mentioned how close, three years ago, he'd been to death, but they led her nowhere, to nothing, the memories she expected to find at their roots did not appear. She began to think, with irrational disappointment, that she had been too suspicious. Drusus was innocent – jealous of Marcus, still half-hopeful that he might somehow find himself on the throne, but nothing more. It must be as simple as that. If he'd planned Marcus' death, surely he could not sit opposite him now and feel no flutter of guilt, nor even a sullen reflection on plans that must have failed.

Was it only arrogant displeasure at being wrong that made her feel so unconvinced, so unsatisfied by this? She thought, uncertainly, that he was somehow not solid. That he must be as elusive to himself as he seemed to her. That it was as if there were nothing to him but *this* mood, *these* thoughts. For a second she thought of Sulien, plunging down from the trap at the top of the Subura tenement, flinging open doors; it was as if she wanted to find her way down through a block of flats, but there were no doors or stairs between the rooms: a structure that couldn't exist, didn't make sense.

After what Drusus had said, Salvius was surprised to see how little part he took in the discussion. As he'd expected, Marcus asked Eudoxius to run affairs in Rome, and Eudoxius, who was fluffy-haired, round bodied and lolling tranquilly on his couch, went through a genial show of reluctance that Salvius found irritating. Drusus raised no objection to any of it. But one glance at Drusus' face was enough to tell him why – he'd given up on voicing any disagreement with Marcus because he no longer saw any point.

Salvius hesitated only for a moment. This can't be allowed, he thought. If Drusus Novius won't then I must. I can't complain if I don't even try. And he said brusquely, 'Your Highness, I don't mean any insult to Eudoxius, but didn't the Emperor mean you to share the burden of your position with your cousins, to some extent? And wouldn't this be an obvious occasion?'

Marcus was silent for a second. Eudoxius smiled in embarrassment as the others turned their eyes to Marcus in startled expectation. Marcus looked at his cousin and said in an irreproachably friendly voice, 'But I hope you'll come with me to Sina, Drusus. Of course our uncle knew I'd need your help. But you can't help me if you're not there.'

Such a possibility had never occurred to Drusus. He raised himself up a little, tense. If he refused an offer that sounded so reasonable, in front of everyone, it would look bad. He said lightly, prevaricating, 'Well, distance means so little these days. We can speak face to face at the touch of a switch, if ever you *did* want to talk to me. What is the time difference? Eight hours?'

'But it's hardly the same,' Marcus objected blandly, still smiling.

Drusus shifted restlessly on the couch. 'It's not for me to comment on General Salvius' suggestion, but perhaps in your absence, and at such a critical time, the people might be reassured to know that a representative of their Imperial family remained in Rome.'

'It's generous and honourable of you to consider staying for that reason,' said Marcus warmly, giving an excellent performance of taking his cousin's words entirely at face value and being fondly impressed by them. 'But there is no greater challenge than this facing the entire Roman nation, and if you stay here you will not be part of resolving it. And I would like you to be.'

'Come on, now, Marcus,' said Drusus, in a low voice, like the first, quietest growl of a provoked dog.

'You will come, won't you?' urged Marcus, all relaxed blond generosity.

'Well – I ...' He felt trapped. Marcus had deliberately trapped him. Drusus cast about for a way of saying anything but yes, and managed to shrug, attempting to make a kind of joke of it. 'Well, whatever I think you should do, you do the opposite, so ...' He cast a grim, humourously knowing look at the men around the table, adding breathlessly to them, 'You know how it is – in families!'

'I know we disagree,' said Marcus, calmly. 'And I can't always act as you want me to. But that doesn't mean it isn't worth your telling me what you think.'

Oh, the shameless liar, thought Drusus, his pulse quickening, and he exclaimed, 'Hardly. You have done everything you can to *gag* me, and the Emperor himself. In his own palace.'

Everyone was looking at him now, and as well as alarm Drusus felt a reeling pleasure at being seen that way, as if each pair of eyes on him lent him a little dangerous weight and force. 'It's true,' he said. 'I know my uncle would want to see me, and you have made it impossible. Isn't it true that you're keeping him in the dark about all these things you're doing?' He glanced at Salvius and felt faintly steadied by the concern he saw in his face. He forced himself to calm down a little, made his voice more level and plausible. 'I tried to see the Emperor this morning. I was prevented from speaking to him alone. You made sure of that, didn't you?'

Again there was silence as Marcus considered what to do. He was aware that this had never happened before; never had there been such loud hostility between them, and least of all in public. And though Marcus was the one in power, and Drusus was so agitated and indignant, Marcus could sense that there was a risk here, and Drusus did have some advantages – not least that he was, largely, telling the truth. He swung himself to sit upright. 'Yes, I did, Drusus,' he answered. 'Because when you last went to see him, your aim was to make him believe he'd done the wrong thing choosing me instead of you.'

'I did nothing of the kind!' cried Drusus.

Una felt such a slap of shock that she forgot her meek disguise and looked up to stare Drusus in the face with frank amazement. She knew he was lying. But only because Sulien had told her what he'd witnessed. If she had walked into the room knowing nothing of what had happened, she'd have been sure he was being honest. All she could see in him was real outrage, no little scattering of escaping truth. He believes it himself, she started to say to herself. And that was nearly true, it was adequate as a shorthand. But it could not be quite right. What had really happened could not be lost to him beyond recall. It was rather that the past seemed to have no existence outside himself. It could not, at least, compete with his commitment to the words at the moment of saying them, a commitment so total as to pass for belief.

'I think it's understandable that you did,' went on Marcus. 'I know you're afraid I'm mistaken over Nionia. I know how anxious you are not to risk Rome's strength. I *do* understand. But you can't go behind my back like that. He's too ill in any case.' He lowered himself down again on the couch, appealing mildly, 'If something I'm doing displeases you, just come to me.' He meant most of this. But he had his own capacity of manipulation, and right now he wanted to keep Drusus angry.

Drusus found he was on his feet, retorting furiously, 'You know well what good *that* would do!' and he strode away from the table, towards the gardens. Before he even reached the steps he realised with a hot blaze of self-hatred that this must have been exactly what

Marcus was hoping to make him do. But by then it was too late to go back.

Marcus felt relieved, watching the senators' unease at the confrontation turn to nervous laughter, but he was left slightly shaken, and before that had subsided he felt a whisk of movement at his side and turned to see Una spring lightly to the floor and follow Drusus, almost at a run.

VIII

DUEL

Drusus walked fast, inhaling the powdery rose scent on the warm, insect-shrilled air. He began to remind himself that Salvius might still be a good ally, but he didn't want to think, he didn't want either to reassure himself or dwell on the damage he'd just allowed. He only wanted to be further away from Marcus.

'Your Highness, do come back.'

Drusus half-turned and the mere sight of Una, tagging behind with an eager conciliatory smile on her face, seemed exhausting to him. He let out a sigh that was almost a plea and went on walking. She pressed on after him.

'Please,' she persisted, her voice urgent but very gentle, soft-timbred. 'Please don't leave things like this.'

Drusus grimaced towards the heavens, uttering a harrassed click of the tongue; it seemed to him not only unfair but distasteful that he should have to detach this pest from himself, but he struggled to be as careful as he could; being rude to Marcus' mistress would not help matters. He said, with stilted patience, 'Thank you for your concern. I would prefer to be alone.'

Una dallied, allowing him a head start as they crossed a paved yard bounded with azaleas, down steps into a sunken lawn. The gold sun burnt in her eyes, making the lids draw together, and she let the softness slip from her face, marching faster again to match his pace at a distance of perhaps fifty feet, structuring what to say to him as he reached an avenue of umbrella pines. Entreating him to come back to the meeting was a good reason to keep close to him for a while, but she was working for more than time. She was composing a way of talking about Leo and Clodia.

Drusus half-realised she was still behind him but he couldn't entirely believe it; he expected at each moment that if he ignored her, she had to go away. And as she did not catch him up, he sank into himself and

135

the warm sun and forgot about her. As he walked, the panicking desperate song of the blackbirds in the arched, steel-skeletoned aviary grew louder and more beautiful, almost drowning out the low crooning of the city below the Palatine hill. Drusus let himself in, hearing the rattle of startled wings as they burst up into the trees. He sat down on one point of a crescent-shaped marble bench. There were all kinds of birds, the blackbirds for music, but there were others far more exotic: bright birds from the tropics, tiny hovering birds like warm malachite-green bees. But he didn't feel like looking at them, he sensed the troubling motion in the air through closed eyes.

When he opened them he found with a light, hallucinatory shock that Una was sitting opposite him on the other point, leaning a little towards him, perfectly still as if she had materialised there. He had not heard her footsteps.

'There is still time,' she said.

Drusus looked at her numbly, without answering. Una remained in exactly the same position, propped on the one hand that she'd slid towards him, her head a little tilted. Leaning like this not only looked sympathetic but kept her head at a self-effacing level lower than his.

She said with slightly overstressed clarity, 'I know you will think it's very presumptuous of me to come after you. To talk to you at all.'

'No,' managed Drusus listlessly, enduring her.

'I'm glad,' she said sweetly, smiling again. She shaded her eyes to look at him and drew her legs up beside her as if trying to make herself a smaller target for the sun. She was still comparatively pale after all this heat; she did not appear equipped to cope under such fierce summers. 'Please be patient with Marcus,' she went on after a while. 'He needs his family. I know how much, because, you see, I don't have any family except my brother. You must almost be that to Marcus. Especially now the Emperor is so ill.'

'I'm afraid I don't think you understand the situation,'

'But why not?'

'Well, your feelings are very ...' He sighed at how stupid it was. 'Very natural, of course it *should* be like that. But it's more complicated. You should be talking to him, not me. He doesn't want my help or my – my friendship. I can't see what more I can offer him.'

'But he just said he wanted you to come with him to Bian.' Drusus repressed a snort and she claimed, 'This is hard on him. It's so new, it's such a weight. If only his father was still alive, he would have been spared this.' She waited

Drusus said, barely bothering to disguise his impatience with her, 'Yes, it's very unfortunate.' And there was a flaring of remembered pain

136

and disappointment, which made Una catch her lower lip under her teeth in expectation, but nothing clearer came and she marvelled again at how little he really seemed to think of it. She let her eyes follow the twitching of a lapis-blue finch near her feet, remembering that she'd made him think of someone, when he'd first met her; there had been a brief comparison with a vanishing face.

She announced, quietly but decisively, as if laying down money on a bet: 'Although the truth is, I'm *thankful* for what happened.'

'To Leo and Clodia?' asked Drusus, startled, reminded unnervingly of his old, cancelled hope.

'I know it's wrong. And I'm talking about your uncle – I'm so sorry. But I can't help it, because otherwise I would never have met Marcus. And I can't imagine that now. Or maybe I can, but I don't want to.'

Drusus nodded, but he shifted on the seat. There was a faint warning in his nerves that something was wrong, that he was in danger, but it was too indefinable to act on.

Una realised her voice had dipped lower from the innocent, faintly childlike pitch she'd been using, because she was telling the truth. She adjusted it carefully again to say, 'And I was only a slave, he could do so much better than me. Someone nearer his own rank. Or just someone more beautiful.'

'Now then, you're a pretty girl. Don't fish for compliments,' said Drusus, smiling uneasily.

'I'm not. I mean, I didn't mean to!' she said girlishly, laughing artlessly and covering her face, and then quietly baring it again, allowing him to look at her.

He'd simply been following the humdrum rules of conversation with a young woman, but it was true, to some extent he could see now why Marcus liked her. He had ceased to focus on the fact that she was a slave, until she reminded him of it. Yes, she might be pretty, but certainly she did not compare with Amaryllis. Or Tulliola.

For a horrible second he could not extricate her, Tulliola, the original, from the surrogate: he saw only a generalised blur of smooth skin and dark eyes. Relief flooded him poignantly as he succeeded, but that made the absence of Tulliola become suddenly overwhelming. She had been here in the aviary. She had been so near.

Una tried not to show anything, not to catch her breath or let her eyes widen at a little jolt of victory, and for a moment could only manage to freeze totally, not breathing at all. She did what she could to relax her body and face, to ease herself back, but for some seconds couldn't get her mind to work, she could only stare at the birds, inanely smiling, as she tried to think how she could go on. To cover the silence she had to reproduce the shy laugh again, beginning, 'Anyway ...' But she was still at a loss. And at the same time, she saw clearly how private it was here, how far away she was from anyone. But why should she not be safe? She still couldn't be certain he'd done anything worse than wanting Tulliola; even if he had, he didn't feel anything more dangerous towards her than boredom and a faint unaccountable unease, which she was doing everything she could to control.

She tried again. 'Anyway, your family has done so much for me. That's why I hate to see this clash between you. And I do know that Marcus feels the same.' She paused. It was difficult to balance her real purpose and her false one; she was wary of telling too many outright lies which might cause trouble later. 'You think he doesn't listen to you, don't you? But perhaps he would if you listened to *him* more ...'

Drusus once more gave a tight-lipped nod, but he was beginning to hope earnestly that she would go soon. A moment before he'd been thinking that she was pretty, if not compellingly so, and being alone this long with a dull, well-meaning, acceptably pretty girl, he would normally have at least entertained the idea of what her body would be like, just to keep from going mad with boredom. But he didn't want to touch her; he didn't know why. If he had, it would have seemed like the odd, fascinated temptation to lay his hand on red-hot metal or into moving machinery. He could no longer understand why he'd thought her so ordinary looking to begin with, nor why the slight organisation of bones and skin had begun to seem sinister, diabolic to him, as if a small wisp of evil had fleetingly assumed the shape of a girl and come gently to light on the bench, its disguise slowly evaporating in the sunshine. Something about her must have changed. The expression was still one of diffident appeal, but it had become stiffened, set. Her eyes were really only a very dark brown, not even an unusual colour if her hair and skin hadn't been so light and washed out; it was only that – a trick of contrast – that made the irises look almost as black as the pupils, the hot colour in the darkness almost red. She did not blink very often. He didn't realise that he had inched back as, very slightly, she'd closed in.

She said, 'You must understand the effect it had on him three years ago, to know that people wanted to kill him rather than let him be Emperor. After that, what could he do but become more ... unbending? How can he help but think, If I don't do what I set out to, then why did I go through all that? It's difficult to *trust* people again, Your Highness, with his parents suddenly gone like that – and to know it was because of people so close to him, someone he must have known for years ...' Her voice had become quiet, even, rhythmic. She now exhaled slowly, shaking her head. 'You know, I can't understand it. Well – it's easier with Gabinius, in a way, he was afraid for his business, he didn't know Marcus. But the Emperor's *wife* ... *Why* did she?' She sat unmoving, knowing this was dangerous. She didn't want to give any sense that she suspected him.

And now he could not help but think of it, though he had cut it out of their story because it did not fit, what counted was that he'd loved her, but now it came: Tulliola sitting beside him on the floor, his body still warm from her touch, but she was hissing furiously: *'I've* done everything. *For you.* Why am I the one paying for it, things I've done for you?' And now there came a hammering torrent of remembered images and touches: the first cool, incredulous kiss – not two hundred yards away from where he sat, but then – oh, he could not help it now – the solitary wonder as the sharp tip of the gold pin he held pierced her heart. Her familiar smooth body struggling under the weight of his. The spilling warmth of her blood against his own breast – and this ache all through him, why did he have to feel this? Why had the baleful thing beside him done this to him?

It was all he could do to answer, 'I don't know. I didn't know her very well.' And even those intentionally bland words stung him with the unwanted memory of how afraid he had always been that this was the truth.

Now, careful, don't behave any differently, Una instructed herself, feeling her flesh beg to recoil, the demand, in the hastening beat of her heart, in all her muscles, to get away. She'd suspected that he'd been part of it, but she'd never had any reason to doubt that Lady Tullia had killed herself. She felt an unexpected strength of revulsion, of contamination almost beyond bearing. She wanted to claw off strips of her own skin, she wanted to wipe off Tulliola's blood.

'Well, I suppose it doesn't make any difference why – it happened anyway,' she said, almost airily, not the note she wanted. She smiled harmlessly again, amending, 'But you don't need me to tell you about Marcus, you've known him all his life. I just ... wanted to help.'

'Yes, of course,' said Drusus, and as he'd hoped, she finally got to her feet to leave.

'Well, thank you for listening to me,' she said, humbly bowing her head.

As she began to walk away towards the aviary door, an inexplicable dread and urgency took hold of him, and an abrupt, commanding voice spoke in his mind saying fiercely: *Stop* her. You can do it easily. Don't let her get out. But it made no sense, so he did nothing.

Una walked out of the aviary at a relaxed pace, barely able to wait to get out of sight so she could move faster. The relief at leaving Drusus behind was wonderful, the air felt clean again. But once she was out in the open, passing the fountains, the golden heat stretched the distance back to the palace, weighed down her limbs and trapped pain in her head. She broke finally into a laboured run, across the grass of the sunken lawn, kept green and flawless even under this sun. Drusus was not following, why should he? She wasn't sure how she could interrupt the meeting to tell Marcus, but she would do it at any cost; beyond all doubt Drusus was a threat to Marcus, and even after three years she felt it could not be delayed a second.

She ran up the steps to the pavilion, between the screens towards the table. She saw the couches were bare, the servants were clearing the dishes away, carrying the cushions inside. She stood and looked at this almost in outrage. Then she remembered that after the meeting Marcus had to go to the Forum to give a speech about the talks. She caught the eye of the boy who'd taken Drusus' glass. She said, lamely, angrily, 'I didn't think I'd been so long.'

Drusus lay back on the bench, sunbathing, trying to let the pain seep from his mind now she was gone. But it would not; too much of the malevolent haze associated with her remained in the air. He got up and left the silvery aviary, glad to realise that already Una was out of sight. He wandered across the grass, but he could not get away from it – he was drifting as if against his will towards the fountains, among rose bushes where he'd first kissed Tulliola. He gave in and went and looked at the same stones and flowers, dipped his hands in the water to cool them.

Still he had the sense that he'd let something go terribly wrong – worse, that he was allowing it *now*, that there might just still be time to save himself, but that he didn't know how.

He saw a woman heading aimlessly across the garden and feared for a moment that it was Una coming back, and thought of hiding. But it was Makaria, so he raised a hand in greeting and she swerved towards him. She was dressed – unusually for her – in a floor-length dress, not the height of fashion; there was a veil hanging back from brooches in her short stiff hair. She looked uncomfortable and hot.

'You weren't at the meeting,' said Drusus.

Makaria dropped wearily onto the seat at the edge of the fountain with a little groan. 'I've been in Veii. Showing the Novians care.'

'Oh, Dis. How was *that*?'

'Looking at rubble and sitting at bedsides? Boring and upsetting in equal measures. Someone had to do it, though.'

Drusus nodded.

Makaria peered at him curiously and said, 'Are you all right? You look pale.'

'I feel it,' he muttered.

'Are you ill?'

'No. Oh, it's just – it's just Marcus.'

'Hmm,' she said, her face tightening slightly in disapproval.

He sighed. He did not want to hear her defending Marcus' plans, he'd had enough of that. 'And that girl.'

'Una?'

'She followed me out and wouldn't go away.'

Makaria made a vaguely sympathetic, tutting sound.

Drusus hesitated, and confessed suddenly, 'You know, it's stupid. But she – she made me feel ... I can't seem to shake it off. Do you know what I mean at all? Have you ever found her ... unsettling?'

Makaria gave a short laugh. 'Yes,' she said. 'Yes, very. Well, I owe her a lot. But, to be honest, yes. After all she is ...'

'What?'

Makaria seemed reluctant to answer. 'A witch, I was going to say,' she admitted at last.

A premonitary alarm inserted taut claws into Drusus' flesh. 'A witch?'

Makaria's face had grown tense, her mouth contracted. There was a pause, during which Drusus felt a fury of impatience, before she went on. 'You know, don't you, that Tullia tried to blame everything on me?'

So many mentions of his love's name in such a short space of time frightening as well as hurting him. He made himself nod. 'The sweets?'

'Yes. I got dragged out of bed in the middle of the night to find that out. That even *Daddy* thought ...' She broke off. Drusus, bawling at her in his mind to spit it out, placed a comforting hand on her shoulder. It worked, Makaria finished: 'And she – Una was there. She was there with Marcus. She knew I was telling the truth. She knew Tullia was lying. And it seems she can do that – know what people are thinking. Someone should have found her and apprenticed her at Delphi or Cumae, or done *something* with her. Because I don't know how Marcus can stand it, really.'

Drusus felt the ground tip sideways, his blood sliding with it, sheets of boiling ice hitting his skin. It did not occur to him to doubt what Makaria said, or ask himself if there could be another explanation for what Una had known. Makaria had mentioned the Oracles, and Drusus thought of the Sibyl and thought of Una, and stark as the physical

141

differences between them were, there seemed something about them that was the same; a kind of remote secretive pride. He felt certain it was true. Reeling, he made himself skim through the innocuously worded conversation with Una, and saw that, yes, it was exactly as bad as he felt it to be. His lips felt numb, as if he were dying of cold, it took such an effort even to whisper, 'I see. That explains it.'

'What is it?'

Drusus just managed to lift his hand, clasping his head as if it ached. 'The heat. I do feel ill.' He was telling the truth. He could scarcely breathe, scarcely keep his balance. He stammered some further excuses about getting into the shade. He lurched across the alien ground towards the palace, tripped as he reached the steps, bruising his hands as he had to put them down to save himself, groaning, 'Oh please, oh no ...'

Why was he going back towards the Golden House? There was no refuge, unless he could get out of his own body. Oh, somebody help me, his desperate self keened. Oh, Apollo, Minerva, please, someone help.

And even before the pavilion came into full sight, he remembered Marcus' speech in the Forum. Una might not have reached him. Surely she could not have done. There was still some time before this disaster took full effect. And the same calm, decisive voice that had tried to help him in the aviary said to him, booming across the gardens so loudly that the earth seemed to shake: No half-measures. No one else to help you. Find her now. Do it.

Only once in his life had he killed with his own hands. The memory, which Una had already scraped raw, loosed tears from his eyes. And to do it again now – so unprepared, with so little warning – 'Oh, no, no, no,' he whimpered pitifully to himself, as his body shook. He didn't know where she was, he had no weapon, the palace was full of people. Even if he could do it, how could he keep it distant from himself – how could he be safe once it was done?

And then it occurred to him then that it didn't matter. If he couldn't kill her, he was finished anyway, so to do it and fail to make it look like an accident or someone else's fault could make things no worse. He would at least have a chance.

The voice continued. It was his own, he realised now, but sounding older and firmer, and it spoke to him like a good father, stern and dispassionate, but on his side. And now it told him the crucial, glaring fact: that it was because of Una that he could never see his lover again. *That* was what Makaria's uneasy gratitude to the girl had meant. *She* had pointed the finger, *she* had killed Tulliola as surely as if she had been the one to hold the knife. To think of Una, sitting there so primly, and a murderer. It was amazing that he could have gone this many seconds without seeing it.

Drusus gasped, shakily, at the blurred grass. 'Oh,' he said softly, no longer moaning. 'Oh.' He took a slow, thirsty draught of the warm air, and exhaled, blowing his panic and misery away into the roses. If the situation had not been so appalling he knew he would even have felt a load lift. With unusual clarity, he remembered the morning before he'd seen Tulliola for the last time, in his hand, the small weight of the jewelled hairpin that he'd kept so long. He remembered scraping away little shavings of gold from its point, knowing he *had* to do it. And that was truer even than he'd known at the time. He could see his anguish as he sharpened the pin, and even the act that had followed, as if Una had been in each room, a poison in the air.

Drusus raised his head to look up at the stark height of the palace wall – a great gold precipice. He walked steadily towards it, under the shade of the awning. The muscles of his stomach twisted in anxious nausea. How could he even get close to her – wouldn't she know at once what he meant to do to her? But he strode rapidly on, as if he knew how he could overcome this. He knew that he *would* know, because he'd never felt this before – this quiet, resigned, chiselled fury. No, not even with Marcus, even though sometimes his cousin's very existence seemed an unbearable check to his own. He had never hated anyone until now.

Una slunk quickly through the palace, her shoulders raised as though she was trying to avoid detection, like a trespasser. Her alarm was more than she could reason away. Not just at the delay, but at how near Drusus still was. She wondered if, in default of Marcus, she should try to explain to Faustus what she knew. But from what she knew of him and his current state, she didn't think it would be easy to reach him in the first place, or that persuading him would save any time. And she knew Drusus had tried repeatedly to visit the Emperor; what if he tried again? She could not stand another encounter with him – the thought made the revulsion itch and shiver across her skin again. And the fear, she thought severely to herself. Even if it wasn't rational, she might as well call it by its name.

She went into Marcus' rooms – she didn't think of them as being in any way hers – and locked the door, thinking, *there*, now control yourself. She sat down stiffly on a chair, but at once found herself on her feet again, stalking restlessly back and forth. Passing the mirror she saw her face looking hard and agitated, flushed by the heat, and she distracted herself briefly by washing her face and repairing her make-up. And it was now that she found the Imperial ring, looking small and unimportant, lying by a basin of Sinoan porcelain. She looked at it blankly. Marcus must have taken it off to wash his hands.

She turned on the longvision to see his face, talking about Bian and Cynoto, to reassure herself that he was still alive. Drusus could have done nothing to hurt him in the past ten minutes. She was aware of servants passing from time to time a few rooms away; still, the room felt isolated. There was no reason to think she needed any defences at all, and yet the lock on the door did not seem enough. She didn't like the fact that anyone looking for her would come here first. She wanted to be out of the Palace altogether.

She went into the next room and lifted the longdictor circlet to talk to the stewards' office in one of the outer buildings of the palace. 'I need to go and meet Caesar when his speech is finished. Can you send a car to the Septizonium?' she said uncomfortably, knowing that she would not be refused, but feeling ashamed of asking, compromised. She would have preferred to simply vanish out of the Palace and into the anonymity she'd felt in the Veii street, but it did not work like that. Arriving in a Palace car, she could be pretty sure of getting through to Marcus quickly.

Still, she felt easier for knowing what to do, and she sprang to her feet with a sudden burst of energy. But she stood for a second more, as if she had forgotten something, and then, before unlocking the door and flinging it open, she seized the gold ring, and plunged it into the pocket of her dress, gripping it there. She would give it back to Marcus when she reached him. In the meantime, it could act as an amulet, a little shield.

On instinct, Drusus raced towards Marcus' apartments, but that wasn't enough, it wasn't enough – he needed something to use against her. But he had something already, she'd given it to him herself even as she was working to trap him, priding herself for it, the little bitch. He ran into a guest room where there was a longdictor hanging in a niche on the wall, snatched up the circlet and pressed it fiercely onto his head as if it were a helmet, as if he were arming himself. He entered the code for the palace's longdictor exchange, tightened his throat, preparing to make his voice a little softer, to alter its rhythm, and said, 'I'm calling from the Transtiberine Slave Clinic. It's very important. I need to speak to Una the freedwoman, you know who I mean? It concerns her brother.'

The young slave – no, no longer a slave, Drusus kept forgetting – answered, 'Leave your details and I can see that your message reaches her in due course.'

A little spurt of inspiration coursed through Drusus. He did know something about the clinic; he'd had his men watch Sulien for a good week, before Veii. 'I understand you have procedures to go through, but she knows me, my name's Aulus. I work with her brother, Sulien. I'm happy to wait while she confirms who I am. But this is *very serious*. I … I can't believe I have to do this.' He said the last words – which after all, were true – in a shaken mutter, as if to himself; and deliberately he let out an unsteady, audible breath. It was easy; he wanted to sound as if he'd had a shock, and he had.

'Well, I'll see what I can do, sir.'

There was silence while, in the exchange office, the young man tried the longdictor in Marcus' rooms, and then, when that failed, someone called across the room to him to say that Caesar's girl had asked for a car a few minutes before, and must be on her way to the front gates.

The voice came back and said, 'She's not in the Imperial suite. But I might be able to find her,' which was exactly what Drusus had hoped for.

'Oh – good, thank you. Yes, please hurry,' said Drusus, in continuing, earnest distress. 'Wait. What are you going to do? Where is she going to take the longdictor? Does she have a private room?' He was pretty certain she did not. Marcus wouldn't have to hoard her away furtively, as he himself had to with Amaryllis.

'No, not exactly,' the voice said. 'She'll speak to you from Caesar's apartments, or the gatehouse, I suppose, if it's that urgent.'

'Oh. No, no. You don't understand. Look – don't repeat any of this to her, because it's better if I tell her everything – but it is very bad news.' He made a snagging, agitated little sound, nearly a sob. 'I don't even know how I'm going to tell her, but I want to try and make this easier for her. That's the least I can do. You have to help me. If people are going to be running in and out – even Caesar himself …'

'He's addressing the Forum.'

'Even so.' He paused, the next part was difficult to phrase – if he was unlucky, or if he was not careful, he'd get only a promise of compliance and no information. 'She really shouldn't hear this somewhere she has to worry about the slaves eavesdropping. I mean the servants. It should be somewhere private. Is there somewhere like that?'

'Yes,' the young man answered. His voice was beginning to catch some of the unhappiness in Drusus'. 'That should be possible. Except …'

'What?'

'If it's bad, shouldn't someone be with her? At least, nearby?'

'No,' said Drusus positively. 'I can tell you from personal experience.' His voice shook with intensity, a little internal scoff at what nonsense this was vanishing out of his memory as he spoke, so that it almost seemed true.

'All right, I'm sorry,' said the operator dejectedly.

'Then where?' asked Drusus, softly, as if it were just a reasonable question, as if the answer could not fairly be kept from someone who was plainly distraught. There were two or three places he was hoping for above all, another few that would be riskier, but still possible.

The man sighed. 'Well, I was thinking, we have some older offices ...'

'An office?' said Drusus doubtfully.

'They're not really used as offices any more. It's more like a little function room. It's quite ... peaceful, anyway.'

Drusus let his eyes close, feeling a moment of rest. He knew the Golden House. Since Faustus had built the glazed oval towers that framed the palace, the old rooms on the top floor, where the lesser palace officials had once been packed, had ceased to have much use. They might have been given over to slave quarters, except that they had access to the palace roof, where Faustus had meant to make a garden around the blue dome. But the garden had never appeared, and the old offices had been reduced to a number of almost untouched reception rooms, decorated with the excess of treasures and gifts from the rest of the palace, where occasionally a visiting governor might still hold a meeting or take a guest up the stairs to look down on the city. Not many of them would still have working longdictors.

'Fine,' he said shakily. 'Thank you. When she's had some time, I'm sure she'll be grateful for what you've done for her. I am, anyway. I'll be waiting to talk to her as soon as she's ready.'

'How can she reach you?'

'It's all right. She knows the code. Thank you again,' said Drusus. And he turned off the longdictor, dragged off the headset and ran. He had only a few minutes to find and prepare the room.

Una walked through the blank blue sunlight towards the high barricade of the Septizonium as fast as the swaddling heat would allow her. She was impatient for the car, which she could not see yet. But already she felt the relief of leaving Drusus behind, that she was out of his reach. But, like a memory of a mistake reluctantly surfacing, she began to realise someone was coming after her – not Drusus, nor anyone she knew – but someone who knew that, against his will, he was going to harm her.

She turned round and stood waiting stiffly, as a boy about her own age approached, jogging unevenly along, unhappy. He said, 'Madam,' and bobbed a bow which made Una recoil a little in embarrassed, apprehensive dismay.

'Don't,' she said, involuntarily curt, remembering Sulien's advice and adding clumsily, 'We both used to be slaves.' She saw how the reminder made his misery worse. And already he was so sorry for her.

'I ... I have a message. That is, Aulus from Transtiberina wants to speak to you, as soon as possible—'

'About my brother,' she finished, blankly enough, sparing him. She could see he had nothing more to tell her. And she could also see that he was sure Sulien was dead, or just perhaps, about to die.

'Yes,' he said, wretchedly. 'Will you ... will you come with me?'

She followed him wordlessly, reduced to one paralysed truncated plea in a rigidly ambulating body: silent stammerings of 'No', 'Please' and 'Not after the factory'. But *of course* after the factory, that was the point – they'd had a good warning something was wrong, of course it hadn't gone away. He shouldn't have persuaded her to leave; she should not have let him; she should not have left. She walked feeling that she could not think, but it was not true, she could supply innumerable terrible things that could have happened to him.

She didn't question where they were going at all. It was as if she were being guided through an entirely unknown house. Finally she seemed to emerge, as if she'd been walking with her breath held and her eyes shut, to realise they'd climbed to the top of the Palace, among dim, cluttered, gentle rooms, and that it was quiet.

The boy showed her towards a door that led into a long, irregularly shaped room, in which all she saw was the longdictor, built into a desk at the far end.

'Is there anything I can do for you?' he asked, almost in a whisper, because these were the first words either of them had spoken since they'd entered the Palace.

'Thank you. No,' she said, faintly relieved that he seemed to be going to leave. Drusus had been right in a strange way, she didn't want a spectator to what she thought was about to happen.

She remained immobile, outside the room until he skulked guiltily away. Then she forced herself in as if the desk was a marathon away, as if she had to pace her strength to reach it. She was halfway across the room when some warning, something other than the agonised apprehension about Sulien, began trying to bat and flutter at her, moth-like, and at the same moment she heard footsteps pounding closer, outside the room. She turned just as the door, which she'd already pulled to, banged shut, with an instantaneous grinding click, as the lock moved.

Drusus had raced, panting, across the top floor, at first throwing open doors, in an anguish of urgency and frustration, gritting his teeth at failures of his memory, but quickly he made himself act methodically. Most likely the boy wouldn't take her too far from the central stairs. And he would surely have chosen the best of the possible rooms. At first, simply looking for function rooms with longdictors, Drusus narrowed the potentials to four, and in two of those he found to his fierce relief that the old, heavy longdictors were dead. Of the final pair of rooms, one, he saw at once, would be far better for his purposes, and it felt more likely too – it was larger, lighter, its furniture a little faded but still handsome, and indeed someone must have been here fairly recently, for on the desk was a vase full of flowers only just wilted.

Drusus had charged in, scrambling to do what was necessary, terrified that Una and the servant would come and find him there in the midst of it, and when it was done he ran out with his arms full of hasty plunder, the vase included. He flung everything into the other room, which – rejoicing that he'd told the operator that Una should be the one to make the call – he then eliminated by finding its key hanging on a hook near the doorway and locking it. He went back to the place he had chosen, took the key from there as well, and then fled down the hall, looking for a safe vantage point on the trap. At last he crouched, trembling, concealed in the doorway of a dusty office, about a hundred yards from the tranquil room. And though he ached with hatred and fright, the next thing that had to be done did not seem difficult to him. Una would be too busy worrying about her brother to notice much anyway, wouldn't she? But until she appeared, until she was inside the room and alone, he had to be camouflaged. He mustn't think.

It did not seem to him a matter of becoming calm, or thawing away from himself into emptiness and peace. Instead he tried to freeze solid every flicker in his skull, and sat staring inflexibly down the passage at the open door to the trap, barely breathing, as if all his existence was in the surfaces of his eyes, two little curved oval plates, which seemed hard and inorganic, like the glass eyes fitted into the heads of statues.

He kept himself like this, rigidly indifferent as she appeared with the servant at the other end of the passage. He saw her wait for the boy to leave, as if it meant nothing to him, as if they were both only flat, indistinct figures on a longvision screen. And then she was in the room, and he was launching himself towards it, the hard little key gripped in his hand, his arm already outflung to reach the lock. He turned the key with a burst of incredulous joy, and ran on at once for the next flight of stairs that led onto the roof.

Una stood absolutely still. The room, which had been an irrelevant haze around her anguish, wiped itself into clean, violent focus. She looked at the desk – she had been glaring at the longdictor from the second she'd entered the room, but it was only now that she saw that it had been smashed, the pieces of the headset laid carefully back together. Unable to find any kind of blade to sever its cord, Drusus had swung the circlet furiously against the wall until it shattered. She observed to herself drily, relieved, as if she'd simply fallen for a practical joke, Well, Sulien is all right.

She felt strangely unwilling to move, to make a sound, because in this first clear moment, all the terror for her brother so suddenly erased, it felt as if all that was facing her was a purely intellectual problem, that she was a disembodied mind appraising an abstract framework of facts. When she had to go towards the door, or call for help, awareness of her flimsy body would force itself and its preposterous vulnerability back upon her attention.

She went and pressed on the doorhandle – not repeatedly, she knew what had happened – to feel the heaviness of the door, to measure if she had any chance of forcing it. No, definitely not. She stood with her back against it, looking at the room. She could see from the depth of the windows how thick the walls were. And she felt silence spreading around her through the palace, for what seemed like miles.

She clambered across the desk to get at the window, hoping only that she might be able to make herself heard through it, for there was certainly no way of climbing down from this height. But the window was locked, moreover it was made up of many little leaded panes; she wouldn't be able to break an opening, at least not with just her fists. And there was nothing else she could use; she knew the next stage must be to look for some kind of weapon, but, she became swiftly certain, the room had been deliberately stripped of them. There was not a paperweight, not a lamp. There were two chairs against the desk, but both were so heavy and unwieldy that it would have taken all her strength just to manhandle one of them across the room. Una pushed one over onto its side, dismayed at the surprisingly weak, insulated thud it made as it fell. Still, she knelt beside it, and began to use the wooden back to knock on the carpet, lifting it and letting it fall. 'Help,' she shouted, grimly, into the swallowing floor. Her voice sounded forced, as if it frightened her to confess, how powerless she was. It made no difference. No one heard her.

She got up onto her knees and began ransacking the drawers of the desk for something with a little weight, with a sharp edge. Her frustration began to kindle the first little glimmers of actual fear, her fingers started, infuriatingly, to shake as she turned out only limp handfuls of yellowing papers. Nevertheless she began to question her instant assumption which was of course that this was Drusus, that he somehow knew and that he meant to kill her. If that was right why had he locked her in, why hadn't he come straight into the room to do it? Then she pulled open what she had assumed was a cupboard, a narrow door set into the wall beside a stiff, high-backed couch, but behind it she was startled to find a cramped flight of stairs, leading upwards to a square of blue sky.

Una crouched on the floor, looking up at it, silent, more afraid than before. It was impossible that the person who had led her here so carefully could have overlooked this; it was not an escape. Someone was waiting for her there. But why did he want to lure her up there, where she would at least be in the open, where it was even possible that someone in one of the towers would see that there was a struggle going on? Because, she answered herself rationally, if she died falling from that height, it would be less immediately obvious, less *certain* that it was murder. And in any case, they were close to the dome, they would probably be pretty well screened from view. But down here, presumably, he'd be forced to beat her to death, or strangle her. Perhaps she would do better to force him to come down the steps, where she could at least be sure of leaving her body as proof of what had happened.

A real cramp of horror ran through her.

She renewed the search for a weapon even more feverishly – there was a shelf of books, all far too light, and the drawers in the desk wouldn't come out of their grooves. But she had decided that even if it meant doing as he wanted, she would soon be going up those steps, she would walk onto the roof to meet him rather than stay here and wait.

In the end she took one of the jagged fragments of the longdictor. It was as slight and breakable as everything else, but there was a length of cord dangling from it, and though the broken points would not kill or disable – unless perhaps she was lucky enough to strike an eye – still they might draw a little blood. There was a sick, cold hollowness in her stomach and in her bones, as she stood up and moved towards the little door. But at least she wanted to leave some marks on him.

150

The flights of stairs from the top floor rose onto the roof in occasional miniature turrets. Drusus stood against the wall, waiting. For a while he managed to keep himself in the solidified, suspended state he'd used to hide himself from her before, but as time passed and she did not appear, he began to feel tremors of impatience and anxiety. Was it possible that she could have got out?

Then with no warning, for she had moved as quietly as she had in the aviary, she burst through the open door away from him, but he lunged and dragged her into his arms. And though they were instantly, bitterly struggling, there was a tiny calm moment of recognition between them when they looked each other in the eye and he almost forgot the harm she'd done and planned to do to him; there was a fractional peace in the fact that she knew about Tulliola, about Leo and Clodia. In another minute there would be again no one else who knew those things. For the moment they understood each other pretty well. For he also knew about *her*, and she understood that too.

But as he pushed her towards the low parapet, all his horror of her returned. She drove all her weight back against him, kicked, stamped at his feet. She had something sharp in her hand which she jabbed at his face, barely missing his eye, so that he felt a scraping pain where his cheek joined the lower lid, and for a horrible moment he thought she'd got a knife. As he struggled to contain her, she put up her hands and somehow managed to join them behind his head, and a cord closed on his neck. But she wasn't strong. The moment of tightness and pressure was terrifying, but he forced her arms back easily enough, driving and twisting the wrist until he got a sound of pain out of her and the thing dropped from her hand. As punishment for that and for everything, he hit her in the face. She began to scream, a weirdly businesslike, artificial sound, a means to an end. He hated the noise, he hated her for making it, but at no point did she speak to him, promise she'd never tell anyone, beg him for her life. And this also chilled and enraged him that she wouldn't acknowledge him as a *real person* let alone someone who could do whatever he wanted with her. He tugged her to him, her back against his chest, and clamped his hand over her face, marching her forward. He felt the base of his fingers grow damp as she manoeuvred her jaw and lips against his hand in a kind of hostile kiss, sucking a little fold of skin between her teeth and biting, hard. He kept his hand in place despite the pain, but she continued kicking and thrashing in his arms and she worked her sharp little teeth back and forth till the blood flowed. A jerk of his hand allowed her to writhe her face free and she screamed again, so he pressed his forearm tight across her throat. He pressed, crushed, feeling her bucking and gasping as she struggled to breathe, and then quite suddenly, she went limp and silent. It was so abrupt that he was not prepared to take her weight and she almost fell through his hands to the paving under-foot.

Una felt herself sink under the changing grip of his hands. It was so hard to hold her breath, to keep her muscles loose and soft. Surprised, Drusus bent to sweep up her legs and swing her into his arms, a weirdly gallant gesture, an aristocrat tending to a lady in a faint. The ease with which he lifted her was appalling. Her eyes were shut; she didn't know, as he took another step towards dropping her into space, how close to the edge they were. But she twisted quickly, like a lizard, spilled out of his arms, and ran.

She dared not look anywhere but at the next stair turret, nor think of anything but outpacing him, but she could feel how huge and bright the sky was, how all of Rome was spread out, imperviously whirring and sighing below this empty, aerial space. The Colosseum, the Circus, above all the Forum where Marcus was, all so close; a pigeon or sparrow, any flying thing set free of gravity, could have reached it in a single plunge.

And he was never more than a few feet behind her; it was only a few seconds before he hurled himself at her headlong, knocking her off her feet, so that the edge of the parapet struck her across the shoulders and she fell sitting on the paving, against the wall, with Drusus crouched over her, his face twisted, his teeth bared with effort and desperation. She had never known this before, she might remember the feel and rhythm of violence as easily as a first language, but never this, such a passion for her extinction. And it was so near now, that a small, un-silenceable voice had begun to quiver through her, admitting, there is nothing more I can do.

Drusus started to haul her up, to push her back over the wall. She continued dragging down, trying to crawl away sideways, to strike at his stomach, his groin; her nails slicing across his arm. Their faces were close and he saw that there was a smear of his blood on her white lips, and it made him feel all the more that he was fighting a *demon*. She lashed against him like a fury, a harpy – the unfathomable malice he was holding almost more frightening for the spikily frail body that contained it.

And as he succeeded in lifting her, in beginning to tilt her back into emptiness, she gave up trying to fight him off or break free, and instead she flung her arms around him, winding herself close and gripping, gripping, so that he felt the insupportable beat of her heart, punching against his own. Oh, please, stop, go away from me, Drusus wanted to plead with her, with that pulse. By now he was longing for it to be over, for the feel of her to be off his skin – he'd expected it to be so much quicker than this. And yet, as the embrace tightened, as her legs clenched around him, he felt a confused throb of physical excitement, not for her, not for her body, but for the ferocity with which she fought him and for the moment, so close now, in which it would all go to nothing, and only he would be left.

She could feel his wild, scared heartbeat as strongly as he could feel hers, and she knew what he felt, the anticipation. And she gripped, mindlessly, tighter, trying to will her grasping limbs into being something more than slight muscle and narrow bone, trying to be a vice, a trap, the jaws of a shark. But of course this could not go on for ever. He was trying to work the loop of her arms over his head, like a tight-fitting garment. Finally, he must get them loose. He would push back her shoulders, her flailing hands would cling to his, to his clothes – that, brief handfuls of cloth under her fingers, would be the sign that it was finished. So, before it came to that, while she still had a good grasp on him, and with as much force as she could, she threw herself backwards, over the wall.

Drusus, intent on unfastening her, felt himself lurch suddenly forward, and at first cared only how almost her entire body was over the edge, that it was done – and then he felt with a ripple of horrified nausea how he was also keeling, overbalanced. She would not let go; his feet were rising and nothing was keeping him from falling but his thighs on the sharp rim of the wall, he was going forward, forward ...

Already her feet were off the ground. The blue sky tipped itself in front of her face, the sun swung up to scream in her eyes. The void broke like a wave against her back, her heavy skull seemed to plunge her downwards like an anchor. The ongoing confession of failure, gabbling through her nerves, soared to a high shriek: There is nothing more! This is dying! And really she only cared about two people, but she'd been afraid all this time to think of Sulien or of Marcus; if she did anything like saying goodbye, took one step towards accepting her own death, she'd felt it would knock away any little chance she might still have. But now, as she pitched downwards – any fanatic hope of saving herself scattering – and there was *nothing more*, she was trapped in her falling body, and that nothing she said to Sulien or Marcus would fly out of her to reach them. Marcus might not ever understand that she was giving him Drusus' death, it was all she could do for him—

In terror Drusus jerked back, let go of her arms to grip the edge of the parapet, finally turning over so that his back was to the emptiness. And, still clinging, still glued to his trunk, Una came up with him – he had

153

no choice but to allow it – so that she was first lying on his chest and then tipped onto her feet, as he sank to his knees, weak with involuntary relief. Una slid free of his body at once.

Trembling, Drusus propelled himself forward, outstretched, to grab at her again, and again she fell. At arm's length, he grasped at her legs, pulling himself towards her, but she kicked brutally at his head, panting, and stumbled up and ran on, and as he began wearily to pursue her he felt dazed, shattered. He should have beaten in her skull on the paving and then flung her down to the edge of the garden where she'd first set out to hunt him. He'd really thought this way would be easier, cleaner.

But now he saw how close she was to the next flight of stairs and it knocked the will back into him. He almost collided with her as she dragged open the door, they skidded down the stairs together, tripping and clawing, Drusus hounding her like an exhausted animal. If he could just pin her to the ground ... The calm, paternal voice spoke again and told him what to do, even how to act after it was done – it was bad because he'd have to involve someone else, but it was the only choice: kill her any possible way, with anything that came to hand, summon a member of his guard whom he could probably trust, have the man shoot a slave and place the body over hers. The guard could say he'd found the slave attacking her.

But they were out in the corridor now, and she'd begun breathlessly screaming again, whenever he managed to touch her. She was leading him, staggering, back the way they'd come, and as they neared the shut room from which she'd mounted the stairs to the roof, Drusus dimly saw a second figure, dithering awkwardly a little way beyond the locked door, moving in shock as he heard the noise. The boy from the long-dictor exchange had disobeyed Drusus' instructions; he'd lingered or come back.

Drusus thought wildly, Well, it must be him that we kill, that's all, he's the one whose body we must use.

And Una called out, not in a panicked scream but a clear, authoritative shout, 'You, bring the Praetorians here now.'

Drusus could not believe what she was doing. He could not believe that the boy did not even hesitate, even though he must have seen by now who Drusus was. But instantly he turned to do as she said, running on ahead along the passage, disappearing down the stairs as Una and Drusus neared him. Chasing them both, Drusus' head seemed to reel with bewilderment, as well as exhaustion and fear. It was true he did not know what to do, how he could kill them both – but the Praetorians were there to protect the Imperial family, he knew whom they would believe over two slaves.

Still he hurtled after them, downstairs, and on the landing he reached her, careering into her and flinging her against the wall, knocking her head back, locking his fingers around her neck and squeezing. He was desperate; he knew the boy was still charging onwards, already down the next flight, and there was nothing he could do to stop him. But he'd got her, he could not think of anything else, could not squander the chance.

He heard shouts, heavy footsteps pulsating up the stairs. He stared silently into her black-brown black-red eyes, half shut now, and could see her looking back, remote, still somehow inaccessible and unconcerned with him.

He changed his grip on her, holding her by the shoulders, pushing her towards the Praetorians as they reached the landing with the boy. 'Help me, she's a traitor; she's a spy for the Nionians. They both are.'

If they put her away somewhere he could surely have someone get to her before Marcus could; it must be possible. She could have committed suicide while under arrest, like Tulliola.

Una shocked him again, as he felt her straightening her body, raising her head, as if the man who'd nearly killed her were not still holding her, as if he were almost beneath her notice. She was out of breath, the streak of blood still on her mouth, her dress torn. 'Arrest him,' she commanded quite calmly, as if it had always been her right to make such orders. 'He is a murderer.'

He did not understand the way the men wavered, why their eyes went from Una to himself, and then stayed on her. And before he could speak again, she stepped forward out of his grasp, thrust her hand into her pocket and raised it again, holding up something gold between finger and thumb. It was the Imperial ring.

'On this authority,' she said.

It could not happen, it was unthinkable. He almost doubted his own flesh as it told him the men were actually taking hold of him, as he saw Una step neatly aside, watching impassively. He raged again that she was a traitor, a liar. He could not accept, as they forced him down the steps, the simple fact that there were more of them, that they were stronger than he was. Worn out as he was, he fought them every inch of the way.

Una looked on, without moving. She wanted to sink to her knees on the carpet, lie down, but she would not within sight of any of them. Only when the Praetorians and Drusus were out of sight, did she even let her body drop sideways to lean against the wall. She looked at the young man who'd come back to wait for her, because of ordinary sympathy, and because they'd both been slaves. His face showed a confused mixture of fellow feeling and shyness, as if he'd been left alone with someone powerful; a senator, an Emperor. She took his hand.

IX

ENDURANCE

Varius passed the very place, the exact paving stones, which had spun and gone dark beneath him as the poison that had stopped Gemella's heart had dragged like a tide on his own. It had been the day after she died; he'd neither seen nor wanted any other choice – just there, before anyone could get to him, he'd almost succeeded in safely removing himself from the world. And only once since then, immediately after he'd been taken out of prison, had he been to the Golden House, and he'd never intended to come back again. But now he had a reason, so before coming here, he'd done everything he could to disarm the Palace, to be able to look at the spot only with dispassionate recognition, only with a very slight cold pull on his blood. It was a long time ago. It had been someone else.

And ahead there was the calm green room where Tulliola, the murderer, had stood, unrecognised. But it was still only a room. Varius listened to Marcus telling him about Drusus, how he'd goaded his cousin into storming out of the meeting that morning, when Glycon appeared and bowed tautly at Marcus, saying cautiously, 'Caesar. Varius. You're going to to the Imperial Office?'

'What's happened?' asked Marcus, tensing.

Glycon hesitated and only said, 'It's not ... I don't think I should ... It's nothing political. Not Nionia.'

Una was sitting on a chair near the desk, calmly waiting for them, calmly massaging her wrist, the way Sulien did, and it was only when she saw Marcus and Varius that it occurred to her how terrible she looked. Wearily she regretted that she'd done nothing to soften the brunt of it. It was foolish, because she'd made the Praetorians take pictures of her, turning her head from side to side to exhibit the marks, hoping impersonally that they were bad, damning enough. But once her appearance was dealt with as an item of forensic evidence, she'd forgotten about it. There hadn't been much time since then, but she could have changed out of the dress with its half-ripped sleeve. Crooked strands stood out in wispy tangles from the surface of her hair; she could have brushed it. All she had done was wipe an unthinking hand across her mouth, rubbing off the blood without even remembering what it was. But of course there was little else she could have done about her face; there was a small mask of muffled pain fixed to one side of it, where the bruises were starting to emerge on her skin, the stained flesh around her left eye swelling and clamping, though it was only her wrist that truly hurt at the moment.

For Marcus the room seemed to boil and ripple around her dangerously as if everything was on the point of bursting into flames, of vaporising. He did not know what to say or ask her first, nor even how he reached her; it was as though he was blown there on a hot gale. He'd never felt anything like it, such a violence of indignation and incensed love; he was dizzy with it, weightless.

He took hold of her, his hands going lightly, helplessly, from her wrist to her upper arms to her face, afraid of hurting her, furious. Her skin was cold to the touch. He stammered, 'What happened? Who did this to you?' but she interrupted him suddenly by pressing her face against his, a tired, urgent kiss.

Oh, thank God, she thought, exhaustedly happy while he was so bewildered and furious. She let her body drop against him, as if onto land against the will of the sea. Small, warming charges of relief simmered through her, as if he were the one who had nearly fallen all that way, who was after all alive. Still, she could not help her nerves registering a quick unpleasant twinge of familiarity: the likeness between Marcus' body and Drusus'.

'It's all right, it's – superficial,' she said.

Varius was retreating towards the door, already surprised that Glycon hadn't prevented him from entering the room, from seeing this, but she looked across Marcus at him and said clearly, 'You shouldn't go. I should tell you –' She was incongruously reasonable and deliberate, given the physical state she was in; she didn't shake, despite how deserted her skin was of blood. Varius nodded at her without speaking, and stood uneasily where he was.

Marcus had resumed stuttering questions that sounded useless to him as soon as they were spoken: 'What happened? How bad is your wrist? You're cold, has anyone—? Your eye – what—?' He was just a little reassured by the kiss. He knew how and why she had once been averse to the touch of skin.

'Listen,' she said quietly. Her throat was slightly uncomfortable

157

when she swallowed. She wished he could know without her having to tell him. She wished she could lie on an untrodden floor, draped over him, all the length of his body safe against hers, asleep. Four hours, she thought, longingly, I want to lie like that for four hours. She said, laying out the words in small, economical blocks because she was so tired: 'Marcus. Drusus and your uncle's wife were lovers. He was behind all of it. Gabinius and the rest had their own reasons. But you know he wants to be Emperor. And he killed her, Lady Tullia. She never killed herself.'

But it was hard for Marcus to listen to the details, even when they were put so simply, for a surge of breathless nausea caught him at the mention of Drusus' name, a dreadful molten compound of recognition and guilt and instant loathing. It was horribly sudden, and yet it was not shock. He realised he felt no urge whatever to refute the allegation. No, he was not even surprised. And that was appalling, that he must have tolerated the possibility for so long, that he'd given Drusus the lease to do this. 'And when you found out, he ...?' he whispered.

'Yes,' she said.

'What did he do?'

She sighed, and began telling them, concisely, sparingly. She felt Marcus' body going rigid with restrained pulses of violence, his hand closing, unconsciously too tight on hers, and wanted to tell him what she'd thought as the emptiness had sucked at her, but she couldn't yet, she didn't want to force him to imagine how close she had been, the embrace in which she'd tried to carry Drusus with her over the edge.

Already Marcus was thinking, Who would have found her? Who would have told me?

She'd called Sulien before Marcus and Varius arrived, and he reached the room while she was talking, his entrance interrupting and complicating the telling, frustrating the others as she was forced to repeat parts of it. Seeing her brother sitting beside her, wide eyed with alarm but untouched by any of the terrible things she'd imagined, brought little weakening prickles of remembered misery. And – it was tiring to be the focus of so much shock – he was appalled in his turn by her appearance. She'd begun vaguely trying to smoothe her hair and hide her torn dress, but with her bruised, pale face she looked almost exactly as she had when Sulien had first seen her, on the prison ferry on the Thames, after they'd been apart so long. She looked unnervingly like a slave again.

Marcus breathed, 'I'm so sorry.'

'Why?' she said.

Sulien agreed, 'You haven't done anything wrong, Marcus.'

'Because I should have made sure – he shouldn't have been able to do this.'

158

Varius had said nothing all this time, nor even moved until Sulien arrived. He was the only one standing now, a slightly unnatural distance from the rest. The painted goddess still stood gently among the flat orange trees on the wall; Tulliola had been waiting for him in front of her, he could place exactly where. 'And so she did it for him?' he interjected softly, across the room, as if impartially desiring information.

'Yes, I think she did it for him,' said Una.

Varius found himself half-wishing the bizarre thing he'd half-wished before – knowing it would have made nothing better or easier – that Tulliola had murdered Gemella on purpose, that it had not been a stupid mistake, a failure. 'Where is he now?'

'He's still here. The guards have him locked up.' There were a few cells, rarely used these days, under the Palace. Una hadn't explained in detail how she'd had Drusus arrested. She did so now, and remembered the Imperial ring, taking Marcus' hand to slide it onto his finger. 'Here.'

Marcus stared at it, finding suddenly that his fury at what had happened also included her. 'Why did you do this?' he demanded. 'Why didn't you *tell* me?'

Una looked at him pallidly, taken aback. 'I'm sorry. I didn't – I didn't expect – whenever I saw him I thought would just know in another minute. It didn't seem like so much to tell.'

'When did you start planning it? When you first met him?'

'I – it wasn't a *plan*, I just – I wanted to be sure you were safe near him, after everything. And anyway – why didn't you *ask* me to do it, years ago?'

'I told you back then,' he answered, though he flushed. 'My uncle. I thought ...'

'You thought your uncle couldn't stand it. But you know it wasn't only that. *You* didn't want to think about it either; you just wanted it to be over, or you would have done something. I thought – if he was part of it, you had to know, but if he wasn't, there'd be nothing to say. Like you wanted.'

'Well, I was wrong; I should never have let this happen, I should have had you find out. But he's my cousin; it's my family, and you should have told me.'

Una had begun shivering after all. 'Sorry! Sorry!'

'That's enough,' Sulien said sharply.

Marcus had broken away from Una in frustration, now he rounded on Sulien. 'Don't you realise – she knew he could be dangerous, she might have thrown her life away and why? To prove a point?'

'I don't care. He almost killed her. Leave her alone.'

159

'I'm sorry,' repeated Una.

'Come here,' Sulien turned to her, ignoring Marcus now. 'Let me look at your wrist.'

Silenced, Marcus watched them as Sulien carefully handled the wrist, put his fingers to the bruises on her neck and face, gently but pointedly. Marcus went back to crouch beside her, remorsefully. 'I wouldn't have stopped you. You're right, you had to do it, we had to know. But I would have made sure he couldn't hurt you.'

'I know,' replied Una quietly, recovering a little. 'But it's just as well he did.'

Marcus stared at her, shaking his head in incomprehension. 'I don't know how you can say that,' he remarked at last, helplessly.

'Because it can be proved against him,' she said evenly, in control again.

Marcus shook his head again, feeling at once that he might have known she would say that and that she was unfathomably strange, exhaustingly strange and precious and reckless with herself. He closed his arms around her once more, and muttered fiercely, 'I want to kill him.'

'Good. Do it,' said Varius suddenly, without raising his voice at all, but much more forcefully than when he'd spoken before.

It was exactly what the incoherent flood of disgust and rage coursing through Marcus had been demanding, but hearing it repeated aloud, approved, was such a jolt that he turned to Varius and his voice sounded small and pathetic in his own ears. 'What?'

'He's killed four people. Four that we know about. And now this; he isn't stopping. You can't allow him any more chances.'

'I know,' whispered Marcus, flinching, holding Una more tightly, while at the same time sharp grief for his parents swept suddenly across him like a blade peeling off a curl of skin.

Varius did not stop. 'And Gabinius getting himself shot – did your cousin do that too? It must have been good news for him, anyway. We could have known all this sooner.'

'We could have done – it's my fault,' said Marcus, scarcely audibly. He couldn't meet Varius' eyes. 'But now I don't think – unless we find something – we can't prove he killed my parents ... or Gemella.'

'Then he falls down the stairs drunk, he goes out hunting and never comes back, it doesn't matter!' cried Varius, savagely, hearing his voice ring in the cavernous room, as if it were someone else's. There was silence afterwards.

'It does matter,' answered Marcus finally, tentatively. 'People would find out. The Praetorians know what happened today ... and where he is. They'd know I did it. And anyway,' he hesitated again and his voice sank even lower, 'I won't ... I won't murder him in secret. It's almost what he would have done to *us*, Varius. I don't want to be ... like that.'

'You aren't like him,' said Varius, almost scoffing, for it seemed such a useless, self-indulgent thing to say. 'There's no comparison. It's an execution. Do you really think you'd have anything to be ashamed of, after what he's done?'

Marcus could feel, with alarming, unfamiliar intensity, what he wanted to do to Drusus: pound his fists into his stomach, smash something heavy against his face and head until the bones broke, stab him. He wanted to do it quickly yet not so fast that Drusus felt nothing, didn't know he was dying. He couldn't imagine feeling any shame afterwards. He managed to say, 'I don't know. Yes. *Yes*. I – Varius, if I start like this – I ...' He felt a sick shudder pass through him, unable to keep the words from forming in his mind: it's too much, and I can't stand it, I can't do it. He said aloud, unsteadily, 'I haven't even been here six weeks.'

Varius said, a little more gently but still unwavering, 'Would it be any different if it were six years?'

Marcus made a trapped, impatient gesture, dragging a hand across his face. 'I meant, if I do this now – before I've done anything else – I'll do it again, won't I? Won't I keep doing it? There will always be someone who's a threat – and we'll discuss what to do, but the conversation will be shorter every time it happens because if I've done it before, why not again? There's been enough of that. I *can't*. And it isn't an execution, you know that.'

'Varius,' said Una. 'There's nothing Drusus can do. He's not going anywhere. It's more than my word against his. There's the room he shut me in. He broke the longdictor – I cut him with a piece of it, it's still on the roof. And there's Acchan – the boy who helped me. It was attempted murder. It can be proved, I know it can.'

Varius sighed and sat down, suddenly tired. 'Well,' he conceded wearily. 'I suppose given he's already in custody it's not ... practical.' But even before he spoke again it was obvious to the others that he had not changed his mind, not in principle. He said, 'If he's alive he won't be harmless. And you mustn't think otherwise. If he has any allies at all he'll always be a threat. Even if he's locked up. Although yes, if you put him on trial, you'll get your way. A court will probably judge whatever they think you want anyway.' Marcus frowned in protest at this but Varius continued, 'It's not a question of proving it to them. It's the Emperor, and what happens if he ever doubts you?'

'But he won't. He won't be able to,' said Marcus.

'But he has to believe all of it. He won't understand this on its own. He's got to be sure about Lady Tullia and everything else.'

'He knew I was telling the truth before,' said Una.

'Yes. That's something,' admitted Varius. 'But there's always the chance.'

'What will happen when the Emperor hears this?' asked Una. She was looking at Sulien, who suddenly understood that it was not only for comfort that she'd called him there.

'Do you mean, could it kill him?' he asked. 'Do you absolutely have to tell him? Because yes, it's possible.'

There was a pause, and then Varius said, 'I don't think that's a real choice. He's going to wonder where Drusus has gone, isn't he? If you do it this way, it can't be by halves, everyone has to know. So he'll find out anyway, and that would be worse.'

'You're right,' said Marcus, reluctantly. He felt another spasm of hatred for Drusus, this time on his uncle's behalf. He asked Sulien, 'Can you be there with me when I tell him, in case?'

'All right. Of course,' said Sulien, uneasily.

'Well, then, you know what you're going to do,' remarked Una.

'Yes,' murmured Marcus. He let out his breath shakily, deliberately uncurled the fist that wore the ring, feeling a slight, temporary relief. His body still felt taxed with unacted violence. 'But I don't ever want to see Drusus again,' he said. He found he was talking to Varius, Varius was the one he wanted to know this. 'If I ever do. If I'm ever in a room with him, I'll ...' He did not say the words, but once again he could feel what he would do.

The rumour of Drusus' arrest had begun thriving through the Palace from the moment it happened, despite Glycon's attempts to quarantine it. As she walked to her father's rooms, Makaria missed the first signals of it – a group of servants suddenly dispersing at the far end of a passage, the sound of doors opening and closing urgently somewhere below her. Still, though she had changed out of her formal clothes, she felt faintly uncomfortable, as if a mistake had been made. She assumed it was only another of bout of anxiety about Faustus and homesickness for her island. On Siphnos, Hypatia, to whom she was closer than anyone else, who could have made her forget the rash of annoyances that always afflicted her in the palace, would be managing the vineyard without her. Makaria was irritated with her father for insisting on staying in the palace, she could not see how he could recover here, he would be better off in Greece, away from everything, but the argument was just not worth having, nor was she even sure how she could manage having him there in her real, out-of-Rome life. But as she walked down a flight of stairs she caught a pair of guards looking at her sharply, as one joined the other and muttered something inaudible, and it seemed suddenly obvious that something had happened, and was being kept from her.

Makaria marched over to them and demanded abruptly, 'What's going on?'

The men looked awkward. 'Nothing, madam. Some routine security issues. That is, nothing to worry about.'

'I saw you look at me; you think it concerns me. Don't lie to me about it.'

'I'm under orders not to discuss it.'

'Then you're disobeying orders by discussing it with each other, as well as *my* order for you to tell me,' said Makaria impatiently.

'Please, my lady,' said the guard in a low voice, so that she was a little repentant. 'I can't. I'm sure Caesar will talk to you soon.'

Makaria frowned, but did not persist. A tremor of anxiety seemed to rise into her throat, silencing her and growing worse as she walked away. And of all things, all possible forms of bad news, she found she thought instantly of Drusus. He had acted so strangely by the fountain. But then he'd said he was ill, which had seemed natural enough at the time, perhaps more natural than it might have been in someone else. For though she could not have said he was unusually sickly, there was always something overstrained and wounded about Drusus. Nevertheless, suppose ...? She began and then left a gap, she could not bear to think it, and yet she could not avoid the guilty logic: if what she'd done was tell him that something terrible about him was known, if he had a secret and had just learnt it wasn't safe, then how would you expect him to act? Exactly as he had.

Why hadn't he known about Una before anyway? He'd been so out of things for the last few years – well, so had she, but for him it was different – he'd spent most of his life barely venturing outside Rome, why had he suddenly abandoned it so totally?

She thought she was reasonably level-headed, perhaps she became sullen or cantankerous easily, but that was not the same thing as panic; she didn't think she was often guilty of summoning up dire consequences on the prompting of nothing. And so she was the more horrified by the sudden gush of possibilities that followed the question: *if all that were so, what would he do next?*

Her fear was compromised all the time by the thought that she was being terribly unfair to Drusus.

She found Marcus walking towards her along a passage with Sulien, both of them seeming to pass in and out of their real ages as they moved: older and younger, they looked worn and sombre, but also pale, scared, as if they were walking through stripes of shadow between bright windows.

'I was coming to find you,' said Marcus.

Makaria had briefly forgotten that Sulien was Una's brother; seeing Marcus with Faustus' doctor she thought she must have been wrong, the news must be about her father. 'What is it, is he worse?' she asked. And then she remembered.

'It's not that,' answered Marcus shortly, and told her where Drusus was.

Makaria put a hand to her mouth. 'Why? He did something to Una, didn't he? Is she dead?' she blurted out, to her own incredulity. The young men stared at her. She was ashamed of being so blunt, so clumsy.

'No, she's not dead,' said Marcus.

'It was you, then,' said Sulien. They'd already decided that it seemed likely.

'How could I know what would happen? Oh no, he can't, he wouldn't, I know he wouldn't,' moaned Makaria.

'It's not all he's done,' said Marcus.

'I must go and see her,' cried Makaria impulsively, sick with contrition.

'She's gone to the baths. You can't. You don't know all of it.'

She could anticipate, unwillingly, much of what she was going to be to be told, but she felt on fire not just with rage but with shame and stupidity, when she heard that Tulliola and Drusus had been lovers. Of course, of *course* it would be that. How could she not have seen when she had always despised Tulliola, had *known*, from the beginning really, how false she was? What Makaria had felt for Drusus would have been only a shared world-weariness that was to do with being a Novian, barely more than a casual liking if it could have been taken out of the fierce complexity of family. She racked her memory now for signs she must have missed, glances between Tulliola and Drusus, times they had been alone together, and she could think of nothing, or at least nothing in Tulliola, always so treacherously opaque. But Drusus – the tension and nervousness for which she had pitied him. 'Oh, it's vile,' she said. 'How could he? So there's nothing my father has that he hasn't tried to get his hands on. He's not human, he can't be. And what is this going to do to Daddy? Bringing it all up again will be bad enough.'

'Yes. But we have to,' said Marcus, firmly – but looking fragile to Makaria, so that she felt a rare twinge of almost maternal pity for him, as she'd felt on sporadic occasions when he'd been a sweet and anxious child.

She had been pacing about with unconscious, caged belligerence:

swinging her shoulders, almost stamping – like a boy younger than Marcus was now, she thought, catching herself doing it. She made herself stop. 'I'll do it, if you want,' she said tersely.

But as they walked to Faustus' apartments, she remained in such a state of enraged panic for her father, so frantic with the certainty that Drusus' betrayal of him was as good as another murder, that she was almost irritated as well as relieved at how patiently Faustus seemed to take the news. Since the morning he had been feeling a little better, he had been sitting near the window eating figs when they entered. The colour left his face as he listened, but still, he was affectionately impatient with Makaria as she faltered through the facts. 'Come on, come on, spit it out,' he said.

When everything was told, Faustus could feel his heart speeding, a thin, dry buzz. But he was aware of Sulien's tactful presence; he could see, with mingled annoyance and pity how they were all looking at him, anxiously, as if at a dropped glass in mid-air, and he dragged ineffectively at his numbed body, trying to lift it higher and straighter in the chair. 'Well,' he said slowly. 'I've always known he wanted to be Emperor. It makes sense of things. I suppose … there was always a chance of this.'

'We didn't want to tell you this, when you're ill,' said Marcus.

'But you had to. Of course you did. Of course you did,' said Faustus, gently. He wanted to say something to Marcus about Leo, but couldn't. 'He … killed Tulliola himself?'

'Yes,' said Marcus. 'He must have got men of his on to her guard. Of course we'll try and find out what happened.'

'I spoke to him a few hours afterwards,' said Faustus, wondering. 'I remember it. He said how sorry he was.'

'He's scum. He's not a real Novian. Drusilla Terentia has a lot to answer for; the gods know there's nothing of *us* in him,' spat Makaria, trembling.

'I don't know if that's true,' murmured Faustus, sadly. Or he tried to; he realised that yet again he had not made himself understood.

Later, when they were walking away from the room, Marcus felt for a moment almost cheerful with relief. He said to Sulien, 'That wasn't as bad as I thought.'

Sulien didn't answer. His right hand had strayed to his left wrist.

'She's all right,' murmured Marcus.

'Of course she is,' said Sulien quickly, with a faint, odd bristle of defensiveness in his voice. 'I know. But if she hadn't been, Marcus. And we wouldn't even have known, I never even thought of someone trying to … kill her.'

'No one did. I certainly didn't. I should have done, if you want to blame someone beside Drusus.'

'It's not that,' murmered Sulien. His eyes were half-lowered, distant. But then he raised his face and looked at Marcus with sudden, jarring urgency. 'There's something wrong. All the time. This happening to Una just … *proves* that. I *know* it, all the time, I can't talk myself out of it. The people from the tower block, and whoever killed all those slaves: we don't even know if they're the same people, but they're still there, somewhere, and whatever they did it for, they still want. And I can't get used to it.'

'We'll find all that out,' said Marcus. Sulien shook his head a little, impatiently, as if Marcus had not quite got the point. 'Look, it'll be alright. Of course you're on edge. This happens after Veii – anyone would be.'

Sullien's mouth pulled into a tight dubious grin. I'm not like this, I never have been. I don't know why I never have been, if I feel like this now.'

'You still often think about the cross, though,' said Marcus softly, and indicated Sulien's fingers, still smoothing his wrist.

Sulien looked down at his hands, which sprang hastily apart, as if of their own accord. 'It thinks about me,' he mumbled, and then, at Marcus' startled look at him. 'Oh, I don't know what I mean by that. It's different.' He thought for a moment and went on, 'It's different, because even when it was happening, I knew what I was supposed to have done. I knew exactly why they were taking me to the cross. It was all in the open. Not like all this. And your cousin – that was just out of nowhere. Or that's how it seemed.'

Marcus grimaced and asked, 'Did you want me to have him killed, too?'.

Sulien was faintly surprised both at the question and, when he thought of it, at the fact that he hadn't taken one side or another. Shouldn't he be wanting to tear Drusus apart? But Drusus, already locked in the palace cells, his actions revealed and explained, seemed removed from the need for anger. He might have been a dangerous machine that had been deactivated. 'No, not really. You really wanted to hurt him, didn't you? But he's already done so much to you. And he's part of your family. Of course you hate him.'

In the pale cell under the Golden House, Drusus felt like a wasp, battering out its life against a window pane: each separate second was so

166

desperate, so horrifying, that sometimes his brain clenched upon itself and he thought he wanted to kill himself, when really he wanted anything but that, at all costs he wanted to live. Sometimes he clutched for comfort at the Sibyl's promise about his death – but there was no comfort, there was nothing he could even bear the thought of. He reeled from corner to corner of the room, in a continuing agony of disbelief, still loathing the fact of having been handled, of being thrown in through the door, of terrible wordless loneliness.

He had no idea how long this had gone on, when he saw that a man – dark-skinned, about his own age – had appeared behind the pane of thick, latticed glass in the door, and was watching him impassively. The man stood neutrally, very still, his hands loose at his sides, with no expression on his face, or at least none that Drusus was capable of reading. Drusus froze, unconsciously ceasing to breathe, even though he was long past recognising Varius. For what seemed like a long time they both remained unmoving. Drusus was slightly crouched, drawn together like an animal, as on the other side the man watched and watched, intently, like a scientist, and the gaze became unendurable and finally, without warning, Drusus flung himself into a forward sprint, cannoning into the glass, his fists raised, screaming so that his throat felt ragged, 'Get out of here! Get away from me!' And without even knowing who the other man was, he would have burst through the glass and torn him apart, if he could have.

He could not have said what he expected; he had no sense of the future any more – but it was dreadful to him that Varius did not react at all. He remained exactly where he was. All that happened was the revulsion showed more clearly in the cold stare, so that Drusus, shuddering, realised dimly that revulsion, or contempt, was what it was.

Varius understood, intellectually, why Marcus had wanted never to be near his cousin again. Perhaps that wasn't so different from the way he himself had felt about Gabinius – or would have, if Gabinius still lived. But he had felt compelled to come here, to look at Drusus with his new knowledge, even though he did not know what he expected to see – nothing that would reveal any new facts about Drusus, or make any more sense of him. And yet in some way Varius did sense how intangible people almost always were to Drusus, how hard it was to believe they persisted when he even shut his eyes or turned his back, that it was all but impossible for him to connect a name that figured in his plans with a solid human, standing in front of him. Varius could see that Drusus didn't recognise him, although he had seen him a handful of times, and moreover must have known of him, must have agreed with Tulliola as to what was done.

167

The door that led up into the Palace was open behind Varius; nevertheless, the weight of the huge building pressed on him. It was impossible for Varius not to remember, to share the feeling of being shut in. Still, he stayed on and on – perhaps it was only a kind of endurance game, another minute, and another. He did not exactly indulge in any fantasy of what he would do if, say, he could bribe his way into that room. He could almost certainly ignore Marcus' decision and take Drusus' life – but only at the cost of wrecking his own, something that might once have seemed a reasonable trade, but did not now. And yet he continued to study Drusus, weighing him up, some part of himself quietly calculating what would happen, what it would take, if the barrier between them suddenly disappeared. And this went on until Drusus suddenly ducked away from the window, hiding, hating himself for it, and didn't know how much longer Varius stood there, a few feet away from him. He stayed huddled on the ground against the door, grateful despite himself that the door was there, that the glass couldn't be broken.

Faustus felt he could sense him through the many floors and walls, as he'd been aware of Tulliola, the one night she'd spent in the same cells, three years before. At least there had been work for him to do back then, and he'd been capable of doing it. He was grateful when at last he got the attendants to leave him to himself. He let out his breath in a gasp, beginning to shake, as he covered his face, remembering Drusus' sympathy as he sat by his bed, then thinking of his own father, and what was left of his three sons. Himself a derelict, blind idiot, stupid enough to let someone as dangerous as Tulliola into the palace for the most trivial of reasons, gullible enough not to see what was in front of his face. Lucius a wreck for years, and his son a monster. And Leo dead.

But when he woke in the morning, his head astonishing him with pain, in a spinning room, among unrecognisable people, he did not remember any of it.

X

NORIKO

Noriko watched the Romans coming through the high walls of this foreign city. Even through the moist and heavy air, the slow column of vehicles, blazing dully with bronze and semi-precious stones, was visible right from the heart of Bianjing. Two broad, straight roads quartered the city's perfect square, crossing beneath the palace, cutting across the lake that lay like a square-cut mirror below it, out through the four gates and away across the Yudong plain. Only occasional variations gently disrupted the symmetry: temples and gardens just inside the walls to the north-east, the old shrine-tower of glazed and moulded ceramic brick that they said looked as if it were made of iron, although to Noriko it looked more like green-tinged copper. Around the central cross the finer streets spread in an elegant, geomantic grid of lines and right angles. Every edge appeared just sharpened, all ancient, all pristinely new.

Only the guard she had bribed to let her pass knew that Noriko was here, on the upper parapet of the outer fortress of the palace. Her hand lay on one of the hot, cylindrical tiles of thick, bubbled glass that roofed the lower fort, and of which no two seemed the same, each modelled with flowers, Buddhas, clouds; the petals and billows outlined with subtle brush strokes of coloured enamel, jewel bright. And yet the detail was only visible this close: the roof swept down away from her and up again, like a wave turned to ice, faintly grey-green and luminous, though not transparent. Riding the cutting peaks at the eaves stood a file of blown-glass dragons, delicately scaled with yellow. All the city was like that, an extension of the palace itself, the blood red of inner walls just visible behind green, flowered pillars, the steep curved roofs heavy with ridged and overlapping glass, strict in its uniform beauty. It glared like a diamond.

At night the electric lanterns lit up and glowed through the watery roofs. Inside the steamy summer air was chilled and fresh. But except for the shrine-towers and the ramparts themselves, none of the buildings rose very high – five or six storeys at the most. On her first day in Bianjing, the polished agelessness of the place, so meticulous and so conservative, had made Noriko feel faintly defensive. Comparing Bianjing with the cities of her home, she felt that it was stiflingly antique, unreal – no one lived here who did not serve the government in some way, there were scarcely any children. But still she was obscurely afraid of finding Cynoto, Nara, Naniwa wanting beside it.

But today the city might have been nothing but a waste of grey brick; its beauty meant nothing to her, she scarcely saw it – only the approaching procession of ornate cars.

She could deflect any questions by pretending her Sinoan was worse than it was. In the plain, dark cotton robe and trousers she was wearing, she could have been one of the maids attending the Nionian Imperial party. She might have lost her way on an errand; the long, tubular, painted letter-case that hung like a quiver of arrows on her back, might have held a message between the pavilions, although she did not know what she would do if anyone demanded to open it. But it was difficult, she trusted, to quarrel with the polite incomprehension she would assume.

From a narrow pocket inside her sleeve she took a little silver telescope, only as long as her hand and slender as a writing brush, and studied the convoy. Through the lenses, each vehicle became distinct, separate. Marcus Novius would be near the middle, but not actually in the central car – not quite so clear a target. She deliberated a little, sweeping the focus up and down the line, until she thought she could even guess which of the glittering roofs hid him.

The dawdling pace tormented her. She swallowed drily, flexed palms grown damp with anticipation, and was wrung by a sudden longing to go home. Before she even saw Marcus Novius step out into the courtyard below, a wrench of nervous sickness made her bend forward, groaning quietly. She could not do it, it should not be asked of her. She tried to master it, but the nausea and breathlessness continued; she could hardly bear to watch as the fleet of gilt-wreathed cars finally passed through the gate beneath her, into the courtyard, as the dark-gowned Sinoan court officials came forward to greet the Romans as they stepped out into the hazy sunlight in their sombre pale clothes, like a party of mourners or priests. Though she stepped behind a pillar to be sure of remaining hidden, she stood with her face turned in silent anguish to the painted wood, her eyes closed, and it was a second or two before she could steady the telescope and look out again.

Europeans, Africans, Indians were all gathering in the courtyard below. Of course she had seen hundreds of Roman faces, but only on longvision screens; very few in the flesh. And the Nionian Empire too encompassed a good deal of diversity, but again Noriko had not seen much of it, there was only limited exchange between the provinces. So now she could not help seeing the assembled foreigners with what she knew was an irrational sense of vague freakishness. It was even fascinating: for a moment – the Roman prince being concealed among the rest – Noriko relaxed a little, almost tempted to waste time turning the telescope frivolously from face to face, enjoying the garish variety, as if she were in a private museum of overstated features, odd-coloured skin and eyes.

But that was not what she was there to do. For a second Marcus Novius came into view and she recognised him instantly. In bleak, funereal white like the rest, he was the only one to wear the Roman toga over otherwise normal clothes – or rather it was a simplified, ceremonial suggestion of a toga, a drape of white fabric with a purple stripe across his body, despite the heat. Without moving her eye from the telescope, Noriko unslung the long letter-case from her shoulder, feeling with one hand for the opening. But she had only a glimpse of his face. As she tried to focus he turned again to speak to someone and a Roman lady stepped into Noriko's line of sight, so that all she could see of Marcus Novius was a fraction of the back of his head, his dark-gold hair.

Screening him, the young woman stood looking from side to side, at the two bronze-cast lions sneering identically across the courtyard, up at the richly painted cross-beams beneath the glass roofs, her lips parted with wonder. She was beautifully dressed in thin, silvery clothes whose folds stirred loosely in the humid breeze, the narrow body that might otherwise have looked too pauperishly bony was graceful under the flow of silk. Noriko examined her face curiously, even though the lady was less bizarre looking than the others in some ways, having too little colour rather than too much. Her fluttering hair was a light, faded-looking brown, her skin ghostly. Nevertheless, although the European bones of her face were as angular and protrusive as any other set of features there, her small mouth was delicate, elegant. She was very young, too – the youngest Roman there. What was she doing here?

Marcus Novius Faustus moved again, but just as Noriko lifted the glass to find his face, quite suddenly the lady raised her head and seemed to look straight into her eye. And her expression hardened, changing from sweet, naive wonder to what looked like clear-sighted suspicion.

Instantly Noriko jolted back behind the pillar, shocked and confused. The little telescope hung loosely between suddenly nerveless fingers. Surely, at this distance, in the shadows, she could not possibly have been seen. Nevertheless her heart seemed to batter so violently within

171

her that she could have thought that alone was causing the shaking of her body.

There were too many people in the way now, the Romans were moving on, inside. Noriko swung the case back onto her shoulder, slid the telescope into its sheath. She ran along the cloistered walkway on the ramparts, down the steps within the wall, to follow them, comforted briefly by the coolness and the solitude. With both the Roman prince and the lady in silver out of sight, Noriko knew who the woman was. Too well dressed to be a servant, and standing too close to the prince to be a lady in waiting; Marcus Novius was certainly unmarried, and he had no sisters. So, of course the girl was a concubine, or a lover. It was only because she had been in such startlingly plain view, standing there with him so indiscreetly, that Noriko had not seen it at once.

Una felt no more weariness from the long journey by magnetway through the endless woods of Sarmatia and Scythia, through the bare grasslands in the north. The cryptic beauty of the city exhilarated her. She felt conscious of her origins with rare absence of resentment or shame: how had she got here, so many thousand miles from London, where she hadn't even had much hope of living very long? Nevertheless, without it spoiling her pleasure in the city, she was was also exercising a different part of the mind, from the moment the car passed through the outer gates, down the avenue across the lake that presented the Palace with a bright inverted image of itself. Who kept it so clean, who replaced the glass tiles even before they ever showed a flaw, who prevented weeds from growing and fed the fish in the almost sterile, stainless lake? They had travelled through Jondum in the north, she knew that not all Sinoan cities were like this, homogenously perfect from edge to edge, without even suburbs, let alone slums.

Almost in the same moment as she looked up at the gates, Marcus did the same, with his own brief, intangible feeling there was someone hidden, watching from a distance. Perhaps it was only because he had caught Una's movement, and understood it without even having to think. They glanced at each other, knowing they had felt the same thing. But there was nothing to be said – there were so many pairs of eyes turned towards them, too many people to fathom, all talking, thinking in a language Una didn't know. But despite the sudden sense of quiet vulnerability, Una felt a twinge of happiness at how easily, how mutually she and Marcus had read each other's thoughts. She smiled at him.

Ahead, between the inner palaces, a group of Nionian ladies went by. They were, it seemed, not meant to be seen, although equally it seemed that the precautions to keep them hidden were more symbolic than actual; four servants flanked the group, carrying portable screens, plain lattices of white paper and unpainted wood, simple against the women's brightly coloured clothes, for there was little attempt at keeping the screens together and few of the ladies remained totally out of sight. They turned their heads, openly, to look at the gathering Romans. There was no great difference now between the Nionian and Roman clothes, except in the colours and fabrics used, and the length and squareness of the Nionians' sleeves. But Marcus and Una were both fascinated by the women's hair, which hung in straight, long falls – unbelievably long to the Romans' eyes – hanging to the knees or heels, or kept from sweeping along the ground by a train extending from a butterfly-embroidered dress. Only a couple of the women had left their hair its natural black; the others – it was a fashion a decade or so old – wore it stained or dyed in deep, bright colours: crimson, lilac, dark indigo, kingfisher blue.

'Some of them have got to be wearing wigs,' Una remarked, to Marcus' slight disappointment. It was the sharper, electric colours she meant, hair surely could not undergo such punishing dyeing and still grow that long and glossy. The women passed and Una heard a distant cry of laughter from behind the paper screens. Why had they come?

They were led on into the complex of gardens and halls, and the feeling of being spied on returned to Una again, like a cool stirring of the air. And again when she turned to look back, and saw numberless faces of guards, officials, eunuchs, all watching the Roman arrivals with blank polite faces and varying secret feelings of fascination, distrust, revulsion or indifference – it was lost.

An hour or so passed as the Romans disappeared into guest quarters on the western side of the grounds, to change their clothes, rest a little after the long journey – and Noriko slipped quickly into the Crown Prince's rooms to speak with him.

Later, she recognised Marcus Novius' new advisor, Varius, striding across a courtyard towards the northern gardens where Prince Tadahito and the Nionian dukes and lords would soon approach. She watched him pass before she followed to hide among the trees.

Varius had barely looked at the lovely apartment he was shown into. He was tired, but he would not be able to relax yet, nor to appreciate any of the beauty around him. And as he walked he was aware of people trying not to be caught gawping at his height and bone structure, and the colour of his skin. He walked impassively, ignoring it, yet felt self-conscious heat slowly filling his skin, lapping from within at the foreign contours of his face: an unpleasantly primal sense that he was outnumbered.

The gardens were full of faintly desperate activity, as in the last few moments before any performance. Among the yellow roses and chrysanthemums, beside a lake shaped in artful, curving imitation of nature in contrast to the mirrory square outside the palace walls, priests and officials and interpreters hurried about nervously and untidily, setting out an enclosure of screens and banners – the Roman eagle, the red Nionian sun – while the daughters of the Nionian priest, wearing white tunics over scarlet skirts, tuned musical instruments. Varius commandeered one of the interpreters to help him talk with one of the Nionian ambassadors, and the three of them, an awkward trio, wandered back and forth across the enclosure, knowing they were probably more in the way than not, checking things Varius knew should not need to be checked. But neither he nor the ambassador could rest: Marcus was about to meet Prince Tadahito and the Sinoan Emperor for the first time.

The courtiers and civil servants of all three nations had been strained almost to madness by attempting to plan this moment: it was like calculating some deadly sum involving three incompatible versions of infinity. How could the three leaders be brought together; how would they treat each other and what kind of treatment could they accept? All visitors to the Sinoan court were required to lower themselves to all fours, to knock their foreheads nine times on the floor before the Emperor's throne. It was equally impossible that Marcus and the Nionian crown prince and barons should do this, and impossible that, as guests, they should not. And how were they to acknowledge each other? Would each one of them not demean himself and his people if he failed to exact the deference which was his due from *every* human being? All three were supposed to be somehow divine: the Son of Heaven; the heir of the goddess Amaterasu; a descendant of Olympians. Marcus' grandfather was only one of a long line of Emperors to be made a god after his death; Varius might not believe in any of them, and he knew Marcus did not believe either, but that was not the point. The Romans might be cynical among themselves about their deified Emperors, but if only a few of them really believed that their rulers were potential gods, how much less could they believe in the claims to godhead of foreign leaders? How could they ever bear the shame if their Caesar knelt down and worshipped another man? And it was the same for the other two. To each of them, his whole nation's pride seemed to dictate that he must insult the others, for to make any gesture of submission was intolerable.

At first the Romans had hoped that a carefully judged performance of simultaneous nods – indicating respect, but not inferiority – might be sufficient. Rapidly, they realised it would not – neither the Sinoans nor Nionians could accept it; the meanings of different bows were so specific that a nod was too glaring a violation of Imperial rights.

Now, the enclosure cleared as the Romans and Nionans took their place on either side, the Imperial envoys still hidden from one another. Varius stood among the rest and watched, anxious, as if even now everything might collapse into bitterness and failure. It was so insane – so childish, that a crisis over the relative positions of three men's heads might have hurtled them all into war, before a serious word had been spoken, but it was true, they'd come that close. Varius had only become involved in the final days before the Romans were due to leave, when he realised how critical things had become.

Dressed in red, her forehead bound with ribbons, the young priestess from the temple of Venus Genetrix in Rome walked out under the willows. She seemed slightly ill at ease, perhaps feeling the same discomfort here that Varius did. She cleared her throat and began to speak:

'Before they meet in the hope of answering the grave challenge before them, it is right that the Imperial households honour their shared divine ancestress. In Rome her name is Venus the Founder, who led her son Aeneas from Troy to the shores of Italy, where the Empire sprang from her bloodline; in Nionia she is Amaterasu, and to the eastern islands too she sent her issue to found a nation. Her heavenly favour passed from the hero Ninigi, to the first Emperor Jimmu, as it passed from Aeneas to Romulus, who laid the walls of Rome. Through her, the Empires of Rome and Nionia are sisters, born of one mother; their citizens, though separated by barriers of land and sea, and of brick, are brothers. Today we pray that the Goddess will guide her children to lasting peace.'

As she finished the Nionian priest rose, clad in voluminous white silk, a high black mitre on his head. Twice he clapped his hands together, loudly, and bowed before he began his own oration, saying, Varius hoped, something along the same lines. Varius let out an inaudible sigh, and smiled with private relief, as if until now he'd really feared someone watching might stand up and decry this as the nonsense it was. For it seemed a precarious pantomime to him, and he was the one that had written it.

In fact the identification of Venus and Amaterasu had never been as firmly established as he had made it sound. He had reached for it when, almost at the point of hopelessness, the inspiration came to him that in this case the only way to circumvent ritual was to create more. The founding stories about the two deities were, as the priestess had

175

said, at least adequately similar, and there was the coincidence that the first syllables of the Nionian goddess' name sounded like the Latin for 'loved', and that the whole of it was not so different from other names Venus had borne, like Astarte and Aphrodite. But still Varius had only noticed the idea of the link circulating among two sets of people: first, as a student, he'd heard it at his academy, where it had been only a playful bit of trivia, intended to be slightly provocative, because hardly any of them there believed in the gods. But oddly enough the idea had been taken up among certain politicians and conservative writers – men like Salvius, waiting for the war they felt so necessary – who would either grumble disconsolately about 'the Nionians' spurious claim of descent from Venus', or, more optimistically, cite it as evidence that it would not be so hard to integrate Nionia into Roman culture, once she had been conquered.

But they'd got away with it; everything went as he had hoped, and he even allowed himself to feel proud. From the Nionian side, bearers carried out a kind of moveable shrine, curtained and canopied, a small, silk-roofed tent over a miniature wooden house, resting on poles over the bearers' shoulders, like a sedan chair. Meanwhile the Roman priestess unveiled a half-size statue of Venus in gold leaf over bronze, standing over a low altar, a bright round mirror – Amaterasu's symbol – shining in her golden hands. It was a feeble, tawdry, simpering figure, for they had had only a few days to find and requisition a statue of the right size, suitable for quick alteration. Besides the mirror, clouds of clumsy-looking gold drapery had been added, swathed around her in frantic haste, after Varius realised the Nionians' acceptance of 'Venus Amaterasu' would certainly disintegrate if the goddess was nearly naked. Consequently, to most of the Romans watching, she did not look like Venus at all.

Marcus went forward without hesitation. Makaria should have been beside him, but resignedly she had stayed in Rome with her father, and instead Marcus was followed by Probus, and Yanisen, the head governor of Terranova, and a few younger noblemen. At the same, precisely timed moment the Nionian lords appeared, and among them was Prince Tadahito, a young man with a long sensitive face, like a hare's, cautious and alert. He was dressed in steel-blue silk, embroidered with stark gold squares; the central lock of his black hair was tied back from his forehead, the rest falling loose to his shoulders. His youth and his clothes made him conspicuous among the older barons and generals – Kiyowara-no-Sanetomo of Goshu, Mimanano-Fusahira of Koura – but Tadahito was not the only one to stand out, nor the only one who generated a silent, thunderous atmosphere of power. In front of him was the governor of Nionian Terranova, Masarus Cato, as the Romans casually referred to him: Seii-Taishougun Kato-no-Masaru, Lord of Tokogane. He was in his late forties, of no more than medium height, but handsome, his eyes sharp under dense, clear-cut, slightly slanted brows, his smiling mouth and heavy jaw framed with jet-black blades of hair. While the young Nionian shrine-attendants in their red and white could occasionally be seen to steal shy glances at Prince Tadahito from beneath lowered eyelashes, the older man had drawn looks of frank admiration from the Roman priestesses of Venus. He walked with such electric confidence that beside him the proud young prince looked almost fragile.

Side by side, the Romans and Nionians bowed to Venus Amaterasu, not to each other; indeed they avoided even looking at each other until it was done. Nothing worse happened than Yanisen's glower at Lord Kato, his counterpart, which was answered with a calm hostile smile. They both offered Italian wine and honey, along with rice, and Nionian pine branches hung with strips of silk.

Beside Tadahito, Marcus was murmuring with apparent quiet piety, 'Let this altar be our refuge. Take us into your protection and defend us, kind Venus. Be not offended with us, nor hold us at fault; consider us not unclean. With your father Jupiter, in whom rest the hopes and lives of all humankind, grant that these days prosper. Venus Amaterasu, may you be honoured by this offering.' He seemed completely at ease. Varius felt affectionately impressed with him – he was so natural. Varius knew he would have hated being under such open scrutiny himself.

Finally the two parties could turn to each other and begin to ex-change polite, wary greetings, but there was still the Sinoan Emperor to be met for the first time. In this case the solution had come from the Nionian side: solemnly, Marcus lifted the *pallium*, the purple-bordered swathe of white cloth, from his own shoulders and put it over Yanisen's, while Tadahito untied a cord he had worn over the sash of his tunic, and handed it to Kato. Thus loosely representing their two leaders, they could, it had been grudgingly agreed, prostrate themselves before the Emperor to spare Marcus or Tadahito having to do it in person. Still, it was strikingly obvious that both men loathed what was being required of them: Kato's faint smile tightened and faded; Yanisen's lips were folded into a stern grimace as if he were about to undergo some kind of physical pain. They both bowed, stiffly, Kato to the prince, Yanisen to Marcus, so that at least no one could say they were honouring the Sinoan Emperor above their own monarchs, before they marched reluc-tantly up the steps, through the high trellis doors into the hall where the Emperor waited. No one accompanied them – the only witnesses to their shame would be the guards, women and eunuchs of the Sinoan court. The rest waited until it was over, and then followed.

The hall was hung with tapestries, set about with large, beautiful, painted vases and ornamental trees, and very bright, filtered light through tall shuttered doors and the greenish glass tiles, high above. Sitting on the yellow throne, the Emperor must have been at least fifty but looked much younger, baby-like almost, with his round, smooth face, plump body in yellow satin robes, and his air of somnolent indifference to the arrival of the foreigners. He smiled with bored benevolence at the Romans, with just the faintest visible trace of listless antagonism at the Nionians, and scarcely spoke. The Romans talked of him as 'the Emperor Florens' – 'Sing-ji' was the best reproduction of the actual name into the Western alphabet, but the Romans preferred the loose translation into Latin since they had long considered the Sinoan syllables barbarously impossible to pronounce. And with curiosity or disapproval, they whispered that he was only a puppet, that the Sinoan Empire was truly ruled, quite openly in fact, by a woman, Florens' mother, the Dowager Empress, whom the Romans called Junosena. But she did not appear in the hall, as the welcoming banquet began. The uneasy guests were seated at long, low, lacquered tables – the Nionians and Romans were given places of scrupulously equal rank, although Florens' throne rose calmly above them both.

As they ate the tension was softened and overcome by a seemingly infinite succession of courses, among them dishes as difficult and epicurean as the most eccentric Roman offerings – stewed bear's paws, turtles cooked with egg yolk, fried swallows – along with fare more recognisable to them – pork, duck, shellfish – so much that even those Romans who baulked at the unfamiliarity of the spices and the combinations of meats could hardly help eating until they felt almost gorged. With silent tact, spoons and knives of gold and ivory had been laid before them, not the bewildering acrobatic sticks manipulated by the Nionians and Sinoans.

Often the Romans laid down their spoons to scoop up their food with their fingers, as was normal in the Empire. Prince Tadahito turned his eyes away in polite disgust.

Singers and musicians appeared. A little dancer or tumbler, standing on a small gold pedestal, curled and looped her spine like a bean stem or an eel; she arched dizzyingly backwards, spinning circles of red felt balanced on her outstretched fingertips, to lift in her teeth a peony laid below her on the floor. Her little upside-down golden face, as it lowered relentlessly back and back, was strangely serene and unreadable, though she could not have been more than eleven years old.

Noriko could just make out a movement of Marcus Novius' head from time to time, watching through the lattices from her slight hiding place behind the steps of the neighbouring pavilion. The young concubine was no longer at his side – apart from the entertainers, this seemed to be an entirely male gathering. But Noriko was too exposed already to improve her view; she had to keep looking around to make sure no one had noticed her.

It went on for hours; the diners were almost worn out with eating. Finally the Emperor withdrew with the same lethargic pomp with which he had appeared, and the banquet came to an end. Outside the hall, in the warm twilight, Tadahito and the other Nionian nobles gathered together on a rounded bridge over a glittering artificial stream, conferring rapidly in low voices. Marcus watched them with faint apprehension. He said quietly to Varius, 'I think I should talk to the Prince alone.'

The Nionian Emperor, Go-natoku, had remained in Cynoto, but he was not an invalid as Faustus was; he remained a real, if remote authority. As far as Marcus understood it the Nionian party would be acting for him, referring their decisions back to him to be approved – or not. Nevertheless, Marcus' instinct was to single out the Prince, not only because he assumed that as his father's heir, Tadahito must have the most authority, but because they had spoken before, and because already he could see himself so clearly through the older men's eyes: a naïve boy hardly out of adolescence. He enjoyed his power over the senators in Rome, but these lords were under no obligation to do more than go through the motions of respect. The Prince was so close to him in age, their positions were so similar. Marcus knew he would not feel so vulnerable and fraudulent with him.

Varius murmured, 'I don't think that one likes us very much,' indicating Lord Kato with a minimal move of the head.

Marcus felt the same thing, although the Nionian lord had done nothing but smile at them. He smiled at them now, noticing Varius and Marcus. But it was neither friendly nor ingratiating, although nor was it insincere. His small, fierce smile was somehow at once courteous and rude, the expression of a glowing self-assurance so strong that it was almost joy.

'He was the one that first requested the troops for their side of the Wall,' Varius said.

'But he doesn't seem to resent being here. Salvius would think it was all a waste of time.'

'He might welcome the chance to decide what he thinks of *you*,' suggested Varius.

Marcus sighed and went over to them. He began in Nionian, out of politeness, although he had never used it to address so many native speakers before, and his middling fluency felt suddenly hampered by an attack of self-consciousness. Nevertheless, this time, to Marcus' faint dismay, as he began to feel he'd been over-confident, there was no taut contest over languages, Tadahito accepted the use of Nionian gracefully, or as if he himself had no knowledge of Latin. 'It's good to finally meet you in person,' he said.

Lord Kato inspected Marcus with calm care. 'A longer journey for you than for us, Caesar. And this city must seem even stranger to you than we find it,' he noted, good-humouredly.

'Perhaps, but I have always thought the Romans and Nionians quite similar,' said Marcus, a little stiffly, hearing in his own voice the instinctive haughtiness he had learnt from childhood. He had become aware of it in the tense days after he first met Una and Sulien, as they crept across Gaul; he knew now how he fell back upon it most when he felt awkward or unsure of himself. His anxiety was increased by how fluid the power seemed to be between the lord and Tadahito: at present the Prince was standing by quietly, looking unassuming and almost deferential. You must do better than this, Marcus told himself.

Lord Kato's face managed to communicate total disagreement and distaste, without its actual expression of civil attention seeming to alter at all. 'Obviously not in superficial things,' he remarked genially.

'Well, we have just claimed descent from the same Heaven, and I have noticed similar stories in the histories,' said Tadahito.

'Yes, Lord,' said Kato dutifully, with slight perceptible exasperation.

'Your Highness, can I speak with you?' said Marcus, growing impatient. The older men contracted a little at this, as if Marcus had been crudely blunt. Tadahito, however, came with him readily, down a long walkway of scarlet columns between mulberry and apricot trees.

As he had hoped, Marcus felt less like a child dressed up alongside the other young man, and the Prince too seemed to become more confident and vivid away from the others.

'Your Nionian is good,' he said, so that Marcus' pride trapped him in that language, and then, 'You want to test some idea on me? Please do so.'

'All things considered, neither one of us has any more right to the territory than the other,' said Marcus. 'We could try and renegotiate Mixigana. Some new patched-up version might work for a while, but the strain on the border will build up again in the end. I want us to take down the Wall.'

Tadahito's pace slowed suddenly, so that it was clearly only self-control that kept him from stopping dead in surprise. His face swung towards Marcus and a quizzical, wordless murmur spooled through his lips.

'We would treat the land as both Roman and Nionian,' continued Marcus.

They walked in silence for a moment or two as Tadahito thought. Marcus felt a tense balance of trepidation and hope, and was convinced the Prince must share it: he *had* to feel that it seemed unimaginable that two people walking reasonably along like this, with no rancour between them, should ever need to be enemies. And yet real safety lay far off at the end of a long file of hurdles, so many and so separately difficult, that they might sink into fighting in exhausted despair.

'How can one be a citizen of two nations?' Tadahito asked. 'To whose laws would one answer? I assume Rome would not want your people subject to Nionian law any more than we would wish ours to be subject to yours. And if we could somehow blend them into one, how would it be administered, and by whom? What responsibilites would we have to citizens of Mexica or Aravacia, whose lives must be very different from those from Yukimichi, in North Tokogane. And then there are – oh, questions of travel, the natural resources. And what would it mean for both our empires, to have this land between them that is not quite one thing nor the other?'

'Of course I can't answer that yet,' said Marcus. 'I only want to know if you would try and find the answer with us, if there is one.'

Tadahito hesitated. 'I hope it is possible,' he said at last. 'And my father ... hopes a way can be found. But whether it *is* possible – I don't know. And even if I think so, I am only one voice.'

'But your father would listen to you over the rest?' pressed Marcus.

Again Tadahito seemed to hesitate, but differently this time, an embarrassed mischief in his face that Marcus could not understand. 'Everything else being equal, perhaps, yes,' he said, smiling as if at once amused and wary at the possibility of saying something tactless. 'If he heard from the others that unfortunately I'd gone out of my mind, probably not.'

Marcus smiled, though he felt the usual Novian flicker of sensitivity at the mention of madness.

Tadahito looked down at the paving.

'He is terribly young,' said Lord Kato, disapprovingly. They were seated in a circular open summer house on the edge of the lake, auditory circlets on their brows. Tadahito's discomfiture had been caused by the knowledge that no matter how far he walked with Marcus, they would never be out of earshot of Kato and the other lords. He wore

181

a listening device, hidden in a tassel hanging on the breast of his tunic. It was simply easier than his trying to recount everything for discussion when this conversation was over, and furthermore Lord Kato was insistent on exploiting every opportunity to study his potential opponent.

'So is our Prince,' answered Lord Mimana.

Kato uttered a snort of dismissive agreement that shocked the others into murmurs of alarm.

'The question is whether all this is a charade to occupy us while they prepare a further attack,' said Lord Taira, after a scandalised pause, trying to steer the discussion away from any hint of criticism of the Imperial family.

'I would say the boy was sincere about it,' said Kato, in thoughtful, but mildly disappointed tones.

'I wish I were as confident.'

'It makes very little difference to the outcome, the war will certainly take place,' said Kato. 'Removing the border altogether! Novius Caesar's attitude is absurd and feeble, but I won't at least accuse him of indecisiveness. I suppose he has been trained up fairly well, for times of peace anyway. But there is no substitute for experience. It's just possible the war may harden him, but he plainly has an extraordinary aversion to it, and more likely he'll be a disaster for them. Well, so much the better for us, but I wish that their Lord Salvius had come here. It would have been worth observing him.'

'We none of us have experience of a war on such a scale as this would be,' said Mimana restlessly.

'I have governed Tokogane for eighteen years,' said Kato, with sudden force. 'And I am not going to give up an inch of it.'

'Still, it does not belong to you,' Lord Kiyowara reminded him. 'And these are not our decisions to make.'

'I have always known what we would face in the end; I am as prepared as anyone can be.'

'The Emperor and his son plainly don't want a war to take place unless all other possibilities have been exhausted, or we wouldn't be here. We are not playing a game.'

'Aren't we?' asked Kato, smiling.

'Lord Kato,' warned Kiyowara, his face locked in an agonised, meaningful grimace.

'We can talk freely,' said Kato, carelessly. He had swept a bronze instrument like a censer around the little bower as they entered it. 'The foreigners' surveillance devices are far cruder than ours, if there had been any I would certainly have found them.' He was intensely interested in advancing technology; Yuuhigawa, his seat in Tokogane, was an obsessively modern city, more so even than Cynoto, and Kato's investment and passion kept innovations churning out of it. That many of them were useful was undeniable, yet many of the other lords found Kato's faith in them disproportionate.

'It is nothing to do with that,' lied Kiyowara, piously and loudly, earning a roll of the eyes from Kato. 'I should always be disturbed by expressions that ... could be construed as disloyal. Although I am sure you cannot have intended it so.'

It was not only the Romans and Sinoans he was worried about, as Kato must surely know: it was perfectly possible that Tadahito wished to spy on them as well as for them.

Kiyowara had phrased the reproof as tactfully as possible, yet he wouldn't have been surprised if another man had grown angry. Yet Kato, for all his fierce unpredictability and outspokenness, could be almost preternaturally slow to take personal offence. He smiled again. 'I believe His Majesty can look forward to victory over our enemies, that's all,' he said, without acrimony. 'It's strange if that's disloyal.'

Lord Kiyowara sighed.

'It makes you uneasy because you don't have the same confidence,' went on Kato, almost tenderly. 'It's true they have greater numbers. Fleets more spiralwings than we do.' Naming these deficiencies so openly was itself enough to make the others uneasy, but Kato seemed oblivious to it. 'Still – I promise, it will all mean nothing.'

'Of course strategy counts for more than brute strength,' agreed Lord Kiyowara wearily.

'Not just strategy,' said Kato.

'Oh,' said Taira derisively. 'These mythical weapons,'

This time Kato did bristle defensively. 'I have seen the first tests. There is nothing mythical about it. Another year and it will be ready for combat. And as you say, strategy is an important weapon, we could certainly hold our own that long; by that time we could have Rome in retreat already. And then, before there could be any chance of it developing into deadlock or the tide turning against us, we would strike with a force like an invisible hammer, a hammer to level armies and cities two hundred miles away. In the near future, explosives will be virtually obsolete! We will use them to prepare the ground, if that!'

'I don't mean to doubt you, Lord Kato,' answered Taira drily. 'And yet it seems to me that I have been hearing how this miraculous thing was on the brink of being ready for years.'

Kato sat, tight-lipped and incensed, as if at first he could not trust himself to speak. 'When we are dealing with such new devices, my

Lord, some failures are inevitable,' he answered at last. 'To have the technology perfect well in advance is a luxury we can rarely rely on. But when the call comes, when the need is real, my people will rise to it.'

Lord Mimana looked at his knees. Something about the way Kato had said 'my people' affected him uncomfortably, even if there was nothing logically wrong with it.

Tadahito and Marcus went on talking. That the lords had missed a section of the conversation was unimportant. Although it seemed unlikely anything else significant would be said, they were recording it – unaware that there was another listener, and that Tadahito had another reason for keeping Marcus so carefully to Nionian.

Una had expected to be ignored while the ceremony and the banquet went on, instead she had been entertained and looked after for hours. She had watched a play, which she could not follow despite the little Latin synopsis someone had handed her, but which she enjoyed well enough because the actors wore glittering, architectural costumes, yet still managed to break into pyrotechnic bursts of acrobatics. She had been rowed out, shielded with parasols, in a painted boat on the square lake; fed little steamed sweetmeats; handed cups of the leaf-infusion that had never become popular in the Roman Empire except in the most unconventionally fashionable circles, so that although Una had read of both Eastern powers' devotion to it, she had never seen or tried it before. She was slightly disappointed. The golden liquid was barely distinguishable from hot water, hot water which just barely retained a scent like smoke, or woody earth, or subtle flowers. She had expected some stronger, more titillatingly exotic taste.

The palace women who had seemingly been assigned to keep her company spoke only a little Latin; Una had learnt a smattering of Sinoan in the camp in the Holzarta gorge, and some more from Marcus and his wealth of books, but it did not amount to much, and the few words she attempted evidently came out wrong, for they did not understand her. So they had been communicating by smiling, and it worked fairly well. But she had been politely smiling so long, carefully mimicking them, so as not to do anything too ridiculous. They fussed over her as if her outlandishness were entrancing and precious; they giggled, and Una tried dutifully to giggle along with them, feeling that their kittenish-ness was, at least in part, a deliberate mode of correct behaviour which she should, perhaps, also follow. But without language it was difficult, and although, when necessary, she could produce the kind of convincing display of gushing sweetness she had used when talking to Drusus, it did not come without effort. She could feel the women's thoughts burring and rustling, loud and yet incomprehensible, although she did know that some of them found her appearance hilarious. They were very hospitable; they treated her as what they reasonably assumed she was, a nobly born concubine.

Even if she'd had the language, what terms could she have used to explain the difference, and what would they have thought if they knew where she'd really come from, the muck she'd scrambled through before she got to them?

She had enjoyed the novelty of it all. And yet, as it went on, she felt hard and heavy and out of place, like an angular stone, a lump of granite or flint dumped inexplicably on a bed of silk. The other women seemed as weightless as humming birds. They had been sent out to play like children. And the men had their own games and rituals, but finally they would begin to make the first tentative feints at unpicking the conflict between them. Did she want to be among them? Yes, but she was aware it was not a very reasonable wish; even if all barriers of sex and birth could be done away with, she was not yet nineteen – what right would she have? As much of a right as Marcus, it occurred to her, with just a trace of sourness, while she wished it would come to an end so that she could see him. A strange tension and rawness fluttered urgently over her skin and in her throat when she looked towards the gardens and the Emperor's hall, as though she were itching to say something, yet did not know what.

But now at last she was alone, in the garden of the inner mansion Marcus had been given, the roofs of the palace glowing icily around her in the warm, magnolia-stained air, and she relaxed again into almost untroubled happiness.

Marcus was looking for her. She had been impatient for his arrival, but she did not move or call out to him. It was suddenly lovely to extend the waiting, and she remained still, sitting upright and self-contained but basking, ready for him to find her.

She was sitting by the ornamental pond, looking at the reflections as if she hadn't noticed his approach, but he knew that she was pretending, and that she knew he knew. Going along with the game, he stood still and watched her.

Since he'd come back to the Golden House to find what Drusus had done to her, every time they met after any separation he'd felt his pulse leap painfully, with dread rather than with desire, as if this were the last time he could expect to see her safe. Even when they were together and everything was fine, he had got into a habit of watching her with

185

furtive anxiety or distrust, as if she might be badly hurt in some way, even dying, without realising it, or without having told him.

Now he felt an unreasoning flow of relief, as if again he'd been afraid something terrible had happened to her, but finally, now she was so far from Rome and from Drusus, the gripping fear had gone. Yet it had left the sight of her sharpened. The familiarity of her face and body was not stripped away, but scoured, made luminous, so that it seemed wonderful that she was just the same. There were glossy lilies on the black surface of the pond at her feet. Once, days after their first grim meeting, cold and filthy, they'd smashed their way into an industrial greenhouse in a Gallic field; they had looked at each other across a shallow pool of farmed lilies, the first snags of attraction stinging between them as he noticed for the first time the grace of the wet limbs emerging from the damp cheap clothes. She was more beautiful now than she had been then; he could see with new, transparent exactness how beautiful she was in her silver dress.

She went on sitting there as if absorbed in watching the reflections in the pond, but she could not – or chose not to – prevent the pleased smile spreading slowly across her face.

Come on, then, look at me, thought Marcus, and still for a little longer she put it off, and at last raised her eyes to him innocently, as if she'd had no idea until now that he was there, although she was obviously holding back laughter, and to maintain the pretence he had to do the same.

Una went into his arms, close but brief; she looked into his face, but she did not kiss him, there was a continued pleasure in delay as well as a faint smart of suspicion that someone again might be watching. She went past him, inside. There was so much red in the bedroom, lustrous red cabinets painted with gold, red glass lamps. The bed itself was like a little internal room, its pearwood walls carved with leaves reaching into a high fretted canopy over the low mattress.

'Is there another city somewhere near here?' asked Una. She shivered slightly; the cooling machines had stripped the air of heat with over-scrupulous vigour.

'I don't know,' he said, kissing her. He gathered her back into his arms, pushed her between the screens of the bed. She let herself fall back onto the glossy cover, and lay stretched out, one hand resting drowsily on the pillow beside her, but her face and voice were as guilelessly thoughtful as if she simply had yet to notice his lips and hands warming her, his progress with her clothes.

'It wouldn't even be a separate city, really – just the ugly half of this one. For the cleaners to live in, butchers, the undertakers ... It should be bigger than this place. And it can't be far, but we didn't see it. It could be on the other side of the Yellow River. But it must be somewhere – like a shadow ...'

Marcus murmured a perfunctory answer now and then, as he loosened the silk cords at her waist. The dress would have come off within seconds if she had helped him, but she still lay as if calmly oblivious, and the cords looped two or three times around her body, not tight, but inaccessible where they crossed at her back. Instead he slid a handful of the silvery cloth upwards, from ankle to hip, baring one leg, leaving the other covered; he separated the layers of the dress above her breasts, kissing the revealed skin. He felt her body arch a little, but she carried on talking dreamily and intelligently, as if the one-sided conversation was the only thing of interest to her at present. He knew at any moment he could ask her to stop, demand her undisguised attention, but that would be to forfeit the game, which was, apparently, to see how long she could keep this going.

'I read about Junosena. Only a concubine to begin with. I wonder *how* – I wonder if she meant to get hold of power right from the start, or if ... But you didn't see her, did you?'

He plucked again at the strings of the dress, and her clothes fell open at last, spread lapping around her naked body, her arms, still in the wide rumpled sleeves, lying loose and outflung. Only the green and silver necklace she wore remained fastened, and still glittered at the base of her throat, incongruous above her bare breasts. He stroked her, running a hand in a slow uncoiling spiral down her body, from her lips, over the hard necklace, down to where one thin knee still rested lightly over the other up again. Una had fallen silent but was still passive, still not conceding, though the half-hidden smile widened again, and he could feel the small, uncontrolled betrayals of her body. He lowered himself closer to her, his still-clothed weight resting half on her, half on the bed, confident she was losing.

Then, because she'd been waiting for a moment when he'd be too absorbed to anticipate the trap, she flung him over in a sudden ambush, triumphantly pinning him on his back, her face gloating as if she'd won a fight. Her open robe hung over him, enclosing them both as she pulled roughly at his clothes, far quicker and more abrupt than he had been undressing her. 'Aren't you beautiful?' she paused to demand, almost severely, as he lay there breathlessly, laughing up at her. Una rose upright for a moment, one hand going from his body to her own throat, deftly unclasping the necklace so that it slipped down to fall from her breast onto his skin, the links of metal warm from her flesh. The silky tent of the dress collapsed around them again as she lowered her head to press her mouth to his skin, printed kisses on him, covered his body with hers.

Watching through her spyglass, Noriko had seen him enter the garden. She saw the lady sitting by the pool, not yet realising Marcus Novius was watching her. She did not understand why the strong feeling inscribed so clearly on the prince's face should seem to include such relief. Although she had been watching him long enough to know otherwise, she could almost have thought he had rushed back here to find that some terrible news about his lover wasn't true.

Well, there must be some reason, and she did not need to know what it was. But something else became obvious to her, in the confidence with which the pale lady looked back at him, in the depth of familiar happiness between them: the lady was not simply a favoured lover – she was the only one, Noriko was certain of it.

She was perhaps two hundred yards distant from them, standing in the shadow of a great bronze urn. She drew closer, keeping the spyglass steady, training it from one face to the other as the young woman rose and went into the prince's arms, and again a physical twist of anticipation and misery churned through her. She drew closer.

A voice spoke just inches behind her, and struck like a pickaxe to a sheet of glass. 'You've been caught much later than you deserve, no thanks to your own competence.'

Noriko almost cried out. It was the caustic contempt in the voice she understood first, as her brain, cringing in shock, limped slowly to translate the Sinoan syllables. Lurching, she turned round.

At first, instead of a person, she saw clothes: a cone of clothes, a tiered monolith of primrose and red satin, topped, at face level, with a nodding oblong concoction of petals and jewels. Lowering appalled eyes Noriko saw the small, elderly woman who stood engulfed within the edifice, glowering at her. The clever, ferocious face looked tiny below her hair, which stood rigidly in a flat, precarious rectangle a foot high, like a large book or a picture balanced upright on her head. The hair was black, but must surely have been dyed, and it was festooned with fresh flowers, combs, and dangling pendants of pearls, tourmalines and jade beads. The thick coating of make-up on her skin was not merely white, but faintly iridescent, and should have made the woman who wore it look ethereally inhuman, as if the entire face had been fashioned out of pearl. But the paint had soaked into the gullies and pleats in the seventy-year-old skin, so that the crumpled, white-stained flesh was marbled with shimmering streaks and rays, around what must once have been delicately elfin features. Her mouth was like a small, scarlet puncture wound. A cut-out gold flower design had been applied carefully to her forehead.

Her upper body was laden with a chainmail of necklaces, draped with plum-sized rubies that must have bruised her chest as she walked. A phoenix in flight spread its embroidered wings across her skirts, which, alone, would have marked out who she was: Junosena, as the Romans called her – the Empress Jun Shen. It seemed impossible that, so ornately armoured in her clothes, she could have moved so soundlessly.

In confused horror, Noriko bowed clumsily, only from the waist at first, and then realising her mistake, began to drop awkwardly to her knees on the hard paving.

'How dare you violate this Palace and these negotiations?' shouted the Empress passionately. 'How *dare* you conduct yourself this way in *my country?*'

Noriko, shaking but reluctant, had finally curled up on her knees with her forehead on the ground. She gestured vaguely at the eastern side of the palace compound, as if she were lost, stammering in apologetic, hopeless Nionian: 'So sorry, I can't understand – so sorry.'

Scowling, the Empress snatched the telescope from Noriko's flinching hand, a startlingly rapid, violent move from a woman of her age. She brandished it so that instinctively Noriko turned her face aside, expecting to be hit with it. 'You barbaric idiot! Liar! Must you shame yourself further and insult my intelligence as well? You can't be stupid enough to doubt I know exactly who you are and what you're doing.' She jerked her burdened head at the Roman prince's quarters, so that the coiffure wobbled and the pendants swung wildly. '*They* may not have seen you creeping around on the ramparts, but *I have.*'

Noriko stared stupidly at the paving, which swung and clouded before her eyes. She could not speak.

'Well, I will call my guards and tell them they have failed in their duty, and after they have killed you, they will be punished,' announced Jun Shen. She was still holding the telescope aloft, like a weapon; it seemed, at the least, she was about to dash it to the ground.

Noriko raised her head a little, although still she could not lift her eyes from the ground. 'You cannot,' she whispered, trembling, in Sinoan this time.

The Empress' eyes narrowed. 'I can't have a spy, or an assassin executed in my own palace?'

'If anyone touches me ...' breathed Noriko.

'Is there a reason you should be spared? Will you tell us all why in front of everyone? Will your so-called Great Lords be able to explain themselves when the Romans discover they have been prey to a Nionian intruder? Your identity and your purpose must certainly be established to everyone's satisfaction.'

Noriko closed her eyes in agony, lowering her head again. 'Please ...' she moaned.

The Empress snorted, and there was harsh amusement in the sound. She poked Noriko with her foot. 'Sit *up*,' she said disgustedly, as if Noriko should have done this uninvited. Noriko, shaking with fury now as well as fear, obeyed. But Jun Shen's mood seemed to have altered suddenly and her creased little red mouth lifted into a smile of malign enjoyment. She uttered another, more meditative snarl, and tilted her head sardonically, like a parrot, as she surveyed Noriko. 'Your disguise is pitiful, it does nothing but tell the world you have something to hide,' she remarked, with a kind of haughty friendliness. 'Better to find a way of doing your work in your own person. You could not have been challenged. That,' she confirmed, with a decisive nod, 'is what I would have done.'

She extended the telescope a little way towards Noriko and dropped it, seeming to lose all interest as soon as it left her fingers – certainly she did not wait to see if Noriko caught it. She swung round and stalked off, trundling silently, erect beneath the husk of clothing.

Aghast and sick, Noriko rose from battered knees to her feet, and almost ran back to her quarters on the east of the compound. In the outer chamber her ladies-in-waiting sat on mats on the ground, the trains of their dresses spreading around them, talking and playing a battle-game on an illuminated board.

Lady Mizuki, the long locks of her jewelled pink wig falling around her pert, cheerful face, looked up at Noriko in her maidservant's clothes and asked teasingly, 'Did the new maid serve my lady satisfactorily?' But Noriko walked through to her bedroom without answering, almost weeping with homesickness, rage and shame.

There was too much stuff in the room, too many tapestries, needless, over-decorated chests and chairs, cluttered, vulgar – she thought furiously – unfitting for a royal palace. She dropped rapidly into a sitting position on the floor, and tears abruptly leapt from her eyes. For a few moments, she allowed herself to sob, before she closed her eyes and exhaled, trying to smooth and order her breath, to be calm. She unhooked the letter-case from her shoulder. It was a beautiful thing, an antique, made of glossy black wood and painted with a gold serpent, its fine coils spiralling elegantly round the polished tube, but what she slid out when she opened the lid was very new: a thin, flexible screen that rolled up into a slender scroll and fastened with a circular silver clasp cut like an aster blossom. Noriko unfurled it and stood it up on top of the chest before her – it spread into a broad, curved vista, three feet wide, a foot and a half high. Noriko touched a silver dial and the screen glowed, and what appeared first was a shining view of Cynoto – Tetsugaku-no-Michi at its loveliest, in the spring dawn, the white blossoms coursing from the dark trees, and the transparent sun rising red behind the city's segmented skyscrapers, stacks of fringed squares and hexagons, filigreed and bracketed like ancient shrine-towers, but rising ten times as high into the glassy air, their pearls and ribbons of electric light still glittering, all so piercingly beautiful that she dared not look at it too closely just now.

She lifted the little telescope from her lap and unscrewed a ring from inside it, slotted it into the narrow column, plated in chased silver, that supported the right side of the screen. With a twist of its drums, the telescope stored the images it viewed. She had recorded everything.

She felt a terrible temptation to look again at Marcus with the girl. It was precisely what she had wanted; to see Marcus Novius off guard, as he really was. The conversation he had had with Tadahito, for which she had the sound as well, had been enough, but this – with a woman, with someone he trusted – was even better. Already, of course, she had recordings of him speaking from the Roman Palace, in the Forum – but she found it peculiarly difficult to watch them. That it should be possible to watch an Imperial prince, the Emperor, flaunting himself on a den-ga screen, like an actor! And not merely did they allow themselves to be so cheapened and exposed, but they looked and spoke nakedly into the cameras; like actors again, they displayed and malleated their emotions, they worked themselves up, grinning or forcing their eyes to fill with tears, exaggerating sorrow or determination to some weird level neither natural nor forgivingly stylised. It set her teeth on edge, and made it hard for her even to keep her eyes on the screen. Oh, she was not stupid, or ignorant of Roman methods, she knew that really it made perfectly good sense within the culture, she could even see the advantages of it: perhaps it helped to inculcate loyalty among the people. But still, it left her with no impression of Marcus Novius except a feeling of strange, vicarious embarrassment, of having witnessed something unseemly and disquieting.

But she felt ashamed of having recorded him with the pale girl, ashamed of having witnessed it at all.

Tomoe, Noriko's favourite among her ladies, a tall young woman with hair stained dark indigo, trailing down the back of a butterfly-embroidered dress, came in quietly and knelt beside her. She began silently unwinding the black fillets Noriko had bound around her plaited hair, to cover it. Noriko let her do it without comment.

At last Tomoe murmured quietly, 'You are beautiful even in these simple clothes, Lady, but let me find you something more suitable. You would not want my lord the Prince to see you like this.'

'He already has, it doesn't matter,' said Noriko, bleakly.

Deftly, Tomoe unravelled the plait so that the hair hung loose and pooled around her body on the mat. Noriko's hair was both conservatively and expertly coloured: untouched black down to below the shoulders, where very gradually it began to shade into deep, deep green – a tint almost invisible except where it reflected light, as if a dim green lamp was shining on the black surface. The colour intensified slowly down the length of hair, until the final foot of it was a cool, bright jade green, the long points of it like willow leaves, brushing on the ground when she stood. Tomoe took a bottle of scented water, poured the liquid into her palm and smoothed it through, trying to straighten and erase the ripples left by the plaiting.

Tadahito came to the pavilion before Tomoe had persuaded her into a silk dress, and Noriko wearily insisted that he be let in at once. She still felt perversely reluctant to change out of the cotton clothes, reluctant to do anything, to consent to any movement forward in time. Tomoe withdrew as Tadahito entered the room. Noriko, too dumb with gloom to ask for it, hoped she would bring tea. The Prince returned Noriko's bow, his own, of course, less deep than hers, and then placed his hands affectionately on her shoulders. 'Did you see what you wanted? Did it help you?' he asked.

'I suppose so,' she said, a little distantly. She did not think she could bear to tell him about her encounter with the Empress Jun Shen, although she was afraid it might be her duty to do so.

'But you don't seem ... reassured.'

Noriko reached out to the curved screen. Her finger hovered for a moment, hesitating, and then pressed one of the silver buttons, deleting the recording of Marcus with Una. She seemed to feel the privacy of which she'd robbed them flow back, submerging them in safe quiet. She felt relieved as if it were she who'd been exposed, glad they were protected, for now.

Instead, the conversation between the two princes on the long cloistered walk began to play. She appreciated that Tadahito had kept the conversation in Nionian; she spoke Latin, but to nothing like the same standard as he.

'Might I borrow that once you're finished with it? I think Lord Kato would be glad to see it.'

'How will you explain its existence?' she asked, wincing again, feeling the Sinoan Empress' tirade resound silently through her humiliated flesh.

'I can say I had a retainer do it and that I forgot to mention it,' he said, smiling. 'If he concludes I may have other spies, I don't think that would do him any harm at all.' At the same time his voice spoke on the screen, saying, 'How can one be a citizen of two nations?' A shudder of grief, a renewed urge to shed tears, reached Noriko's face suddenly before she could stop it.

Tadahito's smile vanished. 'You feel you are being sacrificed,' he remarked, unhappily.

'I *am*,' she wanted to cry out, enraged. Instead she said flatly, 'I understand what is required of me, which has not truly changed, even if its full nature was not clear to me before.'

She felt she was distressing Tadahito with her formality but somehow she could not shed it: inwardly she had already taken a preparatory step away from him and she dared not move back.

Still, when he put his arms around her, her face dropped helplessly against his shoulder and she sobbed again. 'It's only a possibility,' he urged. 'It may never happen.'

'And if it doesn't, it will be because everything has failed, and the war will begin. And I don't believe in Lord Kato's magical weapons. If it comes to it, Nionia will lose.'

'You cannot say that!' Tadahito protested, shocked.

Noriko sighed. Looking away from him, she saw both their faces held in a richly framed mirror on the wall. They did not look much alike, really; her own face was rounder, graver, more still, Tadahito's full of tense, expressive energy. She loved her brother – she was closer to him than to any of her other siblings. And yet she was two years older, the firstborn, and her mother was the Empress, not merely a concubine, as Tadahito's was. As sometimes happened, she could not help reflecting on the advantage over him she had lost by being born female. If she had been a boy, almost certainly she would have been the heir to her father's throne. Tadahito would have been brought up to bow more deeply, taught to defer to her as well as love her. And if he had been a girl, this would have been happening to him, not to her; she would have been offering comfort and regret from her own position of power.

'All right,' she said wearily. 'So we'll win, if that's what we are obliged to say. But only when millions have died. No, I can't even wish my way out of this.' She turned back to her screen, free for the first time to give her full attention to Marcus' face.

When she looked at him it was as if she saw two transparent slides laid one on top of the other, overlapping and distorting each other. In one image – reminding herself that she was an educated woman in a shrinking world, not some insular reactionary – she saw a handsome young man with straight features, the attractiveness of the face only deepened by the occasional faint, touching irregularity: the soft asymmetry at the full mouth, the drowsy heaviness of the eyelids with their load of varicoloured blond lashes. The colour of his hair brightened from subtly tawny brown to gold, his eyes were a seawater grey-blue.

And the other was exactly the same, and yet it was the caricature of a foreigner: a long, knobbly skull, the features as overgrown and gangling as the body; the yellowy hair clownish or effeminate, the bleached-looking eyes eerie or at best hypnotically eccentric.

It tired her eyes, trying to separate one impression from the other. But in time, surely, the ugly second image would fade, leaving only the other behind. He was younger than she was. Well, it was obvious that he'd been made to grow up fast, they all were, it was part of being born to their rank. In any case, there were often discrepancies of age between husband and wife.

'Did you like him?' she asked Tadahito.

And he could not very well say anything other than, 'Yes,' although she knew he might have added, 'If he is as he seems.'

Everything she had said to Tadahito was true; naturally she had always known that finally her father would settle on a marriage for her, on the basis of political alliance, of strategy. She did not know anyone for whom that was different, and it would be absurdly immature to complain about it. But she had never expected it would mean exile. She would be forced away, not only from Nionia, but even from the Empire itself, and to a country so profoundly foreign, to spend the rest of her life stranded in the static buzz of a language she could only half understand. Nor could she have known that her marriage, if indeed it was to happen, would begin with such furtiveness and shame. For it was not just the humiliation of being caught creeping around by the Empress that hurt her. In Nionia – and in Tokogane, doubtless, in Goshu, Koura, Siam – everyone would of course applaud the Emperor's wisdom in setting his daughter on the Roman throne. And many of them would mean it. But privately some would think it a disgrace that their Princess had been dropped into such undeserving hands. She would be a pitiable stain on their pride for ever.

All this she had known before she left Nionia. She and Tadahito had hoped that the private glimpses of Marcus Novius she had won today would help her bear it. But instead, she had the mortifying knowledge that she would not be wanted, something which, secure enough in her own beauty, had not troubled her before. She could not have expected that he would not have lovers. But there was only one, and it occurred to her belatedly that what she felt was partly envy. Not jealousy of the lady, of course not. Noriko could imagine becoming attracted to Marcus in the future, but she certainly had not fallen in love with him at first sight. But that solitary fullness between them, like the fullness of light before evening, intense but lucid, it was not meant to include anyone else, and she would never have anything like it.

And she was sorry for them, too. If everything went as she had to hope, soon she would be driven against them like a bulldozer, and their happiness would be cracked or damaged, or destroyed altogether.

XI

IN NOMINE MEI

Finally the Roman sky had turned brown and puffy with rain. Under the bridges he'd crossed, the Tiber frothed restively, brown and engorged, almost with the same stubborn bulk of the Thames. And the dust was dissolving into gritty mud as, in Veii, Sulien picked his way forward over the ruins of the factory. He wondered what was mixed in the wetted ash that slid away treacherously under his feet.

Here and there he could see the barbed coils of snapped tramlines, standing up from the heaped and pitted earth like small, painful trees. It was on one of those tracks it must have started, he had been told. Any of the buildings should have contained an explosion within it; the first flame, however lit, had to have been out in the open, moving in on the little carriage of explosives like a slow missile, to spray outwards, setting off several blasts at once. Huge and bleak as a battlefield, the place seemed strangely unfamiliar now; he could not even decide for certain just where the barracks had stood in which he and Varius had been trapped. Even the landmarks the explosion had spared had been cleared away; most of the long wall was still there, but the laid open management building was gone, and a couple of large diggers or levellers were moving torpidly, oddly sedate, over the blackened ground. From this distance and through this rain, Sulien could not see the men driving them and the vehicles seemed more like ponderous, trundling herbivores than machines under human control. He knew that a few bodies, or parts of bodies, had been retrieved by the vigiles, but as for the rest – who wanted the scraps and fragments of them, for whom was it worth sifting through so much rubble? No one who was free to do it. It was all being ploughed under. There was nothing to see.

He turned back to the Praetorian who was standing stiffly enduring the rain in a cloak, saying, 'Sorry I brought you out in this, Fenius.' He could not see the rest of them, but they would be near, they would be sure of where he was. He no longer found this unnerving. It was still an embarrassing encumbrance, but he got on well enough with all of them now. You could get on with anyone, if you tried.

Tancorix hadn't wanted to look at the remains but she was waiting for him in a dingy little taverna, though she was complaining about her soaked shoes and the hem of her skirt.

'I'm sorry,' he said again, heavily. 'I don't know what I thought the point of that was.'

Tancorix shivered in her wet clothes, and said, 'You look so sad.' And she looked mournful too, her lovely yellow hair splayed dripping over her shoulders, her face unintentionally washed of make-up whose ruins she'd been dabbing at, discontentedly guiding herself by a little hand mirror.

'I know,' agreed Sulien, mildly.

'You weren't going to get it out of your head. And your minders must have needed the exercise.'

Sulien nodded, swilling his drink around in its glass, blankly watching the pivoting disc of reflected light. Two men, middle aged, were talking at a table behind him: 'Yes, the whole of the kitchen ... I suppose what matters is we weren't in the house when it happened. Just hope they come up with something over there. I don't want my kids going through any more of this.'

The other man grunted with cautious dissent. 'Yeah, but ... I know, but don't you want something done? We *know* the Nionians bombed the place—'

'Oh, come on.'

'And we're not even going to fight back? We're admitting we're scared of them? It's not Roman.'

'But it's different now. It *is* different. It wouldn't be like Mexica again. The *world*.'

They were silent for a while, then the second man said, 'I think this generation needs a war.'

Under his waterlogged clothes, the damp skin on Sulien's shoulders prickled with faint paranoia, an instinct to turn and see if the man was looking at him.

When he did not speak again, Tancorix asked, 'How is the Emperor?'

'I stopped the bleeding in his brain,' answered Sulien, dully, the direction of his thoughts unchanged. Then after a while, he set the drink down decisively, saying with an effort, 'Well. It was a terrible place, and it's gone. They're out of it. And when it went up I didn't feel anything. Nothing hurt until later. It might have been like that for most of them.'

Tancorix's face underwent a sudden, resisted crumpling into tears.

197

Sulien, startled out of his own sadness, looked at her in guilty dismay. 'What is it?'

'I wasn't going to tell you ...'

Inevitably Sulien insisted, 'What?'

'Edda,' wept Tancorix.

'Who? What's wrong?'

'When I was in Epimachus' house ...' Epimachus had been her husband. 'The only person who was even slightly bearable. That is, I was so lonely there and she was kind to me, especially when I realised I was pregnant and it seemed so awful, she was so good. But he sold her after I left.'

'She's a slave?'

'Yes. And I didn't really keep in touch – not this last year, anyway. She would have liked me to. But he sold her to the Maecilii. Or gave her to them. They're in the Senate; he always wanted to get in with them.'

'And their estate was burnt,' said Sulien, remembering reading of it.

'So you knew? *I* didn't know – it was *weeks* ago and I didn't even realise. I never look at the news.'

'She might be fine,' said Sulien, weakly.

'I know. I tried to find out but no one would talk to me.' Her face creased again with a new spasm of tears. 'Because they know Epimachus and I'm some – tart, they've got no reason to tell me anything. I don't know what else I can do. So ...' She wiped her eyes again, and smiled theatrically. 'I look like a wreck now.'

Sulien went and put his arms round her, enjoying the act of comforting her as well as the pressure of her body; it made him feel warmer, more solid, more real. A handful of times since she'd come to Rome, – well, three times, of course he knew the exact number – they had fallen into her bed or his, laughing, excited and alarmed by the knowledge that no one was going to stop them, nothing was going to happen. He felt now like spending all his money on wine, watching her body soften and relax through a gathering haze of warmth, dragging her home through the streets. It seemed almost the only sane thing to do, they would both feel better. But he had to go back to the clinic for another six hours, and there was her little girl, whose presence had worried and embarrassed him after each of those nights. These barriers seemed intensely unreasonable to him just now, although part of him still knew that it was as well they were in place. They'd never spoken of what had happened, beyond making shy jokes while they dressed, and it had never led to anything further; he'd felt always, really, that he'd made a mistake, and had only barely got away with it.

He was not sure what Tancorix felt, but finally she moved away, and said, 'Are we going, then? I'm never living in Veii, we've established that much.'

Sulien stood up, reaching for the hooded jacket slung over the back of his chair. 'I wonder if Atronius lived here,' he said quietly. 'Or further out – I don't know where.'

Tancorix sighed, arrested in the motion of picking up her bag and turning away from the table. She looked at him. 'The man who did it?' she asked, patiently.

Sulien shrugged. 'I don't know if he did it. I'll have to wait for the vigiles to find that out, if they ever do. But in the meantime I think if I knew one real thing, it would be better.'

Wherever Faustus was, it was all fluid, all in constant, dappling motion. And within it he was neither floating nor sunk; he was dissolved into it, no more solid than anything else, less steady than the people who swum or bobbed nearby, recognisable now, chattering softly. The pain had gone on and on and on for a long time, but it had been absent just as long. He did not think this melted region was the only state of things, or that it would always be this way. He might only be asleep. Some time he might harden into dry land.

Once or twice, indistinctly, he'd asked for Marcus and Drusus. Makaria, scared and worn out, was not sure what it meant, of how she should answer. She said warily, 'They can't come. You remember, don't you?'

'Of course I remember,' said Faustus furiously, much more clearly than before, so maybe it was true, maybe he did. At any rate he seemed more himself, and angry with her, for hours afterwards.

Drusilla Terentia climbed the prison steps lightly, trying to draw herself in and upwards as she walked, as if it were possible to keep her full weight from ever resting on the stained concrete. There was a bad smell – inadequate cleaning fluids and male sweat – that had struck her almost as soon as she'd forced herself, tight-lipped, through the gates. It was an insult, it was rubbing it in, placing him here. They might have been content with trampling over his name and hers, and shut him somewhere private, that much had been done even for Tullia. He was at least away from the mass of the prisoners; still, following the oily-looking guard, she'd been compelled to pass rows of cells, and the men were there even if she did not look to left or right. Some of them had seen her, some of them had shouted out, jeering. Even if they didn't know who she was they knew she should not have to be there.

'Mother,' said Drusus unsteadily, rolling at once off the bed and flying towards the bars in a single move. Already he'd lost a lot of weight; his skin was papery, his lips cracked. He tried to blink away the tears that came into reddened eyes. His mother looked at him with a feeling, already, of exhaustion. 'Can't you let her in?' demanded Drusus of the jailer who'd led her up the steps.

'No one is to go in,' said the man calmly.

Drusus gritted his teeth against a cry of rage. 'What do you expect of her? Look at her. In the gods' name. What's wrong with you?'

But the man said nothing more and Drusilla Terentia stood there and did not protest.

Drusus drew back a little from the bars. When she first appeared he had been unable to check a downpour of feeling – panicked relief and childlike longing – but after the first few seconds, looking at her and remembering the facts, he controlled it, straightening his back. 'Why didn't you come before?' he said. 'It's been weeks. I kept sending messages.'

'I am not used to this,' said Drusilla. She was dressed in black as if she'd been bereaved. Her face and greying dark hair had been hidden by a veil, which she lifted as she entered the room. Was she in mourning – for him, or for whatever son or life she might have had instead? Perhaps yes, but not deliberately. It would be her perverse idea of deflecting attention from herself. If she had to come here she would have preferred to do so wrapped in impenetrable fog, invisible and blindfolded, so that even she could not see what she was doing. She looked in fact more stylish than usual, darkly elegant, which would again be unplanned. She was still a good-looking woman, although when she put on jewellery – she never wore make-up – it was seemingly with some other intention than looking attractive, an obscure form of obedience to some internal State. There was a chair. She did not sit.

Drusus caught his breath with anger at what she'd said, and explained through gritted teeth, 'They won't let me write any letters. There are people I must contact and it'll have to be through you. I've been waiting all this time.'

'I hoped it might have been cleared up by now. Or that you might at least have been out of this – hole.'

'Yes, well, I wouldn't choose to inflict it on you,' snapped Drusus bitterly.

'Why have you, then?' cried his mother suddenly, shaking.

Drusus tried not to flinch, but he could not speak; the air was banged out of him. He had not known she still had the power to do this to him. She never could have if he had been free. Finally he whispered breathlessly, 'I didn't do any of those things. They're lies. They're lying about me. You ... you do believe me, you must, Mother.'

'Of course I believe you,' said Drusilla, scathingly. In fact, it seemed too likely that he'd been the lover of that creature, Tulliola, and from there, if Drusilla had allowed herself to think it, she might have concluded that he must have known what was happening, more than that, he must have caused it. But she did not think of it. Though she looked at her son with, for the moment, acute, undisguised dislike, no one could compel her to turn her attention that way. She insisted, 'But at least in here you're spared knowing how we're being talked about. Why did you get yourself into this? Don't tell me you were an innocent bystander. You must have been doing something with that girl. I don't want to know what.'

'Una?' said Drusus, unsteady with shock, flushing with hatred at the mention of her. 'You think I—'

'I don't want to hear,' announced Drusilla again flatly, looking at the wall.

'She's a lying whore,' said Drusus. 'You think I'd want to lay a hand on her?'

'Well, either way, it's done, now,' stated his mother, lowering herself after all with slow distaste onto the edge of the chair. She almost never spoke of Lucius and so she did not say, and wasn't your father shame enough? But the silence bore the same weight as the words.

Drusus had also dropped back, sitting on the bed with his head bowed, so that Drusilla felt an intensification of resentment, ebbing in and out of unmixed pity. Probably he did not even know how much he resembled Lucius when young – a heightened, intensified rendering – although it was true she could see herself in him also; a queasy mingling of them. Still she was aware how people might have looked at him and envied her a son like that, how tall, how handsome he was, even faded as he was now. There had never been anything wrong with him in that way.

He raised his face at last, even paler now, inky pools under his eyes, the dark needles of emerging stubble seeming to injure the frail skin they pierced. 'After the trial will they kill me or just keep me here – do you get any sense of that?' he asked calmly. Drusilla closed her eyes, letting out a long breath. Drusus took a little heart from the sound of grief. He said, 'The trial will be the worst thing of all, you realise that. The Empire will talk of nothing else.'

'You have to remind me,' she murmured, pained.

'I have to prepare you. You will have to face it.'

'I can't bear it,' moaned Drusilla to herself.

Drusus watched her suffering face and thought bleakly, it's only the disgrace, or almost only that. If I'd asked for a blade to open my veins, you would have brought it without question, wouldn't you? You would even have come here sooner. He wanted to say this aloud, accusing her, but did not think he could stand to hear it confirmed. Instead, coming to the point, he asked, 'Is Salvius in Rome, or did he go away to Bian?'

'How should I know?'

'You will have to find out,' said Drusus. 'If he's in Bian you'll have to write to him. And someone you can rely on completely will have to carry the letter all the way, we can't risk it being intercepted. But if you can go to him yourself, then you must.'

'What do you want me to do? Do you imagine he can help you out of here? It's an impossible thing to ask of him. I can't do it.'

'No. No. You mustn't ask him that. You mustn't even hint it,' said Drusus fiercely, coming as close to her again as he could. 'I'll tell you what to say.'

'No, Drusus,' said Drusilla. A faint heat stained her cheeks.

'You only have to ask him to talk to me. I believe that he'll come. I'll tell you what to say and you have to repeat it exactly. You must do it or any life you or I value is finished.'

He sat back, and Drusilla Terentia again looked at him with helpless weariness, as at some enormous task, a quarry of paper to be covered in close lines of handwriting, a whole soiled city she had to wash clean – something so endless and impossible, something for which her whole life would so plainly be insufficient, that she could not even lift her hand to begin it.

Cleomenes unlocked the door to Atronius' flat, saying, 'There. You can have ten minutes. And I shouldn't be doing this, so don't get too talkative about it. But I don't know what you expect to find. There's nothing left here.'

There was only one room. For more than a week, since the desolate trip to the factory, Sulien had been anticipating this, talking Cleomenes into it, waiting for the time to come. But stepping inside he felt immediately foolish and disappointed. He had not hoped to find anything tangible, no real evidence the vigiles might have missed. But he'd thought there might be trace enough of the man who'd lived here soaked into the place to tell him whether it was true – and what it felt like, then, to be such a person. But Cleomenes was right. The flat was not perfectly blank, there were a few signs of interrupted life that the landlord or the next tenant would have to clear away. But the walls were white and bare, and wherever he looked, Sulien saw nothing personal, nothing that showed up a choice made. There was only absence.

'It's not just that the boys stripped everything out,' said Cleomenes, behind him. 'It was pretty empty to begin with.'

'Does that mean anything? That he had so little?' Sulien turned round slowly, trying to read the vacant space. A single window showed only a square of wall. On the cramped kitchen counter that occupied one corner, a half-empty bag of shrivelling onions sagged, and a few flies spiralled weakly over an unwashed pan. Near the bed the vigiles had left open a scuffed chest, which they'd almost emptied: an abandoned pair of thick shoes sprawled in the bottom beside a fallen cotton tunic, clean and blandly ordinary. He said, 'There's just enough that you can't be sure he planned to leave.'

Cleomenes shrugged. 'Well, you could say, he didn't need much, he knew what he was here to do. Or you could say, he never had a chance to make his mark: he'd only been here a few weeks and now he's dead, poor bastard.' He was leaning with folded arms against a wall, watching with unsurprised sympathy as Sulien wandered dejectedly across the narrow floor. The ferocious daubing of sunburn and ginger freckles over the robust features of his large, sceptical face was even more violent after this summer. He was thirty-nine now, and a commander in the vigiles, and though of course he had nothing to do with the factory case, or what had happened to Sulien in the Subura, Sulien had been fairly sure he could get the favour out of him.

Sulien was still picking despondently over the sparse vestiges in the room. He said, 'How's Alexander?'

'He's not too bad,' answered Cleomenes, shortly, trying to keep his face and voice from softening into dumb, amazed joy. After four months, the sheer incredulity at his son's existence remained so strong that he could have begun helplessly burbling out his love, to Sulien or anyone. Partly in order to stop himself, although his concern was real too, he said, 'Is your sister all right? Terrible, what happened. To think that man's been running around for three years without a care in the world.'

'He's been caught now,' said Sulien mildly. 'And Una ...' Was it all right that she should be able to shrug off what Drusus had done to her, so swiftly, apparently so coolly?

He pushed the moment's hesitation out of his mind and said confidently, 'yes, she's all right.'

'And Varius?' Cleomenes asked, anxiously. He was always faintly worried about Varius, whenever he met or thought about him.

Sulien murmured another reassuring answer. He drifted from the counter to a set of empty shelves, thinking about the unknown man moving through the same air, as if his own body might catch specks of information left behind. By now – and he knew it might only be because he was looking for it – he'd begun to see or imagine he saw in the antiseptic plainness of the room, a similarity to the hasty fakery of the Suburra flat. The dark blue blanket on the bed reminded him of the one over the dummy on the mattress in the attic room there. But it was not actually the same. 'What do you think?' he asked Cleomenes.

'Oh, it sounds like he did it to me. He was well placed for it. The neighbours say they scarcely saw him, very quiet, which would worry me if I was working on this. And it seems like he never had any visitors – he couldn't have given anyone a meal or a drink, even, he hadn't got the stuff for it. That doesn't fit what we heard about him from the factory people – the man who gave him the job's still alive, and all he can say is how bright and keen he was, not shy at all. And he was one of ours, a few years back. Got kicked out, which he didn't tell the Veii people, although you wouldn't expect him to.' Cleomenes smiled slightly. 'Finding disaffected officers on the wrong side of the law doesn't surprise me that much.' He looked at Sulien, who made him remember his own disbelief at being in that position himself. Even when his job was safe again, he'd come very close to leaving the vigiles, cursing himself for not seeing sooner what had been so close to him, what he'd been part of. Even now he was sometimes morosely uncertain whether his reasons for staying had really been that good, whether it was honest to tell himself. 'It would be wrong to leave, there has to be someone decent left.' It might only have been that he became so baffled and depressed when he tried to think what else he might do.

He went on, 'And forgetting all of that, there's the simple fact that a couple of weeks before the factory goes up, he arrives out of nowhere, perfect and willing for this job that no one really wants, just when they needed a new supervisor because the last one's gone and had an accident in his car.'

Sulien turned, startled. 'He's dead? I never heard that.'

'No, not dead, but pretty smashed up.'

'And what did you mean, Atronius arrived out of nowhere?'

Cleomenes pulled an untidy handful of printed reports out of a pocket and frowned at them. 'Seems like he gave them the impression he'd only just arrived from Terranova, which wasn't true. He first came here …' he squinted down the sheet, '… four years ago. But there's a lot of time after that still unaccounted for. They reckon he might have been in Byzantium some point this year – illegally, if he was – although not on the strength of very much, I'm afraid, only an old tram ticket from Byzantium. But those things can find their way anywhere. Yes, it had a longdictor code written on it. Could just have been handed to him.'

Sulien nodded. 'The man who interviewed him – he told the vigiles what he was like?'

'Yes. Effective, apparently. Very tough.' Cleomenes hesitated slightly, looking away from Sulien. 'Very hard on the slaves. Had a system of beating the ten least productive in his section – Veii Arms didn't have the best reputation, I hear?'

'It was terrible there.'

'He seems to have been harsh even by their standards. Well, make of that what you will.'

'What else?' pressed Sulien. He had not realised how tantalising the sudden draught of details would be. 'About what he was like? Why would he do this?'

Cleomenes scowled impatiently. 'I don't know what else. This isn't my case. We need to get out before the landlord realises I'm entertaining tourists. And I've got to get home.'

Reluctantly, Sulien followed him. 'Could I look at those papers, please? What is this?' Despite his height he felt like an annoying child, pestering an adult for something held out of reach. But Cleomenes, sighing, let him take the pages. Sulien skimmed hastily through the sheets of print: there was a list, spreading over a sheet and a half, cataloguing the things that had been removed from the flat. After all, there had been some personal items.

'What does this mean, here?' he asked. 'Does it mean pictures of his family? Can I see any of these things?'

'For the gods' sake, no,' said Cleomenes.

In Salvius' house, Drusilla Terentia was no more comfortable than in the prison. The umber building stood out of the centre of Rome, among the pines and plane trees on the wooded hill that rose above the Flaminian Way and the Milvian bridge. In the atrium, Drusilla uttered a little cry of stifled shock as something charged across the room and struck her. She took a flinching step back and looked down to find a breathless boy with dark, curly hair, wielding an elaborate toy gun that flashed and purred. He grinned at Drusilla with easy, bright-faced charm before rushing past, pursuing battle into the garden, sweeping a

few subordinate boys along in his wake, ignoring the smilingly uncon-
vincing rebukes of Salvius' plump, girlish little wife. The boy's bare legs
were so bruised and scraped that he might have been the battered young
slave of sadistic masters, if he had not been so carelessly luminous with
confident health. He could have been nine or twelve; Drusilla had lost
any eye she'd ever had for interpreting the foreign faces of children.

Salvius, kindly and urbane, welcomed her in, led her courteously into
the sitting room, which was squarely dark and masculine, except for the
portraits of four young women ranged on the table – Salvius' daughters.
Salvius put a cup of wine into Drusilla's hand, and she held it, rigidly
forgotten in the air, for long minutes, neither lifting it to her lips nor
putting it down.

'I do sympathise with you. It must be very hard to bear,' he said,
gently.

Drusilla nodded at him in stiff, speechless agony, enduring being
pitied. She had barely said a word since she had arrived. 'Thank you,'
she managed at last, in a harsh whisper.

Salvius braced himself a little, but tried to relax into a friendly,
receptive posture. 'So, what have you come to see me about?' he asked,
pleasantly. He was apprehensive. He hadn't seen Drusilla before; she
lived so privately as to fulfil the old Greek maxim that the best compliment a woman could have was never to be spoken of. And he'd felt it
would have been cruel to refuse to meet her now, but he feared the poor
woman would beg him for something impossible, or begin sobbing. He
knew she'd had a hard life, what with Lucius Novius, and now this.
Even in the public reports over the longvision, it had been made clear
that the actual charge against Drusus, the attack on the girl, was only
part of it. He remembered: the new head of the Praetorian Guard had
made a statement:

'It is our understanding and belief that Drusus Novius assaulted
the young woman after she discovered a close connection between
himself and the Emperor's former wife, who of course died awaiting
trial for involvement in the assassinations of Novius Faustus Leo and
Clodia Aurelia, and the attempts on our present Caesar's life three
years ago.'

And Salvius had seen more than that; there was a file that had been
circulated among the upper levels of power, to senators, governors and
generals – anyone, he understood, whose doubt might cause a problem.
It detailed more closely what had happened, how Drusus had trapped
Una on the roof. Before Drusilla Terentia arrived he had swiftly thrust

it into a drawer of the low table that now stood between them, so that she should not be confronted with the dark, roughly printed images of her son's accuser. He had been studying Una's face, tilted towards the camera to show off her bruised eye, while one hand lifted her hair away from the marks around her throat. Her mouth was compressed, so that the lips barely showed, the dark eyes wide and glaring. One could just see how the loose short sleeve of her dress was torn at the shoulder. Salvius had been more than shocked. The news had destroyed some hope he'd never quite acknowledged. And it troubled him that all this came from Una. Of course there had been no public mention of who she was, how close she was to Marcus, while the confidential reports assumed that it was already known. And he was distressed too that the head of the Praetorians had plainly been used to make known this story about Drusus and Lady Tullia, despite the declared fact that it could not be proved. For the man had gone on, smiling bluffly:

'Now, unfortunately, given the amount of time that's passed, and the upheavals that have taken place since then, it does not seem likely those specific allegations can be pursued in law. But we believe we have strong evidence to connect Drusus Novius with a violent and prolonged attack that was certainly intended to be fatal. It has been decided, given previous lapses such as that which allowed Lady Tullia's death in custody, that Drusus Novius should not be held until his trial in a private house but in a public prison, like any other citizen charged with a crime of this nature. There can be no more special treatment for the aristocracy. The Roman people need to know that no one is above the law.'

It would not have been easy for an official spokesman to say the same thing – he would have had to touch at least on why the Roman people had to be told this, explain how the girl was supposed to have uncovered the secret, something that had never truly been made clear. How could Drusus' trial be fair now, Salvius had asked himself bitterly, with that playing all over the Empire? But none of this meant that he assumed the reports were not true. For one thing he'd never really thought Marcus guilty of anything more sinister than folly. And it was hard, once Drusus' name had been linked with Tulliola's, to dismiss how plausible it was – they must often have been thrown together; they had been young, attractive, close to each other in age when Faustus was so much older. And more damningly, Tulliola's crimes made far more sense if you assumed she'd been acting alongside Drusus, *for* Drusus. And despite Salvius' discomfort about the Praetorian broadcast, he could see that, if all this was true, and the girl really had made some unproveable discovery – if Drusus had perhaps said something to give himself away? – then Marcus could not afford for it not to be known, and would not have had many options. In those circumstances, Drusus was probably lucky to be having a trial at all. Salvius would have had him unobtrusively shot. Leo deserved that much revenge.

'My son hopes you might have time to visit him,' Drusilla told him at last.

Salvius sighed. 'I don't know if I can promise that.'

Drusilla shifted awkwardly to and fro on her seat. 'I know you must be busy,' she acknowledged tautly.

'That's true. And – I am sorry – but given what he's accused of ...'

'It is false.'

Ill at ease, Salvius grimaced. Like Drusilla Terentia herself, he had thought of other possible reasons for some kind of struggle between Una and Drusus that might account for her bruises. The end of a furtive, soured affair? It didn't seem entirely likely; there hadn't been much time for it and the girl, who looked like a canny little thing, would be a fool to risk what she already had. But Drusus might, perhaps, have been stupid and vicious enough to think that being a former slave, she was fair game, there for the taking. This was of a different order from the assassinations, and it was a bad time for Rome if something like that had been pumped up into these terrible claims, but still it remained repellent, sordid. Salvius didn't want anything to do with Drusus if it were true.

'Madam, I hate to say this to you, and I don't wish to anticipate the outcome of his trial, but it does seem that *something* happened.'

'No, there is *no* truth in it,' insisted Drusilla, passionately, her face blazing with strained conviction. She meant it. For the moment she had forgotten her own suspicions. 'He is my son. I should know that my son would not have any part of this.'

Salvius nodded, but with politeness rather than with agreement. 'Even so, there's nothing I can do to help him. You know that. The law will have to take its course.'

'I have not asked you for any help,' said Drusilla, hoarsely. 'There *is* no help, probably. Visiting him is not help. I have done it. It would be – a kind action.' Salvius didn't reply and she stared, mortified, at her knees, which were trembling again, aware that these were not Drusus' words, and she was breaking her promise. At length she ventured tentatively, 'He only wants to speak to you.'

'It wouldn't serve any purpose,' murmured Salvius.

'It would. It would to him.' Away from her son, and now that it came to it, she found she had more confidence in what Drusus had told her to say. 'What tortures him is not that he could lose his life. It's knowing in whose eyes his name is being ruined. Those that truly care for Rome. *You*, above all.'

Salvius looked at her, silently, eyebrows a little raised but not exactly with incredulity, more with a kind of foreboding as he began to sense where his doubts, or curiosity, or discontent, would drive him from here.

'He admires you. There aren't many honest men in Rome, as times go.'

'If hope he's wrong if he says that,' replied Salvius, with some difficulty. It was becoming increasingly hard to find answers. 'You're flattering me. Or he is. And the fact remains, I can't help him.'

'You don't understand.' So much improvisation, then back to her script: 'He has no hopes of the trial. How can he have? And neither of us knows what will happen to him afterwards. But he says, if he dies, at least he won't have to see what becomes of Rome in the hands of that girl. Because – he told me – make no mistake, no one else has any real power these days. And he says, if he had put the truth into your hands, even if you don't believe it yet, he could face what's to come. Even if it's his death.'

By the end of this her voice was shaking, and her eyes were glassy with tears.

In the crook of the Tiber, in the basement of the vigile headquarters, the bare, grey-green painted room was strangely cold. Inside an oblong niche in the wall, still motionless, a scuffed conveyor belt made up of narrow aluminium slats disappeared into unlit cavities of the building. Cleomenes complained, 'Do you get any work done, when you're not hassling me?'

'Yes, thanks,' replied Sulien, needled, because the shaft was at once unfair and accurate. Although by now he was working as many hours as he ever had, he knew that it wasn't the same. It had grown hard to sustain either attention or his usually profligate pity. He could hardly think of Faustus, say, as anything more than a convoluted problem, tediously slow in the solving. And sometimes, even more pitilessly, as he tried to train the cells to repair or compensate, the old man seemed a kind of leech to him, wasting Sulien's time as he wasted the Empire's money and abused its freedom. Faustus would die in the end anyway and might as well have done with it. It was only by thinking of the time Faustus' recovery would buy Una and Marcus, and of the fact that it was these cases – ill rich men – that kept the clinic alive, that Sulien could concentrate at all.

Cleomenes felt remorseful. He had been exaggerating an air of put-upon martyrdom largely out of amused habit, acquired over days of Sulien's persistence. Of the three young slaves into whose long anarchic night he'd found himself suddenly caught up, he'd always thought Sulien the most normal, the easiest to like. Una and the other one, with the horrifying round marks on his wrists that should have been impossible on living skin, had been so desperate, so relentless.

Sulien watched him feed a large card, punched with an intricate pattern of square holes, into a slot in the panel beside the alcove. The mechanism whirred and there was a dull noise of shifting weight in the darkness, as the belt began to move, slowly, finally bearing into view a dark crate and depositing it on the metal-topped table. Cleomenes flicked swiftly through its contents and handed Sulien a photograph trapped between rigid boards of transparent plastic.

The picture was old. The label below it told him it had been pinned straight to the wall, unframed. The sweetness of it surprised Sulien: between his parents, in the bright light, the little boy who must have been Atronius was restrained by each hand as if he could not stand still and might have made a dash towards the camera, but he was smiling. The parents seemed to be laughing, there were pots of hibiscus at their feet.

'Are they still in Maia, these two?'

'Took a while to trace. Dead in the Maia-Mexica uprising,' said Cleomenes.

Sulien felt another flash of excitement at this news, a bright mirage of understanding as he thought of the failed separatist mutiny that Marcus' father had quelled more than twenty years ago. But then he sighed. If Atronius were still alive, he must have been prepared to leave this behind. Did it mean much then? He slid the picture back into the crate and began unsystematically browsing through the other plastic-cased sheets.

'Don't get anything out of order,' moaned Cleomenes.

'I'm not.' Papers to do with the factory that gave up nothing. Receipts and bills. A torn and crumpled sheet of card: a ticket, which he was about to replace – and then stopped, staring at it, feeling as cold and raw as though he were being shaken awake.

Cleomenes leant over. 'That's how we placed him in Byzantium, remember?'

Speechlessly, Sulien handed him the plate. Uncomprehending, Cleomenes looked at it, and at Sulien's face. 'What? What's wrong?'

'That's the clinic's code,' answered Sulien in a soft, flat mutter. His mouth felt parched and rough.

Cleomenes studied the uneven, rather childlike sequence of symbols on the scrap of card. It was hard to read and incomplete; it vanished over the torn edge of the card. There was room for doubt as far as he could see; if it was the clinic's code, he couldn't blame the team for focusing on the ticket's provenance and missing it. 'You're sure?' he said, gently dubious.

'That's my name.'

Above the code was an S, and yes, Cleomenes saw what could have been the first upright of a U. Cleomenes sucked his breath in anxiously, not quite certain.

'I know that's my name,' insisted Sulien, sounding angry and betrayed now. 'You can see it's my name. Think what happened. They called me out of the clinic, by name. And *he* had this at the same time. It *was* the same people. They did want to kill me. Why in hell wasn't this found before? This is a fucking joke.' Unfocused, he turned back to the box and pulled another sheet, scanning it. 'The handwriting isn't the same, is it? One of the others must have written it down.'

'He'd been there for two weeks already, though,' suggested Cleomenes, uncomfortably. 'He couldn't have known you and Varius were going there. That was before you'd decided yourselves, isn't it?'

'I don't know. I don't understand. Veii must have been on their list anyway. Maybe they brought it forward when I got away the first time. I was being followed. They could have found out fast enough what I was doing. They tried twice in one day, Cleomenes.' He began an agitated attempt to retrieve the picture of the little boy. 'He must have hated Leo, after what happened to his family. I guess that includes Marcus, don't you?' The hunt for the photograph was futile; he couldn't remember where it had been; his fingers weren't steady. He brandished the ticket. 'How long had he *had* this?'

Cleomenes shook his head helplessly – it could have been from any time after the ticket was printed, there was no way of telling.

Sulien thought he'd been relieved earlier, when Cleomenes had scoffed at the profusion of bodyguards following him, and sent them away for the afternoon promising, 'I can keep an eye on him.' Now he wondered if all his complaints had been anything more than show, and whether after all the guards had made him feel safe. He remembered the scale of the fire at Veii. What could any number of armed men trailing about with him do against that? He let the ticket fall back loosely on top of the crate. 'Well, whatever else it means, you were right about him. He did it.'

211

Entering the room with its division of bars, Salvius found himself feeling less awkward than he had expected. Of course Drusus' look of physical deterioration was unmistakable, but the young man stood up composedly, as if greeting Salvius in his own home. He smiled, at once confident and self-deprecating, as though he found his own predicament faintly amusing, and extended his hand between the bars towards Salvius.

'The orders are that no one is to touch him,' interrupted the warden, as Drusus had known he would.

'I am General of the Legions of the Roman Empire. You take orders from me,' said Salvius instantly, automatic anger at being challenged overriding any misgivings he might have felt about grasping Drusus' hand.

'Bless you for coming,' said Drusus.

Sulien was growing used to feeling always slightly sick; for hours or days he even forgot the reason for the bands of tension around his shoulders and stomach, was confused to wake up with an ache in his hands from clenching his fists in his sleep. When he remembered he was exasperated: was there anything more he could reasonably do to protect himself? And had anything further happened to him, in the weeks since that one day? No, of course not. And so he should get it out of his mind. And yet it remained in his body, and he kept the printed copies of the picture and the ticket with the fragment of his name, and a later, smudged, unremarkable image of Atronius in the army, the only adult picture the vigiles had been able to find. They were folded into tight squares in his wallet, so that they were always with him. Sometimes, without premeditation, sitting becalmed on a tram carrying him west to Transtiberina, he would mechanically take them out and straighten them, looking at the child's face, at the parents. He knew the scratchy handwriting of the fragmented code so well now that he could see the missing symbols extending over the torn edge, glowing in space. It was not easy to account to himself why he still needed to have them. Perhaps at first he'd had some unlikely thought that someone at the clinic might recognise the handwriting or the face. But he kept them out of some feeling of balancing the scales, of redress. He was making up for the killer's possession of his name.

At least the nausea eased itself slightly whenever he had to visit

Faustus at the palace; he felt, illogically, hidden, insulated among so many rooms and people, so much heaped-up beauty. That must be the real function of a palace, for an Emperor.

In a large drawing room a trio of musicians were playing with dutiful jauntiness while Faustus listened dully, propped on a day-bed before the high windows. A sea-battle played out in fresco across the walls, its ferocious violence disguised and smoothed by the beauty of the painting. A pale missile streaked towards a stricken ship, as lovely as a dolphin. At the other end of the room, Makaria was hissing an urgent, exhausted rant at Sulien. By now she could feel the last dregs of her patience burning dangerously away; she could barely fight off either her homesickness or the wish to be in Sina, as she should have been.

'Considering he's suffered another stroke, I think he's making good progress,' Sulien told her.

'But progress towards what?' said Makaria. 'What about his memory? It's not right. If I remind him of something he says he knows it happened – maybe he's telling the truth, I don't know. But even if he does recognise the facts when he sees them, I don't think he really remembers. He gets so angry with me. How much improvement can I expect?'

'More than this,' promised Sulien, wearily.

'Then how soon?'

Doors burst open somewhere in the Palace, not far off, and a shout of surprise or protest was abruptly silenced. Feet, beating on stone, marching close.

Sulien and Makaria stood fixed, looking at each other, as though they were suddenly complicit in something. Makaria told him, 'Wait,' and ran towards the door.

Quiet, familiar antechambers opened before her, the nearest white, butter-yellow and silver, the next cool twilight blue, with a shy Diana rising above the mosaic floor. At first Makaria saw only Salvius, lustrous and severe, striding at the head of a small column of men. And then she saw, behind Salvius, hurrying awkwardly along as if it were hard to keep up, pale and fragile and sick-looking, but with a hard electric brightness in his face, was Drusus.

An attendant who'd already been making unheeded protests about the lawlessness of this march, dived loyally into Salvius' path saying firmly, 'Look sir, the Emperor's ill, his doctor has instructed—'

Marching on, Salvius muttered grimly, 'Has he?' and one of his men, almost without breaking step, struck the attendant deliberately out of the way, knocking him hard into the wall.

Uncertain if she'd been seen, Makaria darted back into the drawing room, letting the door swing to, and retreated across the shining floor.

She looked at her father, who had heard the approaching noise and was trying to raise himself with instinctive alarm and indignation, and she realised that whatever was coming there was nothing she could do to protect either him or herself.

She gave Sulien a little shove towards the only other door and murmured quickly, 'You'd better get out. Go on.'

Sulien hovered, and then did as she said. He slipped through into a cluttered study, red-walled and cramped, and there was no time even to close the door fully before Drusus and Salvius entered the room behind him. He heard Faustus stutter pitifully in bewilderment, and then shout, with sudden clear rage, 'How dare you do this? So you are a traitor, then, to me and to Rome!'

Sulien was in a corner, just outside the blade of light from the door that seemed to fill most of the room, slicing the space into triangles of bright danger and shadow. Yes, there was another way out, and he tried to sidle carefully towards it, but reached it in the open, revealed to anyone who'd been looking. Now he glimpsed Salvius, and a moment later he recognised Drusus' voice. Hoping the sound would be disguised under Faustus' fury Sulien tried the handle – but the door had been locked hours before, so that the Emperor would not be disturbed.

XII

CONQUERED GROUND

'You coward! Traitor!' How he loathed being able to do nothing but accuse and bawl! The indignity of having no other weapons left! Faustus turned, dragging his useless body from side to side, a crippled worm or caterpillar. 'Give me a – give ...' His voice stalled to an angry buzz. He wanted to demand a gun but could not bear the inevitable, definitive proof of his vanished authority: the Praetorians, plainly, were already answering to Salvius. All Faustus' worst fears were taking life at the same instant; the steady corrosion of these last years finishing in this violent fracture, and after 160 years, he was the one to fail, to see the dynasty break. He would be judged for letting it happen, when he was too unfairly weakened to prevent it. He could not even look at Drusus, who seemed, in any case, merely like a dark accessory or familiar lurking at Salvius' side. Impotently he cried again at Salvius, 'You *will* be sorry for it!'

Only then did he remember his daughter, standing there exposed, a target, and feel terror bite.

'Forgive him, Uncle,' said Drusus tremulously, stepping forward like a dancer on cue. 'He's done this for Rome. Not for himself or me.'

Makaria's instinct would have been to rage and bluster like her father until, she thought, with a cold throb of realisation that this was really happening, she was dragged away or shot alongside him. Instead she was trying carefully to position herself between Faustus and the open door to the little room into which she'd sent Sulien. She had seen the boy's shadow in the thin gap between door and frame; she knew he was trapped there, watching, and after what Salvius' men had done to the servant outside the room, it was chiefly the sense that Sulien needed her protection that kept her quiet. She had seen the small, wounded flicker of guilt that stirred Salvius' face at the word 'traitor' that Faustus, blind with rage and despair, could not. And she saw how Drusus laid a reassuring hand on his ally's arm as he passed, as if to remind him that

215

it wasn't true. With earnest grace, Drusus lowered himself to kneel at Faustus' feet.

'We're not the ones who want to take your power from you. I want to give it back.'

'You murdering little viper, don't speak to me,' snarled Faustus.

With another strange shock, Makaria saw that the flinch that crossed Drusus' face at this was an intensified, less subtle imitation of Salvius' look of pain at being called a traitor. Drusus must have registered and stored the useful expression as unconsciously and immediately as a camera.

'You must listen to him,' said Salvius, stiffly.

Faustus felt too flimsy, too small for his indignation at this; he couldn't find a retort to contain it. He stammered, 'He – he ...' Charges bubbled up to his lips and choked themselves: his poor brother Leo, the betrayal with Tulliola, and yet he could not see these things clearly; everything turned dim and fantastic as he tried to fix on it. He could hardly tell how he knew it all. It was Marcus and Makaria who'd told him, wasn't it? A kind of frantic, poisonous embarrassment smothered him, as if he'd recounted events from a dream thinking they were real.

'I have not come here to commit a crime against Rome,' Salvius said curtly, looking, despite himself, dour and threatening as he said it. 'I would never do that; it's what I am here to prevent. For some time I've feared the danger to the Empire was growing daily, and I'm sure of it now. I – I am not a traitor.'

Faustus gave an inarticulate snarl of anger and scorn.

'Please, Uncle,' urged Drusus. 'I only want you to hear what I've got to say and give me a little time to prove it. I promise, I would have waited to answer in court like anyone else if I thought there was any chance of the truth coming out. But it would not, and it would have been too late. There's still just time.'

Faustus lifted his better arm and clubbed Drusus clumsily across the face. Drusus gasped a little with distress and shock, and Salvius took an instinctive step forward, as if ready to defend him, towering over Faustus. For despite what he had said, it was hard for Salvius to feel any loyalty to the Emperor. He was so angry with him now, the anger sharpening his awareness of Faustus' physical feebleness. Forcing his own sense of duty to Rome to include this man seemed almost a betrayal of the obvious fact that he himself was, in a simply animal sense, stronger.

'Please,' repeated Drusus softly, looking up into his uncle's face.

'My brother ...' Faustus got out. 'All those things. All you.'

Drusus looked angry. 'No. *No*. How can they say these things to you when they admit there's no evidence?' he said bitterly. 'What is it all? Some *vision* or *dream*! Gabinius and Tulliola were picking us off like girls pulling petals off daisies. I don't know why anyone should think it would have benefited me. I would have been next, probably. How do we know what Gabinius was planning? I don't believe he was just worried about some scheme of Leo's that would never have happened anyway. He wanted to buy and kill his way onto your throne, Uncle. That's what I believe. And I was in his way too.'

Sulien moved slightly inside the tiny room, shifting his weight to lean against the wall, closer to the crack of the door. At first he had been unable to see much more than Makaria's back, but she'd just made a swinging motion of frustration and contempt, a thwarted stride, revealing Drusus, who seemed to be kneeling, and Salvius' tense, upright back. The feeling that he was in serious personal danger had slightly diminished, even if the sense of unfolding disaster was stronger. Sulien felt dizzily powerless as he tried to think what would happen now – he could not see an outcome that did not mean chaos. Please, don't listen, he wanted to beg Faustus. But if he did not listen, what would Salvius do? Surely he would not simply subside and let Drusus be taken back to prison. Was it better or worse, Sulien wondered, that Marcus and Una were so far away, unable to answer, but, surely, safe?

Drusus went on, 'So Marcus saved my life in a way, by coming back when he did. And I'm grateful to him for that. But he was too young. It was too terrible for him. He couldn't go through all that and not be … damaged. I know you believed it taught him a lot, all that time knowing his life was on the line, living with drifters and criminals, and I think it did. But they weren't good lessons, Uncle. He should never have had to learn them. But they're fixed in him now.' All this time Drusus had been staring earnestly up into Faustus' eyes. He looked down now, regretful and tentative. He continued slowly, 'I think he learnt not to tolerate anything or anyone he sees as a threat. To be pitiless, even, when he thinks it's necessary.'

'You liar,' Makaria burst out, disgust overcoming fear. 'You're describing yourself and changing the names. You don't even realise. Do you think you can make people forget what they know about you? Daddy—'

'I'm not lying,' said Drusus in a low voice. 'I'm saying what happened to Marcus. You've seen it too, I know you have. He learnt only to trust or listen to the people he relied on during that time. He might as well be deaf and blind to everyone else. But they're dangerous, those people. They don't answer to anyone except Marcus and they know how to handle him.'

Sulien felt his body stiffen. For the first time in months, he remembered overhearing another conversation between Faustus and Drusus, from behind another door. He remembered Drusus' disbelief and fear at what Sulien had heard, at his power to wall him off from the Emperor.

He was aware that for a while Faustus had made no sound.

'What are you talking about? Am I one of these sinister people?' demanded Makaria. 'I never thought you were stupid, Salvius. Do you really believe this?'

'Yes, I believe it,' said Salvius. 'I believe what I've seen with my own eyes. He won't brook disagreement from anyone. And *this* is where it ends.' He gestured at Drusus. 'False charges to clear aside inconvenient people!'

'Oh, I'm sure Marcus believed they were true,' said Drusus quietly. And to Makaria he explained gently, 'Because your own intentions are good, you assume other people are the same. No, I would say it comes down to Varius and those two slaves. That girl. We all thought – didn't we? – well, it's an infatuation, he's entitled to that, especially at his age. But it's far more. And where does she come from? Who *is* she? You said she was a witch, Makaria – that was the word you used. And she was a slave – and a prostitute, probably. And that's as much as we've ever known, nothing about where her sympathies lie. And Marcus is completely dependent on her. There's nothing she could say he wouldn't believe; no suggestion she could make he wouldn't act on.'

In the little room, Sulien had pressed his fists and forehead hard against the panelling of the wall, as if the pressure could numb the flood of complex heat that crackled across his skin. It was not simply an honorific male desire to hit back – although he did, acutely, want to do that – it was intricate, personal, nauseating. That irrecoverable time that he and his sister had been separated in London, when the only thing that was certain was that he'd been no help to her. All his worst doubts about those years – normally so intermittent and manageable – smeared together bloodily with rage at what Drusus had nearly done to her, at the injuries he'd left on her, again with no hindrance from Sulien. Even his clenched teeth seemed to scorch in his mouth, and he felt almost convinced that Drusus was, impossibly, responsible for all of it, even for selling them when they were children. It condensed, painfully, into shame at restraining himself from attacking Drusus now. He was quite unaware of the slight sound he'd made, gasping in his breath through his teeth and holding it. He didn't even notice Salvius turn his head as he heard it.

'You hate her,' observed Makaria, not growling with fury this time but in a cold, scared, clinical voice, which by mere luck caused Salvius to think the short hiss he'd heard had come from her. 'That's very clear in everything you say. Naturally you hate her, given what she found out about you. Quite enough to murder her to keep her quiet.'

'No,' insisted Drusus. 'No, of course not. Yes, I hate her, I admit that – there are limits to anyone's stoicism. I wouldn't be human if I didn't hate her. You don't understand why – you don't know what happened! Please, just let me tell you.' Drusus stopped, and Sulien saw him slowly get to his feet, exhaling, trying to calm himself. He said softly, as if with forced, hurt patience, so that Sulien had to strain to hear. 'Makaria, I think I know why you believed this about me ... so readily.'

'Because it's true,' she said acidly.

'No. I didn't remember for a while. Only quite recently ... I saw how it must have looked, on top of everything you were told. It was that conversation you and I had by the fountain. She'd followed me out of that meeting. She came into the aviary and spoke to me for a while – about Marcus, about how she hoped I wouldn't cause any problems. She was trying to keep me under control, I think now. And when she left, I met you by the fountain and we talked about her. And I think you saw – I was startled by what you said. I suppose I behaved oddly. I wasn't conscious of it at the time – I was only thinking about one thing. But I did, didn't I? And then I left. I went looking for her.'

It was the last thing Makaria had expected him to broach – she had been ready to confront him with it. Her mouth opened slightly, but she didn't answer.

Sulien, listening to the silence, turned away from the door, unable to stand it.

Drusus sighed again, letting his shoulders lower with a first, slow sense of release. He looked at Faustus who was hunched, silent, frowning, tired out already with trying to remember. Of course Drusus had known what he had to say; he had said it once already in prison, to Salvius. But then he'd still felt strained and desperate, lucky to succeed; the memory of the difficulty and anguish with which he'd constructed the narrative still too strong. He'd known there were so many things he must be woven in and accounted for: the locked room, the injuries on Una and on himself, the desperate claims he'd made as he was dragged away. Until now he had been unable to summon the real peace and stillness that came to him now, the luxury of feeling the effort slip away, along with any other version of the past.

No one in Rome, he hoped, knew about his recent visit to the Sibyl. But the first occasion, four and a half years ago, when the promise had first been made – that had not been a secret, although only Tulliola had known what he'd been told. And before he spoke Drusus reached for the memory and this time felt comfort glow from it, and he told himself: I *am* going to be Emperor.

'Probably you've forgotten that a few years ago I went to Delphi and consulted the Oracle,' he began in a quiet, tense voice. 'I didn't take it seriously at the time and I'd almost forgotten it myself. But you reminded me, Makaria. You called the girl a witch and you mentioned the Sibyl. It came back to me.'

'I know she tells the truth,' said Makaria, slowly. 'She was right about me. And about *Tullia*.' She almost spat the word, laden with accusation, watching Drusus' face. But she had not sounded so certain, or so hostile, until she reached the familiar ground of that name. Sulien had heard the hesitancy in her voice.

Drusus nodded tolerantly, undisturbed. The person Makaria had named was not Tulliola, she was some other woman who didn't exist and needed no mourning. He said, 'Yes, I know she was right. And that put her in a very strong position.'

'You talk to me,' demanded Faustus, suddenly, stirring fiercely. 'You tell *me* about this, not my daughter.'

Drusus turned to him obediently, leaving Makaria looking on unhappily. 'After that, Uncle, no one could ever make her account for anything she chose to say. As for what she claimed about Tullia and myself, I can only tell you that it's not true. That I'd never betray you like that. And that the reason I went looking for Una that day was because I remembered what the Oracle told me. First she talked in riddles about a single coal falling out of a grate and burning down a house, that sort of thing – something small growing dangerous and nobody noticing. Then it became clearer; she was talking about a person. A witch, a girl like a Sibyl appearing in Rome. Someone who could uncover others' secrets but keep her own. And no one would see at first how she was gathering power, how she was using it. And she would grow strong enough to wreck the whole Empire.'

Sulien heard how intensely silent the room had become around Drusus, who added almost lightly, 'The Sibyl wouldn't tell me if she could be stopped.'

'You never told anyone,' muttered Makaria. 'You'd have told someone if that really happened.'

Drusus shook his head, 'It was impressive enough at first, but I confess it didn't stick in my mind long. I'd gone in simply as a tourist and there seemed no sign of it coming true. Then years later I wondered if it could have meant Tullia, in which case the threat had passed – although it didn't seem quite right. But that day in the garden, I remembered what I'd seen since Marcus brought her to Rome.'

'I've seen it too,' said Salvius. 'From when I first laid eyes on her. She's everywhere. In almost every meeting, she's there watching. She knows everything that goes on in the Imperial office; she's in the Sinoan palace now. People hardly notice she's there; they don't realise that she listens to every word they say. She reads everything. What legitimate reason *can* she have? Or did you intend that to happen, when you gave that boy all your power?'

There was such restrained, thunderous anger in his voice that Faustus started a little, like a schoolboy at the shout of a headmaster, and only after he'd meekly shaken his head, did he remember that the rebuke should have enraged him.

'Marcus allows it because he's besotted with her,' remarked Drusus. 'She has more power than a girl of her background ever can have hoped for. She's quite addicted to it now. She's tightening her grip.'

'And she needn't look far for support,' said Salvius. 'She has a palace full of former slaves. The boy from the longdictor exchange – even if he wasn't in on it from the beginning, how could he refuse to confirm what she said? Gratitude would demand that much of him. He knows to whom he owes his freedom. Your nephew freed the lot of them for her sake; he scarcely even hides that.'

'I'd have done better to wait – I know that now,' resumed Drusus. 'I should have talked to you. But at the time – it was a compulsion, I *had* to find her. I felt sure that if it were true I'd find some proof of it. And I was right, I did. I went up towards Marcus' rooms, and from the far end of the passage I saw her coming out. She was hurrying, she was ready to *do* something – I could tell from the way she moved. And I followed her. She didn't notice me – or she seemed not to. Maybe it was all a trap. She went up onto the top floor, those rooms that are hardly ever used. I couldn't think of any reason she should have for going there. She shut herself in that room and I heard her through the door, talking into the longdictor. But she wasn't speaking Latin. I'm not good at languages, not like Marcus. But I think – I certainly believed at the time – that it was Nionian.'

Makaria scoffed, 'She's probably barely literate; I don't believe for a second she knows Nionian.' This time she sounded more confident in her incredulity, allowing Sulien fractional hope.

'She wouldn't advertise it, would she?' said Drusus. 'Whatever else, I won't underestimate her intelligence again. We don't know who this gang in the mountains were, what she picked up there. And maybe I *am* wrong, maybe there was some other reason for what I heard. But I went into the room, and *she knew* what I believed, and what I would say. And I think she had already feared I might be a threat. She wasn't going to run the risk. I'm staggered by how quickly she decided what to do.'

Makaria frowned silently down at the floor. Drusus had begun moving around a little now, not nervously but deliberately, occupying more space. For emphasis, he allowed another pause, and, helplessly, Faustus spoke. He asked, 'What did she do?'

Sulien's breath went out of him and for long seconds did not come back.

Drusus smiled a little, not triumphantly, only as if with regret at what had happened, and quiet relief at being listened to. A moment passed before he answered. 'First she just walked across the room and locked the door. I was too surprised – I didn't understand. And then – at first I thought she'd simply gone mad.' Drusus sounded dazed, bewildered at the memory. 'I even almost forgot what she'd been doing. I just tried to stop her hurting herself. But when I touched her she went for me. I never hit her, I swear – I just tried to keep her hands away from me. But she was lashing about like an animal, I couldn't hold her. And all the time attacking her own body as much as me. It was like nothing I've ever seen. Completely fearless, I'll give her that, too, she didn't care what she did to herself. She smashed the longdictor and came at me with it, screaming like a lunatic – as if I was trying to kill her. I did push her away – she fell and the desk hit her face. Although of course, she meant that to happen, too. She hardly even seemed to feel it. And then she ran out onto the roof. I feel stupid for not guessing until she'd gone why she'd done any of it! I was just shocked – it had started so fast I couldn't think. But then I understood. So I went after her – of course I did. Anyway, it was the only way out, she'd taken the key.' He uttered a short laugh, mocking himself. 'But I was already too late.'

It was not only that it sounded true, or his exhausted memory, that made Faustus believe it. It was the choice of either believing Drusus and Salvius, buying their harmlessness with that, or letting them loose with Salvius' troops behind them and waiting to see what they would do in the same room as his daughter.

So when Drusus approached and knelt before him again, appeal in his face and pale with all he'd suffered, Faustus put a hand on his hair and said, 'I'm so sorry, Drusus.'

Makaria lifted her head and darted towards them. 'I'm sorry too, Drusus,' she said remorsefully, and kissed his cheek, so that at Faustus' feet the two of them looked much younger, like loyal children carved on a grave stelae, siblings.

Salvius said, 'They are handing away power in Bian. This can't continue. Something has to be done before the balance swings totally in Nionia's favour. We want to avoid war – but surely not at any price.'

Drusus separated himself from Makaria and raised himself to sit beside Faustus, so that he could look into the Emperor's eyes on a level. He said, clearly, unafraid, suddenly looking and sounding as much like a war leader as Salvius ever had, 'I would go further than that. I would say we have to accept the times we live in and face it. The Empire has been too static for too long. Borders will always break in the end, inwards or outwards is the only question. Rome used to understand itself and the world better. We did not conquer so many lands out of vanity; it was a matter of survival. This is the signal that we should not have stopped. We can climb upwards, or wait to be knocked down. There is no such thing as standing still.'

Salvius looked at Drusus with surprised – even faintly daunted – respect. He said to Faustus, 'At the very least your nephew can't be left as the puppet of these people.'

'At least that,' agreed Drusus mildly, and added, 'The brother should be easy to find, anyway.'

Sulien, waiting, already numb with disbelief at Drusus' words, could almost have given a winded laugh at how true that was. The open study was now a helpless little country with no lines of communication or army, a tiny peripheral state to the subdued land outside. And then, suddenly aware of the folded pictures of the factory saboteur in his pocket, the copied ticket with his torn name, he remembered – Byzantium. He had been staring with blank horror at the wall of books beyond the open door, seeing the titles and the colours of the bindings with strange, lucid interest, like an abruptly detailed memory from years ago, and he could hardly tell if this was a real thought or only a figment of his fear and the ferocious, irrational feeling that there was nothing Drusus was not to blame for. But the thought repeated itself, icy and unemotional as the heightened vision of the books opposite him: it was Byzantium, Drusus had been living there.

'He saved my life,' protested Faustus, but without conviction, waiting for the denial that must come.

'How can you know?' asked Drusus softly. 'Whose word do you have except his? You can't know how well you would be, if he were not here. He controls you. And all of them – him, and Varius, and that girl, that whole circle around Marcus, and Marcus himself – they all depend on your being ill, or dead, for the power they have.' He had a hand on his uncle's arm now; he murmured diffidently, 'The shock almost killed you when they told you, didn't it? They must have known that could happen.'

Faustus asked sharply, warily, 'You think Marcus wanted me to die?'

Drusus hesitated a little, uncertain for the first time of quite how far to go.

'You think they should all be – questioned?' interrupted Makaria.

Drusus looked at her doubtfully and said, quietly, 'Yes.'

'The boy was just here,' said Faustus, and looked around.

Sulien, his back to the wall and rigidly still, nevertheless felt his body ringing like a tapped glass with anticipation of what was about to happen; with disbelief as he heard himself think, as if that was his best attempt at reassuring himself – they can't crucify me, I am not a slave.

'No, Daddy,' said Makaria, steadily, heartlessly. 'That was earlier, in your rooms, don't you remember?'

And Faustus conceded sadly, 'Oh, yes ...'

In front of them all, Makaria walked without hurry into the ante-chamber Salvius had marched through. For a good minute, remembering the unease she had felt in Una's presence, she had wondered if she should not believe her cousin. Wasn't it sad that she'd had so little faith in her own family as not to defend him, didn't she owe him more loyalty than that? But even as she felt this she'd known, truly, that it was temporary, unreal. No. There was the memory of panic and guilt as she had thought over what she'd told Drusus; the fact that really she had not needed to be told what he had done. It was true, that was all. And then that speech about Nionia, about the world. That was whom she had sent hurtling lethally towards Una; and having done that she had an absolute duty to keep him away from Una's brother.

The servants were gone and the doors at each end of the room stood wide, she was in full sight of Salvius and the soldiers. A pitcher stood on one of the silvered tables: as an excuse for leaving the room, Makaria poured out a glass of water, masking the slender drawer with her body as she slid it open and removed the keys to the rooms from the little enamelled box within. She carried the glass back to Faustus, offering it calmly and said, 'Have some water, Daddy.'

'I can ask for it if I want it. Stop treating me like an infant,' said Faustus.

Makaria smiled a taut apology, and placed the rejected glass on the table nearby, telling Drusus and Salvius, 'No, I know where to find Sulien.'

Sulien, still uncomprehending, heard her approach. She entered the little study and, almost without looking at him, put the keys into his hand. He couldn't even mouth thanks to her; she was already at the desk beside him, searching for a pen and paper so that she could come out of the study with a good reason for having gone in, the address of the slave clinic, and say to Salvius, 'Here, he works in Transtiberina.'

She knocked the door shut beside her, as loudly as she dared, to cover the sound of Sulien trying the first of the three keys in the lock. She crossed the room to Drusus and her father, brushing the glass of water off the table to give him another chance. She could think of nothing more and she felt that what she was doing was luridly obvious; she was sure that Drusus did not and could not trust her, and she was actually blushing with self-consciousness, her hot face surely beaconing Sulien's attempts to escape. She should not have been so overtly disgusted so long, she should have been quicker to make a show of being won over.

She saw Drusus flinch with unexpected violence as the glass broke and scattered across the floor.

Sulien slid around the door into some gallery, cold blood pummeling in all the pulses of his body, his vision briefly dappled with unsteadiness and dark. Trying to simulate fast, unremarkable confidence, he walked blindly forward through unrecognised rooms, and as his head cleared it was almost a relief to feel the segments of knowledge about Atronius and Drusus assembling themselves into order, as though they were merely a number game he'd turned to as a distraction. Drusus would always have needed agents: discontented, rootless men who were trained how to kill or spy, or who knew about fire, and had lost the right to use those abilities in the vigiles or the army.

Drusus wanted the war, and he had wanted access to Faustus without interference from Sulien. And what were a thousand slaves' lives to him?

Sulien reached mechanically for an unobtrusive door, painted to match the fresco around it, and started down a flight of the slaves' stairs, feeling temporarily protected there. The shrill self-centredness of fear receded enough to let him think with a jab of alarm of Acchan, the one from the longdictor exchange who'd helped Una – if they lost Sulien they'd find him, round him up, make him say he'd lied.

He bolted down a few floors, feeling how stupidly vast and overblown the Palace was, how superficial was his understanding of its passages and stairs. He had to fly out, exposed on what proved to be a busy landing among offices, and grab the first person he saw to ask directions, assuming a cheerful, hasty casualness that felt ridiculous.

Warm rain flicked against his face as he stepped outside and sped along beside the Palace. The Praetorian escort were waiting for him at the guard-house, still innocently intending to protect him, not knowing yet that they were a threat: he would have to find some other way out. Sulien let out a small gritted moan, a wordless little plea for things to be otherwise, as he dodged in among the smaller buildings at the

225

Golden House's flanks, beside the towers of blue glass. Briefly, unbearably lost, he nevertheless searched for and found – painfully close to his bodyguards at the Septizonium – the stewards' office and the longdictor exchange adjoining it. Faces and names, at least, were one strength of his otherwise lazy, cavalier memory. Sulien plunged through the office until he recognised Acchan, a slight young man with soft black hair around an oval face, carrying a box of papers across the room, looking patiently yet intensely bored, until he saw Sulien, lunging at him out of nowhere, grasping his arm and breathing, 'You've got to get out of here, now, come on.'

Of course Acchan was bewildered, and Sulien was drawing attention to them both, creating a small uproar, but he could see no help for it. Apologising and insisting he dragged Acchan out into the rain and tried to explain, as economically and urgently as possible, what was happening.

The pines breathed wet, dark scent. Outside, Acchan looked away from Sulien at the golden Palace, and out across the huge drenched city, and turned a few stumbling steps – speechless, uprooted. He did not, at least, doubt the danger; he'd seen Drusus chasing Una towards him, pursuing her like a floe of lava flooding down the passage, almost close enough to consume her.

He muttered, 'You're the one he told me was dead, aren't you?'

'Yes.' Sulien had almost forgotten that part of it. He felt uselessly to blame for doing this to him. He confessed, 'Some of the guards at the Septizonium are waiting for me – I don't know how to get out.'

'There's the west gate,' Acchan said numbly. 'Have you got a pass?'

Sulien feared it would mean passing the façade of the Palace again, in the open, in full view, but Acchan led him down an unexpected flight of steps into a long basement corridor that ran beneath it. They said nothing as they approached the west gate; it was small and discreet compared to the high, stark arches of the Septizonium, but still heavily guarded. But no one stopped them passing through, down towards the Julian Forum. He said to Acchan, 'Is there anywhere you can go?

Acchan looked helplessly up at the screens and columns, all running with water, and the streets beyond, rust coloured in the rain, dazed as a small-town sightseer who'd never set foot in Rome. 'I've been in the Palace since I was twelve. If there was somewhere else to go, I'd be there already.'

'Fine,' said Sulien, as if undaunted. The other boy's presence seemed to be forcing his face and voice into an optimism that even he found faintly irritating in himself: he'd just explained how close the danger was and now he wanted to say that it wasn't so bad. 'Come with me, then.'

But he could not go home. He had only enough money in his wallet for perhaps a cheap meal and a couple of short tram journeys. He thought of friends, colleagues, girlfriends, and knew that any of them would have lent him a floor, a mattress or a side of the bed – and also that he could be tracked to any one of them effortlessly, in hardly more time than it would take him to reach them.

Una, Marcus, Varius – he wanted more than anything to be able to go to them for help, and also to be able to warn them. But they were thousands of miles east, and – so suddenly stripped of connections – he had no idea how to contact them.

XIII

THE LEVELLED FOREST

Lord Kato knew that the Go-natoku Emperor could see him, but could not be certain whether or not he could see the Emperor. He had placed an unrolled den-ga screen on a lectern in his rooms, and stood before it with his head respectfully lowered, so that the limited information it offered him was further obscured. His vision was clearest on the dark floor as it stretched to the distant feet of the Chrysanthemum Throne, and the upright figure within it, veiled by the canopy above him. Two flat oval panels, standing on slender ebony stems, were placed in front of him, their carved wooden backs concealing the screens on which, if this were real, the Emperor would be watching Kato in full close-up. He was far off, sitting in shadow; if his lips moved, Kato could not see it. In fact he could see nothing stirring in the long, sparely decorated hall. It could be an old recording, it could even simply be a photograph, and the Emperor might in fact be anywhere – in his private rooms, in his gardens, even in his bath, and yet the clipped, measured voice spoke calmly, in the formal dialect of the court, loud in Kato's ears – it was, as Kato struggled not to admit to himself – unnerving.

'You still believe it can be deployed effectively?' asked the hidden Emperor.

'I will send you the pictures, Your Majesty. We tested it on one of the Kazanshotou islands in the East Sea. It levelled a forest in less than a second – too fast even for our eyes to make sense of it.'

'But only on one occasion out of ten, I think?'

'It is true,' admitted Kato.

'And I believe the attempts to avoid war are ... proceeding well?'

'It is all very well to find a form of words everyone can interpret to their own tastes and then persuade themselves they are agreeing.'

There was a pause, and then the Emperor said, sounding faintly amused, 'So, we *are* finding such forms of words?'

Kato detached himself carefully; not being able to see his interlocutor, it was hard to keep in mind how important it was to control his own face. 'Yes, Your Majesty.'

'You may be right to be cautious, but still, you and the other lords have achieved more than many expected or hoped for. You should congratulate yourselves.'

Kato bowed, expressionless. He was aware that there was a tentative jubilance growing among both the Romans and the Nionians. Sometimes after long sessions Kato saw dishevelled gangs of them, senators and daimyo, out in the courtyards, without their interpreters, trying frivolously to learn each other's languages, and laughing shrilly together like overtired children. Kato's regard for the Roman prince had increased somewhat, having seen how despite his youth and softness he had managed to jolt several meetings past what might have been hopeless sticking points. And Kato had an eye on their Lord Varius too, quieter and more meticulous, who seemed to thrive on the sleeplessness and tension, walking from one fraught hall to another, vanishing into the haggling over marriage laws or integration of the police, or slavery, before emerging to lay out a possible solution, as clever and fragile as a folded paper bird. Kato had begun to think some sort of treaty might be inevitable. But some differences lay too deep to be reconciled. The agreement would do no more than render the opening of the war more complicated, for which Kato was prepared. But increasingly he saw that while everyone wallowed in this illusory fellow-feeling, he would lose Tokogane. They would establish some bastard hybrid council, and it would not include him. And moribund though it would be, he might never get his land back after it. For Tokogane was his. He could admit as much in the privacy of his mind. And he pitied the princess, abandoned in the chaos, as she would be.

'What is it you would like from me, Lord Kato?' enquired the Emperor, indulgently.

Kato looked at the solid ground below his feet, not at the screen. 'We cannot correct the weapon's faults without further resources,' he said quietly.

There was again a short silence. 'You are talking of course of many billion ryo.'

'Yes, inevitably. But the work *must* be completed, Your Majesty; to spend less would be a false economy.'

'We agreed to make no further preparations for war during the talks,' remarked the Emperor.

'We agreed only that there would be no movements of troops,' said Kato. 'We don't know that they are not doing the same thing.' Kato heard the Emperor's breath expelled grimly.

'I wish you to do nothing to risk the success of these talks,' he said, emphatically. 'I wish you to continue whole-heartedly. And I think it is time to proceed as concerns my daughter, as well.'

'Of course, Your Majesty,' said Kato heavily.

'And in the meantime, in Tokogane,' went on the Emperor, calmly, 'your philosophers will have the funds they need.'

Kato lowered his face again, this time to keep it from showing an excess of delight.

'I imagine they can resume, without you?'

'Thanks to Your Majesty, they can now,' said Kato.

'Don't you find the city beautiful?' asked Princess Noriko, stiltedly, in Latin. An opera, largely ignored by the audience, was yowling onstage in the palace theatre and she had just met Marcus for the first time.

Marcus agreed, of course. He was slightly bemused. Tadahito had entered the room a few minutes after him and headed for Marcus at once, saying cheerfully, 'You must meet my sister.' He led Marcus through the crowd and Varius, who almost alone was sitting stretched out, anti-socially watching the opera with tired eyes while the other guests milled around him, looked up sharply as they passed him, approaching a group of Nionian women, whom Marcus had not seen since that glimpse of long coloured hair and wigs between the screens on the first day, and whose presence in the theatre he hadn't noticed until now.

All of them but one melted away as Tadahito, who had up until this moment seemed informal and relaxed, announced, in an oddly stately way, 'The Princess Imperial, Noriko.' And almost at once he too receded, leaving them together in a little lake of space, the shores of people just too distant to be reached, so they could not extricate themselves.

They smiled at each other.

'What have you been doing all this time?' he said. 'I didn't know any of the princesses were here.'

A blank, stricken look crossed her face and he realised that although her last words in Latin had sounded close to perfect, it had been because she'd had time to construct something she knew how to say. He'd spoken too fast. He saw her processing what he'd said, before she mumbled something too hesitant and blurred to be understood, and then repeated more clearly, 'There is only me.'

Unlike the other women's, her dress was very Roman, dark turquoise with a gold sash wound round the torso, the skirt calf length where the others all flowed to the ground, the sleeves narrow. The differences

230

were not so great, nor his eye for women's clothes so sharp that he pinned this down at the time, although he had a vague feeling that there was something incongruous about her appearance. He knew he wanted to stare at the floor-skimming, green-tipped hair, even – guiltily – to touch it.

'My brother wanted me to come,' she explained in a murmur. And she blushed. He didn't know why.

'I always wished I had brothers or sisters,' said Marcus, rather help-lessly. It occurred to him to wonder how old she was – he'd been think-ing of her as his own age, or Una's, but no, she must be four or five years older, and yet still so shy. Perhaps it was only the language.

There was another pause as she prepared the answer. 'If you had, you may wish you are – you *might* wish you *were* an only child,' she said laboriously, for the tenses were complicated, but she seemed pleased with her success once she had spoken, and relaxed slightly.

'Your poor brother,' said Marcus, teasing her.

'Oh – no! I was thinking of childhood.' There was a pause, and his eyes must after all have slid incredulously down the length of her hair, or flicked to that of one of the ladies in waiting beyond her, for her eyebrows lifted and suddenly she leant forward a little. 'It *is* all real,' she confided. 'But, standing behind me, Lady Mizuki is wearing a wig.'

She smiled naturally, even a little flirtatiously, for the first time, and Marcus felt another furtive sizzle of enjoyment at her beauty. 'Then – what's her hair like underneath?'

'Well, not as she would wish it to be, of course,' said Noriko. She laughed, but then, ashamed of being catty, lowered her eyes. 'Would I look very bizarre in Rome?' she asked, in a quieter voice.

'No. Striking. Beautiful, as of course you would anywhere,' said Marcus, with formulaic gallantry, although he meant it too.

But she did not look up again, and once more the conversation stalled: she subsided into mystifying nervousness that fatally encum-bered Marcus' capacity to think of anything to say to her. And yet they remained stranded together, Marcus trying to support an increasingly dull and feeble conversation almost single-handedly. Then suddenly, Varius was at his side, saying urgently, 'Caesar, there's someone you need to speak to now. Forgive me, Princess.'

Thankfully, his entry seemed to cause the empty circle around Marcus and the princess to collapse; the waiting women flowed in to receive Noriko, who gave Marcus a diffidently polite smile of farewell before turning back to them.

'There isn't anyone, is there?' asked Marcus, following Varius to a safe distance.

'I thought you needed an excuse,' Varius muttered, glancing back over his shoulder.

'Thanks. I didn't make it too obvious, did I?'

'No more than she did.' Varius' manner was odd: at once conspiratorial and evasive, distracted.

'I did *like* her,' said Marcus, feeling mildly defeated.

'That's good,' said Varius, disappearing.

Noriko let out a sigh as her ladies surrounded her, safe for a while among her own people and language, but frustrated too. She wished she could have at least expressed herself more gracefully, that she could have been less pathetically timid with someone who was, after all, her junior. Still, the charge between them, brief and tenuous as it had been, would have pleased and reassured her, if she had not known about the Roman lady he was in love with.

She was surrounded by curious chatter. 'He was lost as soon as he began talking to you, Madam!' cried Lady Sakura, exaggerating enthusiasm either to disguise actual distaste for Marcus Novius, or in a real attempt to buck Noriko's spirits. 'I could see it in his face. Poor creature, how could he help it?'

'Without effort,' replied Noriko, tersely. 'I don't think he is in need of your compassion.'

'No, not if you will love him in return, Lady,' said Mizuki, smiling, but with a trace too much mockery in her tone.

'But he was very respectful,' said Tomoe.

'No, more than that, he could not take his eyes off you. If ...' Sakura lowered her voice, 'he *were* to be your husband, you could be sure of his devotion.'

'I would say he looked at me with no more attention than was friendly or polite in a first meeting.'

'But what did you talk about with him?' persisted Sakura.

'We had a very pleasant conversation and I have nothing whatever to say about it,' Noriko answered crossly.

Dismayed they talked obediently of other things for a while. Later, when they had withdrawn a little from the party and were out on a verandah, Lord Kato approached her, his face full of sympathy. 'You must be very anxious,' he said gently.

'Yes,' she said, despite herself.

'I understand. If the marriage *does* go ahead, it will be a great ordeal for you of course, but I hope I can comfort you a little. I will not allow you be stranded among them in the event of war. I will make sure you are rescued: a secret escort can be ready to remove you from the country at all times. And I hope your time away from us will not be long.'

'Thank you,' said Noriko, wanting to let out a wordless bark or roar of fury into his face.

Marcus did not see Varius again that night; he seemed to have left the party abruptly, without speaking to anyone. But the next morning, as Marcus left a meeting with Tadahito in one of the pavilions, Varius was there at the foot of the steps, waiting for him.

Marcus looked down at him. 'What happened to you last night?'

'I had things to do,' said Varius mildly.

Marcus laughed, and headed down. 'Parties *are* the best time to get serious work done.'

Varius smiled, but didn't speak, and he let out a short sigh as if something were difficult, and turned away, motioning for Marcus to follow.

In Varius' rooms, two uneven heaps of paper lay on a table, looking isolated and out of place. For otherwise, although the apartment was as luxurious as any, Varius seemed to have had no impact whatever on it in the weeks he'd been living there. It still looked uninhabited, blank for a guest that had not yet arrived.

'What is it?' asked Marcus.

'Marcus, do you know why Princess Noriko is here?'

Already Marcus was growing uneasy, and the wary gentleness with which Varius asked this made the feeling worse. He sat down, saying nothing.

Varius seemed to subject his answer to some final check before he let it pass. 'If Go-natoku could see his grandchildren as Roman Emperors it would be some compensation for whatever power he's losing in Tokogane,' he said. 'And even now they're not certain all of this isn't some kind of trick to weaken them before a war. A marriage would be a declaration of good faith from us – from you.'

Marcus sat immobile and speechless for a moment, and then slumped back in his seat feeling only, at first, so very stupid. 'How do you know?' he asked at last, dully. Much as he would have liked to, he didn't doubt that Varius was right.

'I convinced one of the Sinoan interpreters to stay close to the princess' group last night. He passed himself off as a waiter.'

Marcus gave a snort of mingled incredulity and despair.

'He was pretty happy to help. The Sinoans generally sympathise with us more than Nionia. He heard Lord Kato telling the princess he'd get her out of Rome if and when the war starts. The interpreter doesn't speak much Latin, though, only Nionian, so it had to go through someone else before I could tell you. I thought you'd rather have certainty.'

'Why – why did you ...?'

'I could have used some kind of listening device, but they'd have found it. I could probably even have asked, but the longer they can't be sure we know, the more freedom we have. Besides, it was faster this way.'

'No,' murmured Marcus. 'You already knew. You were just ... proving it. It was the way they introduced us, wasn't it? I should have worked that out.'

Varius gave a dry, self-conscious laugh. 'No. Wait until this happens to you another couple of times, you'll get to know the signs too.'

Marcus looked at him, startled by the implication, and laughed bleakly, as it occurred to him how little Varius usually told about his personal life, how little, perhaps, there was to tell.

'There are only so many ways of dropping that particular hint,' continued Varius, glancing away.

Marcus pressed his face into his hands.

'Look,' said Varius, leaning forward. 'They can't offer her openly, it would degrade her and the whole Empire if they even appeared to run the risk of your turning her down. They want you to ask for her. So hinting is all they *can* do. It has to be like this – everything indirect and nothing acknowledged, so no one looks bad if it falls through. So they are well aware it might not happen.'

'Of *course* it's not going to happen!' answered Marcus, almost shouting, launching onto his feet. Varius watched him in silence. Marcus paced around for a second or two in an aggressive, desperate ring. More quietly he said, pleading, 'Surely, they wouldn't stake everything else on this?'

'No. If the treaty is too perfect to be thrown away, if they're sure enough we really mean to hold by it.'

Marcus asked, feeling that never since he'd taken the Imperial ring had he been so in need of help, 'What am I going to do?'

'Nothing. Or nothing except work even harder. They can't expect a response to something they haven't said.'

'They'll ... drop more hints.'

'We'll be very obtuse,' said Varius.

'But they won't let us ignore it for ever. They can't offer her, you said, but they can make sure someone lets it slip by accident.'

'Yes,' said Varius. 'And they will. But it's a test. By the time it comes to that, we'll have to be sure you've already passed it.'

Marcus sighed. 'Thanks,' he muttered. 'Thank you for finding out.' He hated the idea of telling Una, but he knew he must do it immediately. There would be no chance of keeping it from her.

Una was not in the quarters she shared with Marcus. She had begun, as she had in the Golden House, to insert herself subtly into the meetings, listening. And yet it was harder. Now she was watching Nionian and Roman delegates argue about slavery through their interpreter, and the urge to speak pressed her; the modest shroud of decorum she used to hide herself was growing stifling, heavier.

In their long robes, the eunuchs glided about, as unobtrusively as herself, tall, with smooth deceptive faces, unctuous and fawning, and all so consumed with familiar rage that it startled her when other people did not flinch at their approach or look, that anyone could think they were not conscious of how they were irreparably mutilated as well as enslaved. Una remembered the refugees in Holzarta. With Delir's money, with Lal's forged travel papers, Sina had meant freedom for some of them. But really what she'd most feared when she'd first climbed out of a London window, bruised and raging and hating Romans, was true: there was no place outside that offered more than a private escape, nowhere that was simply free and safe and good.

The forceful, handsome Nionian lord from Tokogane moved swiftly through the room without seeing her. He placed a hand on the arm of an agitated official and spoke to him briefly before leaving again, but to Una he seemed like a walking firework, scattering generous sparks of satisfaction and excitement as he passed. And when she looked at him, she saw – almost with her actual eyes, like the floating auras of a migraine, an instant dwelled on with eager, meditative gladness, and repeated over and over again – the lower slope of a cone-shaped mountain, a green volcano, rising above a blue bay. And no sound of an explosion, no change in the glittering light; but the long creaking screech of the shattering trees, and the leaves puffing into the air like dust at a breath, as something like a dry, pulsing flood pounded over the ground and up the mountainside, stripping it bare. Sitting there in the Sinoan hall, Una seemed almost to feel a faint impact in her own flesh, such as a ghost might feel.

Una shivered, and looked at the ground, a little more willing to be silent and unnoticed. She was uncertain when or where what she had seen had happened, or what had made him think of it with such keen attention; sharp as it had been, so much else remained hidden in the unknown language. And as she watched Kato leave, a eunuch came up and handed her a crumpled letter. Una was surprised to receive a letter from anyone, but when she took it it fell unrolled in her hand.

'It's been opened,' she said indignantly, holding it up and jabbing her finger at the broken seal.

The eunuch's face performed a perfunctory expression of smiling apology. Una looked at him with a chill, and could not protest any further. She smoothed out the letter and read, feeling a dart of disbelief, '*Lal to her Una ...*'

But the eunuch tapped gently at her shoulder again before she could read on. 'Please you come. Your Caesar,' he urged.

Confused, Una glimpsed another line: '*... and I hope you're with him. Perhaps there's a better chance ...*' before, with a conflicted sigh, she rolled the paper up again to follow.

Marcus was waiting in a small, empty meeting chamber nearby, tense and agitated.

'What's wrong? Why didn't you just come in and get me?'

He moved to her quickly, his hands on her shoulders, spilling the words out in a hurried mess, racing the truth across the little distance between them. He could see her face changing and hardening, the reaction just perceptibly ahead of what he said to her.

When he had finished, she did not move or speak, and though her eyes had not left his face she no longer seemed to be looking at him. She was not aware of the grim, sour smile that had appeared on her face. She said nothing because it was not his fault that she felt like doing something brutal, hooligan-like, the kind of thing a thuggish lowlife off the streets should be relied on to do. She wanted to steal something without understanding its value, she wanted to vandalise something. Within the long expensive dress she felt rough-edged, snide and grimy.

'I'm sorry, I'm sorry.'

'For fuck's sake, what have *you* got to be sorry about?' Una snarled irritably, so that Marcus realised with a jolt just how deceptively innocent and delicate money and freedom had made her look, how a jagged surface in her voice must after all have been softened and worn smooth, for both the word and the sudden abrasive rasp with which it was spoken sounded unreasonably shocking coming from her lips. Una felt the incongruity herself, saw it in him, reflected back at her, and it gave her a small tingle of bitter comfort. She withdrew again into hard, staring silence.

Marcus urged, 'Say something.'

Una gave a harassed sigh, gathered herself competently and said, 'I think Lord Kato is building some kind of new weapon. I think he used it on a forest on some island somewhere – I don't know. I can't understand, but, well, I've told you now.'

'Una,' said Marcus, though storing the information away for later.

She looked at him properly at last and said flatly, sadly, 'We knew something like this would happen in the end.'

Marcus gave a little cry of exasperated misery. 'No. *No*. Why do you have to say that? I won't do it. Under any circumstances. You *know* I won't.'

'That's very sweet,' said Una, the involuntary jeering note returning to her voice. 'Shame it doesn't sound like it's up to you.'

'It *is* up to me, I can do anything I want,' retorted Marcus dangerously. Somehow this silenced Una more effectively than he had meant or expected; she looked down with a kind of flinch that irritated him and he added unnecessarily, 'I wish I didn't have to tell you every little thing, because this isn't even going to matter.'

'I'm sorry I'm so much to put up with,' taunted Una, wanly. She sank into one of the chairs against the table, stiffly, and laid her cheek on its surface.

'Oh, you are! I just love you, I don't know why.'

But the hard, scathing expression had gone and she looked simply beaten and wretched. She muttered, 'No, nor do I.'

Marcus breathed out, and went and enfolded her silently, hanging over her shoulders like a heavy garment. 'You must,' he told her softly at last. 'You must know better than to believe that.'

She whispered desolately, 'I'm just not very nice. I love you. I'm – horrible to you, half the time.' She'd put up her hands to hold his arms in place where they crossed around her.

'No you're not.' He didn't move. 'Listen now. It doesn't matter what they want me to do. No one can make me marry anyone else.'

'No, please don't. You're not to,' Una said, hiding her face against him.

Later, when they were both a little calmer, she remembered the letter, which was crushed to a shred in her fist. She did her best to uncrease it and showed it to him. 'Look at this, can you believe it?'

Lal to her Una,

   I always start by writing the same thing – by counting the letters I've sent to you since we came here, and telling you that I wanted you to know that we are safe. Well, this is the sixth letter, and it's very likely you'll never get this one either. I've never known for certain where you are, and it hasn't been easy to send anything safely. Even if the Sinoan authorities aren't interested in our presence here, there has always been the possibility that the Romans would have demanded our extradition if they knew where to find us. But now Marcus is in Sina. Perhaps there's a chance this one will reach you.

I don't know that you're with him. It's been three years. You said you were interested only in what he could do, as Emperor. But I remember how horrified you were when he left Holzarta. And we know that you must have found him, for of course we heard the news that Marcus had been named as Caesar. And later we heard rumours about something that happened in a sanctuary for lunatics, and about two slaves.

Only two, though.

But Marcus must at least know where you're living now. He would make sure you get this. I can't believe that he is practically Emperor, so young, and I used to know him! Of course that was good news for us. We've begun talking about coming back to the Empire. My father thinks he should start up another refuge, somewhere like Holzarta. But it would take a few years to build a network of people we could trust, and Marcus must be so close to shutting down the slave trade anyway – I almost think it's not worth it. We could settle in Rome, maybe.

You probably know we had to evacuate the camp. There were meeting points in the mountains, mostly on the Spanish side, but we couldn't risk gathering into a single group again, so there are many people from that time that I've never seen since. Of those we travelled with, some decided that with the identity papers I'd made, they'd be safe enough staying in the Empire. Helena and Marinus and their children didn't go any further than Spain – to Caesaraugusta, I think. The last I heard, Tiro was in Lepcis Magna. But some of us continued to Jiangning, where we've been ever since.

We came because we knew that over the years, many of the slaves we'd sent from the camps had made homes here. Some of them still teach Latin – there's always a demand for that – others have set up shops selling Roman clothes and food – that kind of thing. They import some of their goods illegally from Rome, which is how we get most of our news of the Empire. So, the people here were already used to Romans, or whatever we should rightly call ourselves, having no real citizenship and belonging nowhere. They even call these streets around Black Clothes Lane 'Rome' now. So, there, I live in Rome, I have my wish, in an annoying way. I do like Jiangning. When we came through the north we couldn't move without being stared at. Here it's easier.

But my father isn't happy here. Part of it is the language. He can get by, but he can't really have a conversation with anyone from outside these few lanes. He works in the shop of one of our friends, and he hates it. He and Ziye call themselves husband and wife now, although they have never actually married, and even if in general the Sinoans in Jiangning aren't surprised to see us around, they still stare at the two of them. Of course Ziye would draw attention anywhere, and she doesn't look like other Sinoan women. She hasn't grown her hair; she doesn't hide the scars from the arena on her face, any more now than back in the Pyrenees when you knew her. People find her shocking. And the fact that she lives with a Persian man only makes it worse. She seems indifferent to all this, most of the time, but my father certainly isn't. And even Ziye says sometimes, 'I always knew I'd never really be able to go home.'

I told you how I was giving a few Latin lessons in the last letter. I'm not a good teacher, to be honest, I don't think Liuyin learnt very much from me. He failed his Imperial Examination, but that was always kind of a foregone conclusion. He didn't want to be an official anyway. I told you about Liuyin – the official's son, the artist, he said he was in love with me. Why am I reminding you as if you already know? I wish you did already know, that's all. Well, it was fine for a while, but his parents found out and of course I am the wrong class and the wrong … everything. Liuyin made a great tragedy out of obeying them and giving me up. But we still meet sometimes, near the Lady Without Sorrows lake, and he expects us both to be as starcrossed and heartbroken as lovers in an opera, and I find that I can't be bothered. And you would think, from the way he's growing to resent this, that I were the one to have finished with him.

If you do live in Rome now, I wonder what you think of it? You used to feel, I think, rather as Dama did, that it was wicked. Yet you wouldn't want to go back to London. That's part of the reason I'm writing to you now, why I wish so much I could talk to you; I think you must feel as I have in every place I can remember, only as if I'm staying here, not as if I live here, not that this is my home. I should miss Aspadana, and Persia, but it's been eight years now, and my mother died there. So instead I still fix Rome as the place I want to be, even though I've never seen it, because, at least as I imagine it, it contains … everything. Nothing about me could possibly be strange or out of place if I were there.

As for Dama. Of course I've been asking you the same question for three years and each time we had to give up hoping for an answer. Do you know where he is? Nothing we heard about what happened in Rome sounded as if it included him. We don't talk about him any more. My father and I used to pray that he was safe. After about a year we stopped, at least, I did. Lately one of our friends out here died, a woman called Servilia – you never met her. The evening after the funeral, I heard my father saying a prayer – for her, and then he added Dama's name, as if Dama were dead too.

And Ziye told me afterwards that it wasn't the first time. I would never have thought of doing that – how can the dead need our help? But I realised that I had come to the same assumption. I remember Dama when he left – so fierce, as if this were the last thing he'd ever do. But then, he never did anything without giving himself over to it, like that, so maybe that memory doesn't mean as much as it seems to me now. I hope I'm wrong. I wish my father knew, because Dama was almost like his son. At least, he always felt, and always will feel, responsible for him. I'm sorry if this is painful to read.

I nearly went with you. If I had, my father would never have left the camp, no matter how bad the danger. So I can't regret that I stayed behind. But I wish I really knew what had happened to all of you, and that so much time hadn't passed without my seeing you.

I think of you often.

Affectionate, and at times disarmingly astute as this letter was, both Marcus and Una were subtly wounded by it, reading it just then.

'You said that, did you?' Marcus accused Una lightly, indicating the lines about her years-old claim of indifference to him.

'Oh ... something like that. I suppose that's what I thought, though I don't remember actually saying it. You know how it was.'

'Poor Sulien. He might have hoped he'd at least get a mention.'

'Oh, that's on purpose,' scoffed Una. 'Look how she brings up this other person. Sulien should be pleased. If she wasn't thinking about him, she'd say "I hope your brother is well", or something. She can't even write his name without feeling like it looks obvious.'

For that reason Una was a little sceptical of her own apparent precedence in the other girl's thoughts, but still she was startled and touched by how fondly Lal appeared to remember her. It made her ashamed that she had not been more faithful, over the years, in missing Lal as sharply as she had been prompted to now.

'So, if she wrote pages about him it would show she'd forgotten he existed?' said Marcus. They were both aware of exaggerating to ease the tension, pretending not to understand each other when really they did, constructing a rather laborious joke about male rationality and female intuition. They succumbed to strained, shuddering laughter, and pressed closer to one another.

'What can I tell her about Dama?' asked Una bleakly.

Marcus hesitated, feeling, to his shame, slightly threatened by Dama, and Una's complicated grief or guilt for him. 'There was nothing you could have done,' he told her quietly.

Una saw Dama's face, propped in a brittle electric ray of torchlight, against a thundery aura of black and red, on the rock walls behind him were the shadows in ancient paint of punished, fingerless hands. 'Yes,' she murmured. 'There was.'

Dama stared back at her in the memory, so that she felt loaded with a nearly unbearable weight of ardent, blue-eyed focus; he was so painfully bright with – yes, with love, and also authority, a coiled density of will she had not encountered since. Una looked at Marcus to reassure him that her sorrow now, like Lal's stateless homesickness, did not include regret. At least, she loved Marcus, and there was no getting out of that now. But still, a rude, sneering element in her heckled dismally: 'Dama was right; you should've stuck to your own kind.' Because Dama *had* been of her kind, had he not? She had known, back then, that whatever the raw matter of her was, and whatever her life as a slave had made of it, it had been the same with him. And God knew no one could have been pushed between them, like this Nionian princess. And after all she did wish she could see him again, that they could have even just an hour together, talking.

Marcus said nothing and she picked up the letter again. 'Will they be all right?' she asked, as if Dama hadn't been mentioned. 'She tells all this stuff about who they are and where they're living, and someone opened this before they gave it to me.'

'We'll find them,' he said. 'I'll get them to Rome, or wherever Delir wants to go. I owe them so much, and all I've done is cause them this. I even took that money to get back to Rome – I'll make it up to them, I'll give them a fortune.'

But still in his arms, Una caught her breath without speaking, and lifted her head as if trying to distinguish the sound of thunder from the noise of a distant train. He felt her body growing rigid against his.

'What?' he asked her.

She hardly knew how to answer; she was unwilling to understand. This was the dread that had lingered for so long, demanding so many obsessive little private rituals in order to manage it, while all the time she'd tried of persuade herself that it was silly and unneccessary, and what she was afraid of *could* not return to rational, concrete life. It was the knowledge of being tracked down, by a great mass of people, disciplined and intent, and marching closer.

'Oh, God,' she pleaded, not just an exclamation but, perhaps inspired

241

by Lal's letter, a real, miniature prayer. She started to her feet, saying, 'Marcus, I think the *army* ...'

Her voice died in bewildered horror, and Marcus insisted, *'What?'*

As her sense of the approach grew worse she stammered, 'I think they've come for you.' Una gazed at him and thought that whatever was happening, escape would be impossible for him, not only physically but ritually, politically. So many shreds of chances that placing that ring on his finger had tidied away. There remained only the hope that she had somehow misunderstood, or else the satisfaction of knowing the facts as fast as possible. She looked at him a second longer before she shot away from him, out of the dark hall into the light beyond.

Marcus, following her already, heard her call out his name almost at once, a shocked cry of warning.

Outside, it was her his eyes found first, almost before he understood that he was looking down into what seemed like an expanse of red-uniformed men. In reality, there were perhaps thirty or forty. And Una stood, boxed in among them. They did not touch her – not now, or not yet – but contained her nonetheless, and made her body look acutely frail between theirs. She did not look afraid for her own sake, but she was gazing at him with desperate hard intensity, as if she could transmit herself back to him across the soldiers between them.

The only person whose eyes were not instantly fixed on him as he emerged through the door was Varius, whose face was, for the first few seconds, turned away, glaring at nothing, as if there were nothing here he could bear to see. He glanced up at Marcus at last and, oddly, smiled – a terse little greeting. Both he and Una looked as if they considered themselves somehow responsible.

Mechanically, absurdly, returning Varius' flinch of a smile, Marcus took a short step backwards, not so much backing away as keeping his balance, wishing he could at least think of something to say. He looked around at the glassy roofs of the Palace, anticipating the Nionians and Sinoans seeing this, and felt scorched with humiliation at being exposed as the charlatan or child he'd been all along. As if that mattered compared to the risk to the peace. And then – Una, Varius? He couldn't construct an appropriate hierarchy of fear.

The centurion at the head of the squadron announced calmly, 'You are to return to Rome, sir.'

'These are my uncle's orders?' asked Marcus, evenly enough, although he found he could not get much strength into his voice.

'They are, sir.'

Marcus felt more shock flutter across his face before he could control it. Half of him had thought there must have been a coup, and that his

242

uncle was dead. 'It will take time to explain to our hosts, and to the Nionians.'

'That's not possible, I'm afraid, sir.'

'I can hardly just – leave without a word,' said Marcus, forcing his voice to an almost unnatural slowness to disguise the desperation in it. 'The Sinoans and Nionians have been working with us to prevent the most destructive war any Empire has yet seen. The Emperor *must* see that, however ... disappointed he is in me.'

'We're neither of us in a position to tell the Emperor what he must or must not do,' observed the centurion levelly, and the other men did not quite laugh, but a curt, amused rustle of breath flickered across them. Two short files of men strode tidily up the steps to where Marcus stood, flanking him.

'You're arresting me, then?' Marcus heard himself say.

'I hope not, sir,' said the centurion philosophically. 'Not *you*.'

Marcus demanded finally, '*Why?*'

'You'll be told more when you come with us, sir,' the man answered.

Marcus walked silently down the steps into the midst of them, feeling the straight-backed, defiant posture his body assumed of its own accord to be at once ridiculous and the only possibility.

He wanted to keep his eyes on the others, to communicate at least by expression, but the men reorganised themselves so that somewhere behind them Una and Varius were hidden in their ranks. The soldiers marched them efficiently through the pavilions and gardens, and Marcus strained to see the reaction of the Sinoan guards, wondering sickly what they knew, what the Empress had agreed to. Plainly the Nionians at least knew nothing, for he saw Kato appear from one of the halls among his own bodyguards and retainers, and stand shading his eyes to watch, concerned and intrigued. Marcus looked at the other man blankly, unable to let his face explain anything.

Kato frowned as the young Roman prince walked away in the centre of an excessive escort of guards, far more than Kato had seen gathered around him before. 'What is this? Where is he going all of a sudden?'

'I am not sure he's leaving willingly, Lord,' said Sohaku, who had fetched him to see this.

'Isn't he, now?' cried Kato, with a start of curiosity, his face lighting up as if this were wonderful news, although he was, in fact keenly but neutrally excited. 'Then who is forcing him to go, and for what reason, and why don't you have the answers already?'

'Lord, I have tried, but I will have to find one of the interpreters if you wish to press them to explain. Plainly I have forgotten all but the basics of Sinoan and my Latin was always pitiful. Forgive me. But I believe that in any case, both parties were trying to keep the truth from me; I think the most anyone was willing to say was that it is an internal Roman matter which we should disregard.'

'Well, we'll find out for ourselves, won't we?' Kato said with the odd fusion of command and collusive playfulness for which they loved him.

He set off briskly after the detail of troops and his retainers followed. Entrenched in their orders as Kato had expected, the Roman soldiers ignored them.

They came to the great courtyard at the front of the Palace compound. The red gates stood open and Bian glittered frostily beyond. Bronze standards rose within like a field of rigid sunflowers: the upright Roman hand in the circle of laurel, the Eagle. Surely there were at least a hundred Roman soldiers, ranked on the cobbles in two, hard-edged squares and between them, before the heavy, six-wheeled Roman cars, a wide silk carpet from Persia or India had been unrolled, and upon it stood Drusus, all in white. He turned his face towards his cousin, but looked at him almost as if without recognition, although he smiled.

Marcus stopped as if he had struck a wall, too furious and shocked to notice that the troops around him stopped also as if he had been leading them, rather than being transported as if a passenger among them. They had been instructed, in fact, to maintain some distance between the cousins. As the group halted, Drusus' eyes swept across them, and Una, breathing hard, knowing he was looking for her, forced her face and body to obey her so that when he saw her he would see her looking as indifferent and contemptuous of him as when he had seen her last.

A herald swaggered out across the no man's land between them, carrying a stiff, red-edged sheet of paper, rather like the script Marcus had been given at his investiture. As it was placed into Marcus' numb hands and he began to read, Varius was taken over by a temptation so vivid as to be almost an hallucination – of somehow seizing the weapon of the nearest soldier and trying to kill Drusus. He knew too well that it would be impossible even to fantasise success, and yet it seemed to flash instantly through all his nerves, sharpening his eyesight, readying his hands, and he had time to ask himself with alarmed, distant wonder, if he could really be going to do it ...?

And then, as if the impulse had escaped his flesh and travelled beyond him, cut free and devilish in the live air, he heard a triple crack of gunfire. And the next thing he saw was Marcus, felled to the ground under a heap of soldiers, before he too was dragged down.

XIV

MOON GATE

There was another spluttering of gunshots, closer this time, from somewhere on the ground – the first round seemed to have come from above. And then more, and a sense of people running, both nearby, as a number of the soldiers chased forward, and further away, a more scattering flight. But Varius scarcely paid attention to any of it. At once he dragged himself free and onto his feet, and began ploughing through the now-disordered mass of soldiers to where he'd seen Marcus fall, relentless, frantic. *No*, not Marcus, not after everything ...

But Marcus was rising from the ground, shoulders hunched over something, doggedly ignoring the soldiers' attempts to shield him or herd him away. He did not even look round to see what was happening; he seemed oblivious to everything except what he was doing, which was methodically tearing the letter he had been given into fragments.

Bruised with relief, Varius made nothing of that. His attention, which had been fixed totally upon Marcus, expanded slightly; ahead he saw Drusus, bundled back towards the cars in a scrum of soldiers. And the developing turmoil around them came into sudden focus: the Roman soldiers and the Sinoan guards were shooting back at the ramparts, at whoever had been firing down into the courtyard. And two or three Nionians – where had they come from? – rushed past towards the gatehouse, enraged, although charging across the open court they seemed desperately vulnerable. Soldiers from all three Empires apparently fighting one enemy, then, but not united, not remotely. Varius heard an ugly uproar of uncomprehending fury and distrust as the different factions converged at the base of the steps, shouting at each other in their separate languages, weapons raised, each incensed by the shots the others had fired already. Varius looked on, teeth clenching in anticipatory horror, ready to see them break into three-sided battle right there inside the high Sinoan walls.

Marcus scattered the flakes of paper and turned to Varius with a startling look of harsh decision, almost as if he'd expected to see him there. But then his gaze slid past to something behind and his face, which already looked dried out and bone pale, blanched further. Varius turned his head to follow the look: a Roman officer who seemed to have been wounded in the shoulder was being dragged away from the corner of the broken formation. And beyond that, half screened by the Nionian retainers as if they could still protect him, someone lay, face down on the cobbles. Except that there was no face left; the corpse was truncated at the neck in a collapsed wet mess of powdery blood from which Varius' eyes instinctively skitted away, before deliberately he looked again to recognise the body – from the clothes and the behaviour of the retainers – as Kato.

'Come on,' Marcus said to him, suddenly close, lunging past him towards Una and seizing her hand. She too was unhurt, although she had been staring numbly at Kato's body and she moved stiffly when Marcus touched her. Varius wondered with an abrupt jab of pain what it was like for her when someone died close by. Marcus put his hand briefly to her face, a rough caress, and she mechanically brushed his fingers with hers, but then seemed to retract very slightly, looking at him with something almost like distrust.

Marcus turned towards the remaining mass of soldiers, steering Una in front of him, and barked, 'Well, are you going to stand and let us be shot? Get us away from this!' And he began striding urgently back the way they'd come, towards the shelter of the red-pillared colonnade. Already, Varius had realised how Marcus was taking advantage of the confusion to group the three of them together, but he saw now, without understanding why, that he had also managed to position himself between them and the main body of the squadron. Except that he kept Una and Varius ahead of him, he was once again in the lead, almost outstripping the troops around them.

More Nionian soldiers hurtled past into the courtyard. The retainers must have alerted them to what had happened.

They reached the colonnade, but Marcus' pace did not slow, and he said quietly, 'Come on, keep going.'

At first, Varius was too relieved at even attempting to separate themselves from the troops to resist, but Una hissed unhappily, 'No. Marcus,' she had begun to hang back; Marcus was almost dragging her along now.

Uneasily Varius said, 'They're not going to let us go any further.' The closest soldiers continued to follow, not quite chasing yet, but trying to confine and head off their movement, like sheepdogs.

'Oh, I think they've got him,' remarked Marcus in an odd, light voice, ignoring them both, looking back over his shoulder at the ramparts, where he thought he'd seen something falling.

Varius demanded, 'What are you doing?'

'Leaving you here,' said Marcus, in an undertone.

'*No*, you're not. I'm staying with you,' cried Una through gritted teeth.

Varius said, in indignation, 'Do we have any choice in this?'

'No,' Marcus answered them both, shortly.

Varius stopped walking, as much with angry shock as obstinacy. 'I won't let you take these decisions from us. If we choose to go with you we will. We're not your slaves, Marcus.'

'*Varius!*' For a moment Una thought Marcus was going to hit him. He did go as far as shoving Varius a little way, saying with restrained, rapid violence, 'That letter. Drusus is taking my place here. I don't know how he did it but he has. He had to make my uncle think the worst of me somehow and plainly it was easier to do it through you. So you are both criminals and traitors, and I'm – I don't know, a pawn, I'm the puppet whose strings you've been pulling. We're meant to go back to Rome, in *his* power, to answer for it. They're taking me, I can't stop it. But I'll be safer there than you will. Whatever the Emperor's been told I don't think he's going to let anyone torture me or kill me, but it can happen to you.'

Varius had automatically taken a breath to speak, and found he could not.

Marcus turned away from him and looked at Una, his voice cracking when he spoke to her. 'And you'd never get there. I know you wouldn't. You know he'll find a way of killing you if he can.'

'And you?' she said, shivering, barely more than a croak. 'He has no interest in killing you?'

One of the soldiers called out in warning, before Marcus could find an answer, 'Sir, you're safe here. Don't go any further.' And they were closing in more purposefully now.

'Come on, faster,' urged Marcus, driving them forward up the white steps to an octagonal inner gate. The soldier in the lead reached to pull him back. Marcus shrugged off the hand as it touched him, turned seamlessly and punched the man in the face, so that the Imperial ring split his lip and he fell, overbalancing down the steps, back against the troops behind. Marcus stood snarling down at them, unrecognisable, the bloody fist that wore the ring still raised, shouting with unhesitating savagery, '*I still wear this, I am still Caesar; touch me again and I will have you crucified!*'

The man staggered, blood coursing from his nose and mouth, and

247

the rest stalled and hesitated, uncertain. Marcus wiped his hand and added, curtly, 'I will come with you as soon as I can.' And he turned and muttered to Una and Varius, who were both gazing at him, blinking, stunned, 'That's not going to work for very long.'

Without truly feeling that they had consented to what was happening, neither Una nor Varius protested any longer. They moved on with hurried wretchedness through the moon gate, along the path where Marcus had walked with Tadahito just at the point of breaking into a run. Marcus was afraid to look too much as if they were in flight. And Varius realised with an inward tremor of understanding that they were heading for the Nionians' guest quarters, from which, at their approach, a floe of armed men erupted down the steps, weapons rearing and pointing them out like a host of accusatory fingers. Varius and Una could not help but flinch backwards at the sight, but Marcus came to a halt letting out a sigh of strange relief. He raised his hands appeasingly, saying in loud, commanding Nionian which Varius hated not being able to understand, 'I must speak with your prince, now.'

'Murderers!' cried out one of the warriors, fiercely, and Varius and Una could both guess what that must mean: they saw doubt flicker for a moment across Marcus' pale face, before he looked back towards the gate through which, soon, the Romans would appear, and it vanished.

'There are only three of us, we're unarmed. If we make a move you don't like, shoot us. Search us if you have to, but be quick. I need to make him an offer and in another minute it will be too late.'

There was an undecided movement within the group, and then the first row moved forward towards them, weapons levelled, the tips inches from their chests and faces. But behind, one of them had vanished back inside the building.

Seconds creaked by excruciatingly. Marcus could barely refrain from shouting in impatience and rage, and only the fear of provoking the men to shoot kept him still; all his muscles were in an agony of unuseable energy.

Then Tadahito appeared behind his soldiers, at the top of the steps, looking haggard and aghast. He said, 'What have you done?'

Marcus swallowed. He hadn't been prepared for this apparent depth of conviction that he must be responsible for Kato's death; and it meant that the danger to Varius and Una was worse. 'Not this,' he replied. 'Not Lord Kato's murder.'

'The assassin was a Roman. A European, that is. What part of Europe is not under Roman rule?'

Marcus gazed at him rigidly, clamping back the moan of despair that rose in his throat. It was too late to go back, and he was sure in any case that there was no other chance. He answered, 'Whoever he was, I had no connection with him. If I had, I wouldn't do what I'm about to now.' Ahead of him, Una and Varius glanced at each other, tense and humiliated, trapped into an odd, shame-faced solidarity. Marcus said, 'These are – these are the people I trust most. Take them into your custody, send them to Nionia if you want. But only on condition that I have your word no Roman has any access to them until I return.'

Tadahito just stared back at him, bewildered and horrified and worn out. Finally he said with tired patience, trying to sort one strand of information from another, 'You are leaving?'

'I've got no choice,' said Marcus, with as much straightforward confidence as he could. 'I want them to stay in my place.'

'Your place is not with us,' observed Tadahito, dispassionately.

'*They* will explain as much as I can, if you accept. But you don't have much time to decide. After the explosions in Rome, you moved your troops back from the Wall to convince me that Nionia was not responsible. I took your word then. This is the same.'

'So they remain as hostages against your sincerity?'

Marcus shuddered and his eyes closed involuntarily before he could mutter, scarcely audibly, 'Yes.' He felt authority and certainty draining away from him like blood, leaving him cold. 'But only ... mine. I can't ... answer for Rome, at the present moment. Just ... don't harm them. You have no need to.'

Tadahito said nothing.

'Marcus,' appealed Varius desperately, unable to stand there any longer, passive as a token on a board while they bargained over him in a language he didn't know. 'If you must do this, ask for asylum too. Don't put yourself in Drusus' hands alone. You could speak to the Emperor from here, surely.' He had to say this, but he knew Marcus' answer before he gave it.

'I *can't*. Drusus would look right; it would look like treason. If you're here maybe you can keep it all from collapsing, I don't know. But if I seem to change sides and if they refuse to hand me back, it triggers war *now*. And I would give up any chance of being Emperor, of stopping this.'

'If your cousin kills you you'll lose that too,' said Una, turning her back on the guns to face him, and her face looked to him like one drawn in charcoal on white paper, the colour seeming to have gone even from her eyes, so that they looked like wells of appalled black against her skin.

Marcus lowered his eyes to the ground. 'I don't think he can. It would prove he'd been guilty all along.'

'Do you know he's that rational? Or that the Emperor has enough control over him for it to matter?'

Marcus looked at her again silently, his face twisted into a kind of anguished plea, as if for forgiveness for having no answer. And behind him, at the far end of the path she could see the Roman soldiers in their dark red uniforms heading grimly towards the moon gate.

'What is all this?' asked Tadahito impatiently. 'Why should your life be in danger? This seems less like a gesture of good faith and more like a request for help. Or else you have staged it for some other reason.'

'Whatever you believe, it must be an advantage to you, having them,' Marcus pressed, forcefully again, hearing the footfalls of the Roman soldiers growing louder behind him, refusing to turn to look. 'You can't lose anything by it.'

Tadahito sighed, looking at the sky. Then, instead of answering Marcus he gestured to his men and said mildly, 'Well, then, take them.'

The men stepped forward and pulled Una and Varius into their midst, gripping their arms and hauling them back, closing in front of them so that Marcus could no longer have reached them. As if they had had no warning at all, all three of them gasped with the shock of it. Varius felt his body jolt with reflex protest at being held still, his blood suddenly seeming to scrape against the inside of his veins as if full of crystals of ice.

Standing on the pavement below, they saw Marcus sag as if winded. He raised his voice to plead, 'I have your *promise* you won't let the Romans have them?' The request sounded thin and helpless to him. He realised that somehow, despite the urgency, he had not expected it would be so abrupt. He had not even kissed Una, or held her, and now she was straining against the guards to keep her face turned towards him, and tears had finally been jarred from her eyes when the men touched her.

'Yes,' said Tadahito, flatly, turning away and entering the building once more.

Una called to Marcus, 'If you can't come back – if I never see you again ...'

Marcus opened his mouth to assure her blindly, I *will* come back. But as he looked at her the words seemed to crumple, and he knew he would be cheating her if he spoke them, that it was cowardly to try and palm off a hope as a certainty. He met her eyes and told her instead, although he hardly knew what he was going to say until he heard it, 'Then – I don't know what you'll do. But I know you won't waste your life. You mustn't. You matter too much, you *are* too much. And not only to me.'

Una felt her lips move, as if she were answering, but she seemed to have no air to get out a sound. 'I ...' she breathed painfully, as they drew her back like a tide, too quietly for him to hear her, even if she'd managed, in time, to say 'I love you'.

At the top of the steps Varius braced himself for a second against the propelling mass, resisting long enough to look back and say, with willed calmness, 'Goodbye, Marcus.'

Marcus gazed up at him speechlessly and, in Varius' last sight of him as the Roman soldiers advanced, before he himself was jostled inside, he looked totally horrified.

Marcus stared at the empty doorway and drew the back of his hand across his eyes. He turned to the Roman officers and told them bluntly, 'I'm all you're getting. Let's go.'

But he had no more power left, of course, and they must know it too; he could not manage more than the shabbiest imitation of it now. He ducked his head when, finally, the soldiers accepted what had happened and began to march, because more appalled tears simmered blindingly in his eyes. He could not keep them in check; there were too many.

The reasons for the decision remained, it was not really that he had changed his mind: surely it could not have been better to let them come with him back to Rome. And yet he still felt devastated by what he'd done. He'd meant to protect them, and perhaps he had; but what did the intention matter if what he'd actually committed was utter betrayal? And he had taken the risk knowingly. If Kato's assassin was indeed Roman, if they suspected Una and Varius knew and were withholding anything – oh, in the gods' name what had he given them up to? Were the Nionians any gentler than the Romans?

They came to the courtyard again. A cloak, or something, had been draped over Kato's body, but it still lay there, with one of his men sitting cross-legged and straight-backed beside it, his head lowered. The memory of the Nionian princess floated past Marcus, like something unreal – was it really true that only minutes before he'd been hearing he was supposed to marry her? He couldn't believe it.

The worst of the conflict seemed to have subsided, but Marcus could not summon any curiosity about what had happened. It seemed the tiniest mercy that Drusus was nowhere in sight, his Praetorians, presumably, were not yet confident it was safe enough. So at least Drusus was not going to see him in this defeated state. When the shots had sounded and they had both been slammed down, Marcus was sure that under the defensive heap of the guards' bodies, he'd seen his cousin looking back at him along the ground, fixed, elated, despite the violence around them, in the air.

251

And so he'd decided what to do. Yet he was leaving Una in the same city as Drusus, as if the fact that he'd turned her over to Rome's enemy were not enough.

It was at this point that Marcus noticed that he had been promising himself, quite unthinkingly, that if he did regain power after this, and if he found that the Nionians had laid a finger on her or on Varius, he would have Salvius stamp Cynoto out of existence, bomb it into mud. He recoiled from himself with a start of alarmed amazement. How was this unfamiliar self qualified to judge what was safe for anyone?

He let the soldiers lead him to a car. His overloaded brain spared him any images of Una and Varius and the worst happening to them. But the facts banged there like a concussion, or a splinter of fractured bone lodged in tissue – something that should, at the least, have caused unconsciousness, for which Marcus would almost have been grateful.

XV

LADY WITHOUT SORROWS

'Her Imperial Majesty says, "Who knows why the Nionians do any-thing?"' the interpreter informed Drusus gravely, after the loathsome old woman finished speaking. Drusus tried not to scowl in frustration. Junosena sat perched on her broad, yellow throne, encased in a sarcoph-agus of jewelled clothes like a horrible mummified doll. A fine gauze curtain hung between them, which – although it scarcely obscured her at all, along with the fact that the conversation had to be further sieved through the interpreter – kept giving Drusus the dangerous illusion that she was not really there, that he was talking invisibly into a longdictor, and that she was somehow unable to see him.

He said, 'They are Roman citizens. Well, the man is a citizen. In any case they are both Romans, they belong to Rome and Rome requires them. The Nionians must give them over.'

Junosena launched into a headlong, impassioned diatribe under which the interpreter flinched and stammered out hurriedly, 'The Empress says you seem to be under a misapprehension that Sina is somehow a province of the Nionian Empire. You have mistaken the Grand Empress for a Nionian servant. She says, "Not in my lifetime."'

'Yes, yes,' said Drusus impatiently. 'I intended no such insult, as I am sure you are aware. If the Nionians would respond reasonably I wouldn't have to trouble you. But the two ... suspects are still in Bian, in your palace. They cannot be more than a few hundred yards away at this moment. The Nionians are your guests and their custody of these people is completely illegitimate. They must be compelled to hand them back.'

The residue of his earlier exhilaration still remained in him, brush-ing against the inside of his skin, still gently electrifying, but he was growing badly worried, too. The Nionians had retreated into austere, sad intransigence, shut up in their quarters apparently mourning Lord Kato, and in their sparse answers to his demands would only express

253

bleak incredulity that the Romans could freely offer two hostages one moment and call for their return the next.

Jun Shen kicked her little feet irritably against her throne. 'I am not in any mood for this,' she commented crossly. 'I thought I was receiving another Roman prince and his escort, now instead I have a small army rioting in my palace, the bodies of some of my guests are defiling my courtyard, and others have been – disappeared.'

'The term "prince", is not really appropriate, to Romans,' remarked Drusus, but Weigi, the interpreter, left this diplomatically untranslated. Jun Shen waited, listening and watching and thinking how dissonant and uncouth a language Latin was, as the young man continued talking.

'He sympathises, Your Majesty,' Weigi told her, finally. 'But he points out that he has just been the victim of an attempt on his life. That this is not a situation either you or he would have expected or wished for.'

Jun Shen raised her eyebrows and leant forward a little. 'You think the Nionian lord was killed by *mistake*?'

Drusus listened to the translation and replied, 'Of course.'

'What a very bad shot the murderer must have been, in that case.'

'One of our soldiers was wounded,' Drusus reminded her, unperturbed. 'I have been very fortunate.'

Jun Shen sat and contemplated him for a while through the gauze that separated the private female province to which she still theoretically belonged, from the open, masculine world. 'Yes,' she agreed at last, musingly. 'You seem to have assumed all Novius Leo's power, you survive an assassination attempt unscathed, while one of Nionia's principal warlords is killed. You have been *very* fortunate. Although some might consider it a misfortune that your good luck in other things should provoke a war. But perhaps others would not.'

Drusus let his eyes rest lightly on the surface of the curtain that separated them as he considered how to respond. 'Either war or peace will be an opportunity to serve my country,' he said evenly.

The Empress pursed clotted scarlet lips. 'Some opportunities become less attractive when you get to my age,' she grunted, rather morosely, although she maintained her narrow-eyed watch on Drusus. 'There is a great deal most of us cannot attain without time and experience – for example, *rank unpopularity*. Yet here you are, so new to public life, and you say your own people already follow you halfway across the world to try and shoot you. A sad thing, for someone so young. Although I would still rather be you than the Nionian gentleman who bumbles into the way.'

'It depends what you mean by our people,' said Drusus, doing his best not to be provoked by any of this. 'Are you aware of how many

Roman outlaws and slaves have settled illegally in the East over the last decade, most of them in your country? They obviously consider it a soft touch.'

'Of *course* I am aware of it!' Jun Shen bounced a little on her seat, needled. The fringe of gold and coral flowers on her swan-shaped coiffure jingled, and a rich gust of perfume welled from her. 'Nothing happens in Sina that I am not aware of!'

'Yet you tolerate them.'

'If Rome cannot be bothered to keep track of its own, it cannot expect me to do the job for it. As for the immigrants, they've always seemed harmless, and some of them are useful. Well, there they are. What have they got against you?'

'Plainly they are *not* harmless. And this is not a pleasant matter to discuss with an outsider, but you know already that it is not due to concern for the safety of either Varius or the freedwoman Una that I cannot tolerate the Nionians' detention of them. These people have been a dangerous and corrupting influence on my cousin Novius Leo, and they have sought, shall we say, to have me *removed* in the past. This is why we did not wish them to know of my arrival in advance. However, they had agents and allies in the palace, and it would seem we have not been successful in uncovering all of them.'

This was almost true. Sulien had vanished too thoroughly not to have been alerted by someone, and he knew now who it must have been. He and Salvius had constructed a morass of restrictions on communications at the Palace, to prevent anyone from warning Marcus. Finally, but too late, Makaria had managed to dodge through them: in Marcus' rooms, Drusus' men had just found the frantic longscript message she had succeeded in transmitting, an hour after Drusus' arrival in Bian. Drusus was not yet certain how to act on this. As long as Faustus lived, there would be a limit to what he could do about her.

'The girl, at least, must have been warned and taken steps. To protect herself. And she and Varius have longstanding criminal connections, which she must have made use of. A gang of fanatics and murderers who used to be based in the Pyrenees, who are, it seems, now among the illegal Roman presence in Sina.' He gestured and an attendant slave came forward to hand Lal's crumpled letter to the one of the silent eunuchs. 'A letter to her from one of them.'

'Oh, I have seen it,' said the Empress, dismissively, waving it away. 'I had it translated last night. I was interested to know that Novius Leo's concubine was from such a humble background, otherwise there didn't seem much to it. Doesn't the Persian girl specifically mention that she has *not* been in contact with the other young woman?'

255

'Yes she does, and all the more reason to believe the reverse is true. And it may contain any number of hidden messages we don't know how to read,' said Drusus, steadily.

Jun Shen kicked her feet and huffed again, but less violently than before, thinking. Then her bloody little mouth twisted into a smile. Drusus thought it looked horrific. She said, in unprecedently sweet tones, 'If you are telling me that either this man or this young woman was involved in Lord Kato's death, you can hardly be surprised that the Nionians are unwilling to give them up.'

Drusus glanced away, reminding himself of how much, against what odds, he had achieved already, to prevent his face convulsing with anger. He looked directly at the timorous interpreter for the first time and said curtly, 'This is important. Shouldn't Emperor Florens be dealing with this?'

There was a scandalised pause. A few of the eunuchs standing mutely about the room evidently knew enough Latin for this to make them catch their breath in alarm. 'The Grand Empress has spared the Son of Heaven ... the *distractions* of worldly government ever since he was a child,' the interpreter hissed in pained, weak horror. 'She allows him to dedicate his energy to ... spiritual exertion. To tending the higher welfare of the country.'

'Fine,' said Drusus irritably. Power-grabbing old hag, he thought, eyeing Junosena. After a moment's speculation he had guessed, accurately, that 'spiritual exertion' meant playing among the wives and concubines, who were apparently practically infinite in number. The word "decadence" sounded clearly in Drusus' mind.

Jun Shen had watched this exchange and scowled and clucked and sighed. 'I suppose he dislikes dealing with a woman?' she inquired jadedly, swinging her head cynically towards Weigi and lolling a little as she sat.

'No, no, Your Majesty—'

But the Empress had uttered a bored, loud groan, and was already ignoring Weigi again, talking fast, straight at the foreigner as if he could understand. 'Now listen to me,' she said. 'Rome and Sina may not be enemies. And absence of hostility may be as close to friendship as can exist between two Empires. We can both see that if your cousin had handed these people over to me, and if you told me that did not represent Rome's wishes, I suppose I would have had to give them up. He must have known that when he made his choice. An enemy does not have such obligations. But *my* obligations only go a certain way. You are not in the Roman Empire here, any more than the Nionian. The Nionians are my guests, as you say. So are you. And while they are here, so long as they break none of *my* laws, I will not interfere with theirs. What becomes of these two people is a matter for you and them. This much concerns me: a man has been murdered, in my country, in *my* palace. I do not sit and ignore such things. The killer appears to be Roman, whatever we consider that term to mean. You wish me to believe he was nothing to do with you, I am sure your cousin Novius Leo would say the same thing. Well then, *my* police will investigate him. If immigrants were involved, *we* will deal with it. You may be right in this much, we may have been too lenient to them. But they are *my* business now.' She gestured at Lal's letter, still held by a nervous eunuch. 'As the girl says, they are not Roman citizens, are they?'

She had anticipated Drusus' next demand, which was that the fugitives, particularly the girl and her father and the Sinoan woman Ziye, must be delivered into Roman hands. From the moment of reading the letter he had seen what use he might, in a pinch, make of them, that they could almost take the place of Una and Varius, should he really be unable to retrieve them. It was true – they were not citizens, they had no rights. Anything could be done to them, quite openly. No bending or dodging of the law would even be necessary, in order to force the kind of statement he needed out of them.

Yet he sensed the uselessness, for the moment at least, of pushing the old bitch to do anything she was set against. So he said only, courteously, 'Well, I am sure we will discuss individual cases, when it comes to that.'

Drusus left the audience hall, and from the steps outside, he looked out at Bian. He had never been out of the Roman Empire before, and every second he stood on Sinoan ground an unclear sense of something jarring and wrong seemed to palpitate in the warm air. Of course, it was primarily the profound difference of this small, low-lying, enamelled city, with its dragons on the glassy roofs and its slightly built, uniformly black-haired inhabitants. And yet, in a strange way, it was also that it was not alien enough; that despite the green bamboo woods, despite the huge, brown, sky-brimming flood of the Yellow River outside the city, some of the countryside he'd travelled through had not looked so different from wet flat European fields, or stark moorlands. It was that the sunlight made no acknowledging change in itself when it touched this subtly unacceptable place. It prompted a kind of bone-deep incredulity that all this vast land could *be*, and not be Roman.

He ordered the slave to fetch his car, and sat leaning back against the seat's smooth back, across which the eagle spread its gold wings. He looked out at the square, satiny lake scrolling past, as the car crossed the flat white bridge. Through the Roman glass of his window, the city was more palatable, more meekly interesting: Drusus could watch it with touristic curiosity, remote and yet faintly proprietary.

In front and behind, of course, defensive Praetorian cars enclosed his own. But inside, sitting uneasily opposite him in response to his summons, was the centurion who'd apprehended Marcus and the others.

At length he said, 'May I ask where we're going, Your Highness?'

'Nowhere. We are seeing the sights,' said Drusus companionably. He had wanted to get out of the Palace, and also it had seemed to him that the instructions he needed to give would be safer in the privacy of a moving car, away from any listening devices or human spies.

The quietness of the broad, beautiful streets seemed bizarre to Drusus considering that this was an Imperial capital – there was hardly more traffic than in a Roman market town. And what orderly Sinoan cars there were were not quite the same as those of the Roman Empire. Despite the problems it caused, Romans liked to travel in belligerent, implacable-looking behemoths, spacious within and seemingly capable of bulldozing over anything outside. Here they were smaller, lower, some mere dark, glossy little capsules made to hold one person, bearing discreet emblems on their narrow flanks – a bear, a mandarin duck. The larger ones tapered to a single, central driver's cab, which would sometimes be open to the sky, exposing the liveried servant's head and shoulders while the passengers were sealed behind, invisible within red silk curtains. But what was most striking to Drusus was how many were identical. In Rome, only the cars of the Praetorians or vigiles, and the fleets run by a few businesses, looked the same. The richest and most aristocratic families ordered their cars bespoke, but even those Romans who bought the ready-made vehicles produced in runs of a few hundred or had to make do with second-hand, would usually have their vehicles personalised out of recognition: – emblazoned with the family insignia or an imitation of one, decked with stylised leaves, lotuses, friezes of struggling gods – or at the least a few plain respectable studs or roundlets. The designs might even be painted on, if plated brass or nickel was unaffordable, sometimes with trompe l'oeil effects destined to be sneered at by the sophisticated. But you would never see two cars alike in the same street. Here in Bian the same crests, colours and substances kept repeating: jade, polished horn, crystal; a crane, a pheasant, a lion. Drusus did not know anything about Sina's official class, or the labyrinthine civil service and the grades within it, but he guessed that the cars reflected some system of rank more rigid and institutionalised than mere degrees of wealth.

He said, in no less friendly tones, 'Two people, whose interrogation was required by the Emperor himself, somehow passed from your custody into the Nionians'. In itself that merits flogging at the least.'

'The men responsible—' began the centurion.

'*You* were responsible,' corrected Drusus, blandly. 'And I was speaking only of what Rome has lost. When one considers also what the Nionians may have gained, what secrets they may be able to get out of these people, how they might use them when the war begins – then this failure approaches the level of treason. The firing squad at best. Or the beasts in the arena.'

There was silence. Drusus let it last a long time.

'Still,' he said at last, briskly: 'One thing at a time. We may get them back without too much harm done. And as for the questions we need answered, it may be possible to acquire the same information by other means.' He scanned Lal's letter again. 'Look how many numbers there are in this,' he said. 'Six, three, a set of three twos, seventeen … And it goes on. I'm no expert, but that seems more than coincidence, doesn't it?' He handed it over.

The centurion studied it. To his credit he hadn't allowed any fear or any relief to show on his face before and the only sign of it now was a slight thickness in his voice. 'Perhaps – when she says that about counting the letters – it means look for the numbers in this one.'

Drusus had already felt how the gravitational pull of power that he had witnessed at work around Marcus was now benefiting him, how much quicker people were to agree with him, to approve – quite sincerely and spontaneously – of what he said. Drusus smiled a little to himself, barely daring to let himself enjoy this or take strength from it, like the first mouthful of desperately needed water from a bottle that might prove to hold no more. He could see that among the delegates in Rome he would be able to find those who would say, and believe, that they had never trusted Marcus, that they'd always seen something was wrong about Una's influence on him, or Varius', or that they'd suspected Sulien's motives towards Faustus. But that would not be enough. Things were so much more fragile, so much more complicated, than he had believed they would be when he came here.

Still, more than usually able to see the contrast between something he had said and the likely external truth, he was slightly diverted by this invention of his about the letter. He even felt a sort of distant pity for Lal for having written something that lent itself so readily to his needs. He said levelly, 'She must be made to tell us what it means.'

'I see.'

Drusus looked silently out of the window at the strange copper-green tower rising above the low city. He felt himself at the centre of complex orbits, people revolving like planets about him at different distances and speeds, exerting and suffering different degrees of force. How was it possible that Una and Varius could be passing out of his reach? Still he could feel his own pull on them, how his strength negated theirs. Despite Varius' humiliation of him in the palace cell, Drusus had no particular desire for revenge on him, not for its own sake. The incident was just too unbearable to be recalled, and Drusus had nearly succeeded in wiping it from his mind. It might almost have been forgiveness. If Varius had actually been under his control now, Drusus might have thought over what had happened to him between Gabinius and Tulliola the autumn of three years ago, at least to take notice of what had been learnt. As it was, he did not. Varius was just a tipping ground for necessary blame, a tool for levering the ring off Marcus' finger. Lost, for the moment.

But Una. It was hard for Drusus to determine exactly what he wanted to happen to her, and in what order. Certainly *someone* must be made to admit a crooked influence on Marcus, to say something that disqualified him once and for all. Once that was said, Drusus was confident it would be useless for Marcus or anyone else to complain of how it had been extracted: it could not be unsaid, it would fit, it would be believed. And such a confession from Una would surely be more valuable than from anyone else. But she was so strange. The capacities on her side were so unknowable – demonic. Sometimes he warned himself that to get any advantage from her more than her death was a luxury he shouldn't rely on. That however he had to explain it, whatever the risks of not bringing her back to Rome, they were less than hanging onto her a second longer than he had to.

All that left aside the ebbs and flows of what he wanted to do. Sometimes he wanted her utterly ruined, reduced to a rag of shame and pain, whether privately shredded into bloody rubbish and thrown away, or publicly picked bare in some Forum, taught a long and unrelenting lesson for the people to witness. And at calmer moments, a little alarmed by this, he felt he needed no such immoderation, he would not mind if it were instantaneous and painless, so long as it happened, and so long as he was there to watch it.

He had to keep his mind off her, for now, anyway. There were these others, the people in the other girl's letter. They were still small and far off, they still didn't know that he was thinking about them, how they were falling towards him.

He looked at the centurion. 'The old woman in there is being obstructive. She's likely to round them all up on a whim and then we'll never get them out of her. So you must make sure you find them before the Sinoans do.'

The man nodded slowly, but said, 'If we can't move openly . . . it won't be easy. We're all plainly Roman, sir.'

Drusus flicked a hand impatiently. 'Can't you think for yourself? Travel in one of those cars behind those curtains. Yes, obviously you will need Sinoan help. Find it. Pay off whomever you need to. Money is no object. As much as it takes.' Here again he left a pause. Then lightly, as if it were a different subject, he said, 'My cousin is returning to Rome to give up the ring of office, and ask my uncle's forgiveness. You understand what that means?'

The man's body appeared to relax just a little – though not really with rest or peace – into a restrained, understated slump of resignation. He murmured, still looking Drusus in the face, steadily, 'I think so, sir.'

'He could be there within three days. But then, on such a long stretch of magnetway, there could be delays – accidents. My uncle is ill. To tell you the truth I don't think he'll live long. I think it would be better if he were spared the strain of seeing my cousin.'

There was again a silence, but shorter this time. The centurion asked quietly, 'For how long?'

Drusus flexed his hands in his lap, as if he were loosening an ache from them. He could see his cousin, powerless among the soldiers in a car like this one, carried away north, on the magnetway through the floodplains and desert, the crowding mountains, west out of Sina, and into the Sarmatian grasslands. He could see him speeding helplessly mile after cold mile into the steppe, so desolate and so endless, that it almost seemed possible he might simply ride on perpetually, through the dust, until he thinned out of memory and out of being.

Drusus could kill him. The bare clarity of the thought, as it returned to him over and over, was not welcome. There it was. The tiny expenditure of breath, of muscular effort in speaking a word – how totally unchanged it would leave him! And it would take even less than a word. He felt, as a kind of tension on his face, how just a movement of the head would do it now, how by just turning his eyes back to meet the centurion's in a certain way, he could have Marcus gone, flicked off like a switch. His uncle had given him too much power already to retract any of it – too much to save himself from being killed too. The Senate would roll over as limp as a sickly whore. Drusus could declare himself Emperor within a week.

And he would die, almost as soon as the ring was on his finger and the wreath on his head. Salvius loomed, like Jupiter, the largest of the planets. He was the one the army would follow. The power that held Drusus up now was his, really. And at the same time, unknowingly, he was lending a crucial fraction of the same strength to Faustus and to

261

Marcus. For the second he thought he had been deceived, that the rules he thought were in play had been broken, there would be nothing left to hold him back. He would storm inwards, enraged, as an avenger, sweep over Drusus, like a wave overrunning the flood defences of a town, and charge on righteously into power himself. Emperor Salvius.

Drusus let out an inaudible breath. 'Until further notice,' he answered the centurion, and added softly, 'I will have more instructions concerning him soon.'

Emperor Salvius. Emperor Salvius. Drusus repeated this to himself, strictly, as a useful check. For when he thought of Marcus, he seemed so engulfed in emptiness, so hopelessly vulnerable, barely even alive, almost – that Drusus almost felt he could not trust himself *not* to do it.

Despite its name, the park around the Lady Without Sorrows lake was in fact a subdued, gently melancholy place. Though the fumes of Jiangning trespassed in, and laid dusty coats on the leaves of the trees, the noise of nearby roadworks seemed only to tap respectfully against its borders, in the distance. There were swallows looping in the hot, white-grey air over the scummy lake. Half an hour or so before, an old man with a frail twist of white beard and a grieving, finely creased face had shuffled by, dressed in faded grey cotton, with a domed birdcage in each hand, a fawn-coloured bulbul, a blue and gold shama preening restlessly within. He had turned his head to stare at Lal with the familiar puzzled curiosity she scarcely even noticed any more. Then he lifted the cages with painstaking tenderness to hang from the branches of a magnolia and a crab-apple tree, so that among the leaves the birds would be indulged or cheated with the illusion of freedom – a kind of holiday. Beneath them, as they sang, he had stood for a while, swaying and bending with unexpected, confident grace, extending and turning an arm, dodging the slow ghost of the gentlest imaginable blow, practising with the air a poignant combat from which all violence had been stripped. Now he was sitting on a bench, motionlessly regarding his birds with sad love.

Lal was seated on the ground, using the bench beside her as a desk on which she had spread a sheet of paper, a writing brush, an inkstone, although she was not writing but sweeping the ink into smooth coils and swirls, lovingly deepening the black, keeping it wet and glossy for as long as possible, with no design at all, beyond some half-conscious wish that it were possible to draw the motion of the swallows – their movement, not the physical birds themselves. She had learnt from

Liuyin how to imitate, with obsessive, squinting precision, the exact brushstrokes of the old masters outlining a bird in flight or perched on a misty spray of leaves, themselves copies of copies. Beautiful, but stifling, finally.

She was too idly engrossed, and too glad of the illicit break from work selling hybrid Roman-Sinoan snacks in Matho's shop, to be genuinely angry at Liuyin's lateness now, although every few minutes, looking around and still not seeing him, she reminded herself she had every right to be, and should go. She should give up seeing him altogether, in fact, she could not keep responding to these tortured claims that he had something of desperate importance to tell her. He had been particularly agitated this time, it was true, and on the way to Lady Without Sorrows, she had wondered if it might be that his parents were pushing him into marriage. But she'd since decided this was giving too much credit to Liuyin's histrionic urgency: probably it was only that he wanted her to read some book he'd found whose ill-starred hero and heroine mirrored their plight.

And then Liuyin was there, breathless, stuttering slightly, exclaiming, 'Oh, you're just sitting there drawing,' with some hopeless, half-censorious emotion. His hands jagged up and down in distress. He was also seventeen, with a gentle, scholarly face, from which his occasional fits of elegiac drama could be unexpected: 'How can I apologise? Oh, if I'd come here too late and you had gone I couldn't have borne it ...'

Lal, entirely without malice, entirely without realising she was doing it, stopped listening to him. She left her face turned towards him in an expression of sympathetic enquiry while her attention streamed away, whisking accidentally three hundred miles towards the bright, sterile walls of Bian, searching for Una there, for Marcus – and questioning with guilty tentativeness: what was Sulien like, now?

'I couldn't get away sooner. I know my mother suspects. If my parents find out I've told you this they're going to kill me. I'm not meant to know. My father must have known what I'd do. But I heard, he had instructions today from Bianjing. There's been an assassination there. You must leave, you and your family. It's starting this evening. They're clamping down on all you people. I mean Romans.'

Lal blinked, as around the unexpected naming of Bian, the blur of distraught words suddenly hardened into horrifying order. 'Wait – *what*?'

'Wherever you go, you won't forget me, will you?' breathed Liuyin, taking hold of her shoulders.

'No,' said Lal, with mechanical, shocked compliance, not hearing herself. 'I don't understand—'

'Yes you do,' said Liuyin impatiently. 'You've got to get away from here, there's nothing else to understand. But you can't tell anyone except your family, or the police will realise I told you and I don't know what would happen. My father could lose his job.'

'But what has it got to do with us?' protested Lal. '*Who* has been assassinated?'

'One of the Nionian lords, I think. It must have been a Roman who killed him. So, you see.'

'And – you said this is happening *today*?' It was strange that the few, useless words that came to her seemed to express little more than a mild alarm. Of course, in part it was simply that the news was too much, and too abrupt, to take in. It was also Liuyin: Lal could not join in lamentation with him at their parting, and he seemed to leave no other way of even feeling panic, except in this muted, polite form.

'Yes. Yes, it's terrible. I suppose we will never see each other again. I don't know what we've done to deserve this.'

'But Bianjing is miles away. We've been here all this time and no one's bothered. They're really going after *everyone*? You are sure about this, Liuyin?'

'Of course I'm sure! Do you know how I've been able to bear it, all this time when we've hardly seen each other? By telling myself that you are still *here*, that I am still in the same city as you. Do you think I would come here and tell you to leave Jiangning if I didn't have to, if it wasn't to save you?'

Lal wondered guiltily if there were any chance that he might, in fact, do that. 'But you don't think it could blow over?'

'No!'

Lal could do nothing but stare at his earnest, self-consciously anguished face, and say weakly, 'Well, thank you, Liuyin.'

'There is no *need* to thank me.'

'Well – goodbye ...'

'Wait. Kiss me,' said Liuyin, wounded.

Because she was too stunned to question any instruction, and because it seemed the simplest way of concluding the conversation, and out of gratitude, Lal reeled obediently forward to give him an incongruous kiss. And ran, over the damp ground, into the warm soft chaos of Jiangning.

It was late afternoon, but within Jiangning's double corridors of plane trees a dense, illusory twilight fell. The light from the driver's cab went dark, and in the windowless rear of the narrow van, jounced among the sliding cases, Lal and her father Delir could only see each other as huddled, urgent shadows. They were driving north towards the bridge over the Long River, at an agonisingly ordinary speed.

Delir leant forward at the hatch in the van's partition. 'You want to go left at the end of this street. *Here.* What are you doing?'

'There's flooding along the Qinhuai, I'm not going that way,' said Ziye shortly. Being Sinoan she was the only one who could risk visibility in the driver's cab. She had covered her short hair with a scarf knotted under her chin, lending her handsome, scarred face a spuriously quaint look. But of course the scars were memorable, and it was unusual for a woman even to be allowed to learn to drive.

'It'll be twice as long this way. Are you certain?'

'Didn't you hear the rain last night? Where did you think all the water went?'

Delir let out a tense, unconvinced sigh. Presently he said, 'Then it's straight on.'

'I *am* going straight on.'

The van sank into a traffic jam. Sitting crouched in a corner, clutching the little bag in her lap, Lal knocked the back of her head against the wall behind her. The argument parodied some safe, normal crisis, it felt agonisingly irrelevant to what was happening and yet it was not, an hour lost one way or the other really might be critical, and it was unbearable to listen to. She closed her eyes and tried, without even a second's success, to disengage from the noise and the jolting, to meditate. She couldn't even keep her eyelids down, let alone stop her attention from butting, like a moth against *this*: they had left nearly everything, there were checkpoints spread like landmines between them and the Nionian border, two thousand miles to go before the crossing into India after that.

But for a few minutes, flinging the bags into the van, a thrill of unseemly excitement had shimmered through her, that they were moving, that they were heading for home.

Finally there was quiet, as Ziye had begun stolidly ignoring Delir, who slumped back against the wall, his head bowed with a quickly controlled desperation. He said suddenly, 'I am so sorry, Lal.'

Lal looked at him in surprise. She felt slightly responsible for the bad news, having been the one to run back and break it. She was still afraid, on top of everything else, that all this might be for nothing. And of course they had ignored Liuyin's instruction not to warn any of the other Roman refugees. She could not think what it would mean for all those people if he should turn out to have been wrong, or lying. And yet, when her father said that, she knew what he was sorry for. He had never been a slave, he had been an affluent Roman citizen when an eruption of compassionate fury, decisive as a stroke, had made him drag down a half-dead boy from a cross on the Aurelian Way, seven years ago. No one had forced him, as he had forced her, to go and live in driven, furtive insurrection against Rome's cruelty, before she was old enough to understand what she was losing by it.

She did not think she could stand it if he said any of this. 'That's all right,' she said, a little blankly.

'We'll go to Rome,' he promised suddenly, rashly generous.

She smiled cautiously. 'We've got to get a long way before that.'

'Well, we will,' he said.

The van began to move again, which was some comfort. In Holzarta they had been professional in their readiness for flight. They had tried to maintain this in Jiangning: three years with packed cases near the door, always light enough to carry easily, sometimes opened and checked, clothes added or replaced, false papers subtly adjusted by Lal. But sometimes, over three years, things were sneakingly borrowed too, packs of money raided when none of them could find work. And despite the stunned looks they continued to attract when they went far outside the Black Clothes quarter, they were so taken for granted there that caution of that kind had long come to feel more like superstition than anything, a ritual to turn aside bad spirits.

'What have you got there?' Delir asked her after a while, gesturing at the little red cloth bag she had in her lap.

Lal shrugged and muttered, 'Some lip paint and perfume and stuff.' To prompt him to laugh at her, which he did, she had struck a note of faint self-parody: young, sheepish. It was not really true to how she felt, although it was true enough that she hadn't wanted to leave without the make-up. In the same light tone, she said, 'It might help if I look nice. If we get caught.'

'We won't get caught,' he insisted softly.

Ziye manoeuvred the van grimly through Jiangning, the only one of them able to see the city they were leaving: Fuzi Miao bazaar, full of clothes and caged animals; prowed, fish-scaled roofs of loosening tiles above cramped whitewashed houses like the two-roomed building they'd left behind, with so much still there, exposed to thieves. Then the road ducked through grey, sprawling burrows of shacks, botched with sheets of plastic and steel. And the Long River percolated through the city as through the cavities of a warm sponge, the pattern of the streets and markets interrupted by the slinkings of low, flower-lined canals. Then, on the edge of the city it insinuated and intruded, the most wretched of the slum buildings leaning over its floodwaters, suicidal. Then, as Ziye drove into the heavy light from under the deep shade of the planes, beneath the suspension bridge it became a sudden bulging sea, even the great barges and ferries looked balanced precariously on its rolling back, the men on sampans fragile as pond skaters. Then, as the road dodged away from it and the trunk of it was hidden over the horizon, it still soaked the countryside, welling up in rice fields, and green-polished lotus beds and swamps.

Ziye thought about fighting. That is, she became aware of her body beginning, without her consent, to think for her: measuring the remaining strength of her unpractised muscles, coldly priming skills too old to be eradicated. She endured the pain of trying to leave Sina now as if it were a passing attack of illness: the core of her life had been spent outside her country. There had never been any shortage of superfluous Sinoan children, especially girls; rural children who amassed like debts, crowding strained families and exhausting supplies of food. And if they could not be shifted off, on to a relative or employer, and did not die, they were sometimes bought up by dealers, who talked vaguely to the parents of a better life and shipped the children onto the Roman slave market, where the excess of unsupported humans neatly complemented a worsening shortage of labour. The difference for Ziye was the length of time that had passed between her removal from her village, and her entrance into the Roman Empire.

She had been nine when Huang had driven away with her, huddled in a wailing knot with two older girls in the back of his truck. She was seventeen when at last she left him, a fluid, supple young athlete whose hands and feet could whir elegantly through space to crack bone, almost without effort. Huang had made some contacts in the Roman gladiatorial industry, and had an idea to raise the value of girls. He had made a good profit out of Ziye herself in the end, she believed, but, from the three little girls he began with, and after eight years of training, he produced only one marketable gladiatrix. After a couple of years Rong and Mei, the other two, must have learnt something, but they looked only exhausted and heartsick and ill. Having brutally washed his hands of them, Huang must have decided the experiment was too time-consuming and costly to repeat. After that, anxiously watching his youngest girl's progress with her expensive teacher, he would, from time to time, pat her shoulder approvingly, almost like an uncle, if not like a father. When the time came and she was ready to go, as he put it, Huang had tears in his eyes. But whatever emotion that had been, it did not stop him: he sold her anyway. Ziye was, in one way, sharply aware of the betrayal. And yet it was also a graduation, the beginning of her career.

And for twenty-three years she had fought, wheeling across arenas in

Roxelania, Ctesiphon, Tecesta and Rome. She fought in the Colosseum, where cameras swooped on tracks around the pitch and the gladiators cast circles of multiple shadows under the lights. They pitted Ziye against men, and she went to work with her usual fearless, passionate focus, utterly deaf to the noise the crowd made as they watched her. They saw a slim, unarmed, defenceless girl erupt like a firework, flicking blades, maces, nets out of her adversaries' hands, and the sound Ziye did not hear was a sighing, pitching, splashing roar, a symphony of gasps, not just of shock but of adulation and lust. Wherever the lanistas took her, a torrent of starstruck lovers would seek her out, both men and women – she could take her pick. The only impossible choice was no one.

At first, she was marketed as an exotic, lethal ingenue, a heroine. Then, later, as she grew older and acquired more scars on her face, the impresarios who owned her turned her into a cropped-haired, implacable villainess whose eastern skills were barely natural, who did not need weapons to win a bout, or kill an opponent. By the time she was thirty-five her gladiatrix persona had even changed nationality – from Sinoan to Nionian – in order to amplify the hysteria of whooping, booing hatred she provoked when she walked out to face some young, blonde fighter with the crowd behind her. She had believed herself indifferent to this. She would do her job, the promoters would do theirs: what they called her or made her out to be had nothing to do with the privacy of the fight itself. And only as she felt her strength start to tire, her reflexes begin to slow, as she began to loathe the very texture of the injuries she inflicted even as she struck them into place, then gradually it began to tell upon her that in every day of her work, she was surrounded by thousands of people who hated her and wanted her to die. She was ready to retire, it was understood that she deserved it. Escape should not have been necessary.

What she'd earnt over the years could have bought a whole troupe of gladiators at the price Huang had got for her. Sometimes she reflected with something between affection and scorn that Huang could have been a millionaire if he'd known how to manage her instead of selling her. But the company she belonged to had changed hands, and though her right to buy her own freedom was always assured, it kept receding: her value kept climbing, one pace ahead of what she had saved. She thought that surely as her performance declined, it would come to a standstill, but she did not want to wait meekly for that to happen: she pressed, angrily, for a date. The lanistas who ran the company hedged and quibbled. Only one more year, she was told at last, reasonably.

One more year. Ziye had gone back to her barracks and thought about this, and discovered with a chill that the feeling she had taken for anger seemed to be fear. Most combats between skilled gladiators were not to the death – that would have been an unconscionable waste. But over twenty-three years she had fought on more than enough special occasions, her opponents were all dead and she was still alive. She had burnt up more luck than she had a right to. She was not as strong as she had been. One more year would kill her.

And they *wanted* it to. The final, best use they could get from her was not to accept her money and let her go, but to create a satisfying climax to the audience's loathing of her, to feed her whole career, her whole *life*, to some rising star who would swallow it all and be strengthened by it. Whoever killed her would become, at a stroke, a gold mine, a new idol. It was like killing a dangerous animal and wearing its skin.

The news of Holzarta in the Pyrenees had come to her a year before, just as gossip from Galla, whom Ziye could not see or think of now without wondering if she would be the one to kill her – a young, fierce, ambitious gladiatrix, who had heard Holzarta whispered about by the slaves of a fan she'd been sleeping with. Ziye and Galla had been impartially curious, feeling casual pity for the poor souls who'd have to make use of the place. But neither of them had any interest then in a freedom that meant subterfuge and poverty and flight.

And even after this she kept spiralling round the idea as around a drain, in panicked hope of some way of saving the comfortable retirement she'd counted on. And yet she began to think of every arena in terms of distance from the Pyrenees. And then one day she was travelling towards the arena at Pompaelo, motionless in a traffic jam, on a bridge over the Tagus. After twenty-three years of professionalism, she hardly travelled in shackles: she had an expensive car to herself, a bouquet of orange roses wilting on the seat beside her, a bottle of wine, music she had chosen playing. But the doors were locked, and all the money she'd saved was far away. She was aware of the river below. She did not know how deep it was, or how fast-flowing. She might as well die in a way that did not profit anybody. It would be either death, or like death – she could only get out if she went as bare and poor as a corpse. The driver and a single bodyguard sat ahead.

It was the first time she'd attacked someone who was not a trained fighter. She was shocked by the messy simplicity of it, her own trembling and incompetence, despite the fact that it was easy, really, and soon over. The car itself was harder – the locks opened not with a key but with a code she didn't know, and in a moment someone would realise what was happening and stop her. She'd exhausted herself and sprayed her legs and feet with cuts kicking out the toughened glass, and then stood on the bridge, barely hesitating. She'd learnt to swim thirty-five years ago, in Shandong province, in a reedy lake the Yellow River had left behind as it rampaged across the land. She thought of that, stepping into space.

During the three days after that, she'd grown more efficient at spontaneous, unstaged violence, since it was all she had to compensate for her almost complete ignorance of how to live in the world. She'd stolen money, clothes, kicked a man from a farmer's four-wheeled mount, on which she burnt across a few hundred miles of country, until the power gave out. But he was the last, she had touched no one afterwards. She had approached the mountains with certain resolutions. It was not that she wanted to change. She wanted to remain exactly as she was in that hour: calm, clean, and either empty as air or full like a cup of motionless water. She wanted, monastically, only to go on wanting nothing. So she would never fight again. She would never sleep with anyone again. She would never go home.

Already she had broken two of these. When she arrived in the camp, she had been the only woman there, and had had to deflect a lot of crude attention. But after she'd weathered most of that she'd found that Delir was pursuing her with courteous, dogged persistence, which to her bewilderment had worked on her in the end, even though however admirable Delir was, he was also a funny, dainty little man she could have knocked across a room with one hand. And that had brought her home to Sina, although she had always known that she could no more truly return to the aching, absent country in her mind than make herself nine years old again. Still, she had not fought again, since those days in Spain. And if the police caught them now, trying illicitly to cross the Long River towards Nionian territory, what would she do then?

Some minutes had passed in silence. Then Ziye announced, 'There's an official-class car behind us. It's missed a few chances to overtake.'

She pulled the van to a sudden crawl. Unspeaking, Lal and Delir drew closer towards the cab, away from the doors. Delir closed a hand on Lal's shoulder, and she could feel the instinct in the tension of his arm: to push her further back, behind him, to hide her, even though there was nowhere further to go. And the very protectiveness of it seemed to reveal to her in one pitiless sweep how fragile he was: no taller than his daughter, more used up than he should have been at fifty, and less at home in this country than she was. For a moment she felt like crying.

Ziye watched the black polished shell slide by and ahead, scarlet curtains drawn, everyone within invisible. 'It's gone past. They might not want to make a move yet, I suppose.'

Delir sighed. 'They would just stop us, surely. Why make such a song and dance of it?'

Ziye gave a half-convinced grunt. 'We may as well talk about what we do if Mouli isn't there.'

'He's worked there for twenty years, it's only six months since I heard from him. Six months is nothing,' said Delir, looking at Lal.

There was a government checkpoint near Wuhu, at the next bridge on the road south – even in the best of circumstances they would have been unable to cross there. There was a little quay a few miles west of the highway, on the edge of a village. Mouli had a small motorboat there, for fishing and some minor trade between riverside villages. He had helped a few of the former Roman slaves living in Sina who had decided, for whatever reason, to travel further south. But Delir himself had only ever met Mouli once, in what had been a fairly casual attempt to reinforce this length of the chain of promises and sympathy, and friends of friends of friends, that had once led back to the camp in the Pyrenees.

'Delir, it doesn't protect us just to assume everything will be all right.'

'Well, then we pay someone else to get us across,' said Delir, in exasperation. 'What choice is there?'

'We could wait until dark and steal a boat,' said Lal, in a low, tentative voice.

Before Delir could respond Ziye said, 'Yes, we can't afford to throw money away on bribes, and we can't afford to approach strangers. Not on this side of the border, anyway.'

Delir was silent for a second or two. Then he murmured, 'Yes. You're right. If Mouli is not there, we will have to do that.' He had slumped back, his eyes downcast. Under his breath he said, 'God in Heaven forgive us if it comes to that.'

Lal looked at his dark shape and knew that having once been well off, it was hard for him, even now, to believe things could be so desperate as to warrant stealing: he had chosen a life that led to this. The people that lived in the pared, tightly farmed countryside outside had not.

It was close to dusk already. In the back of the van, Lal could barely even see her father's outline in the darkness. She lowered herself to the van's floor, lying in a cramped, cat-like curl, the vibration of the wheels on the road throbbing through her bones.

Ziye left the motorway as the towers of the next suspension bridge rose in the purple air ahead, and the river spread again down across the horizon like a shivering expansion of the sky. She could see the red and white lamps of barges – points of light over feathery reflections in the water. She drove down towards them.

271

The ground seemed sticky under the wheels. Lal was beginning at last to retreat into a kind of suspended torpor, and she felt the van cough to a stop with a kind of vague dismay: whatever came next was going to be harder. Ziye said, 'All right. Shall we leave the van here?'

Delir leant forward again. 'I can't see. Where are we?'

'A track. Can't see anyone around. The quay's just ahead. There are lights on.' She tightened the scarf around her head. 'I can go and see if he's around. If he's there it would save us having to go into the village. You should both stay hidden while I find him.'

'I'm not such a sore thumb in the dark,' said Delir, stretching briskly, smiling. 'I'm not blond. I'll come. I remember Mouli's face, at least.' He groaned a little as he moved forwards, and his hand brushed Lal's shoulder again. 'Lal,' he said softly. 'Wait out of sight until we know it's safe.'

Lal made a provisional uncurling movement, and lifted her head as he opened the door and jumped down.

Ziye and Delir started walking towards the river, exhanging a look, aware that they remained superficially angry with each other, knowing that it was unwarranted and that it would pass.

Then a dark, high van rolled up from the quay and two men jumped down in front of them. Someone said, in Sinoan of course, 'Present your identity papers,' before the torch-beam swept Delir's face. At his side, he felt Ziye tense in a way he had never known before and yet recognised instantly: not simply fear, but preparation, defence. And he had a split second in which to know what a defeat any kind of violence would be for her now.

Then more men emerged from the vehicle, and as Ziye counted them and saw the guns in their hands, she let her body relax, utterly certain that nothing it could do was of use. Some old, unfeeling part of her was even relieved.

But Delir couldn't understand what they were saying to him, couldn't answer properly: his clumsy competence with Sinoan knocked all at once into pieces. Ziye tried, in a flat, reasonable voice, to translate for him, and they shouted for her to be silent, one of them threw a slap at her face which she blocked without thinking, and at that they bundled her to one side. They grabbed Delir and swung him away from her. Three of them headed for the van she and Delir had left, and Delir stared back towards where Lal was and couldn't speak or think or pray. He couldn't even decide what to hope for – don't let them find her, or don't let us be separated – but he was choked as if from his crown to the soles of his feet.

Then they came out of the van without her and began swiping fiercely but uncertainly at the reeds, making Delir's pulse hitch, like a fish hook through his heart. She had to be very, very near, she'd hear if he called to her, he could be sure where she was. What would happen to her if she were left behind with nothing, and here where someone must surely have informed on them? What would they do if they found her?

But he couldn't make a sound, until they came back and shoved at him again, ordered him to say whether there had been anyone else. He understood that, and whispered, 'No.'

Lal crouched, paralysed, among slippery weeds. The air buzzed with insects; her right foot and half the hem of her dress were submerged in sticky, blood-warm water. She felt as if she'd been placed here in her sleep and then roughly wakened – she had dived so quickly, and so automatically into the swamp ground beside the track that she could scarcely remember it. She clasped her hands over her face and cried, shallowly at first, easing the pressure of panic and helplessness as she might have at any ordinary hurtful thing and broke into gulping, messy sobs of desperation only when she heard, without wanting to listen or bearing to look, the van being driven away, the police vehicles following sternly behind. Her father and Ziye were there, somewhere, they were being carried back the way they had come, towards the highway; they were gone. An empty hush flooded everything for a moment, in which she could only hear herself snivelling and trying to tell herself that it was somehow all right. Then the quiet filled with the louder triumphant gloating of the mosquitoes and birds, barges hooting on the river, the roar of the road.

She swabbed wretchedly at her face, wiping her muddy hands on the leaves and on her clothes and waded back onto the track. She had nothing but her stupid bag of make-up: it had been hanging on its long strap from her shoulder. She stood and gasped for breath and sobbed, trying to think of a good reason for going any particular way.

Marcus saw five or six low-bodied, honey-brown wild horses, roaming harmlessly along over the scanty brownish grass, dancing east, past his window and out of sight. They were the first change in this numb, bare, dun-coloured steppe land that he had seen for days, but they made a wrench of anger snag through his muscles, like an inward grimace. Since being taken from Bian, he had been kept, adamantly, from even seeing a longdictor, or a longvision. And outside, change continued without him, things were happening of which he was allowed to know nothing. Even when a train was rushing through the Cazak expanse at three hundred miles an hour, the uniformity grew blinding: the eyes would quail at the absence of anything to focus on, the train's flight would seem like a slack crawl, time dried out. Against towns or woods or mountains, the ten broad, dead straight silver strands of the Silk Road magnetway looked commanding and dominant, a brutal Roman taming of the earth. Here, enfeebled against the vast ground and the pale sky, the track was puny, almost poignant in its tentative attempt on the wilderness, like the extinct royal road of a dead civilisation, diminished to a line of loosened stones, leading to nowhere any more. Like what it would be, one day, for the grass seemed poised to quietly heal over and erase it.

Marcus beat the index finger of his right hand rapidly on the table, keeping up the rhythm for pitiless minutes, aware of a very small, spiteful pleasure at the annoyance the sound must be inflicting on the soldiers standing at the end of the carriage. He felt as if his skin were growing harder and tighter, turning metallic, squeezing ruthlessly on some encased and maddened thing that harried and burnt. Not so much a trapped animal, but an awful, incandescent chemical change.

This standstill was real. First the private Imperial train had lingered for two days just inside the border of Sarmatia, its mirror-like sheen incongruous at a dismal little station of a black, scattered, coal-mining town, which it would normally have shot through obliviously, stranded in the void of landscape. The soldiers explained stolidly that they had their orders, they were waiting for someone of appropriate rank to escort him back into the Empire. Marcus gritted his teeth and refused to waste energy arguing. Then the magistrate of Roxelania had arrived on an eastbound train, a short, glumly self-important man, prone to saying things like, 'Unfortunately my instructions are very clear.' And: 'I wish I had a choice, sir.' Over the following days, by petty increments, the drab gratification the man was drawing from the power he held grew glaring to Marcus, as the train slid on for a few hundred miles west, and then turned slyly down what Marcus thought must be an obsolete industrial line, perhaps serving an old copper foundry or a phosphate works, where it glided wearily to a stop.

'Unfortunately we're going to have to wait here, sir. The magnetway's been damaged further west. Bad flooding.'

'You got here all right,' observed Marcus grimly, not with any hope of embarrassing the man into admitting the lie, but compelled to assert the fact that he himself did not accept it.

'The weather is so changeable in my country.'

The train was appropriately well appointed: an additional, plainer carriage had been coupled behind those for the guards and the servants, to accommodate the magistrate. But in Marcus' living quarters, the floors were carpeted in Bactrian crimson silks; the walls were tautly upholstered with rust-coloured, gold-stamped leather, or panelled with gold-seamed cedarwood, painted with laurel leaves. One car was divided by a silk-padded screen into a bedroom and a handsome compartment called his 'study'. Here an ornate clock stood on a marble-topped desk, there was a gilded barometer on the wall, there were photographs of the Imperial family including Marcus' parents, but no writing materials. In the saloon car, where he now took his meals with the magistrate, the narrow ceiling was crammed with gilt-wreathed murals: a fleshy, bloody painting of Romulus and Remus at the founding of the walls of Rome arched over the dining table. The food served amidst this opulence was dire: daily heaps of indeterminate meat sludge that forced Marcus actually to notice what he was putting into his mouth. It proved, once again, that the delay was deliberate. They must have taken on a large quantity of supplies at the mining town: you would have to resort to compact, long-lasting, packeted food to sustain twenty-four people out here for this much time. He forced the stuff down anyway, watching the magistrate at the far end of the table, squeamishly prodding at it. It was a regular, unpleasant task which he refused to fail. He was powerless enough as it was; he did not mean to let physical weakness add to that.

On the windows the eagle and the motto of the Empire obstructed the empty view. He could not be certain he would even know if war had started. On the seventh morning after leaving Bian, when the brown horses had gone past, he wondered if it were possible they might live out their lives without being affected, whatever happened, without even witnessing any sign of what took place between Empires. There was a kind of palliative comfort in thinking that they could.

On the first stationary day, hastily following Marcus out of the saloon car onto the little balcony that opened to the cool air, the magistrate said his instructions were that Marcus should not leave the train. Marcus slowed the furious impulse to slam his fist against something, striking his hand flat on the guard rail instead. He was as effectively confined by the featureless spread of space as he could have been by prison walls. He could not guess how far he would have to walk towards the frosty horizon to get out of sight.

He said, 'Your instructions are your affair. They and you are nothing to me.' He stepped briskly over the guard rail, jumped down onto the tough grass, and began walking fast. He heard the consternation and anger behind him but did not turn. If he went far enough they would have to use force to bring him back, have to risk hurting him, but just how willing or reluctant they were to do that would be some gauge of his own standing, of Drusus' power. Not that he meant to push them to that for the sake of it. If he could just get away from their voices, if they let him walk the edge off this fury, he would have discovered or proved something.

At his feet he noticed little pink and yellow flowers he had not seen from the train, papery, crumpled. The sky was a thin, distant blue. He thought of himself at sixteen, alone, setting out with nothing. And it felt as if he were looking back across decades, as if half a lifetime of doubt and division lay between him as he was now and something essential, pure. For the first time it came to him why the luxury in which he was being conveyed now made things more intolerable rather than less. It was as though they thought that he could not survive without it: as if they were transporting an exotic fish which must not be allowed to feel its captivity, must be kept in painstaking imitation of its natural habitat, or it would die. He thought, damn you all, I would manage out here, somehow. It's more than you would.

He did not want to wander sheepishly back to the train, like a child returning from a sulk. He summoned one of the men, curtly ordered him to lend him his cloak and marched back ahead with the man shivering behind him.

So he won that round, but the magistrate had his revenge later. Most of the gorgeously bound books in the useless study seemed to have little purpose beyond decoration, but there was a set of atlases among them. That night, Marcus was sprawled at the marble desk with them, first poring over the subtle, vacant charts of the Cazak region of Sarmatia in an effort to pin down where he was, then turning to the different maps of Terranova and Tokogane, studying the distribution of gold and other minerals, fluctuations of climate and the courses of rivers. He could at least refresh what knowledge was available to him, he could insist to himself he would make use of it soon.

'It's getting late now, shouldn't you be turning in, sir?'

It was not yet very late, Marcus was sure of that. The light had only left the sky a couple of hours since. He did not fully trust the porphyry clock at his side – sometimes he grew preoccupied with the idea that it was slow, or broken. It bothered him because it distorted his calculations of the time in Bian, or in Rome.

'You really must go to bed, sir.'

Marcus stonily ignored him. He had good reason to defer lying down, filling his thoughts with the maps as long as possible, until he could be confident of complete exhaustion. The man disappeared for a while and then, as Marcus turned another page, the lights went out. The stars were suddenly huge and teeming outside. Marcus sat unmoving in the blackness, breathtaken with rage. He did not need to try the lamps in his sleeping compartment to know that the power had been turned off.

The magistrate said with satisfaction in the dark, 'I wish I had a choice, but in these circumstances we must save our resources, sir.'

All day, he tried to avoid speculating about Una and Varius. And, during each day, he found to his own unease that he could do so: a cold success of the will that troubled him. But he had dreams, more detailed and vivid every night, from which he would wake to a moment's trembling, shattered relief, before the daylight knowledge of crisis broke in again. He dreamt he was in the back of a car Una was driving at wild speed through wind and sleet in the Pyrenees: he begged her to stop and she answered that she could not, the vehicle was moving malevolently by itself. And at that Marcus was no longer in the car, but standing in helpless safety on the snow outside, watching the car plunge from the road onto dark rocks. Or he saw her vanishing over the threshold into his parents' beautiful Tusculum house, and knew with belated nausea that he could not reach her in time, the house was about to collapse and crush her. Or he was in the Palace and Faustus, healthy and authoritative again, was telling him Varius had been executed, or even more unbearable, had killed himself in custody. Faustus met Marcus' distress with grave, statesmanlike sympathy at first, then by degrees grew accusing, and Marcus, who to begin with had forgotten why this was his fault, would remember with a shock of guilt that sometimes jarred him awake. Varius was almost always absent, always dead, while Una was alive but threatened, or dying before his eyes. Except once when he twisted away in anguish from hearing the news, and the narrative of the dream broke off and began again on other terms, as dreams will, so that he found Varius in a room like his office in the slave clinic, sitting at a desk, slowly filling out columns of figures in a ledger, filing accounts.

'Varius,' Marcus said, faint with relief, though the texture of the dreamt air was cold and charged with horror. 'I thought you were dead.'

'No,' said Varius calmly, distantly. 'Not until tomorrow.'

'Then you can't stay here,' Marcus said desperately, for Varius was concentrating impassively on his work and never looked at him. 'Come on.'

'It's underway and can't be altered,' answered Varius, writing something down, with eerie, impersonal authority. He did not seem altogether human.

Marcus pleaded, 'What about Una?'

'They hanged her yesterday in Edo. Didn't you know?'

The magistrate said, 'We must discuss your interview with the Emperor. While we may be caught here for some time, still, if his health permits, you'll be seeing him eventually. You must be clear in your mind as to what you're going to say.'

Marcus flicked a sharp look at him. 'Use that word to your inferiors or equals, not to me.'

The man lowered his eyes in awkward contrition, but murmured, 'I'm afraid, sir, at this stage, you have no option but to give up the Imperial ring.'

Marcus looked coldly at the gold weight on the still-tapping finger. 'It is still mine to give up. No one has taken it from me. I find that interesting.'

'It's a formality to go through,' explained the magistrate.

'I don't think my cousin would weary himself with such formalities if he thought he could dispense with them.'

The magistrate drew back very slightly and glanced towards the guards at the end of the motionless carriage, and a small, self-appeasing smile briefly tightened his lips. It occurred to Marcus, with a new twinge of unease, that the man was reassuring himself of protection against physical attack.

He said softly, 'I'm not going to speculate, sir, about how much you knew or didn't know about your friends' intentions. What part you had or didn't have in the Emperor's illness. It's none of my business. But the Emperor knows you have been irretrievably compromised as Caesar by your association with people who had other interests at heart than the good of Rome. However innocent you may have been. Or felt yourself to be.'

'Then my cooperation is of no importance.'

'Regretfully, sir, I must remind you that you are not fully aware of the developing situation.'

Marcus grinned bitterly, but felt tension constrict closer, as though a rivet had been turned through another revolution. 'No. I am not.'

The magistrate clicked his tongue mournfully, and hefted a case onto the desk. 'I've been authorised to make certain points to you.'

Marcus looked at the case, trying to disguise his apprehension. He said sardonically, 'Now where has that arrived from?'

The final carriage of the train held the retinue's vehicles – the grand imperial car that had carried Marcus out of Bian as well as sturdy military trucks. On two occasions the magistrate had been driven away from the train in one of these, bouncing over the grass, towards the main line of the magnetway. Marcus knew there must be longdictor stations dotted along its course and had guessed he was going to update his so-often-vaunted instructions.

'You gave over your advisor and your – ah, your mistress to our enemies, sir, which, I'm bound to say, was really not a tactic to reflect very well on anyone concerned. Naturally there have been urgent negotiations to ensure their return.'

'Have they given them up?' The question skipped, by accidental lapse, from his dry mouth.

'Certainly they will give them up, probably tomorrow or the next day, it's only a matter of the conditions in which it happens. In the meantime, they weren't the only ones whose questionable involvement in matters of state during your regency is coming to light. There's also Novianus Sulien.' He took two objects out of the case – a stained and crumpled blue tunic, and a large photograph of three men, like doctors, implements in their hands, bending impassively over a metal table; someone lying on it, half-naked, arms drawn back and strapped down: Sulien. The tunic, which was Sulien's, had been ripped open from the neck down towards the waist, and the torn edges were flecked with darkened blood.

Marcus seemed to register a great, blunt impact somewhere in the world, cold and thick, like a stone-headed mallet hitting wet cement. And yet it seemed that it was not him who was struck, as though some sensory function that should have been there to take it had failed. He sat there still and alert and his mind tried Sulien's name and noted irrelevantly, I can't even feel anything. He said nothing.

'It seems he had some prohibited source of information. He managed to evade the vigiles for a while, but he was tracked down to Tarquinia two days ago. He's been being questioned since then.'

Deliberately, Marcus drew in the breath his lungs had, a second before, omitted to take. He reached forward, and, without looking at it more closely, turned the picture over to lie face down on the table, his hand resting with the fingers spread, light on the blank white reverse. He said, 'I want to ask you something.'

'I've told you as much as I'm authorised to.'

'No. I want to ask if you realise what you're risking. You're here to persuade me to do something. The fact that this is necessary should warn you that, even now, I have more control over things than my cousin would like. And that the outcome is not certain. Things may progress as he wishes, and as you expect. But if not – if *not*, I will again be the most powerful man in the Empire. And I will remember you.'

He watched: the man's short-lashed eyelids lifted a little and flickered once or twice, with alarm. He protested, 'Sir! I have done everything

279

possible to see that you are maintained here as befits your status. The situation is not of my making.'

Marcus blankly studied his features without answering.

The magistrate hesitated, shifting nervously in his seat, and then ducked his head forward as if afraid of being overheard. 'You must understand – Drusus Novius has that power now. What can I do? I can hardly ignore instructions.'

'A difficult position. Yet I could not advise you to rely on my sympathy.'

'It would be me or somebody else,'

'Maybe.'

'I have no choice,' appealed the magistrate, in a low tone, his flat eyes for the moment almost childlike with the plea to be excused, to be understood.

'You have hundreds of choices. You would have a choice even if there were a gun to your head. You have this one I am giving to you now, but don't think it will be offered again.'

The magistrate blinked, and his face seemed to turn blank. Then, almost furtively, clearing his throat, he reached for the photograph and turned it over again, sliding it closer to Marcus and swivelling it fastidiously with his forefingers, so that its edge lined up neatly with the edge of the table. Only then he glanced tentatively at Marcus' face and cleared his throat again.

'Fine,' said Marcus shortly.

And he forced himself to look, steadily, though it was as if he had to push his face through wire mesh to see the page clearly, something that dragged at the muscles and skin. 'This is the only picture of him you have to show me?' he said, not talking to express something he already thought or felt, nor to ask for real answers. He was only grimly thinking aloud, trying to assemble his own reaction in deliberate words, and to control it. 'These men. They look clearer than my friend, in better focus. Why should that be?' He turned the picture so that Sulien's profile went from horizontal to vertical. Briefly he allowed his eyelids to squeeze shut – there was no convincing himself that this was not Sulien's face. The head was thrown back, the mouth slightly open, the lips drawn back from the teeth. In that harsh, monochrome room, it was unmistakably an expression of pain, and yet – Marcus hesitated before permitting himself to ask this – if you removed all the surroundings, would that be so? If Sulien were not lying down but standing, if his body were unbound and clothed against some safe, ordinary backdrop, then it would only be a picture of Sulien speaking – even laughing, maybe. It was the cell, the bare torso, the helpless posture, the awful businesslike remoteness of the men that gave the picture its meaning. One of them was standing level with his victim's neck and shoulders, hiding them from the camera while Sulien's head emerged to the left. If they had inserted an older image of Sulien's face into an otherwise staged picture, onto a posed body, then this figure was positioned perfectly to disguise the join.

But it had been done horribly well, in that case. Certainly he could not look at Sulien's face and say, oh, that's only the picture of him at the first anniversary of the clinic, or visiting me in Athens.

Cautiously he handled the torn blue cloth. He murmured quietly, 'This is his, I remember it.' Sulien must have had it about a year – he'd been wearing it that evening in the Transtiberine flat months before, when they'd fought in play over the decision Marcus had imposed on him. It was an informal tunic made of tar fibre and cotton, a bright indigo-blue now a little faded, the unusual design printed on it slightly cracked: a large, white Celtic knot, violently severed in two now by the slash down the front. Marcus could remember Sulien claiming, not seriously, that he'd bought it to counter Una's shock about the loss of his British accent. It was there in the picture too, hanging open against the arched body.

He said, 'Did he just happen to be wearing the thing I'd be most likely to remember? There are plenty of his clothes you could bring me and I wouldn't recognise them, I'd have to take your word that they were his. And these marks. It's clear what I'm meant to think of them, but how do I know they're even blood, let alone his? And if you could bring this to me, why don't you bring *him*? Why don't you show me you have him, show me what you've done?'

'You'll see him when you get to Rome. Whatever state he's in by then,' replied the magistrate swiftly, and Marcus looked down, silent. He'd talked his scepticism into being, and when he looked again at the picture and the pitiful torn tunic again, he could hardly tell if the things he thought he'd seen were really there, if they had any existence beyond some vaguely possible point of view. There was just a picture of Sulien in pain.

'Coming up with some conspiracy theory won't make unpleasant things go away, sir,' the magistrate advised him. 'This is real.'

'If it wasn't, you wouldn't know,' said Marcus dully.

The magistrate had plainly recovered his confidence somewhat, even felt a need to make up for his earlier moment of doubt. 'I know you don't like confronting the situation, sir, but it is my job to explain. Do you see how this renders a continuation of your rule impossible? People like that, whom you've consorted with, in custody – how everything will all come out?'

Marcus again said nothing.

The magistrate sighed patiently. 'I would advise you to tell the Emperor that you recognise you relied too heavily on untrustworthy people. I think you should say, "I was too young for this responsibility. And I let myself be guided the wrong way. It's better that someone older takes over now."'

'So, you don't think I should try and make it sound in character at all?' retorted Marcus. But then he flung himself back in his seat, swinging up a foot to rest casually on the desk, as it hit him decisively that he neither could nor needed to tolerate any more of this. Almost flippantly he announced, 'Very well. I'll say whatever you like.'

The magistrate eyed him uncertainly. 'It's easy enough for you to say that now.'

'Yes, I get the point, you will murder him if I don't. It's hardly subtle,' spat Marcus, forgetting the languid slouch he'd assumed, springing involuntarily forward.

The magistrate recoiled slightly in a tidy, censorious flinch, grey eyebrows lifting. He said, disapprovingly, 'Not I, sir.'

XVI

SALVAGE

Lal shuffled along in her ruined shoes, as red sunrise spilled like an expensive oil over the Long River. She turned back to look at it, blinking: the lounging, dissolute beauty seemed confusing and difficult. It confirmed she was walking west, which would perhaps somehow help at some point. She uttered a little whimper of exhaustion and shame at how long it had taken her to work that out in the first place. How could she be so lacking in sense of direction, or sense of distance – anything? She couldn't even estimate how far she was from Jiangning. All she had been able to do was force herself to some decisions about what was impossible: she couldn't cross the river, and in any case, without means of getting further there would be no point. The police had intercepted them on the edge of Mouli's village, so she could not venture any further into it, and it was probably too dangerous to head back towards Jiangning for the same reason. So, she must go along this potholed track on the north bank of the river, and find somewhere with a longdictor. This reasoning sounded logical enough every time she repeated it to herself – surely her father would tell her to do something like this. And yet she still felt unconvinced, that she was making bad decisions almost at random only because she had to do something. And beyond reaching a longdictor, she knew her strategy could do nothing but collapse into faith: Liuyin would help her, because he would have to. After that, she would have to be capable of helping her father and Ziye. It was not so unreasonable. If she could only contact him, if he knew what had happened, Marcus would certainly do anything he could. Behind her the motorway soared over fields of water yams and grazing buffalo. She was still occasionally sobbing a little, but almost absent-mindedly now, routinely wiping inflamed cheeks. Sometimes, she found she was muttering inane words of encouragement to herself, just aloud, under her breath: Well then, all right. All right.

She grew achingly hungry. She ate handfuls of raw beans, grabbed from one of the densely planted fields, stuffed more into her dangling make-up bag before workers began to file in among the rows, although what she'd eaten already twisted sourly in her stomach.

As the light strengthened she crouched over her bag and rummaged through it, shamelessly begging God to let there be some money in it. Deep in a corner she did find three very small coins, dirty with neglect. They would not have paid for the beans she'd eaten.

She combed her black hair and let it fall forward, protectively, masking the sides of her face. Her dishevelment felt garish and blatant, calling reckless attention to her foreignness, something aggravated by the grubby, ingrained sensation of not having slept. Well, there was nothing she could do about not being Sinoan – and it didn't seem too much to hope that the peasant workers around her would not know about the arrests of immigrants. A few hours ago it had not been public at all; it still might not be. And there would be no longvisions out here. In any case, surely she would not be the police's first priority, even if they knew about her. She was only seventeen, and alone.

No longvisions. So no longdictors, either.

'Where are you going?' From a muddy field where a few thin water buffalo stood staring, a woman had clambered up onto the track in front of her. Her clothes, colourless cotton hanging from an undernourished body, were as dirt splashed as Lal's own, which gave her some reassurance. To Lal she looked, at first, ancient. And yet the threadbare lines on her skin were shallow, the contours of the flesh not sagged. She might be only in her mid-forties – no older than Ziye, but she still seemed wizened, her thin arms tough and dessicated as if a softer, more full-grown version of her had been condensed and dried down to this corky residue. Coarse, dark grey hair hung lank on her neck, held back with a twist of fencing wire. A straw hat shaded wary eyes.

'I need to get to a longdictor,' said Lal. A *yuan hua*.

'Here?' The woman grimaced sourly. 'We don't get things like that here. Nothing changes for us here, no matter what anyone does.'

'I know. I know. I need to get somewhere where there is one.'

'Are you *wo*?' A Nionian.

Lal was, momentarily, staggered. She gasped, 'No.' But the border was not far off. If the woman never saw foreigners, never or rarely saw longvision … Nionian made sense, as a guess. Lal wondered if perhaps she should have said yes.

'Are you from India, then, or somewhere? Are you Roman? You're not Sinoan.'

'I *am*,' Lal found herself saying, madly. 'I'm not – I'm not Han. I'm Mongolian. In the North. You know? Mongolia?'

'But you don't even speak Sinoan properly.'

'We speak another language there,' faltered Lal. For the moment, she could think of no more lies and the phantom homeland she had conjured provoked another spasm of tears. She didn't attempt to stem them; weeping would excuse her for a while from saying any more.

The woman sighed and came forward to pat and soothe her mechanically, with an air of mild exasperation. 'Never mind. Never mind,' she repeated flatly, until Lal had managed to stop. 'What are you doing here, then?'

Lal stammered something about coming south to look for work, about being tricked and robbed. She could not tell if the woman believed her, somehow telling anything seemed to render its credibility unimportant. It was obviously true that she was lost.

'Well, there's a place in Jingshan, but what are you going to do with no money? Have you eaten, even?'

'Not really. I'll work something out. I just – *have* to talk to ...' Tears threatened again as she considered saying 'my family', but this time she swallowed them back, and said, truthfully, 'I know an official's son, he'll help me. How far is that?'

The woman uttered another long-suffering sigh and grumbled patiently, 'I suppose Geng could take you there on the Sixth Day.'

'Oh!' Lal caught her breath with blended gratitude and anxiety. 'Thank you ...' But she could not say it without hesitation. It was only the Second Day now.

'That's when the market's on. You're not going to get there any faster, not walking. Not like that.'

Lal hesitated again, and then smiled with overstrained brightness and resumed thanking her effusively. The woman nodded tersely, so that Lal could see that her long-winded gratefulness seemed embarrassing and graceless to her, which made it all the harder to stop talking.

Geng, it turned out, was her son, also thin and weather-beaten, already balding at twenty-five. He appeared at about midday by which time Lal, who had been in another tiny field cutting sugar cane with a sickle for six hallucinatory hours, was dizzy with tiredness. His mother called Lal over and began explaining her to him, but she saw uneasily that he did not seem to listen; she fidgeted nervously under his curious gaze.

'Are you Persian?' he asked.

Lal suppressed a flinch of bewildered horror. She said steadily, 'No. I'm Sinoan. I'm from Mongolia.'

But this was terrible. The police must be searching for her far more scrupulously than she'd thought.

'Because there are these men in an official car up on the road. Stopping people and asking if they'd seen a Persian girl. *They* weren't Sinoan – they had someone translating for them. They were Roman. Definitely.'

Still stupefied with fatigue and anxiety, Lal felt her brain stall, her skin flush with confusion, before being electrified by a charge of hope. Marcus must know of Delir and Ziye's arrest. Marcus had sent them. 'Are they still there?' she asked.

'They were when I left. They were flagging down cars. It *is* you, then.'

His mother uttered a fatalistic snort at this, but otherwise looked largely indifferent, but a guarded and uncertain smile had spread across Geng's face.

'I'm sorry,' said Lal breathlessly. 'Where are they?'

He told her. Exhilaration buoyed her along a little way, blotting out her tiredness, but she ran for twenty stumbling minutes over spongy ground before the track reached a bare main road, and she staggered panting among a group of peasants on the roadside, who were raking wheat, spread to dry on the asphalt like reddish carpets. They turned and stared at her.

She saw the car, gleaming darkly in the distance. Three men standing beside it talking, one of them at least plainly not Sinoan. They were just near enough for her to see his light brown hair as he turned and disappeared back inside the car. A battered truck they must have stopped was just setting off again, away from them. Lal dragged her aching body to a run again, waving, calling.

Someone further ahead even guessed who she was, and shouted. But the Romans did not see her, or hear. She saw the car's red curtains flash in the sun as the doors swung closed, and Drusus' men drove away.

Varius stood with his back to the locked door, avoiding seeing it. His heart stammered along breakneck, it pelted and tripped. Each breath was like a shallow handhold on a cliff, it demanded so much struggle for such a little thing. This was, in fact, better than some hours earlier, when as he paced rapidly back and forth across the floor, the possessing force in the shut room and the struggle with it mounted until everything went dim and red, strange sickness seemed to lumber through his body like a wind through power cables, and he had just enough time to reach for a chair, to fall into that rather than to the floor. He wanted so much to be able to think clearly, and for the moment dared not lift his attention above noticing the repeating patterns in the carpet. He was disgusted at his incapacity to control what was not precisely fear, not the anticipation of something to come, but horror at the present. He had been in this room for a day and a night.

So far, at least, he blamed the Nionians for nothing. He'd been treated well enough himself; he hoped the same went for Una, for he did not know where she was. It had been obvious that the Nionians were, understandably, at a loss to know what to do with them. He and Una had been herded among the guards and lower ranking Nionian noblemen into a meeting room and held there, first in awkward silence, then with a lengthy quarrel going on around them that they couldn't understand. Meanwhile, someone must have been finding space for them in the pavilions, for then they had been separated, which was only sensible. He had been taken to these rooms, plainer and smaller but otherwise not much unlike the quarters he'd had on the Roman side of the compound, except that outside was fractured chaos, and inside he could only just breathe.

The bones of his hands were straining the skin, so tightly knotted were his fists. Carefully, finger by finger, he loosened them. There was a broad window seat against locked sandalwood shutters, through which a dim, sifted light fell. He let himself down onto it, resting his head against the wall, closing his eyes. And almost out of simple exhaustion, he gave up ordering himself to be calm. At least being shut in here alone, he could go out of his mind for a while without anyone to see. He almost laughed then, because that last thought seemed to come to him in Gemella's voice, as if she were leaning idly in the other corner of the window seat and speaking to him, so that with eyes still shut, he smiled affectionately at her and murmured, 'Except you.'

It only lasted a few minutes, but the feeling of her company had never been so easy, so close to painless, and even when it faded and he opened his eyes, his mind felt clearer, even if his pulse was still working far too fast and he didn't expect the respite to be permanent.

An hour or so after this, during which he'd been trying to make a dispassionate assessment of things, the door opened, making him start and then scowl at himself. Two of the Nionian retainers entered the room, with the interpreter he'd first encountered at the Venus Amaterasu ceremony.

The interpreter asked softly, 'Lord Varius, would you come with us?'

He got up and followed them. Moving through the open door he felt an illogical pulse of relief and an equally strong, contradictory recollection of being marched through the corridors in the prison, first towards his silent cell, then towards the van that would take him to Gabinius. They

287

went down to a long ground-floor room, walled on two sides with folding shutters of fretted wood, mercifully open to a garden and a courtyard. It seemed bare compared to the rooms in the other pavilions; Varius had the impression the Nionians had cleared away some of the furniture.

The Prince was seated with the other lords – Kiyowara, Taira, Mimana, Sanetomo. All were wearing white mourning, and so looked, to Varius, strangely Roman and senatorial. Tadahito, pale and stern among the rest, said to the interpreter in Latin, 'You may go. I will explain anything the Great Lords need to know.'

The interpreter bowed and retreated. In Nionian, one of the men at Tadahito's side ventured a protest and was answered sharply. 'Lord Varius,' said the Prince, with unsmiling graciousness, gesturing for him to sit.

'I am not a lord,' snapped Varius, much more irritably than was necessary. Tadahito only nodded gravely so that he felt a little ashamed of himself.

He sat down, organising his body into stillness, stifling the nervous restlessness in his hands and making them lie relaxed at his sides. For a second the effort sapped focus out of everything again. He watched the Prince and the lords conferring briefly, automatically lowering their voices in front of him, even though he couldn't have understood a word.

Tadahito said in Latin, 'You will be expecting questions now. It is in your own interest and your country's to tell us the truth.'

Varius judged this speech as pompous and tried to restrain a tic of impatience at it. He said, 'As before this happened, I won't lie to you. As before, I'll tell you the truth or say nothing. It depends what you ask me.' He braced himself a little and said dispassionately enough, 'Can you tell me if you have any intelligence about Caesar's journey? If anything has – happened?'

Tadahito gazed at him, a kind of sad, regal emptiness in his face. 'It is difficult for me to tell you anything,' he answered, and then did not elaborate, so that after a moment Varius realised this meant: 'No. I have nothing to tell you.'

'Is Noviana Una safe?'

'Why should anything worse have happened to her than has happened to you?'

'I would like to see her. I appreciate it's only sensible to question us separately in the first instance. But afterwards.'

'Afterwards, we will consider it.'

Varius nodded wearily, unsure if this was meant as a genuine concession or another coded refusal. A tired, apprehensive reflex shuddered through him.

'Are you unwell?' enquired Tadahito, watching him attentively.

'No,' said Varius looking away through the wide open lattices at the space and the light, clenching his teeth. The weakness was humiliatingly obvious, then.

Without warning, one of the older noblemen – Lord Taira – erupted, shouting at Varius what might have been an accusation, furious hands stabbing at the air, as if a pressure Varius had been unaware of had finally become unbearable. Taira turned to the Prince, bowing, begging something – apologising perhaps – but outraged and desperate. Even more than the violence of it, the sudden tears which ran freely from the man's eyes were unnerving to Varius, for Taira made no attempt to hide or suppress them, and yet there was no edge of a sob in his voice. The other lords looked embarrassed, but Taira himself seemed to have no sense of dignity lost, as if he were at once abandoning himself to the emotion, and unconscious of it happening. Tadahito told him – what? To be silent? That what he wanted would happen in due course? Varius felt jarred, shaken. As abruptly as his outburst had begun, Taira had returned to his seat, apparently composed again.

Tadahito said, as if nothing had happened, 'Two days ago, I thought there would not be a war. It seemed as if the people of Tokogane ...' He paused, reconsidered something, went on, '... as if the people of the world grew safer with every hour that went by. Now, Lord Kato is murdered by a Roman, Caesar disappears without warning, and you are left here. War between us appears only days away and I do not even know that it should be prevented.'

Varius said, 'I only know a Roman was involved in Kato's death because you tell me so. Neither Una nor I will be able to tell you about any government plot against you, because there was none. We came here, all of us, in the hope of peace. That is only what you would expect me to say, and it won't become any more credible by being repeated, but it had better be said once.'

'Yes,' agreed the Prince laconically. 'I would expect that.'

'You said yourself you trusted us until two days ago,' began Varius.

'We were close to trusting you,' Tadahito corrected him.

'Lord Kato's death is terrible, but it is still one man's death. You do not need to let it start something infinitely worse. It has not made that inevitable, even now.'

'It has made some things inevitable. He was much loved,' remarked the Prince blandly. 'Four of his men have already performed self-execution.'

Varius looked up and met Tadahito's eyes, feeling a jolt of disorientating recognition. 'I am sorry,' he said.

'They failed to protect him.'

'I can understand that.'

The exchange had been rapid. Now they were silent, as Tadahito studied him for another second. He had told Varius of the retainers' suicides with a kind of impassive defiance, as if to find it shocking would have been a weakness. But then his face altered, and became simply tired and depressed. He slumped a little, and said bitterly, 'And now I have more corpses to send home, more families to inform. You see? More people have already begun to die. Every Nionian who hears of this will demand revenge.' Varius saw Tadahito hesitate before taking the risk of the next words. 'And, he was a great leader. A great warrior. His loss – weakens us. It strengthens Rome against us.' He leant forward, indicating the other lords with a discreet glance. 'They cannot understand us talking, Varius. They would be horrified to hear me admit so much. But you know it, whether or not you had any part in his death. And in truth, I believe you did not. Caesar would not have left you in our power if he thought you could betray anything. So at least, if you know anything, you do not know that you know.'

'Look,' said Varius. 'Tell me the worst thing you suspect. That he had Lord Kato murdered, and everything else is just smoke to cover his return to Rome. Is it that? And we're here to keep you confused; you waste your time here questioning us for the few days before the attack comes. And he kept Una and myself ignorant so that we would be more convincing?'

'Yes,' said Tadahito. 'Don't trouble to tell me Caesar would not act against us in that way. Tell me if he would do it to you.'

'No.'

'Of course. The only possible answer. Tell me about the lady.'

'Is she expendable? No.'

'Even as a painful sacrifice, if he were convinced it was necessary?'

'No.' Varius remembered Tadahito's sister, the hinted marriage. It seemed to belong to another world, and yet it made discussing Una difficult. He was already aware that to put too much stress on her closeness to Marcus could place her in further jeopardy. He could try explaining that Marcus probably could not have deceived Una in such a way even if he'd wanted to, but the moment Una's ability occurred to him, it was with the certainty that he must not reveal it – it was the only possible advantage either of them held. He said cautiously, 'You must know that after his parents' assassination, there was a serious threat against Marcus' life. He met Una during a time which had a great impact on them both. Even if there were nothing between them now but the past, still, if he were to throw anyone away like that, she would be the last person.'

'And you. Are you as confident of your own standing with him?'

'Yes,' Varius answered. 'He could carry on as Caesar without my help, of course, but ...' He stopped speaking long enough for the Prince to open his mouth to begin a prompting question, but before he could voice it, Varius finished impatiently, 'He considers that I saved his life.'

Tadahito tilted his head, frowning, interested at the phrasing. 'He is ... mistaken, somehow?'

Varius smiled unhappily, already wishing he hadn't mentioned it. 'I don't share his view of events.'

'But in his mind, he owes you that?'

'No. He doesn't owe me anything. And even if he had it's – it's been paid back, that was years ago, but of course I trust him. At least ...' He exhaled a small, harsh laugh. 'I don't want to be here, Your Highness. Caesar put me in this position against my will and I'm not going to forget it. But I do know his reasons. And for them to be as you fear, he would have had to have changed out of all recognition.'

'Perhaps he *has* changed out of all recognition,' said Tadahito. He sighed and without turning away, began to speak in Nionian, evidently summarising what had been said in Latin.

Sanetomo answered, and spoke for some time, quietly arguing his case. He showed none of Taira's earlier passion. But he avoided Varius' eyes.

Tadahito listened and said in Latin, quite lightly, 'Lord Sanetomo says your intentions or Caesar's are no longer the point. If we are to believe what you say of Caesar's departure, then it is this second prince, who demands your return so vociferously, that we have to reckon with now. The peace negotiations are unsalvageable, and we must make use of what advantages we have. Maybe you can't tell us anything about Lord Kato's assassination. But there must be things you do know.'

Varius breathed out. He felt a kind of bizarre relief. They had come to the point. 'And you must know that I won't willingly tell you any-thing that could help you in a war against Rome. And if you attempt to – *force* me to do so, it will no longer be a question of whether you can trust Rome, it will be Rome's certainty that they cannot trust you. And peace really will be unsalvageable. You can't take that chance until you are sure Marcus isn't coming back. But that doesn't mean that there aren't questions you should be asking that I can answer. I will tell you everything, now that I know about Drusus Novius Faustus. Then I want to see Una.'

The lady was crouched in a chair, her knees drawn up and her arms hanging crossed over them. Her head jerked up as Noriko entered with Tomoe and Sakura, so sharply that Noriko stopped in her tracks and felt herself inexplicably blushing. The whites of the younger woman's eyes were scrawled over with red – from tiredness, it seemed, however, rather than weeping. Her skin was greyish, opaque, as if drained not only of colour but of some kind of vital sap. Despite that, she looked almost too alert, feverishly so, if fever could be cold instead of hot. Her movements were all a little too jagged and quick – not actually aggressive, yet with a cornered dangerousness straining in the thin, tense joints, so that Noriko felt she might lunge into an attack. Instead, the lady said, 'Please, come in,' her voice and face faultlessly courteous although the motion of the arm she extended was more commanding than welcoming.

Noriko had spoken at the same moment, murmuring, 'Forgive me. You are very tired.'

The collision of civilities silenced them both.

Noriko glided decorously into the room, thinking that it was either bold or ridiculous for a prisoner – even a prisoner of high status – to offer an invitation into a room she had no control over and could not leave. She settled on finding it rather impressive, and smiled, cautiously.

Una was irritated at the sting of dismay she felt. For God's sake, did any personal thing matter against the brew of crisis lapping outside the room? Or if she couldn't force her thoughts to operate on the clean, rational level she wanted, if she couldn't get her brain clear of agony about Marcus, it remained petty, degrading to be disturbed by another woman's beauty. Nevertheless, she found herself unprepared. Without the glamour of the deep, green-shaded hair, hanging loose to the floor against her clothes like a layer of silk against silk, without the almost equal finery of the women framing her, Noriko might have been no more than pretty. But over the twenty-four years of her life, so many hours of so many ladies and maids must have been poured into her, glossing her hair, smoothing her skin: she was laminated in time and skill, and glowed unthinkingly, taking it for granted. She had not yet identified herself, but Una was in no doubt who this was. And as she registered Noriko's hidden embarrassment, something else struck her – a furtive familiarity, a certainty that Noriko was concealing knowledge she should not have or could not admit to. Una had not seen the Princess before. But the Princess had seen her.

One of the other women confirmed, in low, hesitant Latin, that this was the Princess Imperial. Noriko placed her hands one over the other, before her chest and inclined her head in a nod of greeting which Una, after a moment, returned tersely. She was almost too raw with frustration and pain to be polite and likeable. Already she was aware of the ladies in waiting disapproving of her. Noriko herself was making allowances, though.

'Please excuse my poor Latin,' began Noriko, sitting down on one of the lacquered elmwood chairs. In Nionia they would all have been kneeling on cushions or matting. But they were not in Nionia.

'It's much better than my Nionian,' said Una, after a moment in which she could not understand Noriko's accent.

'No, no. But I have these; I hope I shall manage a little.' She took a couple of books from Tomoe and laid them beside her. Sakura poured out little bowls of the same leaf infusion Una had been given by the Sinoan court ladies. Or no, it was different, a startling grass green. Una stared at it, with a second's blank, exhausted fascination.

'I came to see how you were,' continued Noriko. 'If I can do anything for you.'

Una held back a sardonic grimace, thinking, you came because you wanted to have another look at me. She uncurled, scrubbed viciously at her face, and said forcefully, 'Yes, you can tell me what's going on.'

Noriko smiled sympathetically and busied herself leafing through her language books. But it was a deflecting tactic, Una knew she had understood.

'I've been answering questions all day. They've asked me fifty different ways if Marcus could have had that lord killed, but no one will talk to me seriously.' She was too agitated to speak slowly and Noriko missed a few words of this, but the sense of it was obvious.

'You must be anxious for news of Novius Caesar. But it is too soon for him to have reached Rome.'

Una said bleakly, 'Yes, I know.'

'So perhaps I cannot tell you anything of use. I could have some fresh clothes brought to you.'

'Thank you,' replied Una dully. 'Thank you very much.' She was quiet as she glanced at the Princess, shyly strategising. She subdued her impulse to look Noriko straight in the eyes, feeling that it was the wrong thing to do, but she leant forward and asked in a low, urgent voice, 'But in my place you would find out more. Wouldn't you?'

Noriko shot an involuntary, transparent look at her.

'What is she asking? She is pestering you,' complained Sakura in Nionian.

'It is all right,' muttered Noriko. She fingered the pages of the book broodingly and then snapped it shut. 'Leave us.'

Sakura and Tomoe rose silently to their feet and withdrew. The door shut again from the outside.

'Women are not allowed to know as much as they wish,' Noriko said, balancing her tone carefully, allowing for eventual evasion and at the same time signalling that she knew what Una meant. She smiled again, generously, including Una. 'Perhaps especially women of rank. Sometimes we are so confined in what we may do, aren't we?'

Una blinked. She heard her own short, coarse, incredulous laugh, and thought that alone ought to have been enough to tell Noriko the truth. 'I was a slave,' she said bluntly.

Noriko's eyes widened very slightly in polite incomprehension.

'Not some kind of high-up slave, either. I've been in filthy places doing horrible things you've never even *thought* of. I was a slave until I was fifteen.' Only as it faded did she recognise the tormented spite in her own urge to shock this polished, privileged creature, to rub her face in it. She had even felt affronted – that Noriko should *dare* to think that. She watched, a little angry with herself now, but interested to see how the Princess would react.

Noriko froze subtly. She was indeed profoundly shocked. It was as if with no warning she had been pitched through an invisible rotation in the air, as if the girl in front of her had monstrously changed herself, werewolf-like, into exactly what she had been before. A pale young woman, with a stern intelligent face, fiercely graceful even though dishevelled with anxiety and sleeplessness. A caged, somehow compelling person. 'Oh,' she said, in an unaltered voice, leaning to replenish Una's cup although Una had barely touched it. 'I hope I didn't offend you. So, please – you were saying?'

Una's lips twitched in a half-smile of grudging approval. She thought, fair enough.

'But I'm afraid I know very little about politics,' continued Noriko demurely.

Una nodded a little grimly, sizing up the obstacle. 'I don't want to offend you either, but I don't think I believe you there.' She paused. More hesitantly, in a softer voice, she said. 'I think ... I must tell you something else. I know why you came here with the Prince.'

Noriko started, again shocked into staring openly. And she was silent for a long time, her face slowly staining a clear, dawn red. Una observed again, without rancour now, how beautiful she was. Noriko murmured, 'How?'

'One of our officials worked it out,' answered Una, deciding against naming Varius. She turned her head away. 'I only heard a few minutes before Drusus Novius arrived. Before the attack. So, you must be anxious to know more about ... Caesar. Or at least about life in Rome.'

'I think that will not happen now,' said Noriko in an undertone, wondering how anyone could make such an offer about her lover in such a detached, authoritative way. 'I am sure *you* would not wish to see it, in any case.'

Una clenched her fists against a sudden blast of desolation. He promised me he would not, she thought, feeling her skin remember: the texture of his clothes and his body beneath as she'd pressed her face against him. He would be hurt if he could see this. He would want her to trust his word entirely, to put any other possibility out of her head. 'No, I don't want to see it,' she said, looking back at Noriko. 'This is the information I've got to bargain with and I hope it will be completely useless. It doesn't matter what I think, it only matters whether *you* want it.'

Another silence. 'It's true,' confessed Noriko finally. 'I would like to know more. To be safe. But, to bargain with that, as you suggest ...'

'I'm not asking where Nionia's missiles are! I only want to know what's happening *now*. Drusus Novius must want us back. So what has he said? Has he threatened to attack Nionia if Varius and I are not handed over to him?'

Noriko's face hardened quietly. She asked, 'Would he go that far?'

'Not at first, perhaps,' said Una. 'So far as he believes anything, he believes peace with your country is pointless. But he'll do what he thinks he must to become Emperor. He cares less about a war than that. He's here in the Emperor's name; he might feel bound to go through the motions for a few days. But if he thinks making himself a war leader will raise his chances, that's what he'll do. So yes, I think he will threaten you, and if you refuse, it will give him the excuse to start his war. And I don't think it will take very long.'

Noriko had to open her books again, and it took some time and several false starts before she was able to say what she wanted. 'He has not yet. They say that Novius Caesar had no right to offer you as hostages. We have said – I believe we have said, that still we would expect Rome to honour her pledges, especially since Lord Kato has been murdered.'

'So when he does, how do you think your country will react? Will you let the Romans have us?'

None of the sweetly evasive court mannerisms were left in Noriko now. She said grimly, 'We do not respond well to threats. No.'

Una sighed. 'Then I need to think,' she murmured, largely to herself. 'I need to talk to Varius.'

'I thought ...' said Noriko hesitantly. 'I thought perhaps ... if Drusus Novius has taken Caesar's place, I would be expected ...'

'To marry Drusus?' The girl had drooped a little, wearily, but she stiffened now, her face set with appalled conviction. 'Listen. He might

295

want to string things out longer than I think. I don't know how strong he is back in Rome. He might not mind marrying you. Do anything rather than let that happen.'

'There is nothing I can do. It isn't right,' protested Noriko.

'You can make sure your people know what he is. I promised I'd answer your questions about Marcus. I'll tell you about Drusus, too. If anyone's still considering it after that, think of something, do whatever you have to. Make yourself ill, stop eating. Anything. I'd rather be a slave again or dead than married to him,' said Una.

Lal was tired and humiliated. For the last three nights, Mrs Su, the woman she'd met at the roadside, had let her lie rolled in a musty blanket on the earth floor of her one-roomed house, and given her bowls of cabbage and insubstantial white rice that only pushed hunger to arm's length and kept it struggling and nagging, never more than temporarily weakened. Lal had spent each day cutting vegetables and carrying firewood. Mrs Su treated her with a kind of hospitable indifference, but still Lal felt more like an imposition than a help, and as each day her body ached more with yesterday's work and with the deficiency of food, the work seemed to grow harder rather than easier. Finally, at dawn, Geng had driven with her by slow, rocking cart into Jingshan. The jumbled, dustily blackened town loosely straddled a broad road, dotted with high, flimsy facades of soiled bright pink or red, misrepresenting the drab, low shops behind them. The place had a weak, disorderly, flattened quality, like a grey woodlouse stranded on its back, waggling frail legs.

Beneath one of these garish fronts, an eating house had four long-dictors set around puffy couches in a dimly lit room on the ground floor. But there was no use in going inside yet. In Jiangning they had never felt far from poverty, but affording the use of a longdictor hadn't been any great challenge. Here the price was a good percentage of a day's work. Geng had promised he would pay her enough for a few hours' help unloading and selling the produce from the farm. He didn't speak to her much on the journey and Lal had felt gloomily certain he resented this arrangement. But then as they drove off the road into the market place, a rubbish-strewn plot of scuffed ground, he startled her by suddenly apologising. 'You should have something for all the work you've done already. Unless we sell enough I just don't have it. That's the trouble.'

Lal stared at him, touched, and almost wanted to hug him. As well as the vegetables, she managed to sell her red bag for a few extra *wen*, although she thought the young woman she'd talked into buying it had done so more out of curiosity about the foreigner than a particular desire for it. She was uneasy again about making herself so prominent, but no one seemed obviously primed to spot a Roman fugitive, and she knew she couldn't hope to find the Roman agents by keeping hidden altogether. Nevertheless, when people asked, she said again that she was Mongolian. Geng did not contradict her.

Finally she said goodbye to Geng and walked back along the road with a handful of pierced coins slung together on a string and the make-up and perfume in a crumpled paper bag. It seemed slightly stupid to continue carrying these things, but they were her last souvenir from safety. As long as she didn't look at the contents of it, the sensation of a bag in her hand gave her the illusion of being equipped, comforted the feeling of dreadful vulnerability. Besides, she might be able to sell the perfume if anything went wrong. It wasn't at all valuable, but the bottle was pretty.

She went into the eating house. She found she didn't like leaving Geng behind. He would be in the market for another eight hours, and after that there would be no way of getting back to the tiny farmhouse; she would be alone once again.

She had to wait a long time to use a longdictor. She drew strange glances not only for looking different, but for being alone. No one was talking quietly into a circlet, as she wanted to, instead the sound on every longdictor was turned up so that the crowd around each table could all talk at once with sons or parents or friends, in distant rooms like this one. Families and gangs of laughing women were crammed rowdily onto the couches, eating dumplings and rice rolls, faces flushed with steam rising from pots of scalding tea. Lal thought wistfully that shared between so many people, the cost of the call would not even be that prohibitive. The clamour stuffed the room, bundled the different conversations into an impenetrable mass, insulating each group in a little niche of noisy privacy.

At last two elderly sisters with their daughters and grandchildren trooped out, and Lal self-consciously sidled into their place. She settled a circlet on her head and began trying to reach Liuyin's house.

Liuyin's mother answered. Lal hesitated and turned the longdictor off without speaking. She couldn't speak to anyone except Liuyin – his family wasn't keen on her at the best of times; they'd know she should have been rounded up with the rest, they'd call the police. Better leave it at least ten minutes before trying again.

She sat hunched, the circlet still on her head, eyes fixed on the battered tabletop, but one of the waiters came up to her almost at once, 'Are you finished? There are people waiting.' Indeed, a sullen group were staring at her resentfully from the doorway.

'Can I wait if I order something?' she asked, calculating that she might be able to spare the price of a pot of tea.

'I'm sorry; you must either use the *yuan hua* or let these people have the table.'

Reluctantly Lal got up and went to skulk in the shadows of the doorway, and it took more than three hours and four attempts before Liuyin's voice, sounding harassed and discontented, suddenly answered her.

'You told the other Romans,' he said, flatly.

Lal opened her mouth but said nothing, helpless. This hadn't crossed her mind since Ziye and Delir had been driven away. At last she protested, 'We *had* to.'

'My father could lose his job. My parents won't even speak to me.'

'I'm sorry.'

'You're not sorry or you wouldn't have done it,' said Liuyin petulantly, if accurately.

'Liuyin. They're our friends, what else could we do? It's like how you had to tell me. I'm so sorry to ask you for more help when I've already got you in trouble, but I really need it, I can't call anyone else.'

Silence, and a noncommittal sigh. 'Where are you? What happened?' Liuyin asked, reluctantly.

'They arrested Ziye and my father; I don't know where they are. It's taken me this long just to get to a *yuan hua*. I'm in an eating house in a little place called Jingshan. I haven't changed my clothes in four days; it's been horrible.'

'Oh, no,' said Liuyin gloomily. It was more a careworn moan of despondency than sympathy. He sighed again. 'I can't come and get you, you know. I can't get you any money. I can't travel that far without getting a permit for the checkpoints and I'd have to give a reason and have it approved, and why would I be going somewhere like that? I might be followed. And my parents won't let me go anywhere. Not after all this'

'Oh ... all right.' She shivered wearily. Although she was confident of Marcus' help, she was afraid it would take a while to get her message through, until then she'd hoped Liuyin might be able to spare her finding food and a place to sleep.

'Oh, no,' Liuyin repeated dully.

'Listen,' said Lal, switching decisively from plaintiveness to cheery, jollying optimism, as if Liuyin were the one in need of reassurance. 'It's all right, it will be all right, there are Roman men in a car looking for me. I missed them. All I need to do is let Marcus and Una know where I am and then it will be fine, all right?'

'Marcus Novius Caesar?' said Liuyin in loud, sceptical Latin rather than using the Sinoan rendition of the name.

'Yes, I know him, I've told you before.'

'Yes, but you knew him for a few weeks three years ago.'

'He would help – he is trying to help. I have to contact him, that's all.'

'You can't contact a *head of state*,' scoffed Liuyin. 'And even if you could, you can't contact a guest of the Empress when the police are after you.'

'Just listen. Una is there as well, she's my friend too. She used to sleep in my room back in the camp and there won't be millions of people trying to get messages to her. Your father's an official, you did the exam, you must have some contacts in Bianjing, haven't you? You must be able to get in touch with someone there. They've just got to get a note to her saying the code of this place and "Holzarta". No one will understand that except her or Marcus.'

'Do you *know* she's there?'

An unpleasant, sweaty tremor crawled across Lal, as she considered the fact that she did not know for sure. Sending the letter there had made it seem almost like a known fact. Deliberately, she shrugged it off. 'It can't make things any worse and I *know* the Romans are looking for me. Just try it. Please.'

Liuyin sighed again. 'All right, I'll try. But even if it did work out, what are you going to do until then?'

Lal said, 'Oh, I'll be all right,' and sat there, dazed, as the crowded room filled with yet more people.

Varius got to his feet as he heard footsteps approaching his room. Confinement here had grown less oppressive since the interview with Tadahito. It remained like a physical weight strapped to his body, which his strength to tolerate rose and fell in slow rhythm as the hours passed; it kept him awake, but at least he could think freely, most of the time.

The key turned and a pair of Nionian guards escorted Una into the room. They had not been pushing or dragging her along in any way, and she must have known where they were leading her, yet still she looked breathless and shaken, more fragile to Varius than she had even after Drusus' attack on her. Her eyes were wide and shadowed with the same exhaustion he could feel printed on his own face.

The interpreter followed and said formally, 'You may associate during daylight hours, as long as this situation continues.'

After the men left them alone, a few seconds passed in which they stood unmoving. For a moment they could not say anything, all questions of what these last days had been like seemed useless: the answers were so bald and known. He could not even smile a greeting at her and yet he was intensely relieved and glad to see her there. Instead, although it was rare for either of them to volunteer touch, they both stepped speechlessly into a short, grim, one-armed embrace. As they moved apart it was she who whispered to him, 'Good to see you,' tapping an encouraging pat onto his shoulder that could almost have made him laugh.

'He hasn't reached Rome,' Una told him crisply, almost as though they were picking up a conversation broken by only a few minutes. No need to use Marcus' name. Her voice sounded bruised and raw.

Varius nodded, quietly distressed. No one had told him this. He asked, 'Did they tell you how they're explaining that in the Empire?'

'That there's some problem with the magnetway,' she said, going over to the window seat and drawing herself up into a tense twist on the cushions.

She was afraid he would try and pretend this might be true, but he said, 'Of course they're lying, something's happening. But it doesn't mean Marcus has been killed.'

Una flicked a strained, sceptical look at him, face distorted into a humourless smile.

'Drusus wouldn't stay here, he wouldn't need to press Nionia to give us up if he were confident enough to do that.'

Again her lips curled unhappily. 'It doesn't work – making up stuff to make me feel better.'

'It might work on me,' suggested Varius, managing to goad a more genuine smile out of her. 'Look. I think I've got the Prince convinced none of us were involved in what happened to Kato. And that it's worth not giving up. So we can't. I'm going to work on the assumption Marcus is alive until I get a definite reason to stop. We have to do that. For all kinds of reasons we have to.'

'Varius,' said Una, her voice reminding him all at once how young she was. 'What will happen to us if we're here and the war starts?'

Varius looked at the floor for a second before sitting down a few feet from her along the window seat. 'Well,' he said quietly. 'They would take us into the Empire, of course, probably Nionia itself. And they'd keep us somewhere pretty much like this for the duration of the war.'

'Years,' Una said.

'It could be, yes. Although if Rome had any valuable Nionian prisoners we might be exchanged for them, perhaps. Of course that wouldn't be such a good thing for us if it was Drusus on the other side.'

'What about ...' She hesitated. 'They'd go on asking us questions. Would they ... hurt us?'

Varius gave her a quick, searching look. He did not know, and was not sure he wanted to know, how far his thoughts were open to her. He assumed and hoped it did not go too deep, most of the time. But now he said as emphatically as he could in his mind: *Una. They're probably recording us. Be careful what you say. You're safer if they don't take you too seriously. Don't make them think you've got information they need.*

Aloud he said firmly, 'Of course they wouldn't do anything like that to you. There wouldn't be any reason.'

She had certainly understood, but looked more taken aback at what he'd done than he'd expected. She cast an instinctive glance around the room. 'You mean they would to you?' she asked.

'I don't know.' He felt his heart begin to beat a little faster again at the possibility. He said vaguely, 'Maybe it wouldn't be that bad.'

'What do you *mean*, it wouldn't be that bad?' demanded Una, appalled, in a voice that came out as resoundingly withering.

'You're a very reassuring person to be locked up with,' Varius said, and they looked at each other and found themselves helpless with febrile laughter. Una had barely seen Varius even smile before now, and yet the more unfitting and bizarre it seemed to be laughing in these circumstances, the more they couldn't stop.

When they could speak again, Varius explained, 'They know I'm Marcus' advisor, but I'm not a general, am I? Anything I know would probably only hold for the first few weeks of the war. And the Prince has spent all this time working with us. After that I don't think he would willingly allow – torture.' He did think this was true, but he also thought he would raise the likelihood by saying it, if Tadahito were indeed listening to this conversation.

Una was quiet for a little while. Finally she asked, 'Would they kill us?'

Even if he had been sure he could do so successfully, he wouldn't have lied to her now. 'If they were losing, maybe, in the last stages.'

Una sighed and dropped her head onto her arms thinking how long it seemed since she had seen her brother. There was a small catch of nausea in the back of her throat. Sulien too was not safe from Drusus. At least, she could not be sure he was safe, and no one who came into these few rooms would be able to tell her. She wondered if he had any way of knowing where she was.

'I'm not saying that's what *will* happen,' said Varius. 'Don't tell any-one I said this if we make it back to Rome, but it's not as if a Roman victory is guaranteed. Maybe we can help Marcus run a puppet government. Might be all right.'

She smiled again, despite herself. But she said, 'However it ends, it's going to start now. It will happen before Marcus even reaches Rome. Drusus will threaten them. I can't believe it'll take him longer than another two days. It could be in the next hour. And the Nionians will attack first. There will be nothing for Marcus to come back to, even if he could. We can't just sit in here and wait. And it seems like there's nothing we can do, but there must be something, we've got to *make* there be something.'

'I told the Prince he should stall Drusus as much as he can,' said Varius. 'Ignore him, even. I told him everything Drusus has done. I said he should carry on talking to us – to me, try and come up with something. He said that Drusus is the one with the power to direct Rome's actions, which is reasonable.'

'We've got to do something about that, then,' said Una. But she struck a fist against the seat beside her in frustration. 'Oh, I wish I hadn't been a slave. I wish I knew more.'

'What do you wish you knew?' interjected Varius, calmly.

Una looked first at him, and then into space, thinking. At last she answered, 'About the Sinoan Empress.'

Fine rain dashed against Noriko's face, under the broad silk umbrellas her servants carried as they crossed the courtyard. The screenbearers either side of them hid Noriko's finery from no one in particular. She wore her best, most pointedly Nionian clothes: long, layered, multi-coloured sleeves hanging to the ground, loose ribbons of gold silk restraining her hair. She turned her face anxiously to one of the maids to have the droplets blotted carefully from her make-up, a strand of moistened hair smoothed down. Heavier than usual, the sensation of the cosmetics on her skin comforted her. Beneath it her features seemed controlled gently into an expression of serene composure, like a face painted on a vase. As far as possible, she wanted to look unrecognisable as the girl in dark cotton caught prowling around the pavilions with a telescope in her hand.

She'd received a folded note in Latin the evening before, asking her to come to Una's quarters that night, after the hostages had been separated. Of course curiosity had made her go, even though no one could have forced her. She understood that much about her own actions; she was less sure why she felt so driven now to carry out what Una had asked her, *told* her to do.

She had begun, instinctively, by saying she could not, that it was impossible. And Una had said, putting a decisive hand over hers, 'So far, nothing that you've told me you couldn't do has really been beyond you.'

Many times since, waking repeatedly during the night, Noriko had gone over this, and the effect it had had on her. Did it really amount to any more than self-congratulation on how well she had managed to manipulate Noriko already? And did any of the small prevarications, the small trades and concessions of information Noriko had made so far, compare with this? It was probably profoundly incorrect to have anything further to do with Una, much less allow herself to be influenced by her. Una was significantly younger than she was, too, even if it were acceptable to disregard the matter of her class.

And yet, every time she reminded herself that she need do nothing but wait in her quarters, forget that either conversation had ever taken place, and never see Una again, that voice and that phrase repeated firmly in her mind.

A party of Sinoan councillors came out from the eastern audience hall to meet her, and they acknowledged each other coolly. The chamber they led her to was smaller and more modern than the grand throne room in which Drusus had met the Empress; much of the furniture – small ebony tables, and scrolled marble couches where no one ever sat – was plainly Roman, although every inch of satin padding the seats, hanging from the walls, was the Imperial primrose yellow.

Her attendants stepped aside, and Noriko bowed impassively with conscious, queenly grace. She straightened again as the Empress, who seemed to fill the room with her crimson and peach-coloured clothes and her presence, looked down at her with precisely the smile of sardonic glee that Noriko had anticipated.

'So, *you* turn up again,' she said.

'Your Majesty,' said Noriko gravely, as if she had no idea what the Empress was talking about. She was aware of confusion flickering across the faces of the silent eunuchs and ladies standing attendance around the room. Worse, others smiled with what looked like discreet amusement, as if they understood.

'You look very elegant, Princess. Are you always such an ornament to your country and your station?'

Noriko lowered her eyelids carefully and concentrated on not writhing with embarrassment. 'My brother the Prince has given me permission to come and thank you for your hospitality. Today the elder Roman prince set us an ultimatum we cannot tolerate. So, it will all come to an end, and I will have to return home. I would like to present you a with a few gifts in farewell.'

Sinoan came much more easily to her than Latin, although it was a strain holding two foreign languages at such close proximity in her head. A twitch, that might have been a smirk at her pronunciation or some other mistake, pulled at Jun Shen's mouth, however Noriko saw how gloom gathered over the white face.

'These are nothing, really, but please accept them,' said Noriko, gesturing for her maids to came forward and spread the gifts before the Empress. Fans, robes, carved combs, all to gather dust somewhere, as both of them knew.

'Charming,' the Empress murmured flatly, managing to smile and nod listlessly at the things. Her gaze had turned sad and introspective, and as the will to torment Noriko faded, she visibly lost awareness of her even being there.

'My brother does not know why I am really here,' said Noriko quietly.

A greedy flash of interest brightened the Empress' face: her eyebrows skipped up, her head cocked to one side. She looked so lively with expectation that for a moment Noriko felt almost fond of her.

'I think you should talk with the two Roman hostages,' she said.

They had brought a longvision into the room. Una sat close to it with the sound turned low, managing to keep part of her mind fascinated by the swooning Sinoan melodrama on the screen, sometimes even convincing herself she could understand what the characters were saying.

Behind her, lying stretched on the window seat, Varius sighed and shifted. 'I was asleep,' he murmured, to himself rather than to her, sounding faintly incredulous.

'Not for very long,' Una said. She was sure this was more or less the first time he'd slept since this began. Even now she could usually force at least a few hours' unconsciousness out of each night before she woke in the dark, with her brain clicking along terribly like an automatic loom, manufacturing thoughts she couldn't bear. There was still no news of Marcus. There could not be any news of Sulien.

Varius' eyes closed again, inexorably, as though dark fingers were holding the eyelids down. He felt distantly surprised at how the straining pressure suspended in the walls of the room had faded; he supposed he was just too tired to feel it any more. It was as if the lid of a box had been lifted an inch or two, letting in the air. He said, 'Una. There's something we haven't talked about.'

'What?'

'What you're doing ...' He paused. 'What we are doing. It's treason. It could be seen as treason.'

Had she considered this herself, had she known he was thinking it?

Apparently not, for she jolted round to look at him, and she laughed, a bleak, startled sound. 'Well, who will see it as treason? Marcus wouldn't. And if Drusus gets hold of us, we're in the frame for that anyway, or something like it, aren't we? They can only kill us once.'

'The consequences for us aren't the only reason to think about it,' said Varius.

'No,' she admitted. The amusement on her face died away. She said, 'But I have, I do. And I think it would be treason *not* to do the one thing we can think of. There must be such a thing as treason to the whole world, mustn't there? I've never really thought of myself as Roman.'

'I have,' Varius said, his voice a little remote.

'You aren't disagreeing.'

'No. I only think people should know the possible names of the things they do.'

Una nodded. After a while she smiled again, drily and said, 'Treason. That's good, we can use that.'

Varius' questioning look faded as his eyelids weighed helplessly down again. But it was only a few minutes later that she woke him again, regretfully shaking his shoulder, her face sharp and alarmed.

'I thought it would be hours yet – they're coming.'

Noriko was near, swept along like a leaf, by someone like a weather front storming forward, a few seconds from the room.

Outside, on the landing, Noriko hurried on behind the Empress feeling unpleasantly as if she had been co-opted into the Sinoan Imperial retinue. 'Tell them I can go where I want in my own palace,' the Empress called to her interpreter, as the Nionian guards outside Varius' rooms startled into confused action, reaching for their radios, alarmed eyes moving from Noriko to Jun Shen and back.

Inside the room, Varius dragged himself up, kneading his face with his hands and perfunctorily brushing down his clothes. Una pushed back her hair. They had nothing of their own beyond what they had been wearing when Marcus had foisted them into the Nionian compound. Since then they had been lent clothes clearly chosen to be as Roman, as appropriate to them, as was possible. Still, clean and unfamiliar against their skin, the borrowed fabric was a physical reminder of how dispossessed they were here. The dress Una wore belonged to one of Noriko's ladies in waiting. It felt strange.

The door was opened and the Empress advanced, overwhelmingly, into the room and looked at them. Promptly, Una stepped forward and executed a neat, efficient bow to the floor. Varius lingered for a resentful second and then stiffly did the same. Una was aware of him hating it, and felt mildly exasperated. What did it matter what the body had to do, what convention had to be acted out? They didn't have to mean it.

As they got to their feet, Noriko realised that she had been bracing herself for Jun Shen to mock or belittle the prisoners in some way, and was surprised when she didn't. In fact, the Empress' whole demeanour was, from the first instant of entering the room, different from what it had been outside and from what Noriko had expected. The capricious, fractious manner might never have been more than a kind of disguise. She was looking both Romans over, sharply and carefully, black-painted eyes puckered and shrewd. 'I should like to speak with you both,' she said, with sober grandeur, as if she were the one to have initiated this. She sat down ceremoniously, forcing Weigi to push a chair into place for her without breaking his translation of what she was saying. 'Drusus Novius has been bothering me about you,' she went on. 'I have the impression neither one of you will have anything good to say about him. He accuses you of various crimes – having Lord Kato killed in mistake for him, among others.'

'If I was going to kill him, he'd be dead,' muttered Una darkly.

Varius said, 'We had a chance to have him killed once before. We shouldn't have missed it. But it was Caesar's decision, I accepted it. There was no reason for that to change. We both have strong reasons to hate Drusus Novius, reasons that are involved in why we're here, but we don't need them at this point. He's about to provoke a war we've been working to prevent. I know you're aware how damaging such a war could be to your country. He can't be allowed to do this unchecked. It has to be made impossible for him.'

'I don't hate him,' said Una dully. Varius looked at her in disbelief and she said, 'I don't. I don't know why not. I've hated people who've done a lot less. Him, though … I just want him … *gone, stopped*. I thought he *was*.' She looked up at the Empress, waiting as Weigi's translation caught up with her. 'Your Majesty, if he can't cross Sinoan space it'll slow him down at least before he attacks Nionia. You should close your borders to Rome. Air, magnetways, everything.'

Once again, Noriko expected some kind of affronted outburst from Jun Shen, but it didn't come. There could be no doubt that the Empress was incredulous – she did not attempt to conceal that, letting out a low grunt of frank surprise. But for a long time she said nothing, and only continued to scrutinise Una as if she were determined to commit her face to memory. Una looked back, only a small, shifty contraction of the mouth betraying any discomfort at this.

'You're very young for this,' Jun Shen remarked at last.

Una looked blank for a second, before giving a small, unconvinced nod. She said, 'I don't feel that young.'

The Empress smiled regretfully. 'One never does at the time.'

Something occurred to Noriko: a little knot of snobbery that she had either forgotten or never known she harboured toward Jun Shen came loose, and with it her surprise at the Empress' apparent readiness to take Una seriously. She thought – of course, *she* is not really royal, any more than Una. How old would she have been when she became a concubine? Where does she even come from? She was not born to do any of this. But she does it.

'For such a decree to have any meaning, we would have to be willing to shoot down any Roman force that tried to cross our frontiers,' said Jun Shen, a politician again, the minor softness gone. 'A few shots fired and that amounts to entering the war on Nionia's side.' She gave a mechanical little scoffing laugh.

Neither Una nor Varius spoke yet.

'Do you know anything of the history between our countries?' the Empress went on, with a glance in Noriko's direction.

'I know some,' said Una diffidently, thinking of the books she'd read back in Athens, and the questions Varius had answered for her the day before.

The Empress smiled, mirthlessly. 'Then you know it is not a very happy one.'

'If Drusus remains in power, war will follow,' said Una. 'And you will find yourself against him soon. He will not respect alliances, and he will want total Roman control. So, finally you will enter the war, either on Nionia's side, or alone.'

'But even he will think twice about taking on two empires at once on a moment's notice. Or even if *he* were mad enough to consider it, Salvius isn't,' continued Varius. He'd got his crushing weariness controlled, and he now understood what Una had said to him earlier when he'd been on the point of sleep. He said, 'We've discussed how we may be judged in Rome for advising you to do this. It will keep Drusus contained for now. It could be long enough for Marcus to put right whatever damage Drusus has done to his standing in Rome. If he returns the war can be averted. This is important enough to justify treason.'

Jun Shen played with one of the jewelled pendants hanging from her throat. 'If Drusus Novius is all that you say, what will he do with his cousin now he has the opportunity?' She glowered at them astutely. 'You don't know, do you? You can't be sure.'

'I am very sorry to interrupt,' said Noriko, 'but isn't the point that as long as we do not know, there is still some hope? And so it is still worth trying everything?'

The Empress sucked her lip thoughtfully, slightly smearing the red paint. 'For how long are you asking me to do this?'

'How long could you do it?' asked Varius.

'There would be people left stranded, it would play havoc with trade,' grumbled the Empress. 'And tension with Rome growing all the time …? I can give you a few days at the most.'

'A fortnight,' Varius pressed.

'Nonsense. Perhaps I could stretch to a week, but the costs would be immense – a fortnight is out of the question.'

'That gives us too little scope to be worth the damage. Ten days, or until we hear Marcus has given up his power. Or that he's dead. Whatever comes first,' said Varius, deliberately brutal, but with a barely discernible glance of apology and pain at Una.

Jun Shen pursed her lips again. 'Fine. Ten days, then,' she said shortly, getting crossly to her feet. Standing with hurried respect, Una, Varius and Noriko felt after all the shock of what they'd done, a strange hybrid of relief and anxious dread. Una and Varius turned to each other, almost disbelieving, and Noriko thought of Rome, and the marriage, and wondered how far the work she'd done today had raised the chances of its happening.

Jun Shen gave Una another hard look. 'And I have something for you,' she announced. She took a small card from a little pouch of embroidered silk. 'The message came yesterday. You can have it as far as I'm concerned. So your next job will be to try and persuade your keepers to let you use a *yuan hua*. I dare say you will manage it.'

Una took the card, startled. There were a few columns of Sinoan characters beside the Latin translation: her name, a longdictor code and the word 'Holzarta'.

Lal dragged the stack of pipes she was trying to carry a few steps further and stopped, gasping and dizzy, her legs shaking. She had managed this yesterday, why was she so flatly incapable of it now? She laid half of the pipes down and struggled on with the rest, piled them up against the back wall of the yard and went back for the others. She saw one of the men roll his eyes in exasperation. This was what they had said she would be like, this was why they hadn't wanted to hire her in the first place.

They had lent her some overalls to work in, giving her at least the chance to finally wash her filthy dress, and they let her sleep on a pile of plastic sheeting in a back room. One of them had even brought her some blankets and pillows for the second night.

But they were about to fire her. She was sure of it – she could sense it coming.

She had an arrangement with the eating house. She had told them that when someone speaking a foreign language called, it would be for her, and taught them to say, 'Wait, I will get her,' in Latin. She'd given them most of what was left of Geng's money in advance, both for the use of the longdictor itself and for sending someone to find her in the town. The girls at the restaurant were tickled both at their new ability to speak a few words of Latin, and at the sounds of the words themselves. To be sure of being on hand when the call came, Lal went there for her meals when she could manage it, eating the cheapest, most basic dishes of rice or noodles, and each time she managed to find a day's or a few hours' work she tramped round to make sure they knew where to find her. Whenever she appeared, the girls would chorus at her, 'Wait, I will get her. Wait, I *get* her,' as if the phrase were either a greeting or a string of delectably rude words, and then fall about giggling or tease each other for saying it wrong. They were friendly but it was hard to go on being amused, as her hope of word from Una went on being disappointed.

She had hoped she might be able to get a few days' work in the long-dictor restaurant itself. She felt absurdly wistful about the idea now, as if it represented some kind of paradisal simplicity. But the couple who ran the place had told her that most of their children and a few young men from nearby worked there already – they neither needed nor could afford anyone else. Lal thought her dirty, desperate appearance might also have had something to do with it.

Still, by the standard of the next few days, she'd been lucky the first evening. Her age and sex carried certain advantages as well as certain risks. Trying to guess the meaning behind the bemused stares of men she passed made her frightened and paranoid, but at least there were times when it helped to be unthreatening. In the eating house, after opening her crumpled paper bag of make-up and hopelessly dabbing on some of the perfume in lieu of being able to wash properly, she persuaded a woman to let her spend the night on an absent daughter's bed. But though this small space was free, the house was crammed with a strife-ridden family gripped in a furious, years-long argument, of which certain factions – the husband, the daughter-in-law – were plainly displeased at Lal's presence. Lal took it that she shouldn't come back.

The second day she wandered about desperately, afraid of straying too far from the eating house. She wouldn't have been above stealing if anything she wanted – food, soap – had been exposed enough. But she drew so much interest wherever she went that it was impossible to think she could get away with it. Finally she found a man who had just taken over a dilapidated shop and was dragging dank rubbish out of it into a skip. She helped him empty the place of broken shelves and damp-spoiled boxes in exchange for a few coins and permission to sleep that night curled on the shop floor.

One horrible day she could find no one who wanted any kind of work she could offer, and ate only once before nightfall, when she'd had no choice but to creep away into the fields and try to sleep on a few scavenged sheets of cardboard. After that she'd harassed the men at a builders' merchants into letting her join them in unloading a delivery of bricks, pipes, girders. They had been unconvinced she was strong enough and she was proving them right.

She lugged the rest of the pipes into place, reeled around behind a stack of concrete bricks, and then some black, intangible time later, realised she must have gone to sleep on her feet, her face propped numbly against the bricks. The manager was standing over her, arms discontentedly folded. Lal blinked at him, stupidly, for the moment almost unable to understand the words he was saying. Not that it mattered, the meaning was obvious. She felt strangely indifferent. She changed back into her dress, dropped the coins he gave her into the paper bag without looking at them, and walked leadenly down the road towards the longdictor place out of dull instinct, not because she had any real expectations of going there.

Some way ahead of her, a girl came bounding along up the drab road, long, raggedy plaits flapping as she ran. It was one of the restaurant waitresses, a girl a few years younger than Lal. She skipped cheerfully up to Lal and chirruped, 'Wait! I *get* her!' in an extravagant parody of Lal's own accent, and laughed heartily.

'What? Is it my friend?' asked Lal in Sinoan, startled into something like alertness.

'Yes! Come on!'

Lal struggled to keep up, resenting the unreasonable distance. It seemed amazing that the other girl could dash along so easily having already run all this way. She reached the restaurant long before Lal and stood, bouncing encouragingly in the doorway. Lal stumbled at last into the longdictor room, fell into a seat, one of the girls placed the long-dictor circlet on her head with a comical flourish, and a faintly suspicious Roman voice said hesitantly, 'Who's that?'

'Una!' cried Lal in relief. A hot, dry, torrent of exhaustion thundered over her, and she slumped over the table, propping her heavy head on her hands, smiling. 'Oh, I knew you'd answer, I *knew* you had to be there.'

There was a confused pause, and Una said cautiously, 'Lal?'

'I'm in a village called Jingshan. It's not that far from Jiangning, it's – ah – it's south-west, somewhere, I don't know, but I only just missed them last week. Please, can you tell them I'm here—'

'Wait, wait,' interrupted Una. And this time Lal noticed the tired, beleaguered sound in her voice, the faint controlled hysteria lurking behind it, as though talking to Lal came so incongruously close upon the heels of some difficult or terrible thing, that Una could barely cope with it. 'I'm sorry. It's strange talking to you after all this time and in the middle of all this. I don't understand. Who are you talking about? Are Delir and Ziye with you? Why are you in this place?'

'You don't know,' said Lal quietly, suddenly wary and chilled, listening hard.

'Why? What did you think I knew?'

'My father and Ziye were arrested – oh, more than a week ago now. We were trying to get across the Long River. I got away. The police were rounding up all the Roman immigrants because of that Nionian lord who was killed. You must have known about him. I thought ... I thought you and Marcus must have heard.'

Una gave a kind of moan of tense laughter, as if she didn't know where to start. 'Marcus is gone. He's been taken back to Rome. And Varius and I are with the Nionians. We're hostages, we're trying to – I can't explain it all now. Drusus has taken over, that's the main thing. We hope it's not for ever, but ...'

'But it could be,' finished Lal, in a dazed murmur. She blinked into unstable space. 'But ... there are Roman men in a car, looking for me. I even saw them, I just couldn't run fast enough. They'd been asking people if they'd seen me. Geng said—'

'*Lal*,' Una interrupted with stern urgency, almost in a shout. 'If there are Roman agents looking for you, they're acting for Drusus. He must have your letter. I don't know what he wants with you but it won't be good. You can't let them find you.'

'My letter ...?' repeated Lal, overwhelmed and dizzy.

'Listen. We've got ten days. After that, or if the war starts, you'll have to give up on us. Until then you stay as hidden as you can. If you have to move on, get a message to me again the same way, otherwise, if Marcus comes back, if I get out of this, I will contact you there. And I will send someone and I will get you to Rome. And if you do hear that the war's beginning, then at least it means Drusus almost definitely isn't after you any more. You'll have to – I don't know, you'll have to do what you and Delir and Ziye would have done if they hadn't been arrested. I'm sorry.'

Lal let out an unsteady breath, unable to speak. What answer was there to that?

'Lal,' said Una again, a gentler, regretful catch in her voice now. 'It would be really good to talk to you if it wasn't for all this.'

Lal put the longdictor circlet heavily down on the table. It occurred to her that she was trembling, and she thought with a sense of vague bewilderment and annoyance, but I'm not that scared. That was strange, really – why wasn't she? She was too tired to be scared. She hugged herself vaguely. And then she noticed at last that it made no sense to be so cold in the neutral, muggy air, and then realised that the dull, lethargic weight that had been pulsing in her head and limbs for at least the last two days was pain. For the first time she thought; I'm getting ill.

In Bian, Una turned off the longdictor and leant back in the chair, sighing. 'Well, there's another reason to hope this works out.'

Noriko extracted the little cylinder on which the conversation had been stored from the base of the longdictor. It had been a condition of obtaining permission for the Roman hostage to make a short call that it should be recorded, although by now Noriko trusted Una enough to believe her agitated account of what the word Holzarta meant.

Then Tadahito broke suddenly into the room, his face pale. He stood and stared at Una and Noriko with an expression that hovered between wonder and distrust. He demanded, 'You have done this? This bargain with the Empress – you and Lord Varius?'

'Yes,' Una said, starkly.

'And you?' he said, turning on Noriko switching to Nionian, his voice bright with accusation.

Noriko bowed calmly to her brother. 'Yes. Forgive me if I did wrong.'

Tadahito took a half-exasperated breath and looked speechlessly from the two women to Varius, who had emerged from the inner room where he had been asleep, and remarked to all of them, 'Drusus Novius has already made his threat.'

'Which he can no longer act on, or repeat,' said Varius, standing propped in the doorway between rooms. 'At least not for now. So you pretend you did not see it, or know it arrived. You don't respond. It never happened.'

Tadahito's wary look at him diffused gradually, growing cautiously thoughtful, testing the idea.

Una said, with the lucid, adamant force in her voice again, 'Marcus left us here in his place, to represent him while he's gone. We should go on from where you left off. We should carry on the work, for the time we've got.'

There was definitely a noise in the sky, a steady, drilling rasp, a dull hammering of the air. It had passed the point where it could have been a desperate trick of imagination, nor was it wind or oncoming rain. It scraped away the surface of instinctive fears he'd learnt three years ago, and his blood ran faster, but there was eager anticipation in it now. Marcus pressed against the windows of the carriage, but the sound was coming from behind the train, he could only see colourless sky. They'd locked the door to the saloon balcony days ago.

He had not seen the torn tunic or the photograph of Sulien since that morning four days earlier. Of course he did not need to see them. Day by day the train had remained motionless on the magnetway and the magistrate of Roxelania continued to watch him with vigilant, critical eyes, and Marcus could not stamp the thought of it down into his dreams, as he had done to his fear over Una and Varius. There was no point until which he could safely defer thinking about it; it was too concrete. There was a decision that had to be made. And innumerable circumstances, choices he might make, interviews with Faustus, ways out, acted themselves within his mind as if a dreadful locked theatre had been forcibly constructed there, but all the time he was chilled by the quiet but definite appeal that kept recurring in his mind: 'Sulien. Forgive me.'

But now there were Roman military aircraft out there, flying low, closing in. What did they want with him? If the soldiers on board the train were taken by surprise, as he sensed they were, what would they do?

They landed, shining on the coarse grass, dark-uniformed men bursting out of them just as they had on Siphnos. Instinctively Marcus stepped back as they leapt up in through the doors. A legionary found him at once, and said, 'You must come with us immediately, Caesar.'

'Come where?' said Marcus, noticing the use of the title, unconsciously caressing the Imperial plumb of gold on his index finger with the tip of his thumb.

The officer looked confused. 'Rome, of course, sir.'

Marcus felt a smile of tense triumph wrench at his mouth. 'It will be good to be home,' he said. And as he went forward to join them, he looked back only to stare coldly at the nervous magistrate of Roxelania, and say, 'I told you. I will remember you.'

Marcus never left the aircraft when they stopped to refuel at Trapezus. But they lingered on the ground for so long that his grim excitement began to fade and he wondered if this was only another stage of obstruction. But then he heard the wings begin to turn again and a cold, bracing surge of air flooded the cabin as the hatchway opened and Salvius entered.

Marcus stared at him, straightening in his seat. 'Salvius. Is this your doing?'

'Well, of course it is,' said Salvius brusquely.

Marcus continued to look at him fixedly until Salvius turned his eyes away in impatient unease. Marcus said at last, 'Thank you.'

'Caesar,' said Salvius drily. 'I must in conscience say I didn't do this as a favour to you. Whatever this problem with the magnetway, it was becoming absurd. The situation must be resolved. You must answer to the Emperor.'

'Then I still say, thank you,' maintained Marcus. 'But Salvius, don't you realise Drusus arranged this? He knows he's at risk when I see the Emperor, because he knows how many lies he's told him, and you.'

'Your cousin has been in contact deploring the delay.'

'But he didn't order you to do what you have now. I imagine he said there were other concerns than a few days of my time lost in Sarmatia. Maybe he even admitted that his efforts in Bian would run more smoothly without my interference. But you decided that was wrong. Didn't you?'

Salvius said nothing.

'Tell me something else. My friend Sulien – is he under arrest now?'

Salvius frowned, as if afraid of being drawn into some kind of trap. 'No. Unfortunately, he is not.'

Marcus dropped his head back against the seat with a gasp. And yet the strong, wonderful relief came with an immediate knowledge that in another second he was going to have to let it go. For a second he resisted but the sour awareness remained: there was something wrong.

If Salvius were not so deep in Drusus' confidence that he could not act independently, as he had done, then he might not know if Sulien were being held or not. Salvius' denial only meant that if it had happened, it had not been officially acknowledged. And people could certainly disappear – look at what had happened to Varius three years ago.

And then, in the cold, silent voice he had shrunk from ever since he'd seen that terrible picture, he told himself: Believe what Salvius says – if you need to. Take it at face value. Take the risk. It's the only thing you can do.

Please forgive me, Sulien.

314

XVII

WORMWOOD

'Marcus,' said Faustus. He sounded surprised and uneasy. 'You're finally home.'

Marcus remained standing at the far end of the room, the shut doors behind him, and did not come forward. 'Yes.'

'I'm glad to see you,' Faustus said coolly. Marcus clenched his teeth against an involuntary little spurt of bitter laughter. Faustus' face hardened, and then turned away. He muttered regretfully, 'Perhaps this can wait until morning.'

'No. It cannot.' Tiredness was ground into his skin like a layer of dirt, his clothes felt travel creased and stale. He had come straight from the landing field in the palace grounds. Salvius, at least, had approved his resistance of all protests or suggestions of rest. It was late evening, and Bianjing was five hours ahead. Three thousand miles away, Drusus was probably asleep. Marcus didn't want him waking up before this was done.

'What do you say, then?'

Marcus looked carefully at a detail of the mosaic at his feet. He said quietly, 'You're ill. I must make allowances for the fact that you're ill. Otherwise what you've done would be unforgiveable.'

Faustus hoisted himself up a little, insulted. 'I am not so ill I don't know what I'm doing.'

'Don't tell me that!' Marcus shouted. 'You undermine everything I've worked for. The work my parents died for. You set a murderer loose with two Empires to ruin. You listen to this poisonous drivel about my friends, you risk their lives – you make *me* risk their lives. You'd *better* not have known what you were doing!'

'You be quiet,' barked Faustus, furiously.

'You didn't bring me here to be quiet. If you didn't want to listen to me you shouldn't have signed that letter. What is it you wanted answered, then? That I've let my friends control me, that they're using me to wreck Rome? Well, they're not here now. Whether or not you like what I say, you can at least believe it comes from me.'

He strode closer to Faustus' couch, standing over him, looking down. 'If I were going to betray you. Get rid of you. Do you think I'd have to do it by stealth? I'm young. I'm strong. You've already given me your power. Would I need to dodge around in the shadows to keep it, just for fear of you? No. You're ill and weak – like Tiberius, at the end. Caligula was already the heir. He took the Imperial ring and he smothered Tiberius with a pillow, while he was helpless. What could have stopped me doing that to you? Don't you think that would have made my life easier? If I wanted, I could do it now.' He shuddered with a sudden nausea as it struck him that not only was it true, but that he was actually tempted.

'Give me back the ring,' demanded Faustus.

Marcus stared at him in silence for a second. Then he dragged the ring off his finger and into his fist. 'Drusus had your brother killed. For this. If you give it to him, and then ask for it back, what do you think will happen? And how long do you think *he* will let you live?' He held it out.

Faustus took the ring, holding it between finger and thumb.

Marcus drew back from him a few steps, silent. He did not think, did not even try to read his uncle's face, or his heavy gaze at the ring. But the air in the room seemed to pour out through the space inside the gold circle, like a small puncture in the world, a zero.

Faustus' head fell back on the cushions, his eyes shut, his face helpless. The ring rolled loose onto his lap. Marcus remembered for the first time in months that the band had been changed to let him wear it. They could both see it was too small to fit past the top joint of Faustus' finger, as it was now. Marcus felt a trace of compassion for him, for the first time.

'This feud between you – both of you accuse each other of such terrible things. It can't go on.'

'It is not a feud,' said Marcus. 'There is no symmetry. He's a manipulative criminal trying to take power by any means he can.'

'I *can't* believe that,' moaned Faustus.

'You must. At least, you can't share it out between us. You have to believe either him or me.'

'I can't.'

Marcus left Faustus' room behind, walking an unerring, purposeful course through the hushed palace galleries and lobbies, through doors opened for him by unnoticed servants, skirting the plinths of statues, down flights of shallow marble steps – though in fact, he had no destination in mind, and could not have described a single room through which

316

he passed. The palace remained so deeply imprinted into his brain that he scarcely needed to look where he was going, and yet it seemed as if on another layer of the mind, he had forgotten it. He was only obeying the instinct to get a good distance away from Faustus. It was still early to consider going to bed, and yet he was more tired than he felt he had a right to be, as though it were as late here as it was in Bian. Finally, he cast himself back into a chair without having consciously perceived that it existed, and he laughed, without knowing why. Like a madman, he thought idly, and fell silent at once.

Someone entered the room, to his right. Marcus did not look up, but recognised the other man's bearing and somehow, from that awareness and from some small movement on the edge of his vision, he knew Salvius' eyes went straight to his right hand, before he spoke, or even looked Marcus in the face.

'You still have the ring.'

Marcus stared blankly down at it, turning his hand a little. A tawny crescent of thick light burned along the edge of the boss. 'Yes,' he said quietly.

'As simple as that?' demanded Salvius, alarm and indignation pushing through the surface of his voice.

'It's all you need to know for the moment, Salvius. You took my cousin out of prison on no authority but your own. The only reason I'm allowing you to stand there and speak to me is that I know the trouble you could cause me if I had you dismissed from your position, or if I ordered you arrested, or executed. And though you don't know it, I'm in your debt. So you will come with me to Bian, and you will watch me, and I will watch you.'

There was a long, uncertain silence, in which they both were simply still, Salvius standing tense, Marcus sprawled and unresponsive in the chair. Then Salvius asked, 'What does this mean for Drusus Novius?'

'My cousin ... will not pose a problem,' answered Marcus, distantly. 'You wanted to keep him from standing trial for his crimes. You've done it. You've got away with doing it. That's enough. No more discussion of this. There's only one other thing I wish to speak with you about. You ordered the Veii Arms Factory to increase production, just before it was destroyed.'

'You had given no orders to the contrary,' protested Salvius gruffly.

'Do you think I am too close to the Nionians, Salvius?'

Again, Salvius hesitated, 'Yes,' he said at last.

Marcus nodded, unemotionally. 'I believe the Nionians are developing a new kind of weapon, or they were doing so under Lord Kato. They may have tested it on an island in the Promethean Sea. Nothing further

317

is known than that, so don't ask me to tell you more. You should speak to Falx about reinforcing our intelligence on these matters. You will not attempt to go behind my back again, but, with my permission this time, you will see that if this device exists, Rome can match it. Or surpass it.'

Salvius nodded, speechless.

'Don't get too excited about it. I still don't intend for you to get the chance to use it. Leave now and get ready.' It didn't occur to him that Salvius might not do as he said. He shut his eyes for a moment and did not even watch the general leave.

After a few minutes, he pulled himself up and went to Makaria's apartments. As he approached he found the landings and corridors that led to her rooms pointedly filled with guards, and further in, with silent, dour, watchful servants, none of whom he recognised as having served Makaria in the past. He didn't hesitate, or look at any of them, even when once or twice he ordered them aside, but he made sure the ring was visible on his hand.

He heard Makaria before he saw her, her voice hoarse as if flagging after days of outrage. 'Will you stop following me around like a bloody dog that wants feeding? I don't have to be watched every second! Don't you dare stand there and say you've got no choice!'

Makaria looked exhausted with anxiety and fury, far more so than the servant on whom her rage was being spent. She visibly buckled with relief when she saw Marcus. She flung her arms around him, and, with his head on her shoulder, Marcus crumpled a little too, feeling fleetingly weak and lost and grateful for protection. He couldn't allow it to last and it didn't.

'I tried to warn you,' Makaria cried, swiping at her wet eyes. 'Did the message get through? You never answered.'

'No,' he said. 'No, it didn't. But thank you for trying.'

'It got through to someone, I know it. It wasn't this bad before, they at least pretended not to treat me like a bloody criminal. They haven't let me go out, or use a longdictor, or even see Daddy. I've got no damn idea what's been going on. I'm *so sorry*.'

'You haven't done anything wrong. I'm sorry you had to go through all this. It will be better now.'

'You've seen him then?' She touched his hand. 'And you have the ring. He just ... believed you?'

Marcus glanced around. 'Not here.'

They went downstairs and out into the courtyard where months before he had met with the senators, the day Una had tracked Drusus out across the gardens, the day he'd attacked her. The umbrella pines breathed and swayed in the turbulent dark air, Rome stirred below and around them, spraying noise and umber light against the blurred clouds. Makaria sighed, spreading her arms. 'It's so good just to get outside.'

'I know,' replied Marcus.

Makaria looked at him anxiously. There was a kind of impersonal, level bitterness even in the simplest things he said. 'So what has happened?'

Marcus looked out at the trees. 'He can't choose between us, so he hasn't. I'm expected to share power with Drusus, and we are somehow to settle our differences.'

'That's absurd. That's impossible.'

'Of course.'

'What are you going to do?'

Marcus smiled, or produced a grimace that involved the same muscles. 'Not that.' He turned back towards the palace. 'I have things to do.'

'You have to tell me everything,' pressed Makaria, following him. 'What happened in Sina? I've been going mad.'

They glanced at each other with the half-humorous Novian flinch at phrases such as that. 'I don't have time,' said Marcus. 'If you come with me back to Bian I'll tell you on the journey. You should have been with me all along.' He headed towards the first room he could find with a longdictor, beckoning a servant as he did so. He scrawled a name on a sheet of paper. 'I need to speak to this man immediately. Have someone in the Outer Office find the longdictor code and get the line ready, I'll be here.'

'What are you doing?' Makaria asked.

'Trying to find Sulien. They told me ...' his voice twisted unexpectedly in his throat. 'They told me they'd arrested him.'

Makaria looked stricken. 'No, they can't have done. I got him out. He was here when it happened, when Salvius brought Drusus here. But I got him out.'

'He was here?' Marcus blinked at her wearily. 'I don't know. I was told he dodged them for a few days ... I hope it's not true. Salvius didn't know about it.'

A few minutes passed. Then the bulb on the base of the longdictor lit up and he picked up the headset. 'Cleomenes,' he said. 'It's Marcus Novius Faustus.'

'I know it's you, Caesar.'

Marcus could hear a baby's cry in the background, rhythmic as if someone were bouncing it in their arms to soothe it. Yes – he had known Cleomenes had a child now, he felt a tinge of nostalgic regret at having forgotten it.

319

'I need to ask you to do something for me. There's a possibility Sulien is being held somewhere – unofficially, on my cousin's orders. It may be in Rome, I don't know. If I instruct the vigiles or the Praetorians to search for him in the normal way, I might alert the people who have him. Once it's known I'm in Rome, and on what terms, that will happen anyway, so we only have a few hours. I know this is nothing to go on—'

'Sir—' Cleomenes interrupted.

'—and I doubt anything can be done, but you must know who can be trusted to try, and I have to do whatever is possible.'

'Sir,' repeated Cleomenes, more firmly. 'I *know* where Sulien is.'

Marcus said mechanically, 'What?' in a hoarse voice he didn't hear.

'He's in Ostia. There's a house there we were using for some under-cover work on contraband, underground slave-trading, that kind of thing. It finished a while back. Not many people know about it, even in the vigiles. He's there with that kid Acchan. It was the best I could manage.'

'You took him there?'

'He came to me, yes. He'll want to see you. There're things he's got to tell you, it appears. It was eating him up that he couldn't think how to contact you.'

Marcus couldn't answer. He had to call the serrated feeling that dug through him relief – joy. And yet it seemed to leave an empty, broken swathe behind it: if he could only have known before. If he could only have made his decision armed with that knowledge.

'I'll bring him to you. There's no longdictor it was safe for him to use.'

'Thank you,' Marcus managed. 'Don't tell him – what I've told you. It had better come from me.' After he'd turned the longdictor off, Makaria, watching him, thought for a moment that he was about to break down into tears, but his face smoothed in an instant and he only said, 'Well, I need to eat, and to rest for a while.'

They ordered and ate a short, almost silent meal in the nearest of the many dining rooms. Only as the servants cleared the dishes away, Makaria ventured, 'Una and Varius aren't here, are they?'

'I'll have to tell Sulien that and I don't think I can go over it twice tonight. I'll explain tomorrow.' And she felt remorseful at having asked, not exactly because he looked upset but because he seemed to be sliding so precipitously into sleep, his limbs falling still on the low couch as if he'd been drugged. 'The time difference,' he said. 'It feels like it's midnight, to me.'

'Marcus . . .' said Makaria. 'I am sorry.' It felt as though someone had to apologise.

320

'Why?' he asked, a little impatient.

She hardly knew how to answer. 'You're so different,' she explained at last, gently.

His eyelids lifted once, revealing a detached curiosity in the cold-coloured eyes beneath. 'Am I?' he murmured, before he fell asleep.

A tap on the door woke him. He looked up to find Makaria gone and the room empty. He hadn't slept more than an an hour and a half. 'Come in,' he said, getting to his feet. And as a servant showed Sulien into the room he took nothing in except that it was him, he was there.

Sulien had just enough time to be taken aback by the elated, anguished smile on Marcus' face, although not time to speak, before he found himself tackled into a crushing hug that almost knocked him back against the doorframe. Still, despite being startled, because this wasn't like Marcus, he was in the first second simply very glad and thankful to see him. But then he heard Marcus let out a breath that sounded like a sob, and his grip on Sulien seemed somehow despairing, bereft.

'Are you all right?'

Marcus gave a cracked laugh. It seemed bizarre and unbearable to have Sulien patting his back in concern and asking him that, after everything. He let him go. 'Yes.'

'Are you drunk?'

Marcus laughed again. 'I've been worried about you.'

'I didn't think you'd know there was anything to worry about.' He saw that Marcus' eyes were indeed raw with tears. 'You're not all right. What's happened?'

Marcus knew the best, most honest thing would be to tell Sulien everything unprompted, not to make Sulien question it out of him. But he could not think how to start – his voice still caught in his throat when he tried to speak, both with emotion and, he knew, with simple cowardice.

Sulien continued, innocently, 'Where's Una?' And then saw Marcus' odd, grieving smile cave in, and how he couldn't meet his eyes any more. A horrible possible reason for his distress occurred to Sulien. 'Marcus, *where is she?*'

'No, no,' promised Marcus hastily. 'It's not that. She's ... she's still in Bian.' And he realised that he did not know if this was true.

'What?' Sulien's apprehensive look flared into panic. 'But Drusus is there – he's been there all this time. If he's anywhere near her, she's dead.'

'*No.* He's not near her, he can't hurt her. She's with the Nionians.' Sulien shook his head, his brows gathering into a slow, bewildered frown. Marcus made himself go on. 'I asked them to take her. As a kind of … guest.'

'A guest?' repeated Sulien.

'Yes – yes, look, we only had a few minutes. She was in worse danger if she stayed with me – much worse. I had to.' But he'd tried too hard, and too quickly, to ward off what he'd dreaded seeing from the beginning: incredulous distrust building on his friend's face.

Sulien said slowly, 'So you left her alone, on the enemy side, and in the same place as Drusus?'

'She's not alone. Varius is there.'

'Varius too?' said Sulien, dragged unwillingly along by another acceleration of suspicion and shock. 'Did he agree to this? Did Una?'

'No,' said Marcus, steadier now, more resigned. 'Not exactly.' He took an instinctive step back as Sulien advanced on him, not quite in deliberate aggression, hands not quite raised, but his greater height and reach suddenly menacing as they had never been before, as if the disbelief and betrayal were struggling to earth itself through him somehow.

Sulien was briefly, sickly aware of holding himself back, of reminding himself that this was Marcus. 'And what happens to them now? How sure are you that Drusus can't get to them? What if the war starts?'

'I don't know. I only knew what would happen if I didn't do it.'

'And the Nionians,' went on Sulien sharply. 'Why did they want them? What do they get out of it?'

Marcus cast a hunted glance at him, realising he had not expected this kind of acuity from Sulien, not now. Was it possible he had underestimated Sulien, just a little, all this time? He hesitated a second, provoking Sulien to shout his question at him again, and then admitted quietly, 'A guarantee I wasn't involved in Lord Kato's murder.'

Sulien slammed a hand down on the table. 'And if they think you were? What will they do to them? You don't know what's happened to them since, do you?'

'It's the middle of the night there.'

'Wake them up, then! Why in hell haven't you done it already?'

'Because of the situation with the Nionians,' muttered Marcus. 'It would look as if I don't trust them. And – because—'

'What does that matter?' broke in Sulien. 'How can you even think like that?'

'I can't *help* thinking like that,' answered Marcus, imploring. 'And anyway, I could only do one thing at a time, and I—'

'You were more worried about me,' completed Sulien softly, staring at Marcus, the hard, evaluating look strange on his open face. He looked, at that moment, unnervingly like Una.

322

'I'm sorry – we'll find out now, of course we will.'

They went to the room from which Marcus had spoken to Cleomenes. Sulien stood with folded arms against the wall, avoiding looking at anything. He didn't want to listen to Marcus' voice, level and controlled as he issued instructions to unseen aides in the offices upstairs; he didn't want to imagine the chain of conversations and decisions, of electric impulses travelling so far in the dark, servants rousing officials and noblemen from sleep, halfway across the world. He was aware of Marcus' bleak, stranded misery as he remained in the chair with the longdictor circlet on his head, and because he couldn't bring himself to meet his eyes with sympathy, Sulien couldn't look at him at all. And an hour passed this way, in impassable, frozen silence, although it did not occur to either of them to wait alone.

Then the small rustling of someone's voice leaked out of the longdictor. He heard a shattered little intake of breath from Marcus – a cruelly ambivalent sound, which Marcus himself seemed to notice, and so assured him at once, 'They're still in the city. They're safe. The Nionians promise they're safe.'

'I want to speak to her,' commanded Sulien.

Marcus just looked up at him and nodded obediently.

They settled into another unspeaking wait, not quite as long as before. This time they were both poised rigidly around the longdictor, Marcus gazing at the desk top, feeling that to speak to Sulien until this was done was somehow not allowed, an intrusion.

Then Marcus said eagerly, 'Una?'

'Give me that,' Sulien ordered him fiercely, grabbing the circlet. 'Una, it's me.'

Una's voice laughed at him, wearily. 'Your accent. All over the map.'

'Shut up,' said Sulien.

Marcus watched, trapped into patience. Sulien and Una talked a long time. He could see some of the tension draining out of Sulien as he listened; his shoulders went loose, he smiled, shakily. But he was no less stern and watchful when he glanced at Marcus, saying tersely, 'No, he's here, he's fine. Nothing's happened to him.' Finally he pulled off the circlet and held it out, grim faced. 'She wants to talk to you.'

Marcus seized it. 'You are all right – both of you?'

She sounded tired, a battered relief like his own in her voice, but she was alert, herself. 'We're fine. You can come back, can't you?'

He said unsteadily, 'Yes. Yes, I've wanted to hear your voice so much. I'm so sorry.'

She ignored the apology, whether considering it unnecessary, or rejecting it altogether, he couldn't tell. She was saying urgently, 'Marcus, you've got three days to get back. If you aren't here by then I think Nionia will declare war. You need special permission from the Empress, the borders are closed to Rome.'

He'd known nothing of that. And they began trying raggedly to summarise what had happened in the last two weeks, although they were both so tired, and aware that there were things that had to be said in person.

'I love you,' said Marcus. It was an awkward thing to say, under Sulien's grave, disillusioned scrutiny, but she said the same and it felt like discovering money when destitute, enough to live on for a night.

Sulien held out his hand for the circlet again. 'Una,' he said into it emphatically. 'Come back soon.'

Silence washed back into the room as Marcus laid the longdictor circlet back in place. He said tentatively, 'They're all right.'

'They're all right,' agreed Sulien, unsmiling. He sat down opposite Marcus, the desk between them imparting an air of even-handed formality. His voice was calm now, reasonable. 'And I'm all right. Why were you so worried about me?'

Marcus released a long, exhausted breath, and Sulien felt irritably sorry for him. 'They showed me faked pictures – of you. Being hurt. So that if Drusus couldn't get the ring any other way, there was at least a chance I'd just give it up.'

It was the first time he'd ever found Sulien's expression unreadable; his subdued, complex gaze rested on Marcus' face for what seemed a long time, before it shifted lightly down to his hand.

'But Salvius assured me it wasn't true, and I thought from the beginning the pictures weren't real,' said Marcus quickly, despising himself for offering the justification, and impressed by Sulien's generosity in not saying, 'You were not sure.' For Sulien just remained silent, staring contemplatively at the ring, until Marcus added mechanically, 'I'm sorry,'

'Don't say that,' retorted Sulien in sudden disgust. 'You're not sorry. You did it for a reason. You'd do it again.' He slumped, muttering, 'If it's something you can be sorry for it's worthless even saying it.'

'You have to understand—'

'I *do* understand, I'm not stupid,' said Sulien, but with the rancour gone out of his voice. He remarked with sad wonder, 'You were right. What else could you have done?'

'Then I mean I wish it had never happened,' Marcus said.

'I do take that much for granted,' replied Sulien, and he even smiled at Marcus, but with so much affectionate regret, as if over the memory of someone he never expected to see again, that Marcus felt like crying.

Sulien sighed, pulling himself up into a businesslike stance, reached into his jacket and brought out the crumpled copy of the picture of Atronius. 'I wanted to tell you about this. This is the man that sabotaged the factory. He was in Byzantium at the same time as your cousin. And he had my name and the clinic's longdictor code in his flat. I don't think he's dead. He's the kind of man Drusus used in the past. He could have used him for this. Get the war underway and get rid of me. At a time I wasn't so – useful.'

Marcus couldn't yet feel the murderous anger with Drusus he knew this would generate later. He just said, 'Well. He's more than capable of it. And it would follow he murdered Kato. It was clumsy, but it's the Nionians' chief strategist out of the way and it's a lot of mess between me and him. I'll deal with it. Thank you.'

Sulien shrugged. 'Well, then.' He got to his feet.

'Don't go now,' appealed Marcus. But Sulien's flat expression answered that. 'The vigiles raided your place. You can't go there tonight. Can't I at least – help you?'

'Is anyone going to round me up and kill me if I go to Tancorix?' asked Sulien wearily. Marcus shook his head. 'I'll go there, then.'

'Can you forgive me?' asked Marcus, in a low voice.

'How can I forgive you when you haven't done anything wrong?' asked Sulien, genuinely at a loss. 'It isn't that. I just would never have thought ...' His gaze seemed to slip beyond Marcus, towards the past. 'When we were driving into Rome to find you – Una and Dama and me – I remember thinking, there were things that you wouldn't be able to do. That you couldn't ever ... kill someone, even if you needed to. Things the rest of us could. Even me.' He looked back at Marcus, with the benign leave-taking smile again. 'You're not the same.'

Marcus considered that. 'No,' he acknowledged, in the end. 'I'm not. It's what happens.'

Sulien nodded. 'Of course it does,' he said, with impersonal kindness, before he left.

'I only regret that I have been able to spend so little time in the Empire, among the Roman people. But in returning to the discussions with Nionia, I will act to achieve peace for Rome, peace without diminution of our strength. I will be home again soon.'

Marcus was watching a recording of the broadcast he'd made that morning on a small screen, set in the wall of the spiralwing. It was satisfactory, he decided. Perhaps he looked a little more threatening than reassuring, but that might not be such a bad thing. He looked down at Rome, as it diminished. It was true that he'd hardly time to feel that he was there. The Pantheon already cowered and vanished among the higher domes and towers; Vatican Field shone like a puddle of oil. It all shrank until he could no longer see anything moving on the ground, as if all the city and the earth beyond were sterile.

'So we only have a day's grace?' Makaria was sitting nearby. They would arrive in Bian the following afternoon, one day before the expiry of the ten-day breathing space Una and Varius had engineered.

'The whole thing's always been fragile,' said Marcus. 'And they had fair reason to lay Kato's death at our door.'

'But plainly they realise now you were not involved.'

'Drusus is still there,' murmured Marcus.

Makaria watched the end of the broadcast. 'Tell me more about the Nionian princess.'

'I've already told you everything,' replied Marcus. 'I only met her once.'

'You didn't tell me if you liked her.'

Marcus said nothing. Makaria set her shoulders, steeling herself to say, plainly. 'You're going to have to do it.'

Marcus looked out of the window. 'No,' he said tersely, after a pause.

'You've said yourself how precarious things are now. You just promised in that broadcast that you'd do everything possible for peace. You have to do this, to save what you've worked for. It's simply a political arrangement, everyone involved realises that.'

'How many political arrangements did you refuse to be part of?' asked Marcus, his voice edged with a distant, warning sarcasm.

Makaria sighed. 'There was never so much at stake.'

Marcus shook his head. 'It's unnecessary. And unacceptable. No.'

'Because of Una?' exclaimed Makaria. 'Marcus, if you can't give her up, then fine – don't! Carry on with her as you always have! I'm sure the princess isn't naive. She'll understand so long as you behave with tact. You know this is the way things work. Do you think you're the first man of our class to fall for a slave girl?'

'It's different.'

'How? Why? Just because it's you?'

'I didn't *buy* her,' cried Marcus suddenly. 'I never owned her. I didn't take a fancy to the girl who brought my meals. If I'd had any power to force anything from her, whether I'd used it or not, she'd always have hated me. And even if I'd believed I was in love with her I would never really have known her. But when I met her, I had nothing more than she did – or than Sulien …' His face and voice both tightened, as though the name were a slap, or a shallow cut. He said, 'It *is* different. When we were alone in the woods she was Una, she wasn't a slave. I was myself. That was all. There wasn't any difference between us.'

Makaria sighed. 'I'm sorry,' she said quietly, placing her hand over his. 'But there is now.'

Marcus didn't reply for a while. 'No,' he repeated, withdrawing his hand. 'I'll think of something else.'

Lal lay curled up into a scrawled and icy letter G, cold, cold under the blanket, her body juddering stubbornly like a road drill. There was an ache, like a rancid stock in which her muscles stewed, growing rubbery and fibrous. She'd walked so far, for so long, she'd had to sleep in the open, knowing that when she woke she'd feel worse. And was there any point? She couldn't work, however far she walked it would soon be up to other people what happened to her. But she mustn't – wasn't allowed to let that happen in Jingshan, not now she knew who was looking for her. Although as she paced on, the precise nature of Una's warning kept slipping out of her mind. She knew it was a stupid, fever-thought, but she stopped worrying about being obviously foreign, out of place. She felt she had reached a stage where nationality didn't count or show any more, her clothes and body were dissolving and fading into the international uniform of vagrant. She wouldn't be remarkable anywhere. She'd begged for food a couple of times, without shame. For huge, month-long days, she'd lurched on and on, the ground throbbing and protesting under her feet …

No, no – all that was days ago, it must be over: she must be lying still if she could feel the cold mats under her side, the crumpled blanket drawn round her all the time. The uncertainty frightened her suddenly, and she flung herself over, starting up with a gasp, and looked up at the serene red-robed warriors painted on flaking whitewashed walls on either side of the doorway. She even felt proud that she'd achieved what she'd meant to – she'd reached the next village, asked for the temple, and here she was. There was nothing more she could have done. She wasn't sure what had happened since then – she had some memory of being made to drink something – but it didn't seem to matter. She sank back, relieved. But within minutes she felt herself leadenly trudging again, even if in some way she knew she was still in the improvised bed under the temple portico. The only pleasant sensation, oddly, was her teeth chattering: the rhythm inexplicably comforting, like lightly fluttering wings, like the sound of rain against a window.

Then she was shocked again, because someone was sitting by her; had he just appeared or had he been there for hours? A thin, apprehensive monk – she couldn't understand what he was saying and she wished he wouldn't talk to her, it distracted her from her walking.

He had been there before, she thought, talking to someone. They must have been trying to decide what to do about her. There were government-run hospitals in the towns, they might take her there, and then the police would find her. This thought no longer concerned her very much. It seemed to her it would be difficult for anyone to move her; maybe she would be well again before they could manage it.

Then there was a cup of pungent, watery liquid, splashing at her mouth again, and the monk was speaking to her, reassuring her, sounding less anxious now. Lal choked, and struggled a little, so that the bitter stuff trickled into her hair and pooled in her ears. And when she could not burrow away from him she made a resentful effort to understand what he was saying: '... looking for you. Here they are.'

Her head full of sullen weight, Lal looked up again, hoping it would be Delir and Ziye, half-remembering there was some reason why that was impossible. Two men, giant top-heavy pillars, stood there and swayed over her like masts at sea. One of them smiled down at her pityingly. They were Romans, with a black car waiting in the dusty yard behind them.

'No, no, not with them!' she cried. She was speaking Latin, only the men would understand what she was saying. 'No,' she managed, in Sinoan, and the monk only smiled and tried to soothe her. Panicked, Lal flung the blanket back, and scrambled to her feet. But at once the walls and ground crumpled weightlessly around her, as though everything were made of hot paper. When it all came to rest she was lying, bewildered, in someone's arms, and then laid on a seat in the back of a car. She shivered and shut her eyes, which were too sore to keep open. The car had begun to move, she could feel every stone under the wheels. And she was still walking.

XVIII

INEVITABILITY

'Hey, hey you. Can you tell me your name? Do you know where you are? See? She's out of it.'

'She's quiet, anyway. Just leave her.'

'Yeah, but what if she doesn't even make it back to Jondum? Give her more of the stuff, she's not going to be any use like this.'

'And it's going to be better if you make her overdose on that? We don't know what's in that bottle. She's not due any more until tomorrow. Leave her.'

'Sir.'

Lal groaned quietly in protest at all the talking, turning her head, hunting for a new place to lay her cheek on the seat. For a second the leather would be wonderfully cool on her skin, but then the growing heat in her flesh would melt into it and simmer again, through the surface.

The car swerved as something tore past. There was a disapproving mutter in Sinoan, from the driver's cab. But someone nearer moved sharply towards the windows, shoving past the rest.

'Where'd that car come from? Ask him if he saw it before. Did anyone else see it before – around the temple?'

Murmurs of denial. 'Do you think it's following us, sir?'

'I think I don't want to see it again,' said the one who seemed to be in charge.

An uneasy silence fell. Lal was grateful for it. The cold was unimaginable now, a current was pushing through her, shaking the reluctant atoms of her body into glowing, crimson heat, flow upon flow of it. She rolled over vainly, panting, concentrating on something crucial that kept proving too difficult for her.

Then they were slowing down, it made everything drag like seasickness. 'There's a car across the road. I think it's the same one.'

'Tell him to reverse,' the leader, the centurion shouted urgently. 'Don't stop, don't get any closer. Back, *now*.'

Something punched at the car from underneath, with a great bubbling crack of sound. We're going over a storm, thought Lal distractedly, before shaking the foamy nonsense in her brain away and forcing herself to think, exhaustingly: No. It was some kind of bomb.

The car choked and tripped to a stop. The Romans banged open the doors, dodged out into the sunlight, crouching against the vehicle's flanks. Lal was dragged out and dropped abruptly onto the cracked tar surface of the empty road. Gunfire broke the air. Behind the back wheels, Lal lay on her side, at once curious and indifferent, busy with the molten pulses of heat. Her eyes stayed shut until suddenly, somewhere to her right and ahead, on the far side of the car, an explosion burst like an orange marigold, rocking the car and casting heavy lumps of stuff around on the road. The blast beneath the car had been nothing – the tap of a cat's paw. Even far away and blazing as she was, she had to shrink back and cover her head. Someone shrieked and whimpered horribly. Lal moaned and turned heavily over again, away from it.

'Lal, *Lal*.' Someone gabbling on at her from the edges. She felt like crying. It was too much to spring these things on her and expect her to decipher them, with everything melting and burning. The gabbling at least changed to Latin, but remained more than she could cope with. 'Are you hurt? Get up! Come here!'

Lal gave in and looked painfully across the road at Liuyin, who was lurking impossibly by the edge of the road, beckoning her. 'Lal! Hurry!'

Lal shut her eyes and hours seemed to pass with him still apparently there and begging her to move. Finally she floundered a little way towards him, all her muscles wrenching and melting as she did so, and Liuyin grimaced and scrambled forward, awkwardly lifted and bundled her across the road, tugged her down into a ditch beside it. 'Don't look. Don't look at anything, Lal,' he whispered, as another, smaller explosion opened itself ahead of the car. She could feel him trembling. 'I'm sorry I didn't come before. I should have tried harder. I shouldn't have been angry with you. I didn't know you'd be ill. But you'll be all right.'

Someone called out, in Latin – but the soldiers all were silent. Liuyin hoisted her up onto the road again. A battered grey car swung round, in front of the fire and smoke, someone got out. For the moment Lal felt a composed, lucid interest in how the delirium was progressing, what it might come up with next. She wouldn't claim it was all an hallucination – something must be happening, but surely it wasn't this. The light was beautiful even as it hurt her: pure, replete, like still water held in a bright globe of glass. Within it the fire looked cool, fine, and far off, threads of saffron in water, and the young man's reddish hair glowed carnelian, wine-like. The blue of his eyes seemed scarcely natural, emitting their own light like gas flames. Lal was amazed at how far behind he seemed to have left the day-to-day pastiness she remembered. The light in the air or in her mind compelled radiance from his fierce, soft-featured face and he seemed almost not human enough to be ugly.

He said to Liuyin, 'There – you've done more than you thought you could, haven't you? Come on. I need you to drive now.'

Then Lal was lying half in his lap, in the back of the rubbish-strewn car, and he was murmuring to her, with a kind of soft urgent authority, 'We've got you now. I'll get you out of here – you'll be safe.'

His arms were bare, which was not right – he would always have them covered. One supported her head, the other rested protectively over her, so that his wrist hung just inches from her blurred eyes, the skin stamped with the round scar of the cross.

'You're not here, Dama,' she said, reasonably.

Dama-in-the-vision smiled at her fondly, regretfully. 'That's right, love. I'm not.'

Liuyin drove too fast, still trembling with the physical shock of the explosions and of what had happened to those men, at the sense of accelerating through a strange space alongside the tracks of his normal life. He knew at some future time he would not be able to believe what he had done and seen; for now it did not matter. Sometimes he struggled a little against the overwhelming imperative to do what the stranger wanted, but only in a helpless, fumbling way that felt as meaningless as the kickings of a hanged man – a rather ignoble failure to recognise inevitability. For now, of course everything was real, *of course* he was doing this. There was a kind of exhilaration in it, because it was right. And after all, he wasn't quite unprepared, was he? Hadn't he always wished to be part of some kind of story, some kind of drama, for something to happen? And here he was.

It was only the stranger's silence that was making him more consciously nervous now. Liuyin kept glancing at him, expecting some kind of instruction, but none came. The young man seemed wholly preoccupied with Lal – he was carefully bathing her face with water from a plastic bottle, deftly enough despite his damaged hands. The water would certainly be warm by now, but his look of sad, zealous tenderness was so strong that for a strange moment Liuyin caught himself wondering if he were somehow part of Lal's family.

'What happens now?' Liuyin blurted at last, in Sinoan. He wasn't sure quite how much of the language the other man understood, evidently some. He'd switched into it unexpectedly once or twice, just for a few words, usually at times when Liuyin's resolve was fading.

'I can't take her with me,' Dama said quietly. He was speaking Latin, but Liuyin didn't struggle to understand: the longer they were together, the more everything Dama said seemed to carry a firm, lucid weight that went beyond the simple fact that his voice was very clear. 'I don't exactly go by public transport. And she's too ill.'

Of course, Dama couldn't have anticipated Lal's illness. Liuyin had to remember that. He'd found Liuyin after a few days' searching and questioning around the Black Clothes Lane area, and he'd got the story of Lal's call for help out of him within minutes. He'd made him feel briefly worthless for what his response had been, then just as swiftly fired him up into this state of baffled daring. They'd reached Jingshan just after the Romans did, and they'd been following the car ever since. If they didn't find Lal that way, at least they'd know the men hadn't found her either. But from the moment of his first appearance – cornering Liuyin as he returned home from a painting lesson – Dama had given the impression that he was simply trying to carry out, as quickly as possible, something that was already certain.

But Liuyin was frightened for Lal now. 'Could she die?'

'No,' said Dama instantly, with simple, flat conviction. His better, almost-normal left hand was under Lal's head, and he would not move it; taking infinite pains not to disturb her, he managed with the three functioning fingers of his right to extract a little box from his pocket, remove the lid, and swallow down a couple of pills with a swig of the water. Liuyin had only seen him do this once before, far less openly. It seemed that either he preferred not to be seen taking them, or that he resisted resorting to them as long as he could, or both. He sighed with the anticipation of relief, and murmured, 'I know where I'd want her to be. I know who'd get her there.' He closed his eyes, as if this, unlike anything else in the journey, meant doing something he found hard to face. 'Una will do it. Novius would, too.' His mouth curled grudgingly at the second name. 'But even without him ... Una ...'

'You want to go to Bianjing?'

'Near enough,' said Dama.

There was no way back, and suddenly no way forward, as if he'd been moving up a flight of stairs that had fallen away around him, leaving him stranded in empty space, an unstable column under Drusus' feet, an awful drop below.

Could he get out? His slaves had already packed his belongings, he had been all but ready to leave. He knew Lal was found. It was less to work with than he would have liked, but it was something, and he had been waiting only for word that the soldiers had transported her as far as Jondum for departure into the Empire. But since yesterday, after that news of success, there had been nothing, no response to his messages, silence that seemed in retrospect like a warning. The palace in the square, walled city felt like a glass box within a glass box.

But why should he have to run? He had as much authority as Marcus. No one could simply ignore that, could they? Perhaps they might divide the Empire into east and west between them, temporarily at least; such a split had been contemplated once or twice in the past. It would be enough for now; if he had that, and time, he could claim the whole in the end, he knew it.

But the guards who were stationed outside his quarters were marching away. Drusus, who had moved restlessly outside again, watched blankly for a second as they filed through the darkening gardens, before commanding them furiously to stop. But they did not, even when he roared out his order again and added every threat he could think of. Only when he modified the order to a demand for an explanation, did one of them tell him, 'Caesar's ordered us to assemble outside the barracks, Your Highness.'

'He doesn't have any mandate for this,' shouted Drusus, wanting to keep this hot, bracing anger flowing within him as long as possible. 'We are to share power, that is the Emperor's decision. *Equally.* Read the message for yourself if you don't believe me!'

But really they did not believe him, and no evidence he could provide would make them. Marcus was here. If they knew nothing else, they knew that was Drusus' failure. Marcus had the ring, and the soldiers were frightened of him. The absurdity of it struck Drusus as never before. Marcus was only one person, Drusus was only one person. The soldiers had nothing to fear from either of them beyond what they could be persuaded to do to each other. If they could only have trusted each other to see through the trick, they need not answer to anyone! Why didn't they realise that?

He had not been left totally alone, there were three men who hadn't moved. But he did not imagine it was out of defiant loyalty – they had been told to stay. Marcus had left them there, either to watch him, or as an insult to him.

Drusus slammed back inside the pavilion. But it was too late, the sustaining warmth of anger was leaving him, and he stood there, out of breath and shivering. How flimsy and unprotected it felt in these Sinoan rooms, only floodlit glass and painted wood, the panels fretted full of weak points and holes, between his skin and the world. How did any Sinoan prince ever sleep in peace?

He turned to a slave, and said almost in a whisper, 'Lock the door.'

Una resisted running until the last few seconds. She kept herself almost ceremoniously in check, as the Nionian guards led them unnecessarily across the Sinoan courtyards and gardens, as if too abrupt a transition into freedom might damage them. Varius walked slowly, not speaking, face tilted up slightly towards the sky. They had known for two raw hours that Marcus was in the city, that they would be allowed to go. Now it had happened, after all their manoeuvring within captivity, it was hard to believe that it could be so simple, that accompanied or not, they could just walk back to where they had been and it would really be over, Marcus would really be there. Una stifled the presentiment that this was not only a dazed reaction to change, that it was true. It was not so simple. In some way he would not ever be there.

She saw him, magnified and dark in his purple robe. She did run then, leaving the group of guards behind. They collided, clutched. She'd never wanted to see him so badly and yet not wanted to look him in the face. He lifted her a little off the ground, the pressure of his arms painful around her waist and against her ribs. Neither of them was smiling. But they held on, Una's eyes shut, her teeth clenched, blocking out everything. He *had* come back, that was all. She didn't want to know anything he was thinking.

'It's good to see you safe,' commented Varius, meaning it, but rather coldly. He would have preferred to have walked for an hour, out in the city, as far from the Palace as he could get, before seeing Marcus. When Marcus, one hand still gripping Una's shoulder, took a step towards him he stiffened, just a little. And then he was startled by the expression of nearly desperate appeal he saw flash across Marcus' face and settle into grim, accepting sadness almost before Varius could recognise it.

Marcus said to both of them, 'Thank you for everything you've done here. It was heroic. I won't let anyone go on thinking of you as traitors.'

A soldier approached them, cautiously across the courtyard. He looked somehow drained, pale, his salute to Marcus stiff with an odd blend of relief and dread. 'Caesar. A few of the men aren't in a good way. One's unconscious. A couple of his ribs are broken, I think he may have a punctured lung. I'm uncertain if you wanted ...' He hesitated, and revised the question. 'Permission to administer medical assistance, Caesar?'

Marcus looked irritable and disdainful. 'Fine. If necessary,' he said, gesturing the man away.

Una tensed, incredulously. 'What is this?' she asked, in a low voice.

Marcus' eyes turned blank as pebbles, a faint, defiant smile lurked unhappily at his mouth. 'I've had the soldiers flogged for what happened here. Not only them, of course.'

He'd chosen the Alanian coast as a place of exile for the Roxelanian magistrate. And he'd had him beaten too, kicked and punched along the street and through the forum of his city, thrown into the van which drove him away.

He felt an impatience that approached disgust at the shock on both their faces. Did it really need to be talked over? They did not speak. Una stared at him in unrecognising confusion, lips parted with some kind of hurt concern for him which he didn't want to see. Varius' subtle, withdrawing frown came closer to a look of disappointment. It was hard to tolerate.

Finally Varius asked quietly, 'How did you choose the ones to be punished?'

'I picked the ones whose faces I could remember,' Marcus said roughly. 'That centurion who led them should have been first. No one knows where he is. Lucky for him.'

'Did you want this done before you saw us?' Varius enquired more forcefully, and looked away when Marcus didn't answer.

Una muttered, 'But it was Drusus. And your uncle. And Salvius. They are far more guilty.'

'What, do you think I can snap my fingers and make the world a different place?' demanded Marcus, a harsh, resentful break in his voice. 'I could have had them killed. I *should* have done. I don't respect myself for sparing them. It won't happen again. Are you going to defend them because they were acting on orders? Well, next time they get orders like that I want them too afraid to carry them out. This is how things work.' He swung round and strode away. Una went after him. Varius did not.

They didn't return to the pavilion in which they'd stayed before. 'Drusus is there,' said Marcus, shortly. 'I'd rather keep him there than move him. He's not getting out.'

So these rooms were unfamiliar. Una was literally treading carefully around Marcus, placing her feet delicately as if afraid of frightening him. Marcus told her, 'I have to meet with Junosena – to thank her. And then Tadahito. Try and solve all of this.'

Una nodded, silently. She padded warily about the room. She felt suddenly tired by the fact that even if she was out of the Nionian-controlled rooms, she was still in the palace, still in Sina. She didn't want to think of it as a longing to be in the Roman Empire.

'I don't know what happened to all our stuff,' she remarked. 'My clothes.'

'Yes, what is that dress? It's not yours, is it?'

'One of the Princess's waiting women's.' They looked at each other and mutually shut out the subject of Noriko, there was even a kind of camaraderie in that simultaneous refusal to think about it.

'Your things won't have gone far. They'll be brought over.'

Dragging off the outer robe, he pulled something out of his pocket and gripped it – a small roll of blue cloth. Una recognised it with a confused stir of blindsided feeling: a plain woollen hat, folded into a soft tube.

She'd handed it to him in a graveyard the day after they'd met, terse and unsmiling, just to render him less of a risk, cover up what he was. Still, it was the first thing she'd ever given to him.

Marcus glanced at her quickly, with a shrug and a tight, uneven smile, 'Thought of it yesterday when I was at home, so ...'

But he still looked angrily desolate. Again it flashed over Una what he had done, and that it had not satisfied him, the violence had still not gone out of him. She wished she could say some sweet, fond, mind-lessly supportive thing. She could imagine a different kind of lover for a man in power – a blindly gentle woman that in real life she'd have found unbearable, a human cornucopia of inexhaustible tenderness, someone with no capacity to judge, no concerns except soothing him. She thought it would be much simpler to be like that. Instead she had gone cold, stiff, stern. As she could not speak she willed herself to go and hold him again. She stroked his hair, lightly and tentatively, and though she'd meant to comfort him the smooth familiar warmth of it comforted her. But he must have detected something forced about her touch, for he drew back and said impatiently, 'Do I need to tell you? Do you know everything already?'

'No,' she muttered.

'Well,' he sounded perversely exasperated. 'Why not?'

She prevaricated. 'There's too much, all at once, you're too ... worked up.' It was half true. She wouldn't tell him that she was afraid to see what he might be thinking, or remembering, or planning to do. 'I don't want to spy on you.'

'You've got to know,' he said brusquely, and began telling her about the time stranded in Sarmatia with the magistrate, the choice he'd made, the meeting with Sulien in the Palace. He finished flatly, 'I don't think he'll want to see me again.'

336

'He will,' said Una. And knowing her brother, she genuinely thought this was true, yet reservations wormed into her voice and she could not make herself sound wholly convinced.

Bleakly, Marcus shook his head. 'I said yes to him dying slowly, I don't blame him.'

'Yes, rather than give Drusus the chance to do that to whomever he wants and start a war – rather than see slavery go on for ever. I would have done the same thing.'

He paused and looked at her. 'You would, wouldn't you?' he said, with a kind of wonder in his voice. 'And leaving you and Varius here, would you have done that?'

She hesitated, considering it. 'Yes.'

'But not this.' His voice grew harder. 'Not punishing the soldiers.'

Una said more strictly than she meant to, '*No.*'

Marcus almost shouted at her, 'So what *would* you have done, then?'

Una mumbled, flinching, 'I don't know,' so that Marcus turned away from her with a scathing sound, and then she retorted with answering anger, 'Yes I do, I would have warned them. I'd have told them any orders that didn't come from me weren't valid, so they shouldn't think that was any kind of defence. I'd have made them realise I could do what you did, and then I'd have made them amazed that I hadn't. I'd have made them *grateful* to me.'

Marcus made the scoffing noise again, although with diminished force. 'And you think they'd respect that?'

Una said stubbornly, 'Yes.' Marcus sighed and sat down on a couch, depleted and slack. She looked down at him and whispered, 'You were there? You ... watched it happen?'

'Of course I did. I had to be sure they knew why it was happening.' He closed his eyes and said, sounding more like himself. 'Anyway, it would have been cowardly not to be there.'

They fell quiet for a while, as at some kind of truce. He didn't want to fight with her. He didn't believe her reassurances about Sulien, and he was still wretched and resentful at the memory of the look on Varius' face.

Una discovered and sifted through a pile of messages on a low table, surprised to find a new one for her. She read it and turned round to Marcus, shocked. 'Where's Sinchan?'

'It's across the river,' he said. 'It's pretty much what you said – do you remember? The city where they put all the dirt they don't want in this one.'

'Lal's there. I promised I'd get her to Rome. And it says she's ill.'

'What?' He looked up.

'Delir and Ziye are under arrest, I don't know where. The Sinoan police have been rounding up people like them ever since Lord Kato was murdered, she's been lost out in the countryside all this time. She had a friend who helped her get in touch with me, maybe he got her here somehow. I have to go to her.'

Marcus stated, his voice oddly mild, 'Drusus murdered Lord Kato.'

'What are you going to do about him?' Una asked softly.

'Keep him quiet,' said Marcus, and didn't elaborate. His face, with some small display of effort, brightened. 'Well, if there's anything you need. And I'll do what I can for Delir and Ziye and anyone else caught up in this.'

Una stood with the message in her hand, looking at him with softened, mournful helplessness, until he got up and went to her, kissing her and saying gently, 'You don't have to look like that. Don't worry about me. Don't worry about anything. We'll be out of here soon.'

Dama had seemed to grow more restless as they approached Xinjian, the shafts of influence he emitted became more fitful and less blinding, not to the point where Liuyin seriously lost confidence in him or questioned anything they'd done, but enough for him to observe the other man more clearly. Once they had reached the ugly, centreless town and had installed Lal in a cupboard of a bedroom in a grubby guest house, by the time Liuyin had contacted the minor official he knew in Bianjing with the message for Una, Dama could barely keep still. He prowled around Lal's bed and out into the dingy street, looking south, as if he could somehow see Bianjing through the city's brownish sprawl, across the river. At first Liuyin had assumed he was anxious about Lal, who was worryingly quiet now, but Dama continued to insist with wide-eyed, categorical certainty that she would be well; Sulien – the name irritated some residual prickle of jealousy in Liuyin – Sulien would cure her. And indeed his unsettled mood did not seem precisely like anxiety, he never showed any fear of being arrested, or that anything would go wrong. It was more like a desire to be elsewhere.

'What's wrong?' Liuyin asked, after discovering that Dama had discarded nearly all of his share of the gristly food Liuyin had been sent out to buy. As with the pills, Dama did not seem to like to be seen eating.

'Nothing,' said Dama, in a distant voice. He sighed, and then smiled at Liuyin. 'She'll be here soon. Her or some *servant*.' His lip curled in the beginning of a sneer that melted with surprising speed into a perfect smile of faith, and he murmured, 'But I think it'll be her. As soon as you see her, you don't need to worry any more. Just make sure she's going to the right door, don't hang around – don't talk to her, don't mention me. Just stay with Lal until Una comes, then go. You can trust her.'

'You won't be there? You're going?' said Liuyin, flushing with an embarrassing sensation of abandonment.

'I must,' said Dama, rather dejectedly. 'Don't worry. You're not going to need me here. Look.' He produced a crumpled roll of money. 'This'll get you home.'

'Oh, no, no,' said Liuyin, backing away from the cash, startled and shamed. He was almost surprised that Dama should have or need money.

'Don't be a fool. This isn't anything like enough to pay you for helping me, or helping *her*. You *gave* that. This is just a way back home from this dump, which you haven't got and you need, so take it.'

'How can I go home?' asked Liuyin bleakly. 'My parents ... I just left.'

Dama scrutinised him shrewdly for a second and then placed his better arm on his shoulder. 'You're their only son, aren't you?'

'Yes. And I left them. It's terrible.'

'They're going to be thrilled to see you back, then. You can *tell* them you couldn't rest until you were sure Lal wasn't in danger. You don't regret it. You know that. Even if they're angry with you, you're not going to mind. What's a little row with your parents after all this? They can't frighten you any more. Them or anyone else.'

Later, alone, sitting by Lal's bedside, watching for Una from the blackened doorstep of the guest house, Liuyin wondered resignedly why Dama had really left. He had not said where he was going, but he had said 'I must', with none of the sense of willing mission which had been so manifest in him until then. It occurred to Liuyin that perhaps Dama had not wanted to leave at all. He had wanted to be exactly where he was, and for some reason had compelled himself to resist the temptation.

The meeting had been sombre. They had traced their way along the thread broken by Drusus' arrival and Kato's death, spun it on through with the provisional work done in Marcus' absence by Varius and Una. But there had been a tension in the air, a chilly sense that someone was failing to say something crucial.

'What is Drusus Novius' position now you have returned?' Tadahito had asked quietly.

'He will not participate any further in our negotiations. I have no doubt that he will be leaving the country very shortly,' answered Marcus.

'But I understand he is to retain a share of Emperor Faustus' power. If so, and if he is outside this process, the treaty we have been trying to create with you, Caesar, will be written in the dark.'

Marcus clenched his fists under the table and said, 'Any role he has from now on will be strictly domestic.'

Afterwards, answering Tadahito's look at him, Marcus hung back to join the Prince as they left the hall. He said, 'I must thank you again for protecting Una and Varius.'

'They acquitted themselves very well,' said Tadahito. 'Lady Una is formidable. I am not sure if the world is more fortunate or unfortunate that she was born a woman.'

'Well, it was fortunate for me,' answered Marcus.

Tadahito smiled, but remained subtly grave, averse. 'It is a good thing you did leave them with us. I doubt you and I would have met again otherwise. But still we have barely managed to delay the outbreak of war by ten days. We can't call it more than a delay; we can't pretend things are as they were before Lord Kato was assassinated. I do trust you now when you say you were not responsible; you would hardly have returned otherwise. But your cousin is not you, is he? He threatened to attack Nionia when we would not hand Lady Una and Lord Varius over to him. He does not want the same things. Could he have been involved?'

Marcus felt his throat close, balking at the unexpected pressure to lie for Drusus. He muttered, 'I've had no chance to see any of the evidence about Lord Kato's death.'

A look of cynical understanding flickered quickly across Tadahito's troubled face. He nodded. 'Well, you can see why my father feels something decisive must be done. Rome and Nionia must build a distinct alliance, and there must be some assurance it will be honoured in the future.' He lowered his voice. 'You have only met my sister once, I know; perhaps you did not have time to consider why she was here. Our hope was always that we might see the Nionian and Roman thrones united by a marriage. I am sorry it has come to this, of course I would rather not have urged it so openly. But I think there is no time to be reticent.'

Marcus made an effort not to freeze, to show a proper surprise on his face while disguising the abrupt panic of a creature in a trap. He could feel an aghast stammer building against his teeth and fought not to let it out, not to allow himself the sharp intake of breath he wanted. Yet he had to say something. 'You – you are very generous,' he managed. 'You would still – want that, even with these concerns?'

'I think it is more necessary than ever now,' replied Tadahito.

'Of course, I am honoured,' said Marcus. He thought his voice sounded parodic and absurd, as if he were stiffly reciting lines in a comedy. The conversation must not go on, he could not sustain it. He would make some catastrophic mistake. He smiled as best he could. 'May I – discuss this with you tomorrow?'

'Certainly,' said Tadahito. To Marcus he sounded mutedly displeased, though it might only have been a paranoid trick of his mind – surely the Prince could not have expected an immediate answer.

He walked swiftly and stopped unconsciously on the peak of a round, silver-pale bridge over one of the landscaped streams, not seeing, trying to think and unable to do so, one hand on the balustrade, gripping. He did not notice Makaria following him, and coming to stand at his side.

'Salvius will be here in an hour. What if he wants to see Drusus?'

'What?' said Marcus. He turned and looked blankly at her. He could see a faint thrilled expression in her face that in his current frame of mind irritated him. Makaria was still overcome by the unfamiliar beauty of the city that Marcus could no longer have seen, still dazed from visiting the Empress Jun Shen for the first time earlier in the day. Though she had tried to display a properly Roman aloof pride, it had been shocking – *thrilling* – to see a little old lady, dripping with jewels, perched on a throne and exuding as much authority as any Emperor of Rome.

Marcus irritably performed the adjustment of mind necessary to focus on what she'd asked him. 'Let him. Let him, but be there with them. Behave as if the whole thing were just a family misunderstanding – I don't think Drusus will dare challenge that, and Salvius can't do much if he doesn't speak out.'

Makaria nodded. In a softer voice she asked, 'What were you talking about with the Prince?' with a look that said she thought she knew.

'The weather in Edo,' snapped Marcus, hurrying away from her. It was Varius he wanted to go to first. But after today – after all of this – the only person he could and must tell was Una.

It was late when she came back. She found Marcus sitting alone in near darkness, his chair pushed close into the corner, slightly hunched, very still in the shadows. It was as if he were hiding, but only as a formality; as if something terrible had hunted him down over so many miles that he had given up getting away from it. The knitted hat lay loosely in one hand. He asked, in a numb murmur, 'How is she?'

No, thought Una again, drawing in inside her head. She was very tired, it had been so distressing to see Lal ill, and if he didn't want to face what was about to happen, nor did she. Here they were together, that was all they wanted. They were both free, no one could make them do anything. She answered, 'She woke up for a little while, but she thought Delir was there – she was talking to him. And to – her mother. She didn't know me.'

As soon as Una had stepped out of the car, a young man had jumped up from a doorstep and lunged at her across the dirty street. He looked panicky and breathless, but then, as he reached her, he changed and became suddenly polite, ushering her to the door, smiling, showing her towards a room – and then changed again and pushed desperately ahead of her, to Lal's bedside. Lal, who had always been so softly pretty, so fastidious, was wasted, filthy, slave-like. The youth had stroked Lal's damp hair, and then dashed furtively away, almost without having spoken.

Una went on telling Marcus, in as businesslike a manner as possible, 'But I found a doctor and he said he'd seen worse, at least, I think that's what he said. And I got the doctor's daughter to stay with her. There's medicine that he said would cool her down. But I want to get Sulien to her, or her to Sulien; I didn't think she should be moved until then. I should go back. But I thought you would want to know.' But really she hadn't come to tell him anything, she had only wanted to be with him after these horrible weeks apart.

'Poor Lal,' whispered Marcus, lifelessly.

'Yes.'

Marcus straightened in the chair, as if about to rise and walk over to her, but he did not. He remained powerlessly seated as if getting to her required some skill, like swimming, or driving a car, and he couldn't do it. He told her, 'The Prince told me he wanted me to marry Noriko.' He gave an ironic little smile, lasting only a second. 'So, I can't pretend I don't know any more.'

'Oh,' Una said, very mildly and neutrally, standing still in the centre of the room.

Marcus drew in a breath and held it, strenuously, like a weightlifter. He said, 'If I did ...'

Una turned her head to one side, a small, sharp movement. Her hands closed slowly at her sides, the nails biting bracing little notches of pain into the palms. Well then, now that had been said, he would have to go on and say the rest.

But Marcus couldn't get any further, he looked up at her as if he could hardly bear either to do that or to look away from her, with a wretched expression that seemed on the point of disintegrating; a smile that was not a smile but a knot holding the straining muscles of his face together. He confessed, pleading, 'I don't want to ask you this.'

Una was wrenched with pity for him, but she found she was not kind enough to tell him, 'You don't have to say it.' She could not help him do this; she could only stand there and wait.

'If I did,' said Marcus, laboriously again, one resisted word at a time. 'Would you stay with me?'

It seemed that since he'd begun trying to say this, she too had been holding her breath. She sighed now, releasing it, and felt her body become oddly still, relaxed, empty. She said, 'No.'

'You know it would only be an agreement between Nionia and Rome, it would never change how—' began Marcus, guiltily.

Una interrupted fiercely, angry with him after all for making her argue the point. 'You'd have to sleep with her. Have *children* with her.'

Marcus blanched a little at this; it was something he hadn't let himself think about yet, looking for a moment young and unprepared.

'And you like her,' Una went on, more subdued. She smiled regretfully. '*I* like her. If it wasn't for me you wouldn't think this was so bad.'

'If it wasn't for you?' echoed Marcus incredulously, springing up at last and gripping her shoulders. 'How could it be if not for you? I'm not whoever I would have been if I hadn't met you, I never can be now. I love *you*, I only want you. We should have married long before this.'

There was a fractional pause. 'It's against the law,' Una observed, dully.

'Then I should have changed the law. I *will* change it.'

'Then you'd have been expected to divorce me.' A bleak version of her withering tone hovered in Una's voice and vanished. 'So you would still have asked me this. And I would still have said no.'

Marcus looked exhausted. But then he moved away from her and began talking again, a little too fast, working up a shallow optimism. 'All right. Good. Then that's clear. I'm sorry I had to ask. I'll tell the Prince it can't happen – I'll say the people won't accept it or something. We'll just have to keep working. And then – when this is all over – you and I ...'

Una found this agonising to listen to, but it was her turn to pull together the strength for what she had to say. At length she whispered, 'No.'

He fell silent at once. He turned to her with an anguished, almost disbelieving look, begging not to have understood.

She said, 'It's happened. You've asked me. Now I can't ... stay.'

Marcus shook his head. He said in a low, reasonable voice, 'No. Please.'

Glancing away from him, because it was so difficult to look him in the face and stick to this, Una found she was looking at a trunk on the floor which had not been there before, when she'd left to find Lal. She felt a sob of a laugh trapped somewhere in her throat as she guessed it held her missing clothes. So she didn't even have to pack. It was like a joke. She said quietly, 'I'll take Lal with me, to Sulien. I'll find a room near her for tonight, and I'll go tomorrow morning.'

'But I won't do it, I won't marry her. I promise,' insisted Marcus, his voice rising desperately.

'But you *have* to, don't you?' answered Una, harshly. And for a second she was furious with him for driving her to say that. She muttered, 'At least, I can't be the reason you decide.'

Quite suddenly Marcus seemed to fold up, he collapsed back onto the chair, as if winded, he looked helplessly around the room, then back at her, with tears on his face. He said brokenly, 'I didn't want this. I didn't want to ask you – *I'm sorry*—'

'Oh, I know,' cried Una remorsefully, unable to bear it, going and closing him in her arms, shielding him protectively as she had done after he'd first heard the news of Faustus' illness, and the massacre. She kissed his hair, his cheek, trying with a kind of superstition to avoid his mouth, until from being in a kind of stupor he seemed to come to life and pressed her closer, turning his face to find her lips, winding a hand into her hair, caressing, holding on. Tears spilled out of her eyes at last as she tried at once to comfort him and to pull back, stroking his arms as she tried to slide out of them, his face as she pushed it away from hers. 'No,' she managed to say, but he only echoed the same word, whispering, 'No. No,' and didn't let her go. His hold on her was nothing but gentle, but still it was so difficult to disengage herself that for a moment Una relaxed hopelessly into the embrace, warm, dazed, and Marcus stood up, turning so that they were twisted even more closely together and drawing her further from the door. But then she forced herself alert again, and pushed his hands back, kissing him once more as she held them down, and broke away.

And then she was outside, alone, under the foreign night sky.

There was a firm, rapid beat on the door. Varius was back in his rooms after walking through the city until after darkness fell, letting some of the unease and strain beat out of himself into the clean white pavements under his feet. He opened the door and found Una standing there, hugging her arms and shivering so that for a moment he had the bizarre impression that the weather outside had changed and frozen, and that she was soaked to the skin with icy rain. Then he saw her pale, hardened face, and that she had been crying, and would cry later – but not now, not while talking to him.

'Come in,' he said at once, concerned, but she shook her head, vehemently, as if he were asking her to part with something essential.

'I'm saying goodbye,' she announced, rather roughly, her mouth folding tightly as she finished speaking.

He could see at once that she wasn't simply going home to see Sulien. He didn't say anything.

'He'll marry her. Noriko. He's been asked to. What's he supposed to do? Bound to happen really. So ...' she shuddered again, looked at him, and shrugged.

'I'm sorry.'

Una smiled at him unevenly. She remarked with a kind of fractured brightness, 'I wish you could tell me this was the wrong thing to do.'

He'd really been trying to think of something, as he took in the implications of the marriage being suggested openly, at this point. 'I do too,' he said.

She nodded a few times. 'I'm glad you were there, these last two weeks.'

He held out his hand. She gripped it quickly and jerked her head the way she'd come, towards Marcus' quarters. 'Please can you – please make sure he's – please keep an eye on him.'

'Of course I will,' Varius said.

Marcus stood where she'd left him, breathless, shaking. This rigour, this pain he was in, did not tempt him to rest or sink into it; it was not released by the splintery tears in his eyes. Instead it gripped and rolled with a terrible lacerating energy; it demanded some kind of action, and yet for the moment it would not let him move. His heartbeat bucked and surged and seethed.

And then, as he turned his head, he saw the texture of the wall change. The dark, carved wood seemed to put out tiny hairs, or petals, or tongues. And these lapped and rippled and breathed, and then seemed to melt and crumple down together as if the wall were a rough covering, a *skin*, which was about to slither loose.

Marcus lurched back with a gasp that ripped out of him, like a strip of fabric being torn away. He swung around, throwing an unsteady accusing gaze all round him – and the illusion had gone, it had scarcely lasted a second. Yet nothing looked normal any more. It was what he'd seen, three years ago, under the influence of the drug in the Aesculapian hospital and the Galenian Sanctuary. He'd been made to seem mad – to *be* mad, so that all his claims of conspiracies would appear to be the pitiable onset of the Novian affliction. To protect Drusus – as he knew now.

345

And afterwards, when it was over, the fear that the compound forced into his blood had permanently changed him, that it might trigger the disease he'd learnt to dread since childhood, had shrunk away with time until he'd almost thought it had vanished. And now ...

Marcus' breath was still harsh and ragged in his lungs, but he drew himself up straight. He punched open the door of the room and marched out, unconscious of any servant or guard in his way until he reached the pavilion in which he and Una had only lately stayed, where Drusus was now.

He stood and looked at the guards standing outside the shut doors, and said in an undertone, 'Move aside.'

XIX

SANDSTORM

Marcus approached the door with a kind of predatory gentleness, pacing softly, delicately trying the handle. It did not surprise him that the door was locked; he grimaced, sardonically, and then he hurled himself against it shoulder first, felt the wood quiver under the impact and did it again; once, twice – and then as he stepped back to attack again the door was suddenly unlocked from within and opened inwards.

'Marcus,' said Drusus from inside – a courteous greeting.

Marcus strode across the threshold. 'Out,' he said to the slaves – the one who had opened the door and a few others – standing in meek attendance around the room.

Drusus contradicted quickly, 'Stay where you are.' And Marcus watched the white, panicked flicker of his eyes as the slaves obeyed the first order, darting past him with lowered faces, out through the door.

Marcus advanced into the room, and instinctively, matching his pace, Drusus retreated. Then, sensing how close he was to being backed against the wall, he drew himself up and stood facing Marcus. For the time being, Marcus seemed to accept the degree of space between them; he came to a halt, surveying his cousin.

'All the things you've done,' Marcus said to him, his voice calm, marvelling.

'You've never listened to my side of it,' attempted Drusus, with dry lips.

Marcus gave a hard laugh. 'Not likely to start now, then, am I?' He took another hostile step forward. 'My parents – they were good to you, weren't they? Part of your family. But that wasn't a reason to let them live, not for you. Nothing could have been.'

Drusus felt an apprehensive swell of confusion. Leo and Clodia's deaths seemed so fixed in history to him now that he could hardly remember them alive, hardly imagine that anyone could have been surprised when they were killed. 'I'm sorry you lost your parents, Marcus

347

– I've always mourned that loss. But you know it was Gabinius, *I* had no part in it—'

'Shut up! I'm not asking you questions. I want to make you hear what you've done. You're responsible for their deaths. And Gemella's, just as much as that bitch Tulliola. Everyone I give a damn about you've hurt, you've tried to kill. I know what you'd have done to Varius and *Una* if you could.' He could not keep himself from placing a helpless, furious stress on Una's name. 'When I saw the state you'd left her in—'

'That's not what happened,' Drusus stammered, a cold flush rising to his face as he tried not to react at the mention of Tulliola.

'*I said quiet.*' Marcus shoved Drusus, slamming him against the wall and holding him there. '*Her*. Sulien. I know there's nothing you won't tear apart or wreck. The whole world if that's what it takes, right? Kato. Those fires, all those people in Veii, *all of this now . . .*'

Drusus was pale, open-mouthed, staring at Marcus. He blinked and dodged free, backing away again, even more frightened than before. 'What are you talking about? Veii? My own country? I *love* Rome; I could never betray it.' He'd had Sulien followed for a couple of weeks, and having him killed had been an obvious possible end to the business – but his injuries at Veii had removed him from Drusus' way for a while. And after that there had been Una, and arrest.

Marcus was coming after him, moving in a steadily prowling crescent shape, heading him off. 'My father was Rome. And my mother. And I am.'

'I promise I never did anything against you,' vowed Drusus. 'And – the Nionian lord? I don't understand.'

Marcus stopped, reaching a moment of defeated bafflement. 'What can you possibly hope for by denying it now?' he asked.

'You're mad,' said Drusus, recklessly, and for a split second he was chilled as something like a grin of savage concurrence cut like a blade across Marcus' face.

Marcus hit him in the face with all his strength. A hot spark of peace flew up his arm from his fist to his spine, glowed for an instant and died out, unsatisfyingly, so as Drusus staggered back, clutching his face, his lip already split, Marcus dragged him closer by a handful of expensive tunic, pulled tight around his neck, and hit him again. This time he felt a rubbery crunch of bone under his knuckles, which came away wet. Again the moment of release was gallingly brief. At least he'd made a start.

Bright, black craters sparked behind Drusus' eyes, and pain inflated densely into the hollows of his skull, which felt huge and rocky and full of pressure, like deep-sea caves. A spout of blood discharged from his broken nose, spattering shockingly warm and shameful on his chest; blood splashed unexpectedly in the back of his throat too, and he had no time even to gag and spit it clear as Marcus lunged for him again. But Drusus did not hit back, not at first. He was paralysed with physical shock and terror. All day he'd been able to feel the power gathering unreasonably, like a bank of cloud, away from him, on Marcus' side. If he provoked Marcus to call the guards back with their guns, if he gave him any excuse to have him arrested again, he felt certain he wouldn't survive. He could only hope to get away, or to last it out.

Marcus knocked him backwards twice, driving him against the side table behind him so its edge bit against the small of his back and a row of ornaments sprayed across the floor, smashed. Drusus pressed an arm desperately on Marcus' chest, trying to lever his way past, and another blow landed on the side of his face, shivering through the broken bones and causing a whirling drain of dizziness to swill through his head. He grabbed Marcus' forearms and tried to force them back, propelling him a few feet towards the centre of the room. The pain grew tighter and more solid on his face, like something knotted around it, a blindfold.

Marcus felt the resistance as irrelevant, silly. He kicked, scraping a foot hard down Drusus' shin, then tore free of the hold on his arms and flung Drusus right back over the little table, head smacking against the wall. Drusus crumpled, tripping over the fallen table as he crashed down, but at least further from Marcus now. He kicked the table away and scrambled towards the door, propping himself against the wall, limping. Marcus hurled himself after him.

'*I'm sorry,*' choked Drusus hopelessly, his breath wet, blood filming the words. But Marcus brought him down, fists stabbing at him, so that Drusus, too late, had to try and fight in earnest, clubbing and batting at Marcus, whose hands, clothes and unrecognisable face were flecked with red – and not a bruise on him yet.

At last Drusus succeeded in writhing onto his feet, Marcus still clutching and lashing at him, and strengthened by panic, threw a wild punch that skated across Marcus' cheek, catching hard enough on the bone that Marcus veered back. He felt nothing, no pain at all. He said, 'I'll kill you,' and felt a bright elation of discovery at the knowledge that this was exactly what he meant, exactly what he was doing.

He had no idea what the next blow did to Drusus' face. He grabbed him again, by the neck and sleeve, and threw Drusus away from him once more, and a distant part of him was coldly surprised at how far Drusus hurtled across the room, how hard he fell, plunging down in a pile-up of furniture and noise. He did not get up.

Marcus walked over to Drusus quite slowly, brushing toppled chairs out of his way as he went, unearthing him. Drusus was curled on his side under the heap, silent. Marcus kicked at one shoulder, turning Drusus onto his back. Drusus gulped in a bubbling red breath, but his swollen eyes did not open; he lay with his face white around the dark plastering of blood, his arms outflung. One hand lay loose beside Marcus' foot; Marcus flicked it delicately into position with the toe of his boot, and then stamped down onto it. Drusus jackknifed into consciousness, flailing, tugging at his trapped hand, a weak, rasping shriek of agony forced out of him. Marcus pressed his weight down, twisting on the crushed fingers, as if trying to smear them into a paste on the wood floor. Drusus thrashed, still screaming as he tried to pull away, then clawed up with his free hand, clutching at Marcus' clothes, dragging so that Marcus fell onto him, releasing the wrecked hand, but burying fists and knees into Drusus' stomach, ribs, throat.

But Drusus, frustratingly, seemed no longer to be there. Marcus could feel nothing under his hands; he knocked and pounded furiously as if on a locked door, but the punches seemed to vanish into air. Drusus had escaped him by dissolving, turning insubstantial as smoke. So he leant, gasping, on Drusus' neck, then on the smashed face, damming up the thin flow of bloodied air. He could not feel if Drusus struggled – could not even see him any more.

Someone caught him by the shoulders and swung him away. Marcus, who had felt, with his hands pressed over Drusus' mouth, as he were passing into a kind of sleep-like void, jerked, suddenly electrified again with indignation. He pushed the man back, elbowing fiercely, shouting, 'I said *get out*,' swerved round to get in a more emphatic push or strike, and found it was Varius who hadn't let go of him. Who said, quietly, 'Marcus. Stop. You can stop now.'

Marcus stared at him, panting, baffled. He muttered, 'Leave me alone, Varius.'

'No,' said Varius. 'No.'

On the ground, Drusus lolled feebly, trying to breathe.

Marcus grimaced impatiently and shook free, and surged back towards Drusus. At once Varius seized him again, silently holding him back. Marcus struggled, snarled, '*I'm warning you*,' and threw his weight against Varius, dashing him into the wall as he had done to Drusus. And Varius simply allowed him to do it, without tensing against the collision, without flinching. Not even the still look on his face altered, so that at the last instant Marcus pulled back a little, instinctively softening the impact. He was far beyond forming the thought that Varius must have taught himself this deliberate non-resistance in those weeks of silence in prison, but something like it stirred queasily on the edge

350

of his mind and he said roughly, 'What's wrong with you? You wanted this. You told me you wanted me to do this.'

'I know. I know I did. But you'll lose everything if you do it now.'

Marcus hesitated, but then spat out a miserable laugh. 'Sounds fair.'

He let go then, and would have broken away, but Varius had locked hold of him before he could even make a move, saying grimly. 'No. It does not.'

If Varius hadn't defended himself before, it wasn't because he was weak. Straining against his grip, Marcus began to feel how he'd worn himself out. He lurched exhaustedly and gasped, 'What are you protecting him for?' He didn't know what reply he expected, but Varius only answered with a short, castigatory look at him, and Marcus sagged a little, shamed. No – of course he knew better than that. He demanded instead, 'Why not? Why shouldn't I? After everything he's done.' But he was no longer struggling.

Varius cautiously loosened his grip, his hands still on Marcus' shoulders, but not so much restraining him now as holding him up. 'You could lose your power, for one thing. And then what? What about the war – the slaves?'

But all this seemed unreal to Marcus, something to which he couldn't remember his way back. His breathing came almost in sobs now, dry, raw. He shook his head despairingly and staggered away, over to Drusus. And this time Varius did not stop him, only followed, staying close. At their feet, Drusus twitched slackly, like a parched fish on a beach, a pitiful attempt to slip away. Marcus looked down, trying to coax the strength and rage back into life. He was so tired, so daunted at the effort it would take to finish what he'd done. But he still could do it, he still *must*, even without the force that seemed to have drained away while Varius held him.

At his side, Varius said, 'Remember telling me what it would mean. You were right. This is not an execution. You were thinking more clearly then.'

'Thinking clearly,' Marcus repeated, bitterly. 'It's too late. You might as well – you might as well let me. It's come back.'

'What has come back?'

'What they did to me,' said Marcus. He leant, one-handed, on one of the chairs that Drusus' fall had sent skidding across the floor, then abruptly dropped onto it as if he'd been tripped. 'What I saw, when I was drugged. When I was in the Sanctuary. It's still there. I could at least make him pay for that.'

Varius lifted another chair soundlessly onto its feet so that he could sit beside Marcus. He asked, 'Are you seeing anything like that now?'

Marcus cast a distrustful, flinching glance around the room, and shook his head again.

'How long did it last?'

'A few seconds. One second, maybe. It doesn't matter how long. It's in my blood, it must have always been just – waiting to come back.'

There was a silence, in which he heard himself, and Drusus, both labouring for air.

'One second in three years ...' suggested Varius.

Marcus lifted his face from his hands with a cracked little smile and a look that took in the chaos he'd made of the room, the state he was in, Drusus. He said, 'Doesn't it seem like more than that?'

Varius regarded him, steadily. 'You seem furious – desperate, to me. You've got good reason for that. You don't seem mad. You are yourself, you still have that to lose.'

Marcus was finally still, beginning to catch his breath.

'You know what I want for him,' said Varius. 'I don't want this for you.'

Marcus looked back at him and said, 'Varius ...' But he had no idea what more he could have said even if his throat hadn't closed as tightly as a fist and stifled any further attempt at speech. He bowed his head because he couldn't hold Varius' gaze any longer, and then, as if some scaffolding supporting his body had given way, he slumped, not back into the chair but sideways, letting his forehead drop against Varius' shoulder. He shut his eyes, stupefied with fatigue. He felt Varius' hand come to rest briefly on his arm. And then he dragged himself up and went to Drusus, and got onto his knees beside him.

'Drusus,' he said fiercely, lifting him up. 'Drusus. Can you hear me?' Drusus was limp; his head rolled back, but his eyes opened dully – painful slits in the purpled swelling of his broken face. With a groan of effort Marcus hauled him off the ground and onto a chair, bent over him. 'I'm going to let you have what you want. You can make speeches – you can preside over the Games. I'll give you power. I'm going to give Canaria a new governor. I'm sure your people will love you very much. And every conversation you have will be listened to. Everyone you work with, I will have put there. Each letter you write, I will read. And your first will be to our uncle, to tell him how happy you are with your new post, and how glad we both are to have put aside our differences, like family, as he wanted. Do you understand?'

Drusus didn't or couldn't speak, but his head drooped onto his chest in a kind of spasm that might have been a nod.

Then Marcus heard heavy footsteps behind him on the wooden floor, and looked round to see Salvius coming to a halt at the head of the room, staring at the wreckage, at Drusus. Marcus straightened and faced him, confident at least that the trepidation he felt would not show.

Drusus looked up with convulsive effort, and choked out Salvius' name.

But Salvius stood there in silence and several things were immediately obvious to him. For one thing, he knew Varius had not been involved in the fight. He was too clean, not tired enough. And there was no one else there, the confrontation had been between Marcus and Drusus alone. And Drusus was taller than Marcus, and ought to have been at least as strong, yet Marcus stood there over him, dappled in blood that Salvius knew was not his own. So Drusus had failed, totally, to defend himself, failed to fight. Drusus' pleading look and whimpered pronunciation of his name seemed suddenly repellent to him. A weakling begging for protection. This was not what he had hoped for.

Varius said, 'This is over, Salvius.'

Later, when his skin was clean, and the bloody clothes had been bundled off to be washed by servants or thrown away, Marcus stood waiting in one of the Palace gardens, the low fruit trees around him colourless as water in the moonlight. He was aching for sleep, the need so intense it left almost no room for thought of what he'd done, or would do, or for loss. It was past midnight, but there was still something that must be accomplished before morning.

He knew that given the circumstances and the recipient, the note he'd sent should have been a poem like those he'd studied as a boy; its message should have been elegantly encoded into images of snow or grass, and passing time. But he was far too laden with weariness for that, even if he'd had the skill with the language, and the heart to do it. As he'd held the pen, he'd become aware for the first time of the burst skin on his knuckles, smarting when his fingers moved.

He leant against a garden wall, allowing his eyelids to droop, then lifted them idly as he saw someone hurrying through the shadows on the edge of his vision; a quick, female silhouette – a servant on an errand, he thought. Then he was surprised, and at first irritated, when this figure darted towards him, and only when she was quite near did he recognise Noriko, approaching with his note in her hand. She was wearing a plain, dark cotton robe and trousers, her hair was combed back and covered. Her face, he noticed, was still elegantly made up, but she was far more ordinary and unremarkable this way: just a good-looking young Nionian woman, and as such, she seemed much less self-conscious than she had on the one occasion they'd met before.

'You're in disguise,' he remarked, in Nionian.

Noriko smiled. 'So I should be able to say I was never here,' she explained. 'It only matters that I should be able to say that, in this case – not really whether anyone believes it.'

Marcus returned her smile, very faintly but genuinely. 'I think you must know why I wanted to meet you.'

Noriko lowered her eyes gravely, a silent confirmation.

He asked, 'I wanted to know if you have you been given any kind of choice? Are you ... willing?'

Noriko looked at him with eyebrows raised. 'What can you do if I say no?'

Marcus had no answer.

'We are neither of us free in this,' she said quietly. 'But you need not worry for me. I am not unwilling – not unhappy. I am ready, I think.'

Had he hoped that if she were set firmly enough against it, there would be some way out? A childish thought, if so. He nodded and said, 'Thank you.'

Noriko noticed the row of bloody little cracks on his swollen knuckles, the risen patch on his cheek where a bruise was forming. She could not ask what had happened, but something had, and she felt that whatever it was included the blow she had anticipated from the beginning, when she had watched him and Una through her telescope. She wondered where Una was now. She began, 'I am sorry that ...' and she stopped, unable to think of any way of finishing that was not unseemly, or humiliating. She repeated simply, 'I am sorry.'

'Oh,' he was looking at her with the same lonely compassion as must be on her own face. 'I'll try not to make you sorry. I will try.'

Noriko stepped tentatively closer to him, not quite embracing him but just standing softly against him, her cheek light on his. For a moment, feeling that they were meeting tonight in a kind of privacy that might never quite be repeated, she thought of kissing him experimentally on the lips. But she could feel the shallow unevenness of his breath; he felt slighter than he looked at a distance, and at this moment he seemed acutely fragile to her. So she only let her fingertips touch lightly on the nicks and splits on the knuckles of his right hand, which hung still for a second, and then took loose hold of hers. She whispered, 'We can be friends. I hope we can be friends.'

Una sat on the bunk beside Lal's, her knees drawn up, her sharp chin hard on her crossed arms as the train flew west. It was hard for her to believe she had had any part in causing the chaos she'd jostled through, fighting for tickets out of the country as the travel embargo broke. Swallowed up in a jostling crowd of discontented travellers, she had felt as insubstantial as a drop of water.

Lal was growing quiet again. For a while after the city outside the window gave way to the brown and dried-out hills, Una had thought her condition was improving. She had seemed to be fumbling doggedly against the undersurface of consciousness; there had been a concentrated frown on her face. Sometimes she had opened her eyes to stare at Una with surprised, pleased recognition. But now she was almost motionless, her eyes showing in two unnerving blank crescents under her eyelids. Occasionally she seemed to struggle as if being held down, but with less and less energy each time she moved.

Una straightened the row of medicine bottles on the shelf between the beds, and reread the instructions the doctor had written out for her even though she knew she had already committed them to memory. She was glad that she had been able to pay for all of this herself – the doctors in Sinchan and Jondum, this hard-won compartment on the train, the porters to carry Lal aboard – it was a relief that her money was at last honestly good for something. But she knew that for the present, the instructions would not tell her of anything more she could do; she had administered the latest dose of the wormwood tincture, she could only hope it would go on keeping Lal alive. Sometimes she had the irrational feeling that its potency would be diminished by the fact that although she executed every necessary task with exact carefulness, she felt as if she were woodenly acting the part of a nurse; as if Lal would suffer for the fact that so much of her own strength must be consumed in the effort of holding almost all her mind in check. At least until they reached Rome, she would not let her thoughts name Marcus, or produce his image; she would not look at her own future or his. She would keep ruthlessly scrubbing out the possible hope that something might still happen to prevent Marcus' marriage to Noriko, and it was that continual act of will that cost her most.

'You're not going to die,' she told Lal briskly. 'You *know* you're not going to die.'

Outside the grass was a thin sediment, spread half-heartedly over the sharp, dried-out hills. Then even that gave out, to bare stones and grit, and finally the crumpled formlessness of desert. Una watched blankly. Thin, shadowy ribbons of blown sand began to whip past the thick-sealed windows. Ahead of the train a rampart of dust was rising against the light. And somehow Una could not bear to look at it; she crouched down on the bed, hands and teeth clenched, as the sandstorm streamed like smoke, and the train shot into it. Absolutely against her will, the

355

thought forced itself on her that by now the wedding must be formally agreed upon, when she arrived in Rome it might even be on the news. And with a kind of surprise and disapproval of herself, she found that she was pressing her face hard against the bed, to keep Lal from hearing the stifled cry that shoved itself out of her throat. She beat her fists on the blankets in total silence as the windows went brown, and then black.

XX

FLAMMEUM

Lal's eyes opened without hurry, and traced a leisurely arc across the white ceiling. It stretched off beyond the curtains that obscured her view of the rest of the long room. The noise of traffic and a distant alarm slid in untroublingly through the small high window, just visible above her head. She could hear people talking and breathing on either side of her. Her body felt weak and clean as a dandelion seed, drifted down to the bed through cool air.

Sulien was there. She recognised him instantly.

Lal slammed her eyes shut in strange, embarrassed shock. For the first year after leaving Holzarta, she'd daydreamed intensively about Sulien, until picturing an ardent reunion with him in luxuriant detail had become a habit. And later, when she'd lost serious hope of that, she'd still, from time to time, allowed herself to picture a more poised, restrained meeting. They would both be different. Perhaps they would not say much, just wish each other well. He would see that she was more adult now, and she would have a simple, pleasing memory of him. She had long ceased to really think of herself as in love with him, but he was still the very last person she would have wanted to see her unconscious, dirty, half-dead. For a few seconds she almost hoped he'd go away.

But of course she was curious. She lifted her eyelids again tentatively, observing him while hoping he would not notice yet that she was awake. He was standing at the foot of the bed, looking down at her with a calm, professional concern, but without worry – he must know she was well. He must have made her so. Even now he was still tanned after the long, unblinkingly bright summer, but her memory of the warm, new look of his skin was right. His mouth was perhaps smaller and narrower than over the years she'd come to picture it. Against the characterless pallor of his work clothes, the different browns of his body were warm and clear: his hair chestnut, and longer than she remembered, his eyes

357

surprisingly light – so that in an older or less-prized face she might have considered them yellowish and ugly – but in his like gold, like burnt sugar. The structure of his face was stronger now, his frame more solid. But if it were possible to judge from such a quiet, relaxed expression, she thought there was something a little less direct and candid in the set of his face, something more guarded.

She carefully acted out waking up again, and said, 'Hello, Sulien.'

He seemed to feel none of the awkwardness she did, and perhaps the faint reserve or sadness she thought she'd seen in his face had never really been there. He just grinned, happy to hear her speak, and said, 'Isn't it great that you're here?'

Lal grew aware of her hair straggling in scratchy ropes on the pillow, the hard stripped-down feeling of her bones under the covers, 'That I'm where?' she asked, cautiously, as it occurred to her that she didn't know for sure.

'Rome,' said Sulien, gesturing grandly, as if the Pantheon and the Colosseum lay like packing cases around his feet.

She tried to piece together what had happened while she was ill. But she kept falling asleep. At some point, to her dismay, she must have drifted off while talking to Sulien. She felt so lapped with weakness and with safety that she could not summon the urgency she needed in order to remember. The last thing she was sure she remembered was walking endlessly through the countryside outside Jingshan, looking for the next village and the temple. She was almost sure she must have reached it, although it was there her memories began to shimmer and float apart. Her impression that Una had brought her to Rome would have seemed no more solid than any of the other fluttering scraps of fever, except that the fact that she was here confirmed it. But in between – where had she been? How had Una found her?

She prised herself out of bed, shocked at the effort needed and at how her legs seemed as thin and unstable as stilts underneath her. She crept out of the ward to look for a mirror and a window, in that order. Her reflection was even more discouraging than she had feared. Her skin seemed sunken and patchy, her lips cracked, her body more wasted than she would have believed it could be. Her face looked old, her body child-like. She felt frantic to do something immediate to correct the damage. Her dogged attempts to unpick her matted hair with her fingernails filled her with gradual anxiety about the future. The paper bag of her remaining make-up and trinkets was somewhere in Sina. She did not even own a comb. Where was she to go? She thought of Ziye and her father, and wept a little.

Still, to be in Rome after so many years of wishing it, to be well even if she was so weak, kept her in possession of a certain optimism. She tottered resolutely round to the landing and looked down the stairs towards the lobby.

She saw Sulien talking with a young blonde woman, whose clothes, hair, and way of standing suggested somehow that she was beautiful, even though Lal could not see her face. She held a little girl about two or three, who was complaining vaguely, until Sulien hoisted her up into his arms.

Lal looked at the three of them with her head on one side, and a feeling of abrupt, flat, prudence. She did not exactly make any assumptions, and therefore did not feel wounded. But she did feel herself reminded that it was not her business what he did.

She pulled herself up the next flight of stairs, and, with a struggle, opened the window on the higher landing. She could see no landmark, only a close, reddish-brown building, a bedsheet hanging from an upper window, a house further along the narrow street clothed in red creeper, some dustbins. Nevertheless: *Rome*.

A nurse found her and nagged her back to bed; indeed now she seemed to have come such a huge distance that it was exhausting to retrace her steps, the mere sight of the bed overwhelmed her with relief as she approached it. She fell back onto the mattress and began trying to remember again. 'I'll get you out of here – you'll be safe,' breathed the memory of a voice. But it was all as mixed and scattered as a brightly coloured heap of feathers, and then once again she was asleep.

For the moment, Sulien really didn't give a thought to the past he'd had with Lal; he was simply glad that she was here now. He gave Tancorix back the spare key to her flat, and went off with her to buy Xanthe a bag of sweets. Finally he was beginning to feel safe in Rome again. Deliberately, he relished the good mood; it came like a deserved respite from the confused sadness he felt whenever he thought of Marcus – which was hard to avoid with loyally gushing news of the engagement on every public longvision all the time – and serious worry for Una, who remained as white and tight-lipped as when she'd first arrived. He hadn't yet finished clearing the mess the vigiles had made of his flat, but it was at least habitable enough for him to have moved back in. Una had also spent the last two nights there, but already she was hunting grimly for work and a place of her own. He feared part of her haste was an impulse to get away from him. Stupidly he'd said to her, wanting only to offer comfort: 'But it hasn't happened yet; they might still find some other way.' It was the only time he'd seen her burst into tears.

Sulien and Tancorix sat down on the parapet over the embankment of the Tiber, above the hem of colourful plastic rubbish bobbing against the river's walls. Tancorix tried to get Xanthe interested in the sparse snowflakes fluttering down through the bare plane trees onto the water. On the Bridge of Agrippa, workmen were already – months ahead of the event – attaching a system of glass lamps shaped like white roses and camellias and lilies, in anticipation of the Imperial wedding. Sulien glowered at them vaguely on Una's behalf. He allowed himself to think bullishly of Marcus as nothing more than an untrustworthy rat who'd broken his sister's heart, and pushed him to the back of his mind.

For some minutes, Tancorix had seemed on the point of telling him something, but kept hesitating, so at last he asked obligingly, 'What is it?'

Tancorix frowned uneasily at the river. 'I think I've seen Edda.'

It took him a moment to remember who she meant. The slave from her former husband's house, the one who'd been kind to her – dead in the fire that had destroyed the Maecilii estate. 'What do you mean?'

'I was singing at the bar last night,' she said. 'It was quite a good audience. And I saw her. She was round at the side, watching me. She'd come to see me.'

Sulien was willing enough to listen to this, but not very convinced. 'It wasn't just someone who looked like her?'

'No, it can't have been,' insisted Tancorix. 'It was her.'

'But you didn't speak to her, you just saw her in the crowd?'

'Oh, it's never really a *crowd*, is it?' said Tancorix. 'And I didn't know what to do. I even thought she was a ghost for a second! I sort of went on to the end of the song somehow, and then I called to her and I tried to get down off the stage. And she pretended she didn't know I meant her! She tried to hide behind the people in front of her. And you know I can't move very fast in that dress. She was gone before I could get near her. If it wasn't her, why would she run away?' Tancorix shook her head, bewildered and unnerved, and then laughed sadly. 'But then, why would she run away if it *was* her?'

Sulien still doubted there was more to this than a fancied resemblance, but he said, 'Well, if she escaped when the place burnt, she'd have to lie low. You don't tell the world you're a slave on the run.'

'But I know that, you'd think she could have trusted me,' said Tancorix, sounding hurt.

I trust that you are now well.

I wish I could have done something earlier to spare you the ordeal

I now know you have been through, but I am grateful that I can at last repay the debt I owe to you and your family. Of course you have a home in Rome as long as you need or want it. I know you must be very anxious for your father and stepmother, and indeed for other Romans and former slaves, and I wish to reassure you as much as possible. I have been pursuing Delir and Ziye's case since first I heard of it; I have been assured they are both well, and have been moved into better conditions. I am fully confident they will be transferred into Roman supervision and that the only question that remains is how soon we may expect this. I have every faith it <u>will be</u> soon.

Please make the palace steward's office aware of anything you need.

Marcus Novius Faustus Leo

Lal had a sense of earlier drafts floating like ghosts behind these measured phrases, of missing paragraphs that Marcus had stared at and crossed out. There was no mention of his pending marriage, or return to Rome, and nothing about Una or Sulien. The letter was painfully suspended between intimacy and formality, the warmth of its promises now and then melting through the cool surface of the lines. He had not signed himself Caesar.

This letter was waiting for her when a pair of junior household officials from the Palace took her from the clinic to a stylish first-floor flat at the edge of the Field of Mars. It was close to the centre but also an easy distance from Transtiberina, but in a far safer, more sedate district. It was not large, but pristinely finished, and its soft unscratched colours and clean contours seemed to radiate a calm, affluent safety into the spotless air. A little balcony overlooked a flower market in the quiet square below. Lal could not move to look at it; she stood with tears in her eyes, overwhelmed both at Marcus' generosity and at the fact that she had never even been inside a room like this before.

One of the palace staff told her, 'We thought a place of this size would be best for the time being; when your parents arrive we can look at the matter again. And you will have an allowance, paid monthly.'

So she had money, and she began spending it ravenously. The very thought that it was shameful to be behaving like this when her poor father was shut in some Sinoan prison camp spurred her on and she bought wildly, clothes, jewellery, trinkets, paints. The mere sight of things she could not afford pleased her. The plenty of Rome was even more astonishing than she had imagined, the stock of the whole world seemed to roll helplessly into the waiting city, like goods from a fantastic shipwreck washing up unspoiled on an island shore. Every kind of food, all fabrics; longvisions and cars of all sizes and grades of extravagance. And as she'd dreamt in Jiangning, there were all kinds of people, hurling through the city at speed, and she was as at home as any one of them. She bought armfuls of tropical flowers and took them to Una.

She'd made sure to come on the one day out of each eight that Una was not working. She'd taken a job clearing tables and serving drinks in a gigantic, factory-like bar in the station complex at Vatican Fields, where people drank in brief, crowded solitude, waiting for long distance trains to arrive. Her small rooms were in a tenement block north of the station, not very close to Sulien, or anyone she knew.

There was a pinched look to Una's face, as if all the muscles were braced in permanent effort. Her hair was scraped back into a tight plait. The scarlet flowers looked incongruous in her arms, even more so when she trudged back to her flat with them. Lal was shocked that Una was living somewhere so much more bleak and meagre than she was. In fact, there was nothing really wrong with the flat; it was plain and clean, everything in it functioned. At first it seemed ascetically devoid of any kind of decoration, but there were two Sinoan ink paintings hanging side by side on the wall of the cramped main room: a scene of wooded mountains, and a winter landscape. There was no vase for the flowers; Una began mechanically dividing them and placing them in mismatched cups and beakers, arranging them in a row on the kitchen table, where they looked odd but at least added some life to the room.

Una efficiently offered Lal things to eat and drink, but the guarded silence about her seemed somehow to persist even when she spoke. So Lal talked, trying to empty out some of her own strength and eagerness into the spartan rooms, and into Una herself, like a blood transfusion. 'Una, thank you so much for everything. You've been so good to me. I remember being on the train, I think, and you looking after me. And yet it's still strange that it really happened, because I still remember so much other stuff I thought was going on. My father being there ...'

'Yes,' murmured Una. 'You were talking to him when I found you.'

'And Dama,' added Lal. Una glanced round, startled by the name, but Lal only went on, 'What did happen really? I was at a temple – but you can't have found me there. How did I get to you? Was it Liuyin?'

'Your friend? Yes, I think so. I got a message telling me you were ill, and when I came there was a boy about our age, who showed me where you were. But he didn't speak to me. He seemed frightened, I think. But he cared about you.'

Lal frowned for a moment, remembering Liuyin crouching over her in a ditch beside a burning road, and Dama – but the second she judged

362

the memory as implausible it slid away. She urged Una, 'Let's go some-where.'

'When I'm not at work I just want to sleep,' said Una, sitting tense at the table as if she never stopped holding her breath.

But she let Lal persuade her out, and onto a tram towards the centre, because she felt a tired pleasure in seeing how Lal was thriving in Rome. Already she had recovered at least half the weight she'd lost during her illness; her hair hung freshly cut and glossy around her shoulders, her pretty clothes fitting her like the pelt of a healthy young animal. It warmed Una very faintly to see how magnificent Rome was to her, it was like a reflected light and heat, shops rising into soaring towers and arches, belted with longvision screens, glittering alongside grubby street stalls, the Pantheon crouching low over the crowds of people, the fountains – domes and webs of water in one square, weak trickles in another – the immense statue of Oppius Novius on the crest of the Pincian Hill, arm raised menacingly towards the sky, his face only a little like Marcus'. It was not that Lal did not notice or care when they passed slaves laying new tramlines, or slave children carrying bundles of shopping across town, but that to her these things seemed flaws or wounds on something so vigorously beautiful that it must be capable of perfecting itself. Una herself was living here only because of Sulien, not wanting to be too far from him even if she couldn't bear his efforts at comfort. And some days in the sterile, teeming station bar, the whole city seemed to her an unclean eruption that would be better cauterized.

But Lal was not quite as comfortable in Rome with Una as she was alone. She began trying to avoid looking at certain shops and bars, to dodge the forums with the largest longvision screens, until Una said wearily, 'Lal, it really doesn't matter. I'm used to it. They're even on money now.'

Lal had all but refused to believe Marcus could be going to marry Noriko until, a few days after she'd woken in Rome, Marcus himself broadcast a short, very formal speech about how delighted he was, extolling the lineage of his intended bride. This inflamed the entire Empire's furious communal itch to know what the Princess looked like; for no image of her had ever been displayed publicly in Nionia, let alone in the West. Even Lal, although she was ashamed of it, became invol-untarily curious. At last the Nionian court agreed to let a Roman artist attend when the Princess returned home to prepare for her wedding, and a portrait was rushed out: Noriko standing at a slight distance in an indistinct pale space, regal and fragile in her cloak of green-tinted hair, her hand resting symbolically on a branch of laurel.

And at once, although Marcus and Noriko had never yet appeared together, the couple were everywhere: printed or painted or stamped right across the Roman Empire. They stood side by side on windowsills as figurines in plastic or ceramics. Their faces gazed nobly together from ornamental plaques, on cushion covers, plates, and banners to be hung from windows, on paper fans – a Nionian fashion that Romans suddenly found interesting again, even though the weather was cooling now. There were posters, vases, clocks. More products poured out every week. Not that every Roman response to the news was positive. Some of the posters were defaced, especially a series of them that showed the red Nionian sun and the Roman eagle overlapping. There were sullen, anti-Nionian grafitti outside the centre, such as the vicious, splay-legged cartoon of Noriko scrawled on a Transtiberine wall near Sulien's flat, all lemon-yellow skin, green stalks of hair, slanted black lines for eyes.

But on the giant screens on the Saepta, the Circus Maximus, and outside the temple of Jupiter, festivals and blessings were broadcast from across the provinces as the day of the wedding grew closer. There was even a song about it, patriotic and sentimental, that kept playing in every bar and shop, and lodged irritatingly in the mind for hours after each hearing. And it was true, even the Roman mint was colluding now with this outpouring of celebration and enterprise, and had struck a run of commemorative coins on which the young couple's faces were framed in an Imperial wreath.

And then the treaty was signed, and Marcus was back in Rome. It was strange to Una to hear this along with everyone else, from reports on longvision, and yet at times it began to seem horribly unreal that she might ever have known it by any other means. So he was barely three miles from her, although, slamming through the longest shifts she could get at the Vatican bar as if her work there were of the most desperate urgency, she did all she could to eradicate the feeling that it made any difference to her where he was. His birthday passed. She was wracked with the possibility that he would contact her in some way, the feeling might have been hope or terror. And it did happen. Varius visited Sulien at the slave clinic, concerned in his own right about them both, and handed Sulien a letter for her that Sulien, half-grudgingly, passed on.

For two days she did not open it.

You already know that if you or Sulien need anything, if you ever want my help – but of course that doesn't need saying. I hate to think of you having to see these new coins, and everything, at least all that will be over soon. I don't know what I am writing, Una, I should not do it, I think – what is there to say when I can't ask you to come back? But I cannot come home and know you are just on the other side of the river and say nothing. Do you really mean never to see me again at all? Is it at least possible that at some time in the future – but you will not want to be asked that, and I am not sure I want to hear the answer. If this letter has any purpose it is only to tell you that I never stop thinking of you, and now I write it I realise that I do so for my own comfort more than yours, that I just want to be certain you know. I should rewrite this, or not send it. I don't think I can stand to do either. Goodbye—

    Marcus

Before opening it, Una was certain that it would be better not to answer; it would help neither of them to fall into a correspondence. She thought this conviction was solid, but it was knocked over as soon as she finished reading; she *must* write back to him, not to do so would be unforgivably cruel. But when she had a pen in her hand her whole body seemed to clench; her eyes flinched away from the blank page, and any phrase she began to string together seemed to cut her mind before she could finish it. Days went by, the Princess' Imperial train advanced into the Roman Empire with celebrations in every province through which it passed, and still Una could manage no reply. And all the time he would be hoping, or trying not to hope, and she hated herself when she imagined it.

And the day of the wedding came.

In the morning, Sulien went to the Field of Mars. The square below Lal's building was colourful and fluttering with streamers and banners, like everywhere else. He had put off seeing Lal more than once, without thinking very clearly about why, except that he was busy and too anxious about Una to feel like good company. But the memory of the two of them together in the Pyrenees had grown stronger and more troubling, and he was not certain if he was afraid she would want too much from him now, or too little. But today, all he could think of was what was due to happen. And though it had been three weeks since they last met, she was not surprised to see him.

He was a little startled at how much better she looked. Of course he had known the wastedness and sallow skin would pass, but he had not pictured what she would be like. He said, 'I'm going over to Una. Will you come?'

Lal reached for her keys immediately, but asked, 'Are you sure I should?'

Sulien sighed. 'No. But she was glad to see you before, I think. If I was her I'd want you to come.'

So they both travelled north – slowly, because there were few trams running today – towards the Clivus Cinnae, speaking little on the way. Behind them two women were speculating about what the Princess would wear, whether something Nionian, or decently Roman, or some kind of fusion of the two.

Una opened the door and gave them a pretty, reassuring smile, but made no immediate move to let them inside.

'Can't we come in?' asked Sulien, after a second.

'All right,' agreed Una, but her voice was noncommittal. 'For a while.'

The drab flat had been neat enough even when Lal had seen it last. Now it was punitively clean, scraped of almost every sign of human presence, so that entering it felt forbidden and unnatural. Una's arms were folded tightly against her ribs. She looked exhausted.

Sulien said, 'I don't think you should be alone today.'

'Well,' replied Una, in the mild tone of someone concluding a friendly difference of opinion. 'I do.'

But he went closer to her and, ignoring her continued unspoken signals for them to leave, sat down. 'I'm not going anywhere,' he announced, but he could not say it with quite the bravado it needed – she remained so self-contained and unwavering.

She remarked, 'I'm not sure what you're expecting to happen.'

'Why are you treating yourself like this?' he asked gently. 'Why do you work at that place? You've got money already.'

'I'm saving it. And I need something to do.'

'But you could do better, couldn't you? You've learnt so much – you've done all these things.'

'What?' demanded Una, her voice a little louder, and less steady. 'Should I apply to work in an office and say my last job was being Caesar's mistress? No.'

It became noticeable that she was trembling. Her wrists looked thin and hard where they crossed in front of her. Lal almost felt that her own recovery must somehow have been at Una's expense; since they had last met vitality seemed to have drained out of Una at the exact pace that Lal had regained it.

And looking at Una, Sulien felt a bleak familiar helplessness settling over him that had been gone a long time, and was the heavier now for the fact he had not expected to feel it again. It made him almost afraid to say anything to her. He persisted, hesitantly, 'But you did some work for Glycon. If you mentioned him, or maybe Varius ... '

'No,' said Una, expressionless now. 'There's no need.'

Sulien rocked his head forward in frustration and told her, 'You're running yourself into the ground for no reason and *I don't want you to.*'

Una turned away from him with a short sigh, looking down out of the window. She explained with a kind of hurried patience. 'I'm working where I am because it's loud, and it's full of people, and I can't think straight there. I don't want to know anything anyone's thinking. It helps. I'm learning not to. It's getting easier.'

A drum began beating somewhere below. A street party was getting off to an early start.

Lal, who had hung back quietly until now said, 'But for today, why don't you come with us and we'll get out of Rome? It must be so much worse, being here.'

'No,' said Una calmly. She had shown no reaction to the drumbeat. 'It doesn't make it worse. There isn't a village in the Empire where they won't be dancing in the forum all night. I may as well be here.'

'We could go somewhere empty. There must be a field or a wood we could find. We could just go to the top of a hill and talk, or not talk, or whatever you want.'

Una glanced at her, and wished herself a different person, someone who might have accepted. What Lal was trying to offer – empty space – was very close to what she wanted, but only if it were truly empty; not if she were in Lal's or Sulien's or anyone's company. The anonymity of the Vatican bar comforted her and she could have had twice her usual wage for working there over the wedding, but today she could only tolerate full solitude, not merely the privacy she could build inside her skull.

So she lifted her head firmly and said, 'Listen. It was kind of you to come here, and I know you want to help me. But please believe I know my own mind. I'm not ill. I'm safe. There's nothing you need to do for me. So thank you – no. I'll see you in a few days, or in a week, but not today.'

Sulien and Lal were both silent, at a loss. Then reluctantly, Sulien got to his feet. But instead of following Una's pointed look towards the door he went and wrapped his arms round her, kissing her temple. Una didn't unfold her arms to the embrace; it was as if she were holding something pressed against her chest and did not dare to let it drop, but at the kiss she turned her head against him with a kind of shudder, murmuring, 'I know. I know. I hope it will be better, after today.'

But it was a long day. Until twilight fell, the crowd thickened against the barriers along the bridal route from the Nionian Embassy to the Palace. The Embassy, only reopened since the signing of the treaty, was thickly garlanded with both Roman and Nionian marriage ornaments: its columns wreathed with flowers and ribbons, red lanterns glowing from the windows and the portico. Inside, as the hour came, Noriko heard the cheering surging along the street, and the drums, coming for her.

And at last the attendants opened the doors, and Noriko emerged onto the steps. At once ripplings and flashes of light, a roar of excitement from the crowd broke over her. Noriko swallowed, trying to keep her breath steady. She had attempted to prepare herself for this, but she had never in her life been exposed to so many people – such an unregimented, hooting, bulging mass. The Embassy seemed besieged with cameras. And within the lines of flower lamps that framed the street, beyond the young Roman aristocrats who bore the broad silvered litter towards her, row after row of people came marching, pine torches burning in their hands, as if they had come to build a huge and terrible bonfire. So many of them, until the phalanx of fire stretched out of sight. From overhead, beams of light from the prowling spiralwings raked the ground and the rooftops. Every now and then the grinding noise of their wings would drown out the music of drums and flutes on the ground. Noriko could not restrain herself from glancing upwards, nervously. There were more cameras up there, she knew, and also more vigiles, scanning the roofs for possible assassins. Yet she did not feel protected.

Lady Aoi, a senior concubine of her father's court, had travelled to Rome to act as a stand-in for Noriko's mother. As the head of the procession approached, she took her place beside Noriko and closed her arms around her – very formally and lightly, so as to leave no impression on her clothes. Noriko folded her hands loosely over the older woman's, trying not to feel any poignancy in this representation of a motherly embrace, as two of the men came up the steps, faces solemn and respectful, and made a ritual show of parting Aoi's arms and wresting Noriko away. Roman marriage was supposed to begin with a pantomime abduction, a rape. There was more applause.

A pair of little boys, dressed in white and crowned with flowers, took her hands and led her onto the litter. They stood on each side of her, holding her arms, steadying themselves against the chased silver rails and supporting her, as the young men raised the litter up to shoulder height. The music, which had fallen silent as she descended the steps, resumed joyously, and the crowds echoed the singers, shouting something over and over: 'Talassio!' Noriko did not know what it meant. She gripped the little boys' hands. The upwards swing was less frightening than she had expected, but her stomach remained weak with the feeling of precariousness, and it was more than the simple fear of falling from this height. As they carried her forwards, helpless over everyone's heads, she thought, This is what they did to foreign captives, parading them through the streets.

The ranks of torchbearers parted to let her through, then joined behind her and followed, until the bridal litter reached the final line of flames, to lead the procession back the way it had come, through the central Fori, towards the Sacred Way and the Palace. As they progressed, the jostling hunger of the crowd for a glimpse of her only intensified, and yet it helped her to be what was required: passively regal, still. She was a triumphal prize on display, a religious relic, an Olympic torch. The road ahead was spread with rose petals: white and flame-yellow and red.

Without warning, and almost violently, Sulien turned on the longvision. Lal looked up, startled, for it had seemed totally taboo for either of them to watch any of the wedding. It had not occurred to them to part ways after leaving Una, and they had both withdrawn to Sulien's flat without much discussion. Sulien had poured Lal some wine and for a while he made her talk about Sina and the journey from the Pyrenees that had taken her there. But with each hour the noise of celebration from the streets had intensified, and he had grown quieter, more obviously tense. He stood now, gazing at the screen, his face fraught with angry curiosity.

From the air, whenever the lights swept across her, the Princess was like a comet burning, the convoy of torch flames behind her like a trail of blazing particles. Her fire-coloured clothes had been made to keep Roman tradition, and the red Roman wedding girdle was tied under her breasts, criss-crossing her body to hang in a chain of square knots below the waist. But her head was encircled with Nionian flowers – yellow camellias, peonies and lotuses – and the layering of glossy silks, the long, pendant sleeves of her saffron dress were Nionian. A gold inner gown embroidered with cranes and irises showed at the throat and sleeves, the paler fabric above it patterned with overlapping fans. Three fine plaits of hair, bound with silver threads, studded with narcissi and orchids, fell on either side of her grave face. And under the wreath, and the gold headpiece that rose above it, she wore a double veil: a layer of heavy satin, hanging close around her body that glowed a warm, burnished crimson through the translucent silk above it. The long, drifting flow of amber gauze fell into a pool of delicately geometric points and folds on the litter, and haloed her as if she stood in the midst of a soft, beautiful explosion.

As the procession passed through the Septizonium, the view changed to the inside of the palace lararium, darkly brilliant with gold, and to Marcus, waiting. Within the walls of the high apse, stood the jumbled lines of ancestors and gods, carved in aspects from every reach of the Empire: spiders, swans, elephants, bulls, jaguars – as well as muscular men and women. They flaunted weapons, or lounged jadedly, or flexed claws and trunks. Assembled behind Marcus like a silent chorus, the idols seemed to exert a strange, expectant pressure on him. Marcus, dressed in the full ceremonial toga, seemed also marmoreal, timeless. His eyes met the camera with an expression meant to be read as confidence and serenity, but knowing him, Sulien could see the look of controlled anguish that underlay it, and felt a strong wrench of involuntary sympathy. He slammed the longvision off and said fiercely, 'I wish we'd never met him.'

'But this isn't what he wants,' protested Lal unhappily, feeling the tug of competing loyalties. 'He must be miserable.'

'Then he'd be better off too.'

'He'd be dead, and you'd still be slaves,' retorted Lal, and Sulien was silent. 'Of course – I can see why you can't be friends now,' she added sadly.

Sulien sighed, leaning against the wall beside the longvision, his head lowered. He was still staring into the dark screen. 'I am his friend,' he admitted, in a low, resigned voice. He poured more wine, and neither of them spoke for a while.

'What will happen to her?' murmured Sulien, at last, as if they'd never stopped talking of Una. 'Wearing herself out in that place. And everything she says about it is true, I know. But she'll kill herself if she goes on this way.'

'No, no,' said Lal, alarmed, and the more determined to hope for the best because of it. 'I wish she'd have let us take her somewhere today, but she's borne harder things than this. She was a slave; she spent years and years planning to escape and she did it, didn't she? And she saved you all on her own. She doesn't give up. She couldn't have done all that if she had.'

Sulien smiled, but lopsidedly. 'Oh, if she decides she's going to do something, she won't stop, I know that. And I'd be sorry for anyone who got in her way. But she won't care what it costs her, either. Back in London, she hadn't seen me in seven years; she heard I'd been arrested and she decided she wasn't going to let me die.' He gave a little laugh of some kind; maybe it even was funny. 'And here we both are – it worked. But she might have been killed – we might have been killed together, and as long as she'd done everything she could think of—' he stopped for a second. But he'd as good as said it already, so he shrugged, and finished, 'She wouldn't have minded.'

Lal urged again, 'No.'

'She wouldn't. She'd only have counted it a failure if she ended up alive and I didn't. There were only ever one or two things she cared about – until him. She started changing then.' He didn't want to call his own feelings about Marcus any closer by using his name. 'And now I think it's worse. At least back then there was always something she *wanted*. To get out, to get me off that boat – to stay free, if only to spite anyone who ever wanted to make her a slave. Now ... I'm afraid where it'll end.'

Lal kept quiet and watched him, though she didn't like the silence and had to struggle against the impulse to say almost anything, to keep telling him there was nothing to be feared. But he prompted her in the end, asking urgently, 'Do you understand what I mean?'

Lal hesitated and admitted the truth, 'It reminds me of Dama. Sometimes he was like that.'

Sulien recognised the comparison, and it did not comfort him. He remembered Dama's remorseless determination on that last night they'd seen him, and that it had probably killed him. He agreed bleakly, picking up his drink, 'Yes, like that.'

Lal looked at the blank longvision and said, 'He might be watching this. He must know. I wonder what he thinks.' And she did not notice, at first, that she said this as if fully certain that Dama was alive.

The young noblemen that bore the litter approached the lararium, and again the music stopped, for this was the most important moment of the bride's journey; any jolt or stumbling as she was carried across the threshold meant bad luck. But they went through smoothly, and laid the litter down on the dark, glittering tiles. A group of women approached – all of them married, like the men who had borne the litter, there to guide the couple into marriage. Noriko stepped forward in the crowded silence.

Marcus came to meet her. Varius wasn't far away, among the guests and representatives of the household who stood on either side of this empty, central space, but Marcus no longer had to suppress the nervous urge to glance at him. Faustus was watching from a chair, with Makaria beside him; only Drusus was missing. Marcus had seen to this simply by writing to him, 'I am sorry to hear you are too unwell to attend my wedding,' and dating the letter a week ahead of its actual dispatch.

He duly received a letter that he was able to show Faustus – Drusus explaining with appropriate regret that he was too ill to come.

Ahead, Noriko was scarcely recognisable as the person with whom he'd spoken frankly in the Sinoan Palace garden. She looked like a personified virtue in a poem. Perhaps he seemed no more like a solid human being himself. He didn't, for now, feel any pity for her, and he ceased to feel any sorrow for himself. He was dazed and calm. Noriko seemed to float in her flame clothes. He knew exactly what he had to do, and it did not seem real.

On either side of him, an attendant carried a golden bowl, one filled with water, one with a long wick burning in a pool of oil. He and Noriko came face to face, and he heard his own voice saying clearly, 'You are welcome.' He took and offered her each bowl in turn, so that she might dip her fingertips in the water, pass them quickly through the fire, cupping the bowl in her hands before passing it away.

And then they joined hands, and the the eldest of the women bound them together. The touch seemed to break the trance Marcus had been in; he looked at Noriko, and thought he could see an answering shock in her face, as if they were both only now aware of what they were doing. They kissed lightly, their expressions hidden against the other's face, and in the golden room around them, and in the Fori of Rome, and across the Empire, people began to clap and cheer.

Una had begun moving restlessly from room to room, wheeling and striding, her breath gathering speed on every turn. The noise outside went on and on – pounding drums and shrieks of drunken celebration, always fading mockingly and coming back. For some time she had felt, at least, secure in her capacity to block it out. But it continued for so long that at last she gave a little cry of indignation and incredulity, and dropped into a chair, pressing her hands over her ears. If only there were some kind of distraction, something to do! There was nowhere she could bear to go; to sit and read was obviously impossible, and she wished, now, that she'd paced herself in cleaning the flat, left herself something to work on. She remembered some clothes that could be washed, went and dragged them out, dunked them in water. But by now she was gritting her teeth and shaking, and she could not keep her attention on what she was trying to do. She left the clothes floating, forgetting them instantly, and paced rapidly round the little flat again. Then, without any kind of premeditation or plan, she threw open her door and dashed out. She stood for a second on the landing, with her face against the wall, panting, her eyes screwed shut; and then another swell of the noise from below chased her on, and she ran headlong up the stairs, leaving her door gaping. At the top she wrestled open the stiff metal door onto the creaking fire escape. A steel ladder, fixed to the wall of the building, led upwards – she must have seen it from the ground many times before without properly noticing it. She climbed up feverishly, feet almost stamping on the metal, and scrambled onto the roof.

The street parties below boomed on, the sound was only a little weaker than it had been downstairs in her flat. Yet somehow, there was a difference, the rooftop remained remote, solitary. Up here, the air was rough and chilly; Una's clothes flapped, her hair flew around her face. She hugged herself, and walked slowly over to the far corner of the roof. It pointed south east, towards the heart of the city. She climbed onto the low brick barrier at the edge, and sat down, her knees drawn up. Rome opened below her, the view far wider and clearer than she would have expected: she could see the blue dome of the temple of Liberty on the Via Flaminia, the illuminated towers on the Quirinal hill, even a distant glow she thought must be the Golden House. And as she looked towards the heart of the city, fireworks suddenly broke into the air. First only above the palace, then sweeping outwards, all around her, everywhere. Roses and willow trees of coloured fire, gold javelins, scarlet palm leaves. And the jubilant shouts from the streets, which till now had been erratic and scattered, surged up to a steady united cry that built and built without breaking, applause pulsating under the din from the bursting air.

Una's breath stuck in her throat and her body stiffened; she stared out, somehow shocked even now. She had at least, it seemed, expected some kind of release, for the suspense to end. But no release came, and the strain, and the longing wore on. She lowered her head onto her arms, as over Rome, the sky burned.

In Transtiberina the noise lapped around Sulien's building, and the blaze of light brightened the windows. Sulien said dully, 'Well then, it's over.'

Lal nodded, but her expression had become distant and clouded – it no longer connected with what was going on outside. Then suddenly her face cleared, her eyes widening with something almost like excitement. 'Sulien,' she said. 'I did see Dama in Sina. He must have been there. I called Liuyin before, and he told me he couldn't help me. Something had to change for him to come. And those men had found me. We were in a car. There was nothing Liuyin could have done if he'd been by himself. And I remember it – it isn't the same as the hallucinations. Dama was there. He saved me.'

Noriko was not part of the Palace celebrations for very long. The bride's attendants led her through a short round of congratulations, before guiding her upstairs to the bedroom. After she had gone the party bubbled up bawdily, cheerfully lewd songs erupting here and there, gathering in confidence as the wine flowed. Marcus circulated dutifully, to have his health drunk, his back patted, and to submit to being nudged and laughed at. He might be all but Emperor, but it was still a wedding. Marcus bore it as long as he could keep a semblance of a smile on his face.

'He's keeping her waiting,' Eudoxius observed genially, as Marcus passed him, prompting the men around him to utter wailing sounds of mock sympathy for Noriko.

For some kind of small escape Marcus went over to Varius, who seemed, like himself, incongruously sober among the rest, even though he was drinking determinedly. There was a drawn, enduring look on his face. Marcus wondered if he were remembering his own marriage. He saw Marcus and observed, 'It went well, anyway.' and Marcus almost laughed. 'You did well,' Varius added quietly. 'It was the right thing.'

Marcus nodded, and on impulse told him, 'That letter – she never answered.' He did not really want any spoken reply. He didn't need to be reassured that Una was thinking of him, which was in any case no consolation.

Some of the guests launched into a song about an insatiable woman wearing out all the men in Tarraco. Marcus decided he might as well get out. He threaded through the party for the grand atrium, towards the main stairs. Of course there would be a crescendo of knowing howls when they saw where he was going – better to just get that over with. 'He's going to lead his troops into Nionia!' somebody yelled, to general laughter. Marcus climbed the stairs, accompanied by shouts of encouragement.

In an upper hall, Marcus exhaled, alone for the first time that day. He could hear the repeated thuds of the fireworks outside. If Una were in Rome, she would hear them too. He slid his hands over his face and tried not to think of that. It occurred to him that he need not go to Noriko, at least not yet. But he thought of her waiting, surrounded by giggling strangers who would not leave her alone until they saw him. No, it was not fair to avoid her – and in a way, he genuinely felt he would rather see her than anyone else in the Golden House. They had today in common.

The doors to the bridal apartment were open, and a few of the women were standing outside, evidently looking out for him and chatting. They greeted Marcus with the same kind of jolly catcalls that had followed him up the stairs. Inside the room, the windows, ceiling, and the posts of the bed, were heavily festooned with flowers, fruit and green branches. Gathered around Noriko, the other ladies made arch faces at her and kissed her maternally for a last time, and then withdrew, shutting the doors behind them. Marcus and Noriko stared at each other quietly as they heard their laughter fading down the passage.

Noriko was sitting stiffly on the edge of the bed. The women had undressed her as far as they could without touching the knotted girdle round the yellow dress, which was the bridegroom's to untie. Her veil and wreath of flowers were gone, her feet bare, and her lovely hair fell smooth and loose around her. She looked up at him with a diffident, apprehensive smile. Marcus tried the words *'my wife'* in his mind.

She asked politely, 'How are you?'

'I'm fine,' he replied, quietly. 'Are you very tired?'

'Oh, a little.'

Marcus noted the way she looked at him, the tense way she held herself. Of course, they scarcely knew each other. But she had a more profound air of not knowing what to expect. He knew affairs outside marriage were commonplace at the Nionian court, although conducted in virtual secrecy, by complex and unspoken codes. But he had already suspected that the rules would be different for an unmarried princess, whose choice of lover could not help but carry political significance. He had hoped Noriko would not be a virgin and now felt sure that she was. It made it seem even sadder to him that he did not want any of this to be happening, and he worried, too, about hurting her. He wished that Una were not the only woman he had ever slept with, then perhaps she would not be so sharply present to him in her absence now. She was, as he had written to her, never really out of his mind, but this was different, and worse. He could only begin with what he knew of Una's body. It seemed a betrayal of them both.

He approached the bed slowly, saying, 'Nothing has to happen now. If you're tired, or you'd like to wait for a while ...'

But Noriko stood up and came close to him. Her lips on his were even more flutteringly tentative than their first, ritual, public kiss, but her fingers were resolute as they took his hands and guided them down to the string of red knots. 'We are married now. There is nothing to wait for.'

Marcus said nothing. He nodded, bowing his head against hers.

He unpicked the knots patiently, calm and expressionless, efficient and entirely focused on each one. He did not look up at her. Noriko gave a self-conscious little laugh when he finally pulled the long sash away, and let it fall. Marcus stepped back from her a little and briskly loosened the heavy folds of cloth around his own body, while Noriko plucked at the small fastenings on her gown that remained closed. Marcus, bare from the waist up, turned back to methodically undressing her. He lifted off the dress, and she stood there naked and brave, chin raised, summoning a hesitantly seductive smile. But she was trembling now, he could feel it when she touched him. Detached as he had been, it was a relief to feel tender towards her, to want to be kind. He smiled back, and stroked her arms and her long hair, which still fascinated him.

'It'll be all right,' he said to her. 'Let's just lie down for a while.'

So he took off the rest of his clothes, and they climbed naked into the bed, and lay still together, holding each other for comfort and warmth, as if the bed were a raft on a cold sea.

He felt Noriko relax slowly, and uncurl herself against him. Tired and unhappy as he was, with all his mind stained through with longing for somebody else, he had thought that to lie quietly beside her might be all that was possible tonight. Instead he was distantly annoyed at how quickly his body took over, as if it had nothing to do with him. He took Noriko in his arms, and bent over her, but the intimacy that a minute before he'd felt between them, was gone. He kissed her, gently and minimally, caressed her in the same conscientious, sparing way. Noriko lay passively at first, then began trying uncertainly to reciprocate. She pressed her lips to his chest, ran her hand down his back, then slid it doubtfully round the curve of his hips towards his groin – attempts which remained tentative courtesies because Marcus did nothing to encourage her. Her flesh was smooth and warm, beautiful. He shivered a little, distracted with automatic excitement. It was not her fault that he felt he was scarcely even there. He scanned her face for signs of fear and lowered himself onto her, guiding her legs apart, and laid another blank kiss on her breast, as he began to press against and into her.

She gasped sharply and he whispered, 'Am I hurting you?'

'No,' she insisted, determined, though her teeth were gritted.

And they did not speak any more. She kept her arms around him and Marcus moved carefully, impersonally within her, until he felt himself vanish gratefully into dark anonymity, where even the memory of Una slipped away from him and nothing mattered.

But later, when they'd edged apart, and she seemed to be asleep, Marcus felt dull, heavy wakefulness spreading through him like dirty water through the gutters of a town. He was not quite sure why he should feel so disgusted with himself, but the knowledge of loss intensified minute by minute until to lie in the bed beside Noriko was intolerable. He got up, threw on some clothes, and left the room, feeling some relief as he shut the door quietly behind him. He wandered the upper floors of the palace, and slept only for a few hours, much later, in a chair in a tower room, where he'd been looking out across Rome.

He did not return to bed all that night, so that long before dawn Noriko woke to find herself naked and alone in the strange bed, the flesh between her legs bloody and raw, and for the first time since leaving home for her wedding, she shed tears.

Cold and stiff, Una trod slowly down the stairs. She scoffed vaguely at her own stupidity at leaving the door open, even though she was entirely indifferent at the idea that something might have been stolen. Nothing had been. She should prepare some food – because it would pass twenty more minutes or so of this dreadful day, and because she had eaten almost nothing. She felt insubstantial and light-headed, quiveringly sick. But her stomach and throat seemed to clench whenever she looked at what little food was in her kitchen and the idea of even cutting some bread exhausted her. She swallowed some wine without tasting it, trudged into her bedroom and lay down, without undressing, on top of the covers. The festivities in the streets had quietened a little, but she had no hope that they would stop before morning. The fireworks at least were almost over, although sometimes the isolated bullet crack or hiss of a cheap rocket going off in a nearby street made her start, her tense body feeling the noise like a physical blow. She did not even try to sleep. She tried only to rest; she tried, for a while, to be absent, which should have been possible. She'd done it often enough before.

Only a few yards from her bed, somebody knocked, hard, on the front door. Una was jolted upright, as if the entire building had lurched forwards. Her blood buzzed with shock. It was not the sound itself, it was rather that the sound made no sense. It was true that each day, she had been trying to contain herself more within her own skull, to know and sense as little as possible of other people. And tonight, of all times, she had wanted that. But the space around her felt entirely empty; she had not even the vaguest sense of a human presence nearer than the street. There was no one outside the door.

She had known only one person, into whose thoughts she could not see at all, who could have caught her so completely by surprise.

She remained frozen on the bed, shaking, and was very close to believing that she had imagined it. She must after all have lapsed into sleep, into an odd, short dream that had shocked her awake.

The knock came again. And this time Una leapt up, flew out of the room, flung open the door.

Dama stood there. For an instant Una remained fixed in the doorway, staring at him with hard, accusatory disbelief, before stepping forward with a cry and throwing her arms around him.

XXI

OMNES VIAE

Dama's arms went round her slowly, lightly, so that she remembered with reeling bewilderment how rarely they'd touched in the past. He said simply, 'Oh, I've missed you.'

Una tried to answer and was choked with crying. Her eyes had been dry for weeks, as the wedding approached; now she sobbed, helplessly.

Dama looked pained and sorry. The flat was so small that he found the tiny living room easily, where he sat her down, and tried to comfort her. He hushed her clumsily, took off his jacket saying, 'You're cold,' and draped it over her. Then he vanished briefly to the kitchen and came back with glasses of both water and wine, having been unable to decide which would be better. Dizzily, Una laughed at them.

'I'm sorry,' he said. 'I should have done this differently.'

'Differently?' repeated Una. 'Where have you been? How could you? We thought you were dead.'

'No, you didn't. Not you,' Dama said, quietly, certainly.

'How could I know? I was never sure. Why did you just *go* like that?'

His face grew delicately harder and colder. 'You knew I would,' he said. 'Once it was over. I told you that.'

Una pulled away from him and onto her feet, still unsteady and gasping for breath. 'You didn't care what we thought. You didn't let us know you were alive. Were you as angry with me as that?'

Dama gazed sorrowfully up at her. 'I'm sorry. I've had to be careful a long time. I'm still a criminal. Still a slave. There are still these.'

For the first time she began to take him in, to measure how far he had changed, or remained the same. Now, because softened with concern for her, his variable face was unformed and odd-looking, ugly except in the glass clarity of the russet hair and bright blue eyes. He was clean-shaven, but otherwise so exactly as she remembered that it seemed unnerving, a mockery of the years since she had seen him. But he had now – as he never had when she had known him before – an air of quiet, resolute ease within his own body.

Under the jacket, despite the season, he was wearing a loose, well-worn, short-sleeved summer tunic that left his arms bare. On one wrist he wore a kind of leather vambrace, like a piece of armour, on the other a thick band or cuff of stiff black cloth. As he spoke, he thumbed off the right covering, and then the left with more difficulty, having to use his weaker hand. Una looked on, silent, no longer weeping. She had only glimpsed the scars once before.

He glanced down at them, calmly. 'I'm not ashamed of them now. One day it won't matter who sees them.'

Una shook her head, dazed, not knowing what to think or where to start. Trying to hold onto something solid and rational, she said again, 'Where've you been?'

'Oh,' he said. 'I moved around. In and out of Rome. Germania … Gaul …'

'Rome?'

'I couldn't get much further to begin with,' he said. 'Didn't have any money. It was the easiest place to go, from Tivoli.'

'But I kept coming back here. Sulien was here all the time. We were here.'

Dama glanced away from her, curtly. 'Look. This is how it is. I didn't want anything to do with Novius. I didn't want to see you with him. I said I'd go and that's what I did. I'm here now. I'll go if you like.'

'No,' she said, half-resentfully.

'I am sorry though,' he promised her, cyan eyes wide open with compassion for her. He shook his head, indicating the raucous disorder outside with apparent disgust. 'This … today …'

Una managed a small, deflecting smile and made a kind of erasing gesture in the air. He had not said anything resembling, 'I told you so,' and she wanted to be sure he would not. She did not want to hear him talk of Marcus.

'No,' he agreed, understanding her. 'Better not. But anyway, I had to come.' And he went over to her, urging gently, 'Come on, sit down again. You haven't eaten anything, have you?'

He found the bread and a couple of eggs. She still had no real appetite, and beyond getting food on to a plate for her, he did not nag her to eat. She could not finish the small meal, but she felt stronger – more awake, and better able to stand being so.

'What did you do?' she asked. 'How did you live?'

Dama smiled at her affectionately. 'Stealing,' he said. 'To begin with anyway. Or what they'd call stealing. Not much against what they owe us, is it?'

She was free in law, he was not. She felt oddly relieved to be included by him among slaves, among the outsiders and opponents of Rome.

'I'm pretty good at it,' he said. 'I did try for jobs, but there's not a lot I can do. I can't compete with slaves. Or anyone who's got two hands that work properly.' He looked at his scars again. 'And I can't do anything where people get to notice now these match up neatly with a cross.'

'Crucifixion's over now,' Una murmured, remembering sitting at Marcus' side in the Palace, the day he had announced it to the senators.

Dama nodded, a little grudgingly. 'Yes. That was good of him. I'll give him that.'

Una thought of Holzarta: the cabins hidden against the flanks of the gorge, the walkways across the stream, the sophisticated network of alarms and cameras. Dama had designed it all. 'You should have been an architect,' she said, 'Or an engineer.' Distantly, she wondered what she should have been.

Dama seemed faintly startled, and he was silent for a while, contemplating a life that had never been allowed. 'Well. Maybe I will – maybe I'll build things, one day.'

'So,' said Una, rather drearily because it seemed so bleak. 'Is that still what you do?'

Again Dama smiled, the effect on his face disconcertingly pure, transfiguring. 'No. Scavenging and keeping myself alive with no reason for it – I don't care about stealing from Romans, but it's a sin to let your life just drag on and do nothing with it. I couldn't live like that.' He looked at her, a look that seemed to lodge in her like a blue dart. 'And you can't either, can you?'

Una said in a whisper, 'No.'

Dama nodded, satisfied, and got up. 'Are you up to going somewhere?'

Dama had parked an old, nondescript car a few blocks away from her door. A fire-cracker flashed a street away, but the noise and laughter no longer impinged on Una. It had become part of the background.

'How did you know where I was?' she asked.

'I had a friend look by at the clinic, he found out you were working at that Vatican place. I'm sorry if it all sounds a bit sinister, I don't know how else I could have done it.'

'You know the clinic?'

'Oh yes, everyone knows the clinic.' He sounded proud. 'I'm glad Sulien's there. It's a good thing – it's what he should be doing.'

'Are you all right?' she asked, as he settled his hands on the controls. 'Driving hurts you.'

'You know I can manage, if I need to. And it's better than it was, the muscles are stronger.'

'I don't like sitting beside you and knowing you're hurting yourself.'

'Well, can you drive? And I mean properly, I'm not risking my neck with you making it up as you go along again.'

Prompted by anyone else, the memory of the long drive into Rome, hoping to save Marcus' life, would have been painful. From him, it almost amused her. She said frankly, 'No, I didn't get round to it.'

'Then that can be one of the first things you do next,' said Dama.

He drove north-east, onto the road by which they'd entered Rome, years before, but as they left the city limits on the Via Salaria, they no longer had to pass crosses ranked along the highway. Rome seemed to slide away behind Una like a weight. In the centre of Rome it was sometimes impossible to believe that the roads led to anything but more city, that it was even possible to emerge into dark countryside. She was amazed, looking up as the car shifted onto a rough track thirty miles outside Rome, to realise she'd been asleep.

'This is where it is,' said Dama.

The track extended downhill through scrubby fields, into a shallow valley. They seemed to be approaching a cluster of farm buildings within a thick barbed wire fence. In the dark at least, it seemed a forbidding place. As they reached the gates, Una glimpsed a sign that read: WARNING: DOGS LOOSE.

Dama laughed at the sight of it and said, 'They're only imaginary dogs, so far anyway.'

There were many people ahead, within the fence, and they knew Dama was coming.

Dama stopped the car and turned to look at her. He began, 'You trusted Novius to abolish slavery, didn't you?' His voice was stern, formal.

Una stiffened, wary and disappointed. 'We shouldn't talk about him, Dama.'

But Dama pressed, 'Tell me why it hasn't happened.'

'It will,' said Una tiredly, beginning to regret coming here after all. 'It's impossible now with the Nionian situation. And he doesn't have the full powers of Emperor. When he comes to the throne he will.'

'So it's not convenient to do it now,' summarised Dama. Una sighed and did not answer. 'Fine,' he continued softly. 'Maybe that's all true. But there are people dying *now*. They're being crippled, raped, murdered. It's happening every day all across the filthy world. And you know.'

'Yes, I know,' Una said, but she no longer felt that she was being forced to bear an attack for Marcus' sake. Instead, she felt a strange, anticipatory excitement.

'But not these,' said Dama. And he got out of the car and led the way towards the low, concrete buildings, from which throngs of people began to emerge into the bare yard. All were adult, and none was old, but otherwise they were of all ages, both sexes, every race. And as they saw Dama a blaze of intense, spontaneous feeling flashed from them, like hot light bouncing off a mirror. They loved him – all of them. Dama raised his better hand, the left, in greeting.

'In Holzarta we used to wait for people to escape and come to us. There were never many who could do that, but it was better than nothing. Now I go to them, and I get them out. After that, it's up to them what they want to do, but these choose to be with me. We don't wait. We're slaves; it's our business to put slavery to an end – one person at a time if that's what it takes.' He faced Una. He did not touch her, but again his look at her was as emphatic and as intimate as if he'd taken her face in his hands.

'You should be with us. I want your help.'

'I remember him – I know I remember,' insisted Lal, after Sulien's first unconvinced response. 'He wasn't wearing those long sleeves like he used to. I saw the scar on his arm. And he held me in the back of the car and told me I'd be safe. It was him. He's alive.'

Sulien hesitated another second, but then broke into a laugh. 'Well then, that's wonderful. But why didn't he stay? You'd think he could have guessed how worried we all were about him.'

'I don't know. It might not have been safe. He wasn't meant to be there at all, any more than we were. And I suppose I can understand why he might not want to see Una.'

Sulien's smile faded at the thought of her, alone and unconsoled in her austere flat. 'But she'll want to know,' he said, trying to calculate when best to tell her, and sighed. 'I wonder why he was in Sina.'

'Well, we thought it was safe – safer, anyway. You know we sent a lot of people there.'

'It would have been difficult for him. If he was still alive after that night, he had nothing with him.'

'He can't have been there all the time. If he had been, he'd have found my father long before. Perhaps he managed to get by in the Empire for a while, until … I don't know, something went wrong and he had to leave. He must have been looking for us. I hope he's all right.'

Just for a second, Sulien experienced a strange, pivoting feeling that passed before he could have put any name to it. 'How did he do it?' he asked, more quietly. 'If Drusus' men had found you, how did Dama get you out of the car?'

'Someone must have ...' said Lal, beginning eagerly before the bright mess of memory had settled into sense. And she stopped, startled to remember the rumbling noise and impact under the car. She started again, slowly and with less confidence. 'He attacked the car ...'

'How do you mean, attacked it?'

Lal felt again the surface of the road under her cheek, she saw the gorgeous colour of the burst of flame. 'There was an explosion,' she murmured. 'More than one. The first one wasn't big. It just stopped the car. Everyone jumped out; they dragged me out of the back and dropped me on the ground. And I just lay there. But they were shooting ... at Dama. At Dama's car. But then there were the other explosions – much bigger. Liuyin was hiding in a ditch beside the road. He pulled me across. Then there was Dama, standing on the road, and the car was on fire ... and there was fire everywhere.' She looked up at Sulien, and finished clearly, 'Dama had put a mine on the road, and after that I think he used grenades, to draw the soldiers away. To finish them off.' The memory of the screams she'd heard ripped open suddenly in her mind, and she imagined, too clearly, what Liuyin had urged her not to see as he crouched over her by the roadside: scattered lumps of scorched flesh, landing wetly on the cracked asphalt. 'Oh ...' she whispered, and bent forward, hiding her face.

Sulien, guessing what she was thinking, said sternly, 'Better than what might have happened to you if Drusus had got you. If that's what it took, thank the gods Dama managed to do it.'

'Oh, I know. If I see him again, how can I ever thank him? And Liuyin too – it must have been so hard for him. But it's horrible to think of. Oh, I wish I knew where Dama was.'

They were silent for a few minutes. But while Lal, released from the pressure of remembering, began to relax, Sulien felt himself growing tense. He got up and walked about with one hand wrapped around his unmarked wrist, saying with an uneasily admiring laugh, 'So do I. I'd like to know how he did it. It must have taken some doing. I wouldn't have known how. Even if I could get the explosives, I couldn't have used them like that. It sounds like he was pretty precise with them. How was he capable?'

'God knows,' said Lal, wearily. In fact, struck by one of the fits of overwhelming tiredness that she'd suffered since her illness, she did not want to think about those miserable days in the Sinoan countryside any more. She began to notice for the first time how long she'd stayed in Sulien's flat, and to worry about getting home.

Sulien's hand ran slowly up from his wrist to the place above the elbow where the bone had been broken. The great column of fire bursting above the ruins of Veii Imperial Arms. Varius lying on the dust, as if dead. Fire all around them, wherever they turned for escape. Scraps of fire snowing down on their backs. A thousand people.

'What is it?' asked Lal, for the rhythm of his breath had audibly changed, and he had gone white.

'Oh,' said Sulien, with odd dismissiveness, as if it were hardly worth talking about. 'I'm just thinking of when things happened, when the fires stopped.' He smiled, shakily. 'And Tancorix says Edda's alive. I didn't really believe her.'

'Who are Edda and Tancorix?'

'Edda was a slave,' said Sulien, and there was something almost like a laugh in his voice. 'They were all slaves.' And then he did laugh, announcing wildly, and, to Lal, inexplicably: 'The beds were empty. They had to sleep in shifts – Proculus and his bloody superiors wouldn't have paid up for everyone to have their own bed. He wouldn't have wasted space on buildings to stand empty half the time. You could tell by the state of the mattresses. There should have been someone on every bunk all the time. But when we went in, there was no one there – *they'd already gone.*'

'What are you talking about?' asked Lal.

'The slave barracks at the Veii arms factory,' said Sulien. 'That's where Varius and I were, when the place went up. I thought they bulldozed the bodies away under the mud. But they weren't there – like Edda wasn't there when the Maecilii place burned. I thought Atronius was working for Drusus. He wasn't. It was for Dama.'

Lal stared at him, simply anxious. He had become so hectic and pale, fevered with what was either horror or exhilaration, that it was hard for her to know how to take what he said.

Sulien thought of the deception that had lured him into the Subura tower block the day of the Veii explosion, pursuit down the stairs, the gunfire, and for a moment he could not make out the connection that must be there. Then he lurched and grinned breathlessly as he understood. 'Dama knew I was going to be at Veii. It was *Bupe*. She came from the factory. I told her we were going. She'd have known what was going to happen. Atronius must have had them all ready for the day. Poor thing – she had a detonator go off in her face just when she was supposed to escape. She even told me not to go.'

'Sulien,' ventured Lal, 'Calm down. I don't know what you're talking about – it doesn't make sense.'

But Sulien paid no attention. 'The factory staff never bothered with injured slaves. We never knew who brought her to the clinic. But it must have been one of Dama's people, she could have got a message to him. But they didn't have any time to change their plans – just a few hours to try and stop me going there.'

Of course, none of the shots fired in the stairwell had hit him. The three tense people there, the young woman who had told him she was a slave – they had never wanted to hurt him. Their business had been simply to keep him there, by any means necessary, until the escape, and the destruction of Veii Imperial Arms was over. They had been trying to protect him.

He put his hands to his face, gasping out a breath through his fingers. Lal asked cautiously, 'But why do you think this was anything to do with Dama? You think he blew up a factory just because he blew up a car – months later, on another continent?'

'Not just that,' said Sulien, forcefully, looking up and rummaging for his wallet, emptying its contents onto a chair. 'No, it's not that. He took you to Una because he knew she'd take you to me. If anyone was ill or hurt, he'd always send them to me, if he could. He'd tell other people to do the same.'

He found the sheets of folded paper, separated them delicately with unsteady fingers: the image of the young Atronius with his parents, the copy of the tram ticket torn across his own scribbled name. Sulien stared at the broken sequence of crooked letters and symbols, and reached blindly for a pen he'd knocked onto the floor. He folded the two smallest fingers of his right hand around it, trying to grip while keeping the thumb and other fingers loose and limp, and wrote his name. The letters wobbled, legible enough, but jagged, childish.

'What are you doing?' Lal ventured.

Sulien thrust the paper into her hands. 'My name. The clinic's long-dictor code.'

Lal studied it, bewildered. 'Yes,' she said at last in a low voice. 'That's his handwriting.'

Sulien regarded her blankly for a second and then abruptly sat down, looking drained, sick. He said in a dull voice, 'Someone's got to stop him.'

Lal sprang up, confused and indignant. 'What? Why? You're saying he's rescued hundreds of slaves – that all those people you thought were dead are alive. If it's true I'm proud of him. What better life for him

386

could there be? What do you suspect him of? You owe him more than that, and so do I. He saved *my* life too, for God's sake.'

'And he tried to save mine,' agreed Sulien listlessly. 'Not Varius, though. Not all the people who had to live near that place. There were sixty dead. And that's just at Veii – I don't know how many died in those other fires.'

Lal subsided a little, uncertainly. 'Yes,' she admitted. 'But to save a thousand people ... stopping something so terrible ... is it so different from what he did for me? You said yourself that was right, even though those men died.'

Sulien shook his head. 'You don't understand. It was nearly taken for a Nionian attack – Rome nearly hit back. And it was an *arms* factory. If Dama could get people out, he could get explosives out too. Why was he in Sina with a ready stash of them? The fires didn't stop because Drusus was under arrest; they stopped because there were peace talks in Sina, and Dama followed them. He saved you because what happened to your family was down to him. He had Kato killed. He's trying to start a war.'

XXII

INNOCENCE

Una looked up at the patchy white ceiling, and drew her breath in through her teeth, knowing it was the morning after Marcus' marriage to someone else. Yet she had slept well, and she had a sense of clarity and purpose that only a few hours ago she expected never to feel again. She got up briskly and went out. There were bunks and mattresses stowed all over the compound, in former cowsheds and stores, as well as the central farmhouse. But Dama had given her a bedroom to herself, upstairs. Una felt faintly diffident at the luxury, but when she ran into a woman on the landing, she did not seem remotely resentful; instead, she startled Una by seizing her hand and saying, 'I'm so glad you're here.'

Dama went past on the landing below. He called up to her, 'Come and eat with me, when you're ready. We need to talk some more.'

A window over the stairs looked down into the yard. Una was, again, overwhelmed at how many people were here. It seemed the place did, at least to some extent, function as a farm: a woman was dragging a low cart loaded with sacks of something – chicken feed? – over to a barn in a far corner, closer to the house men were chopping up logs. But on the other side of the yard, a group of people were throwing a ball around, focused and animated. Others again, more obscurely seemed to be practising some kind of unarmed combat.

Downstairs, there were yet more people crowded into the large, shabby kitchen, jostling companionably and eating. Una hesitated in the doorway, and before she had so much as spoken to anyone, Dama reappeared, pushing a plate of bread and fruit into her hands and gestured her across the hall into a little room, scarcely more than a cupboard, where a few mismatched chairs stood around a small table, under warped shelves, bare except for a heavy old-fashioned longdictor on the lowest one. It looked a drab and claustrophobic place until Dama was in it.

Deliberately, Una made herself begin, 'Listen. I'm ready to do anything I can to help. But I have to know if what you expect of me is ...'

Dama looked down with a crooked little smile, and finished, 'Anything personal.' He sat still, eyelids lowered, his face quiet. 'I haven't changed,' he said softly at last. 'But no, I'm not asking anything like that. I want you to *work* with me.'

'Fine,' she said. And as if in compensation for having asked the question, said, 'I've got money. There's money that belongs to you, rightly. It's the reward for ... for what we did, at the Sanctuary.'

'Well, we can always use that,' he said, pleased.

They ate for a while in silence. There was some awkwardness, but it faded quickly enough. The bread was good, and Una found she was hungry. Dama fidgeted with his food, losing a little of his new physical confidence, and she knew this was probably not normal for him, to eat in anyone else's company, even though he had asked for hers. He had never liked to do so before, although he was scarcely hampered by his injuries now.

'You're so close to Rome,' she said, wonderingly.

'We need to be for what we do. We keep our heads down, but as far as anyone in the area knows, it's just a farm. We produce enough to make it look real, and it brings in some extra money.'

'But how many people are there here?' asked Una.

'A hundred and ninety-six,' he said at once. 'Counting the two of us.' He grinned as her mouth fell open, and took a cheerful bite of his food, enjoying her amazement as he added 'And that's not all of them. Pretty much everyone here is new. Here they're just learning how to be free, before they learn anything else.'

'Then how many—?'

'How many?' said Dama, suddenly electric, shining. 'Thousands. Millions. They just don't know it yet. Do you know there was once a plan in Rome to make all slaves wear a uniform, so the free citizens couldn't be tricked into thinking they were dealing with one of themselves? Do you know why it never happened? Because they realised that the slaves would be able to identify each other too. That they'd see how many they were, how strong. That they'd see they were already an army. That's almost all it takes – for people to *see* each other.'

'How do you do it?' she asked, almost breathless after this.

Dama sat back, and became relaxed and practical. 'Oh, well, every project's different. Smaller places – it isn't hard, really. Sometimes people aren't really so much physically trapped as hopeless. You know. So it's a question of a few wire-cutters, if that, like an ordinary burglary.'

389

'I suppose you'd want me to warn you if anyone was coming, that kind of thing?' she said.

He smiled at her. 'Yes. But you could be more than that, with time. If you led, people would follow. That's why I've always known you should be here, why I've always missed your help.'

Still feeling herself all but used up, worn out, Una could only equivocate, 'I don't know.'

'I do,' he said, confidently. And he paused, watching her with a guarded evaluating look, before continuing evenly, 'Sometimes we'd infiltrate a place some time in advance – get someone bought in as a slave, or employed as a steward – coach everyone there, get them out, and then burn the building down. It keeps everyone busy while you're getting out, and if you do a few little things in advance, like sawing through a couple of beams, knocking holes in the corners of some floors, the whole place crumbles up. And no one comes looking afterwards.'

She stared at him. She understood at once. 'All those fires over the summer – were they you?'

'A few of them,' he admitted calmly. 'Of course in weather like that, a lot of fires happen one way or another, and get out of control. Which we took advantage of, obviously.'

Una hesitated. 'Don't people get hurt?'

Dama was quiet for a moment. 'If you're careful,' he said, 'no one gets hurt who doesn't deserve it.'

Una considered this and then, coldly, accepted it. People like those who'd used her, who'd ploughed up and fed on the first fifteen years of her life – no, she did not care what happened to them.

Dama's eyes slid away from hers again, but again his gaze returned to her, steadily. 'There's been one exception I can think of. The biggest thing we've ever done was Veii Imperial Arms. One of my best people was there – we got a thousand people that day. And yes, I know. Sulien was there, and he was injured.'

Una had drawn back, her muscles stiff as stone against the wooden back of the chair. She seemed to feel her face harden like clay into a mask, her eyes fired open and fixed on him.

Dama went on. 'We heard he was going to be there, just a few hours in advance. We'd have postponed it if we could. But by that point we were in the final stages, and there wasn't any communication in or out. You can't abort something involving that many people that fast. So we tried to keep him out of danger, and I believed we'd succeeded until after it was done. But we hadn't. We failed. Of course I was ... horrified, but I know that doesn't matter. It doesn't change what happened. He was there, he could have died, although thank God, he didn't.'

'He nearly did,' she whispered. 'I thought he had.'

'I'm sorry.'

'Not just him. Varius,' Una said thickly, remembering going into his room to thank him for saving Sulien's life, his hand, briefly on her shoulder. 'He dragged Sulien out of that place. He built the clinic. You didn't even try for him. He's a good person. Doesn't that count for anything?'

'It does,' murmured Dama. 'But we had very limited time to react. There was only so much we could do.'

Una pushed her chair back and got up, demanding bitterly, 'Would you still have come to me if you'd killed them?'

Dama said simply, fiercely, '*Yes*.' And he leant forward, the contrition and humility gone, not as if he had not meant it or had lost patience, but simply as if the time for it had passed. 'What you have to ask yourself is do you wish it undone? Would you have that place still standing? There's a girl called Bupe who's with us now; she's only got one hand left, with four fingers, and only one eye. There was a man we sent to that clinic who died, most of his skin gone.' Dama shook as he spoke; there were tears of empathetic rage standing in his eyes by now. 'Would you have that go on, for however many years, until it went up in a real accident and killed the lot of them?'

She scrubbed her face angrily with her hands and said, 'No.'

'No, of course not. But what if it was worse, what if Sulien *had* been killed there? You'd want him back, you might want to agree to anything. But there are people *here now* who worked there, dying on their feet every day. Whatever you might want, if you had the power to do it, could you justify putting them back there?'

Her shoulders dropped, and not only with defeat but a kind of relief. 'No.'

'No,' echoed Dama again. And the luminous, sad authority that had possessed him faded away, and left him looking young and frail, innocent. 'That's why I would still have come and asked you to help, even if Sulien or Varius had died that day, and I had to tell you why. Even if you couldn't forgive *me*, it doesn't matter. The things you could do, the people that *you* could help – you couldn't just leave them.' He smiled, very tentatively, blinking away the urgent tears that remained in his eyes. 'So, are you still with us?'

He held out his worse, half-ruined hand – the right – she exhaled, and took it. She said, 'Yes.'

But as Dama smiled again, more broadly, she broke away, saying, 'But I want to talk to him – I have to talk to Sulien.'

There was a pause before Dama answered, and he seemed to shift a little, warily. 'All right,' he said reasonably. 'Of course. But I'd rather you didn't mention exactly where we are.'

Una gave a short laugh. 'Except that we're somewhere north of Rome, I don't know where we are. I fell asleep.'

'And just tell him you're with me, for now. Don't say yet what this place is. It's not that I don't trust him, but ... you know. It's not something to discuss over the longdictor.'

'I understand.'

He pushed the longdictor across to her and stood back, but did not leave the room.

Sulien answered instantly. She had barely said a word to identify herself before he demanded, sounding half-hysterical. 'Where are you? Where have you been? We've been calling your flat since last night.'

'I'm sorry,' she said, taken aback. 'I'm all right. Listen – I'm with Dama.' There was flat, breathless silence, which she might have expected, but it went on until, thinking he might not have taken it in, she repeated, 'I'm with Dama, he's alive.'

'I know,' said Sulien, his voice low, grim. 'Come back. Come back now.'

'What? How did you know—?'

'You don't know what you're getting mixed up in.'

'He's told me,' said Una, baffled and unnerved that he could know anything of this.

'Oh yes? Did he tell you what he wants? What it's all for? What about Veii? Una had no time to respond. 'And Kato? He wants a war, Una. He's trying to bring down everything you and Marcus worked for. Unless you've decided you want that too, he's dangerous. Get away from him.'

Involuntarily Una turned her face towards Dama, who had opened the door but stopped there, watching her. Their eyes met for an instant, then she looked away sharply, and said into the longdictor, 'No – it's not like that. That can't be true.'

'*Una*,' cried Sulien, desperately. 'Who do you trust more, him or me?'

'Oh, come on,' scoffed Una, uneasily. But the question hung, frantic in the longdictor wires, until she said impatiently, 'You. Of course, you.'

'Then *listen* to me and get out of there. I'll tell you everything when I see you.' And then his voice changed. 'Is he there now?'

'Yes.'

'Can he hear me?'

'No.'

Sulien was silent again, and Una felt she could hear him thinking,

392

as she was thinking herself, what she had said, what Dama must have heard. Finally he asked carefully, 'Can you tell me where you are?'

'Not really,' she said, trying to sound casual. 'I don't know.'

'All right. Then just try and seem normal and get away. Please.' He added, like an additional warning, 'I love you.'

'I love you,' she repeated, like a countersign.

Slowly, she laid the headset down. And then she had to turn round again and face Dama, who asked quietly, 'What did he say?'

'Oh,' Una said. 'Nothing. He's just worried about me, after yesterday. He called the flat and I wasn't there; he thought something might have happened. He wants to see me.'

Dama blinked irritably, disregarding this. 'You said "that can't be true". What did he tell you that couldn't be true?'

Come on, make something up, Una urged herself. She was good at this, good at keeping her face under control. But with him staring at her, she found she could think of nothing, and she heard herself uttering a feeble, wordless stutter that nearly panicked her. At last, she managed. 'He said, he had a dream this would happen. Last night he dreamt you'd come back.'

She knew the lie sounded as laboured as it was. Again, Dama's face made a rejecting little twitch. He came closer to her, his voice still quiet. 'And you said, "how did you know?" And you weren't frightened before you spoke to him. What are you frightened of now?'

Una made herself smile, which she knew she could do convincingly. 'I'm just ... sorry I worried my brother. That's all.'

Dama sighed. 'Una,' he said softly, reproaching her.

They stared at each other, a silent conflict thickening the air between them, a clash of pleas not to be disappointed. She had no advantage over him; she felt they were, equally, trying to read each other's thoughts, equally resisting. But at last, trapped, she whispered, 'You can't really be trying to start a war, can you, Dama?'

In a strange way, Dama seemed to relax, drawing in a long, resigned breath and letting it out, as though, little as he had wanted this, it had happened now and he would face it. Almost lightly, he asked, 'Why not?'

Una almost laughed at him with incredulity and horror.

'Why is it so unthinkable?' he persisted.

'Let me out,' said Una, and started towards the door. She anticipated him moving to obstruct her before it happened, but still could not quite believe it would come to that, and Dama himself seemed to flinch at what he was doing. His face, as he stepped quickly between her and the door, was wide-eyed, tender with regret.

It was he who said, 'Oh, please don't.'

'Why?' asked Una helplessly, not trying to push past him, not yet. '*Why* would you?'

'Because there's nowhere to go,' Dama answered her. 'Nowhere in the whole world, the way it is. We get free – we set other people free. But it's not *real*, it's not true. Even if we find some safe little hole to hide in and scrape a little life together, we're still slaves. The Roman Empire's still smeared over half the world, and we're still trapped in it, breathing in its dirt. And there's nowhere outside that's any better; I know that now. I used to imagine this perfect place that must be out there, even if I couldn't get to it. But it's not there; not yet. You've been to Sina – so have I. And you must know something about Nionia. There's just as much tyranny and corruption and evil in all of them. They're diseases on the Earth. It all needs to be broken down and cleared away, and it'll take a war to do it. The empires will wear themselves out against each other, until they're weak enough to be pulled down. And then we can build something better.'

Furious with him and with herself, Una retorted, 'And you'll be in charge, will you?'

A quiver of offence went across Dama's face. 'I don't matter,' he replied coldly. 'Not in myself.'

Una implored, almost unable to believe he had really understood and accepted this. 'But – so many people, Dama. Millions. You can't even imagine how many. That's what it would mean. You can't know what would be left.'

'You didn't mind a few people dying a minute ago, if it was for the right reason,' Dama said, his voice beginning to ripen with contempt. 'So how many is it? What's the upper limit?'

It seemed desperately important to be able to answer, even though it would alter nothing. At last she said, 'I don't know. But I know there is one. What about you?'

Dama grimaced, let down and angry. He did not reply.

'And you knew what I'd think of it,' she went on, with more force now. 'Or you'd have told me it all when you came to my door. How proud can you be of this, that you'd hide it from me?'

'I thought it might take a while ... for you to understand,' said Dama.

'What would you have done? What would *I* have done by the time you told me the truth? I'd have killed already. Wouldn't I? Done too much to go back. I suppose that's what you do with everyone. But Marcus and I – we've already given up *so much* to keep this from happening. *I wouldn't do this.*'

Dama looked away. 'Always Marcus,' he said wearily.

Una meant to give up, then, but instead found herself crying out, wild with some hope not to lose him altogether, grabbing his hands, 'In God's name, Dama. It's wrong. It's evil. You don't have the right. You must stop. You're worth more than this, you *must* be. What's *happened* to you that you'd do this?'

Dama jerked back from her violently, wrenching his hands from hers, spreading them out into a stunted approximation of the cross. Here, among all these people who loved him, he did not wear the coverings on his wrists; the round scars glared like eyes. He shouted in a furious, agonised voice she had never heard from him before. 'You *know* what happened to me.'

There was a stillness afterwards. They let their hands fall, as if one were the other's reflection.

'I'm going,' she said.

Dama smiled sadly at her. 'You can't. You know you can't, now.'

'I won't stay here.' She pushed towards the door again, and he set his back against it and tried to hold her back. He was stronger now than he had been, though they were both, for a time, hampered by a reluctance to hurt one each other. But at last she began to drag and claw at him in earnest, and he shouldered her back into the room.

'Una,' he urged gently, holding her almost in an embrace. 'There are two hundred people here who'll do anything I tell them.'

'Tell them, then,' said Una. She was still more agile than he was; she twisted away quickly, out of the little room and ran into the yard outside the farmhouse, right into the midst of the slaves' game.

'All of you,' she called out, as loudly as she could, swinging around, scanning their faces. 'Did you come here to set people free or to murder them? Your leader wants to bring about a war, the most terrible there's ever been. Do you really want any part of that?'

She saw Dama following her slowly from the house. He looked so sick at heart and miserable that she could not understand why the crowd around her did not see it at once. As she finished speaking, he announced, ringingly audible though he seemed scarcely to raise his voice: 'Rome's corruption is more insidious even than I thought. Even in someone I trusted. She'll betray us. We cannot let her leave.'

And the slaves turned on her with such hatred that for an instant she expected them to tear her to pieces.

XXIII

WARFARE

Dama had them take her back to the room she'd slept in. It wasn't ideal, nothing about this was. There wasn't even a lock on the door, one would have to be canibalised from somewhere else; for the next few hours it would be a matter of keeping it barricaded shut and guarded. But she needed to be somewhere out of the way, somewhere they would neither hurt nor listen to her. There was nothing in their daily routine to bring more than a few of the former slaves onto the upper floor, and he hoped the prohibition against going near her would be strengthened if she were close to his own quarters. There were things she'd need if they were to keep her reasonably comfortable in there, someone must be sent to find them. He had the shutters on the single window locked, they were heavy; he didn't think she'd be able to force them, and he posted a couple of his recruits on the ground below the window to be sure. He didn't expect her to give up trying.

Dama left himself no time to think about what had happened and was happening. He went back to the longdictor, quickly. 'Mazatl,' he said. 'How soon can you get to Transtiberina?'

Mazatl didn't ask why. 'Half an hour.'

'I need you to go to a block of flats near the Janiculum ...'

'Sulien?' supplied Mazatl, interested.

Dama sighed, feeling his breath hitch, jaggedly. He was trembling; aches were beginning to harden like rusted wires along his arms, dragging in his feet. Of course Mazatl knew who Sulien was – he'd known for years. And he'd known where he lived, too, since shortly before Veii. 'Yes. You need to bring him here. He won't come willingly. There could be someone else with him – a girl. If she's there, she needs to come too. You'll need to take a big enough team to do it, but not so big that you make yourselves memorable. It needs to be clean, and simple.'

A thunderous, chaotic pounding began overhead, surprisingly loud and jarring, even down here. How was she managing to produce so much noise? But she couldn't get out; the din itself confessed as much. He tried not to be too concerned.

There was a pause; he could hear Mazatl's confusion in the tenor of it. 'He's not ... joining us, then?'

'No. He's become a threat. But I don't want him harmed. There's no time to discuss it, this needs to happen now. You shouldn't have any trouble getting into the building. Just go upstairs, and knock on his door. Get them under control in the flat, and take them down one at a time at gunpoint, as quietly as you can. If he doesn't open the door straight away, tell him you're the vigiles, and that you've found his sister.'

There was a small garage, filled with junk since they took over the farm, which they'd never used. But it was sturdy; there was only one entrance, and no windows. There was a cellar, too, under the house, if he needed another impromptu cell. He had the garage emptied, he'd have to find some way of getting a light in there, for it was terrible to think of anyone trapped in such total dark. He watched it turning into a prison under his eyes, as the broken farm equipment and rotted furniture were carried out, and felt gouged and scraped through with fury against Marcus Novius. Who was the cause of this, who had set Una against him, sabotaged what she should have been? She was out of earshot now, yet Dama still seemed to hear her.

He joined in the work, gathering up what he could manage, fiercely, almost enjoying and welcoming the tugs of pain in his shoulders. Half of him was expecting to be called to the longdictor to hear that Mazatl had failed; Sulien and Lal had known what was coming and fled, called the vigiles. And when minutes passed and it did not happen, he began to think Mazatl would not come, must have been arrested.

But then he heard the van, coming down the long track. Some of his followers were beginning to gather near the gates, watching it come.

'Go back to what you were doing,' he said gently – no force was necessary. They were passionately grateful to him, and they were used to doing as they were told. It was a tendency he honestly believed he wished them to unlearn, he wished their loyalty to be freely given, but it was undeniably useful now.

The van drew up beside him and stopped. And as Mazatl and the others began to get out, there was the bang of something striking the wall of the van from inside and Sulien's voice, thickened with rage, crying, 'Dama.'

'Was he alone?' he asked Mazatl.

'No, we brought the girl, like you said.'

Dama leant his forehead on the van's side, close to where the impact had been. He didn't have to see them. He could just order them to be shut away. Then he walked purposefully round to the doors. 'Get them out.'

Their hands were tied behind their backs. Sulien must have slammed his shoulder, rather than his fist, at the wall. It was a sensible precaution; Mazatl was right to have restrained them so, yet Dama had to still a little shiver of horror at it. They looked frighteningly vulnerable as the light hit them: crouched together, both their faces made strange and alike with indignation and fear: a pale, underground look, their eyes unnaturally large and black. Lal was crying. And Sulien, who'd given him back so much strength, undone so much pain – Dama was not sure he'd ever even seen him angry, there had always been a leniency and gentleness about him which was part of the reason Dama had never considered him as an active ally. But now, when he saw Dama, as he and Lal were pulled out of the van, he seemed splintering apart with anger, as if it were altering the very substance of his body. He shouted, 'So what are you going to do? Are you going to kill us?'

At this, standing behind Lal and Sulien, Mazatl levelled a hard look at Dama. But Dama refused to show he saw it.

Lal wept, 'You can't, you wouldn't.'

'No, no,' Dama said softly. 'Of course I won't kill you.'

Lal pushed towards Dama, beseeching, 'Dama, how can you be doing this?'

She still seemed wholly incredulous. But Sulien, who had seen Dama kill, found that there was some part of his mind that kept refusing to be fully surprised, that said, yes, this is what he would do. He cried, 'What do you mean "of course"? Do you think there's anything we can trust you on now? What have you done with Una?'

'She's fine,' answered Dama, shortly.

'Where is she, then? Let us see her.'

'I'm sorry. No. I'm not taking chances.'

Sulien lunged forward as if, restrained and absurdly outnumbered though he was, there might still be some way of attacking Dama. He scarcely felt that he was being held back, he was only disgusted that Dama should stand there looking on, sad and motionless. 'You bastard, you ungrateful, sick … How dare you? Look at your hands. Who did that? You could hardly lift them when I met you. I helped you. Lal's father saved your life. How dare you do this to us?'

'I haven't forgotten, Sulien,' said Dama in a low voice, looking away from him. 'And I'm sorry I have to do this. But I can't risk the safety of everyone here. And I can't risk the cause we're working for. I'd like you to understand that. I don't know if you can.'

'Understand?' cried Sulien. 'I don't care why you're doing it.' He was perversely glad to see Dama begin to look angry, it was better than the sorrowful patience he'd shown up until now.

Dama said, 'You don't care? You must care. You have to care.'

'A war. Murder.'

'It wasn't murder when I killed that man in the Sanctuary, to *save* you. That's what I'm doing now. That's what it takes.'

'But *innocent people*,' insisted Sulien.

'Innocent people!' exclaimed Dama. 'People who think they can own a human being if they can only afford it, people who live next to a disgrace like that factory, and do nothing! How are they innocent? And even if they are, what about the innocent people being bought and sold and worked to death? Or do you only care about free Romans, now you're one of them?'

Sulien blinked, for a moment so taken aback as to forget how angry he was. 'I never said that,' he protested, 'Dama – for the gods' sake – how can you ask me that?'

Dama said violently, 'There's only one God.'

All of them were silent.

Flatly Dama resumed, to his people, 'Him, there in the garage, her in the cellar.'

'What?' Lal said, automatically straining closer to Sulien. 'Dama! At least keep us together.'

'You have to,' agreed Sulien, quickly. 'She's been ill.'

Dama, whose eyes were focused now on some undefined point beyond them, eyelids slack and listless, said wearily, 'Sulien, I know she was ill. And I know when she reached you. She's been well these two months.'

'She's relapsed twice,' said Sulien, without knowing he was going to say it.

'Well. One thing at at a time,' muttered Dama and turned away.

Sulien and Lal were dragged apart, but a rapid, urgent look went between them, like the flash of a lamp, a signal across a dark valley.

Sulien hardly noticed where he was being taken. He stared at the man who was marching along, oddly fascinated. 'You're Atronius, aren't you?'

Atronius smiled thinly. 'That's a Roman name. Forced on my family, one way or another, once upon a time. I'm Maian. I go by Mazatl, now.'

'What have you got to do with Drusus, then?' Sulien asked, recklessly curious. 'Why were you in Byzantium?'

Mazatl stopped, and dragged Sulien closer by the shoulder. 'What do you know about me?'

Sulien smiled harshly. 'You know who I am. You know where I live. You brought me here. It's hardly fair to ask me that.'

Mazatl glowered, suspicious and uneasy. 'I've got nothing to do with Drusus Novius. He had a lot of slaves, he wasn't known for treating them well. And an Imperial target was one option, at that time.'

Sulien nearly laughed. 'You might have killed him? Instead of what you did at Veii?' Mazatl didn't answer. Sulien persisted, wondering, 'But you were never a slave.'

Mazatl pushed him forward, as one of the others threw open the heavy garage doors. 'My whole country's a slave.'

The air felt powdery and stagnant, and smelt of soot. Dama had plainly prepared the cellar as thoroughly and humanely as possible in such time as he'd had: there was a mattress on the floor, tidily supplied with blankets, a bucket, a large jug of water, an old, faded dress to change into, even a little pile of books. Lal paced the blackish floor, sometimes hearing herself crying as if it were somebody else. The idea that had leapt between Sulien and herself as she was pulled away seemed far less potent now. Would it not be obvious what she was trying to do? Certainly it would be if she made any move immediately. So how long should she wait? To get free was as much a responsibility as an instinctive, tormenting need: they would have to tell what Dama was doing, where he was. She wept again at this new loss of Dama, whom she had known since she was ten years old. Oh, no, she could not stand to be here for any time at all, thinking these things – not by herself. Being trapped might be bearable if there were somebody with her, but not alone. And even if she could reach Sulien or have him brought to her, what would it achieve? They had no plan, and no way of communicating one.

At first she scarcely noticed the irregular hollow ringing noise, down here it was so faint, and she was so agitated, that she dismissed it unconsciously as part of the workings of the heating system or water supply. But finally it occurred to her that the sound resounding in the pipes that ran along the wall and up into the ceiling was being deliberately caused, and that Una must be causing it. Lal darted to the pipes; they were painfully hot on her knuckles when she knocked on them. She drew back and tapped harder with her foot. There was silence for a second, and then a reply: an imitation of the sound she'd made. Lal laughed foolishly and tapped again. Una replied again. There was still no way of saying anything useful that Lal could think of, but nevertheless, any contact with either Una or Sulien seemed a small triumph.

She sat down on the mattress, still weeping and shuddering a little.

There was a book of scripture among the rest, which she had expected as soon as she saw the little stack. But below that, of all things, were a couple of fashion magazines, both more than a year out of date. Lal stared at them in disbelief. What on earth were they doing in this place? It seemed absurd, even insulting, that Dama should draw from his memories of her, to try to be kind. He should treat her as a stranger now.

But she read a few verses, and looked at the magazines, and felt very slightly comforted.

Dama went to the kitchen for some water, and gulped it down with a painkiller, furtively. Una was still at work overhead, drumming something against the pipes. It was quite plainly not the sound of an attempt at escape, nor an expression of hysteria; it was a message to him. She meant to keep him aware of her, she meant not to allow him a moment's comfort with what he had done. Dama started up the stairs on furious impulse and shouted, '*Stop it. Shut up.*'

Of course, there could be no clearer means of telling her that she was succeeding in unnerving him, and of course the sound did not stop.

Mazatl appeared in the main doorway. 'So, what is this?' he asked.

Dama took him into the little shelf-lined room he used as a kind of study or retreat, and explained, shortly, the gist of what had happened. Una had learnt their plans from Sulien, too soon, too unprepared.

Mazatl glanced drily up at the ceiling. 'So, she's up there making her feelings known.' And he watched Dama, troubled, admonishing. At last he said, 'What are you doing, Dama? You *know* what has to be done.'

Two and a half years ago Mazatl had been a bored and resentful night-watchman, working at a mansion on the Caelian hill, who had caught Dama in an early, inexpert attempt to release a handful of slaves. Dama, who should have been appalled that he had been stopped before he had even begun, had instead been elated by the almost instant certainty that he had, providentially, met exactly the right person. And so he had begun to speak, in total confidence.

The handover of authority that had happened then had lasted ever since: although Mazatl was older than Dama, and though his experience had given him skills that Dama had had to learn, he had accepted Dama's leadership from the moment there had been a movement to lead. And part of his value to Dama was that he could, occasionally and without lasting ambition, take the upper hand, in order to question Dama or tell him what do, like an older brother, while continuing to trust him. This was the first time Dama had seen such obvious doubt displayed on Mazatl's face.

'I'm not going to hurt them,' Dama said.

'I'm not talking about *hurting* them,' said Mazatl grimly. He took his gun from under his jacket and laid it on the table between them, his hand resting beside it, ready. 'Look. It's not as if you've got to be the one to do it. You can leave it to me. I'll get them out in the woods, one by one. It'll be quick, you can trust me for that.'

'You'll do nothing,' Dama retorted.

'What, then? Do you think we can keep them here for the rest of their lives?'

'Of course not. Until the war begins. Then it won't matter.'

Mazatl made an impatient, clicking sound. 'If they're a threat they're a threat. And even if we can hold them here, there's a good chance they'll disrupt what we're doing. It sounds like that girl's doing her best to do that now. What if our people here get curious about them? It's taken us years to reach this point. It not right to let them get in the way, just because you know them. It's selfish to put our own feelings first. That's what you've always said.'

Irritably, Dama slid the gun away from him, but as his fingers rested on the metal, he knew that Mazatl was right. Of course he was right. Dama tried not to hear the thought, tried to forget it. He said, 'I've made my decision.'

Mazatl grunted and got up. Dama added, 'You can go back, now. There's no need for you to stay here,' as lightly as he could. With a sudden pang of sickness he had remembered that he should not have let Mazatl get so close to Una.

Una seemed not to sleep; certainly she intended that no one else should. If the pounding and stamping from the top floor stopped at all, that first night, it must have coincided with whatever fragments of sleep Dama caught without noticing. Sometimes it seemed merely stupid, ridiculous, like a child's tantrum, except so much more relentless. And yet it was insidiously frightening, too. He thought of a mad beggar he'd seen once, banging his head methodically against a wall, over and over again. Some time before dawn Dama flung himself out of bed, and raced upstairs to do – what? He stood outside her door, a few yards away from her, incensed, powerless. No, he must not give in, he would not speak to her.

There were twenty people sleeping in the farmhouse, beside himself, Lal and Una. Some of them were too accustomed to sleeping in the clamour of factory machinery for Una's efforts to trouble them much, but others were hollow-eyed and irritable in the morning. One of them, a large, tough man in his thirties called Baro, suggested, 'It's like she's laughing at us. Shouldn't we tie her up, or something, if we have to keep her here?'

Yes, he could have her tied up, except that the knowledge of having done that to her would be harder to bear than the noise.

The continual temptation to go to her, to try again to make her see, overcame him. After all he had to find some way of controlling her.

Una was flushed, breathless, lit with the perverse energy on the other side of exhaustion.

Dama said, 'Listen, I'm leaving. There are things I need to see to; I never stay here that long. So you may as well stop. I'm not going to be around to hear you.'

Una seemed to smile oddly. Her eyes were hard and feverish, and looked very black. 'How will you know what I'm doing, if you're not here?'

At the time he didn't know what she meant, and went away without saying more. But it was true, much as he resented it, she'd made him dread leaving the farm.

He behaved as if Una were far more dangerous than the others, as if she could turn herself into smoke and pour away through a crack in the door, as if she were a muscular giant who could fight her way out. Repeatedly, he checked the patrol under the window; his fingers kept straying nervously to the key from the newly installed lock. He kept it on him, in his pocket, and handed it over only when someone took up her food, which he had directed to be done in silence, with at least three men ranked outside the door. Yet Dama avoided talking about her with any of them, and so two days had passed before he learnt of the next phase of Una's campaign.

Already the atmosphere at the farm had changed. Mazatl was gone, but Dama thought he saw the same doubt in everyone. They did not distrust him yet to the extent of disbelieving what he had told them, on the contrary. Every precaution he insisted upon strengthened their belief that the prisoners were to be hated and feared. But they could not understand why Dama did not do more to thwart and punish them. And so Dama did not seem quite so strong as he had, and the farm did not seem so safe with the three traitors contained within it. The upper floor of the farmhouse, the cellar, the garage all radiated malevolence. The freed slaves were all under threat, Dama along with the rest.

On the second day, Dama found two of them, Cosmas and Anna, who had taken the midday meal up to Una, standing on the stairs and chatting, both of them picking idly at a plate of bread and cheese.

'What're you doing?' Dama asked sharply. 'Isn't this ... hers?' He hadn't spoken Una's name since she'd been shut in the room upstairs.

They looked guilty. 'Seems like she wasn't hungry,' said Anna, with hostility towards Una in her voice. 'We didn't think you'd mind.'

'I don't care what you eat,' he said impatiently. 'Did *she* eat anything?'

'I don't know,' said Cosmas, lamely. 'Nothing much.'

Dama felt a bright blast of instant, surmising anger crackle through him like as if he'd touched a live wire. He strode out of the house, leaving Cosmas and Anna confused and dismayed.

He found Paccia in the chicken-shed. She was a poor, beaten-looking thing, she'd never be good for more than packing grenades one day, never a real fighter. 'You took her food up this morning,' he said aggressively, accusing her. He had made sure that no one person had carried food twice to Una or the others – less chance of them striking up any kind of rapport. 'Did she eat it? Did she eat at all?'

Paccia shrank back, bewildered. 'No.'

'Why didn't you tell me?' demanded Dama, so fiercely that Paccia flinched as if under a whip.

Once more, he felt the urge to rush to Una immediately, though he hardly knew what he wanted to do or say when he reached her. He looked towards the farmhouse and thought ferociously, commanding her, *give this up*. He seemed to feel the force of his own will, something coiled python-like around the building, around her room, invisible muscles and tendons pressing, gripping. And he thought he could feel her, out of sight, but pushing implacably back.

Well, it still might possibly be that she was simply too tense and wretched to eat, as she had been the day of Marcus' wedding, in which case it would pass. Dama had little confidence in this comforting idea, but he forced himself to wait until evening before giving it up. The hours dragged. He stayed out of the house, instructing some of the slaves who'd been there longest in engineering and controlling a fire. But he could not keep his thoughts away from her, clutching at the idea of her with something that felt like hatred. And sometimes his eyes were pulled to the little concrete box of the garage, where Sulien was. He was increasingly nervous that the prohibition that kept the former slaves from talking with the captive spies among them would at some point be broken. It would be terrible if Sulien heard of this.

Finally evening came. Improvidently, they'd killed some chickens, as if they were celebrating something. Dama opened the door of the kitchen while they were being cooked, so that the smell would carry up the stairs. He checked the food tray before it went up to Una's room, and felt scarcely able to hold a conversation until it was time for the little team he appointed to go and bring it down. There was no need to inspect the food carefully; it was immediately obvious that nothing had been touched. The whole tray had simply lain on the floor for an hour.

Dama did nothing. She wanted him to come to her. This was an attack, with such weapons as she had, and though he had so many people on his side, so much more power here than she, he had little defence against it except trying to pretend it did not frighten him. But increasingly he longed to be able to see what she was doing, what state she was in. He found himself picturing, in angrily wistful detail, the kind of observation hatch in the door that would be in a real prison. It did occur to him that he could have a spyhole drilled in the wood, but even to do that seemed a defeat, a concession of territory to her. Before this he'd thought of moving her, perhaps placing Sulien in the upstairs room and Una in the garage, getting rid of the noise. Now, though, he needed it, he depended on it. Every knock and thud that came from above seemed to fall separately on his nerves, but he was always listening out, wincingly anticipating the next one, afraid of not hearing it.

And over the following days, hideously, he could hear her getting weaker. The dogged blows against the floor or the pipes grew slower, duller. He could feel the aching effort it took, as if in his own joints, he felt the fluttering heartbeat and breathlessness which sometimes forced her to pause, summoning strength. At night, the onslaught was punctuated by abrupt long silences, which kept him awake more effectively than the noise itself, he lay helplessly straining his ears for it to begin again.

Then one day he came into the house and there was nothing, she was silent. She had been silent when he woke that morning. And there was a flatness about this quiet that chilled him; he felt somehow certain it had lasted all day, as if a more recent cessation would have left palpable janglings in the air.

He told himself that she could hardly have died, that would surely take weeks. But this thought seemed to fly away, weightlessly; it was not enough to hold against the wrench of panic that dragged him upstairs.

And in the first moment she did look dead. She was on the ground, her legs lying skewed, her back propped against the wall like a bit of broken furniture. Her hair and skin looked dimmed, altered in texture, as if she'd lain there long enough to be covered in a film of dust. Her head drooped to one side; her eyes were shut; her mouth was a little open as if in a gasp of exertion or pain.

For a paranoid instant Dama imagined that it was a trick: she would spring up and charge past him, tear out of the farm in broad daylight.

But despite this he was already running to her, trying to lift her, horrified. Almost by accident he felt her pulse working, slow and muffled under his fingers. 'Una – please, for God's sake ...'

Una seemed to come awake with a little shudder. Her skin was very cold, and there was a strange smell about her, a stale chemical scent on her breath, like solvent fumes. She looked at him through her limp hair and said, in a surprisingly normal voice, 'Let me go. Let us all go.'

Dama gave a little sob of relieved laughter. He realised she was not as wasted as he might have feared – thin enough to look ill, certainly, but not yet grotesquely so, not skeletal.

'I can't,' he said. 'I will when I can, I promise. But not now. So why do this?'

'Because I don't consent,' she answered, emphatically. 'I will not stay here. I told you that.'

'So you'd rather die? You're going to kill yourself just to get out?' asked Dama desperately.

She sighed, with a kind of weary patience. 'You'd be willing to die, I should think, trying to make something happen? For this new clean world you think you can make? Or maybe you wouldn't.'

'Yes,' he said, in a low voice, suffering a sting of hurt at the idea that he might be willing only to sacrifice the lives of others.

Una shrugged. 'So, then. Would you rather I died than let me go?'

'Of course I don't want you to die,' he whispered.

'I know you don't *want* it,' she said contemptuously, 'But if it's all fine and right to start this war, it shouldn't be such a problem, should it? Not one person. How can you justify *that?*'

Dama grimaced. It was chiefly for her sake he'd been trying not to hear or think such things, it was horribly bizarre to hear them coming out of her mouth. 'I still ... I wish ... I want you to understand.'

'Well,' she said laconically, 'then we want the same thing from each other.' She shut her eyes again and let her head fall back against the wall, conserving energy. It made her look worse, that numb stillness. A sunkenness around her mouth and eye-sockets became more prominent.

He looked away in exhaustion and urged, 'Please eat something.'

Una nodded mildly. 'When I'm out of here, I will.'

'I'll let you see Sulien,' offered Dama, rashly.

There was a pause, and she looked up. But she said, 'No. I'm not bargaining. I won't stay here. You can let me go, or you can kill me. That's it. That's all you've got.'

Dama said, 'No.'

Una got up, a slow painful-looking movement that seemed to turn her dizzy and made him grit his teeth to watch, and walked away from him. She climbed stiffly onto the bed and curled up, with her back to him, shivering again.

'If you won't eat,' Dama warned her, 'I'll force you.'

Una lay huddled among the blankets as if she'd gone to sleep, and didn't answer. Finally Dama left quietly, as if trying not to wake her.

Lal was crouched over the pipes, listening. Between the silent entrances of the people who brought her food, the only way of measuring time in the cellar was against the activity in the house above. She was trying to gauge how long the pipes stayed hot, and how much time she needed.

She pulled her sleeve down over her hand for some protection, and laid her wrist against the hot metal until she had to pull it away with a hiss of pain. She felt the heated flesh anxiously. Did that feel like a feverish warmth, or was it clear what she had done? It wouldn't be enough just to lie on the ground and moan. It needed something more. Perhaps if she could wrap herself in hot cloth. She pulled off her dress and draped it over the pipes. She had wedged a cup of water as firmly against the heat as she could, and left it there for hours, but clearly it was not going to heat up enough to raise her own temperature if she swallowed it. Experimentally, she flicked the lukewarm water onto her face and into her hair, instead. While her dress warmed she dropped back naked onto the mattress, letting herself go limp, trying to remember the helpless, stewed lassitude of her illness.

It was at least worth trying.

She scrambled up to reach for her dress, and knocked questioningly on the pipes. It was a long time before any reply came: a single, weary beat. Una had been so quiet lately. Lal drummed a rapid little tattoo to her, thinking, don't give up. We're going to get out.

No more water was taken to Una's room, unless it was mixed with sugar. If she was thirsty, she'd have to drink that – or milk, or fruit juice. Dama couldn't think of a way of physically force-feeding her, at least none that he could bring himself to attempt but he could do that. Yet he was afraid he might provoke her into refusing to drink, too. But to his surprise and brief exultation, Una seemed to accept that she'd lost a round. She didn't take much, but those mouthfuls of sweet liquid surely must do some good, must slow the deterioration a little.

But they wouldn't stop it. Each day of this would go on diminishing her. Worrying about her frustrated him to the point of self-disgust, now. But he could not help dwelling anxiously on the fact that she was clearly trying to drink as little as she could bear. He became rawly conscious of every drop of liquid he swallowed himself; he thought of

407

blood thickening, drying up. What if he were making her worse, rather than better?

Often, now, he would go and open the door a crack and stand there, unspeaking. He was no longer shy about it. Una was always lying curled on the corner of the bed, where he'd left her, as if she'd never moved. She didn't look at him, and there was no more noise. From hour to hour she hung over him, like an unpaid debt, but she was silent now. In some ways, he told himself, things had settled down. He didn't think about what she had said to him. He only had to keep himself safe from her, and her from him, for a little longer, before the turning point came, and history changed.

Then three nights later, after midnight, he heard her again, knocking on the floor, like a returning ghost. Four dull, sluggish blows. Then a long silence. Then four again, a little louder now, but still so muted, so much enfeebled, that if he'd been asleep the noise might not have woken him. And he was awake already, even after three quiet nights sleep had remained so unreliable that he hadn't yet bothered going to bed. But this was like an awakening, a drench of cold, lucid anger, not the panic she'd brought him to before. Why had he allowed this to continue? Mazatl – his own conscience – even Una herself had told him what was right. He'd said that she had been corrupted and it was true, what he'd seen in her once was either long gone or had never been there. She was his enemy. He owed her nothing at all.

Mazatl's gun was still locked in the little room downstairs, lying beside the longdictor on the shelf. Dama let himself in and seized it, jamming it into his belt and closing his jacket over it; he ran lightly up the stairs. Baro was outside the room, on guard duty.

'You can go to bed,' murmured Dama. Baro got up, in silence, but he cast Dama a quick look that might have been one of approval and relief.

Dama stood there with the key in one hand, the gun in the other. He had to use his left hand to fire. He wasn't a good shot, of course, but he wouldn't need to be. He was breathing hard, but he didn't feel it.

Inside the room the pounding broke off, and he heard her shuffle closer to the door. She said, 'Dama?' Her voice sounded hesitant, frightened. She was not certain that he was there.

Dama launched himself at the door, gasping in frustration as his weaker hand struggled briefly with the lock. He dragged the door open, levelled the gun. He thought: there is nothing between us.

Una was on her knees, her eyes wide and fixed on the opening door, her shoulders raised. At the sight of the gun she recoiled, convulsively, and for a second the structure of her gaunt face seemed to break down in hopelessness, like a lump of spent coal, falling to ash. Then she scrambled up, closing the distance between the muzzle and her forehead, her body clenching combatively, and she said in a shrill, ragged voice, 'Do it, then! You're killing people who've got as much right to live as me!'

Dama was almost bewildered at not hearing the shot, not seeing her fall. It seemed to him that he had, absolutely, made the choice, and that signal had gone from his brain to his hand. And yet nothing happened, as if the scars on the nerves had grown and thickened, obstructing it. He braced his arm, taking a small step towards her, and the gun skidded down over her face. He felt the contours of brow and cheekbone, transferred through the tube of metal to his hand, as again he ordered his fingers to move, and somehow they did not. It made her shake, and her mouth contracted, but she kept her eyes open, staring fiercely at him. The gun quivered between them. And then he had jolted back, slamming the door, dragging with his whole body's weight on the handle to hold it shut while he wrestled again with the lock. He heard her fold onto the ground, fighting for breath, as his own legs weakened too and he sat down, helplessly, with the door at his back

Just a little longer, he thought. Only a little while that he had to go on bearing it.

XXIV

BEACONS

There was scarcely a flower out that Noriko recognised. These grey-ish trees were olives, of course. Sparkling heaps of unnameable yellow flowers spread below them. The garden was pleasingly overgrown, unlike the controlled, symmetrical grounds of the palace, but still the geometric structure was there under the spilling leaves. Over a long, rectangular pond stood a watchful row of white statues – maidens with drapery clinging and flying around bare breasts and arms, curls piled high above square, upright foreheads. Noriko turned back and thought how strange Sakura and Tomoe looked below them, with their finned dresses supporting the falls of their tinted hair. But Sakura and Tomoe were leaning down to feed ruby koi in the dark water. And there would be roses everywhere, in the summer. There was an orchard of apples and cherry trees ahead, where pale petals were beginning to open on the dark branches. Noriko went towards it.

This was the first time since their wedding that Marcus and Noriko had been separated by more than the length of the garden, for they had left the following day for his family home near Tusculum. Eudoxius was to handle things at the Golden House, to give the young couple time together. Noriko hardly questioned what could have happened for Marcus to have been called away so abruptly now – she was, guiltily, too much relieved at his absence for that. Not that she had anything to blame him for or liked him any less; as he had promised, he was trying not to make her unhappy. They spoke in a fluctuating pidgin that no one else could understand, and he was scrupulously interested in everything she had to say. Of course, she had intensified her efforts with Latin, but sometimes she felt that being with him was making her mysteriously less fluent, more tongue-tied. She stammered over simple words she'd known for years. Marcus thought of things that might make her feel more at home. A rock garden, to be built somewhere in the grounds, wherever she wanted it. A teahouse. Most of all, he tried not to seem miserable, as Sakura and Tomoe tried to disguise their homesickness. Justice required the same effort from her. They were considerate to each other; they were sometimes almost friends, and they were afraid of each other. The nights, which were part of the fear for both of them, were in some ways the simplest, most innocent part of it.

In another week, they had agreed, they would begin a tour of public appearances, introducing Noriko to some of the sights of Rome. After that they would not be expected to spend quite so much time together, perhaps it would be easier.

She hid herself among the flowering trees until nothing she could see was unfamiliar. But the butler was coming after her from the house. He bowed and said, 'Madam, if you would come to the longdictor, his Highness Prince Tadasius wishes to speak to you.'

Noriko began to be apprehensive now, because it would be late at home, nearly midnight. She hurried into the villa. 'Is something wrong?' she began into the longdictor.

Tadahito said fast, but very clearly, 'I will speak to you at the Embassy. There is a car outside the gates. It will take you there. Go and get into it now.'

'Why—?' But he had gone.

Noriko felt almost as much irritated as alarmed, but dutifully she went out of the house and down the gravel drive.

The guards on the gates were mildly surprised to see her strolling off alone. 'Do you wish to go somewhere, my lady?' one of them said. 'Wait a moment while I call your escort.'

She waved him away. 'The Embassy has sent a car for me. They will protect me.'

The car was unusually plain and discreetly marked to carry someone of her status, though it was sleek and shining. There was an unsmiling young Nionian man dressed in crisp black, already holding the door open for her.

Noriko slipped inside and said to the driver, 'Why must I go to the Embassy?' The driver was slow enough in answering to unnerve her. 'Explain at once,' she commanded crossly.

The young man who had opened the door for her settled briskly in the seat opposite her. He looked past her to check that the Novian villa was out of sight.

He said, 'We are at war.'

Noriko parted her lips in soundless confusion and outrage.

'The Crown Prince told you you were to come to the Embassy in order that you should be able to say so naturally, and in case your conversation was being monitored.'

'But ...' Noriko craned back in the seat to look back towards the vanished house. The car was moving swiftly and purposefully. 'What has happened?'

'Our troops in Tokogane were withdrawing from the Wall, in accordance with the treaty.' His voice dipped, bitterly. 'The Romans have attacked three military trains in Enkono and Iwatougen, and destroyed them.'

'No,' Noriko protested, almost mildly, as if he might admit he could be wrong.

'Three military trains,' repeated the agent. 'And a passenger train was derailed too; it was following one of the others. They may have killed fourteen hundred of our soldiers, perhaps three hundred civilians.'

'When?' breathed Noriko.

'Moments ago,' the agent said, almost angrily. 'They have betrayed us once again, and we have very little time to remove you from their hands. We will be taking you to a safe house where your appearance can be altered. Clearly you cannot travel safely undisguised. I regret that your hair is too distinctive, it will have to be cut. You will be driven to a launch at Napolis; there is a secret airbase in northern Mauretania from which you may return to Nionia. Let me promise you, Your Highness, that we will not fail you. You will soon be home.'

Noriko fell back against the seat, dazed. 'What about my waiting women?' she asked weakly, after a while.

'There is nothing we can do for them, Your Highness, but they are in far less danger than you would be.'

Noriko sat mechanically fingering a strand of her condemned hair and gazing blankly at the cypress-covered hills as they sped past. Her mind was numb; she could not make it contemplate either this journey or those terrible numbers. But of course, it did not matter what she thought. In the first stunned minutes, this was almost comforting to her. Nothing was being asked of her, everything had been decided already. All she had to do was be carried onward; it would not matter if she were asleep, or unconscious. Her body was being reclaimed like unpaid-for furniture, a little used, but still essentially the same.

'This cannot be right,' she ventured.

'Your Highness?'

'What was I married for, if we only go to war after all?'

'Rome has betrayed you, also, madam.'

'But this is not what Caesar would do,' said Noriko, with rising urgency. 'I know it is not. There has been a mistake.'

'Unfortunately, there is no mistake,' said the agent, sorrowfully, though she was sure she heard the note of exasperation he was trying to suppress.

What would it be like to go back? She could only imagine it as a matter of creeping home to hide, disgraced and shorn. Or perhaps her marriage woud be treated like a short, serious illness, which had altered her, but from which she was convalescing. Or perhaps it really would be simply as if she had never been married at all. Was that not more or less what she wanted – she and Marcus both? She had been gone so short a time.

The road veered around the flank of the hill and fled on, down through the trees. Noriko had very little sense of where they would be going, except that she knew Rome was a little way north and Napolis a long way south.

'Turn back,' she announced peremptorily. 'I want to go to Rome and speak to my husband.'

Nothing happened. The young agent lowered his eyes and gazed at her shoes, his expression sad and deferential. Noriko jumped a little in the seat with indignation and strain. 'I order you to take me to Rome.'

'I know, Your Highness,' the man said, softly. 'And we are your servants in all other things. We will die for you and consider our lives well given. But our orders are from the Emperor. To bring his daughter safely home.'

Noriko opened her mouth to speak again, and then closed it. She dropped back once more and glared out of the window. She felt the sullen expression on her face and, grudgingly, smoothed it away. Finally she said stiffly, 'I apologise. Your duty is very clear.'

He bowed his head. 'You are most generous, my Lady.'

They had descended into Tusculum itself. The traffic was heavy, and the car slowed and stopped. Noriko sprang for the door and hurled herself out into the road.

Everything seemed to reel and swing. She had come close to plunging under the wheels of an oncoming car, but that was almost the least of her terror. This was unthinkable; it was as if she had dashed onto a battlefield. Noriko charged headlong up the ordinary little street, hair flying, her knees weak, her breath already coming in deep, jagged gasps. The traffic strained to avoid her; somewhere a hostile shout died away in confusion. Noriko turned back and saw the Nionian agent following her, wading through the traffic, but his face was pale with shock; his eyes indecisive as he scanned the street. He could hardly kill everyone who'd seen it happen. She'd been recognised. It was already too late.

Noriko staggered, half-deliberately, into the path of another car, putting up her hands as it skidded to a halt in front of her. She banged on the window, drew herself up as the man inside stared at her.

'I am your Empress,' she said grandly and inaccurately, in Latin, to the astonished driver. 'You must take me to the Palace as fast as you can.'

By the time she reached the Golden House, her faith in Marcus' innocence had weakened, and with the aftershock of her escape still ricocheting through her, the possibility that she had made a catastrophic mistake filled her with heady, invigorating aggression. She stormed through the Palace looking for Marcus and almost wanted somebody to try to stop her, so that she could rage and bully her way over them. But it seemed they had already discovered she was unaccounted for, and the servants and aides she encountered were frustratingly willing to guide her on to a huge noisy room she had not seen before, windowless and inwardly fortified with ceiling-high maps: Europe; Africa; Terranova and Tokogane; Asia; the world. There were more maps and papers spread over the long table, and on Tokogane, three red points showed what must be the sites of the attacks, and at the far end of the room, a crowd of men were watching aerial footage of blackened, broken-backed train carriages scattered under a fallen bridge at the bottom of a ravine. And something else froze Noriko as she strode towards Marcus. Other maps were ominously pocked with little dark spots, and there was another busy huddle of people, pointing and muttering around the map that showed Nionia, which was heavily flecked with black. The marks were clustered over Edo and Cynoto, the ports. Targets.

Marcus had been bowed over the charts on the table. He straightened as he saw her. His face was stern, taut.

'Did you do this?' she demanded in Nionian. 'You can't have done this, can you?'

He caught her hands. 'No. No, of course I didn't,' he said quietly, in the same language, and a discomfited silence expanded around the foreign syllables. He murmured an excuse to the men and hurried her out of the room. Then they were in a small ante-chamber, incongruously holding hands.

'You were missing,' he said. 'They said someone came from the Embassy.'

'I was supposed to run away,' she explained impatiently. She saw Marcus' face alter, amazement unfolding slowly across it, but still felt too agitated and fatalistic to be bothered with his reaction to what she had done. 'Well, you didn't do it. Then you don't have control of your army,' she said. 'So it makes no difference.'

Marcus sighed raggedly. 'Salvius called me here as the news came in.

He knows nothing of this, I'm sure of it. We're trying to find out who it was, of course – so far as there's time.'

'Then you must stop it,' she said, her body stiffening as she thought of those black circles on the maps.

'Did you see those pictures in there? They fired on the spiralwing that took them.' He sighed again, but not exactly wearily this time: as if about to gather a deeper breath, preparing to dive underwater. 'The Prince won't speak to me – no one will. It's a good thing you're here.'

He was leading her somewhere else. 'What do you want me to do?' she asked.

'He'll talk to you.'

She knew Tadahito would be furious, but she was still angry enough herself not to be apprehensive about this, almost to look forward to it. She and Marcus were alone in the beautiful green Imperial office, she sitting at the desk like the Emperor of Rome.

'So you were intercepted,' he said, flatly.

'No,' she replied. 'Please do not be concerned on my account. Naturally when I heard the news I wished to consult my husband. I came here entirely freely.' Politeness was a delicate, transparent container into which she released the aggression, a piece at a time, still meaning it to be wholly apparent.

Tadahito dispensed with it, however. 'Then you are a fool.'

'No. Will you please talk to my husband? He's here.'

'Stop calling him that,' snapped Tadahito.

Noriko beat a pen vengefully on the desk like a drumstick. 'That's what he is. By your doing, as well as others'. And he has not attacked or invaded Tokogane. If he had intended anything of the kind, he would not have married me.'

'He married you to use you as a pawn, you stupid girl,' Tadahito cried, in exasperation.

'No, he did not. Everything between us would have been quite different if he had.'

Tadahito sighed, heavily. 'I suppose you have fallen in love with him?'

'No,' she said, looking at Marcus with a mixture of detachment and perverse protectiveness. He had gone right to the end of the room and was leaning against the peach tree painted on the wall, his eyes shut, as if trying to think while blocking out some deafening noise. He did not look encouraged by what he could hear of the conversation. She did not love him; she loved her brother, though she felt like hitting Tadahito at that moment. 'But I am in a position to be sure he is telling the truth.'

'Either you are too infatuated with him to want to leave, or you are being forced to say this to me.'

'How am I being forced?' she cried, openly angry and injured now. 'Nothing they could threaten me with would make me lie to you. Is it not enough to send me here for a treaty you give up on almost at once – you have to call me a coward as well?'

Tadahito said, shakily, 'Noriko,' and she began to forgive him a little, he sounded desperate, lost. She missed him. 'I can't go on talking to you. I don't know what can be done. I hope we have not lost you. I wish we had never, never thought of marrying you to him. Please try and forgive me.'

And the line cut out. Noriko gave a desolate little cry. 'He's gone. He doesn't believe me.'

Marcus came back over to the desk. 'Nothing anyone can say will be enough,' he said resignedly. 'It'll take more than words.'

Noriko looked up at him, and around at the room, with a kind of orphaned incredulity, as if she didn't know how she had come there.

'Don't worry,' he told her softly. 'Tell me what happened when we couldn't find you.'

She explained in a disjointed way about the plan to smuggle her across the sea, about leaping out of one car and commandeering another. She saw Marcus smiling with amusement and admiration, and it did begin to seem comic to her, which steadied her a little.

Marcus said, 'Your family want to see you safe, and they can. You can go home – you *must* go home, as fast as we can get you there. In a Roman spira, not hiding or disguised, but as yourself.' A fragment of his own hidden flight from Rome flashed with wounding brightness in his memory: himself, dodging in fear through a marketplace, darting into a clairvoyant's stall to hide himself, where the fortune-teller lifted her hands away from her face to give him his first sight of Una. He finished, his voice tightening, 'As my wife. When they see you face to face, they'll know you are not a prisoner, and that I didn't marry you as some kind of trick.'

'They'll think it's another attack. They might shoot me down,' said Noriko, shivering.

'They won't shoot you down. We'll tell them you're coming, and that you'll land away from all the obvious targets. They'll think it's a lie, but they can't take the risk that it's not the truth. Not over you.'

For the second time that day, Noriko contemplated a return home. It was imaginable now. She could picture herself, meeting her parents and siblings. 'I will go. But it still won't be enough.'

'No. Perhaps not,' said Marcus. 'But you can tell them what I mean to do.' He looked at her lovely anxious face, and felt with a pang of regret that he would miss her, and yet he would be relieved while she was gone. He told her, before she could ask, 'And if we succeed, you'll return. If you wish, of course.'

'Our obligations remain the same,' she said, rather stiffly.

'You're the only person who could do this. Thank you for coming back,' he said.

She laughed. 'I just didn't want to cut off my hair.'

More than twelve hours later, she was so giddy with weariness as to be glad to lay her forehead on the dark, shining throne-room floor, as she bowed to the Go-natoku Emperor. Within the the canopy, while she prostrated herself and said, 'Your Majesty,' he was a faceless, motionless figure, composed of silk and shadow. Then, as she had known he would, he came to life, he rose from his throne and became a real person: a slender man in his late fifties, his height extended by the black crest of his lacquered crown, a narrow face like Tadahito's, but secretively humorous and at ease, without Tadahito's tense vigour. It was as if her father had simply not been in the room before and had just entered. But an unworldly grace remained with him even as he left the canopy behind; after so many years of habit it never left him altogether. He took her in his arms and said tenderly, 'My little girl.'

'Oh, Father,' she whimpered, and burrowed deeper into the embrace. The Emperor rocked and shushed her easily. He showed no sign of being personally distressed about the crisis; Noriko was not sure she understood this about him any better than a stranger would, but she was used to it, and his apparent calm comforted her.

Finally she pulled herself together enough to speak again. 'Part of my message is just being here. Please may I explain the rest?'

'Go ahead, Noriko,' he said.

'In three hours the Wall dividing Tokogane and Terranova will come down,' she said.

Later, on an ebony-mounted den-ga screen, they saw the first watchtower fall together, on the Anasasian coast. It collapsed inward, and as the view of the land beyond opened up, the screen of dust and flame unrolled up the first length of grey wall, and brought the next tower bowing down, and the next. And beyond that they could not see, as the soldiers, farmers and townspeople of Tokogane and Terranova saw, the fire chasing past on the horizon, across the continent. As the Wall fell, it became a line of beacons, carrying a signal all the way to the Atlantic.

XXV

THE KNIFE

In the clearing among the stone pines, Dama heard nothing now: not the rustles and calls of birds, nor the intermittent rasp of the road. He was no longer on his knees but lying down, the dusty earth and pine needles under his back. The cool spring sky gaped, a vault of pure space that seemed to stretch as he watched it, so that he felt that gravity had reversed or had never till now been understood: he was a tiny doll, fixed with loosening pins to the ceiling of the universe, staring down into the blue gulf. Around him the branches of the trees hung down, above the depths, like icicles. It seemed a long time since he'd taken or released a breath. The movement of his heart was a remote detail, he could not feel it. He had killed more than seventeen hundred people. If he had done so in the course of a failure – if he kept failing, what did that mean?

He stood up, and the world swung over, the ground lunged down below his feet. Sound flooded back. He forgot the prayers he'd said. While whispering them he had felt an emptiness that might have been peace or strength, but if it had been, he forgot that too.

He was on the crest of a hill near the farm. The respite from being there had not lasted very long. He walked back.

Of course, none of the freed slaves here knew what had happened, or if they heard of it, they would not know a disaster on the other side of the Atlantic had anything to do with them. He neither wanted to be among them, in their ignorance, nor with those who understood what the news meant. He could think of nothing he truly wanted, not even victory. Nevertheless, he would keep on; whatever giving up was, he would not do it.

The van Mazatl had been using was parked in the yard, near the garage where Sulien was. Dama stopped, with a little jolt of indignation and anxiety. He glanced at the garage doors, on an uneasy impulse he did not understand, but everything seemed as usual; Pallas was on guard duty, leaning against the wall, looking bored. Where was Mazatl then?

Nowhere in sight, not in the yard. Dama hurried into the house, heading straight for the worst place for Mazatl to be.

And he was there, right outside Una's door. And there was no one guarding it. Although he had turned at the sound of Dama's footsteps, Dama had the impression Mazatl had been experimentally trying the handle.

'What are you doing here?' Dama demanded.

Mazatl withdrew still further from the door and answered mildly, 'We've got to talk, haven't we?'

'Come away from there,' said Dama. 'I didn't send for you. You shouldn't have come.'

Mazatl followed him obediently down the stairs. 'I wanted to see how things were going, that's all.'

Dama muttered, 'You should have called. You should have asked permission. Yes, we've got to talk, but not here.'

He breathed a little more easily once they were outside, not only for having drawn Mazatl from Una. Going that close to her now was like descending into a mineshaft, deep enough to feel the weight of the air. The former slaves were busy across the farm. They had their instructions; they could manage for a day without him. Una would stay alive that long. He said, 'I'll come with you back to Tarquinia.'

He let Mazatl take the controls of the van; there was no need to hurt himself driving. As soon as they passed through the gates onto the drive, Mazatl said, 'I hear that one's starving herself?' Dama nodded, tersely. Mazatl hesitated, then said in a loud, falsely jocular tone, 'She wants putting out of her misery.'

Dama didn't answer immediately. Then he said, 'We need to discuss the future of the project, not her.'

'I mean it, Dama. The strikes in Nionian Terranova should have done it, but they haven't. Nothing's happening. It'll be a while before we can try anything new. On any reckoning these people you're hanging onto are going to stay dangerous, at least until we succeed, and we've got no way of knowing when that'll be.'

Dama felt his teeth clench. Mazatl didn't know of Una's ability, and so didn't know that he had made this more true by coming here today. Yet it felt almost like an act of deliberate malice. Mazatl went on, brutally, 'And if she keeps this up, she'll be dead by then anyway. And as far as I can see, she's asking for it. Why spin it out? And in the meantime there are the other two to worry about.'

Dama's head was turned to the window; his eyes seemed unable to focus on anything close; he let his gaze push up through the transparent sky, at the white sun. He murmured, 'No, Mazatl.' And he knew that really he had no more to say, no argument that could stand up to Mazatl's. But he found himself protesting, 'Is it such a bad thing, to try and protect someone? Out of gratitude or – kindness? Is that so terrible?'

Mazatl made a discontented scoffing noise in his throat. But when he looked at Dama, it was with something close to compassion.

In the cellar, Lal was panicky with boredom and loneliness. Even Una's phantom company seemed to have left her. Two nights ago she'd woken thinking she'd heard a voice that might have been Una's, crying out, and a door slamming. And since then, there was no longer even any response when she knocked on the pipes herself. It frightened her to be left alone this way. Sometimes she found terrible conjectures going through her head. But they weren't rational, she insisted to herself – they weren't likely. It was being alone: thoughts seemed to go bad, like milk, when left for too long. Dama would not hurt Una; that much must be true.

She pestered everyone who came to bring anything or take anything away. 'Oh, please don't go. I'm not as horrible as you think – you don't *know* what I'm like. Please just stay and talk to me.' Most of them stoically ignored her; but a few, in the last couple of days, had mumbled apologies or asked if there were anything they could bring her. Today, at breakfast, she'd even managed to lure a woman into a very short, banal conversation about the weather. But as she'd never yet seen the same person more than twice, she had little hope of achieving more than a tiny reprieve from the monolithic boredom of the day. It had almost goaded her into carrying out her plan already. She had held back because although it seemed she had been here an unendurably long time, it had not really been so many days since Sulien had warned Dama she might become ill. And there would be only one chance. Despondently she had calculated that it was almost certain no one was looking for them seriously yet. She had begun to make a few tentative friends in Rome aside from Una and Sulien, but no one who would be worried by not seeing her for a while. The staff at the clinic might have reported Sulien's absence to the vigiles, but when the vigiles realised Una was missing too, and that Una had been Marcus' lover, they would probably think Sulien had taken his sister out of Rome for the Imperial wedding, as indeed he'd tried to do. He should have called the clinic, but anxiety and thoughtlessness on his part would surely seem a more likely explanation than abduction at first.

A door closed upstairs. Lal picked one of the magazines off the floor, opened it, stared at words she could have recited by heart, and then hurled it across the room with a grunt of fury.

Then the pipes rang, with three loud, urgent blows.

Lal started, and leapt eagerly towards them. 'What happened to you?' she cried aloud, as she knocked her response.

As on the first day, Una mimicked the rhythm of Lal's signal back to her. 'I was worried,' remarked Lal, settling down on the floor by the pipes, and striking them again. She laughed foolishly at herself for talking as if anyone could hear her.

But Una repeated the same sound once more, and then again, harder. For a second or two Lal thought Una was not trying to talk to her after all, but resuming her solitary protest. But then there was nothing until Lal reached out hesitantly to tap again. She had barely touched the pipes when Una pounded out the same beat again, violently.

Lal snatched her hand away as if the heat had burnt her, unnerved. She sat still for a moment, looking uncertainly up at the ceiling. 'What is it?' she murmured, self-consciously. Would Una know what she had been planning? She had been rehearsing it diligently for days, laying the scene, adding new details – would Una have picked that up? The idea was at once hopeful and disconcerting. She rapped again, questioningly, and said, 'Now? Today?'

There was an outburst of hammering from the pipes. Lal caught her breath.

Indecisively, she pressed her hand down on the hot metal, wincing. It was still possible that she was misunderstanding what Una was telling her, perhaps even that there was no message to be understood. Whatever had kept Una quiet all this time, by now she might be as desperate as Lal for a sign that someone was there.

But, before she had even finished this thought, her own words seemed to sound again, as if she had repeated them aloud without realising it, or as if someone had recorded them and was playing them back to her: 'Now. Today.'

Lal heard herself let out a thin, maddened laugh. She felt as if her attention had been compelled back to those words, by a will that was not hers. The next instant, the fancied pressure on her thoughts was gone, and she had no way of telling if it had been more than a jitter of her mind; she knew that every day she was left alone her thoughts were less normal, less her own. But she began to get ready.

Some time around noon, she thought, a man came in with a tray of food. Lal looked up at him forlornly from the floor. She was sitting damp-skinned and shivering on the mattress, clutching a heap of blankets around herself, and whispering, 'Please, stay, I'm not well. Please, it's so cold.'

He looked at her in alarm, but withdrew without saying anything or coming near her. Lal remained poised on the mattress for almost an hour, in suspense, ready to carry on her performance if he came back, or sent anyone. But no one came. Lal had planned for this: indeed, they would have far more chance of escape at dusk. But now it was actually happening, she could not help growing agitated and tearful at the possibility that her simulated illness would meet only indifference. And whatever chance Una had tried to tell her of was passing, it would be too late.

At last she flung down the blankets impatiently, and crept up the cellar steps to listen to the noise of the house. She wished, as she had wished many times, that there were a clock. She could not act more than a few minutes before someone came; the heat wouldn't last long on her flesh. She sat hunched on the top step, for hours, chewing her lips and the skin around her fingernails in an agony of mingled anticipation and boredom, waiting to hear people gathering and crockery being moved.

Then she ran down the steps and dragged the sheet from the mattress over to the pipes, bundling it up against the heat along with her hastily stripped-off dress. She had a cup of water, already jammed against the heat and luke-warm. But that was not enough. She straightened a layer of the dress, draping it to protect her skin, and wrapped her palms around the pipes, and then pressed them to her cheeks. The last part was the hardest. She shifted onto her knees, forcing herself to grip the pipes again, twisting her face into a preparatory grimace, and lowered her forehead onto the hot metal, holding it there as long as she could.

They had left him a lamp, standing on the concrete floor just inside the garage doors. Sulien sat against the wall, waiting for someone to come for the empty plate, and watched a crane-fly bobbing jerkily through the dusty light. The food had always been reasonable, and Sulien tried to get as much pleasure out of it as he could, as it was about the only point of interest of the day. Like Lal, he made attempts to talk to the people who came, but he could not make himself appear as sweetly harmless as she could; they knew he'd tried to push and fight his way out twice, during the first couple of days. He tried to seem resigned and conciliatory now. He was waiting for Lal. But there was little he could do to prepare. It was possible that she had already tried and failed to convince their captors she was seriously ill. Even if not, he had no way of knowing what they would do.

The crane-fly sketched out a predictable pattern as it flew back and forth: a kind of drunken pentangle. He was not yet so desperate as to feel actually fond of the few creatures he'd discovered in the garage, as he'd heard that prisoners grew to care for rats or moths that came into their cells, but he was bored enough to try and count them, and to place endless bets with himself as to which way the spider in the rear corner would build, or how long it would take a woodlouse to run across the floor. He was uncertain if the crane-fly could live on anything here, or if it was also trapped and would starve, or blunder into the cobweb. Its lumbering, angular flights seemed as purposeless as his watching it. It staggered through the air, apparently neither looking for food, nor trying to escape.

Then the doors opened. It was his last view of the outside for that day, and Sulien looked at the sky first. It was strangely double, the sheets of cloud on the horizon dark but lucidly blue, as if a torn strip of a different day or a different time were pasted roughly over the evening light. Then he glanced dully at the two men who stood there, expecting one to take the plate while the other remained poised to tackle him if he moved.

But they both came in and grabbed his arms, pulling him up. Instinctively, Sulien tensed and struggled, convinced that Dama had decided to have them killed after all. But one of the men shook him and said, 'It's your friend, that's all. You need to come and help your friend. Don't try anything.'

Sulien went quiet and docile immediately, but cast an anxious look back at the farmyard gates, as they led him towards the house. It had never been very likely, but he'd hoped it might be the other way round, that they might carry Lal to him. His senses strained in a kind of panic, he walked terrified that he was already failing, he wasn't seeing his surroundings with the right clarity. There weren't many people in the yard now; most of them should be eating, and it was growing dark. That much was good. But the farmhouse itself was clearly full. Sulien knew nothing of what the place was like inside, only that Lal was in a cellar. If the entrance to it was through the kitchen or any other room in continual use, there would probably be nothing he could do.

As they hurried him into a hall he glanced around at the doors on either side. They led him to a narrow door under the stairs. A couple of people came out of the kitchen, and stared curiously at Sulien, as the men unlocked it. He thought they went away once he was ushered inside. So people might be going back and forth often, but perhaps not all the time.

Lal was sprawled across her mattress, hair spread over her hot, flushed face, shuddering and moaning. A jug lay dramatically overturned in a spreading puddle of water, beside one outflung hand. For a moment Sulien felt like smiling, until he heard the key turn in the lock, at the top of the steps. One of the men had come down into the cellar with him; the other was presumably standing guard outside the door. Lal glanced up at Sulien surreptitiously through her hair, but then shut her eyes again. For now, they had no way of communicating.

Sulien bent over her, checking her pulse and temperature. 'Lal,' he murmured, urgently. 'Lal, it's me. Can you talk to me?' Lal, dutifully, only turned her head restlessly from side to side and did not respond. Sulien allowed the tense breath building inside him to escape, letting it sound like a sigh of concern, as he tried to think what to do. 'I knew this would happen,' he began, prevaricating. The pretence seemed, briefly, bizarre. He could feel his blood, the muscles of his face working treacherously to signal the truth. He fought to convince himself that Lal really was frighteningly ill. 'Look at this place. Can you expect anyone to live down here?' There was a single bulb over near the steps; it didn't throw light very far. 'It's too dark in here. I'm going to need more light.'

'I thought you could just touch people, and—'

'If you wanted that, you should have brought me before,' said Sulien, fiercely, trying to hector the man beyond the point of asking questions. He jolted to his feet and glared down at him, trying to make intimidating use of his height. 'She could die because you left her like this. Get me some kind of light.'

The older man grimaced uncertainly, and still resisted. 'I don't know – maybe when Dama gets back.'

Dama was away, then. It was good news. Sulien hid a flash of optimism. 'When will *that* be?'

'Tomorrow morning, I think.'

'That'll be too late!' cried Sulien. 'You brought me here to help. Unless you want to explain that you let her die, get me what I need!'

Finally, the man shrugged and left. Sulien could see Lal listening as the door was unlocked, and locked again. He dropped with a sigh to sit on the ground beside her. 'Hello,' he said.

Lal pushed her hair away from her face. 'What are we going to do?' she whispered.

'I don't know.'

'At least he does what you tell him. Is he the only one?'

'There's at least one more outside the door. And he's the one with the key.'

'Have to get him in here, then,' said Lal.

They looked at each other. Sulien nodded.

'Now?' Lal suggested, hesitantly.

Sulien lifted the jug, trying the weight of it, and put it down again. He got up to make an exploratory turn around the room. 'I don't know. No, not yet. There's no time to get in a fight with him; everyone'll come running. I'll have to just try and knock him out. I don't think there's anything here I can use.'

'Have you done that to anyone before?'

'No,' said Sulien, continuing to prowl apprehensively around the cellar. Lal had crawled to the pipes running along the wall and was kneeling over them, heating her face. So that was how she had done it. He smiled.

She asked, 'What can I do? Should I do something different?'

'You're doing fine.' He climbed up the first couple of steps towards the door and then paused, turning back and looking down at her. 'Wait,' he said. 'Throw your head back.'

Lal obeyed mechanically. 'What am I doing?'

He came back over to the mattress. 'Have you ever seen anyone have a seizure?'

She shook her head. His attempts to show her what to do, and hers to copy him, brought them both to the sharp edge of frantic laughter.

'Not yet,' he whispered to her, as they heard the door opening. 'Like before.'

She shut her eyes and began again to breathe shallowly and fast. The man came down the steps, carrying a solid electric torch. Sulien held out his hand for it. 'Thank you,' he said, sternly.

He took the torch and made a show of scanning Lal's face by its light, checking her pupils. He laid his hand over her forehead and made himself still and remote for a while, as if he were concentrating.

'Well?'

Sulien looked up wearily. 'I think I can get the fever to start coming down,' he said guardedly. 'But she's dehydrated.' He gestured to the fallen jug. 'You've got to bring some more water. I just hope she can drink. You're not going to set up a drip for me, are you?'

The man took the jug without protest, this time. But fetching water wouldn't take long enough. Sulien added hastily, 'And get a sponge or something. And she'd be better off with fresh sheets.'

The man looked irritable, and trudged off without answering. Sulien did not feel confident that he would do everything he'd been asked, but did not see how he could manufacture another opportunity. At best, they'd have only a few minutes, and they'd have to allow enough time for the man to get out of immediate earshot. Lal lay stiff on the mattress, staring up at him. Neither of them could speak.

Then Sulien rushed up to the door, shouting to the man outside, 'I need help. Help me, she can't breathe.'

He drew back, staring at the door with clenched fists. The second man came into the cellar, taking the time to lock himself in. Sulien had placed the torch on the ground near Lal's feet, so that the face from which the horrible throttled sounds came was hidden in half darkness, and the motion of her jerking body seemed amplified by the violent shadow thrashing on the whitewashed wall. Urgently, Sulien beckoned the second man over, pulled him down to crouch beside her. 'She can't breathe. You've got to hold her still while I ...'

He was reaching for the torch as he spoke. He flinched a little as he touched it, but once it was in his hand, his reluctance seemed to drop coldly away and without hesitation he brought the butt of the torch down on the back of the man's head. He fell face-forward onto Lal, who gave a little shriek of panic and revulsion, and scrambled away from under him. A few drops of blood had splashed onto her face.

'Where's the key?' she gasped at once. Sulien didn't move to help turn the man onto his back, until Lal was already struggling with his weight. Lal started searching through his pockets with shaking fingers. 'I've got it,' she said, her voice still high and fierce with shock.

Sulien remained stooping over the unconscious body, looking pale and sick. 'I think he'll be all right.'

'It's too bad if he's not, we've got to *go*,' she cried, dragging him by the arm towards the steps. She ran up to the door and unlocked it, pushing it open a crack. They could hear the blurred noise of multiple conversations from the kitchen and other rooms, treading feet. They peered out as best they could, but there was little choice except to push out, all but blindly; Lal locked the cellar door and they fled across the hall. It was only as they reached the front door, that they realised there had been no one there to stop them, not yet.

'Where's Una?' whispered Sulien.

'Upstairs somewhere,' said Lal, distractedly, warily opening the door and looking out from the threshold across the darkening yard. She could see just a small number of silhouettes moving in the faint light, some around the chicken shed, herding the hens inside, others carrying crates of dishes towards the house. 'Only a few of them have ever seen us,' breathed Lal, craning towards the gates. 'We can get there.'

But to her horror, Sulien was turning back, away from the doorway, towards the stairs.

'They're going to *find* us,' hissed Lal, clutching at him. 'That other man's going to be back any second.'

'I've got to get up there somehow. I'm not leaving Una here.'

'Yes you are,' said Lal, in a kind of stifled shout. 'We get out and call the vigiles. That's how we help her. Otherwise we all stay here.'

Sulien looked unhappily up the stairs. 'When they realise we've gone—'

426

'Dama won't hurt her,' said Lal, firmly, forgetting her worst thoughts. She gripped his hand with all the coercive force she had and slipped outside.

They began walking swiftly, not straight at the gates but obliquely across the concrete, towards one of the unlit sheds. Sulien picked up the handles of a wheelbarrow standing near the house and pushed it purposefully forward. At his side, Lal was instinctively skulking along, her head lowered, shoulders raised.

'Don't do that,' Sulien murmured. 'If we were just two people who lived here going to get something, we wouldn't be keeping our heads down. You'd be talking to me.'

Lal, with an effort, forced her body into a more casual bearing. 'I can't think of anything to say,' she whispered breathlessly. 'For once.'

'Tell me a joke,' said Sulien.

They were halfway across the yard when they heard the shouts of panic and anger from the house. They swerved into the shadow of the old feed-store building, as people began to gush out of the farmhouse, and, in response, from the barn and cowsheds. They abandoned the wheel-barrow and ran along in the darkness behind the building. They reached the gates. And there was someone there, a figure walking out of the dark on the fields, coming home to the farm. At first a sexless, featureless shadow; then an anonymous woman; a girl with one eye, one hand.

Sulien and Lal stopped, grasping each other's hands. Bupe turned her head, an unsettling movement, for it gave the impression she was look-ing away, when really she was levelling her single gaze at them. She said nothing. Sulien opened his mouth to begin some kind of appeal and felt the words collapse on his breath, he could only stare at her. Her expression appeared impassive and grim. It did not change as she stepped forward, and turned her head again, but this time so that Lal and Sulien were on the side of the scarred flesh where no eye was left, and they were invisible to her. And as if they were not there, she walked slowly past them towards the house, leaving them behind as they ran stumbling up the valley's flank, away from the lights.

Una was stretched in the bed, her arms loosely spread, the blankets lying over her face like a layer of snow. Her bones seemed somehow painful to themselves; her cold blood seeped slackly through her aching veins. There was a chill in her flesh that would not disperse, even in sleep. She dreamt she was lying face-up in a field of stones, staring into the snowflakes settling over her, and woke without realising it, expect-ing to look up at black sky, and orchards of bristling stars. Sulien and Lal had been gone for perhaps two hours. Outside the room was panicked turmoil just barely restrained and ordered; she could hear doors banging, vehicles drawing up and speeding off. The evacuation was well underway. Una lay still, smiling under the sheet, into the dream-snow, with indistinct, sad triumph.

People were coming. She pushed the blankets away, heaved herself up on her elbows as the door was unlocked. Dama came in, with a heavyset man behind him.

She would have expected him to be luminous with rage and vengefulness. He seemed more fragile than that, his face tired.

'You knew,' he said to her, flatly. It was not a question, nor even exactly a reproach.

No one at the farm knew of the location of the other groups, or could have contacted him; it was not information to entrust to newcomers. Before now the farm's inmates had often gone weeks or months without seeing him, or hearing his voice. But this time he had called the place almost as soon as he had reached Tarquinia. The tension that had its source in this room had followed him all the way there.

'They're gone,' Una said. 'It makes no difference if I go too. You don't need to take me with you. Just leave me here.'

Dama stared bleakly at her. He could have left her had Mazatl not, twice, come so near her. She might possibly know no more than Lal or Sulien, but there was no way such a safe ignorance could be proved. He thought it was likely that at the least, she knew about Tarquinia. 'No,' he answered curtly, and turned to Baro. 'Get her up.'

Una swung her legs wearily out of the bed, and sat up. She made no protest as Baro picked up her wrists and fastened them together with thick tape, and she got to her feet docilely enough. But once standing she swayed and stumbled, so Baro caught her, and lifted her briskly into his arms. Una flinched into abrupt, violent life, twisting and struggling, disproportionately aghast at being held this way.

'Don't touch me. I can walk. I can't run away, but I don't need carrying.'

Baro would have ignored her, but Dama muttered, 'Let her walk if she wants to.'

Baro let Una down, and shoved her along behind Dama, out of the room and downstairs. The dizziness had passed now; she was out of breath almost at once, and her heart whirred painfully as Baro jostled her across the yard, but she did not again feel close to falling.

Already the farm seemed almost deserted; there could not have been more than thirty people left, and they were on the point of scattering. Dama had seen detailed evacuation plans conceived and fine-tuned before, with Delir in Holzarta; Una did not doubt that everyone here would be gone before the vigiles came, and most of them would not be caught.

They were heading towards the anonymous little car that had brought her here from Rome. Baro opened the door and pushed her in.

'Don't you want me to drive?' asked Baro, as Dama slid in quickly behind the controls.

'She's with me,' said Dama. Baro looked uncertain, shrugged, and ran off to join another group piling into a truck. Dama watched them leave. He was glad not to have to explain his need to keep Una with him, not to trust anyone else with her, for he could not have done so. He did not know what to do with her, but whatever decision to be made was his concern, his business, and he would make it alone. He waited until the truck was gone, and began to drive. The familiar pain set in, from wrist to shoulder, his breath changed to accommodate it, pain and silence simplifying things.

Una lay in the seat beside him, exactly as Baro had let her drop, limp and unmoving. She murmured almost dreamily, 'Where are you taking me?'

Dama cleared the drive and turned the car up into the woods. Una looked out at the darkness.

'Have you decided?' she continued in the same soft, far-off voice. 'Are you going to do it?'

Dama frowned, and did not answer her. Una closed her eyes with a tired sigh and was so quiet and passive for a while that he wondered if she could have fallen asleep.

At last she spoke again, with more urgency. 'Dama.'

'What?' snapped Dama, finally.

'He'll kill me,' she said.

'What are you talking about?' He made himself concentrate on the road.

'The man you left with today. The one who was outside my door. He will. As soon as he can.'

Dama's hands clenched on the control sticks of the car, as tight as the numbed fingers would go, locking the pain along his arms. He said fiercely, 'He won't touch you. He won't disobey me.'

'Won't he?' she asked drily, and Dama grimaced again. Una looked away at the trees. 'I don't know what you're thinking, Dama, or what you're going to do. But with him it was very clear. And you can't stay with me all the time.'

'God help him if he comes near you. I'll kill him.'

'Yes,' agreed Una. 'He knows that. But he'll still do it; he'll do it for you, because you can't.'

Suddenly the car stopped, jolting them both forward. Dama gave a little gasp, but remained gripping the controls, staring at the road, as if he had not noticed what had happened or did not know that it was he that had caused it. But then he let his hands fall into his lap, and slumped back, his eyes shut for a moment. 'You should have come with me when I asked you to,' he said, turning to gaze at her without lifting his head. 'You should have said yes, in the cave near Wolf Step. You'd have understood the task we face, you'd have been ready to do anything to see it done. You'd have stayed on my side.'

Though he believed this, she had been so adamant in refusal all this time that he expected her to deny it. But she became, if possible, more still, her gaze clouded and turned inwards, and at last she said very quietly, 'Yes. Perhaps I would.' Her eyes cleared again, focusing on him. She whispered, 'Or perhaps you'd never have come to this.'

Dama reached, left-handed, into his pocket, and drew out a knife. Una shivered faintly as she recognised it, a clumsy, heavy-handled thing he'd carried from Gaul to Rome. Dama had wanted her to take it once, and kill someone, a spy in the hills outside Holzarta. 'I was there already,' he said. He made his voice light, quite unconscious of the look of despair that caught at his face as he spoke. He cut the tape on her wrists.

Una glanced up quickly from the severed tape to his face, and then could not bear to look at him again. She muttered, 'Goodbye,' and slipped out of the car.

Dama looked back and watched her go. Tarquinia would have to be evacuated too; it did not seem to matter as it once had. Una's steps were unsteady and laborious, but she marched doggedly on, back up the road. She would keep going. Dama did not start the car until he could no longer see her.

Then he drove swiftly, heading north, soothed by the mindlessness of following a plan made before he'd come to Una's door. But an hour later, between flat cornfields, he stopped the car as abruptly as before by the side of the road, and sat there in the dark, he did not know how long, with his face in his hands.

XXVI

FIRELIGHT

Una crept along the dark road, her eyes on her chilled feet as they inched forward. Once she toppled onto her hands and knees, and had to remain crouched there, panting, for almost a minute before she could drag herself up again, pulling clumsily at the thin branches of a bush to help, and stagger on.

The blurred lights of a car swam in the dark. Una had been expecting this a long time, so long that she had almost ceased to think about it, as she had long ceased to think about food. She stepped forward, raising her arms.

'I'm Noviana Una,' she said to the vigiles inside

Almost as soon as she had told her story and climbed into the car, she slid into either sleep or unconsciousness on the back seat. Some time later she woke, shocked by the two strange male faces staring down at her. The car had stopped and the officers were bending over her in concern. The urgent lights of other vigile cars were streaming past, towards the farmhouse.

'They were starving you?' asked the young sergeant, indignantly.

'No,' she said. 'I did it myself.'

They looked confused, and she could not find the energy to explain further. One of them said briskly, 'Well, it looks like about time you stopped, miss.'

They took her to a small vigile station in the nearest village. After some confused fuss in the background to which Una, sitting vacantly in an interview room, paid no attention, they gave her a bowl of wheat porridge. Una stared at it for a while. She'd spent most of her life fearing and hating the vigiles. It was hard to make sense of their being so kind to her.

'Go on,' urged the sergeant, watching her. The spoon was lying loose in her hand, as if she didn't know what to do with it.

Una smiled up at him heavily. 'I was hungry for the first two days.

431

After that it goes away.' To her surprise, though, the first few mouthfuls tasted wonderful. Still, it took her a long time to get through the food, and for a while afterwards, instead of feeling stronger she felt even more tired and sick than before.

Another officer came into the grey little room. Una was blinking at a short summary of her evidence, her head pillowed on one arm. 'Caesar has asked for you to come to the Palace.'

Una raised her head, hesitating. 'I've already told you everything. He doesn't need to hear it from me.'

'Yes, but he would like to see you. Your brother and your friend are already with him.'

Una shut her eyes, feeling tears rise against the lids. She could not argue with anyone. Of course she wanted to go to them, she was not strong enough to withstand that, no resistance left for anything. 'All right,' she said. 'But only if I can go home and change my clothes. And go to the baths. I don't want to go to the Palace like this.'

As they drove into Rome she began to feel the food doing her some good. Her brain cleared, the exhaustion lifted. In a large bathhouse on the Field of Mars, she bathed intensively and at length, steaming, scrubbing and oiling her skin, washing her hair, lying in the caldarium until she felt the heat begin to thaw the empty cold in her blood. It was some time before she went near a mirror. Finally, when she had done all that was possible, she surveyed herself sternly, sighed, and looked away. Well, it was bad, but not to the point of being shocking, and not irreparable. Some of the women in the baths had noticed her gauntness with curious pity or distaste, but not all of them. There were plenty of slaves who looked worse.

She did not know what had happened to the key to her flat; the sergeant broke the lock for her. She looked around the blank clean surfaces she had left, feeling as if she had broken into a stranger's home. As if she were stealing, she found a long, elegant blue wool dress she had not worn since leaving Marcus, and put it on, belting a loose tunic over it. It was heavy wear for spring, but the layers would soften the sharp contours of her attenuated body, and a quiver of grateful pleasure at the warmth ran over her skin. She approached her reflection again to pluck her eyebrows, put on make-up, and tie back her clean hair. It was not that she was trying to look attractive, or even trying to hide the evidence of her fast, which would not be possible. But she wanted to look self-possessed – not weak, not a refugee.

It had begun to rain. The vigile car carried her across the Tiber, past the Colosseum, through the palace gates. Una looked up at the round stained-glass images of the gods, who all looked like Novii, like Marcus.

Someone came down the steps to meet the car. It was Acchan. He did not bow this time, but he smiled at her, and said, 'I'm glad to see you again.'

She followed Acchan through the palace towards Marcus' apartments, to the room painted with the orchard of the Hesperides and Atlas bearing up the sky, where she and Sulien had watched Marcus' first broadcast as Regent.

Una was crushed against Sulien as soon as the door opened. His body hid the room beyond, she saw no one else. Then he stepped back, hands still on her shoulders, taking in the state of her, and until he was finished Una stared rigidly at a loose ruck in the cloth of the borrowed tunic where her face had been pressed, unable to raise her eyes to his, or speak. *Please. Don't ask me.* It was more than she had any right to expect from Sulien, after this.

He let go of her softly, and said nothing.

Then she went into Lal's arms, and over Lal's shoulder she glanced warily into Marcus' face. He was hanging back, almost guiltily, and behind him were a man and a woman that for a tired second she did not recognise, before seeing that they were Delir and Ziye. For the moment their presence, too, seemed too baffling to cope with.

Lal let her go, and Una finally met Marcus' eyes. She wondered if she had thought marriage would somehow mark him visibly, like a dye. Certain tiny changes did strike her sharply: the length of his hair, the fact that she had not seen these clothes on him before. There was a second of raw indecision on how to greet each other; then, looking away again, Una held out her hand. Marcus pressed it loosely, briefly, but as he let go his fingers skimmed over hers, in a kind of restrained caress.

'What happened?' cried Lal.

There was a wide, bright fire at the far end of the room. The evening was cool enough to make it comforting, if not really necessary. Una moved quietly to it, sinking huddled onto a footstool and spreading her thin hands over the flames. Crouched there she felt a little safer from any exclamation at her appearance; she continued trying to ward it off with the set of her body and the expression on her face. Sulien had followed her, his stance close beside her masked her a little from the others, without his even realising it.

She said, 'He let me go.'

Delir looked up at her quickly. 'Did he?'

A painful eagerness brightened his face for an instant. He had given Una a jaunty, encouraging smile of welcome as she came into the room, but he had not got up, or spoken until now. He sat on the couch near the fire as if he had been thrown there, and had been too badly hurt to move. The smile burnt itself out immediately.

Ziye said, 'It's been a long time, Una.' She seemed little changed, either by time or incarceration. But though she nodded politely at Una, and seemed to have her back turned slightly to Delir, all her attention was really on him. She was alert, standing guard over him, ready to handle Una or anything else that came through the door for his sake.

'When did you get here?' asked Una.

'Two days ago,' said Ziye. 'Marcus has been wonderful. But then, of course, we couldn't find Lal ...'

Lal had wedged herself between Delir and Ziye, nestled thankfully against her father. Delir put his arm round her, fondly chafing her shoulder. But his face remained blank, desolate.

'But the important thing is that you're all safe now,' finished Ziye firmly.

Una nodded, and turned her face toward the fire. She whispered, 'Have they caught him?'

'No.' Marcus, apparently being careful not to trespass too close to her, or Sulien, was isolated in the centre of the room.

Even more quietly, she asked, 'What has he done?'

It was Sulien who answered. 'He destroyed four trains in Nionian Terranova. 1,716 people, all together.'

He laid a hand on her hot hair, as she let her head droop forward. She found enough voice to mutter, 'But we are not at war.'

'It was close, as you can imagine,' said Marcus.

She was not surprised. But her body was soft and hushed with guilt. And for Delir it was the same, but worse. He burst out, ostensibly informing Una but really helpless, protesting, 'The Nionians want him.'

Marcus was still and grave. 'He killed a great many of their people. Lord Kato, for one.'

'I know. I know,' said Delir, anguished. 'But what will they do to him?'

'They'll execute him,' responded Marcus, quietly.

'*How?*' Delir breathed the question like a sob, and when Marcus said nothing, he supplied, 'They will crucify him. Or something even worse.'

'If the Nionians can be persuaded to let him be dealt with here, given the change in the law, he would most likely be shot.'

By the fire, Una shuddered slightly. She did not know why she should shrink at the thought of Dama's death. She remembered the smooth point of the gun, sliding over her face. But intimacy survived, against her will.

'And if not, you will let them do what they want with him,' said Delir. But it was not an accusation, more like a groan of pain.

Marcus looked at him soberly. 'It may not be in my hands. My uncle's health is much improved. If I am responsible, then I will do what is necessary. I think it's – premature to torment yourself. He has not been arrested yet.'

Delir rocked forward, a cramped, trapped movement. 'Of course he must not escape. I don't hope for that. But how can I wish him dead?'

Ziye said with sudden fierceness, 'You don't have to think about it at all. Forget about him. He has nothing to do with you any more. You're not responsible for him, or whatever he has become.'

Delir shook his head blindly. 'We can't be sure what made him into this. Surely it could have been prevented. Surely something could have been done.'

'He's not a child. And he's not your son. He did these things by himself. It's been almost four years since we even saw him. You did more for him than could be asked of anyone, and what does he do? He abducted your daughter.'

Delir clasped Lal tighter, and moaned, 'Please, for God's sake, don't repeat what he has done.'

Ziye subsided with a sigh of concerned impatience. Marcus came closer to him, compassionate but subtly reserved, cold. 'She's right, Delir. He's in your debt, not you in his. He can't repay it now. But you've helped more people than him. All of us here.'

Delir murmured dully, 'It began with him.'

'It's late,' said Marcus, gently, after a pause. 'Stay here tonight. At least you have Lal back, whatever else has happened.'

Delir's eyes shone, wetly. He blinked and smiled, trying to make a joke. 'Just a minute ago we were in prison, and my little girl was locked in a cellar; now here we are staying the night in the palace. How fast we are going up in the world.'

More tentatively, Marcus turned to Una and Sulien. 'You both must be so tired. It would be easier for you to stay than go home now ...'

Sulien looked Marcus over: this calm, professional politician whose cautious gaze at them was loaded with silent, subdued appeal. A kind of exasperated awareness that he had missed Marcus tugged at him, and he muttered, 'All right. Thanks.'

Marcus smiled so openly and gladly that Sulien was more touched than he wanted to be.

Una had not responded to Marcus' offer, but she rose passively to follow Sulien and the rest, when the servants came to show them to the guest rooms. But suddenly Marcus reached for her, catching her wrist and saying in a low voice, 'Una—'

Tamely, mechanically, Una stopped. Both Lal and Sulien glanced back, curious and anxious, but they let themselves be guided on, out of the room.

In silence Una and Marcus turned towards each other, though her head remained a little lowered; she would not quite focus her eyes on his face.

She said, 'I could never see what he felt, or what he was thinking. He didn't want me to; he stopped me. That's what I think now. And yet I did think we understood each other. He said to me ...' She was thinking of what she and Dama had said in the car, before he cut the tape that bound her wrists, but found she didn't want to repeat it, and her voice trailed off.

Very cautiously and slowly, Marcus touched her, running his hands over her arms, feeling through the sleeves how close to the surface were her bones. 'So thin,' he murmured.

'Yes,' she said, wearily. 'I'll be better soon.'

Again she felt too tired and overwhelmed to explain, but Marcus said quietly, 'You were trying to force his hand. Kind of ... holding yourself hostage.' Una looked up at him, startled, and he insisted softly, 'I *know* you.'

And he slid his arms round her. Una sank forward against him, feeling her diminished weight as he supported it, as she'd felt the slightness of her own fingers, weighed in his when he took her hand. The solid warmth of his body was better than that of the fire, it sheltered her. She could not ask herself to step away; it was too much. She rested languidly in his arms, almost half asleep.

Then at last she whispered, 'Where is your wife?'

She felt Marcus tense slightly. 'She's in Nionia, with her family.'

Una hesitated. 'Is she coming back?'

He held her more tightly, willing her not to pull back. 'Yes,' he admitted. 'I think so.'

Una sighed, and put up her hand to stroke his face. 'I couldn't answer your letter,' she whispered. 'How could I? What was there to say if I couldn't see you?'

'You're here with me now,' he said firmly, and kissed her. Una became even more limp than before, her arms falling loose from his back, but her lips softened against his, parting in a soundless little gasp. Marcus held her up, half-carried her into the bedroom. They undressed and held each other, nothing more. Una lay warm against him, her fingers spread on his chest, asleep almost at once. Marcus dozed, though not being as exhausted as she, he could not quite relax; he kept waking to look searchingly at her pale, drained face. And he stayed very still, not wanting to wake her.

But once her eyes flickered open, and he whispered, stroking her hair, 'What will you do tomorrow? Is this the last time? Will you leave me again?'

Una shut her eyes again with a small protesting moan. 'I don't know. How can I know? I can't bear it.' She turned over, kissing the base of his throat, hiding her face from him.

XXVII

HOLZARTA

A week afterwards, Sulien visited the new, larger flat in the Field of Mars where Lal was staying with Delir and Ziye. As the doors of the lift opened on their floor, he was surprised to find Delir waiting on the other side, with a bag in his hand. He had an agitated, fidgety look; he rose almost onto tiptoe, and smiled up at Sulien, but in a bright disordered way if he couldn't quite see him clearly.

He said hurriedly, 'You're here to see Lal. I never thanked you for getting her out of that place. I was hard on you when you were in Holzarta; forgive me. You're not of our religion – well, nor is Ziye, what matters more is the kind of person you are. You've shown you're capable of protecting her.'

Sulien stared, and shuffled, trapped like a rat in the lift, feeling redness sweep across his face. 'Well, ah, thank you, but ...' he stammered. 'But I just came to – and anyway, with what happened with Dama, I couldn't have got away alone, she helped me as much as I helped her.'

Delir blinked and looked bewildered, and to Sulien's intense relief the almost manic glint cleared from his eyes. 'Of course. Well. You're a good boy.' He clapped Sulien on the shoulder as they changed places, Delir entering the lift.

'Where are you going?' asked Sulien, relieved by now that Delir was leaving.

'I don't want to go on scrounging off Marcus for ever. I had some friends who were keeping money for me before we scattered from Holzarta; it wasn't possible to collect all of it. And one of them has an idea about a textiles venture I might get involved with. I have to catch a train.'

He shut the door of the lift. But through the grille, Sulien could see his expression turn hollow, void, as he sank out of sight.

The trees were just coming into leaf, scraps of piercing green crumpled and wet like the wings of newly-hatched moths. The damp air was full of birds – thrushes, blackbirds, woodlarks – shouting above the white blast of the river. Yet the Holzarta gorge seemed unutterably silent to Delir, as he climbed along it, upstream, silent on some dark, nerve-deep level of memory. What he had said to Sulien, as well as to Ziye and Lal, had been true. As he headed to Gaul he had convinced himself that this visit to the remains of the camp in the Pyrenees was only a whim he might perhaps allow himself, after he'd completed the serious work of reclaiming his money and speaking to Eonus about importing cloth. And so he had felt no need to tell anyone – it was too irrational and private to speak of. But now, wading his way through the undergrowth, he knew differently. This return had always been his reason for coming, and he was certain of what he was going to find.

It took him a while to find the first ladder down to the hidden walkways. They had always been invisible below the edge of the low cliff until you were almost on top of them, and all the landmarks by which Delir had navigated had altered, fallen down or grown in the years since he'd been here. Now, when he found the ladder, the rungs were clogged with grass and brambles. Delir crouched and kicked away at the weeds until he was able to struggle down.

He knew what the vigiles and time would have done, but still it clawed at him to see the ruin of the camp. The doors, even the walls of the cabins had been smashed in, the broken boards waterlogged and rotten. Young saplings were growing up through the fallen roofs of some of them. Lal's paintings were still visible, but blurred with moss and decay.

There was a thin wisp of blue smoke rising from a further turn of the path. Until now it had been hidden among the trees.

Dama, hunched over his little fire, did not seem remotely surprised to see him. One corner of his mouth lifted in a joyless smile of greeting, while the rest of his pale face remained heavy, unresponsive, dead. 'What did you come here for?' he asked, calmly.

Delir stared at him. Composed as Dama seemed, there was something exhausted, hunted about the crouched body, the eyes that were fixed yet not focused on anything. Delir clung to this as a shred of hope. He answered softly, 'So that you could tell me why you have done these terrible things.'

Dama sighed. 'You must have heard my reasons. What else do you think I can tell you? What other reasons would there be?'

Delir shook his head. 'Don't you feel anything for those people? Any remorse?'

Dama gazed at his damp campfire, or through it a mile deep into the earth. 'It doesn't matter. What I feel.'

'It does matter. And you must tell me.'

'Won't bring anybody back,' said Dama tersely.

'No. Nothing you can feel or do will ever be enough, that doesn't excuse you from offering it.'

Dama gave another mirthless half-smile. 'Do soldiers feel regret for the lives they take?'

Delir grimaced. 'Soldiers aren't the ones who start the wars.'

'All right, then. The leaders. The emperors.'

'What about them?' snapped Delir. 'How does anyone else's wickedness justify anything you have done?'

'If there's wickedness in the world, maybe someone has to risk being wicked himself,' whispered Dama. 'Take it on, so that it can be cleaned away from the future. So that people will be spared.'

Delir watched him coldly for a while. He said, quoting, '"How is it that a mortal can wish for another mortal the annihilation of his body, or of his soul, if he has sense enough to know that he himself is mortal?"'

Dama slumped, his head drooping, his eyes hidden. He conceded, 'I didn't plan for the people on the passenger train to be killed. Not that it makes any difference. We did it. I did it, I am responsible.'

'Yes,' said Delir, edging closer to the fire. 'I believe you *do* know that. I think you *are* sorry for it. Or why aren't you with your people? What are you doing here, all by yourself? The vigiles will come here. It's such an obvious place to try, no one would really expect you to *be* here. But they would have to look.'

Dama looked up, smiling, a wide, frightening crack across his face. 'Oh, they've been already. You know I can hide, I can get away, if I have to. I didn't want them to find me. And people do what I want. Almost always. Except for a few.'

Delir drew back a little, disconcerted. 'I don't think your life can have gone as you wanted,' he said, quietly.

Dama shook his head, first slowly, then more and more vehemently. 'Not what I mean,' he said. 'But the things I want people to do ... if I want them clearly enough – one at a time – they happen.'

God help him, he's mad, thought Delir. Gently, he ventured, 'Did you want me to find you, then?'

As before, Dama stared down into the invisible subterranean space, without answering. Finally he glanced around at the ruined cabins and muttered sorrowfully, 'Look at what they did to this place.'

'They will find you. They'll give you to the Nionians.'

Dama nodded. 'And then what will happen?' he asked, a fractured

440

lightness in his voice. 'Will they finish the job?' He lifted his wrists, then let them drop.

Delir shuddered inwardly at the memory of the tortured young body, almost a corpse, he'd pulled down off the cross; the life he'd freed to do these things.

'What are *you* going to do, Delir?' continued Dama, a flicker of challenge bringing some life into the blank blue eyes. 'Here I am. You've found me. Are you going to let me escape?'

A fugitive, desperate feeling began to press on Delir, as if it were he who was the hunted criminal, trapped in a corner. There was no escape. He pulled himself up to answer grimly, 'No. People have to be safe from you.'

Dama said in a tiny wisp of a voice, 'Maybe that's true.'

'You must give yourself up,' said Delir.

'To execution?' murmured Dama, his eyes hooded again. 'To *that?*'

'*No,*' insisted Delir, fiercely, and fell silent, his fists and teeth clenched. 'I will do it. I will keep you somewhere where you can't harm anyone else. Where you can begin to redeem yourself.'

Dama looked at him, startled and cynical. 'What?' he asked, blurting out a laugh, his hands trembling. 'You're going to lock me up somewhere and keep an eye on me – for ever?'

Delir said, feeling as if the word were a cliff from which he was hurling himself, 'Yes.'

Dama stared, his mouth a little open. 'How do you think you can do that?'

'I will do it, and you will come with me willingly. Because it is your only chance.'

A distant tenderness came into Dama's face. 'You're twice my age.'

'And you'll outlive me?' said Delir, strained and breathless. 'Well, I hope by then, these terrible intentions will have left you.'

Dama shook his head. 'I had your daughter pushed into a van at gunpoint and locked up under the house,' he said in a low, tense voice. 'Why would you even think of doing this? What about her, and Ziye, anyway?'

Delir let out a long, snagging sigh of distress. 'I will write to them. I can send money. And I *will* see them again somehow. I can trust my wife and my daughter, and there are people I can trust to protect them. But how can I trust you? And where will your soul go if you die now?'

Dama was silent. Then he said softly, 'You can't give up your whole life for me, Delir.'

Delir said, 'Somebody has to.'

441

The letter had arrived at noon. It was long, and at times incoherent with apologies, endearments and promises. It explained that Delir had also forwarded to them two thirds of the money from Eonus. It told everything except, of course, where he had gone. Curled motionless in a chair, in the pretty living room of their flat, Lal read it over from the beginning again, turning the pages silently with slow, careful fingers. I'd only just got him back, Lal's mind whimpered, groping for something to keep from being blown away into panic, she gripped hard onto the thought of the solitude in the farmhouse cellar, the escape with Sulien. She didn't want to cope without her father, but the implicit claim of the letter was true; she could.

Ziye was pacing rapidly back and forth across the floor, her face set. Abruptly, in furious mid-stride, she flicked the pages out of Lal's hands and tossed them into the air.

'Don't,' said Lal, in a low, reproachful voice, quietly retrieving them, refolding them carefully. The two women looked at each other, guarded and frightened, assessing each other. Both of them were thinking cagily: we are not mother and daughter. And Ziye was a stranger now; Lal had never seen her like this, uncontrolled, recklessly angry, weeping.

'He's betrayed us,' said Ziye. 'Abandoned us.'

'Don't say that.'

'What else would you call it?'

'I can understand why he wants to save Dama.'

Ziye stared at her in disbelief, which gave way to tired exasperation. 'I can't. Dama's made his bed. What happens to him is not our problem. Why can't Delir leave it at that?'

'I can see why,' repeated Lal, in a whisper.

Ziye flung herself into a chair opposite Lal. She said drily, 'Heaven help us. No doubting whose child you are. Next you'll be telling me you want to let him keep it secret.'

'No,' said Lal. 'We'll have to tell Marcus. Only ...' She stiffened. 'People won't think too badly of him, will they? It's not as if he's joining Dama. He wouldn't be punished – not much, anyway, would he?'

'He's got friends in high places,' said Ziye grimly.

'Then we'll tell everyone. And they'll find them.'

And what would that mean, what would happen to Dama then? It was too awful to think of. Lal steadied herself again. One thing at a time. They could not possibly have the right to keep this hidden, she had to start with that.

Ziye sighed. In a voice more like her own, she said, 'I don't believe that.'

XXVIII

ISLAND

On bright days they could see the dark cliffs of the nearest island, looking close and clear in the cold grey-green sea. But they were five miles distant, and though there were a handful of caved-in stone houses on the hills beyond, there were no people left, except for the occasional visits of lobster fishers from islands closer to the Caledonian western coast; Delir could sometimes see their lights moving in the dark, across the sound. He had arranged by longdictor and letter for the fishermen to come out of their way every three weeks to deposit packs of flour, meat and powdered milk on the pale beach, in exchange for the bundles of money he left out on a stone. Some day he might leave a sealed letter beside it, for Ziye and Lal. He had put it about that a hermit had moved onto the island to spend his life under a vow of silence and isolation, never to be seen by anyone. It was almost true. He had some hope that they might even learn to live without these visits quite soon. There was so much red dulse in the shallow water to be boiled up, lobster and crab were so easy to catch on the boulders at the base of the cliffs. There were eggs, although not from chickens or ducks: as spring came the stacked cliffs became riotous with nesting guillemots and kittiwakes, screaming all day from the first hint of dawn. He had a pouch of wheat and barley seeds to plant later in the year. It might be possible to be forgotten. In the rain the little scrap of earth and rock seemed enclosed in immeasurable walls of opaque glass, so thick that from the sea outside the island must be as invisible to the world as the world was from its shores. The wind did its best to erase it. There were no trees.

Better to think no further than the end of each day.

But the rough slopes and shoreline were Imperial with gold and purple: violets, saxifrage, tormentil. Seals lolled on the beach and cartwheeled blissfully in the water. The comical little puffins uttered plaintive creaks to one another on the rocks. On blue summery days, Delir thought it was a more beautiful place than either one of them deserved.

They had spent the first few nights in a tent, ripped at and pounded by the wind, the first days clearing out and fixing plastic sheeting over the least dilapidated of the tiny abandoned cottages. Once it was stable enough to offer them some kind of shelter they began work scavenging from the carcasses of the other buildings, and from the wreckage that had long ago fallen into the shell of this one, to rebuild the roof properly, and fill the holes in its walls. Delir was not certain the results would not crash in on them one day, but it kept out most of the rain. They burnt peat to cook, and to keep warm. Delir fixed cradles for a heavy bar either side of the door, on the outside. On days when the fishermen's boat was due, he locked Dama in.

They did not speak much. Dama seemed to have retreated into an adolescent inarticulacy. He scarcely volunteered a word, answered most questions with monosyllables, though he did whatever he was told with tongue-tied promptness. At first Delir did not resist the silence. He was not sure he particularly wanted to talk to Dama, not yet.

But later he began to worry. It was as if Dama were being hollowed out from within. On the clearest days he sat on the clifftops, staring west towards the discs of silver light that lay on the sea, the meadows buzzing with colour all around him, and he saw nothing. Delir was certain he saw nothing. There was a blindness, a deadness that seemed to claim a little more of him every day, like an infection, like the tide on the rocks. Delir tried to hope this was for the best – for the distant, incomplete best – this closing down, the forming of a pupa in which something new could take shape. How else should he be, now? Wasn't it inevitable, and necessary, that Dama should suffer? Yet he began to fear that Dama's point about the likely extent of his life was not true; one day he would simply stop moving, sit down nervelessly on the dense, salty grass and forget to eat, to drink, to breathe. Watching him up on the cliffs, Delir became aware too of how high they were, how sharp the rocks were below.

There was nothing more he could do to keep Dama physically safe. But he tried to treat him with a little more gentleness, to give him some encouragement.

'I think it is good that you are here,' he said, one night, as they cooked cockles over the fire. Even huddled close to the flames, they could not quite drive the pervading damp of the day out of their clothes. 'You did a good thing, agreeing to come.'

There was a pause in which Dama seemed wearily contemplating the energy necessary to haul a breath into his lungs and speak. He muttered dully, 'I will never be any good to anyone, staying here.'

'There's me,' said Delir. 'You can help me to live here. As you are doing every day. That's enough for now.'

'But you shouldn't be here at all. I'm keeping you here and it's wrong. It's bad for you.'

'I chose to do this. You didn't force me to it. And maybe some good will come of being here that we can't see yet.'

Dama nodded, with another dutiful effort.

'Try to ask only simple things from yourself,' urged Delir.

They did without news-sheets, without a radio. Better not to know, Delir felt. Dama acquiesced to this, as to everything. He tried, he genuinely tried to do as Delir encouraged and not let himself think beyond the close of each day, through the tasks that would keep them both alive. In a way it worked. In a way his problem was the reverse, that he could not think even that far. His thoughts could not get off the ground, and so could not attempt to escape the island, but nor could they live here, even if his body could. It was not boredom, there was plenty to do. He waded in the shallows, scraping limpets and mussels off the rocks. Spring had scarcely warmed this sea, the cold gripped like two garottes around his calves. He could work, he could concentrate as necessary, but even the shells he touched, the knife in his hand were laminated away from him. The world was one endless glass surface, into which nothing could put down roots.

He carried his harvest onto the beach and sat down near the waterline, once again letting his gaze lie like driftwood, inert on the waves. He leant forward and scored a curve in wet sand with his knife: a letter U. Then he scowled in dull scorn at himself, and scrubbed it out with his foot, unable to wait even for the next wave to come and smooth it away.

A wooden packing crate still lay on the stones further up the beach. The fishermen had been, three days before. Dama had never seen them, and he wondered how many of them there were, how old or young they might be – though he knew he was making himself think about it; he was not really curious. He'd seen the crate before, but had not been been able to stir himself even to move it. Listlessly, he got up to do it now, and as he moved it he saw that under the straw that had padded a couple of cartons was a lining of old news sheets.

Dama picked them out, his hands slow with the habitual lethargy and with a kind of tired reverence for anything from the world outside. The news-sheets were not international. They seemed to cover only the inner islands and a corner of the mainland. There was nothing of what he knew Delir wished to avoid: Nionia, or the hunt for himself. All the bulletins, more than a month old now, concerned lambs to be sold at market, a wedding, a few natural deaths.

445

On the reverse of one, far down the page, there was an alert about a slave, a young man, who had gone missing from a villa by the sea. There was a small picture of him.

It was a while before this seemed to have any impact on him, there was such a distance for the short sentences to travel in order to reach him. Even when it did, it was faint at first. Dama glanced guiltily up the beach, towards the cliffs. He had left Delir mending nets near the house, though he would probably appear soon. He did not like to let Dama out of his sight for long. And Dama did not know why he was behaving furtively; he was doing nothing wrong. Then he turned the news sheet over to look at the date. Yes, it was one of the older ones. He flicked through the others with the dim beginnings of tension, arranging them into order.

The slave was still missing a week after the first news sheet was printed. Dama grew hesitantly, painfully excited for him. Go on, he urged him silently, through the print. Don't be afraid, keep going, you can do it.

But a later sheet announced he had been caught, only a few miles from where he had begun. There was little indication of what had happened to him. Probably no more than a whipping, from the sound of it. Probably he was not dead, however weakened and in pain he might be; he would be back at work for his master again, right at this moment.

Dama screwed the paper into a tight ball and buried it under the stones.

He carried on as before, of course. But he was not the same. He was angry. At first the feeling was negligible: a small restlessness that nagged at him from time to time. Delir saw only that he was now sometimes able to plough little spasms of energy into tasks where he had invariably been mechanical and lifeless before. And Dama would not tell Delir what he was thinking. He did not want it to seem that he was bearing his confinement with anything but patience.

It had felt as if all the ordinary corrupted world were as distant as another sun. It was not, it was obscenely close, and alive, only a barrier like a breaking eggshell held it out. Had he not said to Una that there was nowhere to go to escape from it? Why should that have ceased to be true, even for a penitent recluse, or whatever he was now? No one could get out of the world except by death; it was cowardice and feebleness to try.

Three weeks later, the night after the lobster-fishers had been again, he had a dream.

He dreamt he was exactly where he was, curled up asleep, close

446

to the remains of the fire, on the little bed opposite Delir's. But Delir was awake, sitting rigidly on the edge of his bed, glaring at Dama with bright, furious eyes.

'Wake up!' he insisted, in a voice like rushing wind or flames, only far louder. 'Wake up now!'

Dama thought he woke reluctantly, frightened.

And it was not really Delir; Dama understood that almost at once. He looked as normal: a small, rather fragile-looking middle-aged man, but this being was as incandescent and dangerous as melted steel, on fire underneath his skin. He was full of hot, terrible light, but this was hidden, miraculously contained by the body that should have been scorched away in an instant. Dama understood that his eyes were not made to perceive this brightness, which was revealed to him in an awful, fitful smouldering, melting away some intangible barriers of consciousness that flinched and shrivelled like membranes of flesh.

Dama whispered to him, terrified, 'I'm sorry.'

And the terrible voice said, as he had known it would. 'That is not enough.' Dama twisted away, burying his face, and heard: 'There is no hiding from me, or what you have to do.'

Then he was no longer in the cottage, or on the island. He was in Rome, which was also Bianjing, and Cynoto, where he had never been. The cities were heaped on top of each other, in layers that fused and floated apart, and drifted through one another. People waded and fled through the multiple streets, and tried to hide themselves, but they were also burning, not in the contained and perpetual way of the figure ahead of him, but simply blazing and staggering. So they shone, and were discovered, or curled themselves up in crevices, and burnt away into ash.

'You have not finished here,' said the bright, punishing authority, who was with him.

Dama tried to say something, either a confession that it was true, or a protest, or a plea, or all of these. But he could not speak in this place, he found; he could not even move. He choked, and strove, appalled.

'If you stop,' said the spirit, 'then you murdered them. Unless you go on, they died for nothing.'

Dama wanted to say that there was no more in him, that every attempt had failed, and there was nothing now he could do. Of course, he did not need to speak, his thoughts were instantly known.

The voice was low and dreadful as an earthquake now. 'Do not dare abandon them,' it warned him.

And then he was alone, and somewhere among pine trees where he was able to think normally, clearly. And he thought that he had come very close to tugging the future down to earth, many times, and it was Marcus Novius, each time, who had prevented him.

Then a kind of turbulent roar, like the noise of aircraft, surged through everything, and then he really did wake.

At first he could not move. In the first half-stunned seconds of awareness, he began to cry, shuddering and stifled, so as not to wake Delir. His body felt weak and defenceless, and he wanted to pull the covers more tightly round him and allow the sobs to come more freely, to comfort himself. But instead, he slid out of bed, and reached for his clothes, gathering them into a bundle under his arm.

Before turning for the door, he looked down at Delir. Asleep on his side, he seemed even more small and vulnerable than Dama had remembered, older. Very carefully, Dama bent over him and, as lightly as possible, kissed his cheek.

Then he crept out of the little house, and down the slope towards the beach. The wind scraped the remaining warmth of his bed from his skin. Dama lowered his head and lunged along into it, shivering, struggling into his clothes as he went; he pulled a waterproof jacket over everything else, drew up the hood, and tightened it. He slid down the stones onto the sand, walked straight towards the sea.

He could see a dot of light, far out in the dark. The fishermen were still working, close to the opposite island, or camped upon it.

Dama stepped into the black water. It was so cold that he could feel his blood shrinking away from the skin in protest, the dry flesh above begging to be spared. He forced each inch under the surface, gasping, until he was heart-deep in the cold, then made himself drop forward, lifting his feet from the bottom, and begin to swim.

At least the sea was calm. He'd learnt to swim haphazardly as a child in Rome. Before it had been discovered he could sing, when he had still been with his mother, she had sometimes accompanied her mistress to the baths, to be on hand with scented oils, strigils, towels. Sometimes she'd been able to take him along and teach him for a little while. As a slow wave lifted him to its crest, he remembered her, more clearly than he had for years. He never normally thought of her. And it was almost as long since he had been in the water. His body should have been strong, sturdy, but of course he was no athlete; he didn't even have the full use of both arms. It was easiest to float on his back and kick along that way, but then the cold licked hungrily through the hood of the jacket, against his head. He knew little about the sea, nothing of where the currents would pull him, but he had known before he touched the water that he was probably killing himself. He doubted the chances could be above one in ten that this was escape, rather than suicide. There was no getting used to this cold, it fed mercilessly on him. Soon the fingers even on his better hand were blunted and foreign to him, his feet two vague and unwieldy blocks. Though his mind was still clear enough under the ongoing shock of the cold, that would go numb too, in the end. And when he pulled himself upright in the water, and tried to look back, he found the island he'd come from was lost in the dark. Even if he had chosen to, he could never find his way back now. Everything was utterly formless, featureless: he could see nothing except the surface of the water, black as oil, and the lights in the distance.

In the morning Delir woke to find himself alone in the little house. At first, of course, he assumed Dama was somewhere nearby, outside. But when his first call went unanswered, panic suddenly hooked at him, and he ran to the cliffs, scanning the rocks below in desperation, shouting Dama's name. He searched on, praying that in a moment Dama's voice behind him would release him. But soon the silence confirmed to him that he would find either a body or nothing. Finally, he sagged onto the stones on the beach, staring with tear-blurred eyes at the steel sea into which Dama had vanished.

He was free; when the fishermen came back he could go home. But he would have to take this failure with him. Imprisoned on the island until then, alone, all the slow patterns of survival were snagged and warped, it was torture now to try and capture the patience necessary for starting fires or preparing food, while struggling with a rage of frustration and loneliness. It was two days before it even occurred to him that Dama might possibly be alive.

A sudden jolt of dread, worse than grief, impelled Delir down to the beach. He lit a fire on the stones, signalled to the empty sea with a mirror. But he knew there was no one to see it, and it would be eighteen days before he could even tell anyone.

XXIX

COLOSSEUM

Drusus regarded himself disconsolately, half-naked before the mirror while the slaves stood around him quietly, proffering choices of clothes. He supposed he had to believe that the web of scars across his left cheek, and the ones under his chin and at the corner of his mouth were invisible to other people, as everyone told him, but to him they still seemed disfiguring and vulgar. There was no sign his nose had ever been broken; it had been set, and had healed as straight as before. The grid of hard white scars on his hand was certainly visible, left not by the attack itself, but from the surgeries to repair the damage. The hand was sound enough now, but he had a weakened grip, and the beginnings of arthritis. There was sometimes a ringing in his left ear; he was convinced he was slightly deaf there. His consciousness of all these things was never far from the surface, but it was redoubled now that at last he was in Rome again.

He selected a dark blue tunic, motioned to the slave to drape over it a blue pallium bordered with green.

'It's a pity you have to go to the Colosseum,' said Lucius fretfully, behind him.

Drusus rolled his eyes as the slave knotted and pinned a white fascalia around his neck.

'I think it's dangerous,' complained Lucius.

'Well, I assure you, I don't feel remotely like going, and except for Uncle Titus, nobody wants me there. But it would be ridiculous for there not to be Games and it would be ridiculous for me not to be there. The only reason you can get out of it is because you're an embarrassment.'

Lucius looked at Drusus' reflection with wide-eyed anxious hurt, forcing from Drusus the familiar, irritable twinge of pity for him. His father was too easy and exposed a target for the load of bitterness within him.

'There, never mind,' he said roughly.

'I suppose at least you like the Games,' suggested Lucius timidly.

Drusus sighed. 'Not in this company,' he muttered.

A car came for him from the Palace. Drusus, feeling stripped and raw to any slight, thought it insultingly old and plain. There was a reception to get through, before they went to the Colosseum to celebrate Faustus' resumption of duties. Drusus steeled himself for it.

He was aware of the driver watching him. He knew he was being watched wherever he went. Even in his father's house on the Caelian, there were guards and supposed slaves who had not been there before, and who were never far away from him.

The party was centred in the gallery where the painting of Oppius Novius subduing the Nionians had once hung. Drusus looked for it, but was disgusted to see it had been removed, doubtless out of tact towards the sensibilities of Marcus' new wife. Not only that, but it was the new portrait of Noriko, commissioned for the wedding, that hung there now. Faustus stood below it and beamed benignly at his guests. The ring of State was on his finger.

Drusus wondered where the original painting was, and if there were any chance he could have it. He sighed, wandered further into the room and, looking for a drink, encountered Varius. They were both unpleasantly startled; Drusus recoiled a little and Varius reacted with a restrained twitch of aversion, but looked at him squarely. Drusus felt a humiliating desire to flee mingled with a quiver of masochistic power. He hated the knowledge that his life had hung on Varius' action, but it occurred to him that Varius would be no happier at having saved him, or having to see him.

'Varius!' he said, forcing a defiant friendliness into his voice. 'Are you coming to the Games?'

'No,' said Varius, shortly.

'What a shame. Marcus looks well, doesn't he? It must be a weight off his shoulders.'

'Perhaps.'

But Marcus was in the centre of the room with Noriko, self-possessed and professionally good-humoured, surrounded by people, and noticing everything. He caught Drusus' eye for a fraction of a second, smiled, and thereafter continued to observe him quietly without seeming to do so. Stupid old fool, Drusus thought, looking back at Faustus, who gave him a wave and a confused smile. Why bother with this? Can't you see you'll be an irrelevance? Marcus will be running everything.

'No progress catching that fanatic?' he asked. Varius looked past Drusus impatiently, his teeth gritted. Drusus felt a little glow of perverse

451

triumph. He took a drink from a waiter and continued pleasantly, 'Well, I suppose sometimes there's nothing you can do.'

'Drusus,' said Varius calmly. 'You seem to think that because of what happened in Sina, or because you're not in prison or dead as you deserve, I must pretend I don't know what you've done, and what you are. You can go and sit in the Colosseum with people for whom that's true – for now. But I have nothing to say to you, and you are nothing to me.'

He turned away. Drusus gulped resentfully at his wine. Marcus moved into the space Varius had left and asked, politely and inevitably, 'How are you getting on in Canaria?'

'Fine,' muttered Drusus. He felt a film of sweat coating his skin at being this close to his cousin. Marcus stood there looking so polished and civilised, his presence made Drusus' nerves replay treacherously the sensation of his bones cracking under those fists. His mended hand clenched painfully.

'You haven't met my wife.'

Noriko inclined her head, decorously gave Drusus her hand, and said nothing. She was dressed in the freshest of Roman fashions, her hair gathered up into a lovely mound of loops and braids, hanging in long ringlets down her back. With her dark hair and creamy skin she reminded Drusus just a little of Tulliola. He smiled at her wistfully, suddenly moved. Startled, Noriko smiled back.

'Are you sure I can't get you to come?' said Marcus to Varius, later.

'I don't like the Games. And I don't like your cousin. I'm not Imperial, I can get out of it.'

'Then how are you going to celebrate the Emperor's return to power?' asked Marcus, with veiled irony. 'Are you seeing your family?'

Varius smiled. 'I celebrate by avoiding them. They've found someone they want me to meet. Again.'

'You could,' suggested Marcus. Varius' face went still, closed. 'I'm sorry,' said Marcus hastily. 'Stupid. You don't want to. Don't do it, of course.'

Varius looked down and Marcus thought he would change the subject. But at last he muttered hesitantly, 'Maybe it's not as bad an idea as it was.' He hadn't looked up. 'But it's still not good.'

'Then of course you're right,' said Marcus. More darkly he added, 'No one can force you.'

Varius glanced at Noriko, who was behaving faultlessly. 'Things are bad?' he murmured.

Marcus also turned to watch her. 'My parents' marriage was perfect whenever there were people watching them.' He looked back at Varius. 'It's not her,' he said. And he went back to join his wife.

452

The weather was bad for Faustus' celebrations. They had hoped for a blue summer day; instead the city was wrapped in rain. Varius drove out of the city on the Via Ostiensis, into the countryside between Rome and Acilia. He knew the way by heart, although this was only the fourth time he'd ever travelled it. He had had no say in Gemella's place of burial, of course. He hadn't been there, her funeral was long over by the time he was out of prison. Not that there was anything wrong with the quiet necropolis along a minor road that her parents had chosen.

He sat in the car for a little while, prevaricating, and hoping the weather would clear. The rain only thickened, and finally he emerged into it, shoulders raised, irritable that the day should be so dismal. But he poured half a cup of wine onto the earth of her grave, and drank the rest standing over it, and stayed there long enough to miss what happened that day at the Colosseum.

Lal suddenly pulled away, pushing back the covers and sitting up. She said, 'I can't.'

Sulien sprawled back on the pillows. 'What is it?' he asked quietly, trying to sound patient, harmless.

Lal was hunched forward on the edge of the bed, her face in her hands. When at last she answered her voice was a blurred, shamed mumble. 'We're not married,' she whispered. 'It's wrong.'

Sulien lay silent for a while. 'Lal,' he said at last. 'It's hardly *murder*, is it? When you think of all that's happened, all the killing, how wrong can it be?' He sat up and stroked the tumbled hair away from her neck, pressed his mouth to the warm skin, dragging the kiss across the pulse, whispering, 'How wrong can this be?'

In his arms Lal seemed to stiffen and relax at once, helplessly, tension and languor rolling through her in waves. 'I don't know.'

Sulien gathered her closer. 'This isn't hurting anyone,' he murmured into her hair. 'This is the opposite ...' He slid his hand inside her dishevelled dress, stroking down from her throat, drawing splayed fingers across the nipple. He could feel her breast strain against his hand with her breath. For a second she softened so totally that he worked to pull her down again onto the bed. But she dragged herself free, panting.

'No, I don't know. I can't. I'm sorry.' She pulled her clothes together and fled home.

Ziye and Delir were both there. Delir was working silently on an invoice for some silk he'd sold. Ziye was still barely speaking to Delir, and all her movements around him were sharp and violent, though whenever she looked at him her eyes were hollow with unforgiving and involuntary concern.

Delir noticed nothing strange about Lal, as she hurried past into her room. He looked up, but scarcely saw her. She was relieved, on this occasion, but it saddened her too. He noticed little now. He was too absorbed in guilt, and in suspense.

When the fishermen had returned at last to the island, he'd been too desperate to care about their surprise at seeing the recluse at all, let alone signalling and beckoning frantically on the beach. Had anyone crawled out of the sea, on the other island, or been pulled from the water, three weeks before?

The fishermen had seen something splash feebly in the lights of their boat. When they looked, they saw it was the body of a man, no longer stirring in the water; indeed the movement they thought they'd seen could have been no more than the rocking of the waves. No one had wanted to enter that cold sea for a corpse, but for decency's sake they had hauled it up the side of the boat in a net, before it went under. To their astonishment, once on the deck, the frozen body choked, shuddered, and turned its drowned and ice-pale face to them, blue eyed, blue lipped.

They heaped their coats over him and took him home to the large island they'd embarked from. One of the fisher's wives had tried to undress him, to put fresh clothes on him, but he'd cried out in protest, twisting away with his arms gathered tight against his chest, and begged so distraughtly not to be touched, that they'd left him alone, huddled on a mattress near the fire. Even after they'd got him warmed up and let him sleep, he'd spoken very little. He'd said his ship had sunk, everyone else was drowned, and even if they hadn't found him in the sea, from the empty, horrified look on his face they could have well believed it.

The following day he'd talked urgently of getting to the mainland. They tried to calm him; he was still scarcely strong enough to stand. And they had banded together to pay for a doctor, but when they brought him to the house, the young survivor was not there. They expected to find him collapsed within fifty yards of the house, but they did not. Alarmed and rather hurt, the fisherman's family had checked to see if anything had been stolen. Nothing. They decided the shock of the wreck and the cold had turned the poor youth's mind.

Delir had also made his way as fast as possible to the mainland, and alerted the vigiles. He had not been able to bear to break what he wished bitterly he could have shared: the fishers' ignorance of whom they had saved.

454

'What's wrong?' asked Marcus. Noriko had become very quiet and still as they entered the car for the tiny journey down to the Colosseum.

'Nothing,' she said, with convincing mildness in her voice. But she did not quite look at him, and they were both speaking Nionian, so that the driver and the guards could not understand them. They had something to hide.

Presently she asked, 'So, I am to be entertained by a massacre now?'

'There'll be acrobatics and so on first. And there aren't any prisoners involved today. These are the best gladiators, they don't throw their lives away. Unless something goes wrong it shouldn't be a bloodbath. Just a display of skill and courage. Some bears may die, that should be all.'

'I think it's barbaric to make a spectacle of such things,' remarked Noriko.

'It's traditional,' said Marcus, not sure why he was apparently defending the Games, which Clodia had taught him to dislike and avoid, when possible.

They left the car. Escorted by the Praetorians they walked with the rest of the Imperial family through the private passage that led below the ranked seats of the Colosseum into the Imperial box. As they emerged, Noriko and Marcus first, then Drusus and Makaria, and finally Faustus, there was a flourish of drums and trumpets, and a halo of golden fireworks burst from the arena perimeter. Sixty thousand people rose to their feet, cheering. Noriko applauded Faustus graciously and smiled to the crowd. She was inured to such exposure now.

'Will you be at home tonight?' she asked, still in Nionian, as they settled into their seats. The pillars that supported the bullet-proof screens around them were wreathed with red and white roses, golden rugs were spread under their feet. A camera swept past them on an internal track around the arena below. They remained smiling.

'No,' answered Marcus. He hesitated and said, 'I will be in the Palace. With Una.'

Noriko sighed, softly and lengthily. 'It isn't necessary to tell me everything,' she said.

'I don't want to hide anything from you.'

'Marcus,' said Noriko. 'I know when she can't stand to stay away from you any longer, and when you're afraid you'll never see her again. If you think you are able to hide that, you are deceived. Not from someone who lives with you, and has very little to do except observe you. I know you think about her, *all the time*. I know quite enough. I don't need the exact details.'

Marcus stared at the Colosseum sand. He said, 'You don't love me, Noriko.'

Noriko gave a graceful, hard little laugh. 'I suppose not, no. But sometimes perhaps I forget that I don't. You're the only person here that I *know*. It's not as if I have recourse to anyone else.'

'I'm not stopping you,' muttered Marcus. It was at once an attempt at an honest offer of freedom and a muted retaliation.

'Would you like there to be any doubt who fathered your children? Whether it was a true Novian who inherited the throne?'

Marcus knew he had no answer to that.

'So, she is coming to see you again. Have you reached some arrangement that might last, now?'

Marcus still did not reply, partly reluctant to provoke her by talking about it further, but also because he did not know the answer. Noriko was right, Una consumed his thoughts. Something must happen; this couldn't go on. Yet neither one of them saw any escape from it. If Una could not find some way of enduring his marriage to Noriko, the possibility of children, then they should stay away from each other, for good. But after those months apart, after the clutching, frail relief of that night in the palace, how could they bear it, how could they force that on themselves a second time?

'I wish you would,' said Noriko.

'It's starting,' said Marcus, as there were more bursts of light and noise, and a flood of dancers and tumblers poured out through the gates into the arena. Above them, the panels of the glass roof had contracted shut against the rain, and the Colosseum was sealed in the semblance of a bright sunny day. Marcus looked at the show in attentive silence and relaxed into seeing nothing but the fact that later Una would be with him.

They were watching in a dirty room in an abandoned house on the outskirts of Rome. They saw the Colosseum crowd erupt into applause, the Imperial family take their seats, the show begin on the old long-vision, and several minutes passed in appalled suspense as they tried to convince themselves that the chaos they expected might still be about to happen, any second now. They could not look at each other.

At last one of them whispered, 'What happened?'

'It didn't work,' said Dama calmly. He felt flat and unsurprised.

'All that work,' breathed Ananias.

Dama got up and went into the back room. He'd reached Rome at last to learn that Mazatl was dead. It seemed he'd taken with him at least one of the vigiles who'd cornered him. Better for him than to be taken alive, Dama thought, further grief somehow lamed in him. There were others dead, or imprisoned, or vanished, or extradited to Nionia. But not everyone.

Erastus and Ananias followed him into the store room, slow, baffled. Dama, already kneeling over the equipment, looked up at them. 'I can do it,' he said quietly.

Erastus shook his head, confused and guilty. 'It's my fault,' he said.

Distant and composed, Dama replied, 'It's not your fault. It is an accident.'

'But there's no time now, Dama,' cried Ananias.

Dama shook his head gently. 'The Games go on for hours.'

And Erastus muttered, 'Even if it was possible, it shouldn't be you.'

Dama's expression had not changed. He said, 'Yes, it should.'

Una walked through Trajan's Forum. The streets were full, even in the rain, people making the most of the holiday, hurrying between shops, stooped under hoods. Like the rest, she had the day off in celebration of Faustus' return to power. But she bought nothing, and she moved slowly, wet hair uncovered. The rain was not cold, it tingled on her skin, marking out the boundaries of her body, wearing the worst edge of impatience away. Her thoughts felt like Marcus' thoughts. You can't spend your whole life like this, she said to herself, and the voice in her mind sounded like his. Although he would not have said that, not aloud, not to her.

She had tried. A week together until Noriko's return from Nionia, chaste until the last night. After that perhaps they would write to each other sometimes, but not see each other. They had convinced themselves, painfully, that they had agreed to this. She had begun working at the clinic once she had recovered enough strength to work at all. She was glad to be near Sulien now. Her work, filing papers and taking down letters, was dull, but it was a more gentle dullness than the relentlessness of the Vatican bar. Sometimes she still wondered if that were a mistake. She envied Marcus the work she could no longer have any share in. It was worth giving yourself entire to work like that.

But Marcus' letters filled up with requests, pleas to see her, and forced her back into wondering what on earth she thought she was protecting by torturing them both. Had she thought staying with him now would make her unhappy? How much worse could it be than being without him?

But even now, as restlessness drew her closer to the Colosseum, wishing the time away, feeling the free hours were useless for anything but to lead to Marcus, there was part of her that kept imagining him some time in the future with Noriko's children, whom he would love.

She could have waited for Marcus in the Palace but these days, once again she felt like an intruder with no rights there, at least until Marcus was with her to stop her caring. She looked up at the Colosseum's belt of screens, which displayed the scene within, so that it was as if a round band of wall had vanished and turned bright and transparent. She looked up, blind to whatever was happening on the sand, searching helplessly for the Imperial box, for Marcus. And of course, at last, the camera revealed him at Noriko's side, and made her turn away, flinching. She must have inflicted that sight upon herself deliberately. It was a kind of warning, or pre-emptive self-punishment.

Finally, the rain was too much, it drove her to look for somewhere dry to kill the time. She hurried now, past the Colosseum, onto the Via Labicana. She was about to turn down a sidestreet towards a little taverna, when something seemed to change in the air, as if a switch had turned and halted the rain as it fell. Her gaze was pulled a certain way, as if pulled by an unknown kind of gravity. She looked at a man a little way ahead, coming down the road towards the Colosseum, his face half-shaded by the dark hood of his jacket, a heavy bag slung over his shoulder. His eyes met hers, round and hard as window panes, and terrified. The recognition stopped them both and locked them together, staring, as if they were each caught in a hard shell of glass. And for an instant she felt the barrier there had always been between them was glass too – transparent. And she knew what he was going to do.

Still Dama's stare, the invisible casing of shock, held her motionless. Then she heard her own breath pulled in, and she broke out of it and pushed through the first door she could find. 'The longdictor, I need to use the longdictor *now*.'

It was a fashionable jewellers', pearls glowing on pristine pale surfaces, and the man behind the counter looked at her dripping hair and rigid, desperate face with confused disapproval.

'Oh, God, please,' she cried. 'I need to call the vigiles, you must help.'

She hardly knew what she said to the vigiles, or how long it took. She rushed out into the street again, lurching on the wet stone. Where was he? She forced her rough way back along the busy pavement towards the Colosseum. Her legs had turned numb, trembling. She struggled for enough air to move fast, each breath a tearing, famished swallow.

And she saw him, glancing back, nervously over his shoulder, straight at her. To her surprise he darted off the main road, into a smaller street.

458

Una tried to call out for someone to stop him, but could not force this drowning fight for breath into sound. And she felt she could make no one listen anyway. They'd think she'd only been robbed, or that she was mad, in some trouble they would want no part of. She shoved even more fiercely past them, and ran down the street where Dama had vanished.

The smaller shops here were mostly shut, the pavement almost empty. Dama was hurrying along in front, head lowered in its hood, an anonymous dark figure. I'm faster than him, she told herself, forcing strength into her cowering body, dashing forward, teeth clenched. She went on as she saw Dama stop. Unbelievably, he turned and came running back to meet her. He caught hold of her as she collided with him, gripping his arms, his clothes, silently.

'Get away from me,' he said urgently, but his voice was not violent but pleading with her. 'Don't follow me. Don't you understand? You must get away from here.'

Una could not answer. There was nothing to be said, no language for him left. She clung onto him with all her strength, trying to force him still, drag him back, as once long ago she'd tried to do to Marcus. She stared, speechlessly, into his eyes.

'Oh, God!' he moaned, struggling with her. His face was twisted in anguish; he was scarcely recognisable. 'Let go. You must let go.'

Una gripped and gripped.

A groan or sob pushed through Dama's teeth. He turned his face away from what he was doing, shuddering, and suddenly drove his weight against her, slamming her against the wall beside them so that her head was knocked against the brick, and she fell.

He knew he should move at once but for an instant he could not, he stood paralysed, looking down at her. Her eyes flickered weakly, but then her head drooped forward, and he saw streaks of blood on her hair. He prayed she was only half-stunned. He wanted to crouch beside her, stroke her face or her wet hair in apology, but it seemed false, forbidden, one fragmentary thing he knew he had no right to do.

Whatever happened now, she would be safe.

There was a narrow alley ahead that led into the open space around the Colosseum. He straightened, and ran towards it.

The was a short lull in the Games. An orchestra struck up as the attendants came to drag away the corpses of a couple of Arctic bears. A gladiator, raked by the claws of one before his comrade had speared it, had been borne away on a stretcher. Noriko rose to her feet. 'I'm going home,' she said to Marcus.

'Please don't. It's only another couple of hours,' said Marcus, who had no sense at all of what he'd been watching all this time. It might have been a blank screen.

'I cannot face another hour of watching this. And everyone has already had their fill of watching us. It will be all right, say I don't feel well. It's quite true.'

Marcus let her go. Makaria leant towards him quizzically as Noriko slipped past, but then the lights rose again.

Dama looked up once at the band of screens as he reached the Colosseum. Some kind of high, dome-like steel frame had been erected in the arena and two teams of fighters were dancing and swinging their way, acrobat-like, over and through it. A glimpse of the Imperial box showed him Noriko was gone and his body clenched in a spasm of panic that his chance was passing. Perhaps five minutes had elapsed since Una first saw him. He was racing against her message to the vigiles, in another moment the signal would come to evacuate the Imperial box, clear the Colosseum.

What was he thinking? He didn't wish the Princess any harm.

The Games were free, there were many still trying to push their way in. Bags like the one Dama carried should be checked, but the guards were stretched, trying to keep the crowding within the Colosseum from growing dangerous. Dama took a deep breath and made for one high arch manned by a harrassed pair of guards, trying to fend away a drunken and argumentative scrum of people. Dama moved quietly, through the group, and *knew* a moment would come when the nearer guard, remonstrating with a noisy ringleader of a small belligerent gang within the larger mob would be too preoccupied to stop a smaller, less obtrusive man from slipping past.

And the moment came. The guard even saw that he was inside, turning in exasperation as if to try and catch him back. Dama gave him a cocky, disarming smile that seemed to cost him a great sum of strength from the very core of his bones, and confidently plunged deeper into the crowd.

The lower levels were for the aristocracy and the rich, and were more firmly cordoned off and more closely guarded than the outer arches. The invading surplus audience surged up the steps towards the upper terraces, gathered in the arches that led down into the aisles. Dama ran in quickly at one of these, looking over the spectators' shoulders, fixing the position of the Imperial box in his mind.

Then he ran on upwards. No one was watching him; they were watching the Games. The Colosseum boomed with a great cry of excitement that swilled and spiralled round the huge bowl of space within its walls.

Dama dragged open a door and fled out onto the maintenance level of the retractable roof, the upper rim of the Colosseum. And suddenly he was alone again, out in the open air.

He threw back his hood. The wet wind pulled at his hair. Rome seemed to press near to him through the rain. The Palace, the temple of Saturn, the Circus Maximus were so close he felt he might have touched them.

Dama climbed out onto the panels of wet glass. It was faintly warm from the lights below, and his hands looked black against it. He pulled himself along by a great hinged steel strut that reached out over the arena, a little spider on a huge web. Beneath him, though another great rumble of sound quivered the glass on which he moved, the illuminated ranks of surging people seemed as distant as a drowned city, under a frozen sea. At last, right above the Imperial box, he felt calm, clean again, acting methodically, no longer so frantic and pursued, not thinking of Una. He packed the putty against the strut, and connected the detonator.

Una lifted her head. Her body was a sick, trembling weight that had nothing to do with her, would not obey her. Lights scattered and wobbled across her murky sight. She *must* move. She managed to steer one drifting hand to the back of her skull, felt the blood there, located the centre of the pain. A little focus came back. She pulled herself up against the wet wall, and began again, staggering, to run.

Drusus was bored to death. The Games were bland and insipid, as he had known was inevitable given his uncle's delicate state of health and his cousin's prejudices. Faustus at least seemed to be enjoying himself. Drusus watched with his face set into a look of tolerant mildness, and knew that Marcus, sitting as far from him as possible within the box, was using the same faintly smiling Novian mask to hide his own lack of enjoyment, but Drusus avoided looking at him.

Instead, because Noriko had reminded him of Tulliola, he began to think discontentedly about his slave girl, Amaryllis. Trapped and wretched in Canaria, he needed her too often, and his hopelessness and fury increased every time he finished with her. He'd left her rather bruised and torn, the last time. Now, he found himself weighing up the old idea that he should purge himself of her, let her go. And today he went so far as to picture himself doing it, imagining signing the papers, smiling down at her as he put a present of money into her hands. He would watch her as she left his house, a freedwoman, with a name to show for it: Noviana.

461

Drusus, his eyes still fixed on the arena, jerked back in his chair as if in shocked reaction to a gladiator's fall. The imagined name had struck through him like a piece of shrapnel.

He had long given up any faith in the Sibyl's prophecy. If any flicker of belief ever came back to him it was to think bitterly that she must simply have been telling them that he might have a chance to be Emperor, if Marcus did not ruin it, and Marcus had.

But now again, in his mind, he repeated her words as exactly as he could.

She had promised him the Empire, and she had warned him of someone who could bring him down. The Novian stem. Of course, he had thought of a family tree, the newest branch being the youngest member of his family, Marcus. But if she had only meant the Novian name?

He had never heard Una or Sulien called by any longer, more Roman name, they had never been slaves of his family. But they were free, and it was a Novian who had freed them. Beyond doubt they must carry a form of his name. Noviana, Novianus.

In that stark, frightened shock of understanding, he felt as if he too were an oracle, as if a thread of fate were trying to pull itself into human sight, through him. When Salvius had taken him out of prison he had gone to his uncle with a warning he'd pretended came from the Sibyl, about Una, a woman like a sibyl or a witch, growing to terrible power, threatening the dynasty. It seemed to him now that he had been very close to telling the truth, that there was a second prophecy, about Una and Sulien, hidden within the first, and he had almost uncovered it then. No Novian but one: Noviana Una – not a true Novian, *Una*. It had been a play on her name. But it was not only her. No Novian but another. Drusus had missed out her brother when he'd told Faustus what he'd thought was a lie.

What would the Sibyl have said to them, if they'd ever been to Delphi? Drusus felt now that he knew. She would have told them about him, and that they were made to resist and ruin him. Their very natures, their witch-like powers were the sign of it.

For a second he forgot how powerless he was, that his every move was watched. Bright, vengeful certainty exhilarated him, burnt itself instantly into a passionate resolve that no obstacle would stop him, and nothing could protect them from him now.

Then he remembered. They had already won, he thought, lapsing back into the familiar bitterness. He was not Emperor. This had come too late to make any difference.

But then a Praetorian came rushing from the passageway, shouting a warning, and the guards around the Novians rose, reached to bundle

462

them to safety. Words floated strangely in Drusus' mind: *'There's glass on the ground ...'*

Fire punched open the roof of the Colosseum, and steel and glass rained in.

The blast flung Dama over, throwing him across the plates and struts of the roof. Something ripped through his shoulder, slashed at his face. A spray of small glass blades broke over him, scattering him with cuts. The noise seemed to plough up the sky.

Then it died. Dama lay still for a moment on the darkened panels. Ahead of him the crater opened and spread. A column of screaming rose through it like hot smoke.

He was not too badly hurt to move. If he had sent someone else to do this, Dama would have told him to to get off the roof now, to go and try and lose himself in the panicked crowd. They would be coming for him now, too late – the vigiles or the Praetorians. But this did not seem very pressing to Dama. He felt as if he had infinite time. And so he pulled himself closer to the gulf, as the cracks and splits stretched to meet him.

He looked down into the broken arena. He was too high up to tell what had happened to the people in the Imperial box, but he did not even think of looking. He stared sick, bewildered, at the mass of horrified people that heaved and writhed within the walls to escape. The turmoil was too vast to comprehend. Second broke from second, so that each moment of his life that had brought him here, each sight before him now, seemed utterly separate and unfathomable. He crouched on the creaking glass, and if nothing else, he understood that he would never know what it was he had done.

He heard them come, rushing up onto the wounded rim. As he understood the sound it did not seem worth turning his head to look.

A slab of glass and metal broke away underneath him. A black thrill of recognition caught him as it dropped, twisted, as he was kicked into space. But there had been something he meant to whisper, in his mind, before his life was struck away, and there was no time, it was not as he had thought it would be—

END

A SHORT HISTORY OF THE ROMAN EMPIRE
933 AUC TO THE PRESENT (180 AD–2004 AD)

'To heal, as far as it was possible, the wounds inflicted by the hand
of tyranny, was the pleasing, but melancholy task of Pertinax'
Decline and Fall of the Roman Empire, Edward Gibbon

AD	AUC	
180	933	Death of Marucs **Aurelius**.
		His son Lucius Aelius Aurelius **Commodus** succeeds as Emperor.
192	945	Commodus' bloody and extravagant reign leaves Rome impoverished and riddled with corruption. He is murdered by a group of conspirators including his chamberlain, concubine and Laetus, the head of the Praetorian Guard (the urban army whose formal function was to protect the Emperor).
		The conspirators claim that Commodus died of apoplexy, and install as Emperor 66-year-old Publius Helvitus **Pertinax**, the son of a freedman who had risen through merit to become a General, a Senator and minister of justice.

HELVIAN IMPERIAL DYNASTY

192–204	945–957	Early in Pertinax's reign, Laetus, disgruntled by Pertinax's independence, encourages a plot by the Praetorian Guard to assassinate him.
		The plot is discovered,* and Laetus banished. Pertinax disbands almost all of the Praetorian Guard, hand-picking the remainder for loyalty. At the same time he increases the powers and numbers of the Vigiles to create a counterweight police force, reasoning that any future conspiracy against the Emperor in one body will be detected and exposed by the other.
		Pertinax remits Commodus' oppressive taxes. He halves the expenses of the Imperial household, grants

---

* This is where my history of the Roman Empire departs from the usual one. In reality, the plot was successful. The talented and conscientious Pertinax (who planned many of the reforms indicated here) was murdered after only eighty-six days in office and the Praetorians auctioned the throne to the highest bidder. Didius Julianus bought the title of Emperor, but was deposed and executed shortly afterwards by Septimius Severus, who returned to Rome from Pannonia to avenge Pertinax.

Severus corrected many of the problems facing Rome and at the time his reign could be viewed as a success. But he stripped the Senate of authority and allowed corruption and indiscipline to flourish in the army, whose power undermined the stability of the Empire. Gibbon says of Severus 'Posterity, who experienced the fatal effects of his maxims, justly considered him the principal author of the decline of the Roman Empire.'

		tax-breaks to farmers and lifts restrictions on commerce. He taxes the urban aristocracy more heavily, but the cities benefit from the wealth generated by the farms, and restores to the Senate some of the authority it had lost.
204	957	Death of Pertinax. After the disastrous succession of Commodus, Pertinax was relictant to name his young son Publius Helvius Pertinax II, '**Venedicus**', as Caesar and heir to the Empire until just before his death. The senate approve the succession.
204–220	957–973	Pertinax II continues his father's economic reforms, gradually rebuilding the Empire's finances. When the economy permits it he restructures the army, detaching the legions from the frontier garrisons to create a mobile force. He ties pay to the rate of inflation, stablising the income of the soldiers and rendering them less susceptible to bribery, whilst attracting a higher standard of recruit.
225	978	Ardashir, the Persian king, kills the last king of Parthia and creates the Sassanian Persian Empire, with Zoroastrianism as its state religion.
238	991	Renewed attacks from Germanic tribes along the Rhine and Danube. The revitalised army resists and pushes the barbarians back. To deal more fully with the threat, and despite protests from Roman Britons, Pertinax II pulls the legions out of Britain and leads a massive force into Germany and Sarmatia.
230–240	983–993	Ardashir invades India, and Roman territory in Syria. In 240, his son Shapur succeeds to the Perisan throne.
238–242	973–978	Pertinax II completes the conquest of Germany and Venedia, pushing up into Fennia and Gothia.
242–256	978–992	Skirmishes with Persia over Armenia. Roman recapture of Syria.
256	992	Death of Pertinax II, accession of Lucius Helvius Pertinax **Sarmaticus**. Rome's victories over the Eastern European tribes continue into Sarmatia and Alania.
260–265	996–1009	Still feeling the elation of their German victory, Roman troops, augmented by huge numbers of German barbarians and with support from Palmyra, attack and conquer Shapur's Persian Empire.

265–291	1009–1044	Occasional Persian uprisings and fluctuating borders in Roman Persia, but Rome's grip remains generally firm.
291–313	1044–1066	Under Sarmaticus' adopted son Gaius Flavius **Sulpicianus**, Rome loses Persia and Mesopotamia.
313–345	1066–1098	Marcus Flavius Sulpicianus **Cruentus** reconquers Persia and Mesopotamia. Slaughter and enslavement of thousands of Persians. Persecution of Christians, Zoroastrians and Jews throughout Empire. Invasion and conquest of Arabia. Cruentus exports the Roman religion, or a Roman interpretation of local deities, to the enlarged Eastern Empire.
347–447	1100–1200	From here on it will be convenient to summarise the major gains, losses and technological advances of each century. SECOND FLAVIAN DYNASTY 1066–1234 AUC Reconquest of Britain, with Hibernia and Caledonia. There has been a revival of Celtic culture, but a sustained British nostalgia for Roman rule makes victory fairly easy. Sporadic incursions by Huns, but they are either repelled or absorbed by Rome, resulting in gradual, unsystematic Roman expansion into Scythia.
447–547	1200–1300	ACILIAN DYNASTY 1234–1618 AUC Continued conquests of territory in Scythia. Expansion through Persian territory into India. Lengthy wars to secure it. Romanisation of Indian Gods.
547–647	1300–1400	Quelling more uprisings and rebellions in India and resulting instability in the region keep the military fully occupied – no expansion.
647–747	1400–1500	Attempted expansion into Sina (China) unsuccessful, and there are continuing problems in Syria, Persia and India.
747–847	1500–1600	Border disputes with Sina. India and Persia subside into uneasy peace, but tensions will flare up at any sign of weakness in the Empire for centuries to come. By this time the once-significant Christian sect has more or less died out of existence. Active persecution of Jews and Zoroastrians has ceased, although they are still denied full citizenship.

| 847–947 | 1600–1700 | CORDIAN DYNASTY 1618–1836 AUC |

Libya and other Roman states in North Africa attempt to devolve peacefully from the Empire, but Africa is essential to feeding the Roman world. Heightened military presence there.

| 947–1047 | 1700–1800 |

Song Dynasty unifies and stabilises Sina. Rome is initially concerned about Sina's growing power, but the Emperor feels that Rome is now unassailable, re-attempted conquest of Sina would be costly and futile, and that therefore there is no need to jeopardize profitable trade with Sina. Relations remain cordial – especially since Sina supports Roman rule in India.

| 1047–1147 | 1800–1900 | BLANDIAN DYNASTY 1836–2176 AUC |

The Romans defend the Song against the Jurchen uprising.
Rome introduces various Sinoan innovations, such as paper money, banking, Romanised versions of certain fashions in clothing – and gunpowder.

| 1147–1247 | 1900–2000 |

Quicker to see the military application of the new discovery than its Sinoan inventors, Rome sides with Sina against the Mongols, saving the Song Dynasty. First Roman contact with Nionia (Japan), and welcomes the new source of coveted oriental goods, but Rome has little political interest as yet in the chain of islands, which is riven with internal divisions and wars.

| 1247–1347 | 2000–2100 |

Armed with canons, Rome invades Ethiopia in Africa. Sina watches this new phase of expansion with concern.
The Nionian Emperor Go-Diago visits Rome, learns about Roman exploration and conquest, and brings the secret of gunpowder back to Nionia.

| 1347–1447 | 2100–2200 |

Go-Diago leads the Kemmu Restoration, using firearms against the powerful Hojo regency. The new firepower helps him to see off opposition from his erstwhile ally, Ashikaga Takauji. He restores the powers of the Emperor and unites Nionia.
Continued exploration/conquest of interior Africa runs into difficulty when Roman African states unexpectedly turn against Rome.
Roman explorers return from an attempt to circumnavigate the globe with news of a brief landing on a huge landmass in the West. They call it

467

Terra Nova, but this is no time for a military adventure there.

Plague in Europe and in parts of Sina. The Emperor Blandius **Postummus** dies suddenly and there is a struggle for power unprecedented in over a thousand years.

| 1447–1547 | 2200–2300 | The first electrostatic machine. |

After a succession of short-lived Emperors, the Senate votes Sextus Vincius **Sacerdos** into power.

VINCIAN DYNASTY 2204–2509 AUC

Sacerdos is still trying to secure his position when Nionia invades Corea and attacks Sinoan territory. Sina appeals to Rome for help, but the call comes at exactly the wrong time. Rome is struggling to survive in the face of its internal rifts. African entanglements, renewed Indo-Persian problems and the decimating effects of plague. The Empire is in no position to assist.

Sina battles Nionia alone but concedes large tracts of territory. Roman relations with both Sina and Nionia are damaged.

Rome tries to repair the damage of the last century. In an attempt to rebuild Roman solidarity, Sacerdos extends full citizenship to all free inhabitants of the Empire, regardless of nationality or religion, withholding only the right to hold office from freedmen.

| 1547–1647 | 2300–2400 | Meanwhile, Nionia is still in the ascendant. Nionian explorers sight the Southern island continent and call it Goshu. |

When Nionia begins to colonise Goshu, Rome becomes seriously alarmed. Nionia is beginning to look like a serious rival to the Empire. Rome puts pressure on Nionia to cease expanding and urges Sina to do the same, but since becoming a buffer state between Rome and Nionia, Sina has become increasingly introspective, and the Sinoan government refuses to get involved.

Rome completes the conquest of Africa.

More experiments in electricity and magnetics.

Rome at last begins a serious invasion of central and southern Terranova, spreading cautiously into Mexica, Maia, and inland into Aravacia.

Nionia follows suit, entering Terranova in the far north. Rome is more uneasy than ever and begins seriously to debate war but for the moment, and to the dissatisfaction of many, does nothing; there is

		still a huge amount of land, with its own peoples to contend with, between the two powers.
1647–1747	2400–2500	Nionia pushes south, until Rome's fears that she is not only allowing her rival to claim valuable territory but that her existing Terranovan provinces are under threat become intolerable. Conflict is now inevitable and is to dominate the next century.

The two armies sweep towards each other across the country – the Romans pushing north from the south-eastern coast of the northern continent, each trying to cajole or force the indigenous peoples to side with them.

The ensuing sequence of wars, although they vary in intensity and are divided by short, unsuccessful peace agreements, is brutal and often chaotic, with naval battles in the Atlantic and around Nionia itself.

Tracts of land change hands several times, at vast cost in Roman, Nionian, and Terranovan lives. The Camian peninsular in Mexica is of particular importance since for Rome to allow the Nionians to claim it would amount to their being permanently flanked.

The Emperor Vincius **Arcadius** dies in suspicious circumstances and his brother, **Nasennius**, seizes power.

The Roman military and economy has been damaged. During a brief lull in the Roman-Nionian conflict, the final years of the 25th Century, the first African Uprising takes place in the province of Lundae in Africa.

The first – very slow and inefficient – electrically powered vehicles to run on magnetic rails.

1747–1847	2500–2600	Madness first appears in Novian family.

The Africans are temporarily subdued.

In the second African Uprising of 2503, a poorly equipped Roman legion is massacred near Musitania (Mosi-oa-Tunya) Falls. Nasennius is widely blamed for the disaster.

Oppius Novius, Nasennius' nephew-by-marriage, gains in popularity in the Senate.

After an outbreak of smallpox in Rome, Nasennius commits suicide leaving no children. Oppius Novius takes power.

NOVIAN DYNASTY 2509 AUC–PRESENT

Rome secures Northern half of Africa. Southern Africa claims independence.

Although bringing the conflict to an end and holding

onto Northern territory are significant successes for Rome, this is the first serious loss of territory for the Empire in centuries. Cracks appear elsewhere in the Empire: there is conflict in Terranova, and old tensions in India stir again.

In 2512, Oppius' brother Servius succumbs to family madness.

Oppius works to rebuild international stability. He succeeds in reversing Roman fortunes in Terranova, where the Romans advance north. His task is eased by new technology such as longscript – a method of transmitting codes through electric pulses invented in 2511. This allows direct government of overseas territory. Longscript lines are laid under the Atlantic, and through Africa. Thirty years later come longdictors. Rome will be able to respond far more swiftly to any future unrest.

There are accelerated attempts to find a reliable form of air-travel.

Rome's military might is, just, superior to Nionia's, but it looks as though it will be impossible to ever expel the Nionians from the Terranova altogether. Therefore, Rome finally comes to grudging terms with Nionia and northern Terranova is divided between the two Empires. Under the Mixigana Treaty, a huge wall is built across the continent to separate them. Trade between Nionia and Rome resumes, but there is a persistent distrust and rivalry. Rome develops new high explosives. Nionia seems always on the verge of catching up with Roman technology.

Rome begins to expand through Southern Terranova. Rome works to improve the network of roads, whilst simultaneously building a vast system of magnetways throughout the Empire.

1847–1947	2600–2700	Development of flight using circling wings powered by engines – the first spiral-wing. Continued colonisation of North and South Terranova. The arms race with Nionia goes on.

RECENT HISTORY

1943	2697	Titus Novius **Faustus** born.
1949	2702	Lucius Novius Faustus born.
1958	2711	Tertius Novius Faustus born.
1969	2722	Titus marries Julia Sabina.
1971	2724	Julia gives birth to Novia Faustina ('Makaria').

1977	2730	Lucius marries Drusilla Terentia.
1979	2732	Drusilla gives birth to Drusus Novius Faustus.
1981	2734	Lucius succumbs to hereditary madness.
1982	2735	Gaius Novius Faustus **Rixa** dies. Titus succeeds as Emperor. Tertius Novius posted to central Terranova. He quells an Aztec uprising and his courage gains him the agnomen 'Leo'. He is hailed as a hero, but sees hundreds of previously free Aztecs enslaved and is shocked by the experience.
1983	2736	Faustus divorces Julia.
1984	2738	Leo marries Clodia Aurelia. With Senatorial approval, Faustus names Leo as Caesar and Imperial heir.
1988	2741	Clodia gives birth to Marcus Novius Faustus Leo.
1996	2749	Faustus marries Tullia 'Tulliola' Marciana.
2004	2757	Leo and Clodia are murdered after their car is sabotaged to crash in the Gallic Alps. After surviving an attempt on his own life, their son Marcus Novius goes into hiding at an illegal slave refuge in the Pyrenees. Leo's aide Varius is publicly accused of his murder. On Marcus Novius' return a conspiracy to prevent an opponent of slavery becoming Emp--- is uncovered, including the Emperor's wife Tullia Marciana and construction magnate Gabinius. Vigiles kill Gabinius as he attempts to escape. Marcus Novius is confirmed as Faustus' heir. Nionian provinces are badly affected by a tidal wave after an offshore earthquake.
2005	2758	In January, before she can be tired for treason and murder, Tullia Marciana is found dead under house arrest. Extensive investigation into and restructuring of the Praetorian and vigile forces. Heightened tensions between Rome and Nionia.
2006	2759	Nionian ambassadors at Rome are arrested on suspicion of spying and deported. The Emb--- is closed.
2007	2760	A hot summer brings a spate of serious fires across the Roman Empire.

Thanks to—

My parents, who have both been wonderfully supportive and helpful.

Maisie Tomlinson. I made her pretend to be a victim of crucifixion while researching *Romanitas*, and dragged her across the floor as a necessary experiment for *Rome Burning*. I'm trying to think of something to do to her for Book 3.

Pat Cox, and his colleagues at The Fire Service College in Moreton-in-Marsh for invaluable help in understanding the mechanics of fire.

Frances Ward especially, as well as Jonathon Partington and Jenny O'Keefe at The Royal Arsenal, for their help regarding arms manufacture.

Momoko Abe and Wang Tong for checking over the Japanese and Chinese elements of the book respectively and offering important suggestions. Yasuhiro Yamada also assisted me with place-names and other matters.

Richard Dawson and Robert Low for advice on Roman culture and history, etc.

Everyone who helped me, in all ways, in Rome and in China.

My agent Simon Trewin for his continuing encouragement and good humour.